STAF
AF4

D1586447

SANDRA NEWMAN

The Country of Ice Cream Star

VINTAGE BOOKS
London

1 3 5 7 9 10 8 6 4 2

Vintage,
20 Vauxhall Bridge Road,
London SW1V 2SA

Vintage is part of the Penguin Random House group of companies whose
addresses can be found at global.penguinrandomhouse.com.

First published by Vintage in 2015
(First published in Great Britain by Chatto & Windus in 2014)

www.vintage-books.co.uk

A CIP catalogue record for this book is available from the British Library

ISBN 9780099554653

Typeset in Sabon LT Std by Palimpsest Book Production Ltd,
Falkirk, Stirlingshire

Printed and bound in Great Britain by
Clays Ltd, St Ives plc

Penguin Random House is committed to a sustainable future for our business,
our readers and our planet. This book is made from Forest Stewardship
Council® certified paper.

For Helen Trickett

IN MASSA

Tober 2–Vember 1

I

MY TROUBLE ITS BEGINNING:
TOBER 2

My name be Ice Cream Fifteen Star. My brother be Driver Eighteen Star, and my ghost brother Mo-Jacques Five Star, dead when I myself was only six years old. Still my heart is rain for him, my brother dead of posies little.

My mother and my grands and my great-grands been Sengle pure. Our people be a tarry night sort, and we skinny and long. My brother Driver climb a tree with only hands, because our bones so light, our muscles fortey strong. We flee like a dragonfly over water, we fight like ten guns, and we be bell to see. Other children go deranged and unpredictable for our love.

We Sengles be a wandering sort. We never grown nothing from anything, never had no tato patch nor cornfield. Be thieves, and brave to hunt. A Sengle hungry even when he eat, even when he rich, he still want to grab and rob, he hungry for something he ain't never seen nor thought of. We was so proud, we was ridiculous as wild animals, but we was bell and strong.

In my greats' time, we come up from Chespea Water; was living peaceful by Two Towns until the neckface murderers come. Then we flee onward to these Massa woods. Here we thieve well. We live as long as Lowells – sometimes twenty years or twenty-one years. Every Sengle have a knife, and we together possess two guns. Driver got a gun that shoot, and Crow Sixteen a broken shotgun, still is good for scaring.

This day my story start, we been out scratching in the evacs. These evacs be house after house that face each other in twin lines. Houses shambledown and rotten; ya, the road between is broken through with pushing weeds. Get fifty houses in a street, and twenty streets in one hour's walking. When these houses all was full, it been more people here than squirrels. Ain't nobody living now.

Loot here be older, but is rich. We find every kind of thing – pharmacies, can food, clothes. Find cigarettes, be old with mushroom taste, but still can smoke. What I love most – can of Beef-a-roni. I eat that cold. I eat Beef-a-roni any way. The person invented Beef-a-roni, that person was a valuable genius.

This raid, it been Jermaine Fourteen, Asha Badmouth Fifteen and my brother Driver Eighteen, who been Sengle sergeant then. Ya, my favorite little, Keepers Eight, been there on scouting task. We come out with two horses, my own finicky spotten pony Money and Big Smoke who pull a sledge.

Ya, this been a feary day, because we find a sleeper house. Been two sleepers there, they lain together in a bed. One been grown, one eightish size. Both gone with years to stain and bones. Skeletons mix their ribs, their ghosty hair caught in one tangle.

In houses with these dead, we take no loot. It be unlucky wealth. Nor is good taboo to leave the house. Must rid it with clean fire.

Driver, Jermaine and Asha Badmouth gone to set the fire, while I keep hunting through the houses round with scrambly Keepers Eight. We scout the flooden cellars barefoot, then scratch upward through each room, until we meet the broken roof its sunlight. Then the next-door house.

This be grimy task. Ain't matter how perfect anything look in a closet. When you take it up, dust fly. Hurt vicious in your eyes. Times, be flittering moths, look like they born from dust that instant. But the clothes, they often still all right.

That day, ain't scarcely nothing worth the carry. Food is rotten,

2

cloth be mold, books crumble like dry earth. Ain't no metal but is rust. Keepers frustrate well, go swearing like a mally baby. Child be feroce to want, will rob the laces from a digger's shoe. But this evac street be poory gone. We scratch out five houses, then slop tired in a raggity bed, upstairs of this cold house with scarce no windows. We waiting on the fire across the street to catch correct. Then we can go out staring, warm our face.

The only loot we find:

- 5 cans soup, 2 cans corn, 1 can condense milk, clean and bone. Other cans been rusten useless.
- 1 box allergic pharmacy, 1 Robitussin coughing drink.
- big coat for Asha Badmouth when her pregnant belly grow, ain't prettieuse for nothing but it smell right.
- 1 bottle whiskey, 1 bottle gin. Other bottles unseal and the booze gone stank.
- these sleepers' evac notice.
- a plastic baby, sort with arms and legs that you can turn. The painten eyes so worn, it make your eyes feel scary. Look the way dust in your eyes can feel.

A plastic baby be bad luck. The little children say it mean somebody going to die. Truth, littles always be inventing superstitions. One little say it, they all go believe, and tell it onward. Sometimes, I think the digger gods was starting from a little's maginations. 'They got a man inside the clouds that punish you if you is lazy.' Dribble talk from ungrown heads. However that be, now my Keepers frighten.

On her neck, she wear the lastic string left from a candy necklace. Now, in fretting nerves, she wind the lastic round her pointer finger. Watch the fingertip swell bright, is like she strangle her own fear. Other hand got a cigarette. She been smoking this, and shake the ash on her own head. Be ash all in her bushy hair, for she believe ash kill nits. Keepers never had nits. This be proof to her it work.

And Keepers such a warry dirty cub, she hurt my heart. I ain't know what other children feel, but I swear I feel more. See my Keepers frighten, and it feel like swallowing ice. Yo, the child so vally proud, it hurt her arrogance if I pet her, if I touch her any way. She sit on the scurfy bed and look her miseries, I going to want to pat her head. But cannot pat no proud eight's head.

Ya, beliefs be catching. Soon my nerves go jittery self. Somebody going to die – yo sho, somebody always going to die. Ain't been a year that I remember when nobody die. Only Keepers too little to die, every child I love too needful, and my Sengle people be too few.

'Damn you, Keeps,' I say. 'This person can be dying anywhere. Can be some Mass Army dying. More of them that die is wonderful.'

'Nay, it got to be somebody I know. I find the baby.'

'Yo sho. Maybe it be Mouse.'

She startle, and look up joyeuse and warry-eyed. But, thought by thought, she quit believing.

'I ain't never be so lucky.' Keepers gripe her mouth. 'Bet you Mouse gone find a baby. He want me to die right now. He want me to die sick.'

Now we smell the kindling fire across the street, a hoarsen sweetness.

I say, 'You going to stop with that now, foolish.'

'Ain't no fool, I knowing right.'

'You act like Keepers Two, sometimes.'

'I ain't. I act like Keepers Twelve.'

'Keepers Noisy, all it is.'

'You hate Mouse. Say you hate him and say I ain't going to die. Somebody old like you die.'

'Damn, quit that,' I say. 'Or next time Asha Badmouth stay with you.'

Keepers make a fart noise with her lips and swear again. I turn and grab the evac notice, start to read it loud, try to distract her into reading practice. But she only shut her eyes and yell the evac notice words. Remember almost all. Then we both go laughing,

4

yelling. Rival to say this faster-louder. Every Sengle know a notice of evacuation well.

When we finish, Keepers quit her screaming and pronounce, 'Then sleepers gone evacuating and they go to Europe.'

'Certain, gone to Europe.'

'But where this Europe be?' she say. 'You never seeing Europe.'

'Shoo, is farther distance, cross the ocean.'

Keepers frown in littlish scorn. She put the plastic baby on the floor, she done with dying. Dying finish now. 'You ain't know. I bet nobody cross the ocean never. Ain't no Europe.'

'Shoo, is Europe. Seen no maps?'

'They pictures. Ain't no Europe real.'

'Bone, it ain't no Europe. Sleepers all be hiding in the woods. They coming now, be angry how we robbing all their soup.'

'They sleepers wanting us to have their soup. They leave it here. Nor it be no Europe. You lying and you ignorant and I be Keepers Twelve.'

Truth, this Europe mostly be a tale for pacifying littles. Most older children think the sleepers all be dead, but ain't no proof. If sleepers gone to Europe or to hell, they leave the same bad silence.

What we knowing certain of them be a shorter list. We know their looks from pictures left on walls, from paper magazines. They had straight hair like fur. This grown in any different colors – yellow, orange, black and white. Skin was pinkish mostly, like a plastic baby or a roo. Some faces wrinkle up and baggy. Some lost most their hair. How Lowells say, this be from years – these sleepers living old as parrots.

Yo, be seldom pictures where the children looking normal brown, with person hair instead of fur. What we think, these been our greater parents in the Times Before. Ain't sleepers but is children right.

We know the sleepers fled from sickness, a killing fever callen WAKS, some eighty years before. We know their goods, we guess some facts of their abandon life. But their evacuation be a rumor of a mystery.

Most we can learn be from the evac notices themself. These notices all the same, is only numbers and the street names different. They say exactly this:

NOTICE OF EVACUATION

This is a final notice. The Massachusetts Department of Public Health has ordered the evacuation of your street on **MONDAY MARCH 15TH**. A luxury air-conditioned bus is scheduled to stop at **1 SLEIGH ROAD** at **3PM, MONDAY MARCH 15TH** to transport residents to temporary shelter. Your temporary shelter is **RAMADA INN, WESTFORD, MA**. Residents should not drive cars to the temporary shelter. An allowance of two pieces of luggage per household will be strictly observed. Each piece of luggage must be no more than 70 pounds. Both pieces together must be no more than 120 pounds. Additional luggage cannot be accommodated on buses and will be left at the roadside.

Medical checks will be required before passengers are invited to board. Residents suffering from WAKS **will not be allowed** to board the buses. This is for passenger safety. WAKS sufferers and their families should report to the Department of Public Health at 617 256 2412 for further information. Abuse of a medical inspector, verbal or physical, will be punished with no less than 30 days in prison and a fine of up to $5,000.

Emergency Coordinator for Middlesex County,
Victor Espinoza

We got no knowledge of this WAKS, the sickness that destroy them. Been eighty years of quietness. No memory reach that fact. Some children think that WAKS be posies, but nobody know. Dead sleepers left so long, they got no skin to see no posies on. That body tell you nothing but: 'You frighten like a digger, child. You shivering and weak to look at me.'

And no one like to find a house with sleepers dead inside. Be a sleeper there, we burn the house with all its goods. Is glorieuse always when the house consume to fluffy ash and sticks, it make you happy in your eyes. The orange windows flaming out. Then it fall to its knees. Trees shivering around it, gladden with its crazy heat. And after, all be blackish fine. Inside a year, is growing flowers. Make you proud to be a Sengle, cleaner of the sicken world.

So now we watch the fire begin, me and Keepers Eight Fofana, standing at our upstair window. The burning house stand kittercorner to ours, in easy view, and Driver and Jermaine and Asha Badmouth come out, done with kindling. They stand watching, by a pile of water bags and soaken blankets, kept in case the fire escape. Truth, no fire will spread this day. Is soggy wet from morning rain. Still Driver make each hold a bag and blanket. So be drill.

House begin to look a little itchy, before the firelight come. As the flickering raise, it show clear in the bust-out windows. Is like it be a life we woke inside. Then the roof go staining black and fire squeeze through the stain. Fire make a hole and flames push through the roof like angry hair.

The flame and sky two different kinds of bright. Sun look tame and sleepy while this fire go left and right so huge. It make us big and bright with nerves, although we Sengles, kin to burning. Keepers settle staring to the fire, her mouth agape. I settle to my fire trance.

Then Driver look back and catch sight of us. He startle disapproving. Next, he stalking back toward our house, with angry face.

Keepers look to me. I say, 'Yo Driver going to give me talk.'

'Heed him, sure,' say Keepers. 'Got to be obedient.'

'Like you be.'

'Ain't be obedience, town go fall apart.'

7

'You wise as something. Ain't know if it be dirt or wood.'

Keepers make a fart noise and she grin.

I say, 'You wise as dirty feet.'

Then Driver there behind us in the open door. He nod me out, and I come peevish, sorry-tail. We go on down the hall, cause Driver guard his business from the littles. Everything a dignity for him.

Only been a year my brother Driver be the oldest. He sergeant in our wolfen time, when Sengles thieving rich. Girls all go in love for him. Hounds and ponies fear and trust him. Driver give four babies that I know, and three of them is living. And he got a liking strength, is like a big warm house that you can punch and kick on, and it never shake. It standing there despite you, knowing what it known before.

Now he easy kept, although he come to rule me down. I gone glooming at the carpet. Carpet mostly bone and clean. Is only a wedge of shadow by the window, made of mold. Mold show where it raining in. Everything smell green from that, and moody like my thought.

My brother say, 'Must be responsible, Ice. Ain't like to see you dabbit round with Keepers like a small.'

'These poory houses, ain't find garbage here or nothing. Ain't about responsible.'

Driver never heed a foolish saying. You speak a foolishness, he act like this be forest noise that ain't concern him. So he say, as if I never spoken, 'If you ain't work, no little think to work. You be third oldest.'

'Ain't third. Crow be third.'

He skew his eyes at me. 'You counting Villa, babyish? Villa senseless as a moth.'

'I count in numbers, it be three before me. You and Crow and Villa. Make me fourth.'

Driver get his seriose eyes. I look away and spot the bathroom only then. Ain't notice this before, nor Keepers notice. Can see two towels there, is hung and perfect. Mostly Sengles got some towels, but these towels hard to keep. Every winter some of them get mold and cannot clean. Be towels in that bathroom, maybe there be soap and Robitussin, anything.

8

I only rile worse then. Ain't justice that Driver right.

He saying, 'You gone heedless something. Hothead round the place. Be fifteen years and got no plan for babies.'

'I do what being true to me. I ain't do nothing cause of something false.'

'You ain't do nothing cause you lazy.'

'Ain't getting babies with no Crow or no Jermaine.'

'Ice Cream!' my brother say, and his eyes fury. Then he halt and everything too still. I hear the fire like snoring sleep.

And Driver cough. Cough hard, and look surprise. He put his fingers to his chest, then he lift away his fingers, checking at the fingertips like he expect to see blood there. As if blood going to leak out through his skin. Sure, nothing be.

But I see clear, that cough hurt. And Driver gulp and suffer not to cough again. He frown his nerves.

'Driver, you bone,' I say in sudden fright. 'The smoke do that.'

'Sure.' But Driver cough again, and catch his chest the same.

'Ain't got to breathe no smoke, goddamn.'

'Been no smoke. Nor ain't your problems.'

'Sure, it ain't my cough. Damn me for caring. Going to stop from caring.'

'Nothing be to care about, Ice Cream,' say Driver shortish. 'Care about your lazy self.'

Then he turn and go downstairs and I be standing shaky.

Ain't nothing happen, but I know. Driver gone eighteen and mostly children live to eighteen–nineteen. Then they get their posy sickness. He look at me with knowledge in his eyes, he let me spy his feary knowledge.

I want to go downstairs and fight him worse. My brother got no need to tell me who third oldest, second oldest. Driver staying oldest. I tell him in my mind, *You cannot die. I die before you die. Crow be sergeant if you die. Crow be a poison well and maggot, what he do to Sengle town you fear. My brother, keep with me.*

*

Then Keepers Mouthy yell my name. I got to go tend Keepers, who ain't got no brother nor a sister. Who grown in loneliness feroce, without no brother's loss to feel. Ain't fear nothing worse than her own death.

In the room, my Keepers got a chair up to the window. She standing on this chair, and hold my oak bat in her hands. Aim upon a square of glass left in this window's upward corner. 'Going to bust that glass,' she say joyeuse.

'Yo sho, you seen it first,' I say, and my throat haze with uncry tears. 'Make war on it, go on.'

'You ain't want to?'

'Sure I want to. Only said, you seen it first.'

Keepers twitch her freckle nose. She see how I ain't care about no glass. And she throw the bat down on the floor. It make a bigger noise than I expect, a sounding blammer. Noise make me startle weak. My heart keep saying, *Nay, my Driver cannot die,* and then my mind remember it can be true. The loud noise seem like all the things on Earth that ain't care if you frighten.

I say in careful voice, 'Ya, better you ain't break that. You get glass on you. That glass can hurt.'

'You got to stand with me,' say Keepers. 'You keep going somewhere and then I ain't know.'

So I get up on the chair and stand. Keepers lean back to my warm. Fire carry on, it going to go an hour now. The house's upper part look darker as the roof fall into scraps.

Driver walk across the street to Asha Badmouth. He put his hand upon her baby belly and she push his hand away. This happen in the bottom of my vision, but I watch the fire. I get a watching trance upon me. Keepers gaping by.

All children glad to watch a fire. It help you feel the things you need to feel, like drinking whiskey do. So now I slip toward my grief and watch a finicky flame around a window. It move like restless water there, blue and gold and white. I feel my trouble, but I think of NewKing Mamadou, the boy I dream upon. Think how he kill me with his knife someday. And I feel crying like a painful coldness in my jaw. But I ain't cry.

Then the burning house's door flap open, staggering wild. Smoke come hazy out, and from the smoke, a person run.

I yell and Keepers yell. I terrify senseless for my Driver, every fear flash white in me. But Driver, Asha Badmouth and Jermaine stood screaming just like us. It ain't our people in the fire.

Be a stranger boy. At first he looking like a shadow, black, against the fire's bright. Then he come out whole and running strong. He the only one ain't scream.

Ain't no fire on him when he come out, but Asha Badmouth frighten. Splash him wild. He startle, skid and fall. Then Driver tackle him. My brother never wonder if a person be a risk. He warry and particular, will stop that person first.

He wrestle with the frighten boy until he get a throat-lock on. For a breath, is quiet. Only fire still rush and snap. Then Driver shout, the boy gone kick again.

Keepers swear and say to me, 'Ice Cream, it be a sleeper. Ain't in Europe.'

'What?' I try to hear what Driver say. 'What ain't?'

'Sleepers ain't in Europe.'

The boy twist, and I see him clear. I breathe cold into me. The head got yellow furrish hair. The boy got plastic baby skin, he be a yellow roo. Driver holding on a roo. Now panic grab my breath.

I run downstairs before I think. Somewhere Keepers shout at me, all high and frighten, till I shut the door upon her voice. Outside the day stripe hot and cold from fire.

2

OF ROOS BEFORE

I be the only living Sengle ever seen a roo. Sure they ain't trouble Massa woods for years until this day. Only jones children, of thirteen and more, still known this fear.

It been a month before, by Tember when the summer still prolong. This night, I gone sleeping at the library, alone except my mare and hound. I like to be alone from Sengles, and I like to take my pony and my hound indoors. Be sweet in separateness to feel their faith. Driver give me talk about this habit – he say I be unmanageable since I got a horse. This saying true, but he ain't recognize that I be better so.

The library a prettieuse and cleanish edifice. Been a place for books in sleeper times, but now the books is gone. We scratch them all to sell to Lowell in my mama's time. Got one upstairy room at that library, it be round. This round room be my favorite joy.

My Money stubborn for no stairs. She want to stop, she clamp her hoof. But if you switch her, she will trot up fast and sudden like a going-upstairs horse that only bred for this. Room stink remarkable from her, but with the windows open, still can breathe without unhappiness. Yo, my hound ABC eat most her shee, in cleaning help.

Below the library window be a road, is mostly gone to bush. Become a shaggy meadow with bald patches where the street remain.

Across this meadow road be Friendly's, which say Friendly's on one sign, and Friendly's Ice Cream on the other. This been a store for trading food. But I ain't like to be called Friendly's anything. I know it ain't myself the sleepers meant, but it just feel disgusting. Then I remember ice cream been a food I never taste. I wonder what my mama dream to name me for this food, as if she name me Something Lost.

This Tember morning that I seen the roos, I woken early. Smoke my waking cigarette by the library window, looking out, and piney breeze come in to touch my face and brighten on my eyes. A sycamore grow close. Between its fingery leaves, can spy the Friendly store in bits. ABC stand by to whine. She think my cigarette be food. Ain't never learn, she watch it going to my mouth.

Yo, into the meadow road below, a doe-deer walk. She snuff the bushes, in a worrying way like deer will do. I watch her, wish I got my bow. Ain't guess I make my mark from here, but always be some lucky hope.

Then come a cracking loudness. It come again, it be like ripping, or woodpecker pecking hard, but twenty times as big. In the field, that doe rise up and buck lopside. Then she curling over and I see the beast shot through and through. Got blood more than hide.

And a boy jog into that bushy waste.

Then fear walk over me. I feel black water in my head from fear. He be a roo. Got brown furry hair upon his face and throat. He wear a roo suit – gray-green dapple thing, ain't satisfy to be one ugly color, it be ugly twice. Creature mostly twice my size. And his skin whitish like a no-luck sky.

Then some dozen roos with furren face and ugly suit come out and gather in that road.

My heart flee, scrabbling in my chest. ABC take breath to bark and I catch at her muzzle quick. Tug her nose down, press my finger to her brow. Her boogly eyes stare at me. I shake my head, but she still strain her mouth. So I keep her snout fast while I spy the roos go swarming, through that sycamore I watch.

Roos got cattish hair that never curl. All be males – or else their girls be square and bearden like a male. Children say they grow to seven foot, is bigger than no person. Yo, all roos wear the same. Ain't even deer got the exact fur that each other got. Roos all got one clothing, same as Beef-a-roni do.

They run in packs and hunt our people. In my foaly years, it been three children took from Massa woods. Ya, once a Lowell child found dead with gunshots. That been roo work. They slavers, maybe – or they eating children, how the Christings say. Nobody know. So roos coming for some mally years. Nobody know from where, they come from air and going into nowhere. All we know of roos, they take our children and the children ain't come back.

I stand and watch the roos. Be extra dozens now, they swarming to the bleeding deer. Then they go past in twos and threes. Is like a creek that gather round a boulder, then it slipping on.

Each one got a gun that is a rifle, long and black. One roo taken off his jacket, wear his rifle at his skin. Ain't got fur below his neck, despite what children say. Ya, they roos be talking, though I cannot hear particular words. All wear packs behind. A few be smoking like a person. And it inkle in my mind, the roos be roaming scratchers also. And I see that they be bell and vally in their shaggy sort.

Then I spy the blackish children come, the stolen. I count seventeen. Ain't bound, they walking free, but got no rifles. Be naked helpless with these jumbo roos. Then I fury with my pity in the hot palms of my hands.

Children ain't be Sengles, or I going to war for them, against a hundred roos or more. But these stolen children all be strangers to my eyes. Nor they look scary none, they got no blood nor blemish on their face. They walking leggy, strong. One be drinking Pabst, or can be water in a Pabst can. A roo talk one blackish child, and that child laugh. Yo, the child be mostly tall as roos, is only skinnier made. Calm my mally nerves to see, the roos ain't seven foot for nothing. Is tallish, but still person size.

In this, the roos gone took the deer apart, and wrap the meat and insides. Flowing roos just like an ugly dapple river, wash that unluck deer away. And they pass along and vanish. Is only scattern guts and hoofs remaining from that deer, and red confusions in the flatten grass.

They roos ain't seen again. A week behind, we keeping close to town, then we forget them mostly. Is only times I hear a stranger noise and hold with breathless nerves. Will only be a blackbird landing clumsy – but I magine hundred roos behind the hiding trees. Then our familiar woods look like a dream. Look like the safety you remember, sweet particular, as you fall into grandy death.

3

OF TOBER 2, PROLONGING

Now I be running to this roo, the day of Driver's cough. Evac door slam loud behind, and I run out where Driver strifing on the yellow boy. I catch and hold one stride away, beside Jermaine and Asha who be balking. No one want to be in Driver's trouble. My brother proud, ain't thank your help.

This roo so grandy, look like Driver wrestle with a pony. But Driver got an arm about his neck and strangle well. Roo reaching with his mouth to breathe and cannot. He seem to grow and grow, straining, then he slacken weak. Driver saying, 'Kick at me, I cut your goddamn throat. Lie quiet!'

Then Driver let up and the roo gust air, but he look beat and tame. He muttern words that ain't words. All his voice ill-shapen, rough. When he raise his arm, my Driver choke his voice again. Roo hush and gasp his breath.

Lying so, the boy be eerie. Got a face ill-shapen as his voice, flat like an owl's. Feary bluish eyes, and the color in his skin only starting to be born. Be like worm skin. But he thinking in his eyes. His arms and legs be like a person's. Is jeans and shirt like any.

In this quiet pause, Jermaine say nerviose to me, 'Ice Cream, you bone? Ain't find no strangers?'

I look where Keepers smoking in the window. I yell up, 'Be any living sleepers there with you?'

Then I got to laugh cause Keepers vanish from the window, can hear her feet come pounding down the stairs. I tell Jermaine, 'You watch, Keepers sure ain't frighten. You go ask.' My voice be high and scary and my laughter also.

'Going to frighten,' say Jermaine, surprise. Then he catch my meaning, and he laugh. 'Ya, Keepers proud as hatred, sure.'

Keepers scramble out and yell, 'You got to kill it, Driver! It a roo!'

Jermaine and me laugh wild. Jermaine tell Keeps, 'You violent, small! You fearing me!'

Then Driver say, his voice all booming nervy from the fight, 'Ice Cream? This a roo?'

When Driver look at me, the roo look also. He cannot turn his feary yellow head, but his eyes turn. You know then all they children look at me.

'Ice Cream,' Driver say again, 'a roo?'

How it is, I got no cause nor sense to help that boy. But his eyes be living. Eyes mean something at me, and I feel that Driver kill a roo. It be the only person he can kill.

'Ain't so like,' I say. 'Can be some other thing. Some alien thing.'

I fix the roo's weird eyes with mine, expecting he be thankful. But they eyes watch back unknowing. Comprehend no word.

Driver tell the roo, 'Be easy, child.' He loosen up his arm.

The roo jolt free and run. Run like a frighten person run from enemies. We all roar surprise. Roo sprint and cross the road in one thin second, running like an arrow. Keepers calling, 'Kill it! Chase it!' Then Driver pull his gun and fire. A string of grass and wet fly up.

Jermaine and Asha Badmouth swear. And in the broken road the roo crouch, balling down, and turn to face us. A gun look from his hands. The gun look back at Driver's face.

I go screaming 'Nay!' and swearing. Then I run to catch that roo,

I run all dreamy-legged and tired. Hold my empty hands up, and they feeling naked, frighten. Like if he shoot them, it hurt more than anything.

I keep between my brother and the gun the best I can. I be too feary to think of anyone but Driver. I ain't think at all.

The roo look at me first. I get his gun on me, and something happen in his dazy eyes. I think, *You see me. Kill me if you hungry for a death.*

The roo shout, jerk the gun. I slow to walking and I walk to him and he be flinching bad. He die to stop me. Ya, he closer, bigger, as I walk. He stand up to his feet, and he be grandy like a bear. The gun will take my hands in pieces. The gun will take my head apart.

I close the gun nose in my hand and all my children scream and call. I pull the gun nose down. Aim to my heart, my gut. The earth. My fingers gentle and I say, 'Let go, let go. Ain't going to kill me, fool.'

The feary roo be staring at my face. I notice I be crying. Crying for us all who got to die. And when the fire so huge, the sky so huge, and we be minnow small and loving. So I feel. The metal simple in my hand.

The roo let go the gun. Jermaine run up, and Driver run up, and they grab the roo away. We shouting back and forth, I ain't know what we shout. Next, my noisy Keepers punching at my legs and skree, 'You moron! You ain't get you kilt! You goddamn moron shee!' I laugh, eyes nervy on the roo, as Driver and Jermaine begin to tie him. He ain't resist, is soft bekept – like the pistol been his final strength I taken from his hands. Ya, his queery eyes keep to myself.

They bind him, then they lash him to the sledge. Keepers lose her fear and climb upon him, ride home on his chest. I be on Money, Driver sat behind. He hold me to himself protecting, his big arm about my waist, and I ain't push him loose. I ain't desire to. Big Smoke in front is prancy from the nerves of everyone.

This be how I take my pistol, first of any guns I own. This be how my Pasha Roo come into Sengle town.

4

OF CROW MY ANIMOSE

Riding home, we trace Road 27 through the older woods. This be an hour at a walk, and ain't no trotting on they broken roads. Be only holes and humps. Horse walk akimbo like a drunk.

Is dusking, and the birch trunks glamour white like paths of moon. A birch leaf yellowing here and there, for autumn now begin to start. Maple crowns patch red and orange, and Road 27 sprinklen somewhere with these color leaves. Be houses on this stretch, but all got ruin roofs, insides gone rotten. Telephone poles still leaning in their rows, but all the wire been scavenge. Heren there a blackness show where we been burn a sleeper house. Some already gone to aspen, some be starting meadow flowers.

Where we turn off 27, stand a sleeper sign, bright orange metal with black letters: 'BLIND CAUTION CHILD'. Behind it be Blind Caution Pond. This night, the frogs all creaking loud. Where there be frogs, is twenty times mosquitoes, and the night gone chill. We dabbit here to put on jackets.

My jacket's sort be Patagonia. This word stitch upon its chest. Be light, but unroll to a greedy size. Can wear two shirts beneath. Now I got my pistol in my jeans, nose chilling underneath the belt against my skin. When I tighten Patagonia's string, gun poke my belly. Then I feel the gunfire that there was, and how this gun been pointing at my face.

When I turn to look, the roo lie still as sleep. He bound upon the sledge from foot to neck, with rope and orange cord. Only be his fingers loose. But his ghost eyes look and blink. He be cold color like a gun. A feary birchen child.

Keepers been riding queenish on him. When we start, she perching backward on his chest, watch to his face. She guard our safety so. But Keepers quick to bore. Soon she climbing up and down; stand on his thighs precarious. Roo, he got no choice but to endure. So Keepers warm to him in sympathy.

Now she get a blanket, tuck it round the roo against mosquitoes. But this blanket wet for killing flames. The roo begin to shiver.

'Roo suffer,' Keepers notice.

Asha Badmouth saying to Driver, 'Been some blind child drowning in the pond. Become a caution to the others, ya. Blind caution child.'

'This sign ain't make no sense,' say Driver. 'Mean nothing, be like writing on a shirt.'

Jermaine go whistle in disgust. 'Foo, you said that last time. Told you then why it be wrong.'

Driver cough, but keep on talking. 'Sure I say it twice, and it be true both times.'

'Be foolish every hundred times,' say Asha.

Keepers shout, 'My roo be suffering!'

Everybody look. The roo lie in his ropes and shiver. Ain't look so grandy, lain like that. But his face got a spookery. Bluish eyes look like they knowing thoughts a child ain't made to hold. I get a shivering fear myself. Driver tense behind me.

'Ain't necessary he a roo,' I say. 'Can be a sleeper or nobody know what.'

Keepers frown her dignity at me. 'This one alive, ain't sleeping. And cannot call it sleeper. This give children fear.'

'Children name of Keepers,' say Jermaine.

I say polite, 'He need a jacket, ya.'

'Yo sho,' say Keepers, and polite me back, 'this be a kindness for myself and for my roo.'

I laugh. 'Be Keepers' roo, nobody touch this roo without permissions.'

I unzip Patagonia. All my skin dislike this notion, but I throw it to delighting Keepers. She pull the sogging blanket off the roo, and all his body ease. Is like the shiver strip from him. Then the jacket make his face go kind.

This be the moment that he speak, his birchen eyes on me. The word so simple everyone must hear. He say it clear. 'Spaseep.'

We all frighten then, as if this talking been a weapon. Driver close his arms about me hard. I breathe against his strength.

Only Keepers ain't concern. She shake her moppy head. 'Nay, you must say, "Be thanks," my roo. Or must say, "Be gratty."'

'You ain't know what his blablabla mean, small,' say Asha Badmouth, cricket-sharp. 'He saying, "I go kill you, I go eat your head with sauce."'

'My roo be thanking,' Keepers say, contain and lofty. 'In his words, this be spaseep.'

Driver laugh. Then everybody laugh, and Keepers shout, 'I got a keeping roo! My roo can speak! My roo go eat up Mouse's head with sauce!' We all giggling breathless. Horses shift and snort confusing. Asha Badmouth laughing in her warry melody; the girl can sing her voice into a valley of space. Ya, is always breathlessness in dusking woods somehow. Is everything insane and starry fine.

As the laughter ease, my Driver got me in a pinching grip. I buck my head against his chin. He laugh and loose me, swat my head. I want to laugh again, but all my laughter gone somehow. Be only conscience, how our laughter small in all this night. Gun chilling at my skin.

Then Driver take his jacket off for me. We wrestle some, but I allow the gift. Will not insult his care. When Money pick up walking, I got his Carhartt on, can feel his warm still in the cloth.

Our path go by and time walk with us. Soon the light become all moon. Yo, this been an hour to ride, and Driver only cough but once. I hold this in my mind. Mind make a fist on it. Some time, I think on my ghost brother, Mo-Jacques Five. When our mother Shasta die, I had him to my keeping – scrambly piglet with a mouth like Keepers. He been the brother of my arms. A small child die of posies quick, ain't ugliness nor hardly pain. Yet now tears swim down my face. Feel like they fill with moonlight, feel like they be sadness color.

Where the aspens done, is open night. The farming fields of Christing Tophet show in squares of different dark. Their home and barn got sleepy looks. Windows wave a reddish light that mean a fire lit, and wisty smoke come from their chimney. Sky be full with coldness, and this smoke go warm into its heart. Ya, John of Christ, their husband, be standing on the porch to greet whoever come, as Christing husbands do at dawn and sunset. These times be callen guesting bells. But we ain't turn down their road.

Then Sengle town begin to smell between the trees. It be a sweetish stank, as comfortable as my own farting, or as Money's farting. Smell puey in a friendly way, my town.

Sengles be unmannerly with trash, ain't civilize on this. Got cans and apple cores and papers, mix with leaf and piney needles, every-color on the ground. Though we dig privy pits at distance, be some littles fear to use them. Stray off paths near town, you put your foot in something you regret.

As we come into this townie smell, I loose the reins. Money pick her feet up, trotting glad. The path go sleek and clear, and soon can smell a campfire through the pue. Because it be no noise, can know the littles gone to nighting camp. Ain't nothing waiting but the stank and dark and Crow Sixteen.

Crow be stood with my hound ABC beside the fire. Fire is banken low. Its minnow flames go crack and smoke. Crow eating Nillas from a box. My ABC be munching one herself and got some lain between her paws. They two look sleepish in the shallow light.

Crow an uggety child, all froggen mouth with scarce no chin. Yo, his eyes be prettieuse, black-sweet and lashy. Face look like his heart, sly and wrong-made. But my ABC love Crow, and he keep kind to

22

her. When she been a puppy, Crow and I been animoses. Friends be close as grass and clover; animoses close as grass and green. So been our truth. We eaten every breakfast from one bowl. We set our snares together. Both was warry children: my bones rung with Crow's beating and his skin been always sore from me. We slept in one hammock, tangle-fashion, loose as cats.

Then he gone doing sex with Mari's Ghost. Mari get an enfant from this, when she been only twelve and Crow fourteen. Then Crow ain't speak to me no more. I set my snares alone.

Ain't no bitter like an animose is lost. What Driver say, it ain't no love like hate. Be days, I crave to look at Crow to hate his boogly face. I never want to murder Crow, for once he die, my hatred left alone like me.

Now Crow be fire-blind a minute, while my ABC come run to me, then wheel back to her Nillas – Crow standing, squinting at the roo. We all dismount but Asha Badmouth. Be a fine relief to come down to the sparking warm.

Keepers curlen on the sledge still. Got a cigarette lit. She smoke and give it to the roo to suck. Roo smoking glad. His winter-color eyes look round at everything; the fire, Crow, trash.

Now Crow swear quiet. He say, 'First I thought you fetch some Army back, but this.' His uggety head be tense. Then a strain come over all.

Keepers say, 'It be a roo or sleeper. Found it in a sleeper house.'

'Sleepers dead. Yo why you bring it here?' Crow grin, except the grin be angry.

'Can be living sleepers,' I say sharp. 'Be science that they know.'

'You bring this here,' say Crow, and half his face be grinning teeth. 'Ain't want no roos nor sleepers. Going to eat it?'

Keepers suck her cigarette, and speak a blast of smoke: 'My roo go eat your head with sauce. Crow head with crow sauce.'

Then Driver step towards the fire, and everybody ease. Yo, soon as Driver speak, it be like no one spoke before. We heed. He talk to Crow in quiet friendship, tell about the fire and roo. Crow nodding like a thoughtful horse; he love my brother yet, despite his ruin heart. Only when Driver telling how I take the gun, Crow look at me and his black prettieuse eyes go wide.

Then Driver talking on, but Crow ain't listen. And when my Driver finish, Crow say vicious, 'Expect the girls will save a handsome male. Yo, Ice Cream got eyes for this.'

Inside my stomach and my head, my hatred scratch. Crow look at me, Crow look away. My animose, he know my evil, but forgot my good. My skin be hot and thin with being known.

Keepers say, 'This roo be mine. Ice Cream be here nor there.'

Then Driver laugh the most of all. Jermaine and Asha Badmouth hoot and call to me, while Keepers looking strict. She keep one hand upon the roo his shoulder. Shake her head while every person laughing through her pride. Roo look far-off with frosten eyes and grief on his pale mouth.

When people quiet, Crow look to my belt. He say, 'I like to see the gun.'

I give the gun like Sengle give to Sengle. Give for asking. Driver there, it never worry me what happen next. Crow take my pistol. Lay her blackish nose across his palm.

Crow's evils be: vain, blame others, liar, make plans, ain't worry if somebody hurt. Give Mari's Ghost a baby when she only twelve, she hurt each morning of her life from this. Crow never care for Mari's Ghost, he ruin her without no heart. Crow's good I ain't recall, his good be doubt and mist. One day Crow brought a trout and say, 'Fish got a diamond in his gut.' I ain't believe him, so he throw the trout back in Blind Caution Pond. We watch for it to float up, but it never come. His good be like that diamond lost.

Now my mood fall in with Crow's. The jolie gun lie to his palm, warm from my belly. His fingers curl to grip it and his other hand slide out the magazine. That sliding click, delicieuse exact. He free a bullet, hold it to the firelight. Crow and I smile. (Crow a locken door in winter, Crow a poison well. Crow lost. I call him in my mind: Crow Ruin.) Behind me, Driver cough.

I say whispern, 'Be one prettieuse gun. Ain't try yet if she shoot. What you believing, Crow?'

Then be silence. ABC look to my face and wag, but Crow ain't look at me. He narrow on that bullet. Then his fingers shut on it and his eyes go to Driver.

'You be oldest,' Crow say.

Driver say, 'Is truth. And so?'

'Oldest choose his weapon.'

'I be oldest, got a gun already.' Driver give his nod to me.

'Second oldest be myself,' Crow say. 'My gun ain't working.'

'Villa second oldest,' I say. 'She deserve this gun. She shoot your legs and drag you to her hammock, greedy.'

Jermaine and Asha Badmouth laugh hard. Villa live for males and nothing else. She cannot hunt her foot if someone tie it down. Cannot hunt a roasten fish.

Crow say, 'Driver favoring his sister, all it is. Gun should be mine.'

Jermaine say, 'Damn, you wasn't there.'

'Villa need that pistol, Crow,' say Asha Badmouth, laughing yet. 'She hunt your meat, be sure.'

'I give the gun to Ice Cream,' Driver say. 'Can finish with this talk.'

Then the fire dip and darken. The forest seem to grow and lean towards us, angry dark. ABC make noise inside her throat.

Crow slip the bullet back into the magazine. He fit the magazine into the gun. All looking at the gun, and Crow say, 'Driver choose to bring a roo back to the town. Choose to give a gun to little sister.' He say this with sucking anger. ABC shy from his voice. Crow shy himself and look at ABC with nerves.

Then he turn sharp, and aim the pistol toward the roo. Keepers squeak and duck. Then pride hold her still. Feary Keepers strain her body away, but make herself stay on the sledge.

The roo go shut his eyes. If he frighten, it ain't show. Likely, he been frighten all this time.

Driver say, 'You shoot a stranger who be bound and cannot move. What you being then? You be how vally then?'

Crow's hand ease from its aim. Driver standing quiet, though I see him swallow. He say, 'Crow, give that gun to Ice Cream. Ice Cream, Jermaine, you tie the horses. Can leave the roo tonight. I be at nighting camp.'

His voice be angerless and tired. Then he leave, my brother pass to darkness in the farther trees. Nobody else hear, but I hear him cough a minute down the path. I hear him coughing hard.

Crow reach the gun to me. I take it careless. When our fingers touch, I look at Crow's face. Someday I look at Driver's face, when Driver been already dead. Everybody lost.

And Crow turn away and follow Driver down the nighting path. I slip the pistol in my belt.

'Ain't go to nighting camp without my roo,' Keepers say with pleasure.

Asha Badmouth say, 'Myself, ain't go without Big Smoke. Ain't walking on my feet.'

'This be different cases,' Keepers say. 'I love my roo.'

Asha scoff her breath. 'He loving you, I guess?'

I say, 'Cannot take no roo to nighting camp. He go escape and eat us all.'

'With crow sauce,' say Asha Badmouth.

'I fetch us hammocks,' say Jermaine. 'We sleep here and keep the fire.'

Then Keepers joying in her eyes. She say in happy voice, 'Spaseep, Jermaine. Mean gratty in their rooish.'

Our nighting camp be kept a minute's hike from town, clear from its trash unpleasantry. Summer grown thin then, so we strung hammocks in the reddish maples back of Christing Tophet. Hammock high enough, mosquito never think to go. Brook nearby, and everything the pure reverse of town. Is wild and tall with star bellesse.

But this night, is comfort sleeping in our townie stank. All person smells be warm somehow, surround you with their unwant life. Yo, is Money by in friendship, and my ABC. Even the roo seem kinder in my fear, now Crow dislike him.

Jermaine bring back four hammocks, but we only using three. Keepers nest up on the roo, where he be on the sledge. Yo, she start to speak roo language. Any word he speak, she parrot. Then me–Jermaine go parrot after, we all rooing to the stars. *Spaseep. Ott vyazee mnya. Bolna, syo takee.* But soon the roo gone silent, he look starward with his birchen eyes. Keepers curl against his ribs. His grandy hand be held in Keepers' hands and they be snug as twins.

5

MY PARLEY TO THE CHRISTINGS

No child ever know a time be happiness until it gone. Time Pasha come, when we still raiding in the Massa woods, I swore to worry. Yet this been before the Nat Mass Armies took no Massa child. Driver bell and vally still, he rule and never weaken. We live wolfen through our wars.

This morning when my trouble wake, Driver send me out to beg a housing for the roo. His judgment be, this perilous beast ain't safe to keep with Sengles. Must go where there be walls to keep him. Ya, the Christings own a cellar built for prisoning. Kept Armies there, in murder wars that been. So this morning I leave my Jermaine to watch the roo. Ride to see the digger folk at Christing Tophet house.

Before the murder wars, it been ten Christing homes in Massa woods. These people mostly fleeing north, whoever can survive. Now only Tophet stay. Ya, in time before and time remaining, Christings live the same. House got one husband ruling it, with any-number wives and every enfant that they breed. And all believe a god who live in two sticks. Each Christing wear around their neck a string with two sticks crossing – and truth, is healthy people. Can think, this god do something, they live fatter than no Sengle child.

They growing corn and tato and got apple trees and milking cows. They can make cheese, and Sengles bring them venison to smoke for winter. We catch them parrots also – Christings partial well to these. Parrots through the Massa woods caw 'Repent ye of your sins' and 'Jesus save'. Yo, Christings gave me Angry Bitch Cub, my Vermonter Stalking Hound, when she was a puppy and I been a puppy child of nine. Anyone give me ABC, that person treasure in my mind. I going to go and love the Christings then, and never stop.

I ride out by whisker morning. Worries be my company; about the roos, about my brother's cough. But most, I fix my mind upon my ask. Can know without no questions, Christings want no housen roo. So is problems, how I trick them to this unwant gift. It be a sort of mischief I accomplish any times, and soon my Sengle heart be brightening, grin its wolfen lies.

Then Tophet's edifice and barn show whitish in their pastures. Red cows look up with one feeble mind. I canter Money at the lower fence. She jump it easy as a cat, and all they cows come bumble to her. She put head up pickety. Act like cows be itchy, and go trot sideways away. Then John of Christ call from the step, where he got cider on the table in a glassen brock.

John of Christ a kindly man, and slow with pleasant life. Child keep thirteen Christwives dutied to his single love. These wives the same that chosen John, is how all Christings choosing husbands. Wives pray three days to Jesus for advice, then vote a male. Ain't know what Jesus say, but every husband of Christ be cake for eyes – is catly-faced and tallish bell. But Jesus never care for brains. A Christwife told me once, John telligent enough to hear advice, and they ain't need no more. I never met the person who cannot like John.

I dismount and tie my Money up, go climb their cleanish steps. Always I get shame for Sengle pigliness when I come here. Be no showing litter. House smell only of new food. All be painten white as white, and this the story's end.

John say, 'Greeting in His word.'

'His word enduring,' I polite him. Then I nod at that glass brock.

'Somebody told you I be bound here? Sure you ain't pour cider mornings for your only self.'

'You my second visit.' John get face like bad reminders.

A moment, I get curiosities, what this visitor been. Must be awful persons, if it giving John unhappiness. But I fix back to my need. 'I come with parley to you, brother. Thinking, is business you can like.'

'Be gratty heard,' John say, distracting still. 'Christ's welcome to our home.' He pour my cider tall and lead me to their sofa room.

Sofa room be where the Christing enfants spend their day. So it be enfants round your neck and grubbing on your leg, their fingers worming in your pockets. At Tophet, I known all these littles since they was a fatly belly.

This day Boy Japhet tend them. He be a seriose twelve with Tophet's copper skin and cow respect. Now he running desperate among the scarum enfants. Unpick their fights, tell disapprovals, answer screamen questions. When I come in, he line them up and make them say *Peace on you, sister*. Then they fall to strife again, and Japhet chase behind.

John call to the kitchen wives, require a guesting meal. Sit me to a fatty sofa, and he start in slow politeness, asking on my hunts. But all my conscience heeding to the kitchen, guess which wife will come. Can hope it be their kindly Hannah, or Jane Moron, slow to argue. Worst be Beanie, who dislike all Sengles and all asks.

Yo, when Susannah step into the room, I discourage well. This girl be the crown of wives. Got plum lips and thinking eyes, is never stepping wrong. She born the May that I been born myself, we be moon kin. Both love salty more than sweet. We both is handy quick. Been occasion, in our twelvish years, we riding cows together. Do races, and we talk into the dusking hours, like friends.

But she the smarter brains of Tophet. Try no trickeries, she name them to your face with easy laugh.

She bring a plate of apple fritters. Sit by me, and littles gather round her knees for food. Then all must thank the two-stick god before we eat. The thanking go: 'God be great and God be good, and we thank Him for our food.' I know this saying well, and say it firm. Ain't loss in good respect.

Then I say, 'These apples vally fine. Sure, your god bless all they trees with luck.'

Susannah leave this flattery heedless. Nod straight to my belt and say, 'You wearing pistols now, Ice Cream?'

'Ho, is right,' John say. 'This pistol new. Ain't notice this correct.'

'Ya,' I say with hasty thought. 'So be my business to yourself. Is where I jack my gun, be vally tales.'

'Ain't bought from Lowell?' John say frowning.

'Nay, my John,' I say. 'We catch a roo. This gun been his.'

Susannah fold her hands and mention Jesus.

'Shoo!' Japhet spit into his palm. 'Ain't no roos, it be a story.'

'Ain't existing,' John agree.

'Nay, truth,' I say. 'We catch a boy, look like a roo or yellow sleeper. Skin as white as teeth.'

'Christings got some light-skin people, sure.' Susannah doubt her mouth. 'Aaron of Christ been so. Was callen Aaron Sleeper, also.'

I shake my head. 'This be two differences. Roo's hair got no curling in it. Be like wolfen fur.'

'Ain't be a wolf?' say Japhet.

John laugh, frighten. 'Sengles catch a wolf and think they find a roo.'

'May be a sleeper,' I say. 'Run out from a sleeper house we burn.'

'Foo,' say Japhet. 'The littles hear. You spook their dreams.'

'What we hear?' say Baby Leah, curiose. Some other littles perk and ask what they did hear.

'Hush, hush, be a rabbit in the bush,' Susannah say.

'Yo sho,' I tell the littles, for I now feel mischief. 'Been a boy who fall asleep, and sleep a hundred years. Then come a fire that wake him. He run outdoors, and poom! Your vally Ice Cream thieve his pistol.'

31

Susannah laugh. 'Is bone, you found new friends to rob. It save our eggs. But how this be no business?' Now Baby Peter crawl up on her knee. She take him to herself and jog him there. Her eyes keep sharp on me.

I make a scouty frown. 'How Driver say, we must consult. A roo be every person's risk.'

'Can kill it?' John say nerviose. 'Is beasts or thinking people?'

'Foo, is people,' I say. 'Can talk. Been murder, if we kill him.'

'He talk?' say Japhet. 'What he said?'

I nay my hand. 'Be different words. Like fisher Panish, or . . . ain't English.'

'How he kept?' John say unhappy.

Now my trickery scent its game. 'Kept? Ain't know. I guess he been in ropes, when I depart.'

'You guess?' John say. 'How, you ain't know?'

I wave my hand dismissing. 'Villa there to watch. Ain't worry this.'

'Villa?' Susannah laugh in disbelief. 'You try to breed this roo?'

'Truth, Villa ain't responsible,' say John with worry face.

'Foo, most our children hunt these days,' I say. 'But if you fearing, you can take him. Got your cellar there.'

John flinch. 'Our cellar?'

'Ya, he safer here,' say Japhet exciting. 'I can watch him.'

'Nay, shoo,' say John. 'A roo ain't Christly beasts, to live with people.'

'We only thought you worry,' I say unconcern. 'Your cellar safest. Driver thought you maybe want him there. But if you ain't . . .'

Susannah give me narrow glance. 'If we ain't, he watch by Villa?' She swipe her finger through the fritter plate and offer it to Peter to lick.

'Today he do,' I say. 'But what we thought, if you ain't want him, we go sell him to the Lowells.'

John blink to this. 'You sell him? How, this roo be something worth?'

'Yo sho.' I make impressing face. 'The Lowells curiose for roos. They sure to want him awful.'

'And what the Lowells pay?' say Japhet.

I shrug. 'What Driver thought, they pay a horse.'

'A horse?' say John. 'Is worth all this?'

'Be sure.' I make surprising eyes. 'A roo be scarcer animals. But how you friends, we give good price.'

'Can pay you something.' Japhet turn to John. 'What we can pay?'

To this, Susannah break in laugh. Say through her giggling breath, 'You heed, Ice Cream? We take him, and we pay.'

Japhet frown. 'Nay, how this being jokes? Can sell him after.'

Susannah nay her finger, grinning. 'If Lowells going to buy him, Ice Cream been at Lowell mill this hour.'

John sit back frowning. 'Nay, she said . . .'

'Be Sengle sayings.' Susannah nod to me. 'Ice Cream want to rid him, so she try to fool our simple brains.'

Japhet think a moment, then turn indignant face to me. 'No sho?'

'Foo,' I say discourage. 'Sure, I try to fox you something. But truth, we got no walls to keep him. Ya, our children . . . how they is.'

'Ho, Sengles got some badness?' Susannah laugh. 'Be new discoveries.'

I shrug. 'Ain't careful people. And truth, your cellar bone for this. Kept prisoners there, when it been wars.'

'And now we keeping apples there.' Susannah shake her head, put Baby Peter from her knee. 'The apples you be eating, sister thief.'

'Be right.' John ease his face. 'No person wanting roos. Ain't natural beasts.'

'But he safer here,' say Japhet.

Susannah scoff her breath. 'Roo living underfloors? And all our littles roundabout? No sho, we–' Then she catch her voice. Fold hands and turn to John respecting. 'But it be your judgment, husband. Must ask Jesus word.'

33

To this, John get important looks. He mention something from their Bible book and close his eyes in thought.

This shut-eye posture mean a Christing pray advice from their stick god. But truth, their Jesus only tell them answers they already like. So I wait with plain frustration. Ask be lost, and Driver sure to blame myself somehow.

But as John bow his head, the kitchen door bang open loud. John look up in startle, ya Susannah–Japhet stiffen harsh. Only the littles keep their jumble noise, chase without care.

Child in the kitchen doorway be their posy wife, Jemimah. This girl gone in sickness. All herself be thin like winter branch. Face swollen out of shape, and cover thick with crusting sores. Only one eye be showing – ya, it got no white, no seeing color. Is only bulging red. Her breath come scraping, short, and she peer round her awful face, like seeking in blindness for her air.

By Sengles, when a child be took with posies, they be callen dead. No person talk to them, nor use their name. Is bad taboo. So when Susannah speak to Jemimah – like to any person – I get superstition chills.

'My sister, rest yourself,' Susannah say. 'We care for this.'

Jemimah say in wheezing voice, 'He gone?'

'He gone, be sure,' Susannah say. 'Was only trading here.'

'Ain't talk like I be brainless,' say Jemimah. 'Know why he been here.'

John say, 'Was buying cheese, for truth.'

'Cheese! He seen our Hannah?'

'No sho, he ain't,' Susannah say. 'You rest.'

'Rest? Ain't going to–' Then Jemimah choke. Cough and wheeze her air, a sound like strangling. And something happen in my heart. Driver's cough remind, all terrors of this passen night. I cringe and stare unbreathing to her face, her struggling chest.

Then, like she feel my dread, Jemimah push back. Slam the door behind. Can hear her wheeze, her dragging foot, as she go slow away.

Susannah put one hand soft on my shoulder. 'Be sorry, Ice Cream. Jemimah never known you here. She blind these days.'

'Foo, ain't no matter,' I say shaken. 'Be your house.'

'Nay, you guests,' say John unhappy. 'Wish you bone respect.'

'Be no disrespect,' I say. 'But who she fearing for?'

To this, all change their looks. Get faces of disliking memory. And John say heavy, 'Who been here before, was NewKing Mamadou.'

'Ya,' Susannah say in quiet voice. 'Their Army queen be dead.'

Take me a breath to comprehend. Then hurt change uncanny in my blood. 'You going to lose a wife, can see. Be sorry.'

'Be right.' John sigh. 'He come to see.'

'Choosing.' Japhet scowl disgusting.

Susannah frown to Japhet, like she warn him from some misbehavior. 'Be what it is. Ain't tell them nay.'

'He ain't take you,' say Japhet. 'I nay him, if he wanting you.'

'Ain't ours to choose.' John shake his head.

'Can give him Mary,' Japhet say. 'Or Beanie, no one want her. John, you told him he ain't take Susannah?'

Susannah stand up now. Her face be tired like regrets. 'Child, we cannot tell him how he do. It be the Long Agreement. But sure, ain't guess the NewKing choose myself. I got two enfants born.'

'Ya,' say John. 'If Armies take her from her enfants, this been bad respect.'

Now Japhet break in rage. 'They care for no respect! He ain't! He staring at our girls like animals. Ya, their queens be bell, and all it is. Ain't care for us!'

The littles hush, look scary to Japhet. Become a troubling silence. Then Baby Leah laugh at last and throw her fritter to the floor. Susannah stoop and take it, with her eyes still brooding on Boy Japhet. I grit my jaw and breathe in deep. Hold this sorrow breath.

'Foo conversations,' say Susannah soft. 'Ain't know until we know.

Now it be guests, you going to hold your mouth. Our husband pray decision.'

Then I must wait John's pointless prayer, if they will take the roo. I use this time to breathe myself to semblance, though my heart be knives. Heed their last refusal of the roo with patient face.

Yo, when I leave, the sun be scarcely risen to its height, although the morning feel so long. This day feel old and tired of me.

6

OF PASHA ROO

I tie Money in our horsen field. Then I go to a briar gully, overgrown and lonely, for first testing of my gun. Ain't brave yet for Sengles. Fear they asking on my visit. Ya, ever my troubles be, this pistol be a simple goodness.

First I check the magazine, and wonder on its missing bullets – if these been children shot or meat. I pick one out to learn their make. Is parabellum nines, a common sort the Lowells keep. Yo, I allow myself five bullets for this testing practice.

I shot my brother's pistol before, and this gun be like; is almost disappointing normal. Still, she shooting where I aim, her trigger flighty quick. Spring back to my hand with leap joyeuse.

But through this, my mind keep turning back to posies, find its hurt. Remember Popsicle and Lily of Gold, dead in this passen year; Abel of Christ who been the Christing husband before John. All been nineteen when they gone sick. Ya Sticking-bone live old, was twenty-one in posy dying. And my mind go through all dead I known, remind their posy age. Be some friendly twenties in this list, ya most be nineteen years. But be eighteens enough, and these names gather, sticking in my dread. Ya, Jemimah self be eighteen years, the same as Driver.

Ever I pull my mind from this, the NewKing waiting dark in mind.

Time I shoot the final bullet, my hand trembling awful. Gun mostly leap out of my grip. The bullet skew to nowhere.

Then I swear in underbreath. Poke the gun into my belt and head to Sengle town.

Town be a sally mess. Tents up since the yester rain, their orange color gone in grime. Is mudden trash around, and ashy circles from the evening fires. Across the town from me, one trickle fire still be lit. All littles scramble round it, and our hounds in bark delight. Some brats camp beneath the eating table, some hunt bluey caterpillars, some play war. Hate You Fourteen watch all these, while Mari's Ghost boil soup upon the flames. Yo on the easter side, two trees from me, be Keepers and the roo.

Keepers got a yo-yo and a cigarette. She blow smoke rings and send the yo-yo upward through the rings. Ain't successful, but this been her aim. The roo lean on a piney trunk and smoke a cigarette self.

The roo stand free. Ain't bound. Ain't guard except by petty Keepers. Like a prideful mouse go guard a bear.

Keepers spot my coming, and she run to me with grinning face. Drop the yo-yo at my feet and cry, 'Roo's name be Pasha! I been speaking roo all morning!'

I hold my speech. Be studying the roo. Standing, he goliath big, is sure a glory animal. Though his ghosty color spook me yet, he shapen normal. And as I look, he nod, the way a Christing will in greeting.

I nod back with skeering heart. Recall the children took by roos, for meat or slavery. But pride insist, must show no fear. I fetch Keepers' yo-yo from the dirt and cast it down. It rise fleet and fit my hand, while I ware on the roo.

Keepers say, 'I learn his talk so quick, it been like science. Next I go and learn the talk of deer. I go convince the deer to come be meat for us.'

'Deer ain't talk language, small. Be brainless creatures.'

'Ain't. Nor I ain't small.'

Here her victory ain't contain. She break, run pelting to the roo. He brace his arms and toss the cigarette. My heart freeze hard. His hands as big as Keepers' face. He going to go and squash her ribs, he throw her at the tree. Be late to shoot, my Keepers kilt in blood.

She run and raise her arms and leap. He catch her in the air and sault her high above his head. Keepers screaming in her joy. He turn her high above, and set and seat her to his shoulder. There she perch, grip with both hands upon his furry head.

I swear at her like any baby. My pistol wakeful in my hand, I ain't remember how.

Keepers call out, 'Roo's whole name be Pasha Sleeper! I invent him this last name.'

Roo fix on my gun, until I put it back into my belt. Then he ease. Smile up at Keepers, houndish warm, like any another child.

I say, my heart fresh with relief, 'He cannot be both roo and sleeper.'

'Ain't so,' say Keepers. 'Roos the same as sleepers, I figure this.'

'Sleepers all been roos?' I laugh thin and walk to them. 'Is curiose and wise. You be a well of truth, my Keepers Eight.'

'You guess how old he be?'

'I guess that you untie him.'

Keepers close her fingers on his hair and pull. The roo go startle, then he laugh and swat her fingers loose. Lift her to the ground, then go complaining in his rooish talk. When he grin, it be a thing to see. Child lack half his teeth. Be science how he going to chew.

Keepers say with knowledge face, 'Must guess! How old?'

'Nay, think what you do. You risking danger, but be older children face the danger. How I going to tie him now, without no Driver here?'

'You guess, then give me talk.'

'Where be Jermaine? I left him here to watch.'

'Roo eaten him. Jermaine done talk too much and never listen.'

'Keepers—'

'Roo be thirty years! Pasha Thirty Sleeper, older than nobody else!'

I chill down to my ankles. Put my hands behind me like this thirty be a catching fever. Yo Keepers look up at the roo joyeuse. Her eyes shine and convince. Is like she see the number thirty written on his brow.

'Nay, he lying,' I say weak. 'Or you ain't comprehend. Must teach him how to speak in words.'

'Roos live longer, ya. We been discussing well in roo.'

'Each beast live the same. Horse and hound and person live their eighteen–twenty years.'

'Parrot live more longer.'

'Parrot be a bird.'

'So roos be birds.' Keepers shrug. 'Hair be a kind of feather.'

I try to scout the roo for age, but ain't know how to look. Sure this child enormous big. Can be, he grown ten extra years.

'Why he ain't got posies?' I say rough.

'Ain't know,' say Keepers unconcern. She reach for the yo-yo and I give it to her palm.

'How old roos being, when they die? They die from posies like a person?'

'Will ask. Be many tricky questions.' Then Keepers turn and run across the trashy-bottom town. Hate You pouring soup, my Keepers go inspect. Ain't look back at me, nor at the roo. We be the past.

Roo smile after her. He scurfy with unwash, his shirt all dirty spots and torn. But his face bell enough, now that the strangeness grow accustom. Be a marvel in his bluish gaze and catly hair. Yo, as he smile, I notice webby wrinkles by his eyes. Across his forehead go two lines alike, is sketchen thin.

Ain't uggety to see, like wrinkle sleepers be in pictures. But I remind how Lowells say that wrinkles come from age. I scout along his other skin, heart beating furiose, but find no more. Is only stubble beard and smooth.

I get my cigarettes out. Is sleeper Marlboros; be stale, but smoke, if you ain't finicky. I pull a cigarette and show its filter to this Pasha. Must wait before he trust my gift.

He say soft, 'Be gratty.' The words pronouncing strange, as if his mouth was made for different sounds. Yo, we both smile, like this pronouncing been a friendly joke.

Bolden, I reach up in curiosity to touch his cheek. He look peculiar to this handling, but hold himself in stillness. Only squint embarrassing.

His skin be warm. Look frosty, but feel warm and soft like any another child's. I take my hand back to my side, and in my heart, an inkling rise.

If he thirty, this can mean that roos ain't get no posies. They live like sleepers, for uncounten years, until their skin be old.

But can also mean, they know a cure.

Now I remind the blackish children with the roos in friendly field. Ain't bound, nor they been feary. They gone with roos in willingness – and it gleam vicious in me, they been going for the posy cure. I magine how I find the roos and learn this healing craft. I see the cure like Robitussin, reddish sticky in a bottle. How it taste metallish, taste numb. How Driver grown to thirty.

But children took by roos ain't come back never. They be gone and gone.

I say in choken breath, 'Nay, truth, you thirty?'

Roo frown confusing, shake his head.

I point to him and say, 'You. Thirty years?' Then, three times, I hold up all my fingers.

Roo's face complicate. I try my gesturing again–again, but he frown only worse. At last, he say in his unshapen speech, 'Nay comprehend.'

He smile again, but I ain't smile. Frustration whisper: *Got to comprehend. Is lying simple.*

At last, I force a smile, say weak, 'You bony met, my roo. You bone.' I nod correct, and turn from him with spooken reveries.

I think to tie the roo again, but sure it be no use. If Keepers want him free, he going loose. She sneaky pests. Ya, be a mally satisfaction, how they Christings terrify, if they known. So I leave my gun with Hate You. Tell her sharp instructions, how she shooting if the roo start violence; how she threaten if he try escape.

Then I head back to horsen field. My duty been that I go hunting – ya, my heart regret its simple mind and quietness. But cannot leave my closer need. Must find more bullets to my gun, yo I must parley thoughts with El Mayor.

7

AT LOWELL MILL

Most my way lie through the wood. Be friendly ride, in company with gnats and peeping birds and squirrels. Only the last stretch lie through Lowell City, strange in emptiness. Here the houses reddish brick, three times the height of evac houses. Every street you pass, it be a thousand shatter windows. Blind windows fill half the sky, and all the streets be sparkling dangerous with broken glass. Ain't any a child live in these homes. Be no life here but sleeping bats.

Time I come to Lowell mill, that spooken city tire my nerves. Be glad to see their lectric lights and hear the cryer calling up. Be glad to see a movement in their windows, hear the larm of life.

Lowell mill a jumbo bricky edifice, long as a street. Got Lowell River on one side, and green canal the other sides; an island sort of building. Is five floors tall, and be five minutes walking to go past. Inside, be doory hallways, long enough to run full pace. Walls groan and groan, this be their turbine wheels that make lectricity. Lowell River turn these wheels, and Lowell River never rest.

Each Lowell got a room all to themself, got springy beds and blankets. They grow tobacco through the winter in a glassen house. Have water toilets, and they can make paint and tiles and furniture. Got ninety horses of their breeding, and they selling these as far as

Nampshire and the fisher coast. My Money been from them, flirtation gift of El Mayor himself.

No Lowell use a name. Each Lowell calling by their task and rank within – be Second Plumber or First Gardener or Thirteenth Custodian. Yo, as they grow in worth, their calling name be always changing – and if you call them by their younger rank, they insult furiose.

Now sun be bright upon the green canal. The river's sound of wish, wish, blend with the coop-up voice of Lowells. Even by sunny day, their windows glown with lectric light. Third Cryer perch above, on stony wall, and call her challenge to me. As I step to easter gate, I shout my name correct, and my requirement to their El Mayor.

Third Cryer call this news. Other cryers yell it on, the farther voices sounding sore bereft in all that hard indoors. A stabler come out, hurrying his steps, to take my mare. Then I come across their bridge. The door be open into goldish warm.

El Mayor be waiting in his workenroom, door 123. The door hang open, and he lying careless on a sofa. Wear cottonish pajamas, bluish stripe, with silken robe. On the floor, is papers cast about, and straddling books. Though El Mayor possess a desk, he shy from using this. Be a lain-down man. Can think, he only use his feet to walk from bed to sofa. Yo, with his slug behaviors, he boss two hundred Lowells smart correct.

El Mayor been Sengle born. We trade him as a seven with the calling name of Girl Egg. He suffer from the gasping illness, and his eyes been poory – be no use for hunting work. But sure his brains been healthy meat. The Lowells took him glad, and give us Villa Moron in his place.

Now he be eighteen, and he grown long in body, gracile. Got a face like to a handsome horse. Ain't the sort to please a Christwife, but he well enough, if you do take him for himself. Sure, been no girl egg in his making; child is male as bulls and bother.

When I enter, El Mayor go rummage up his limbs to stand. Look sleepyhead and glad.

I say, 'Ain't need to work your legs. Ain't going to chase you nowhere.'

'Foo,' he say. 'Stood up to get my arms around you, noisy. Got to squeeze your rudeness out.'

I dodge, but he come quick and grab me. Lift me off my feet, so all his chest be hard against. Can feel his lips' heat in my hair.

I say, my talk squish up and nervy, 'Got business to you, companiero. Leave your goating rest.'

He loose me slow, stand back with mischief grin. 'You rule my goating, Ice Cream Star. Ain't rest until you leave.'

'Goat on me another day, Girl Egg.'

He laugh to hear his Sengle name, and say in wistful flirt, 'Sure a spoon of you be better than three bowls of any another girl.'

He flop back on his sofa and unfold his easy body. Point to the end where I must sit. I perch on sofa's arm.

'How it is,' I say. 'We catch a roo.'

El Mayor go stare. 'You ain't, you lying package.'

'Tame and kept at Sengle camp. Smoke cigarettes like any person. Speaking words, is truth.'

Then I tell how the roo come to our hands. Give every detail of his looks, and I repeat his rooish words. Ya, El Mayor fix on this story like a hound will track a smell. Smell drag the hound behind it, into bushes, through the thorns. El Mayor almost sitting upright, how the thing enthuse his mind. Only thing I keep behind be Keepers' tale of thirty years. Be complication talks. Good sense decide, I get my bullets first.

When I end, he say with fever, 'Damn, why you ain't brought this roo?'

'Rich be lazy,' I say, laughing. 'Come and see him with your feet.'

'Who given you a pony?' he say, grinning. 'Fickle sort you be.'

'Shoo, I bring him soon enough. Unless . . .' Now I make fretting mouth. 'It be one worry, ya. Crow try to kill him, first he come.'

El Mayor's eyes narrow. 'Tell me better news. The roo tore Crow into his parts?'

'Nay, the roo been tied. Crow aim to shoot him, what it been. Sure Crow never wonder what this roo may have to tell.'

This be the way to catch the Lowells, children curiose as flies. Yo El Mayor grit his annoyance.

I say on, 'Crow gone worse, can swear. Child been my animose, I cannot hate him every way. But be wrongness there, ain't trust him now.'

El Mayor still frustrate in his head. He nod but listen poory.

'What worry me, be this. What happen . . .' I take frighten breath. 'What be in time to come, when Driver sicken?'

'What you saying, bell?'

'My Crow be sergeant, how it be.'

Now disgust change in El Mayor's face. I scent my trick's success. The Lowells never liking Crow. Ain't know the bottom of this circumstance, but truth be fact. Once, Crow give his shotgun to the Lowells for repair. When Lowells fix a gun, you know that gun be shooting forward. They fix every gun and pistol, even Nat Mass Armies can get service for their guns.

But they telling Crow his shotgun broke beyond their skill. Say it need a finking pin, and they ain't got no finking pin. 'You find a finking pin, come back,' they tell unhappy Crow.

I ain't expect no 'finking pin' exist in all of time. Believe these Lowells laugh about this joke all night and every day.

Now I say, 'Crow must be sergeant. He the oldest male.'

'Sergeant never need to be a male. Sure Jennifer been last.'

'But this be common for a leader. Children tell me even you is male.'

'Can prove you this.' He smile again. 'Wait only for permissions.'

I shrug. 'Ain't your problems, sure. Is only scary to myself. Crow want me for his sex. Fear it be violence, once my Driver gone.'

'Damn he do,' say El Mayor. He rummage up himself to sit.

'Damn is truth,' I say more fortey. 'Crow a mally wasp, ain't fear to hurt.'

'He try this with you? Seriose?'

'Nay, with myself. Got fear of Driver. But this be the secret truth of him and Mari's Ghost. Been force. And sure his pants be hungry for myself.'

Now El Mayor go balk. He look at me with weaken faith. Yo, I remind unhappy, El Mayor know Mari's Ghost. No male forcing Mari's Ghost. Her only word be yes.

Then a grin start on El Mayor's mouth. He shake his head and laugh.

Here my show of anger weaken. Cannot help, I start to smile. El Mayor leap on me, shouting, 'Lying fox! I teach your mouth to lie!' Downstairs he tickle at my ribs. Upstairs he try to kiss my mouth. I kick him every which way. At last I bite my teeth into his chin, and he give room. Flop back to the sofa, gasping breath.

'Bad I took that bait!' he say. 'Goddamn. The roo been truth?'

'Foo, it all been truthful mostly. Got an aim, but . . . nay, the part with Mari's Ghost ain't true.'

'Crow bother you for sex?'

'Nay, but–'

'Honest as a Sengle! You an honor to your people.'

'Shee. You be a pinching pain to all my Sengle people, Girl Egg.'

'Sure, they rid my painful self. So what you want? Can guess you foxing me for something.'

I sit up, arrange my face into some dignity. 'How I said, I take the gun.'

'For your defense from Crow.' El Mayor laugh.

'Shoo, need bullets with–without no Crow.'

'This be some bullets of mine, I foresee.'

'Parabellum nines. I like to pay, but it be hungry seasons. Winter coming soon.'

'Ice Cream, you be a Lowell in your crafty head. Be a loss to joy that you ain't trade to us.'

'Foo, say yes. Need no suspenses.'

'Yes and yes. Sure I give you any foolish riches, every child know this.'

My heart clear in relief. I put my hand upon his ankle, for it be closest to. 'Be gratty well.'

A moment, we only grinning to each other, happy from our jokes. Then he look to my touching hand. Can see he think to reach for me. But I say, sudden out of nothing, 'Keepers said the roo be thirty.'

A moment, El Mayor still yearn his eyes. Then he flinch sharp. 'Thirty? Thirty years?'

'What he telling Keepers,' I say breathless. 'She talk to him all morning. Was rooish that they spoken, so she ain't learn much. But this been certain.'

'Keepers?' El Mayor's face ease. 'Been tales from only Keepers?'

'Foo, I know when Keepers lie.'

'So you believing this?'

'Ain't know. But roos be other people. Can be sleepers, any strangeness.'

Now El Mayor sit back in puzzle. 'So if they sleepers, sleepers ain't get posies?'

'How they ain't?' I scoff my breath. 'They getting WAKS. I thought your Lowells say that WAKS and posies been the same?'

'No person knowing certain.' El Mayor pooch lips in thought. 'But white people dying quick from WAKS, ain't living extra years. It been our children mostly live. Had some resistance to this pox.'

'Then roos must have some cure. They white themself. Should all be dead.'

El Mayor nod like this be usual notions. 'Or they from a place that ain't infect. Can be this.'

'Nay, thought it been the world entire.'

'What we think. Ain't seen the world ourself.'

48

'But every evidence say, it been the world.' My voice come thin. 'Most likely be, roos got a cure. Ain't see?'

'But why they kept this to themself? Roos coming here before.'

'Goddamn, they got no reason they will help! Yo think! You only contradicting!'

El Mayor look surprise to me. Ponder on my face a moment, then his eyes change sorry. 'Ice. Keepers be eight.'

'So she eight,' I say in weaker voice. 'And so?'

'Ain't get excitements, from some eightish tales. You think. She learn his rooish speech in hours?'

'Was only numbers. Can learn numbers. And if it being right?'

El Mayor look down, discomfort. 'Ice . . . you thinking of your Driver?'

I startle queery. 'How you meaning?'

'I know he got his posies.'

'Nay, how? Who saying this?'

'Ain't no one saying. Driver come to me for papa tea, to ease his hurt. Sure, he ain't want everyone to know.' Then El Mayor's face painful, like his memory see someone suffer hard.

I watch his sadden face, and cannot get a breath inside. 'Ain't posies certain. Nay.'

El Mayor look startling to me. 'You ain't known? Damn, Ice, I speak this to you first?'

'Nay, ain't certain. Cannot be.' When the tears come up, they rush like breath. My head be stars and hurt.

Then come a blind and sobben time. El Mayor come clutch me to him, and I weep against his shoulder. Try thinking of my pride, but misery wash my mind in circles. Can only think of Driver. How he keep this silent, and the months he going to sicken. How he going painful, going to die, and every grief be rain.

Posies take each person in their sort. Popsicle cough his spirit out. Jay-dee's belly swell and hurt until she claw it to the blood. Mailman strangle in his throat. He strangle once, then find his breath. Strangle again, and beg for help. Then he cannot bear to wait, he shoot himself in desperate fear. Jennifer been sergeant last. She scream but she forgotten words. Ain't recognize our faces. Scream a week, then she ain't speak no more. She stare and dribble her mouth.

And all their face and skin eat up by red and blackish posies. Posies scabbing and they open into sores and horrors. Posies grown inside and outside, blackish death put roots into your body and its flowers bloom.

My death must come before his death. I start a murder war, and all my Sengles die in blood. I blind my eyes and never see the posies come. I shoot my heart.

El Mayor be muttering, 'Damn, I hate to see you cry, goddamn.' His voice come through my panic, and the sobbing soften in my chest. I open eyes, and there be his cat Radio, perch on sofa's back. Be a whitely kitty with one crinkle ear. Sniff at me curiose. I laugh a teary laugh, and El Mayor touch to my cheek. He say, 'You going to kill me, you keep crying.'

We sat up on the sofa now, press close. All the room seem big and light. The bricky wall look warm; the yellow painten wall look clean and kind. Yo Radio hop over to the windowsill. There she arch and say her yorry miaow. Behind her in the window go the river through the tumbledown bridge. River slip around the beams, the metal splay and twisten. I watch the blackish bluish brownish water till my spirit settle. Radio sit in my view and lick her rosy pawpad.

Cat's name be Radio because this be El Mayor's present work. He get a dozen radio machines, and swear to make one talk. Before this, been a cat name Gypsum, and a cat that change its name from Plumbing Joint to Insulator. So El Mayor intend to puzzle back the world of sleepers, cat by cat. And all the Lowells copy after him, got cats name Coffee Plant and Airplane, things these children sworn they will create.

It come to me that cats ain't live no twenty years. Be luck that Keepers ain't remember cats, will be one gloating little. I think now to tell El Mayor about the roo his wrinkle brow. But he lean to me then and kiss my lips.

Be something like a gift how I forget to tell him nay. A minute we been kissing, then five minutes it prolong. What happen in my mind and blood be dizziness and sparks. His fingertips stroke feather-ish on my nape.

He gather me to him. Pull me down, and we lie out along the sofa, front to front. I feel his hardness at my thigh, a fever wake into my skin. The kiss slow and feroce, this kiss contain all feary luxury.

But my panic wake. Cold prickle all my hairs, and without thought, I push him rough from me. His hands pull me back, refuse to notice. I say, 'Nay. Leave me free, goddamn!' Be shaking, sweat go bright along my nape.

He freeze. Pull sharp away and scramble awkward to his sofa side. There he sit with wretchen face.

He say, 'Some strange dislike you got to me. Can say this.'

'Quit, quit.' My trembling ease. 'Beg you gratty, quit this.'

'Ain't never quit to hunt you, bell. I go find you a room in Lowell mill tonight. Can stay with me, and damn this Crow, whoever being sergeant. Here you be anything you like. Be a Sengle, all I care. Lowell First Thief Sengle, be your name with us.'

'Lowell Seventh Girlfriend, be more like.'

He smile but his eyes darken. 'Ain't need they other girls, if you been here. Can swear you this.'

'I cannot help your want.'

'Why? You got someone? No sho, you ain't.'

There be no why. Ain't know what tale to tell. I think of NewKing Mamadou, the enemy I yearn upon. How he capture me in guilty dreams. But my spirit seize resentment, how I care for this when Driver sick.

I shake my head. 'Sadness, all it is. I got no feeling to this now.'

'Sure, comprehend,' he say with poor belief.

Then no more parley can be spoken. He call a runner down to Lowell First Contractor for my bullets. We wait, and El Mayor tell nonsense of his loves with other girls. Sure he boast to rid his shame, but that ain't make it joy to hear. I mood myself to leave.

Soon I say my parting words, and El Mayor polite me wisty. The noise of Lowell mill slip back from Money's trotting hooves. The dusking sleep of Lowell City take my loneliness. I ride home to my full-grown trouble, to my people few and feary small, my Sengle town.

8

BY DRIVER'S HIDING MEADOW:
TOBER 3–15

These be the Sengles in the time I speak of, when my trouble grown. Of baby children, be Bother Zero Tool, the Answer Zero Ka, Fine One Ndiaye, Bell Eyes One Ndiaye, and Lolina-tina One Diouf, Crow's child with Mari's Ghost. Be healthy screaming babies, they got grandy rolls of fat. These all got mothers living but the twins Bell Eyes and Fine.

Of littles, there be Dinty Moore Two Fall who cannot hear, Naomi Two Forgotten, Maple Two Diop who be a son of John of Christ, Mohammed Three Insulting, Story Four Duval that has got reddish hair, Problem Four Tool, Luvanna-Lana Five of Lowell, Best Creature Five Wang who is misname and be annoying, Mustapha Five Insulting, Dollar Saver Six Fall, a fine enchanting little who can sing, Baboucar Seven Grandpa, Jeep Cherokee Seven Skips and Foxen Seven Fall. The mother of all three Falls be alive but gone to Lowell, now name Lowell Second Plumber and got posies bad.

Of the eights and nines, there be my vally Keepers Eight Fofana, worth all other children, and her favorite hatred Mouse Eight Wang. Progresso Nine Wilson and My Sorrow Nine Wang been solo-animoses for some years, ain't speak with never another child.

Then come Marlboro Ten Tete-Brisee and Kool Ten Tete-Brisee,

53

twins, birdcatcher-age and lean. Shiny Eleven Angels be a prettieuse and flirtish girl that give bad sign of wisdom, for she dabbit after Crow. Shiny chosen her own name, this be the measure of her wits. Redbook Twelve Ba, Bowl Thirteen Tete-Brisee and Cat Fancy Thirteen Ba all go ridiculous in love with Driver. They tend the littles and tell reveries one to the other, all day long. Jonah Fourteen Feet the only weakly jones, and scary since his brother took to Lowell two years gone. Then come Jermaine Fourteen Uptown, Christing born and Christing seriose in gentleness. Jermaine be wisty for my love, and many Lowells also and some Christings sleeping hungry for my love.

Next be Tequila Fourteen Tool, Mari's Ghost Fourteen Diouf, Hate You Fourteen Ka, and Asha Badmouth Fifteen Feet. Then come my place. Then come malicieuse Crow Sixteen Doe, and Villa Seventeen Insulting, fool infatuate for any male. When she ain't bother males, she eat, that be the list of what she do. Last come my Driver, which make thirty-eight in Sengle town.

These been my Sengles in the year when Driver been our sergeant; time that kindly John been husband of the Christing fellowship; when the Lowells' El Mayor been Sengle born and Sengle brave. Mamadou was NewKing of Mass Armies, savage like his people – yet the child have dignity and sense, best of the worst.

Fat luck been the story of this year. Snares ever struggling full, and every arrow find a turkey. Any a sleeper street we did maraud, that street give food. We war like twenty guns, but no one injure. Sling our hammocks in the crowns of sycamores like secret birds, and rest there, chattering and smoking, noses to the stars. Children forgot the taste of hunger and the touch of fear.

Yo when Driver sicken, this the happiness we lose.

These early Tober weeks, my Driver woke before us all. He walk out to his hiding meadow in the frosten dark. Half the day he leisure there. Brew papa tea against his pain and drowse beside the fire. Times, he lie down on the ground to cough. Hurt him less so. Then he work at coughing like a task. He try to cough the wrong out, but that sticky wrong ain't shift.

In a brook that dabbit by, he wash himself – for he ain't going to show his body in the stream at Sengle town. Got posies on his leg. They only be a few, and ain't disgusting. Only is blackish spots. Yet no one can see this, or all children going to know his sickness. And how it is, the posy sergeant must be callen dead. He go apart to useless silence, and another sergeant must be chosen this same hour.

Become my habit that I gone to meet him in the hours of dew. I bring ABC and Money, led on leash and halter. Feel they know my trouble, feel their caring hid in beastish tact. We pace the morning damp together, and our silence knit in one. All the morning birds sing with our feeling.

This meadow set behind an unroof house. Been three sleeper hounds dead there, most reason that the field abandon. No child love this place. House got wooden sides, once painten yellow, now be any color. From the house's understep, a frazzle hose come out, is greener than no grass, look like a snake in corner-eye. The day that Driver name our trouble, I feel something evil here. Is like a ghost remainder from the evil times before.

'Town been feeding thin these weeks.' So he begin.

We sit frogleg in the grass beside a low tea-fire. I still be sleepy-head in thought, watching Money graze and twitch her skin against the flies. So I say distracting, 'Meat gone cautieuse, and all it is.'

'Meat come back, but scarely be no Sengles fit to hunt.'

'I been hunting rich.' I scratch my fly-bit neck and yawn. 'Had some owes to pay, but now they done. Be fatter now.'

'Cannot feed only from yourself.'

'Is Crow ain't bringing meat to town. Child pigging to himself. What I suspicion–'

Driver's voice raise up. 'Nor I ain't hunt this week.'

My eyes stop on his face. He sad as water then. His blackish skin be grayly, and his looks lost their bellesse.

'I go ask John of Christ for corn,' I say rough, 'if worst become. They Tophets wait for pay, they ain't particular in this.'

'Ain't no John I know myself, who trade you corn for nothing.'

'Trade for promises.' I shrug. 'He easy for a tale. Must only go when their Susannah missing.'

'Sister, cannot pay with lies forever.'

Then Driver breathe in sudden, and he cough. Cough take him hard, it look like something kicking in his ribs. My nerves go thin. Yo, while he suffer, ABC come nosing round, stick in her mouth. Her tail aloft and glad. I swat my hand in air beside her nose, and she go off low-held.

At last, my Driver quit to cough, stare empty at the fire. And he say low, 'We be too few.'

I shrug discomfort. 'When Jonah grown to size, be better seasons.'

'Nay, child. We be too few.'

'Sure, our jones be few, but we had skinny years before.'

'And Crow be sergeant? What this be?'

'Ain't no joy,' I say uncertain. 'But he strong. Can hunt.'

'Nay, heed,' say Driver. 'If I be gone, you go to El Mayor.'

I hunt his face for meaning, but his patience be like unmark snow. I say, in nervy joke, 'This be some going that result in babies?'

'Ice Cream, sister. Go and stay. El Mayor will take our Sengles. Take even useless children for your love.'

'Stay?' I huff a disbelieving breath. 'We all be Lowells now?'

'You all be fed. Be safe to live.'

'But ain't be Sengles. We be some worthless beggars in their mill. Ain't no hunger worth this loss. Nor Crow allowing this. And he been right, we Sengles. Be ourself.'

Driver shake his head. Bend to the fire again with painful frown.

I glance at that hose, my eye mistake that it been sneaking toward. Shiver and feel, this be a ghosten place my Driver chosen. Is like I visit Driver in his death.

Then Driver say, 'Your hound be foo, look there.'

He point. I look and see that ABC been took her stick to Money.

Set it down before her hoofs, expect the mare to throw. Money stare uninterest, a sprig hung chewing from her mouth. ABC bark up, instruction in her voice. Then she feel us watching. Hound look to us, confuse and panting. Look back at the stick, like she get conscience that she been mistake, but ain't see what is missing yet.

I laugh bold and sweet. And laughing make our quarrel easy. Driver told me sense for years, and never I give him yes. No reason that this talk be different, laughing make me feel.

But when he take my hand, I fear again. My heart gone small.

He say, 'My stubborn, heed. Been talk, the Nat Mass Armies want to take you. Once they knowing I be sick . . . ain't only hunger that you need to fear, Ice Cream, is slavery.'

9

OF NAT MASS ARMIES

When Sengles come to Massa woods, it been three peoples here already: Lowells, Christings and the Nat Mass Armies.

With the Christings and the Lowells, we had truce from the beginning. Never our tiny thefts and misbehaviors hurt this peace. But with the Nat Mass Army kings and featherboys, been war. Yo, war be ever our respect to all their cockroach hearts.

How Sengles will rob eggs and corn, the Armies robbing girls. They take them to do sweating work, and for unwanten sex – for any nasty use that be. These slaves be callen simper girls, and they lose every other name. Ya, every Army baby born from these unlucky children. The Armies give their own girl enfants to the Christings, when they grown. Trade for Christing males, whichever ain't been chosen husband. So Armies all be boys, and any females in their town be slaves.

Sengles hate a slaver worse than our bad luck. We hate their sally smell from drinking, and we hate their feather heads. Will raid their chickens for this hatred, or we run to skirmish. Ya, they raid us like a stenching wind, come wild and evil. From twelvish age, all Sengles harden to this war farouche.

When our greats arrive in these wood forests, this been murder war. In they times, the Armies stolen girls from Massa woods. Now, for years and lives, the Armies slave afar, from fishers and Vermonters of the north. Will travel off two days, then stalk and rob a child while her town sleep. Only the Army queen be took from Christings, by their old agreement.

Yo, as our woods grown soft in peace, our Sengle wars grown soft alike. In my time, our war knives sharpen only at their tip. Make cuts prettieuse and reddish but ain't take no life. Our wars be beating-wrestling strife, for pleasure of our hate.

Armies come to war with feathers braiden in their hair. Be like fighting with a hatred bird, no pity in this case. Your one hand have its knife, it hurt from holding on so hard. You slash and beating at his head until you breathing hard and tired. Until it feel a kind of lonely. And close, you smell that feary unwash slaver who dive his knife at you. Can smell blood when you cut him. On a colder day you feel his warm.

Been one occasion, in my younger memory, we fight to murder. A Sengle girl was taken careless for their Army rape, and in wars of vengeance, Dogness Fofana was kilt. They been the years of NewKing Hak, a spider-hearten wretch. But he become the OldKing now, is gone in posy sickness. Already he kilt his queen and burnt her gods.

Now is NewKing Mamadou, as honest as a knife. He Army, born without a gentle turn, but keep his slaves in fatness. Yo, he bell to love. My own heart's secrecy been his, my cat insanities of night.

But he die seven deaths before I capture so, I swear my heart. Be ever a hundred Armies, I go shred them all to blood despair. Be screaming on this land to them and broken dreams, be hell and hell.

The sun be risen now, is cold and feary in the sky. Where I stare across that poory yard, the sun's bright ache. And Driver's hand be hot in mine, his skin unhealthy dry.

I say hoarse, 'They insects capture nothing. Kill them all, they try this.'

'You stop them how? They got twelve boys is grown to size. Without myself–'

'Who even saying they will take me?'

'Better you think, who fight them. Ice we be too few.'

'But Lowells–Christings fight them also.'

'For Sengles?' Driver set his mouth. 'Cannot expect this, sister. If you gone to Lowell–'

I flee my hand from his. 'I go defeat your Armies, weakness. Who fight them, be myself.'

Driver clench his hand into a fist. 'Can leave your mally pride. How you will fight twelve boys?'

'Who–' My voice choke in my throat. 'Nay, who will take me? Mamadou?'

'Is Armies. Ain't no who.'

'Nay, how this be about myself?'

'Shoo, my sister. Ain't about yourself.'

'Nay, Mamadou ain't try this. Is only talk. Is only how they insects talk. They never dare.'

Driver shake his head, frustrate. Turn back to his fire. My weakness dry while he reach out and bed a new log in the embers. Now he grow a silent anger, sure I know him well. I crave to tell him what he need. But Mamadou be red in my hurt conscience.

At last, I say, 'But while you strong, they leaving us?'

'Ice Cream.' His shoulders tense. 'Must think beyond this.'

'But if you keep–'

'I ain't. You cannot think this way.'

'Nay, posies is our trouble, brother. Can be help for posies. Children live to seventy in sleeper times, you know this tale.'

Driver stand up from his fire, his lips gone tight in rage. 'Ain't sleeper times.'

'Yo sho, the roo–'

'The roo. He give you pharmacies for this?'

'Nay, but–'

'You know he ain't.' He spit into the fire. 'Beast telling lies and baby children go believe these lies. Can leave me from your noise. This talk be done.'

'Ain't even listen. If we—'

'Nay, can go. Go on!'

I stand up to my feet. 'Ain't be no slaving. All I say.' Driver start to me in anger, but I turn by quick and stalk to Money. I catch her mane and mount, kick her into a hasty trot. ABC come chase behind, and bark her worry bright.

Yo while I ride, my heart be clear. I know what I will do. Be something Driver ain't forgive, what no good child forgive. But if evil can save Driver, I will love all filth. And I heel Money to a gallop. Already be pulling the pistol from my belt in readiness, as I ride hard to fetch the roo.

10

OF PASHA ROO HIS LIES

It been two weeks since we found Pasha Roo, and he accustom well. No one think to fear him now. Is horsen in his mild respect. He townie with our littles, ya, he doing tasks his own. Nor he ever budge to leave. Is there and there, like rooten plant.

Yo, every day of those two weeks, I ask him on his age. At nighting camp, the roo must talk to me or he ain't smoke. Most meals I give him from my hand, nor any a bite he take without an answer. Keepers taking gifts from me to teach him English speech. The roo be duteous to this. He always trying, asking words, and soon can talk as good as threes.

But all my trials end in frustration. Be English or be rooish, he ain't know one truthful word.

Our first talk go like this:

'Where your other roos be?'

'Far.' He give me friendly smile. 'Ain't fear.'

'Ain't fearing, only wondering. And every roo live thirty years?'

'Nay,' say Pasha, eyes gone careful.

'How you live so long?'

'Ain't kilt.'

'Nay, why you ain't got posies?'

'Posies?'

Here we snag and go no farther.

*

I tell Keepers to explain him posies.

Keepers sniff and say, 'He know this well. You seen his teeth half gone? Was lying rot them out.'

'Nay, he truthful in this case,' I say, for I ain't know him yet. 'Explain him posies, little. Will be cigarettes for you, and meat.'

Our second parley sound like this:

'Roos all living thirty years?'

'Nay, been lucky, me.'

I given him a bag of raisin cakes, he eat this vally fast. The sparkly noising of the plastic bag pick at my nerves.

I say, 'What luck? You ain't get posies how?'

Pasha concentrate on cake. No thought be in his face. His hand slip in the bag, flee to his mouth. Mouth labor like a mill.

'How you ain't got posies? Hear me speak.' I reach and grab the bag. His careless hand hit mine and all his body startle.

He study how I tie the bag. At last, he lick his lips and say, 'An insect.'

'Insect?' I stop my tying.

Pasha start to talk all speeds, his eyes still watching to the cakes. 'Yo insect living near. Be brown with legs. Eat him, be no sickness. Sickness go.'

Joying, I give back the bag. Ain't scarcely breathe for want. And sure my pity warm to him. Every Sengle must be fed before the roo can eat. Now Pasha's face gone tired with starving, any a child will sympathy.

He discuss the insect, its brown color and its lair. Which part contain this pharmacy. Discuss and eat. Cakes finish, and his eyes be fat joyeuse.

Take five minutes of this gabble. Then my mind go bright. I say, 'Yo lying cockroach!'

'This ain't cockroach. Nay.'

'Admit your lies, ain't be no curing insect.'

Pasha look his thinkless way. 'Ya. Ain't insect. Be a fruit.'

Here I realize, this child ain't care for being liked.

I say, 'You trust me too far, Wish-To-Die.'

'Ice Cream bone. I trusting, yes.'

'Ice Cream will beat your head to soup. I feed your liver to my hound.'

'Ain't comprehend.' He wipe his lips in good content. 'Words crafty.'

I try asking where roos be from. One day, he say they live west of the mountains. Other day, they live beneath the sea, and roos breathe water.

All roos be boys, he go agree with me, one day. Another day, roo girls be prettieuse as pocket-flowers. In their country, be moths as thick as rain, eat clothes right off your body. Roos ain't die at all. Roos die at nineteen, just like any a child. A roo will grow to fifty feet, when he been live a hundred years. Was giant roos built all the houses. Other children cannot reach the roof.

Roos feel no shame, this be the only fact I learn in all this talk. And days go by, and ain't come back. My Driver looking gray and thin.

I tell Pasha, 'Never you be thirty. You be a three, a nonsense enfant. Ain't got sense to chew.'

'Cannot chew,' he say. 'Ain't give me food.'

Ain't that he shy from talk. Be only meaning he dislike. Roo will blablabla with glad respect. Learn English faster than no sense, got noise for every company. And any a painful child can spend their boring talk on Pasha. One day, Best Creature and Baboucar play at throwing dirt into his hair. Roo shake it off and smile. Dirt soon be dog shee, dirt be rotten bones. Pasha never bother. Hour pass, he shake it off and smile. Next day, Best Creature and Baboucar feeding Pasha from their meal, they be his fetching hounds. Then Pasha go friend Mari's Ghost and Villa – girls that chase for any male. Pasha never mind their giggling foolerie. Be no boring word he ain't lick up, and look for more.

When I been still of bookish age, before I burden up with task, I read a book called *For My Country*. Be memories of a person, Jack Devont, who call himself a spy. He ain't succeeding well at this. Soon in this book, he capture, took to solitary prison. There Jack Devont must count his steps and shave to keep from madness. Truth, this prison boring for myself. Like Lowell mill with worser food. Nor I ain't so rich that talk of maudy food will interest. I chew some rotten food all weeks of life without no talk. The early, spying pages been my pleasure.

Been in a town name Soviet Union. Sleepers there be callen Russians, and he acting like a Russian. Jack Devont wear Russian clothes and speak their Russian language. Got some papers saying he been born in Soviet Union.

Now, be times I wonder if this Pasha spying for his roos. Ain't move to leave us, though he left unbound. And no one tolerate Baboucar's talk – yo, for their country, spies will suffer. For their country, spies be quick to learn a stranger's speech.

Can think, no child will need to know a thing Baboucar tell. But come a time, I long for some Baboucar Roo, who spill his truths unthinking; a Villa Roo that hunt my sex, and tell me any wanting fact. Never a roo be boring to my mind, no roo will tire my love.

One other thing I learn from Jack Devont. Someone ain't answer sense, can torture them to make them tell. Use burning for its pain and drowning water for its fear. This a matter OldKing Hak once practice on his Army slaves – yo Hak is callen Spider-heart, Disease, by his own people. Never a Sengle do this filth. Ain't done in jalousie nor war.

But for Driver, I forgotten honor. I will love all wrong.

From the hiding meadow, wild, I gallop hard to Sengle town. ABC ain't keep our pace, she go off in the bushes. Yip her disapproval as she go. I ain't wonder, I ain't look. Hate fill my eyes like night.

In town, be morning meal. All children round the folding tables, yappit and larm. Got rabbit fry and wheaten cake. Hounds sit by to beg. This be the scene of morning, as familiar as my hand.

Pasha stand by Villa's place. She hand him up her plate to share. Her motion freeze, the way I scream his name. The noising halt, and they all turn to staring frighten cats as I ride in. I almost gallop over the tables, and I yell my hate.

Soon as I be down from Money, I get Pasha by his shirt. My Sengles start to laugh and shout. I never see, I never care. Pasha's collar in one hand, in the other I have my gun. Let Money go where Money please, I ain't got time to rule her. I only drag the roo and warn my Sengles back with yell.

Last thing I see in town is Crow. Child coming down the Lowell path, two rabbits hanging round his neck, strung from a bloody shoelace. Got his hunting face, of arrogance and impish joy. He see me come, his joy run out like water.

'Going to fix this roo,' I call.

He say, 'Fix it to death. I hate its sight. Ain't coward out, Miss Weakness.'

I walk on, my strength ain't falter. But his words stick to my nerves. *Fix it to death. I hate its sight.* Be rushing, never-thinking, but these words repeat in mind. Soon I be breathing thin. Air weaken, like I got the gasping sickness.

Is nothing faithful in the world. Air itself betray. I walk down careless, let the briar thorns tear up my arms and ankles. Ain't even Ice Cream Star be worth to trust, myself be trash. Crow and Ice Cream twins in evil. But ain't no otherwise to do. I drag big Pasha across the stumbly ground, the gun dug in his ribs.

This be the gully where I test my pistol, bramble-grown and lonely. No one see what happen here. No interfering child will help. And I let Pasha's collar free. He stand fast, but be a Pasha lost his owlen peace. His face besweaten pink, and all his jaw gone tense and feary. He say soft, 'Truth, I ain't . . . I ain't hurt.'

I take breath. 'You ain't hurt yet.'

'Nay. Ain't hurt *her*.'

'What her?'

'I ain't hurt Villa. Villa ask.' His face be foaly seriose. Any a time beside, will make me laugh like twenty hounds.

'Ain't caring who you do your sex with, roo. Villa do her business anywhere, she do it with a stick.'

His face ease. Be like a smile begin. That light my fury new. 'Tell how you ain't got posies! Say the truth, you yellow spew! My brother–'

Here my voice stop thick. I stare and breathe.

He say, 'Cannot.'

I aim my pistol at his feet. He look, and something flinch inside him, though I ain't seen that he move. I say, 'You can keep secrets, this be all you do.'

His boots be warpen, uggety. Roo boots, must be all roos wear this. The leather thick, but never stop a bullet.

I say, 'You can keep secrets?'

'Yes.'

'Be secret from my people. My brother sick.' The heat of tears come in my throat. I swallow it away.

'Ain't know this,' he say.

'You know now. I do this for my brother. Be his life.'

'He sick?'

'Got posies. Now you know. Now you must leave your lies.'

Fright inkle in Pasha's eye, the bluish eye-round nearly white. 'Cannot.'

Spite blaze, my hand go nervy on the gun. 'I shoot your foot. Then I bust in your eyes, I use my hands. This be my brother's life.' My voice go sicken rough, my stomach twist. All I see is blood and bone, thrust out of dirty leather. Face got blood for eyes. The words themself be foul.

'Cannot.' His voice be small and dry. 'Cannot.'

I stare and swallow. Must shoot his foot. Be pain, but it ain't death. Ain't posies. No one spare my Driver's foot when he be dead.

The gun drop from my hand. It strike the dirt and lay, ashame and helpless. I be saying, 'You can save my brother. Why you will not help us? All your lies be weak.'

'Cannot.'

Pasha look on my bandon pistol. All himself be gratty soft. Relief look at the gun, and his relief increase my sickness. *Ain't coward out, Miss Weakness.*

Then Pasha duck and take the gun.

I step back, my footing slip.

He say, 'I cannot save no child. Trust my word. Ain't bone you know more.'

My courage rouse again. 'Cannot go back without I know. You can well shoot me, evil.'

'Nay.'

'Will murder you in sleep, goddamn.'

Gun in his hand look at me well. His owlen face consider. Then his hand ease, the pistol pointing at the dirt again.

He say in undervoice, 'Ain't bone.'

He finger in his pocket and pull out a box. Marlboro Red. One-hand, he open it and get a cigarette. Hold the box to me. His other hand go easy, pistol loosen at the dirt.

'Shee,' I say, 'how you got cigarettes?'

His bluish eye go clever. 'Villa ask.'

'Foo! Villa pay. Dirty-habit females.'

Want to laugh, but all my worry stick. My feeling follow the pistol, while I take a cigarette. He light us with a Lowell match. Still I focus on the gun so much, I startle when he speak.

'Cannot tell, is sorry. Ain't bone to know.'

Fear loosen in my chest. 'Truth, you thirty?'

'Leave this. Ain't bone.'

'Be my brother's life.'

He shake his head, go careless in his eyes like he unlisten. Then he smiling at the gun. He shift it in his liking hand.

I try, 'Must ask this gun, my Pasha.'

'Gun like me best.' He lower the pistol to his side. 'Gun missing Pasha.'

'Gun working for our food. Been talk that Pasha learn the eating habit, also.'

A thought go past his eyes, it bloom and fade. He say, 'I know to hunt. I hunt, can eat more?'

I catch, surprise. The notion tease my hope. Roo can be a yellow Sengle, hunt and scratch like any a child. Yo in war, no Nat Mass Army will resist his size. Give the beast a knife, they featherboys run in scream confusion.

'Can show you places,' I say careful. 'Where to lurk for deer and turkeys. Yo, must hunt with bow, ain't every Sengle have a gun.'

'Bow? This be with arrows?'

'Kill more meat if you use arrows.' I laugh. 'I teach you. Ain't no craft.'

'Ain't know arrows.' His face discourage. 'Better hunt with gun.'

'Driver never tolerate a roo with guns,' I say, eyes on my pistol. 'Ain't even going to like you using arrows. Gun ain't to consider.'

I hold my hand out for the gun. The roo miscomprehend, he put his hand in mine and smile. His hand be warm and heavy in my hand. I catch my breath, surprise.

Here be when Crow crash from the bushes, shotgun in his hands. He scream, 'Let go that gun! Ain't touch Ice Cream!'

Pasha toss the pistol in the dirt again, as quick as flies. He lift his hands above his head – a foolish deed, it make him taller, feary worse. Crow flinch back and shout, 'I kill you twenty times, you dirt!'

'Calm, calm,' I say. 'Been giving back my gun.'

'Be fool yourself!'

'Roo ain't hurt me! Calm your mouth!'

'Hurt you myself, you giving guns to roos!'

Then Crow take angry breath and hush. A nervy silence pass. Little tawny rabbits hung on either side of Crow's neck, their bloody shoelace crusten stiff. When he stir, their helpless paws go kick.

69

Crow's face twist, hating vicious – but this be my Sengle own, who dare himself with empty gun to fight for Ice Cream Star.

Then Crow turn his head and swallow. I look at Pasha, where he frozen sad, his hands above his head.

I say, 'Can rest your paws. Nobody shooting you today.' Roo put his hands down slow. To Crow, I nod my head. 'Be gratty for your care, my Crow.'

Crow work his jaw. 'It need no thanks. Roo touching you for your own want.' He spit at the dirt and raise his shotgun to his shoulder, glooming.

I shake my head. Go bend and take my pistol from the dirt.

When I gesture Pasha to depart, Crow walk ahead. Go up the trample bushes, shotgun held to him like cherishing. Keep his back to me, but lag until he feel me in his shadow. Pasha come behind, and we walk silent, Crow–me–Pasha, through the gully, up the Lowell path, the way to Sengle town.

II

BY HUNTS WITH PASHA ROO:
TOBER 15–29

This time of Pasha Liar, autumn start its naked cold. Leaves be Tober colors, changing with the turns of wind. Frost glitter sometimes, then the sun speak up and it be gone.

This also be the time me–Pasha start our friendly hunts. I even give up mornings with my Driver for this enterprise. Ya, Driver's temper sour to me behind our strife about the Armies. He chafe to any word I say; his face relieve when I be rid. So I pursue his help apart, in chase with Pasha Roo.

Walking out to hunt at sunrise be like stepping straight from your own dreams into birdsong and dew. Trees seem higher. Gray shy dawnlight fill their rushing crowns from underneath. Pasha stalk beside, my monster fabulous and tame, and be like fleeing every worry to a secret hush.

And truth, it be a secret. Driver hostile to no roos. Ya, the roo hunt with my gun, a recklessness no child forgive.

How it is, the roo be mostly thumbless with a bow. His arrows wiggle in the air, they strike like feeble worms. Nor he can tie a snare for much. Go fishing, and he noisy restless, like an unschool ten.

Only business that the yellow mess do right, is shooting guns. He scarcely seem to aim. Wherever Pasha look, his bullet go. Can pick a firefly from the air, can throw a stick and split it. When our bullets still been plenty, Pasha teach me gunly craft, and soon I can shoot firm and clean. But fireflies safe from me, I never rival Pasha's skill. So, because time hurry past, because my children hunger – I accustom to see my gun in his big hand.

And Pasha be a bony companiero, come to find. Hunting be unspeaking task, and we spend chill-foot mornings hid together, quiet as the sky. Stare the same direction, hear the same commotions in the leaves. If his shooting hit, he say in rooish underbreath: '*Tock vote.*' When he miss, he say, with sorry twist of lip, '*Blyat.*' When I ask what *blyat* will mean, he say, 'This ain't explain.' But he teach me bits of roo, and I will talk in rooish sometimes. Always be surprising, that these words work just like speech.

Again-again, I ask him how he live so long, and ain't got posies. Ask in anger; ask in helpless beggary. Ask in vain. Yo, in this time, his age begin to feel to me direct. In every detail of his face, his hands, is something worn and tired. Be in his size somehow. It be particular as a smell. But ever I turn my mind, it be no sense. Roo grown affections to myself, can swear. If he known a cure, he never left me dying sick. So can think, cure ain't exist. But, in all his fool denials, never he say *It be no cure.* He answer sticks and nonsense, or he give unhappy silence. And secrets look from his blank eyes.

Once I threaten him again. Go grab the pistol from his hand, and press it to his throat. But Pasha only tense and wait. Blue eyes be mostly sorry. He grit until my fury tire, then say his same, 'Cannot.'

So when at last he tell some use, ain't on the posy cure. Ain't on the roos, or WAKS, or nothing from the world beyond. It only be an unexpecting fact of Crow his treachery.

We walking home from hunting, rainy day without no luck. Rain strike thick, and we go ducking underneath a pine. Tree got a set of boughs that overlap, the needles thick. Almost can pretend that it be dry.

I make my accustom talk about my dying brother – sicken without help, because some children got no heart to use. How Driver raise me from an enfant, when he being small himself, but Pasha never care. Ya, soon Crow be sergeant, bad in ways.

Then Pasha say up curiose, 'When the sergeant change?'

Almost, I react annoying. But then I only shake my head. 'Whenever the sergeant showing posies, he be callen dead. New sergeant ruling this same hour. Truth, ain't lawful, how we doing. Should be changing weeks before.'

Pasha shrug, our broken laws ain't worry his composure. 'New sergeant rule. Old sergeant doing what? He leave?'

'He dead,' I say unliking. 'No person talk to him except the sergeant. Ain't use his name, must call him "our good child". Be like OldKing then.'

'OldKing?'

I sigh and find a cigarette. Rain thick as hair. 'This be an Army definition. Nat Mass Armies got two kings. OldKing and the NewKing. When the NewKing sicken with his posies, he become an OldKing. Then they choose a new NewKing. Sound complicate, but truth is simple. Only the NewKing ruling. Yo, only the NewKing keep a queen.'

'Queen?'

I shrug nerviose. 'Queen be the NewKing's wife. Ain't got no power. With that filth, is boys the only people. But the queen the only girl they taking from the Massa woods. Ain't like a slave, she keeping fat. But when the OldKing sicken bad, he kill her with a knife. Be all their filthy manners.' Here I stop and light my cigarette, my heart be beating queery. Snap the zippo shut and say, 'NewKing Mamadou must take his queen soon. He tardy in this. OldKing kilt his queen four months before.'

Pasha's face go disapprove. 'He kill his . . . girl he sleep by?'

'Ain't sleep by no one, child. The NewKing keep his hut alone.'

'Nay, I thinking . . . sex.'

Here we both laugh, embarrassing like any enfant children. I say, 'Yo sho, is sex. Most bell be stolen for their queen.'

Mischief brighten Pasha's eyes. 'Be sad to lose you then, Ice Cream.'

I see he ain't meant disrespect, but still my mind go vicious red. I suck my cigarette without no breath and feel despicable.

'Will overlook this speech,' I say. 'You ain't to understand.'

His face go wary. 'What I say?'

'No Sengle taken queen. No Sengle kept by Armies since the murder wars. Nor will be. Never going to be.' I spit into the dirt. 'Queening be a matter for the Christings. Always them is took.'

Pasha looking at me careful. 'You pain with me? I say some mally?'

'Nay, is only feeling.' Ain't know why, but then I say, 'Got history with NewKing Mamadou.'

Then I sure regret my words. My cigarette taste weak, and all the rain be falling shame.

'History?' say Pasha. 'What this history?'

'Shoo. Forget this talk.'

His eyes grow mischief back. 'Ho, love history. Comprehend.'

'Goddamn, you hush. Be crime to love some Nat Mass Army.'

'Be crime you feel? Is sorry.' He laugh loud, his head tip up and hit the bough above. All piney rain shake on our heads.

I swear and kick his shin. This only make him laugh up worse. And the piney wetness break my vanity, I laugh myself. All the woods is private with the darkly rain, I feel uncanny.

'Damn your yellow brains, you see too much. Yo shaggy dirt.'

He laugh again and say, 'You kick me more, yo criming girl?'

'Goddamn!' I try to smoke, but cigarette been soggen from the rain. I throw it down. 'Must teach your mouth respect. Can go too far, this rooish freedom.'

Pasha's eyes shine through my shame. 'NewKing, how looking? What his face?'

'Ain't concern yourself, what face he have. Shee for your questions.'

'Nay, think I seen this NewKing.'

'Foo, how your NewKing look?'

'Prettieuse boy, got feathers. Greenish feathers here.' He sweep his hand behind his neck.

'Ain't Mamadou,' I say, relieve somehow. 'The NewKing's feathers black and red. This been some featherboy.'

'Seem like NewKing.' Pasha shrug. 'He talk to Crow like. Bossy.'

Then disbelieving prickle on my skin. I narrow at the roo. He looking unconcern, inspect the wet spots on his cigarette.

I say, 'This feather talk with Crow? They two alone been talking?'

'Ya.' He ware at me. 'Ain't bone they talk?'

'Be . . . ain't normal that they talk. Is sergeant's business, parleying with Armies. They talk how? Was friendly?'

'Ya. They walking arm with arm.' Pasha put his elbow out to show the linken arms.

'Foo, boys linking arms. Is Army manners.' I squinch up my nose. 'What they said?'

'Ain't comprehend the speech good then. Been weeks before.'

'They spoken friendly, though? Ain't been dispute?'

'Ya, they laugh and friendly. Like we be.'

I press my back against the piney trunk. Sap sticking at my jacket, and I feel my hungry nerves. Sure this be why Crow ain't bring meat to town. He give his meat to Armies, trade to them in secret crime.

Reason be no science to explain. When Sengle boys go to the Armies, be for simper slaves. Male who cannot please no girl, will go where he can pay. The slaven girls cannot refuse. Nor these girls ain't get the loot; is for the Army filth to keep. Crow be Crow, but never I thought my animose do such. The child my arms remember never do this cruelty.

I say, 'For crime, this be the worst. Ain't to know, what this Crow do, if Armies capture girls from us. If he be sergeant . . . shee!'

'Ice Cream. I ain't–'

'Nay. Hush.'

Pasha turn his eyes away. I take and loose my sadden breath. Try thinking how I tell my Driver, but can see no help. Crow be our only male full-grown. He sergeant, or we ridding him, the Sengles lost the same.

At last, I only reach my palm into the chilling rain. Breathe and feel its trickle cold until my sense return.

As I think and Pasha hush, the rain go slow and lessen. Soon my palm feel weak beneath its course. Sun brighten through. I put my chill wet hand against my throat.

'Is tardy,' I say soft at last.

Pasha stir. Look at me sleepyhead and faraway. 'Ya, be evening meal.'

'Foo, ain't dusking yet. You see the sun?' I point and feel a glad frustration. 'Teach your leaky brain to tell the time, goddamn.'

'Be crafty,' Pasha say, and laugh.

We set forward easy-foot, our empty packs be light. But as we find the path, some running footsteps sound behind. Come a Lowell runner breathless through the splashing mud.

Sprinting to, he cry out, 'Ice Cream Sengle! Word from El Mayor! Must come and bring the roo!'

The runner wearing Lowell jacket suit and flat cravat. Is eight, an older age to be a runner, and his face be panic. All this show importance; El Mayor ain't going to hear my nay.

Runner start again. 'Be urgent. El Mayor himself require.' He yappit on about the need, while all his eyes stare at the roo. Ya, my heart exasperate. I got no moods to El Mayor, nor I got time for Lowells now.

'Cannot come,' I say. 'Tell El Mayor he ask some other day.' I nod to Pasha and set off. Roo come behind, and runner last, must jog to keep the pace, while crying, 'El Mayor be seriose! Ain't heeding, companiera!'

At Sengle town, they got a rain-sheet spread from tree to tree. All children yappitting beneath, the raindrops chatter on its plastic. At the corner where we come, stand Driver and Crow Doe.

Crow standing normal like all days. His froggen face resent and brood; arms cross against his chest. And I feel a knifen pain. Mind babbit nonsense, how it be some explanation, all can fix. But my heart know, and miss him like a thing forever lost.

The runner dash up straight to Driver. 'Sergeant Sengle! Sure your Ice Cream want to never heed! El Mayor call her to business. Tell her, companiero!'

Take me a breath to gather thought. Then I say thin, 'Brother, I got parley to yourself. Ya, El Mayor will handle me, be all his mally business.'

'Yo injustice!' the runner cry. 'And El Mayor been give you bullets! You never bring his roo, is all his talk. He angry on all Sengles.'

Then Driver speak, in voice like steel. 'You go, Ice Cream.'

'Ain't wish to visit El Mayor,' I say, quick from my feeling. 'Can keep his dirt for his own Lowells.'

'Foo!' the runner say. 'Yo disrespect!'

'You go,' say Driver. 'Be no talk.'

I turn on him with every cavil noisy in my heart. But then my brother cough, and seize in pain through all his body. Yo Crow flinch like he cough himself. Bowl Thirteen step back, like she beware some sudden threat. And all the children round unhappy kept, look maudy at the dirt.

Then can feel their knowing. And I see my Driver's eye gone plasticky from papa tea. His breath come wheezing, thin for life.

I say, 'Sure, your decision be my work. You be sergeant.'

Driver swallow at his throat. 'Ya, El Mayor keep loot for me. Can ask him for this also.'

My heart know, loot be papa tea. But I only say, 'Will ask. Forgive no disrespect.'

12

TOBER 29 ITS FEARY NIGHT

We come to Lowell mill at roofen sunset. For hastiness, we take both horses – though Pasha be a stupid rider, Big Smoke follow Money sans no help. Still, be a long way through the city, where shadows lie uncanny stiff among the bricky homes. Never a breeze make any shadow shift. Is set like paint.

Be gratty to reach the mill at last, its windows gold joyeuse with lectric light. A dozen children scramble to the gate to see the roo. All come noising, pushing, asking if the roo be danger. I be calling nay and shoo. Underfooten Lowells barely give us room to dismount.

At the door, these leave us in respect. We pass inside. Soon the only sound is groaning turbines and our patting feet. We walk in this loud quiet to El Mayor's workenroom. Here, windows show the purplish sunset on the glassy river. Lectric light be shining. All is neat and sugar clean.

El Mayor be frogleg on the floor. By his knee, a radio sit. This be a plastic instrument, with metal grill upon its face, and tiny numbers painten by. Now it give a snoring noise. Snore rise and fall as El Mayor tweak at its side. His nosy face intensify, his long hands work.

Radio been El Mayor's delight and duress, six months long. Child expect this plastic box will tell him every mystery. If any a city still exist, the radio will speak its voice. But no word come from this object, ever he rearrange its wires.

Now El Mayor put down the no-book he been writing in. Eyes concentrate on me, and his mouth narrow on no smile. In this chilly look, can see the days that I avoid his friendship.

'Is bony that you come,' he say.

'Your sight be welcome,' I polite him.

El Mayor tweak the radio again; it hush its snore. He rise to his feet, regard my Pasha head to foot.

Pasha say, 'Be joy to meet you, El Mayor. Your mill be bell.'

'Yes, be bell.' El Mayor slant his eye at me. 'Love of bellesse a Lowell weakness. Our strength be weakness, weakness be our strength. Is such a saying.'

'What this meaning?' Pasha ask.

'Mean nothing,' I say. 'Nonsense be their sense, sense be their nonsense.'

'Ice Cream ain't love weakness.' El Mayor look at me hard. 'Wolfen female, loving trouble more than featherbeds.'

'Be well,' say Pasha. 'Mill be fine.'

El Mayor turn back to Pasha, careless in his face. 'Hearing you is thirty. Can believe this tale?'

Pasha shrug. 'Ain't never count my years.'

'Count now, my ox. Be wrong by two or three, ain't figure.'

'Roo ain't smart to count,' say Pasha. 'Like tree. Live hundred years, grow into sky. But tree got stupid head.'

'Tree got no head,' say El Mayor.

'Truth be right,' I say. 'Here great Lowell science speak.'

El Mayor wave back my talk. 'You come from far away? Or is there roos born here in Massa?'

'Born . . . I ain't remember this. Been born before my memory.'

'Shoo, where you live, before the Sengles catch you?'

'Live in this house they burn. Remember now, I borning there.' Then Pasha laugh, like his own saying please his ticklishness. I laugh myself. Be good relief, some other person bear his nonsense.

El Mayor ain't rile. He never mind no disrespect, is only untying in his mind. Can see him circle round this knot, seek an end to tug. When this ain't appear, his face distract. 'A yellow Sengle, shoo. Got better trouble than your lies.' He turn to me and say, 'Heed this. My radio been talk.'

Take me time to hear his meaning. Is Pasha wake my sense.

'Radio talk?' say Pasha.

'Ho, this object talk?' I say bewoken. 'Talking words?'

'Talk and talk,' say El Mayor. 'You hold. I find this speech again.'

El Mayor crouch to poke the radio, and it repeat its snore. He pinch its belly, twist his fingers. Noise go boo, then shrink and crackle.

'Speech start out on ninety-one point five,' say El Mayor. 'But then it go to ninety-one point seven. Then I gone to evening meal. Been lost when I return.'

Pasha watch with narrow eyes. Listen like he know what all this Lowell babble mean.

I say, 'What speech the radio been doing? You talk to it any?'

'Nay, cannot talk back,' say El Mayor, his voice impatient. 'Said some sleeper English. Hasty speech, ain't comprehending much.' He look up from the radio at us. 'Then it spoken fisher Panish. And it spoken something else. Was thinking, can be rooish.'

'Rooish?' Pasha say. 'You speak in rooish?'

'Nay,' say El Mayor. 'You speak in rooish. Be rooish, maybe you will understand. For this I fetch you.'

My nerves waken, bright joyeuse. I kneel by El Mayor. A green line move behind the radio's numbers as he twist its dial. El Mayor be scowling hard, as if it take all hungry strength to catch this voice again. Pasha crouchen by. And now I see, the roo be frighten. Can wonder if he fearing science inventions, like some children do. But ain't got time to ponder this before the snore break into talk.

El Mayor's hand lift from the dial. Pasha lean in hungry-eyed, and we all heed this voice.

Can guess, the speech be fisher Panish. Got its hopping sound. Ya, be uncanny how this box speak out in boyish voice. Cannot guess how the voice be made – I seen these radios' insides, and be no throat nor tongue. Voice sound bored and priding both. Be like it tell a lesson, and ain't hope much for our telligence.

Then the voice go finish. A different boy begin. Take time before I recognize, is sleeper English. Some words comprehend, but nothing weave into a sentence meaning. El Mayor been grab a pen and scribble in his no-book. Write fast as hand can move, but this voice pippet hasty on.

Some bits untangle as they pass. 'We ask that . . . give aid . . . do not . . . safety . . .' Pasha listen hard, and press his fist against the tilen floor. Voice drop at last into confuse, a gabble that ain't comprehend. But one word come clear: 'Lowell.'

Here the voice is finish. Only hushen fuzz go on.

'Said Lowell, ya?' say El Mayor, glad feary. 'Heard this before.'

'How these strangers know our place?' I say. 'They speak to us?'

'Ain't know.'

The radio crackle break to voice again. Is rooish – sure I know from Pasha's face before I hear.

The slushen talk go draining past, sound bored and vaunty like the rest. Pasha follow on, ain't breathe nor stir. His face be rotten white.

As it jabber onward, Pasha rise up on his feet. Stand tense, his face gone deaf and strange. His hands join into angry fists. Arms biggen with their hate. Is like he see this talking boy, and gather for his murder. Yo, now it realize again, the grandy beast he be. I crouch tense to help, but sure I fear his size. My bones go fear.

But as the radio hush again, his anger pass like blown-out flame. Is like a child who lose a fight and stand in beaten misery.

I stand up nerviose. He inhale sharp and look at me. Is like his pain been on myself, my heart react uncertain.

And Pasha say, 'We all must leave. Must go from Massa woods, as far as . . . far we can.'

13

OF THE RADIO SPEECH

'Leave where? Ain't sense. My Pasha, calm.' But panic flutter in my chest.

El Mayor say slow, 'Why we must leave? What they said?'

Pasha shake his head. Go rub his eyes with fisten hand. Where the hand pass, dirt be smear. Eyes blaze their suffering.

I look at El Mayor. He stand up waring, making fists himself.

'Got booze?' I say. 'May help.'

'Is sleeper brandy. Can–'

Then Pasha speak up harsh. 'This radio talk be from my people. Say they help, but ain't to trust.'

'Your people?' I say frighten. 'Roos?'

'Is what you call us, yes.' Then something in his face be skew. Like laughter wake, but ain't no happy joke.

'Ain't to trust?' say El Mayor. 'Roos will steal our children now?'

'Roos kill you all.' Pasha clench his jaw, consider on these words. Then he nod, like he approve their truth. 'They kill you all.'

A minute we three breathe our hush. Radio gabble fisher Panish, keep up its unrest. Yo, my thoughts be like all frighten mice, run everyway and blind.

'When we must leave? Tonight? Or this can wait to morning?' El Mayor's voice sarcasty, but his face be stiff with nerves.

'Can get a week,' say Pasha, sans no humor. 'But be sooner better.'

'Why these roos will kill us?' I say. 'Eating children like they say?'

Pasha shake his head, impatient. 'Nay, is like your murder war.'

'War?' I laugh up thin and scary. 'Got no war to them. Ain't even know these roos.'

'*You* know these roos?' say El Mayor to Pasha. 'These your townie folk?'

Then Pasha show his silent face. The meaning dim out of his eyes.

'Sleeper brandy,' I say nerviose. 'Need this myself.'

'Yo sho,' say El Mayor, his voice gone shy. He step to a cabinet, take out a chubby brock. His hand be shaking as he reach the brock into my hand.

I drink a sip that burn my throat, make heat behind my eyes. I magine a folk of shaggy Pashas. All got long-nose guns, wear ugly-color like the roos I seen. And I recall the deer shot through and through in friendly field. Roos pool around this unluck deer, is noise and size and many. They pass on and nothing left.

The radio go back to sleeper English. El Mayor grab up his no-book. Hunker down and start to write. Pen pause like it think, then scramble. Most is single words. *Can, must, is* – mean nothing by themself. Further be writ *safety will . . . only sixteen days.*

Pasha turn away, his gaze go frowning to the window. I look along, see where the fallen bridge crouch in the water. River fat with rain. Sun below the gray horizon, only give a thimble light.

The speaking mumble to its end. When I look back at the no-book, words is writ: *treatment for waks.*

Here my heart misgive. I say low, 'Treatment for WAKS?'

'Ya,' say El Mayor in catching voice. 'What I heard. Ain't certain.'

I look at Pasha, and his eye meet mine in painful meaning. 'Pasha, it be WAKS? You know?'

'Is bait,' say Pasha cold. 'Is bait in snare.'

'What bait?'

A moment he resist. But then he say in careful voice, like every word must comprehend, 'Roos say, we give help. Come to us. When you come, is different tale. Must fight for them before they give. Nor they allow you leave. You fighting for them, or you kilt.'

'Fight for them?' El Mayor scoff his breath. 'Who we will fight?'

'Fight . . .' Pasha rub his face again, the dirt smear thin. 'Be farther place. Ain't nothing you will know.'

'If we fight,' I say, 'they give us cure?'

'You die.' Pasha's voice come rough. 'All die in war.'

'Nay, why you ain't said before? Been weeks.'

Pasha shake his head impatient. 'Ain't think they coming here, so far. I think, was safe.'

I start to cavil more, but El Mayor say through, 'If we ain't go?'

Pasha grimace. 'If you ain't go, they come and take you. Or they kill you here.'

El Mayor whistle in his teeth. 'Ain't to escape these roos.'

'Why any child do this?' I say. 'Peculiar in itself.'

'Nor I comprehend your wars,' say Pasha. 'Argue this, but leave. You still can run.'

'WAKS is posies?' I say. 'Tell me truth.'

He look misery tired. 'Is posies. Sure. All that you ask.'

I take my breath and say in brave unbalance, 'Treatment for WAKS. This mean the roos got treatment? Can help posies?'

'Yes,' say Pasha bitter. 'Now you run to them, be kilt.'

The radio begin in roo again. Pasha light his eye toward the box in jitter hatred. My mind beset with roos and posies. Cannot think nor pause from thinking. I shut my eyes and drink again, the brandy lighten in me. Driver can be breathing full, can live. Roos kill us all, but Driver breathe.

The brock flee from my hand. I open eyes and El Mayor got the brandy. Though his grooming nett, he look unkempt with tired thought. Ears themself look crooked on his head.

El Mayor drink twice and thrice, then crouch down to the radio. He tweak its side, and its voice halt in silence. Then I surprise how my own fear relieve. Radio voice been like the voice of flies when your best child is dead.

El Mayor say low, 'Find what it say ourself. Then we consider.' He look back to me like checking, but I only stare. He make a forcen smile, then stand up to his feet with stiff respect. Walk to the door and call like normal bossery, 'Report!'

Room beside El Mayor's workenroom be Mailroom One. Here First Runner wait. As his voice be finishing, can hear her scurry foot. Second's blink, she standing in the door neat and exact.

This child a tennish paragon, is quick as dragonflies and light. Was born an Army girl without a name; now she learn science under El Mayor himself. Got braiden hair and her own sleeproom, princen in respect.

El Mayor say, 'I need all my firsts and seconds here. First Electric must bring radios. First Library bring the dixonaries. Rush.'

Any a ten be curiose, but runners must not question. Yo First Runner never blink. She only say, 'Is done.' Before I can expect or watch, she gone. Feet hurry to their silence.

And El Mayor turn back. Make painful smile to me, and slip misliking glance to Pasha. Then he crouch by the radio. Touch it scary like he touch a flame. Turn on its voice, and flinch as it begin. Reach for his pen.

Yo, as he start to write, can hear the mill begin to sound with feet – all Lowells running hasty to our help.

Time behind be like a waken-dream. Room fill with noisy Lowells; El Mayor yell orders furiose. Radios plugging everywhere, and Lowells gather thick to them, go write with all their hands. Yo, always be that grinding voice of flies. It jeer from every part.

When the radio talking Panish-rooish, they all join to Pasha. Ask any questions they can think. But Pasha's answers be the same: We stay, roos kill us all. We go to them, we took to wars afar, where never a child can live. Yo, when Lowells ask him where the roos be now, he losing tempers. Go ranting on the rooish guns, and how we small comparisons. Ain't fight them anyhow, must flee without no stupid wait.

And ever they ask him how he know – ask any question on himself – he only grit and hush. Eyes blank.

When they go back to the radios, Pasha look at me. He always look at me, face grieving. And I watch my fury back, my beggaries of blame. But I ain't try to speak. Be waiting till we can depart. And I fear this talk its future, and I fear the waiting moment. The radio voice ache in my ears. Be like the voice of Pasha's scary eyes.

Yo, this time seem like one minute somehow, that hold still in agony. But it been three hours before the speech be written whole.

Is this:

This is an emergency broadcast from the American mission of Russian Federation. We are asking all people over the age of 10 to report to [word nobody recognize, is probably a place] for registration and treatment for WAKS. Please give all help to the security operations of the rescue mission. Your safety will depend on your compliance. Report any people who stay behind to local troops of Russian Federation.

The final date for registration is November 15th. After this date, all unregistered people of 11 and older are in violation of emergency laws. For the safety of other citizens, they will be subject to punishment action. Repeat: the final date for registration is November 15th. Only 16 days are left for safe registration. You can request transport and information from troops in your own area.

Please tell your friends that treatment for WAKS is available. This will be given free to all people over the age of 10. The treatment is safe and effective. Please help us to accomplish the great mission Russian Federation has undertaken for the aid of her American allies.

This announcement is in force for the listed areas: [more words nobody recognize. Here the word 'Lowell' come.]

14

THE PARLEY ON THE ROOS

Time me–Pasha leave, be starrish windy night. First Library writ me out the radio speech. This fill my jacket pocket. In this zippen pocket, also be a fattish bag of papa tea for Driver's use.

The way through Lowell City, ain't no sound but crickets and our crunching hoofs. Moon hide around the edifices, stalk us in the snaky alleys. Yo be stretches where the dark go blind. Here my terror rise. I feel my Driver's death and all our threaten murders as one truth; how we come to darkness without help.

Where the light shine clear, the broken glass make paths of sparkling moon. Then the bricky walls gleam warm, and all my courage wake. I think: *Roos got this cure, we rob it. For my Driver, I face guns and hells, this be my treasure chance.*

As we leave the city, we pass through a birchen evac. One tumblen house stand closer to the road, look friendly in its ruin. Wooden sign stand skewish by: *Lowell Family Dental.* Here I pull Money to a halt. Big Smoke stop behind.

When I turn, the roo sat like a person lonely in the night. Eyes turn to the prickling stars. He got a Lowell cigarette, its brownish scent come to my nose.

I say, 'Tock vote.'

He blink but never look. The moonlight show him whitish cold.

I say, 'The cure be real? Can cure my Driver?'

Pasha hold in stillness for a moment, like he never hear. Then he say, resenting soft, 'Truth, they got cure for many things. Can send a voice on radio. Can fly. Can burn you from the air.'

'Roo, I ain't fear their killing. Learn this fact.'

'I learn this fact, you be a fool.'

Nerves begun to sing around me in a cricket voice. Be nerves or cold. When I speak again, my voice come rough. 'How many be these roos?'

'Nay, you think, how many be their guns? How strong their guns?'

I let my hand run on the saddle's leather, feel its scuffen marks. 'Ain't hope to fight them, bone. So how we do?'

'Ain't do.' Pasha's voice come bitter. 'What I say of killing – I seen this killing. Ain't prettieuse nor easy.'

'Shee, if they take us, we fight for them. Live all days by them. Be sure, can rob them sometime.'

'Nay, ain't rob. You die in war.'

I scoff my breath. 'Why we must die? They fight to only lose? Ain't sense.'

'Sense different there. Yo, where I fight before, the taken children been worse than roos themself. Kill and kill, for nothing. Nor they live much time, is kilt.'

'Your wars be curiose. All murder and no war.'

Pasha shrug and ain't object. He leave this saying in the air.

Then something inkle in my mind. 'You fled from them? You hiding somehow?'

'Ya.' He shrug. 'I hide.'

'So if you bring us to them, they will punish you for fleeing?'

His eyes fix mine. A minute pass while hope flame keen in me. I say feroce, 'You fear these roos, ain't need to go with us. Can tell us where they be. We never speak of you, be certain.'

Then Pasha laugh. His untooth mouth show spooken in the night. And he say harsh, 'This be my task. Bring children to the roos. I giving you to them, my fear be gone.'

I let my gaze sink to the darken ground. The moon pick out the bitty grass, can see a balden dandelion gray with night. And now first consider what become of Pasha's missing teeth. Children can lose teeth from hunger. Teeth bash out in war. No glad adventure lead to gappen teeth.

At last I say, 'But you ain't bring us?'

'Nay.' His voice come low. 'Cannot do this work again.'

This *again* hurt in my mind. Think how he said, he seen their killing. Come in my mind precaire, if Pasha done this killing self.

I swallow and say, 'Yo, why you never tell me? Asken you these weeks.'

'I try this in one town. Tell everything. And seen they children die. Run to their death.' He laugh. 'Cure for posies, cure for posies. There they say, *la cura. La cura para la sarcoma.* Nothing hearing, but this *cura.*' He toss his cigarette to the grass. 'I show them where is roos. Cannot say nay. They threat me with their guns.

'So we go there. I bring children, is good. Good task I done. But all the time these children living, I fear they tell about my warning.'

I take my breath. 'They told? Is why you left?'

'Nay,' he say cold-voice. 'They dead.'

He get another cigarette from his shirten pocket. Take out a lighter also – object that I recognize. Be Villa's priden joy, a pinkish lighter, sparkle in its plastic. Words on its side say *Hello Kitty.* Now my heart seize somehow, seeing this thing from simple days.

I say, '*La cura.* This be fisher Panish? You seen the ocean?'

'Is many things I seen, Ice Cream. Been war for fifteen years.' Then he add, in careless anger, 'Ain't you think, what come to littles?'

'Littles?'

'Be no use for war.'

'Yo sho,' I say uncertain. 'Ain't thought this question.'

Pasha light his cigarette. I watch the tiny flame twist and go out. I say, 'The roos kill littles.'

His words come in ghosten smoke. 'Roos tell the jones, we keep the littles safe – if you obey. But littles never keep. Most times is left, can die themself of hunger. Be times, roos hunt them with guns. Kill them with hands.'

His hands tense on the reins he hold. My eyes go to them, feary.

I say, 'Yo, taken children do this work? You said, be worse than roos. They killing littles?'

'Sure. Is pleasure game for some.'

My heart disgust and shrink. 'I ain't do this.'

'I know. Crow do this, maybe.'

'Nay. Never a Sengle do–'

'Here you mistake,' say Pasha cold. 'Surprise be yours.'

I turn my eyes away in private feeling, look up to the stars. When I been small, once Driver told me cricket singing was the voice of stars. Now I watch the stars and hear their voice be frighten shrill. Stars call the fear of all our helpless life.

I say, 'What happen, when I come to them? What happen first?'

He toss his cigarette away half smoken. Never speak nor blink. Be like a creature cannot talk.

'Heed, my Pasha,' I say thin. 'Ain't only Driver die. Myself, can live two years, three years, before my posies come. El Mayor eighteen, life wearing thin. We dying in your eyes.'

'Ain't take you,' he say angry. 'Forget this.'

I swallow hard. 'Nay, need your help.'

'Ain't help.'

'You lead me to their camp. Where I can see this camp.'

'Nay.'

'Goddamn, I go without you! I will find their camp, be sure. Ain't justice that you choose my death!'

He grit his mouth, get his bethinken look. I look to the stars again, my need wear through my nerves.

And I think of Driver sick. The plastic baby Keepers found, and all the children I seen dying, all their frighten voice. How I carry Mo-Jacques to his burial with straining arms. Flies gather to his open eyes, and I been trying to blow them off, but all my breath been weak. How I sat weeping while he bury in dirt.

I stare around myself, ain't hardly see. White stars and grayish dandelions – is dozens of these balden dandelions tremble in the nighten wind.

Then Pasha answer slow, 'The roos ain't bring cure here. Ain't bring in Massa. Going to be in south.'

A moment I only hold, uncomprehending. Then hope chill in me. 'The south?'

'Where they go after Massa. Steal more children. Far in south.'

'Far? Yo, where?'

'Washington,' he say in queery softness. 'Where it going to be.'

A second, my heart falling glad. I remind all maps I seen, the roads drawn clear. Word *Washington* writ. Then I feel Pasha's eyes on me, his queery grief upon.

'Washington,' I say soft. 'I heard of this. A sleeper city been.'

He nod like tired conscience. 'Ya. Be bigger war there. Roos will come from every part. Come by . . . things that go on water. Ride on water?'

'Boats,' I say with choken need. 'And cure be there? On boats.'

'Yes. At Washington. Ain't lies.'

Only when he saying this, I realize it can be lies. I try to spy his face correct, but it be lost in shadows. Only his white hands lighten clear, fist hard upon his reins.

Then he say, 'You can obey my telling?'

'Obey?' My breath catch sharp. 'Nay, why? You bring me there?'

'Cannot go in their camp alone, yourself. Ain't safe.'

'Is natural I obey.' I laugh up nervy. 'Truth, you bring me?'

'Ya. Must think how this can do.'

'You and I, my Pasha. Sure you be my hunting shadow.'

'Sengles still must leave. Ain't bone to stay here.'

'Sengles flee, ain't no affair,' I say in loving voice. 'Be wandering peoples.'

He shake his head misliking. 'Must think. Can talk of this tomorrow.'

'Tomorrow, truth. Be gratty well.'

I turn forward nerviose, ain't want to hear no changes. I fumble the reins in sweaten hands. Tug at Money's head, where she nose down to crop at dandelions.

Then I take a hungry breath. My courage fill with night. And it wake inside me, the enormities we do. All war shrink before this deed, all science done by Lowells. Yo, I swear myself, if we succeed, I roam the Nighted States. Give cure to every needing child, and never a person die for Ice Cream Star her failing heart.

I heel Money into walking, and my life gone sweet and fearless as we leave to Sengle town.

15

OF CROW HIS TREACHERY

All great works start with mistake. Ain't no exception in this fact.

On the nighten path from Lowell, I been planning so: Tomorrow I wake early. Go to Driver in his hiding meadow, tell him every news. At morning meal, he speak to all, convince them to escape. Then I talk apart with Pasha. With his help, I plan to rob the cure from these nefasty roos. I go with him to Washington. Can leave by risen noon.

Morning come, I wake alone. As I open eyes, my aching know the hour be late. The forest warm and woken, feel myself outside its busy life. All other hammocks bandon – ya and Pasha's hammock empty left, it ripple loose with breeze. Must worry where this yellow creature gone. Why he ain't woke myself.

I scramble down the tree with clumsy sleep in all my limbs. Drop and land unbalance, come away with scratchen wrist. From a lower bough, I fetch my Patagonia jacket. Feel the papa tea, fat in its pocket, as I pull it on. Fish down my white Adidas, where they hung from laces by. Socks inside is healthy cold against my seeking finger.

Be hunkern down to clad my socks when, in the corner of my feeling, tickle a creeping motion. I look to watch this creeping, and my startle eye find Crow.

Behind the woodstack, he go sneaking. Subtle as blackish light that change in trees, he slip to Nighting Brook. Stoop by the water's edge. Can see, he washing something there, his arms move picky to.

He stand and shake this something round. Shiny drops go flung. He turn and it be a dangling rabbit. Collar of blood show in her tawny fur where she been bled. Crow go busy to the ground, swaddle this rabbit in some plastic. Fit her in his pack and zip it. Stand and sling the pack upon.

Then I see Crow's shape walk shadowy behind the branches. Hop the brook, and crash up through the bushes to the farther path.

This path be overgrown. Ain't kept since Popsicle been sergeant. Got brush, ya ladyflowers growing where the path be wet. It be the Army path, a way no Sengle take except in war.

Then my anger comprehend. Crow go trade his meat for simpers. Fetch our wealth to Army camp.

A moment, I still catch on need, how I must chase the cure. But Crow burn in my furiose nerves. Ya, I think how Pasha said, it be a week before roos come. And Crow be disappearing now, he steal our food to Armies now. My littles hunger while our enemies fatten on their meal.

Then my better task forgot. Ain't even pause to clad my shoes. Sling them by laces round my neck, and I stalk over Nighting Brook. I track my animose.

No easy step be in this journey. Army path untend, is rich with sticks and leafy bushes. These be Crow's scouts, they wait to give a warning noise. My bare feet ache from cold, and times, my heel land on an acorn peak and pain light all my bones. But cannot stumble. Cannot pause. Ever must keep Crow in my hearing, but cannot walk into his sight.

Where the trees be thin and small by Army camp, Crow halt his step. This I ain't expect, and I come careless up behind. I stop with one foot raise, hold like a hound that point a bird. Be sure he going to turn and see me, but he peer down at himself. Can see his nervy breathing, how he tug preenish at his clothes.

Then he spit into the dirt and go accustom into camp. Move among the huts without no thought, no worry sneaking. Step to a hut of green bepainten hide and speak his voice.

Hut open mouth. Crow stoop and gone inside.

Green hut mean Karim, a boy who wear green feathers to his war. Ain't know Karim's looks sans this feather gaud. Child broken Jonah's wrist in war, is all I know of him. Now be bitter to think this green fly eat our townie meat.

I creep forward careful. Find my familiar hiding, in a clutch of enfant spruce. Here I hunker low to watch. The camp weigh on my eyes.

Army huts be tallish cones, cover in scrappy fur and deerskin. Huts painten every color, and they drawn with Armies' birdhead gods. Behind, disgusting like no shame, there stand the simper house. This be a warehouse sort of building, flattish to the ground. Sides be dismal metal, warp along its grayish stripes. Got two doors that roll up from the ground, and locken from outside. Here the Army horses winter with the simpers and the enfants, bed by pissen straw.

In campen center stand the god chair. This be a grandiose tree trunk carven with the faces of their gods – Shango, god of rain; Musa, antlered bird of thinking; Ayesha, goddess of their rape that Armies callen love; and Allah, god of gods. No person sitting in this chair. In the seat, where no one see, is heapen skulls of OldKings past.

At the feet of this strange ugliness go twitching hens. A gross-head rooster threaten among them, like a staring OldKing. Every distance smell like boozy spew and piss and chicken shee. In this place, no good thing smile.

Now is hunting hours, and camp be mostly empty left. Only, from the godchair's pit, the smoke of sacrifice go by. Here stand a simper, wrappen in black godclothes, head-to-heels. Ain't got no person shape, her face be cloth. Her front look like her back.

From her nothing face, she sing. Be a whine that change and wasten on the passing breeze. She raise her hand above, a bloody joint of chicken dangle there. Then she bend down from the hip and lay it on the sacrifice. Rise singing, and unwrap her godclothes, till she remain in simper garb, of scants and naked skin. Smoke grow with the taste of food.

I be gritting hungry, when something startle in the trees beside. Second that I look, the NewKing stalk into the camp.

Then every wisdom be behind. I stare my lonely eyes.

NewKing Mamadou bell severe like blackness in a starry night. His every move go graciose as fire. He seventeen, and tall in height, large in ferocious strength. Wear godscars on both his cheeks. Got one tooth broken from our wars. In him, this also be bellesse. Yo girls think upon him, like all boys think on myself and suffer in sleep. I think upon the NewKing, Ice Cream Star that love like ten hearts.

He walk, loose in his scorn. The feathers at his braids lift reddish blackish in the troubling breeze. His deerhound Terrify Courage jaunt behind and woof in steep delight. Hound nose to the chicken fence as Mamadou look back.

Pasha come behind him, laughing. I shock hard. My legs begin to rise, all risk forgot. Voice join to call his name.

But then the roo turn by. My voice choke. I crouch back in my hiding, sweat bright on my nape.

Ain't Pasha. Child bigly made with yellow hair, but ain't got Pasha's face. Nose small and perchen, like a hound's. Pink cheeks is fatly loose. Yo, half his ear been cut away. Only show a curlen scar, where normal ear will be.

Now this roo bring out a shooting pistol, twin to mine. Roo focus and he aim. Gun fire and all noise startle in my head.

A hen leap sideward, spraying blood into a cloud of risen dust. The roo laugh pitchy high as Terrify Courage yap and dodge away. Hen come down scrambling, spending out her blood. Wheel and scrabble another puff of dust before she hush in death.

Mamadou speak, displease. He beckon Terrify Courage, who canter to and stop beside his feet. Look up with chasten eyes.

Roo smile unconcern. He reach the gun to Mamadou.

Mamadou take the gun. The roo go talk in undervoice, pink face be grinning teeth. Ain't hear particular words, but I can hear his voice be drunk. Ya, Mamadou only do, is hold the gun. Ain't even part forget the gun. Seem like this gun be thinking.

Then Mamadou tuck the gun into his belt, like my gun poken in my belt. I feel it there as Mamadou smile back at the roo, smile hard and angry.

And Mamadou turn, go to his hut and duck inside its open flap. The pink roo follow, hound come jog behind. The hut close its black lips.

Everything fall silent calm. Only the smoke go thoughtful by, the chickens twitch their heads. I ease onto the ground, my hand held hot on my gun's cold.

I never been in Army camp by day. But I known these huts by sneaking darkness, lorn in moon. Yo, I often seen the NewKing's hound in guilty night.

Once Terrify Courage come beside, place his bearden snout between us two where we been lain. Hound look up hopeful in his eyes. Ain't myself can make the NewKing laugh, but Terrify bring this laugh. Hound sit back and pant joyeuse.

'Terrify Mice, should be his name,' I say. 'Hound got no hate.'

Mamadou frown. 'A picky hound, can terrify who he wish.'

'Can terrify who be mice.'

Then Mamadou call me mice until my spirit rile. I slap his head. He catch me rough, we war in wrestling, war in scary love. We wake again by blackish night in Mamadou's smoken hut.

I walk out lonesome to my shame. The moon watch like a skull.

Now I recall the sleeping furs, the reddish light of his birch fire. Lips linger on my throat, a crime, a crime, but honor shed like clothes. Every pain be gold.

Once, in folly of this love, the NewKing say he steal me queen. Some sleepy night I wake in slavers' nets. Queen gems be mine. So Mamadou say, and twist my braids around his fingers.

Since any time remember, been the Christings given queens. Never a Sengle bear their filth. Queen be a slave that boss the lesser slaves, she live without no name. Sengle song about this say: 'Queen go in tears and rubies.'

I tell Mamadou: Send your feathers, sure I fight beyond all love. Your feathers die in screams before I rest. They die in blood. Mamadou say: You die in blood, yours be the throat is cut. Queen ain't the chooser, girlish. You the choice.

Arrogant death is been my choice. I said: Death be my choice.

Then weeks passing when I sleep unquiet. Wait for featherboys and nets, the wrestling bruises and the gag. I watch hard for my war. Curl beneath my tarp on rainy nights and hear within the watery storm. Dry nights, I hear the quiet air.

Weeks pass in breeze and nothing. Lonely weeks turn into summer. Then my listening be my need. Windy nights when sorrow race my blood, I heed my pain.

No one know this quiet business but myself and Mamadou. Ain't Driver know, nor any a Sengle child. This been the pain I choose. And sure no Nat Mass Army draw another tear from me. Been my heart's downpour that I shed before.

That time been gone. My every love be gone.

Be sorry minutes then I wait for Crow. The fire of sacrifice burn out and quit its smoke. I try to think of roos, how Armies friending them somehow. But my mind stray and stray to Mamadou's hut, insist its memories.

At last, to rid my awful nerves, I sit and put on shoes. Lacing my Adidas tight onto my feet is comfort. Like a bone child hold your hand. I zip up Patagonia, and my shivering fill its warm.

Then a voice rise from the quiet. Laugh up bright and long. This friendly noise uncanny in the beak unlife of camp.

Crow stand out from Karim's green hut. He straighten himself and stretch his bigly arms, his face excite and glad. Pack hang flat and empty from his hand. His meat be gone.

My animose come toward me. Trample by, uncaring spiriteuse.

Yo, I stand to my feet and follow. Ain't no thought betook, nor I attempt to hush my footsteps. But he ain't heed my noise. Lost in himself, he walk his strut joyeuse.

Scarce been going for a minute, when he turn off from the path. He step through the twiggy berries down to Passing Brook and crouch along its stony margin. Bend himself and splash. He wash his uggety face, the lips still smile. Eyes far in selfish joy.

I think of Armies warring for the roos, Crow bringing them his catch. Yo, I be starving from this morning. Hungry feel like angry; it be natural these words sound kin. My hungry anger stare at Crow Sixteen, his beardskin washing in the brook, his strong respect. And he shake water from his head and stand. His eye meet mine.

His face go stiff. I want to pull his hair and cry my voice. I want to skree his guilt.

And we be so, eyes met. Plight and blame share in our eyes.

Then Crow leap off, he spark away. Crow gone in sprinting flight.

Too slow, I chase behind. Go swearing, calling his unluck name. Name sting him faster on, and we go tumble scarra-barra, running until the chase be pleasure. The forest soft in its gold afternoon, pine needles kick behind. Arms catch flying boughs. Sun jewel in the patchy trees. I course with all my breathen power, but Crow be fast and long, begin to pull away in distance.

Past the 110 broken road, he leap a bracken gully. Be near to Sengle town, can think he head there, seeking home. But before the town smell come, Crow dash sideways. Go duck through branches into blinding clear. I leap behind and sun be whitish everything, is grass and air. We run into the powerline.

Powerline be a road of grass. Is shot with gnats and crickets that skip up and blend with light. Lectric towers stand above, shape like giganty children with arms out. Be steel and wire and ruin. Feet concree, and heads is set about with hawken nests.

In this big sunlight, Crow weaken. Like a stricken deer that feel its arrow, he lose stride. Slow and stagger, until he only stand with hands on thighs and gasp his breath.

Panting, I stop by him. We gobble air, squint sun, like both been struck by sudden sickness. His face be sweaten ugly in the bright, his teeth flash strange.

Then, from his wheezing breath, Crow hiss, 'Yo poison! You the worst thing that I want!'

I shout breathless, 'No one care what Shee-heart want!'

'Ain't got to follow people who ain't want you!'

'Nay, you give Karim our meat! Why you done it? Why?'

'Why you gone to Mamadou they nights?' His voice go high. 'Be sure I know yourself, more than no Driver know!'

My spirit sting, but I yell furiose, 'Know from Armies!'

'Know from eyes. I seen! Yo, why you gone?'

'This ain't the same, goddamn! Be stuff of feeling.'

'Why it ain't the same?' Crow's sweat show helpless on his face. 'You only saying. How it ain't?'

Then everything shift in my thought. Be like in hunting, when a turkey hid in dapple sunlight. See nothing but the goldish leaves, until the turkey twitch its tail. Then all the shapes go into different meaning.

A chill rise in my nape. 'Is business of amour with you?'

'Ain't yours to know.' He grit his mouth. 'Ain't need to sneak behind me.'

'Nay, ain't girls? Be this Karim?'

Crow spit into the dirt, frown sharp away. 'Cannot be Karim. This act forbid.'

The answer bitter in his face, and my eye shy from it. I look up at the steely towers. Wind fly rough above. The grassy trash, caught on the towers' wire, flutter like clothes. My mind see sly Karim. His head bend toward me, feathers flutter. Is bent to kiss Crow Doe. Here my thought fail.

No Sengle do this crime. Is Army manners, boys who love with boys. Been so with NewKing Akh, a prince feroce, but boyish in his love. He stolen boys to serve this greed. These boys been clothe like simper girls, in scraps and beaden chains.

No Christing tolerate this; nor a skewish boy remain at Lowell mill once this be known. No enfants bred from it, its get be death. Is selfish loves. Their hearts envy and their bodies pain – so say be the Christing Teachings.

I gone staring at Crow's hands, how they make and unmake fists. Press small, then they release. Wind kick hard again, my braids blow round like trash.

'Truth, you liking boys?' I say in whisper.

His voice come low resenting. 'Can be so. Ain't felt no girlish love.'

'Thought you gone there buying simpers.'

'Sure you be an imbecile fool.'

I laugh short. 'I guess.'

His eyes come up. He seek my face, eyes narrow against the sun. 'How it begun with you and Mamadou?'

I shrug unliking, look away into the blowing grass. 'In war. Been chasing him . . . yo sho, begun how things begin.'

'Chase your enemy?' Crow scoff breath. 'Karim must chase for me. I hunt no Armies, nay.'

'Karim come hunting you?' I look up nervy.

'Seen what I am.' Memory darken in his eyes. 'Seen and want. This day, been following deer myself. Karim come follow me.'

'This green filth disrespect yourself?'

Be a breath where Crow stare at me. Seem he try to understand. Then he say, 'Your thought the filth. Karim the only child in all this world that love myself.'

My stomach tweak inside. 'No Army love a Sengle, blindness. Be your own people love you.'

'Nay, I be my crime to them, they known.' His voice break soft. 'Go love this, I ain't think.'

'Been crime the same with Mamadou and me. Can be forgot.'

'You and Mamadou be forgot, is nothing. Be your gain. All things for Ice Cream Star is gain. Go with an Army, gain. Go with a yellow roo, is gain.'

'Ain't gone with any roo—'

'Yo heed! My heart be dirt, is Army meat. But I ain't leave this heart.'

My voice come feary thin. 'You go to them?'

'Been gone these days. You know my hunt be theirs.'

'When you be sergeant—'

'Hear me, fool. I cannot be no sergeant.'

Cloud put its hand upon the sun. Can feel this dark upon my skin, and I pull back my Patagonia cuff. Find my shirt's cloth and wipe my sweat. Behind my arm, I watch Crow's face.

His lashy eyes more prettieuse than deer's, his no-chin face. But his ugly closer to my heart than no bellesse. Be the face of all my memories.

Then I get a sickly doubt. I say careful slow, 'Ain't want myself?'

Crow staring long. The grassen route change color in the wind.

I say, 'You want myself, I do this with you. Ain't need . . . ain't need boys.'

His breath stop deep. A moment pass while we both hurt and hush. Then his mouth twist up feroce. 'Nay,' he say rough. 'Ain't your blame. What I become, you ain't no part of that.'

First moment, I relieve. Then grief rise again, I say, 'Ain't need to go to them, you ain't.'

'Can quit this empty noise. You never even miss myself.'

'Damn, you my animose. I always miss you.'

'Been littles then. That business gone.'

'Nay, this business of Karim be gone. Never a person know. Can be forgot.'

'Argue be a waste. I ain't expect to come home from this walk.' Then his eye skit sideways from my looking, and he turn away. Stalk hasty toward the shadow woods.

My step be ready to pursue, but some conscience hold me still. Heart sprint and weaken as he walk on. Yo, as he reach the woods, I call, 'I love you like no damn Karim!'

Crow ain't heed nor startle. He go on feary through the blowing grass, he step into the forest. Something crunch and something shift, but then his catly foot find silence. Soon he only be a changing dark, a dark that I remember.

16

OF PAPA TEA

My heart see backward to the powerline, as I walk forward home. See Crow returning to that feathern hut, to slaving and to roos. How green Karim receive Crow in his arms. The hut flap close and shiver.

Walk forward on. Walk forward on. Ain't no way else to do. Yo, I must do all work that I neglect. Must plan to steal the cure. Must bring my Sengles safe from roos. Ain't got rest to do, ain't time for feeling in my life.

Yet, ain't Sengle town feel like no home without Crow's angry self. Ain't Ice Cream feel like me.

Near nighting camp, there stand a sapling oak is yellowen with fall. Show clever like a flag. Where this oak appear, I stop and take a leaf between my fingers. Ain't pluck this leaf. I roll it tight. Let go, and there the leaf spring up. Is curly on its stem.

When we been eights, my Crow and I writ messages on leaves. Been one moose oak we chose. We curl the leaf was writ upon, in signal. The other then go check our tree, and find the curlen leaf. It say 'Come robbing eggs at Tophet', or 'Villa got stank breath'. Pluck this leaf and write upon the next. So we kept our secrets ours, before we had no secrets.

Then winter come and bald the trees. This writing game forgot.

Now I pluck my curly leaf, and put it to my lips. Stay thinking, quiet.

Be unworth, to choose no love amour above his people. Ain't done this for myself, ever I want. Want like no living pain. But my children eat before my heart can eat. So I must feel. Yo his love be skewish – worse than evil, lower than beneath.

Yet my spirit say: My Crow, my Crow. My sorrow weak and kind.

Then ain't no help to do. I take my breath. Walk forward on.

In town, it be our higly-pigly stew. Trash left in every catching place; clothes hung to dry on branches. Fawny littles scream and chase, play war among themself. Tequila Fourteen Tool sit by to watch. A squirm of babies sleep around her, hounds curl in among.

By the cookfire, Hate You Fourteen Ka and Driver sit. Got folden chairs toward the burning warm. I spy them, and my news feel dirty somehow in my blood. Want to turn and leave, feel like I bring a catching fever. But Hate You see me, and reach hand to Driver's hand. He also look.

This Hate You be a quiet-kept fourteen, responsible in ways. Now, how they sit cahoots, I mind that Driver been her enfant's father. My brother never chase no girl, ain't choose between them in his feeling. Yet these two pair well.

I come toward and say low-voice, 'Salue.'

'Bone salue,' say Hate You.

Driver get his brother face. 'Slept far, my Ice. The morning meal be by.'

'Nay, been away and back.' I come and hunker to the fire. Its woody breath come to my nose.

Driver reach and touch my head. 'Hair grown beyond its braids. Be some old centipedes you got.'

I shake my braids to shoo him, smile up weak. 'Sure, I look like any rotten log. Males going to fear.'

'I fix your braids,' say Hate You. 'If you ain't go hunt.'

'Nay, nay. This misery wait.' I pinch some piney needles off the ground, toss them in the fire. Watch them worm and brightly shrink.

Be thinking how I tell about the roos, but feeling cringe. The fact be sudden in itself.

At last I say, 'Where be my Pasha Moose? Ain't stole my horse and left?'

'Been fetch to Lowells,' Hate You say, eyes close on me. 'Their First Runner come.'

'Is so?' I breathe relief. 'Been wondering where he took himself.'

Driver say, 'You keeping late at Lowell yesternight.'

'Truth,' I say with conscious nerves. 'The owls been sleeping, when we come.'

'Owls done more than me,' say Driver soft. 'Been waiting here.'

'Ain't slept for me?' I turn to him, surprise.

Before I speak again, my Driver cough. Cough hard, and he go on. From toe to hair, he wheeze his strength. Ya, when it exhaust, his breathing still be noisy in his throat. Long body looking hungry strange. Nose shapen like a bone.

Then Hate You say in undervoice, 'Got Driver's loot? From El Mayor?'

'Nay.' I recollect myself, sit back. 'Got business past no loot.'

'Ain't papa tea?' Hate You suck her breath. 'Sure El Mayor–'

'Ain't tea, is said,' say Driver thin.

A moment, I be only startling, Hate You know about this tea. Discuss my brother's need like any fact. Then memory recall the papa gift of El Mayor. Hand go to my pocket's fatness – but with the tea, I feel the folden page from yesternight. The radio speech writ down for Driver's eyes.

I slip my fingers in my pocket and pull out the paper. Guilt react, but I go on. Sure Driver take this tea off to his hiding meadow, sleep all hours. My need ain't wait this time.

'Yo heed,' I say. 'Ain't loot but news. Been spoken through their radio. Is word about roos.'

Then my talk travail, it haste ahead of Driver's sickness. I tell about the radio speech and Pasha's scary warning, how we need to flee our woods. Yo, I tell what Pasha spoken on our homeward journey. How we plan to thieve the cure, save every yeary child. Last I read the speech itself. Paper gone damp in the night, is limp when it unfold.

My voice start weak, but it gain certainty as I read on. My fingers shiver, and beside them, I see Driver's hungry face. His tired sickness breathe. His eye go empty at the fire. My eyes turn from this truth, and I speak louder, till my voice rasp dry and scrape, and every word is said.

I fold the page. Driver watch the fire where it burn low. An orange tracery scab the logs. One flame squirm, nerviose and white.

I say, 'My brother, treatment for WAKS. You hear? Is real. The cure be real.'

He watch the fire, ain't seem to think. Only his frown be carven deep. Then something tremble in his face. 'You ain't go to roos.'

'Nay, be well,' I say, surprise. 'My Pasha help me, sure.'

'You be fourteen, ain't got your growth.'

'Been fifteen all these months, my brother.'

He look to me, face harden in its hurt. 'Should be myself.'

A moment, I relieve. Will Driver go, ain't mine to do. Then I see Hate You clutch her hands. I hear his gasping breath.

I say rough, 'Ain't everything your task.'

'Nay.' Driver shake his head. 'Crow do this work. Ain't skinny girls to send.'

'Ho,' I say, frighten. 'Crow—'

Here my voice fail. The fire wave its light.

I swallow and say, 'Sure Crow, he . . . you know how.'

I hook an acorn from the packen ground and toss it in the flames. In the earth, this acorn left the imprint of its pointy head. I put my finger in the hole, and feel the earthen cool, the sandy wet.

'Something been with Crow, Ice Cream?' Hate You's voice sound simple nerves.

I shrug. 'Ain't nothing mally. Crow our child, he bony in himself. Yo sho, he got some reason he be gone.'

'Be gone?' Now Hate You's eyes is black with scary feeling.

Driver sigh. He turn his face away, but I see where his hand move up. Rub at his eye.

'Gone to Armies.' Tears hurt in my chest, my voice sound all of nose. 'Some boys do so. Ain't nothing in it. But, brother, Sengles going to leave? What it needing first, we flee.'

'Ain't know,' say Driver, face low-held. 'These roos . . . be only tales.'

'Nay, brother.' I clutch fingers in the dirt. 'The radio been.'

Then Driver shift, he look at Hate You. She reach her hand to him. He take it soft and say, 'You go to Lowell for me?'

Hate You say, 'Yo sho, must get this tea. Ain't wait no day.'

'Ho, your tea!' I say. 'Ain't meant to leave you hurting, sorry.'

My hand find the bag. I cast it hasty to my brother. Throw clumsy, and it land short from his toes. Take a second till he comprehend. Then Driver scramble to the dirt and grab. Eyes gladden before they shame.

Then anything in his face, be that he look if he can leave. Eyes got no self, like plastic baby's eyes. Sweat brighten on his skin.

I stand shaky to my feet. 'Go, brother. Use this gift.'

He clutch his tea against his chest. 'Will think on what you say. This threat of roos. Will think.'

My voice ain't mine, his voice ain't his. Is lies speak to each other, while we watch foreign in our eyes.

Then Driver turn away. Walk off to easter path, his step go hasty through the bushes. And my pain know, time left my brother.

We only know one pharmacy for posies: papa tea. Is grown by Lowells, in a glassen house of fatly leaf and reddish flowers. Walk through their Pharmacy House, its smell be drowsy in itself. Be beary smell, like monthen sleep.

Tea ain't changing what occur from posies. It besleep the pain. Turn agonies to dreams; it dull a cough into a tickling swallow. Yo, some children with no hurting sickness use it for its joy. Drink it once, and every love be thankful. Pain seem tiny. Sleep tumblen on yourself, and never bother with no pride. But you drink every day, your need begin. Ain't get that tea, you took with shaking sweat and itching fright. Is mostly simpers fall to this, or Lowells working in the Pharmacy House. And a Sengle, when his years is gone, may slip to papa need.

When my death come, I face this death. Got courage for my pain. But I ain't strong to see my brother weak.

Standing by this fire, I break in crying unashame. And Hate You cry herself – she come and cling on me so hard, be like I carry her somehow. Her crying sound close in my ear, a yip is like a fever's voice. Behind this everything somewhere, I see the tallish day, our trees. A Tober leaf fall lazy down, slip in and out of long sunlight. Below, our littles shout and chase. Is blind to just themself.

Then in my sorrow dream, there come a rustle up behind. Something cold poke in my back. Turn icely at my spine.

'Foo baby manners! Quit.' Be Keepers' voice. 'Will shoot your head!'

Hate You stand away and gasp her breath. 'Ho, where that object stole?'

I look around and blink my tears. Round Keepers' neck be strung three candy necklaces. She wear a rooish jacket, gray and green, is mostly twice her size. And pointing upward at my nose she hold a rooish pistol. Got two fingers on the trigger, and she grin like every joy.

17

Of ROOISH GIFT

'Damn!' I grab the pistol's nose. 'Shoot me, you shooting all your meals, my Keepers Two. Who hunt your meat?'

'Go wipe your nose. You snailing on yourself.' She laugh high in her voice.

'Where you got that gun, annoying?'

She tug it from my grip and step back dodging. 'Kit of Pasha Roo. You tell him I can keep my pistol. Been stolen fair, now he say it ain't mine.'

'Point that garbage down! Can hope that pistol ain't got bullets.'

'Tell him! It only be a stranger roo. I be your Sengle.'

'Ain't eights is wearing guns, my fool.'

'I ain't no fool! Where Driver at? Sergeant decide this gift.'

'Calm your fight, biggety,' Hate You say. 'Ain't girlish sounds.'

'Girlish shee!' say Keepers loud. 'Girlish maggoty shee! Shee eaten by a hound, and he go spew it on your head!'

Here Pasha Roo walk from the woods. He wear an under-tee with rooish, dapple-ugly pants. Ain't seen these pants before. My Pasha only worn but jeans. Yo, the tee be whiten fresh, like something found in plastic. A roo-pack on his back, be near as grandy as himself. Yo, on his shoulder slung a rifle, black entire without no wood. Gun be new as morning.

He see my teary eyes, and something happen in his face. Ain't know why, I gladden well. I call, 'What angry loot be this?'

'Salue,' say Pasha, careful-voice. He come toward, his step go heavy with his packen load.

When he coming close, can smell he washen. Lost his stank. His whiff be Lowell nice, of herb savon and bathing water. Can guess, they treat him to a bathing room at Lowell mill. But Lowells never give the roo this gun.

He say, 'You cry for what? What doing here?'

'Some worm fall in the fire,' say Keepers. 'Ice Cream crying for this worm. Is weakling tears.'

'Give Pasha back his pistol,' I say.

'Hungry tears!' say Keepers. 'That worm the only meat Ice Cream can hunt!'

'Give his gun, rambuntious.'

Keepers throw the pistol on the ground, run stamping off. Best Creature Five come in her path, and as Keepers pass, she reach one hand and catch Best Creature's chest. He topper-bottom down and skree, ain't notice how his hurt begun.

I bend to take the pistol, hand it up to Pasha Roo. He pull off his pack. Settle it down and open its main partment.

Inside be any loot. Most is carboard boxes, brown without no markings. Among be candy sucks and boxen cigarettes. Can see a rubber lizard toy, the kind that stand on its back legs. A radio there, is black with hearing spike fold down upon itself.

All is plastic-wrapt, and none of this got normal looks. Candy ain't crumble nowhere, nor the plastic ain't got blackish spots. Be simple like a picture drawn. Nor the cigarettes ain't any sort I known from scratching. Got crabbish writing with all weirdo letters. Roo and roo.

Hate You suck her breath. 'Loot prettieuse, ya.'

Pasha twist his face. Take a yellow cloth from his pant pocket and wipe the gun. Find a carboard box and set it in. This go back in the pack.

Now can see, the other boxes be the same. Is guns.

I say, low-voice, 'Can leave us, Hate You? Need to parley with my roo.'

She hold a lingering moment. Glance at Pasha Roo, unnerve. Then she wipe her tearen face and walk off toward Tequila.

When Hate You gone, I say, 'Curiose, where you attain this wealth.'

He grimace, still waring on my tears. 'Is only mine. Was left, hid by that house you burn. Keepers come with me, show place. I ain't known how to go.'

'But . . . most be guns?'

'Twelve guns. Thirteen with rifle.'

'And why you keeping thirteen guns? You got no thirteen hands to use.'

'Is from our politics.' He shrug. 'Give gifts, the children come for war. Give guns and candy and . . . ain't know this word. Gero, we call.'

'Gero. What this definition be?'

'Is dust. Can smoke, it make a child joyeuse. Ain't fear.'

I flinch, my thought see Driver by the fire. 'You brung this gero?'

'Nay,' he say. 'I smoke all this myself.'

'Foo! You ain't!'

'Nay, is joke. Been left in house that burn. I smoke some then, ya.' He get a sorry look, shake his head.

'How, you got some sickness?'

'Nay, be so. For nerviose.'

Ain't help my mouth, I say unkind, 'Who like that trash, ain't got no sickness?'

Pasha grimace and muttern roo. Reach in his pocket, get a box of rooish cigarettes. Fish one out, is white and perfect. Look like something grown.

And now the Army roo remember – how he hand the gun to Mamadou, grin his uggety face. Can magine easy how the feather-boys will preciate these gifts. What they do with dozen guns.

I look to the pack again, feel every kind of mally. 'Pasha. Be others like yourself? Roos that come to children . . . give this trick bonesse?'

'Sure be many. I ain't only.'

'Heed, I seen a roo at Army camp. They got a roo their own.'

Quick, I tell about this roo. How he and NewKing friendly met; the pistol given. While this talk continue, Pasha's face go through some differences. He grip his rifle nervy.

When I finish, he say, 'How this roo look? How his face?'

'Yellow fur like you. Is bellyish, like he bear a tardy enfant. Yo, he lost one ear.'

Pasha shake his head disgusting. 'Deema.'

'Deema?'

'Child name Deema. Who it be.'

'How, you know him?'

'Ain't bone sort. Be fool soldat. Ain't bone for nothing.'

Here first, it realize to me that every roo got names. Can know each other, and can say, *This roo be bone, this roo be stank.* Obvious be so, and yet this fact ain't want to comprehend.

'Truth is right,' I say uncertain. 'Ain't bone acting. So I feel.'

Pasha say his rooish *Vote*, deep-sounding in his body. Then he say, 'I best go back to Lowell. Tell this.'

'Lowell, right. And what you doing there this morning?'

Now Pasha's face clear into warmth. 'I talk to El Mayor. Is vally child. He choose to leave.'

'The Lowells go?' My heart pause in walking. 'When they go?'

'What he said, five days. But now is Deema.' Pasha shake his head. 'Must leaving quick.'

'Ho, for this Deema? Why?'

'How Deema work, the Armies going to help him. Help take children.'

I startle mally. 'Foo, they help. The NewKing help no roos.'

'Help,' say Pasha flat. 'For promise cure. For promise . . . how the Armies stronger. Deema, be his work so. Yes.'

'Can promise, sure. Ain't mean that Mamadou heed.'

'Ice.' Pasha tense, his face distress. 'Ain't time for . . . for be moron. I go talk El Mayor. But Sengles leave? Tomorrow best.'

This word *tomorrow* come to me like tired impossibilities. I feel my tearen face again, the stiffness where it dry.

'Tomorrow,' I say rough. 'Ain't know. Is Driver got to say.'

'Driver?' Pasha flinch. 'Ice Cream–'

'Nay, heed. We go to Washington? We get this cure?'

Can hear my noisy fives behind, is fighting sticks and laughing. Pasha's mouth gone grim. His bluish eyes be tired distances. 'Ice, roos ain't in Washington now. Ain't be till January.'

'January?' I suck my breath. 'Nay, be two months to wait.'

'Ya. Can go then.'

'Ain't no chance they being sooner? We gone sooner, best.'

'Nay.' He grit his mouth. 'If I ain't flee roos, I gone to Washington also. How I know.'

I swallow, look back to the fire. Now it only got one clinging flame, creep frail beneath.

'Must leave this place,' say Pasha wishful.

'Yo sho,' I say in choking voice. 'Will talk to Driver. He going to heed.'

Roo's big arms tense up and grow, like he intend some obstacle. But he think again, say low, 'I go to El Mayor. Come back soon.'

I shrug. 'Driver live two months. He can. But we will rob the cure? You and I, my Pasha.'

He stare at me without no answer. Then something liven in his frosten eyes, like water stir by fish. He reach into his pocket. Pick a paper out, hand this to me.

Then he duck and hoist his pack. Lumber and unbalance while the burden settle its weight. 'See by,' he say in undervoice and turn with downward mood. Soon his yellow grayish greenish colors mix into the woods.

Folden paper be a page of El Mayor's no-book. Is writ:

Hope you know my writing. Roo ain't lie about their killing. Ain't know what lies he tell, but killing all be real. Seen proofs. I can explain this when you come.

Our mill depart in petty days. I ask you to come with my Lowells. Send Driver to me if he give you talk. Sengles share our food while there be food. Trust this word.

Also yourself can share my tent. Bony tent, good company. I save my goating for this hope.

I fold the page again. Slip it in Patagonia pocket with the radio speech. I try to wonder on this killing, how it prove to El Mayor. But I keep seeing Driver seize the papa tea with skinny hand. His eyes gone empty, false.

Other children now return. Middy meal be soon, our numbers thicken like a rain. Jermaine and Jonah come from hunting. Got a pigeon, all they carry. Ya, thirteenish girls come back with fishing poles and nothing caught. My hunger's expectation think of Crow, of Crow Doe's hunt. Then hope misgive. Crow never hunt our food again, nor Driver hunt our food.

Yo, as my grief occur again, come Mouse and Foxen from the woods. They see myself and scramble toward, exciting in their eyes. Mouse cry, 'Ice Cream! Must guess the secret!'

Then both these moron eights be chanting, 'Guess the secret! Guess the secret!'

'Want no secrets!' I shout through their noise. 'Yo leave me rest!'

They hold with disappointing face. 'Want, if you known,' say Foxen airy.

'So tell,' I say. 'It need no guessing.'

'Nay!' Mouse scream. 'Must guess!'

Foxen peal a giggle. 'Be one hint. Is from the Christings.'

'Here be a hint for you.' I show my fist. 'Yo leave me rest.'

'Shoo,' say Mouse. 'You only stupid. Or you guessing normal.'

'Cannot guess! You shaming cause you stupid!' Foxen blow her tongue.

Then come a sound like cows. Be low and high at once. Mouse press his palm against his mouth. Foxen say, 'The secret!'

It blare again: ain't cows but horns. Be the Tophet trumpets, now can hear their plaining tune. When the blaring pause, beneath is christy-nonnies sung. John of Christ's good basso come familiar through the trees.

My first thought be gratty. Bugling mean a church been called, for meeting of all towns. Any a child can witness at their churches, though I never done. But this be needful time – can warn them everything we learn of roos. Sure Christings heed, ya Driver heeding better in their company.

But when the Christings ride into the clear, my gladness choke.

18

OF TAKEN QUEEN

Four riders come. Is John in front, on their big plough-mare Tribulation. Boy Japhet ride behind with Beanie Christwife on a fatten mule. Trumpet hang round Japhet's neck. These three sing low and weary. Yo their hair be wet, in sign of grief.

Fourth rider be on Mamadou's buckskin stallion Beg-No-Pity. NewKing's feathers, crow-black cardinal-red, is worn in mane and tail. Rider be a girl, is wrapt in gauzy black from head to toe. Black drippen from her feet themself; her head misshapen with thick cloth. Only her brownish eyes reveal. These eyes be scary blank.

The song die to its final sound. John of Christ remove his hat.

'Be met in Jesus name,' he say. 'His greeting on your town from Tophet graced. We bide the Long Agreement.'

'Salue your home. Salue the queen,' I say. My face feel scalden tight. 'Was this Susannah?'

'Ya, Susannah been,' say John. He got spent weeping in his speech, voice sounding all of nose. 'She sacrifice for all our peace. The Long Agreement stand.'

My littles gather, curiose. Be thrilling sights to these. Even Villa join this crowd, with plucking pigeon in her hands. And my heart beat slow and weak, bemisery my blood.

*

The Long Agreement be the bad remainder from our murder wars. Until this law been made, the Nat Mass Armies took slaves in our woods. Been Sengles taken, and it been occasion, even Lowells took. But mostly these been Christing girls – unwarry people, easy caught. In the simper house, these stolen children lose their name.

At last, the Christings take a fellowship that they destroy all Armies. The Lowells and the Sengles join in this revenging creed. Then killings follow killings; every day be sad with burials. In these wars, the Lowells build their steely gates, build walls about. The Christings' cows been murdern, and their fields grown up unkept; most their homes gone fleeing north. Worst battle that there was, been fought about the Christwife Sarah. In this, the Armies burn a home, the Christing Showcase Cinema. There fifty children die in sleep.

Then was made the Long Agreement, soil of all our better years. Now Armies take their slaves in distant towns beyond all friendship. In Massa, girls be living safe. Our wars lose all their death.

But in this Long Agreement, be a clause about the Army queen. Christings let one girl be taken for every NewKing made. This queen traden strict in law. Two featherboys ride out to Tophet. Bring godclothes and queenly gems, and name the chosen wife. Then in consenting show, the girl must clad these gauds and veils. Her husband ride her to all towns, and call a queening church. No child must talk to riding queen, nor she can speak her voice. Not till this cloth unbound by NewKing, when she taken in her flesh, can she return to life.

Return without a name, return apart from all her people. Return to Mamadou his hut. To blood of Ice Cream Star been left upon the NewKing's furs, and listen to the voice I known, the only love I choose.

'Took queen be praise to Tophet,' I say rough. 'Be honor in this choice.'

'Be honor,' John repeat, and Beanie Christwife say up bright, 'Be honor.'

Boy Japhet grit against no words. He scowl and stroke the mule's brown neck. Behind me, Foxen's voice say clear, 'Is wearing chains, beneath. Her nose cut off.' Keepers reply in hiss, 'Ain't so. And you ain't speak.' Foxen say, 'I speak. I speak,' then everybody hush.

I make the two-stick sign in air and say, 'Is well. We will respect the queen for Tophet's sake.'

John put his hat against his chest. His eyes blink hard. 'Church gather tomorrow morning at Tophet house. At first of dawn, be welcome prayer. Follow this with honey meal, for sweetness granten by Our Lord. Then be speech from any child who witness . . .'

As he speaking this, reminders inkle in my thought. John tell on – about the later meals and music songs – while it needle in my mind how I must witness on the roos. Yo I can tell about the roo at Army camp. Never the Christings give Susannah to Armies, once they learning this. Ain't send her to no camp of roos. Is time, still can be right.

Then John of Christ conclude, 'We call your Driver Star to churchen meet.'

I startle from my thought. 'Driver? Only he?'

'Ain't church for friendly talk.' John shake his head. 'Queen church be holy met.'

I look at him, at Japhet and Beanie. A moment I confuse, feel they should know that I must speak. Then I stumble in my words, 'Sure, myself . . . I wish to come. Be good respect in this.'

'Only leaders and Christings come,' say Japhet low. 'Ain't happy feast.'

'Must be ceremony,' say John.

'I keep this ceremony,' I say. 'Sure, will keep with any rule.'

'Nay,' Beanie Christwife say. 'Ain't extra children. Cannot feed all Sengles.'

'Queen church written in the Long Agreement,' Japhet say. 'Can feed whoever eat but–'

'Ain't feed all they Sengles,' Beanie muttern.

'Sure, the Long Agreement,' John repeat with better certainty. 'Determine by our fathers so.'

Then, in my feary watching, Japhet rein his fatty mule. John glance at Susannah, his good face blur with grief. Every slightish motion say they leave.

I feel how this church will pass. Nor I can trust what Driver do. I feel his sicken face in all my nerves, his papa speaking dull. Then all my panic join, goliath bright inside myself.

I say, 'Driver taken with his posies. I go in his place.'

Then my Sengles staring bright. Their fright be turn to me.

'Must be the sergeant come,' say Beanie Christwife, sharp.

John raise hand to Beanie. 'Driver taken? This be said?' He squint at me. It seem he try to hear my words in memory.

'In His name, be said.' My sight be dark, but voice speak clear. 'The sergeant gone in sickness. I take his place.'

Can hear the muttern voices of my Sengles, start objection. Keepers' voice go hissing, 'Hush, ain't hear. I got to hear.'

'Driver Star is dead,' say John of Christ in careful sadness. 'Heaven call his honest soul.'

'Driver Star is dead,' I say.

Story Four Duval begin to cry. I ain't look at her face. I wish to swallow back my words, but I stand cold. I mouth these words again, in silence, like this stop their meaning.

Then Shiny Eleven Angels spit into the dirt. She turn and run, yell Crow Doe's name. All flinch and watch. She run up in the woods, her feet hit crunchen through the sticky briars. Voice weaken in its running.

John say nervy, 'Crow ain't in this? Must this telling wait?'

'Crow be gone,' say Hate You, shy-voice. 'Is gone to Armies.'

'Foo!' Villa sniff. 'No show, he gone. He sergeant, if no person be.'

'Crow?' Jermaine say loud. 'Found what to want! He gone, is better luck.'

'Ain't Driver dead,' Cat Fancy Thirteen say. 'He ain't so sick!'

Story Four yell at me, 'Want no other sergeant! Ain't want you!'

'Nor me neither,' say Cat Fancy. 'Ain't so sick, he ain't!'

Best Creature panic and skree, 'Where Driver gone? You rid our

Driver?' Now Problem start to cry, and every nervy little catch this wail.

Cat Fancy shout, as her own tears begin, 'Driver must be here! Ain't to decide without him!'

Then every child be noise and mouth. Susannah's mount, the buckskin Beg-No-Pity, shy back from this tumult. Susannah sit this graciose in silence, her strong body bow. I call through the reeling larm, 'I must be sergeant! How it is, my Sengles. Wish it ain't, goddamn!'

Then around behind me, silence start. It cast and darken. Soon is only enfants wailing. All faces turn to watch behind.

Is Driver come back from his hiding meadow, slow with tea. His sicken eyes stare at myself. All his respect be tired.

My fear see nothing but my fear. Ain't speech come to my mind.

Cat Fancy call out nervy, 'Driver! Make her go!'

Driver flinch, but keep his eyes on me. Yo Kool Ten begin to call, and Redbook shout her voice. Driver stare beyond this jabber to myself. Take breath, take air in deep. It come back coughing. Chop in parts.

One and one, my Sengles hush. Ain't hear but Driver's cough. Be a helpless sound, like moth that kick against a tenten wall. And Driver look beyond. Look where his sleep remain and can forget.

He turn away. Put hand up to his face, like he will guard his privacy. Walk to the farther woods.

My strength go with my brother, leave unsteady to the darken pines. Yo I turn blind to John.

I gasp the parting words: 'His grace be on you. Grace go with the queen.'

John take reins up nervy. 'All gifts be good from Christ our Lord.'

They heel their mounts, the horses pick their hoofs toward Lowell path. Beanie start the christy-nonny as they reach the branchen shade. Sing though Japhet never join, nor John of Christ be singing. Her voice sound feary wondering as it dismiss and thin away.

19

MY SERGEANT TIME BEGINNING

I sit to middy meal in Driver's place at sergeant table. Ain't notice how we eat. Ain't know, was this meal cake or wood. I sit and think, nor any child require me with no question. Tequila Fourteen weeping careless, all our girlish thirteens weep – but ain't no child objecting more. No voice pronounce the name of Crow.

And when this grim meal finish, I first speak to them as sergeant.

All it need, I stand up to my feet, and every child go hush. Look to me like I being sergeant always, safe in every help. Only at the enfant blanket, skree go forward, and Hate You's hushing. This skree be in my heart, is like my feelings' crying voice.

First I say, roos come to Massa woods. I tell this careful calm, ain't make these roos particular risky. Just be so, like we got termites in some chair. Ain't worth to keep.

The next words I remember mostly. They repeat again in memory like jeering after. Been spoken in my wildness, in my courage born of grief.

'This move, we wander farther. Leave these woods, like time ago, the Sengles voyage here and prosper well. Our greats been roam for daring miles. Come up from Chespea Water, nor they ain't had horses like we got. Yo this journey we will take, the Lowells be our trusty help. Tomorrow I request the Christings also. Hope these all be company in our deed.

'Be bell wandering to expect. Can see the stony mountains, see the waters in the leaping ocean. We wander till we seen each inch of sky, drink all its shiny rains. Beyond, we find another woods. Some country where the tatoes growing wild, and every evac full. We go and choose a life joyeuse from every life that be.

'Ya, beyond the farther south, it be a cure for posies. This truth discover past no doubt. Loot dangerous to find – ain't bring you all to face this risk. But ever it take, I going to rob this pharmacy for . . . for our good child.' Then I stop in weakness, watch their feary faces' hush.

A wondering moment pass, then Jonah Fourteen say, 'What be this cure?'

Now can notice, all my older children watching perilous. I say, 'I only know it being there. And it fix posies.'

'Fix like papa tea?' Now Jonah's face be clenchen with mistrust.

'Nay.' I say. 'Fix it entire. Child live sixty years, can be. Ain't die of posies nothing.'

Be another quietness. My jones all frowning inward. Is like they seek within themself, to figure if the cure be real.

Then Mouse call out, 'What happen for the Armies? They be bring?'

To this, all laugh up nervy. Some littles hooting, calling nee-naws at Mouse seriose. Asha Badmouth say, 'And we bring spiders. Bring diseases also. What we need!'

'Foo,' say Keepers. 'Must bring Armies. Who we fight in these new woods?'

I say loud, 'The Armies gone to roos.'

The jabber stop its voice. Their stares bewilder. Can hear Cat Fancy keeping at her crying, through and on.

'How they gone to roos?' Jermaine say. 'They becoming roos?'

Foxen laugh and call, 'They go turn white!'

'Hush,' I say in sergeant voice. 'Will see this at the morrow church. Learn what these Armies do.'

Before no child can give new problems, I start them to pack the camp. Is complication task, ya every child belabor me with questions. I ain't get peace to feel my sorrow more.

And work go to its finish, day walk down to tired night.

Been thought to wait for Pasha, but he slow in coming back from Lowell. And when the final sun be gone, is sure that Driver sleep. Ya, sergeant be the only child can parley with the dead-among. So my heart insist toward my brother, need his living face.

I leave Jermaine my deputy. Give him instructions, how the town depart to Lowell mill by morning, while I be at church. Then I head to Driver's hiding meadow, through the Tophet woods.

My foot know every hill and stumbling hollow of this walk. Know where the owl will hoo, and where the rusten bicycle been left. On this path, when I been five, I catch a toad and try to teach him speech. Here I drink my first rat booze. I known the mosquitoes' fathers and their grands and greats; I known the cardinal birds that eat these parents.

But now my townie woods become a temporary place, a picture where some past life been. I walk through memories gone.

As I come to the evac roads, a crashing sound break out. My ABC leap from her houndish nowhere. She run left–right before my path, her tongue laugh sideways down.

'Shoo, every creature,' I say. 'Every creature in my trouble.'

Hound trot in front then, looking back responsible and bright. When we come to the hiding house, she dash ahead. Vanish through the tween-yards, where the shadows make a path of blindness. Here I go cautieuse. Can smell his fire.

Cloud hug the moon as I come to the meadow's grayer dark. By the dying fire, show Driver's tent. Tent flaps tied open. ABC sat by, look scouty like she guard this meeting.

'Brother,' I call low.

A shadow change inside the tent, but ain't no word return. I take my breath in this reproach. Say the words is drill: 'The sergeant will bespeak the sergeant been.' Then my heart repent, my throat ache with my sorry love.

But Driver say, 'Come by.'

I walk toward and hunker by the tent, go down on knees. He lain, head to the tenten opening, wrap up in a felty blanket. Is only hair that show. His face turn down toward the ground.

'Thought we can parley,' I say clumsy.

'Be gone night. Was sleeping.'

'Sure, is tardy. But, brother . . . I can sleep here?'

His head shift, but he ain't look. Can only see his cheek, cut by a shadow from the tent. 'You be sergeant. Yours to choose.'

'Is what I wish,' I say weak-voice. 'But I respect your wish above.'

I wait on haunches, all my thinking shame. Feel where ABC be watching, and think about the sleeper hounds is dead inside the house.

Then Driver sigh, 'Expect, be rain. You like a tent this night.'

'Sure be rain. Is right.'

He ain't say more, but shift himself, make room. I creep inside. Tent scarce is big for two, it take some spidering before I can lay down. A sleeping bag unzip and spread upon the floor, but cold creep through. Can feel the chill of earth. I lay behind him, pillow my head down on my open palm. But nothing in my body rest.

Then cautieuse, I reach and lay my other hand on top his blanket, on his ribben side. When I touch, my Driver flinch. Be careful held against my feeling.

I say low, 'We move the town.'

His head turn slight, like he present an ear. Can hear him swallow.

'We go to Lowells,' I say. 'Like you said, when we been fearing Armies. Yours been right. El Mayor ask this himself.'

'Been right from him.' His voice come tired.

'Sure. He a trusty goat enough.'

'He fit you, sister,' Driver say uncaring. 'Both be birds of hotness.'

'Ain't fit me while I still can fight.' I try to laugh, but Driver wait in stillness. Can feel, he wait to sleep.

I swallow against my guilt and try, 'These roos be coming. Must be changes round.'

Driver shake his head against the tenten floor. 'Talk ain't war.'

126

'Yo sho, but if this be. Remember how you say, "Do more than less." You mind this saying?'

'Can be.'

'Is yours. Cannot be foolish.'

Then his shoulders tense up quick. My hand upon his ribs can feel his cough mount, how he hold and still. Struggle at this weakness, like his body straining at some weight. Then it only cough beneath his breath. His body ease.

He say, 'Foolish be a child who sleep without no blanket.'

'Sure, but, brother—'

'Going to sleep here, sleep,' he say with almost laughter. 'Less your noise.'

Been meant to tell him all my plans, but now I give my talk up gratty. Take the blanket, pull it careful till it cover both. Then, though my sadness crave to hold him, I leave him good room. Ain't bone taboo to lie held with no brother. Nor my Driver love exceptions. Be a plain-lawed child.

Then I lay and watch his breathing. Is simple one and two, though he cough sometimes, or stir his limbs and rearrange. Yo, soon his breathing slow and gruffen gentle into sleep. In this my spirit comfort. I go drowsy to my brother's warm.

In my beginning dream, I see the NewKing in a broken road. His back to me, and all himself be distant like a sun. Yo, gunfire noise ahead. My conscience suffer and insist: *He cannot hear. Is roos. He walking to his death.* I try to call, but cannot make no voice . . . and I wake, and soothe again, and drowse again in fretting, now Mamadou be there at the morrow's church. If Armies leave with us, if I can save him anyhow. And this mingle into dreams, my brother's struggling breath, his warm.

When last I open eyes, outside the tenten flap, a snow begun. Sparkle airy over the ember fire. One crumb of snow caught in a dab of clover, near outside. And there it stick, against the moving night that blow behind, until my eyes close into dark.

20

THE SPRING WHEN I LOVE MAMADOU

First ever I come to Mamadou, been war. I chosen him for hate before I wanting him in love.

This been our Sengle–Army wars, a clobberie joyeuse. Been skirmish for its wildness, good as laughing to no breath. Knives sharpen only at they point; can make a braggery wound, but do no worser injury. Come back in a feast of body gladness, ravish in your strength.

These scuffle wars, we fight our match. No eighteen want to beat a skinny twelve. Be coward victories. So ain't sense that I will try to fight no Mamadou. Is only bellicose pride – must catch the biggest fish and shoot the biggest deer and fight the NewKing. And I confuse in feeling, all that year that Crow gone cold to me. My loves become an anger. War been my only good relief.

This war when I chase Mamadou, they come on us at middy meal. I been fighting a reddish brownish feather I call Bigface, striking dangerous like twenty cats. But when I see the NewKing, where he turn to leave, I lose my care. Then Bigface cub me heavy to the cheek, go kick my leg from under. I scramble falling to my hands, and he cry victory on me.

So I take my hurting pride into the NewKing's chase.

Mamadou walking heedless, leave this squalling fight like boredom. I run toward, he never even look. I catch him once behind, and he fight back with half attention. Call me pest and enfant, bat away my blows but never strike. Yo, I fight beyond my sense, feel my beginning shame. And ever he see my tricks before, like he control myself.

Through this, he dodge back in the woods. His only interest be to rid me. In last insult, he catch my stabbing wrist. Break my knifen grip, and throw the knife into the farther bushes. Then furiose in shame, I catch onto his hand and bite.

Ya Mamadou laugh. Ain't even seek to free himself, he laugh uncaring in my face.

My pride go stark. I stand away. He watching at me, grinning, godscars gone deep in his cheeks. Then he shake his head and turn again, pick up his careless step. Go off like I ain't been.

At fourteen, I been shy in wanting, late to boyish love. Done kissing mostly, and my thoughts of sex was misty never-beens. Magine what you saying after; how someone suffer for my need. Infatuate on Popsicle sometime, but he callen dead before no flirting grown to use. Never I think of Mamadou so. My heart to Armies be disgust.

But the following nights, I stalk the NewKing lonesome to his camp. Nor I tell any a child about this habit.

No girlish Sengle go into the Army camp alone. Ain't their feather honor that a girl depart without no shame. So I hunt the NewKing by weak moon, and spy from distance. Climb a tree beside, or find a hunting hide in bushes. Watch for Mamadou to come out to piss, to roam in sleepless temper. Plan how I knock him footless unawares, get kicks into his face. Best worth, can cut him with my knife. Bring back his blood in victory.

But Mamadou be a morning-risen child, he fool my need. See simpers going in-and-out his hut; or he appear some seconds, talking to a feather. But mostly it be empty in the camp by starlight hours. Hounds sniffing round, and sometimes chickens rouse in cluck disturbance. The whinnying snuff of horses by, no differences to see.

So these nights become a thinking loneliness. Lie belly-down on some fat tree bough; wonder on Crow's malignant ways, or how all children loving Hate You Ka more than myself. Look at my legs in moonlight, deciding if they prettieuse or stalky. Through this, I feel a savage missing in my flesh entire. The Army camp, its pointen huts with feathers stirring in wind, seem like a picture of my need. All evil be inside these huts, the evil that bemisery me. Evil I desire to know, in all its maudy powers.

I begin to come by sooner, in the second hour of darkness. Watch the evening business there, feel how this settle back into my quiet thinking time. Sometimes the NewKing passing round, can hear his angry voice. See his sharp bellesse of movement, and every change wake in my furiose blood.

Here I begin to talk to NewKing Mamadou in my head. Explain my need; how it be natural we war together. We be the same in heart feroce. And this thinking stray, until I telling all my moods to him, about Crow Insect and my brother's disapproving talks. Tell dreams I got of roaming to the mountains, lonely with my horse – how I will saddle Money with a puma skin, ride to the wester ocean, fight wild strangers into fear. Yo, in my dreaming mind, the NewKing answer with respecting coldness. Tell me every evil wisdom, and I gather this in strength.

Gone weeks in this strangeness, till one night, when camp be empty in its sleep, Mamadou come out. Terrify Courage trot behind, the NewKing going in his stride. He walking lost in silent angers, got a flask of booze he carry. Yo, the hound come sit beneath my tree. Look quizzy up, wag friendly to my scent. Mamadou pass on thoughtless, stop apart with back to me. Lift up his flask to drink, ain't heeding nothing. And I curse my cowardesse. Must go, must make my actual fight, but every blood in me be cold.

I creep careful down, be gratty for this time of only climbing. Can hope the NewKing pass back into camp, that something cheat my war. But nothing be. I get my knife in hand. Check on the goodly rock in my front pocket. Yo, as I put my feet down in wet leaves, Terrify Courage bark.

Mamadou look back sharp. See me, then ware around, expect a raid – some dozen Sengles wilding from the trees. But ain't no breath of people there. Be only myself in foolish venture, staring at him with no hope.

And it realize I fear to touch him. Fear his hands on me, without no sense. I grit against myself. Go for pocket quick, and peg my stone crisp at his face.

He duck in almost time. Stone glance against his head. Then he come hawken straight and angry, bigger than I remember. Cannot breathe before he be upon – ya in the final second, as he swing his fist, I scrabble quick. Catch him in the chest with my good knife, and he get in a clobber to my head. I trip but catch myself. Come back warring with both arms, but Mamadou catch my wrist. He catch my hair.

I got my knife hand clear. Must stab him, but my body lose its knowledge. Can only feel his hands on me, the starting heat of tears.

He stare at me a furiose minute. Clenchen hand hold painful in my braids while he look at my face, look with uncomprehending scorn.

Then his hands ease. 'Driver's sister?'

I ain't answer, but my face go painful to this question. Known, but never felt, I ain't no person he can name.

He say low, 'You here alone?'

'Yes.' My voice come out in whisper.

'Cannot be here.' He glance back to the camp, unwoken still.

I say, peculiar soft, like telling secrets to my Crow, 'Ain't fearing them.'

Then his hands flee from me. 'Want no problems. Damn, you rid yourself. You crazy.'

'I leaving when I choose.'

He shake his head, some wondering wise. 'Go. Go on.'

Then he turn and leave, snapping his fingers to his hound. Hound look at me sorry and they two depart with haste unliking, noisy in the leaves.

★

Following nights be stank. I keep to Sengle nighting camp, but be a dirt humiliation. Is always littles screaming, fool Jermaine come bothering round. Crow stare past myself, is all the ugly problems of my life.

Three nights past, I lose my reason. Go back to Army camp, and dress particular to this. Wear some tighter jeans I never use for their discomfort. A strappy tee that show my breasts. I think of this like some distracting powers I can use in fight. And I bring my hunting knife, is sharpen all its length. Bring everything that cannot help me in no real world, and walk off like I go into some fantasy I can rule.

Come to the camp in normal stalking. This time, I never climb my tree, I only hide below. Hour pass in watching, while the camp go nightward slow. Simpers fussing round and all their usual grossness talk. At last, they slip into their huts, like mice that disappear in holes.

Their troubling passen into stars when Mamadou come out. Stalk careless from his hut, straight to my tree. He look up at the branches, get a humor look. My heart beat in my skin, and every fear gone into knowing shame. Yo, as he come to shouting distance, I stand into sight. Hunting knife hide close against my leg.

Mamadou pause his step. Shake his head, and come on tired. But his eyes be on me, he see my body in its clothes. Now my anger wake, and as he come in reach, I break and go for him with simple rightness. Dodge sudden as he ware, I swing. Knife catch his naked arm. I take my knife back frighten glad as he cry in his throat. Almost, I pelt away, but he leap fast and catch my braids.

I come off my feet, be jerking agony from this hair. Get my footing back with healthy panic. Yo I stab my knife, but he hit fury hard against this hand. It loose in numbness, almost free the knife. In this distraction, Mamadou get my face a solid punch. Feel good as need, but then he grab me to him hard. Capture both my arms, and peel the knife from me like easy practice.

I stiffen. Look past his shoulder to the trees with showing

carelessness. No consequences weigh for nothing. Can cut me how he like. Was vally done, I win my aim.

He raise the knife and poke its point into my underchin. Lift my face upon this pain, until I look into his eyes.

Then he say low, 'What you think happening to you now?'

My heart go queery to this. Gladness changing to some unknown thing, some unbearable brightness. Yo our bodies breathe against each other, harsh from war. Can feel his muscles shifting as he put the knife in his back pocket. And he say, soft in mockery, 'Think it be war? You thinking this?'

My thoughts gone terror white, but I say, 'Ain't nothing to me, what it be.'

'Ain't nothing to you.' Then his face come toward. First I think he going to kiss me, and I brace myself to bite. But he brush his cheek past mine, until I feel his heaten breath against my tender throat. I go weak in my blood, unwanten sorrows how is good. Run through myself in scary trembling, and when his lips rest to my neck, I take my breath in startle love.

He lick there, taste my sweat, and say, 'Think I can want your nothing. But what your brother say to this?'

A moment, I catch perilous. All my body weak with questions. And I say, 'He never going to know.'

So Mamadou bring me to his hut, he take my blood in fair return. Be hells and mysteries in this, and I feel shame like nevering worms. But when I leave into the starren nakedness of after, I ain't want to leave. Be gone five steps, and all my body weep. I want the NewKing cruel.

Forward weeks be stumbling madness. My every breath drink Mamadou, his hands on me, his angry use. I love him like a death, as hard as black behind the stars. Day become a boring strangeness. I look at my Sengles like they be unmeaning dust. Like Mamadou be the first thing that I ever truly known, the only life in this stale world.

Most nights I never go to him, I keeping scary back. But I lie in my hammock with my hunting knife. Strip off all my clothes and lie without no blanket in the searching air. Lick the knifen blade and touch my body with my other hand, and pass through every second of our loves in angry sweetness. And then a night will come that I decide. Sneak out in perilous want. Stalk through the Armies' sleeping huts, and magine how he can be with some simper. Yo, I duck into his hut with fearless loss of human pride, and he be lying how he sleep, in stripen blanket on the furs. But he ain't sleeping, got no simper, and arrogance know he wait for me.

His eyes give me one second of his pleasure. Then he change in usual coldness, and my heart relieve. I say, 'How your arm is healing?' and he say, 'Come here and see.' And we tangle into this, a scary underwater of our bodies on the furs, the ground beneath.

Be nights I stay for hours, and Mamadou teach me love till I jalouse his unguess histories, the taken simpers who been here before. Yo, be nights we lie together when the fire gone to ash. We talking in this secret dark. Feel the coldness gather, and Mamadou tell of wars in sleeper times, of generals and their thousand children run to burning fight. And I tell my roaming maginations of the wester ocean – but we never talking of our lives, our daytime self. Is always dreams and tales from books.

Then come a night, from passing word, I realize his books of ancient wars been read to him by slaves. He never learn to read, is girlish to their Army attitudes. Then I laugh at him unnerven, all they insect morals, but Mamadou catch me vicious in his arms. My laughter frighten into need. He say my name into my ear, like he give me this name. Yo, in this lost fight, he say, like daring me to fail, like mockery: *You love me, Sengle?* And I feel, this ain't no love, we be like ghosts in hell – like after death you lose your thoughts, but keep your body in a bliss of nightmares – and I say furiose, *Ain't going to lie, I do.* He press me down beneath him, say my name, and say he love me also. Then every terrify hate be gold. Darkness better than no light, and I creep out to solitary night and think of killing him, or how he kill me in some madness. Feel it ending so, is like a war must end with burning death.

In this, I come fifteen, and my bellesse become a gossip of the Massa towns and homes. Jermaine begin to fear me honest, and Driver start his talk how I need enfants, time be late. Yo, these feary months, I sometimes wearing dresses to my hunt. Wash myself with perfume soap, weave beads into my hair, gone hot in vanities. Sometimes I stare into an evac mirror, seeing what Mamadou see, a sultry perfectesse, and love this Ice Cream Star who ain't myself, who only be a dazing looks, like starry light on water.

And as these weeks pass into memory, I become his given creature, past no separate freedom. But I going to him less. My guilt begin to struggle alive. With Sengles, I feel like a sounding crime, a smelling dirt among. And I begin to know, some day I grow a baby from these evils – baby who be an ugly question. So I keep alone these days, sleep at the library apart.

Then come a time, ain't been to Mamadou in various weeks. Will go, I promise to my need – but I promise to my pride, the night I go must be the last. Become two weeks, become a month, and summer be in flower while I dream in grief of this last night. In Sengle town, I cry strange tears at nothings. Driver frustrate at my tempers, and I gripe at him to feel my anger, how my love be bright. This also be the time I start to visit El Mayor. We fight our goating battles while my need be terror black. Be fighting Mamadou's love – yo when I leave, I walk into this missing love. I breathe its lack. Can feel it in my teeth themself. Will draw an arrow in my bow, but what I shoot be love.

And then, one morning I be hunting, with my bow and no belief. Can scarcely notice well enough to find the deery trails. Come to a sunlight patch of woods and I stand there in dream, one tender palm against a tree. Feel its rough bark on my skin, like every cruelty I love, and I look by and there be Mamadou.

No Army come to Sengle hunting places, ain't in custom. So I know he come for me. Can guess, he see my second's joy, before I find my pride. Then I say cold, 'You needing something, NewKing?'

135

He walk to me with graciose and casual scorn. Pull the bow out of my hands, he take the arrows from my shoulder. Throw all this aside, and we be kissing like we love each other in some other way, until he take my braids into his hand, hold me apart. Keep me fast, like he cannot say words without this mean security. And he say, 'Come by tonight. I got a parley to you.'

'Got a parley, you can tell it now.'

He ain't answer, only look at me with thinking eyes. Like he consider me again, make some decision in his pride. I say, 'You parley or you leave? Be hunting food myself.' My voice be almost truthful, and he smile the way he sometimes do, with simple liking. Nor he leave for nothing. Be an hour, with sunlight on our skin in woods, and all our crimes of night be strange. And real again, like never known, beyond all fear and comprehending. And when he go, I think, that been our final time, is done. But I know, will go this night. Will bring myself to him, like debt I owe to his bellesse.

This be the night he say he take me queen. I meet this furiose and blind. Stand in their camp of rape, in NewKing's hut itself, and tell the filth his people be. Mamadou watch with hatred as I give his crimes their names. And my scary blood feel how these words be simple truth. He be a slaver, ya, is natural that he keep me slaven. I terrify when he fight me into love – say all hating nonsense while I hold him desperate, weeping breath. But he let me leave. He only saying, *Sengle, you be back some night to beg for me.*

Yo I never done. I only wait in vanity for this queening raid that never come. For his killing knife I need, this ending.

So been the hauntings of my sleep, this last day of my younger heart. So I bewoken to the NewKing's memory. And he follow me in thought, the morning of Susannah's church, last morning that it been no Sengle town.

21

TOBER 31 ITS EVIL

For church, each braid must wear some bead, dress must be graciose and clean. Slow hours be took in hair and painting for a grandy church. So, before the sun begin, I creep from Driver's tent. Do a freezing wash in Nighting Brook, and I wake Hate You to my help.

Groom be an houry task of hair unbraiding, braiding, dark and cold. Only is the fire to see, the moon in tired cloud. Hate You tug and work and time take in my fever thought. Be reveries of roos and Mamadou, of Washington afar; the grandy war my Pasha spoken of, and how we sneak there. Worry if I survive somehow – and how I ain't told Driver that we leaving. If he can forgive me. If he can survive.

Time my braids is done and beaden prettieuse, the east gone soft. Then Hate You paint my eyes with some cosmetic, while I squint its tickling. We scout some shoes, black heely nonsense things that cannot walk. Last work be gowny dress, and this become a seeking complication. We open packen bags, clothes toss around. Still every dress be wrong. They thin from moths, or falling loose, or be too tight for decent looks. It seem like sleepers only made all dresses to defeat this purpose.

Yo at last, one zip close to my waist. It take my flesh up in itself like glad embrace, and settle warm. Hate You take her breath and say, 'Yo right.' She fetch a standing mirror, edgen rough without no frame. Hold it up herself, and nod with smiling expectation.

Any a Sengle Star be bell. We long and careful made, got prettieuse faces sweet with mischief. Myself, in dress and hundred braids – is easy truth, be bell. Dress be silver cloth, is bright and slender to my waist. Legs show to the knee, is clean in elegance like stepping mare's. Skin perfect black. My lips be formen like a purple bloom. Eyes clear like knowing, and their color got a raven shine, show even in this whisker light.

Yet these eyes fear.

Can only see, how I be small. Be gracile and glitter, is a dragonfly of nothing. Look like a twelve, ain't grown to bear no child. Ain't big to fight.

'Is vally done,' I say. But my voice halt, it sound like breath.

Hate You look at me uncertain. 'Can be more bell with lipstick.'

I see her hurt, and I say stronger, 'Feary bell. Give diggers envy. Only, it feel like nuisance on.'

Then I leave Hate You to repack all clothes. Run to the horsen field. Ain't bear my nerves for haste. Yo, when I ride out on Money, still is only darkness birds that sing. Be night in every quarter but the east as I take Tophet path.

Riding, skirt must hitch up to my thighs, my shoes caught in one hand. Nor this dress be wintry garb. My chicken skin be lively, bare feet ache and yearn toward Money's warm. And now I riding to, my mind skip headlong to the meet. I magine the Christing churchroom, how I stalk there silvery in dawnlight. How all eyes will turn and startle to my shine bellesse.

Then, in my magination, NewKing Mamadou appear. I give him proper greeting, but our hatred love be in my eyes. Yo, the sermon pass, the time of every witness come. I rise to tell about the roos. The NewKing watch with every child.

Then any speech I do, be choice. Can swear damnations on the Armies, how they join with roos. Describe how they will steal our children into rooish slavery. Then Christings keep Susannah back, reject these Army lice. But Mamadou's arrogance scorn my word. He stay in Massa, stay by roos and lose into their warry death.

Or I can speak without no blames. Ain't mention Deema Roo; tell only warnings, and the cure its promise. Invite the Armies to our brave departure. Then can be, the NewKing leave with us – and take Susannah queen. His treachery love walk always in my eyes.

My freezing mouth make shape of Mamadou. My prickling breasts recall his touch, and half my mind remember nights was tumblen in his furs. My skin remember Mamadou, his weight and strength, my mouth upon his sweat, and never I see how I can do this choice.

Be at the Tophet's farther pasture, where the open land begin, when Money shy up wild. She buck away beside the path, yank vicious at her reins. When I pull back, my selfy mare break stubborn to a gallop. I rein and wheel her round, but she still pick her feet in backward mood.

Then in the snow, I see a humpen shape behind the railing fence. I shush at Money, stroke her neck. Let the reins draw gentle till she ease and stand, half off the path.

I swing down from her back bare feet painful in the snow. Ain't pause to fuss with shoes, I step quick forward, let the reins play out until I stretch like hound who pull a leash.

Dark shape be huge ungainly. Squinten in the dawn, can see is Tribulation, Tophet's plough mare. Lie on her side with hind legs thrust out strange. Her neck curve sharp, nose tuck toward her knees. This nose be still as wood.

Beside her neck, like musty smoke, a reddish grayish stain be spread. I think of hounds, of bears. But she ain't eaten none; is dead but whole. Be like this bear come by for killing only. Rabie mad.

A shivering take, deep in myself. I shush in honey tones, lead Money on beyond this prey. She trot with prancing motion, hasty.

Take a minute's going in barefoot snow before she ease and walk. Then I grab into her mane and hike to mount again. Kick her up, and heel to gallop. Then our two fears join. We sprint together from this death.

We driving hard along the fence, face to the yellow dawn that look at us from steely distance. At the hill, I gather her to turn. Look up expecting Christings, brace to warn them of their loss. Yo where we clear the barn, the shapes of Tophet house appear, its narrow windows and its peaks. These show in dashing light, and give a restless crackle sound.

This light be fire. Is set beneath the step, and by the long east side the flames slip up. White smoke rise slow away. Nor ain't no person by. No child be in the fields, no light in windows. Fire play lonely in this spooken place.

I slip from Money, throw my shoes apart. Ain't feel my chillen fingers as I tie her reins on their near fence. Money whicker and pull disliking. Yo, I feel feary strange. Ain't any a child be here, my heart repeat. It ask, where be these children?

I step toward the burning house. Breathe and think in Sengle mind, what happen in this burning. Can notice, fire ain't crafty set, gone dead in any a place. Yo, the easter side be flaming well. I go and yell with all my lungs, 'John! John of Christ!'

A moment, I only hear my breath, the fire's patient working. Then above, as pale as wishing, come an enfant skree. My body flash in weakness, everything be hard for me.

Then this skree repeat, in double voice.

I grit myself and leap the step, jump over its petty flames. Go touch the door. This be drill, must feel the door. Ain't open if the door be hot. Be thinking how I break some window, enter from the farther side. But door be normal cool. Then the metal doorknob sticky with its cold, it open well. In the house, all things be simple like they ever was. A sleeper magazine lie open on a fatty chair. Be wheelie toys on their yarn rug. The clock tick unconcern.

But in the room behind, a fire sway toward the open door. Fire fall back again and find a curtain, climb in watching time. Smoke prick my nose.

I call out, 'Where you be? Be people here?'

A voice go scream, 'Susannah?'

This cut loose a buzzing cry of every Christing little. Be nonsense fright and larm, and it come from the floor above. I break to run.

I trip once on the stairs, and fall onto my scrambling palms. Shin strike a corner with full weight. Hurt keen, but I run on. The air be thicker here, got scratchy taste with rising smoke. And all the littles' voices seem to boil against the wooden walls. I get to the upstair floor and here my breathing stiffen. Must go down crawling, all my mind think drill, drill, and I go to the howl that draw my need.

Noise come from the enfantroom. I grab the knob, well knowing it be locken. Yet when it hold against my hand, I swear. Throw my shoulder to the door, wild in headless rage. But this door ain't open in, must pull. Nor I got tools to break it.

I yell through the door, 'You keep down to the floor! Keep low!' Turn and rabbit down the stairs into the airy cold.

The morning give reluctant light, be like it shrink from this unkindness. I jump the steppen flame, and pause to kick some snow back over it. It hiss and change its smoke, but ain't no time to check my work.

Then I run looking, cursing every Christing who ain't leave tools astray. The garden and fields be bare of nothing. Money neigh reminder at me, back herself and pull her reins. Ain't got breath to call to her, I run on toward the shed.

Every gratty nerve respond when I see its door open. I find a ready hoe, and turn again. Is something sobbing in me, want to think how this become. Want to sit into the snow and think. This drag in my mind as I run onto something dark.

My foot misstep on softness, I go tumble. Hoe fly beyond, and I turn back, sit up in icy mud.

Japhet lying on his back. Legs drawn together tense. Got a shotgun lain across him, one hand clutch its stock. Blood run from his corner mouth, his face got flecks of gaudy red. White shirt be soak in this bad color. Eyes stare dull surprise.

I leap and fall on him, like I will wake him from this death mistake. Grip his head in hands, scream help in they uncaring eyes. Then I press my face to his chill face. I breathe in once and taste his normal sweat. He stank of life. Yell again, but he stare his same death. Surprise and cold.

I rise with panic through my flesh. Grab the hoe and gasp my sobben breath. I sprint back to the house.

Now the sofa room be bright with wriggling lines of flame. Walls begun to blacken, scraps of fiery curtain blowing round. On the stairs, the smoke show gray and real. I take good breath before I run. Stairs taken jumping. This use all my air, and at the top, I duck down to the floor and breathe again. Is dirty air, ain't right. Lungs gulp with panic. But I crawl on, and in one concentration, rise and raise the hoe and wedge it in the door. I swing my body's weight against. The wood crack loud. Be gasping at the poory air, as I go strike again.

Be some twenty times I strike. Must tear the lock surround, be digging into simple wood. Ain't know how many times I drop, and take my inch of smutty breath. Call my orders, breathe again. Be gratty to hear the yawling skree, can guess these children walk themselves. Ain't hope I carry all.

And then the splintering grow until I see the metal through. I haul the doorknob, and the door fling by.

Be every dozen littles in this room. Enfants in their wooden pen, and clumsy twos in diapers. Be a storm of eights run at my legs, and forcen past. I skree myself at this. I shout, 'You take the enfants! Ain't got sense to live! Yo digger trash, goddamn!' Then I be kicking through their fear stampede. I catch a running eight and whirl her back onto her heels. She scream and beat at me, but I go grab her by both shoulders.

I yell into her face, 'You heed! You take an enfant. Ain't be asking, you will do this thing.'

Then something waken in her fear. Her struggle pass, she nod.

Behind, the littles empty through the door like thunder. Some been tumble and they call as they go crawling on. The thinnish smoke come lazy over their heads, turn with a picky motion. Air begun to look a grayish blank.

I turn to the enfant pen, a grandy bed with wooden walls. Be six crawler enfants in this bed, all squallen breathless. My sight go harsh. I bark down to my eight, 'Ain't run nowhere,' and loose her arm. She stand there sobbing air as I reach in and take the tiniest chit. Heft this, reach it down to her. She take this enfant well. I grab another and another. Every smoke be aching in my head this weary time. Ain't carry more than two myself, these enfants struggling fat.

My eight be stood, forgot no reason. Hold her babe and stare. I yell some hollow word, and when I go, she run along. Then we be scrambling down the stairs into the ravish air of life. The open door be heaven, and outside some littles is hurling snow into the struggling fire. They scatter as we come.

I crouch and let my enfants into snow. They scream a different note, like this the peaking insult. I laugh in panic and turn back. There a boyish ten gape at me. I shout, 'As big as that and never help! You come with me, you trash!'

Child shout in frighten rage. He turn and run off toward the field.

Be no time for hate. I cast around, and there my trusty eightish girl be waiting. She grin and run before me, looking over shoulder, toward the step. So we go again, and now the air is cotton thick. Must have a wetten cloth, ain't drill to enter smoke without no cover. But ain't no time for drill, and every nerve remember we almost finish. Only three remain, is only three.

I let her run before, watch her steps for weakness. But she go up vally. At the top, I grab her from behind. Force her down to crawl. But ain't no proper air remain. We coughing every inch. Be thinking, ain't no matter. Be only minutes. Yo my head now agony, a dark exhaustion start in me.

The rest be strange confusions. Can know how I stand in the enfantroom, eyes run blind with smoke. The enfants quiet dull, but move themself when they been took. Next, I be running, and I swear my arms flop at my sides. But when I reach the stairs, some grace become – both enfants kept. Arms held right, though they ain't know. Next I be lying on the outside step, cheek heavy on grateful wood. Smell burning but the air be sweet. My mind repeat, no smoke. Then I be sitting up and scream, 'You eight! Where be my eight?' Be weeping foolish, never known her name.

Someone pull at me, and I be walking, though my legs go craze. Breath is scorchen in my throat. It hurt feroce when I cough out, but thinking say, *I ain't be ruin. Going to be the same, will live.* And then I see my eight, she stood like nothing been. Her straggle hair got ashen scraps atop. She look staring to me, saying, 'You be Ice Cream Star, yo sho?'

And there my Money come and shove her nose at me. Most push me over. Her reins come loose, or some child free her reins. I laughing wild. I say in tears, 'What be your name, my little?'

Girl laugh back nervy. 'Got no name. I waiting on this now. Myself been Army born.'

WHAT BEEN AT TOPHET HOUSE

First work, I send a tennish girl to fetch my Sengles to. She ride off cantering on their mule, start yelling for Sengles before she find the path. Then my No-Name Eight begin their tale, yo every brat give help. They tell this backward forwards, say the middles on the ends. Be work before this history understand.

First event been yesterday, when Riding of the Queen reach Lowell. There El Mayor tell John about the Armies' roo.

Can be, ain't nothing come from this. John a lawful servant, ain't want nothing out of custom place. But Japhet break in anger, insist they keep Susannah back. No Christwife give to camp of roos, he say. Ain't in the Long Agreement, nor is morals so.

This argument continue all their journey back to Tophet house. There, they call the wives, and all go in the sofa room. Start talking, drinking cider booze. Is natural, the littles sneak onto the stairs to spy.

Most they hear be hennish scandals – calls of coward, calls of fool. But when the night be old, Susannah come out armen-arm with John. Her face beweepen, and the godclothes torn down to her naked shoulders. Braids shine and swing with Army gems.

She say, 'I still can go. Until the church, it still be time.'

'Nay,' John say, in boozen voice. 'The NewKing need to learn. All Massas stand by us, ain't only us.'

Here Susannah spy the littles, where they pressing back in shadows. She cry up, 'You waking? Ain't enough to worry? Go!'

Must grumble to their sleeprooms then. But from their high room windows, they see John ride out to Army camp.

This night pass into darkness morning, and he ain't return. Wives go to their beds, but their low squabble never hush. Yo, they rise before the dawn. Been arguing in the cookroom – littles peeking from the stairy rail – when Nat Mass Armies come.

Been ten Armies. They ride on horses, wearing feathers as for war. Yo every Army got a shooting pistol. With them come the roo.

Roo hold a rifle, and this rifle use before his horse can pause. He fire against the house, this shooting chatter like loud teeth. His frighten horse buck under him, he laugh. His gun swing, firing wild. A window busting in, glass fly and bullets fly. All children dashing for some hiding. Armies self been duck.

When this shooting rest, the NewKing shout Susannah's name. Yo, before no other child can move, Susannah go.

The eightish No-Name spit when this part come. 'Ain't seen no cowards like these other wives,' she say. 'Should go with her.' The other littles give this hot dispute: ain't cowardesse, been sense. But all agree Susannah leave alone.

She go out barefoot, in her ruin godclothes. Hair been unbraiden from its gems, be shaggy loose like littles' hair. The feathers call their dirt at her and laugh. Mamadou watch her come. Ain't say no word.

She go to his horse, stand by, and there be talk between. The littles never hear this. Nor can tell Susannah's mood, her back stay proud. But when this speaking finish, she turn back from Mamadou. The Christings all give breath with joy. Boy Japhet say, 'She talk some reason there! No Army argue our Susannah!'

But she walk to a feather. He put his hand down grinning. She grasp this, spring aloft. Go mount behind him on his horse.

Then Japhet swear, is lost with blindness. He break and run

outside, sprint desperate down the steps and out. Ain't go to Armies, he run longside the house like he go flee. Can see the Armies laugh, some feather fire his pistol loose at Japhet. Ain't never strike, and Japhet reach the shed. Here he go in. Then, watching in the kitchen, Hannah Christwife say, 'Oh no. Oh no.' She keep on this 'Oh no', while Japhet come out with the shotgun.

Nobody seen who shoot him. Ain't seen him hardly fall. When this bullet fire, Hannah Christwife turn, scream to the littles. Dash, herding them with feet and hands, and heave a two up by the arm. Scream till other Christwives give her help. They chasen all the littles, fighting–swearing, up the stairs. Catch every one, and wrestle those resisting, without talk.

So the littles lock inside the enfantroom. The wives go stamp back down, and can hear Hannah wailing thoughtless, 'Oh, my Japhet, got to be alive. My Japhet.' This her brother born.

Windows of the enfantroom look only to the back. The littles never see what happen more. Nor they ain't hardly hear above the larming enfants in this room. Can only hear some gunshots, slamming door and female shouts.

When the enfants' larming ease, been silence. Ain't no voice, no step. Hear nothing, but be soon, they smelling smoke.

While this story dabbit and confuse, the fire complete its work. House get jacka-lantern looks, be red in all its eyes, before the flames die into black. The roof collapse with noisy sparks, can hear the falling floors within. Soon the fire be only drifting smoke.

In this, my healthy breath return. Head clear into simple pain. Be scrubbing my hurt palms with snow, my Money's rein caught to my arm. Gentle her on her neck with these cold hands, amid the littles' squabble. Yo, I think where these Christwives gone. When I remember Japhet dead, my fury waken dark.

At last, I say, 'Yo hush. The Sengles coming, they bring you safe.' I take Money's rein in hand.

'You going?' cry my No-Name Eight.

'I wait for Sengles, shoo. But then I go. Ain't leave this crime to breed.'

'Crime?' a frighten seven ask. He shivering in his whitish jams. 'What crime?'

'Foo,' I say. 'Can see, the fire.'

'And Japhet shot,' a little say, in helpful voice. 'Be other crime.'

'What you leaving to?' This say a troubling six. Can recognize, this be young Cora, child I known since crawling years. Is grown grasshopper thin, and now got soot along her nervy face.

I set my hand in Cora's hair. 'Ain't do nothing, never a thing but talk. Come right, you see.' But my hand tremble stubborn.

Cora say, 'Will Japhet heal? Where Japhet now?'

Before I answer, sound of gallop come. All the littles spook. They skree, push close around my legs. Money snorting, prance back from the noise. Some children run when Big Smoke come around the barn, Jermaine astride and whipping him like devils.

I yell, 'Ain't fear, be Sengle help! Ain't fear!'

Jermaine rein in so harsh that Big Smoke stumble, kick his heels. Then Jermaine fling to the ground and run. Make path through all the screamers and I caught into his arms. Money back away, her reins cut into my raw hand.

'Nay, let me free!' I say unthinking. 'Nay, I got to–'

'You ain't hurt? You hurt?'

'Foo, how I hurt? A fire like any. Let me free, goddamn!'

He hold me back. 'How this become?'

'Ain't no time, I got to go.' I break off from his hands. 'You take these littles into Lowell. Be my deputy in this.'

'Where you going? Ice Cream! Cannot go! You ain't got *shoes*!'

'Heed, you bring them into Lowell! Bring our Sengles also. Damn, we leave this mally place, been said!'

This balk him, and I step back free. Turn to snorting Money. Take some nervy steps before I settle her to mount. Then my head catch pain as I spring up.

Jermaine call, 'Ice, you come to Lowell mill? Ice Cream!'

I ain't say nothing back. I call out to the littles, 'You see, ain't got to fear no more. Be right. Wives coming back!'

Yet their staring follow with reproach as I heel Money off.

23

OF RESCUE DESPERATIONS

The morning come up blue and strict with cold. Day made for careless deeds. In the final hiding woods, I pause my Money and
unmount. Go find a stick of firewood weight, is fortey for a bat.
Then I sault back on Money. She break in canter for some strides,
bright-foot like she approve my act. I say to her, 'Bespeak him, all I
do. We flee if trouble come. Ain't leave you to they Army rodents.'

Can hear the camp before I see its huts. Make its booze music,
howlen song and mally-strung guitar. Child shout some anger while
the others jeering, hound yip up. Yo, when I see the feathery points
of huts, my fear take bright. Then hatred rise above, hate that these
grubs cause fear to Ice Cream Star. I heel my Money into gallop,
swearing my heart that Crow be there, will speak for my protection.
And my mare run willing forward, jump a log and scatter dust.

Got time to see the Armies standing round, their faces dumb
with booze. Trailing feather ornaments look dull in this blue light
of morning. With them stand a simper. Wear a yellow shorty dress,
been torn across her belly. A glittering cloth wound in her hair, and
she lean to a feather's shoulder. Wave a bottle in one hand. Yo the
sun stare unconcern on this disgusting life.

Seem like a scene I watch forever. Like something in my starting
dream, as I fall into sleep. Ain't Mamadou nor Crow be by, and this
seem like some normal doom, a certainty I expect. But it come

peculiar in surprise when all these feathers startle. Ain't right that they run toward, ain't human that they carry guns. And I be galloping hard. I hold my bat at waisten height and call for NewKing Mamadou, and call again, I skree his name.

Been plan to gallop past these Armies, gallop round again, the times it take until the NewKing come. Use my bat if this require. If bullets come, ain't turn to meet this death, but gallop on feroce. Ain't figure in my mind that Money never seen no war.

As these dozen feathers scatter and jeer, my Money fright. Plant hoofs and wheel. My weight go forward loose, I let the bat release to catch her mane.

I jolt onto her back again and we been rearing wild. Dust rise, but feathers running through. A bottle thrown, fly past my head. I shout again for Mamadou, kick Money hard. But where she turn, a feather raise a pistol. He fire into the air, and Money scream her neigh. She rear again and paw her hoofs.

Then someone caught my dress. I feel my balance leave me, all my body seem to leave control. I fall and fall hard back, jar pounden on the dirt. Money kick again, her hoof go huge above my head. The feathers gather to me, and my heart feel gratty as I see my pony jump beyond. Can hear her gallop off, her neigh trail panic as she go.

Then my every part grab by some sally feather. I wrestle, but can get no purchase. I scream Mamadou again, but my voice waste, my every scream sound nothing. Feather kick me in the back, and kick again with fortey pain. I cough and scream again. Next clobber catch my jaw, some ringen hand. This be a metal feeling, like a door slam sudden in. Their insults start to hear, and other kicking jolt my ribs. But I ain't feel no single pain, be all a rain of hurt. Some hand be pushing in my dress, fingers hurt my breast. Their laughter go.

Then something cry behind. All their bruising holds release. I fall. Bones rattle on the ground, head strike a sharpen hurt. I see their bodies rise away. Can feel a wet pain in my hair.

A high and girlish voice come jeering. 'She Mamadou's Sengle bitch, ain't see? You steal your trouble, fools.'

Some feather swear and stamp upon my hand. Be sideways crushen, and a whine escape my mouth. His foot remain there, its weight ache through my nerves. I puke slight water in my mouth. And bitterness waste in me, that I shown weak. I swallow my gross taste.

Above, they argue quick. In my corner eye, can see the yellow-dress simper, fist on hip. Be like she float above my pain, a tiny yellow ghost. The feathers be a stanking everything, all things I must escape. I writhe against my squashen hand, but nothing come. Then despair sink cold. Be only breathing through my sickness.

I feel the cold dirt underneath. Stare on my stampen hand, the heel of sneaker shoe on warpen fingers. Cannot tell, if they be broken. The hurt confusing big. Yo my head be whole, can feel this with my other hand. Is only bloody wetness there, grow sticky in a braid. And my breathing come, my body live. Ain't ruin, can still live.

Their sneering fight go on. Most be toilet swears, their voice be filth. Cannot help my body, it go flinch at louder words. Yo, all my thinking wait for my escape. Ain't see no way, but I watch quiet. Listen to their angry garble passen overhead. See the simper's heely shoes. One heel lift and scratch her other ankle, while the feathers calling insults, and she spit return. My attention sharpen when she say, 'Ho, get some rope, you dregs. You waken Hak, I like to see your sorries then. I see this gratty!'

One feather and another tell her she must get this rope. Their voices peevish high. Yo, her shoes turn. She laugh another sewery word and go. A feather call, 'And bring yo booze! I drying here!'

Then their laughing come again, and hands in all my dress, fingering my nakedness. I close my eyes, I grit my jaw. Be only thinking of any way I flee. Where Money going to wait. Some Sengle come for me and they distract. We fight like normal, fists and knives. We flee. Must be, I going to flee.

Then something land beside my head. I open eyes to see a dirty whitish rope, loose in its coil. All hands flee from me. Sneaker on my hand release, and I be scrambling up – and knocken down. And caught again, however I slip and scratch. Be caught and hit in jaw again. And hit in every place, ain't know how much.

My tears come only when they tie my hands. Rope scraping in my skin. Ankles tie, the rope cut in. Be draggen by this ankle rope, my shoulder rasp in dirt.

Then some other calling rise across the camp, impatient. The feathers hush their voice. Step over me and step around. Like miracle wish, they pass away, be like all pain depart. They pass away, is real. Their faces gone.

I look up feary, seeing only sky. Seem like it fall away from me. It move like gasping, dizzy. I pull my wrists against the rope. I stretch my ankles, struggle every careful way. But the rope stay tight, ain't give enough. I only hurt my hand.

Then steps jar in the earth. I look up, there the yellow-dress simper stand. She bend to me. And she pull from her dress, between her breasts, a bladen knife.

Will cry for help, but ain't no help. Close, can see the simper's eyes, weird in nefasty gleam. Seem a beasty soul contain within a person face.

She bend past me, like she reaching for my bounden hands. Her plumpen breast touch at my shoulder. Then I feel some coldish metal slipping at my back. I gasp my voice.

She say at my ear, 'You hide this now. The NewKing come. Be safe, ya.'

My injure palm hurt on some harden object. Simper form my fingers to it, wait until I hold. It take a breath before I comprehend, she give her knife.

Then she stand away. Rise up like anger, turn her back. 'NewKing. Got your loot. She here.'

Come Mamadou's voice, is sleepen dry. 'Hak waking, fatty. Call for you.'

'He call for me, he call for me. Whatever else he do?'

153

She go forward. I watch after her in sickness. Ain't want this sudden friend to leave. Ain't want this knife my bound hands cannot use. Yo, she pause in walking, like she feel this inward cry.

Then her back notice, baren where the yellow dress hang low. First I think some mud crust up in ridges there. Back show every color but the healthy color of good skin.

Is scars. No inch be whole. Is ridgen scars and fresh red hurt. She sigh and reach behind to scratch, her fingers reach this injure patchwork with accustom grace. Then she ease, walk on.

My eyes watch through their water. See Mamadou's tall shape approach, and then my nerves react. Behind myself, I turn the knife. Hide it beneath my hurting arm.

His naked feet stop by my head. Feet long and simple-boned, he wear a golden circle on one toe. It show a bird head, lightning in its beak. Shango, god of rain, of flashing war.

Above, he huff a laugh. 'Prettieuse. Sengle grooming.'

I look up his body. Is wearing jeans and nothing. All his body show in dreamen glare.

My head speak pain, but I go answer, 'Yours, be what your insects do.'

'Do worse than this. Your luck I wake.'

He hunker by my feet. I feel him tug my ankle ropes, they pull into my skin. These slacken, and the hurt go chill and loose.

Then my hands is wary. Expect he free their ropes, the knife discover.

But he leave his hand rest on his knees, sit back. My eyes go scary to his face.

Mamadou's thinking eyes be soft from sleep. Skin shave to a glisten, how he do in vanity. His locks tie in a tail behind, and godscars blacken in his cheeks. Nothing in him prettieuse. Is only bell, is vicious bell.

His hand reach out. I flinch back, but it find its place. Finger touch a scrape on my top lip and gentle there. His mockery smile be felt in my own mouth.

He say, 'Cannot keep yourself away from me.'

My heart be kicking in my side. I shut my eyes against him. Yo in this dirt, with all my trembling wounds, I love the thing I love.

He say, 'Come on, get out of this.'

He reach to grip my arm, but I pull back. Twist up myself, with knees and shoulder, feel my struggling hurt. Yet my legs work.

I walk beside him to his hut. All my conscience ware the knife, where it tuck at my arm. But nothing happen in this walking. Yo, his reddish blackish hut stand, same as ever be. He lift the flap for me. I duck inside.

NewKing hut be grandy as a Christing room inside. In shape, it be a jumbo cone, made of poles and curen hide. Floor be curly sheep-skins, thick enough to sleep without no bed. Ain't furniture to sit. Armies never sit but on the ground, they scorn this wooden help. To one side, there be a patch of naked earth. Here stand his personal idols, wooden children with beak heads.

Never a wall be bare. Is hung with every ready object. Be pots and clothes and cutting scissors. Books hung by a string deep in their pages. Mamadou's red spear and bow hang there, his feather trappings. Crow-black, cardinal-red, they trail down, longish in peculiar twists.

And hang a rooish rifle with a curven magazine.

Mamadou let the hut's flap close. Then light be only from the fire, this moving darkness comforting like sleep. He come before me, look down where my dress be muddy, wet with melten snow. Some pleasure working in his face.

I flinch back and say, 'Can like some whiskey.'

He narrow eyes at me. 'You like this?'

'Been said.'

'Ain't brandy you prefer?'

'Take what you got.'

Be no other guesting they believe, but Armies will give booze. So I watch upon his thinking face, and misery grow in me. Can fear, I be no guest in this. I lose this final hope.

Then he shake his head like disapproving, but he turn. As he reach to a flask, I let the knife drop from my hand. With a seeking foot, I scutch it underneath a sheepskin. Put one foot lightish on the bladen shape, and breathe relief.

Mamadou find two handled shopes. Uncork the flask with teeth. Check me with his eyes, a second late, and he pour standing.

When he bring the shope to me, I tug my arms against their ropes. 'Yo how I going to drink this so?'

He bite his lip in smiling, and his chippen tooth show there. He stoop to rest the shopes down on the floor.

Then he come behind me. My skin along my whole back waken, feel him there. He take my wrists, begin to work particular at the rope. I tense against his touch. Think on Japhet dead, the red specks on his face.

Ropes drop lazy off. My hands chill as the blood return. Crushen fingers go and boom with hurt.

'Your head been cut,' say Mamadou. He touch lightish at my nape.

I flinch away. 'I know. It be my head.'

Can feel his breath of laughter pass my shoulders. Then he come and fetch the ratten shopes, his eyes on me. I move my injure hand, test its fingers. Knuckles, wrist and palm be bloody skinned, all sting in air. But the bones is whole. Ain't pull a bow with strength, but can hold reins. Can steady a gun.

Here my eye glance to his rifle hangen. Arms tense before I think.

Mamadou see my glance and nod. 'Go try this plan. Recall, we wrestle any a time. I ain't refuse this chore again.'

'Ain't come for that,' I say unpleasant. 'Got business.'

'Business, call it this.' He reach a shope toward me.

I take the shope, hold it against myself. 'Truth. Be sergeant now.'

To this, his face change inward. He take a drink of rat, swallow it like a thought he take. 'Your Driver sick?'

'Be so.' My throat stick, and I say on weaker, 'Gone from us.'

'Be soon for this. Ain't known.'

His fingers move like pondering on his shope. Then he shake his head. 'Think, you sergeant now, you can come into camp like that? Ain't those times, girl.'

'Ain't fearing this.' Nerves rise in me again.

'Come into camp like that. Ain't think you likely going to leave. Going to expect, I keep you here.' His eyes look up like this a question.

'Shee to this.' My voice rise hoarse. 'Dirt, what you done at Tophet?'

Mamadou's face surprise, then it go settle in annoyance. 'You come for foolishness like this? A waste.'

'Nay, what your feathers done at Tophet?'

'You and me, we got a parley, right. But it ain't this.'

'Goddamn, you answer. What you done?'

'Done what I like. And so be done to you or any. This story tired.'

'Done what this Deema ask. Been order by some animal roo.' I spit upon his furs. Some spit go fly and strike his foot.

Mamadou tense. Face lost its bell, be gritten as my feeling. Can see the muscles change across his chest. But he ain't answer.

I say, 'John of Christ ain't kilt?'

A moment, I expect he answer nothings like before. But he say cold, 'Nay, this digger run. A speedy coward.'

'And where they Christing wives?'

'Be in the simper house. A cherry take.'

Then something closen in myself. Ain't thought to this, their simper house. Been hours since these Christwives took. Sure every child guess what these hours contain.

When I speak again, my voice be rough. 'Susannah? She your queen?'

His mouth thin down, distaste. 'Susannah ain't no name to me. Got some newer simpers. Expect I know the one you miss.'

'You know.'

'Yo, been remember. Give to Deema's use, she doing for this animal now.'

Be times, the NewKing tell me any unheart thing, to rile my hate.

157

Like to bring me hot and yelling, his arms receive my fight. But he never lie. Ain't think to lie. Is straight as blood.

Now his bitter stare return. Eyes watch with all their thinking, and ain't no amuse in his respect.

I say flat, 'This rape bring murder.'

'Myself, I never like no struggling girl. Some meat that suffering while I eat, this be sad work. Deema, he ain't bother.'

'Sure you die for this.'

'Girl ain't wish to be no queen, can be a simper like another. Choice been chosen by herself.'

'Yo tick of all disease! You kilt their Japhet! Try to burn their littles, enfants in a locken room. Ain't know how you can live. How you go live beyond—'

'Slow, slow.' He put his fingers toward my mouth.

I flinch back, and booze flash from my cup, sting on my scratchen hand. I swear in underbreath. Switch the cup to other hand, and I suck at this crawling hurt.

'Sengle,' Mamadou say, 'ain't be no littles in this case. A boy been kilt, he got his gun to thank. That girl with Deema, she my goods. But ain't no littles in this.'

'Littles been lock inside. You light the house. Been burning when I come.'

Mamadou watching on my face, like he inspect some lie. 'Ain't nothing done like this.'

'I know a fire set.'

'Been no fire. Can spare your talk. Expect you set some fire behind. A Sengle habit, like your boring lies.'

Then something freaken in my heart. I yell with all my breath, 'Ain't lies! Yo unheart cockroach! King of filth, you be the shee of Hak! Your blood be piss! Can see you die, this blood stank every tree of woods.' Then I catch my breath, go suck my hand again.

He watch this speech with face surprise. But when I suck my hand, he break up grinning. All his anger pass, he laugh out hard. Yo, he step toward and take my chin in his big hand. Hold fast.

'You ain't change none, my Sengle. Seen you beaten, worry this will calm you.' He laugh again.

I put my hand up to his chest, like I will push him back. But my hand remain there, like a fact.

I say uneven, 'Beaten, shoo. Your feathers fighting weak.'

'Sure, is slaving work. Wish the girls to fear, not that they spoil.'

'What fear? Been like our normal wars.'

'So this handling by my feathers been your joy, can comprehend.' He grin, his broken tooth appear mischieviose. Godscars go into deep furrows.

Under my hand, can feel the muscles shifting in his chest. Then my body remember him, ain't courage can forget. My feet themself awaken, fur feel sweetish in their toes. Knife shape feel sweet.

And he say with low particular softness, 'Hold, I clean yourself.'

He step back toward his hanging stores. Go hunting through some various clothes. Reach about, he go as graciose as naked shadow.

Yo I drink my whiskey, feel its burning and my stinging hand. Force myself to think of what I do, and what I owe. The whiskey feel like weakness in me, and I think of leaving here. How I get this knife. But it ain't magine somehow. Ain't seem like nothing going to happen after this.

Mamadou take a cotton tee, a flask. In by-thought, he turn to the hanging rifle. Yank away its magazine and toss this in a farther corner. My mind distract at this, can feel his thought. I may reach the rifle, but ain't time to run for both. And I feel some gratty strength, he fearing me somehow.

Then he come back. Open his flask and splash its wet onto the tee. Can smell, is low rat booze.

I waken from my thought. 'What this be for?'

'Clean your hurts. Is what we use.'

'Yo, I can do this. You ain't got to touch me nothing.'

His fingers tensen on the tee. Look in my eyes with something bitter. Ain't know what happen in me then, but when he take my chin in his sure fingers, I go calm. He sigh, say low, 'Got cuts behind, ya. Better I do this.'

He start upon my face in silent mood. Rat sting malicieuse. Yo, this cotton tee come back with any dirty streaking. He clean along my arms, and find new hurts I never known was made. Bend my head and take time with the sticky cut left in my hair. He hold my injure hand in his, and work in tiny gentleness. Face show but what he do. Then he hunker down, his hand go searching up my scrapen leg.

Cannot even say how I become in this. I think of pain while I can try. But my body be one seeking memory. And when he leave his work and stand and watch into my eyes, these eyes tell every story. Mamadou's face be cold without no joy.

Then, how it begin – how it beginning every time – he say my name.

Ain't words for what this be. Be something make all honor small. No life nor honesty remain, and every strangeness, every stopping pain, become bellesse. We speaking words like *love*, like *you*, that ain't mean nothing. Words waste in air. Nor ain't knowledge of this losten hour, is gold you cannot see. Cannot find out what it been. Yet this blind thing be more real than life.

And then it finish. I lie upon the sheepskin like I done, yo twenty nights of evil. Lie naked in myself.

Mamadou lie, one arm upon my belly. Ain't sleep, but stare beyond. Nor I ain't look to see him. Wish this been forgot.

I watch the changing firelight. How it catch on points of objects on they walls. Every object seem like some sad proof. A string of books. A leather jacket with a rip sleeve.

Outside the hut, the feathers sing. Can hear this dim and eerie. Be a simper song, weak with all feeling feathers never get. Tell of the pain they cause. Song repeat: *ain't no kin, ain't no help, ain't no help remain.*

And I think of Driver knowing what I done. Susannah with the roo, left in her misery. How something in me come to Army camp for this. I stood before the littles at Tophet house, and squawk my lies, while in my heart, been wanting this.

Ain't be the hero of my mind. Ain't even normal made.

And all my losses wake, and every task I ain't perform. I grit against this, but it rise with every pain that breathe inside my flesh. The howlen singing. All the helpless things that I must help, that going to waste.

Then inside this misery, something inkle. Be looking straight at Mamadou's rifle.

Magazine in farther corner. Ain't going to get this magazine now. Mamadou catch me easy. Be only one act that can work.

Then it be careful work to get my knife. Knife lodge by my lower shin, ain't reach it, how he hold myself. Yo, if I move from under, he will rise and watch on me.

I hook my leg around, show like I scratching on this knee. In this, I work the knife out with my toe.

My mind repeat, this must be killing. No Mamadou threaten by a knife, can laugh at this small weapon. Take this knife before I strike. Must kill him while he never fear. Be for my freedom and the Christings' freedom. Be for Susannah's rape, and for the littles capture in this fire. Be done and then consider.

After, I will take his rifle. Drive the feathers off with bullets, or I die in this. If I ain't die, I go to the simper house. If it be feathers there, they ain't wear guns. Can hope they ain't. Tophet Christwives free, run in the woods. Be done if I ain't die. Then I must find this Deema Roo. This be a second murder, must be done without no thought.

I bring the knife out with my foot. Be finicky work, to catch it so. Begun to sweat when I bring it into reach.

Then it go without no thought. I grab it with my hand and turn. But as I go to strike, is like the knife catch in some cannot. Ain't hurt him. I pause in air, when Mamadou's hand fly at my hand.

Knock it wild, and I pull back, but he grab quick and catch my wrist. Hold on and grip feroce.

First his face surprise. Then it clear to a bitter preciation of the knife. He rise and force my arm back. I fight my other hand, but this be caught, he pin me on my back. Straddle over me, his hands go painful on my wrists.

Then I ain't help myself, I smile. Be my relief, this task been took from me. Ain't mine to help this now.

Mamadou watching cold. He shift his weight on my knife hand. Work at the fingers, dig them loose, and take the knife himself. Look at the blade, like he inspect its sharpness. My freed hand go to his throat.

There it rest. Ain't try no hurt. I be smiling helpless, like this been a pleasure game.

He rest the knife blade flat against my nose. 'Sengle, you ain't never disappoint.'

'Christings be my friends.'

'Been told, I never burn their house. Ain't got no listening sense.'

'Be thirteen girls you keep.'

He stroke the blade along my cheek. 'Agreement broken by themself. Be murder war this is.'

'Shee, found a thing to want.'

'Ain't liking war, I guess. You ain't.' He make a face, and rest the knife point at my beating throat.

I swallow against this knifepoint. 'Every fool see how you thinking. Roo bring guns to you, your prowess rule.'

'Truth easy. How it be.'

'You trust this Deema, you be blind.'

'Ain't trusting any a child.' He raise and waggle the knife before my eyes. 'Shoo, you be one can speak of trust. You funny, Sengle. Noisy, but you funny.'

'Yo,' I say in scorn, 'and what these roos will gain from this? You know we got a roo ourself. He tell me of this gain. Your end be pity.'

Here his thinking pause. Eyes narrow, and he reach behind and find the flask of booze. Uncork and drink, still watching on me. 'So, what the roos will gain?'

I try to make my spirit think. Mamadou watching me with hate, with interest. Drink booze and watch me past his knife.

I catch my breath and say, 'I trade this news. You let these Christings–'

'Shee.' He sit back cold. 'My trade be this. I feel too lazy tired to kill you. Be tired with this discussion and your knives and nonsense talk. Going to tell you what will be. Can be my queen now, Sengle, this the final time I give this chance. Then you *tell* me what I ask, because you *doing* what I ask. Or you be a slave like any. Can try your luck at fighting feathers, will be cherry entertainment. But you never leaving here. Must know this be the end, when you come running to this camp.'

I chill in my blood. 'Choice of worm and cockroach. Ain't no different to my mind.'

'You see the difference when I let my feathers take your precieuse self. You feel some difference then.'

'Fool, you got a nothing brain, same as you got a nothing heart. Be no death I fear. Go kill me, ya.'

'Got no killing mood. Nor I ain't mention no third choice.'

Then we staring, hate to hate. Can see the muscles tensen in his neck.

I say, 'Prefer to be a simper. Will be bone variety.'

He raise his arm behind, and bring it down with all his force. My head ring false, can feel my teeth. Sight go in hurting blur.

He say in weaken breath, 'Ain't want no girl I got to beat. Ain't like sad work, been told you this.'

'Go kill me, fool. Ain't slap me like an eight.' But I be trembling, cannot tell if this be fear or rage.

Then something come, be stranger than no blows. Mamadou's face go stark. He put his palm flat to my cheek and hold the place he hit. Ain't stroke nor press, he only feel me, like he ain't certain it be me.

And tears shine in his eyes.

My heart beat uncanny. I reach up to his face, but he push hard, rise up and stalk away. A moment he only stand, his back move with his angry breath. Then he fling the knife back to myself. It land beside my knee. I ain't look to it, I watch the NewKing with all beating fear.

'Goddamn.' He wipe his eyes hard, like he want to tear them out. Walk to the wall, look at the rifle like this thing ain't recognize. Yo, when he speak, he speak toward the gun.

'Ain't let you go, should know. Nor my feathers accept this weakness. Come running here, you going to be my queen, if I must keep you bound. For truth, I never leave you to them. You ain't for that.'

He put one hand up on that gun. 'I know the things you say, you talk to me like . . . damn, I ain't no fool. Know well this roo ain't honest. Got any roos behind, I know they ain't want nothing good for me.'

I catch breath to this. 'Nay, what he promise you, your Deema?'

'Now you asking questions.' He look at me feroce. 'Tell you this, ain't going to be no Sengles or no diggers here. People be mine or took by roos. What you thought was happening, if you even do no thinking?' He turn by and hook some jeans down from the wall, begin to pull these on. I watch, feel how I never seen him do this normal task before. Resent my own insisting love, and I say, 'So, roos help you to this power, you think?'

Mamadou finish with his jeans and look back at me cold. 'Nay, I know. I helping them. But cannot see how power can hurt me. You going to fight them with that knife, I guess.'

'Can leave. Ain't got to stay by them.'

He make his scorning face. 'Thought you been smarter. Leave, they find me in my weakness. Then it be no promises from them, be other stories. Think you going to flee from them, you need to find another world.'

'Better chance in this. You let me go, we see who living longest.'

'Nay, you heed. You going to be my queen, because I want you, all it is. Fight me if you like my beatings. Guess you prefer to be some rooish keep. Talk like you knowing something. You ain't even knowing what you be.'

'I be some goods, I guess.'

'To Deema? Yo, can meet him, you begin to comprehend.' His face change into different hatreds. 'Tell you this, some chance become, we war against these roos. And sure, if war be made, mine be the people gain this war. They digger rabbits die in easy blood without myself. Your Sengles, sure be enfants, going to die.'

He shake his head, reach up and lift the gun off of its hook. Cross to the magazine and fix it on. Then he look back with measuring eyes. 'You bone? Ain't hurt too much?'

'How you meaning? Sure, ain't nothing.'

His face go easier. 'Yo be right. I going to fetch this Deema. Best he understanding who you be, before he do no grossness. And heed, you ask him on the fire. Deema stay behind at Tophet, but he never spoke of fire. Be truth, this interest myself. And be easy with your knife. Deema ain't so soft with noisy females, like I be.'

I watch his eyes, and my heart waste in hurt. I say without no thought, 'Ain't wish to kill you, for yourself. Sure you know.'

He swear some filth beneath his breath. Show his tired grin and say, 'You be a year of misery, Sengle.'

Then he duck outside the hut. Can hear him swearing as he go.

24

OF DEEMA ROO

Belief be food to courage. Yo, never been my courage hungrier than on this day. I crave for any madness hope, so it be hope and not despair.

So it become that I resolve to be the Army queen. Will beg the Christings' freedom for my love, all I can do. Then I make war against the roos with Mamadou the NewKing. Can fight the rooish cure from them, my Driver healing quick.

This endure for wishful minutes. It last while I put on my filthen silver dress, inspect its ruin. Yo my strange belief continue while I drink the last of my rat booze. Cut a hiding for the knife into the silver skirt, can hold it ready by my thigh – and I believe. Believe while Mamadou return, and yo I wish to speak, to tell him that I stay. Ain't no love been like what I desire, while he come watchful in. His rifle slung upon, it hanging careless at his naked chest. He say, 'Is coming. Mind my word,' and every shame be gold.

But when Deema come, this madness die.

He come with arm around a feather who bear up his drunkenness. Roo wear only whitey underpants and mudden boots. Paunch show sweaten hairy, and his face be pink as ugliness. Ruin ear look like melt wax. Got a knife himself, thrust in these underpants, the lastic hold it sloppy to. Yo ain't this grossness spoil my faith.

The bearing feather be Karim. He got his greenish feathers, loose untie and straggle down. And his face can recognize, though I ain't thought that I will know his face.

Be handsome made, but low in height. This height mark Crow's Karim, and how his beard be shapen on his chin. Eyes is careful nervy, like he struggle with his patience. He look at me with knowledge, and I look at him with hate.

Then everything I feel be nothing in this visible sight. Cannot go the sinking path of Crow.

And here it recognize how I be caught. I been a hundred fools that I come here. Even if someone guess I be here, all they Armies wearing guns. Ain't nothing Sengles do against. Mamadou said, *You never leaving here*, he spoken with true meaning. Been my stupid pride that I ain't heard this seriose.

I feel the world be shrunken to this hut, these men in flickering dark. Ain't no future out of this. No Ice Cream ever be beyond. Is almost pleasure when the roo distract with his bad noise.

'Mamadou! My king!' call Deema Roo in slushen voice. Then he laugh like this been enfant joke. Hunt his hands around himself, surprise when he find only skin. Mamadou understand this, reach the rat flask out.

'I thank gratty,' Deema say. Grab the flask and put it to his mouth, try drinking through the cork. Then he look annoyance. Pull the cork out, drop it on the floor. Drinking go in pulses down his neck.

Mamadou look intention at me, like he show some point. Yo Pasha's speech of Deema remind: *Be fool soldat. Ain't bone for nothing.* Now I struggle in thinking all this *fool soldat* can mean.

Deema finish his drink and hand the flask to green Karim. In this, he notice me. Come toward sway-foot and stop at talking distance. Ain't so tall as Pasha, but is grandy size enough. Yo his fattish sides make weight.

And close, I see his face be ruin queer. Got creases in his brow and cheek, the skin bag loose below. Pink color in his cheeks ain't regular. Be tender lines of purple branch along his cheeks and nose. Be like a face in sleeper pictures, looking all disease.

He say, 'This girl I never saw. Where you hide this one? A good take, almost good as mine. I think–' He point up at my face, scribble the air before my mouth. 'Think she was hurt. No, this girl you use yourself, I see what happen now.'

Mamadou say in careless voice, 'Told you of Army queens. This my queen, you heed. She got a question to you.'

'Queen?' Karim say sudden. Look to Mamadou, and his hand touch his feathers finicky. He glance at me with spitting face.

'Queen,' say Deema. 'Queen I know, is like you say before. But questions is the wrong time. Bad time. Children, I drank.'

Now my love be cold, and all I feel is how I can escape. But I say in shaken voice, 'Ain't trouble you with much, but just one question.'

Deema blear his eye at me. 'Got pretty breasts,' he say. 'But too black.'

I feel the hating eyes of green Karim inspect myself. He pick at his feathers, say low-voice, 'Queen ain't insult.'

'Truth,' say Mamadou cold, 'quit your familiar games, my brother. Myself ain't slept one hour this night.'

'Bad,' say Deema. 'You must sleep. We all sleep! You with Karim, I take this girl.' He laugh high in his voice.

Karim swear underbreath. Look back at Mamadou with pleading, like a cheaten little.

Roo drink from the flask again. A shadow rise up grandy on the wall beside, snake there in firelight. When he lower his arm, the shadow drop, like it suck back into himself. And I recall again, I never leave this place. Myself be by.

I take a feary breath, and my hand gather on the knife. 'My question this. Why you burn their house at Tophet?'

The roo turn sudden, leave his back to me. 'Got more rat? I go to find more rat.'

'Got more,' say Mamadou. 'Sure this wait. Queen been ask a question.'

'Question?'

Mamadou say like carelessness, 'She ask about some fire.'

Roo seem to wake alert. 'Fire! Ya, I light a cigarette. Match go down. Comprehend? This wooden house, it go–' He raise his hands up overhead. 'Never to make a house with wood, my king. In my country, we make stone material. Many houses, very high. No fire.'

I force my voice. 'No fire beginning so. In snowy morning, I ain't think.'

'Begin,' say Deema with back to me. 'Wooden house.'

'Yo littles inside this house.' I say up harsher, 'It been killing work.'

Karim go swear again, and look at me with new intention. I feel my boldness spark, I say to him, 'You hear, Karim, was littles there. Been an eightish girl the Armies' own, your child.'

'No,' Deema say, but I say through this harsh, 'Yo, Deema kill them all.'

Mamadou flinch. His eye look wary at me.

Roo stand and scratch his face. Karim watch on him now, got trembling looks. Then the roo say, sour in temper, 'Cigarette. Can give me?'

'Be sure,' say Mamadou. He pass along the wall toward me, holding sharp onto his rifle. Reach a pouch above, retrieve a fold of Lowell cigarettes. As he turn, his eye look at me warning.

He handen Deema Roo a cigarette and zippo. Roo light, make noise as he draw in the smoke. Muttern to himself, 'Talking. Bore from this.'

Then Mamadou say, 'You burn this house, my Deema? Ain't no harm to me.'

'Is politics.' Deema turn to him with injure face. 'Ain't burn no children. Politics to burn a house, you see. Be fear to others, you keep this fear. They come like . . . for slave to you. You know this politics.'

'Sure, cleverish thought,' say Mamadou. 'Only wonder be, why you ain't spoke of this.'

Karim look at the roo, look back at NewKing cautieuse. Bite his lip in mally attention.

Deema point his finger at Mamadou, then swing it by. He shake this finger, saying, 'You must learn by me. Ain't only guns. Going to give you learn. Can rule like–'

'Rule like science, sure you said.' The NewKing fish a cigarette, shape it in his hand. Look at it considering, then narrow eyes back at the roo. 'But how I going to learn, if you ain't tell me what you do?'

'Ain't listen to your girls, I learn you this. Ain't take this talk.'

I say cold, 'My only wonder be, why you will do this act. You try to win these Armies to your use. Then burn their eightish child.'

Roo turn to me with painful face. 'Was no child. No person in this house. Girl lying, fire was small.'

'Ain't believe she lie,' Karim say nervy. 'Chosen queen ain't lie.'

'Expect that I can lie,' I say. 'And sure I like this lie above the truth that all these enfants dead.'

Now can see this Deema's mood gone stank. Is drunken riling. And in my corner-eye, I see the NewKing watching disapproval. Put cigarette in his mouth and shake his head.

I look away. 'Nay, roo. Be honor that they kill yourself.'

Deema turn toward me squaring. My hand brighten on my knife. He say, 'Be pretty to look, but this bitch lie. This allow?'

Mamadou staring on me hard. 'She going to learn some honesty. And you can learn respect, my Deema.'

'No,' Deema say, his eyes on me. 'Was no enfants. Girl be filth.'

I say in frighten hate, 'You lying. I seen these children dead.'

Deema's face twist up. Then, like some despair I magine, his hand go to his knife. Karim swear underbreath, and Mamadou say, 'We finish now, be done.' His voice be angry cold, and Deema's face flinch insult at this. Yo my burning fear be on my knife and Deema's knife.

Then Deema yank his head back sharp and spit into my face. I startle back, raise my free hand and wipe my face off rough. Mamadou saying hard, 'Can leave your knife,' and Deema yell some rooish drunkenness, at Mamadou or anyone. Look at me, and I can see how I become an object to him, like a cup a little throw in tantrum. And in one rearing motion, Deema punch me in my breast.

This be a weaken hurt. My breath go queer. Feel all the beatings of this day, and see like evil certainties how I can die in this. Then the world go slow as all my feeling gather in one curse insistence that I live. Yo as he spit again, I pull my knife. I dodge back, but he come grab at my hair. His knife flash in my terror, and gasping wild, I stab him in his gut.

Knife go in like a punch, ain't easy took. Yo quick, the roo jump back. Knife fall loose away between us. Then this Deema yelling healthy noise as he look down.

All my thinking be, how he ain't die. Ain't die for nothing. Scarce be blood. Then the beast wheel yelling and punch my face. My footing lift, be lost. I fling back heavy on the furs, one arm fly up and strike some hardness. My sight go black. Be fighting in this sleep, and wake to Deema struggling Mamadou away, his knife be out. I think how I must crawl, but ain't be nothing I can hide behind. Arms weak.

And then a different light appear. A shot go deafen hard.

Deema hike up harsh, his back arch queer. His head lost its side part, and blood be streaming, sprinkling. He fall onto himself, slop in the furs.

I look at Mamadou, heart alive, but yo his rifle hanging loose. He stare by, looking where the hut flap open.

Pasha stand into the tent, like some unknowing dream. He rise and his long rifle held in shooting pose at Deema's ruin. Darkness fill my blood, be like I see all things through blackness.

See how Mamadou lift and aim his rifle. How Pasha turn at him. The shot been gone before I fear. Mamadou fall and small Karim cry out and crouch beside. Tears look greasy on his face.

And Pasha point his rifle at Karim. Pause and hold. Karim hunch. Guard his face with naked hands. His mouth move without sound.

Pasha say to me, 'He also?' His voice be shaken cold.

And I look blind at nothing and say, 'Yes.'

25

OUR FLEEING

When murder happen, ain't no time to know. Must run, must fight. Must do more murder, flee again and fight. So it happen in this day of sickness.

I stare at dead Karim, the blood that slither on his greenish feathers. Everything be calm and dead. But Pasha call to me.

Cannot know the words he say. I know but what I done. I go in simple madness to the NewKing, kneel beside. Touch where his blood spread on his chest. Then Pasha crouch by talking. I want to speak of something, feel is something I must say. But nothing and nothing be.

Only when Pasha take the NewKing's rifle and unhook its strap, my weeping blindness start. Then my thought come plain and distant. Think how I must breathe through sobbing. Must have eyes is clear. Must run, I got to see. I blink and wipe my eyes in working movements, like I clean a dish.

Then Pasha hold the rifle to me. His face be tense like rage. He whisper, 'Can hold well to shoot?'

I take the rifle. Its cold be mally. Something in me wailing, but I cough and snort my nose. I look at Pasha's whitish anger and I say, 'Can shoot.'

Then Pasha shift the rifle in my hands until I hold it right. Guide my finger to the trigger soft. I nod. His jaw shift, Pasha touch my head.

He whisper, 'Ain't go out till you hear quiet.'

He take his rifle up again. Go to the flap and listen. Be only then I hear the voices. Be all cackeny shouts and running. Angry yell beyond. And Pasha breathe in deep and dive outside.

Bullets jabber like a chattering jaw. Be deafen so, it almost comfort how it never pause. Can clutch my rifle to myself in this bad darkness. Feel my tears go cold. Hear the jabber and wait for quiet. Wish this quiet never come again.

And it stop. Be silence like a simple falling. Can see in magination how my Pasha lain there dead in blood. Feathers standing to, wait every gun upon myself.

But I go to the flap. I swallow, push the rifle nose between. Follow it out.

Pasha there, is standing whole. Heart only beat again when I see, ain't no person by. No dead. Be huts and dust and sunlight. Nervy chickens hopping in this dust.

'Where they gone?' I say dumb.

'Run,' say Pasha flat. He pull the magazine off his rifle, shove it in a pocket. Find another out, fix it in place.

'Run.' I feel my face be grinning, though my tears still go. Be like more tears than I got in myself.

'Your Money there. I catch.' He jerk his head toward the nether path. 'Ice Cream, you can ride?'

'I bone. I got . . .' I swallow at my throat, and peep a sob. 'Must get the Christings.'

He sigh out hard. 'Nay. Ain't time. Fool.'

'You come with me?'

Then I stare at him until he nod. His eyes got all frustration, but he follow when I go.

Simper house's door be risen open. Can guess, from here the feathers come out when they first hear Pasha's gun. Come out, rush around, and flee when this gun turn upon themself.

As we approach, Pasha pull me behind. Go forward stalking. I keep back and feel my rifle gangly in my weaken arms. Be tired work to keep it steady. Yo my head begun to agony. All my sickness wake. Sight fuzz in eyes, keep blinking at its changes.

He lead me to the blank side of the house. We listen there.

Ain't known what I expect. What we hear, be crying enfants. First I panic senseless, think this be the Christings' young, was brought somehow to join the wives. Then I know, these be the Armies' get.

Then something in me disbelieve, after all been done this day, that enfants can remain on any world. That Armies can be squalling littles, frighten from a noise.

I whisper, 'Enfants.'

Pasha look at me with his frustration. He turn, creep forward. I stalk behind, and every nerve go hurt with his loud feet. Can hear each step, ain't nature how is loud.

At the corner, he stop up. Look at me angry still, and say with only breath, 'Keep here. Behind.' He wave his hand around the huts. My nerves react, and I turn staring, like all feathers rush on me.

Then Pasha rise and shoot around at nothing, at the standing huts, the trees. Noise blinding loud, can hear the enfant skree behind like silent thought.

Shooting stop. The skree rise up. Dust and flying chickens. A plastic sack blow round among.

And I hear the footstep sound of Pasha running. I chase him to the door unthinking, gun held clumsy to myself.

Simper house be strewn about with sheepskins. Each lain separate with some personal objects to their head: china dog or mirror, a sprawl of sparkling jewlerie. One wall got hooks with hanging clothes; these spread across like crusten stain. In the nearer corner, floor be bare where water risen through the floor.

Is any struggling girls inside. All push together to the farther wall, clutch littles to their legs. Wear every kind of dress. Be girls is nothing but a blot of blackish godclothes. Girls in shorty dress or unders. And by, where light come in an upper window, be a girl in Christing nighting gown. Beanie Christwife, sobbing while she clutch her chest. Yo, behind her gather all the Christwives in their nightclothes.

Stood before me, Pasha yell out, 'You! Come here!'

Among the huddling simpers, lurk a boy. Ain't but fourteen, got whitish grayish feathers round his neck. These feathers ruffle on one side, and he clutch himself, push back among the simpers.

'Come! Will shoot you there! Will shoot!' Pasha gesture with his gun.

And now a simper panic, push the feather from herself. He stagger forward, staring on Pasha's gun. Begin to gabble frighten curses, and he pulling at his jeans. Like he hide himself with these. A simper reach toward him, and he strike back at her hand in panic.

Pasha flick a switch upon the gun. My nerves go calm. Be thinking, gun on safety, we be done.

Pasha shoot once. Boy wheel on his feet, and sink away.

Then come a scream like never heard. Be any panic simpers, rushing from the blooden feather. Go back like a wave, then this wave turn and come again. Scatter of simpers fall upon the boy and hunch there wailing. I grab at Pasha's shoulder. 'Hold! Goddamn, goddamn, what help this be?'

He stare at me, his jaw be set. Be stupid anger in his face. I say high-voice, 'Be safe enough! Goddamn, you go, you guard behind. Go back!'

Then something falter in him. Pasha nod and turn away. I watch until I see him at the open door, sharp cut in sunlight.

I turn and stare upon the girls. I breathe heavy, looking if there be no other feather. My head be any pain. Sight queering worse, it churn and flicker. Simpers cry their begging words and curses, but they ain't come toward. Be careful time before I know, is only females there.

Then a girl step forward. I turn wary at her, and she halt. Raise a hand against the sun. 'Ice Cream?' Behind her, all the simpers start to quiet, heed to this event.

Take a second before I recognize her face. Is Hannah Christwife.

I say in hoarsen voice, 'Yo Christings, come away. Ain't fear my roo, he go protect you. Go. Can trust my word.'

One and one, the Christwives stumble out. As they come, they watch me feary. Hurry past my gun. I feel a shame like icy wind at this, but I stand fast. Yo, in some nether misery, I see Susannah ain't among. Must be, she kept apart in Deema's hut.

Now the simpers watch me. I see a twelve who stand unmoving, face besobben wet. Behind her, an older girl go press her face into this twelve's thin shoulder. Another and another, all these dreaden shapes of girlish slaves.

Ain't courage left for this. I say in weak, ungiving voice, 'Can come. Ain't stay in this. You free. You hear me? You be free.'

They stare, and only larming enfants carry on untired complaint. Never a child move forward. Ain't no answer in no face.

I call with angry hopelessness, 'Can go to Lowell mill. You come!'

Then I turn and run, my last fear chase me from the house. Run into hurting sunlight, where my Pasha wait alone.

Huts and dust. Pasha stood, gun looking at the empty trees.

'Where the Christings?' I shout foolish. 'Where they gone?'

He turn angry. 'They run off. You come now. Now!'

I gasp frustration, look around like I will see their path. Can hear some scrambling noise, but ain't know who been making this. And sudden, I realize this can be feathers stalking back. When Pasha push my shoulder, I go run.

My running limp in clumsiness. My head be misery, all my vision gone in busy light. Pain sicken in my gut as we come to the nether path.

Aside, among the trees, be Money. Come nervy when she see me, pull against her tied-up reins. Whinny and leer her rolling eyes.

Pasha shy from this, and I go forward, coaxing thoughtless. Money skit at first, and my hand go sloppy on her neck. Pain blur all my body. Be like I sleep afoot, my hand rub weaken on her fur. Then I open eyes, and Money gone down calm. I grab some mane and leap. Ain't get no strength, I fall back loose, and my head ring with hurt. Annoying tears fill up my eyes.

Pasha come to, careful. He hand his rifle to my clumsy hand, go mount. Be pleasant done, I thank all gladness that he learn this task. He take the rifles from my thoughtless hands. Last he reach for me.

I give my hand, and go up liften. Scrabble around with leg, come up and slip on Money's rear. Pasha reach back wild to grab me. Yo, I clutch to him.

Be myself who kick the horse. Kick and kick until she gone into reluctant canter.

This cantering hurt in sicken waves. I clutch and press my face to Pasha's back.

Then blackish madness come and pass. Be times, I hang with face press, and ain't know where we be coming from. Want to beg my Pasha that we quit. Be times, I think he taking me to roos and be in scary minds, ain't know if he can trust. Then I wake again in sharpness, skew my eyes behind, look for the feathers that may come.

At Sengle town, this agony jolt and jolt and stop. I slump at Pasha for a string of shuddering breaths. Lean sideways and puke rat booze. Then, when my eyes open, I can comprehend, ain't no one here. No enfants, nothing stirring in the camp.

Pasha breathing hard like fear. He say, 'Ice Cream, you bone?'

I take a grainy breath and say, 'They gone to Lowell.' Want to make an explanation, sure these explanations crowd my head. But I ain't speaking somehow. I shut my eyes and see the NewKing grin. *You be a year of misery, Sengle.* Ain't know at first, when this been said. Then I know, and start to cry.

Pasha reach back clumsy. He find my arms and pull them, one and one, around himself. Say, 'Hold. Hold to me.' I hold and cry on gratty, like Pasha been the one I miss.

As we come through Lowell City, everything begin to ease. The pain become familiar trouble. Got no strength for feelings, and I look up at the bricky buildings like this be a casual day. Notice a sparrow on a step; she turn her eye at us. Then she flight away, and there be blue above the bricks. So I be squinting into blue as we come to the Lowell gates.

Here come a yell, is long feroce. Can scarcely see above my Pasha's shoulder. I stretch my painful head to look.

At the easter gate, where petty cryers keep their watch, now stand a grown eighteen. Got a long-nose rifle in his hands. And yo upon the walls, more jones aim various guns at us. These Lowells call their frighten voice.

I take my breath and yell in weakness, 'Here be Ice Cream Sengle!'

Then every voice break out, call to each other. Money pick and drop her feet, shift back. The sun stare bald around.

A jones voice call out hard, 'What roo be this? Identify!'

I scream wild, 'It be our roo, goddamn! Be Pasha Sengle!'

Then I weaken down. Exasperate this whole event. Pasha pinch my arms to him with elbows as Money start again. We come among the noisy voices. Hear them boss and question. Then it be a queery feeling, how I be loosen off the horse and handle down. I struggle at a hand that touch my hurt. And I be swung and loose again, come folding to the ground. Lie on their concree lot. Sun's heat fill my skin, the ease of stillness chill me.

'Ice Cream? Companiera?'

When I open eyes, there stoop a girlish jones with croppen hair. Ain't know this child to name. She be a fattish child enough, I think of food. Then puking feeling come in me. I shake my head. Close eyes again.

Her voice come niggling. 'Companiera, I be First Physician. We get you fix. Can walk?'

I say, feel angry at this imbecile, 'Ain't walk. Where Pasha at?'

'Ice Cream, I here,' say Pasha.

'Yo get me, get me.' I open eyes and look for him. He stood with happy on his face, ain't guess what he feel happy for. I say, 'Ain't leave me, foolish.'

Shut my eyes, and I hear Pasha laugh. I go talking on in darkness.

'Hurting well, this ain't no nonsense. Yo, can walk. Nay, why you pull me?'

Can feel how he collect my knees. Then I be dizzied up against him. Swaying start again. Some worry fret in me, I open eyes.

We rocking down a Lowell hall. The doors and numbers stretch like work. Yo beyond, stood at one open door, be El Mayor. His face look enfant scary, like he hear some horror tale. Wear his silky robe like any a day.

Then life begin again in me. I struggle, say, 'Can leave me down. Nay, seriose. Be bone.'

Look up at Pasha's face, he frowning like he disapprove. Hold on me firm.

Then can hear how El Mayor come stamping down this hall. The sound come hard on all they simple walls.

El Mayor say close, 'You leave her down. She say to leave her down.'

'Ain't bone to walk,' say Pasha.

'Leave her. We attend this. You go with my runner. Answer!'

'Nay. She–'

'Answer how I tell you. Ain't hear nay from you!'

I look to El Mayor, surprise. He staring at my Pasha with untemper fury, brow grit deep. Ain't seen him in this mood before. A thought suggest, this ain't my normal El Mayor. Be some dream person.

Here it panic in me, that I never left the NewKing's hut. Be still there, and dreaming. Pasha ease my legs, while in my terror Deema smile his bags of face. Panic rush into my blood, and I fight onto my weak feet. Hold Pasha's arm to steady.

Then my mind come clear again. Is quiet real. We be in the center hall, is all their squarish tiles and walls. Door to Carpentry be there, but ain't no sound of work. A grayish cat sit by this door, look at myself and swish her tail.

El Mayor got both hands up, like he prepare to catch me. First Physician with her croppen head look weary kept. Got duty on her face, and now I recognize a purplish spot on her top lip. Her posies start.

I swallow and say, 'My Sengles? They–'

'They here,' say El Mayor.

'Yo Driver?' My voice peak. 'He here?'

'Sure, Driver here. He bone.' El Mayor look past my head and say somewhere, 'Start a room. Room 209. We come behind.'

Then misery concentrate in me, like lightning find a tree. I look round at Pasha, grab his jacket. 'Susannah! We leave Susannah!'

'Hush.' El Mayor push in somehow. He staring at my Pasha, who go melt away. Can see him press his back against a wall.

I swear in voice, reach back for Pasha. Struggle El Mayor away, but this fight ain't go far. He arm me round, and I be like a caught bird in a cloth. I say begging to him, 'Christings here?'

Then something happen at my back. El Mayor hug me at his chest, so hard my face press hurting. He yell, 'I told you, go! Get off! Ain't want you now!'

Pasha's voice say, 'Ice Cream, I go down now. I be by.'

'Nay,' I say in muffle squashing. Yo a pain rise in my head, and all my arms go feeble. Cough somehow, and nose at El Mayor. Then I be liften rough. Some hand be pressing in my hair, poke like it checking fruit. We moving then, must swallow not to puke. My head careen, my pain go blind.

Yo, somewhere in this handling, I remember NewKing Mamadou. The fire cast shadows up, the shadows flying on the hanging objects. Dead Karim lain by. My hand on Mamadou's warmish blood. Then be like my hurts gone far from me, I crave them back. I grit my jaw and try to fix my mind on nothings. Pains. But through between, my skin keep saying Mamadou and death and never happening again. In this, can hear a door come open, light change painful on shut eyes. Then the world drop by, and nothing be.

26

FIRST RUNNER, ARMY BORN

Be a foolishness of life, how we forget our hurts in sleep – like they unmade there, taken back into the time before. We wake in stupid innocence. Then all pains flash to memory, and every cruelty be fresh.

Yo when I first woken, I lie careless for a minute. Feel my bruises like a sleepy question. Then I startle up in fright. Ware and raise my hands, like I can fight this evil back. Breathe while every knowledge come, and place its separate weight on me.

Feel like I slept a beary winter, but the windows daylight blue. A wooly blanket cover me. Beneath, be bare to unders. Been sweating in the Lowell heat. When I look down myself, be sticky bandages on my hands, like messages from some world that I ain't want.

On the bedfoot, slung that silver dress. Be like a cloth of murders, draggen here from Army camp. First act, I rise on aching legs and snag this in my hand. Go to the window, open it and cast the dress into the yard. It struggle down on wind, and settle tired on a wiren fence.

Then I lean against the wall and breathe. Say to myself, *Is done. Ain't need to think on this. Is done.*

Head lost most its pain. I go to the door, feel how my injuries be stiff. Had these limps before, from war, from Money's bucking ways. Be familiar like a boring friend.

Outside the door, First Runner stand. Even in stillness, child seem quick. Braids tie back particular, and she wear a pockety jacket that lie smooth as polish wood.

She say in duty voice, 'Companiera Sengle, how your head?'

I swallow nerviose. 'Ain't mally.'

'You seeing clear?'

'Sure, can see.'

'Confuse? Ain't get no trouble thinking?'

'Foo, leave this.'

'Nay, I got instructions. Confuse?'

'Goddamn, ain't nothing with me. I be bone.'

'You rest some more?' Her eyes look hope. Can feel, this save her work.

I sigh annoying. 'Shoo, must see my Sengles.'

'Nay.' She shake her head. 'Ain't go till El Mayor come by.'

Now, farther down the hall, I hear a rush of dozen feet. An object dropping heavy, and a boy shout thin, 'You packing what? Is rocks? Ain't carry this.'

'You clumsy, what!' a girl say back. 'You got no fingers? Hold!'

Then it remind, we leaving Massa woods. I say in worser nerves, 'Goddamn, I got to see my Sengles. Be all chores to figure.'

'Chores be doing.' First Runner nay her hand. 'Yourself must wait for El Mayor.'

'Foo, what I can do? Ain't going to rest. Be bone.'

She sniff her nose, look some embarrass. 'Certain . . . you can wash.'

Truth, I stank of booze and sweat. Can trust, this warry scent offending all their nice indoors. And now that it remind, I feel this pue myself like smelling guilt.

I shrug. 'Ain't argue with no wash. Be bone.'

'I fix this, ya.' She nod. 'Instructions.'

Bath be inside the room, it got a petty room itself. Be Lowell kept, so clean it hurt your eyes. First Runner fill the bath for me, and tell instructions while she work. Explain how I ain't wash my hair, the cut there be too deep. Put bandages by, explain their boring use. Explain the bath savon itself, how it must wet before it work, like she believe I ain't seen soap before. Every insect detail been in orders, and she speak these orders. When the orders finish, she stand by with no affection. Watch her eye upon the growing water.

I look to the checker floor, see one tile chip away. Start wondering how the Lowells fix this chip – except they ain't. All going to leave this place. Will be an evac, left to ants and weather.

When I look again at small First Runner, she be watching me. Drill passen from her face, and she say shy, 'Yo injuries be cool.'

I take my breath. This be a word of Armies, *cool*. Now it recall, this child been born by them. Run here from the camp, two years before, when she been a troubling eight. Can guess, she raise to love of wounds. All scars respect in Army camp.

I say low, 'Is truth, they brave.'

She nod, her feeling pass back into duty. Yo I stand there scary. All my thinking run and run, like bees inside.

At last I say, 'My companiera, sure you known the Armies.'

She flinch, frown on the bath. 'Ain't got much memory.'

'Nay, I only wondern. Simpers liking featherboys? Feel for them like a townie child?'

Her face be solid nothing. Time pass, my question freeze into her stare. Then sudden, she grab into her pocket, take a wrap of cigarettes. Without no word, she slip past to the sleeproom. Come back with a glassen shope, she hold this up and say, 'For ash.'

I make a sorry frown. 'Ain't meant no insult with my question.'

Her eyes come birdly sharp on me, and she say hot, 'Simpers like the feathers, nay – they simpers *love* the feathers. Simpers slave themself, is *wormen*. Birthing featherboys and give them to this, so they slave . . . slave someone else. They simpers hating any girl who free, ain't wormen like themself. Hate their own girlish enfants. They ain't *people*.' She spit upon the tilen floor, an act no Lowell do. Then she turn to the bath, frown furiose.

183

I say careful, 'Sure, be sorry.'

'You ain't known.' She drop her cigarette into the shope, unfinish. 'Sengle, easy life.'

'Be pardon.'

First Runner shrug. 'Ain't theirs no more myself.'

She crouch and reach her fingers to the water, test its warm. For a minute, she hunch there, tense. Her fingers dabbit in the water. Then she look back and say in stiff respect, 'Ain't guest you to a cigarette. Was ugly courtesy.'

'Be no fault. Yo, I take one gratty.'

She leave her wrap of cigarettes and Lowell matches on the bath side. Set the shope beside, explain how ashes must go in. Pause to wipe her spit off of the tiles and go off, upright quick.

In the heaten water, my cruel morning recollect. I concentrate my work on soaping arms, cigarette in my mouth. But still the skree of littles in the fire return, the feathers swarming. Deema's ruin head. Mamadou handling up his rifle, falling. Noisy death, and death, and fear that come when fear be too late. Last, my voice say *yes* and small Karim be shot.

Savon stop in my hand. I stare beyond.

Child ain't done no wrongness to me. Never I say this *yes*. Yo, I sit and live this voice again. I live this *yes*, but in my mind I ain't say *yes*. Say *nay, he bone. Can leave him. Child be right.*

He frighten, crouch on Mamadou. Here the tears come angry through myself. I huddle in the bath and sob hard grief. Heaten water be a comfort that my flesh resist. Ain't take this lying help. I cry, and frighten how this crying going to stop, and I be left.

Only when I hear a voice outside, I catch my shamen breath.

The sobbing hiccup in my gut. A knock hit at the door.

'Ice Cream?'

Is El Mayor. His bossing sound.

I say in raggety voice, 'Ho, you. Been something happen?' I start to rise, the water slush around.

'Nay, stay. Ain't nothing mally.'

Silence pause. I sit back in my water. It start to cool, feel like a disappointment on my skin.

He call, 'I come to say, the Christings here. Susannah also.'

'Christings?'

'You finish, come by my sleeproom. 124. I tell this story.'

I take a halten breath. 'I come. Wait – yo, bring me some clothes.'

'Clothes? Why you need clothes?'

I hear his laugh as he go by.

I leave the bath, and use the towel careful like instructions tell. Use germ wash, but ain't put on new bandages. Be itching pests. Yo I wash the shope out in my bathen water. Cigarette ends jam stubborn in the drain. I leave them there. Sure, ain't mattering now, this bath ain't never use again. Can be, this been the final heaten bath in all the world.

27

BY EL MAYOR HIS SLEEPROOM

'John of Christ been drunk.' So El Mayor begin his tale. 'If he been in normal minds, can be these miseries never start. But Christings argue through the night, and they all drink like buckets. Nor John accustom to this, sure. Gone big and foolish, time he riding out to Army camp. Walk in there yelling wild damnations, how no Christwife live by roos.

'Can magine how they liking this. Mamadou say, John break the Long Agreement. Now every wife be took.' El Mayor grimace sour. 'Then John try hitting Mamadou.'

'Ho.' My laugh come scary. 'Christing war his hands? Like angry rabbit.'

'Truth, ain't war for much. The NewKing beat John seven ways. Time John escape, he scarcely stand on feet.'

I fidget at my scabben finger, try to magine this. 'So where he gone? Ain't been at Tophet when I come.'

'Gone nowhere.' El Mayor shrug unhappy. 'Was lain in bushes there, all hours. Been only luck, Susannah find him.'

'Susannah? How, she fled?'

El Mayor nod, troubling. Look to the bed, like he avoid my eyes.

I say reluctant, 'She been hurt?'

'Ain't hurt that we can tell. She cry more than she speak, can comprehend. But got no injury.'

I sigh out perilous. 'Roo ain't rape her?'

'Nay, he rape her,' El Mayor say heavy. 'Be no other injury.'

We sitting frogleg on the floor by El Mayor's fat bed. I be in Lowell working cottons. Skin feel bright with wash. El Mayor wear a silky robe and jeans, look like himself on any a day. One hand stroke nervy on his whitish cat. She rumble in her chest, blink lazy pleasure.

This be a scene of quiet. Simple painten walls and clean. Bed got seven covers, and a fatty chair sit by – is Nampshire goods from Lowell's farther trading, made with carven paws. Ya, both chair and bed is places El Mayor prefer to corner me, in goatish moods. Ain't never laugh so well as I been laugh in this sweet place.

Be labor to believe there ever been an Army camp, its booze and chicken dirt, its rape.

And El Mayor say, from his clean respect, 'It been a day, I tell you this. Shoo, when you come in. All like you was.'

'Was normal war.' I touch to my cut lip. 'Bruises, mostly.'

'Glad this never come to you. That . . . they ain't rape yourself.' His voice be hoarse uncertain then. Is mostly like a question.

I tense against this. 'Pasha said they ain't?'

'Said he figure this.' El Mayor look to me wary.

'Sure, ain't been.' I shrug. 'They roaches never bother me this way.'

His face soften with relief. 'Truth, Mamadou ain't do this foulness to you. Been honest sort.'

This 'been' go ugly in my mind. I fumble for the wrap of cigarettes First Runner given me. My hand be bruisen stiff, is careful work to strike the match.

El Mayor say on nervy, 'Ya, I know he done this crime. But still be sorry work, his killing. Been a friend to me, some time.'

I look by at the cat, she blinking there with preyish joy. 'Ain't known him for myself. Fought with him in war, is all.'

'I known him years. Gone trading there most weeks. Child was honest as a drum. An enfant for all tricks. Shoo, one time, I bring a china cup to him for trade. Got a tint I make myself, was green. Been any work to get this green, yo I been Lowell proud.

'I take this out to Mamadou. Can see the man confuse. He say,

"It got some better use?" Mischief in me, you know how. I say this green be pharmacy. Put water in, the water greening. Make you drunk like papa tea. I tell him he must try this. He drinking water from it, and when he say he ain't feel nothing–'

My voice break loud. 'He been allow this foulness to Susannah. Been allow this foulness, any a time, to all they simpers.'

'Ice Cream, sure–'

'How they less than me?'

'He ain't hurt you? Truth?'

'Nay, how they less than me? I ask this.' I hear the weakening in my voice. Hold nervy, suck my cigarette.

El Mayor's nosy face be tight in thinking. Silky robe and shaven face uncanny on him then. Like his outside clean, but inside live all grieving dirt.

Then his voice come rough like mine. 'You asking, how they simpers less than you? Most children less than you. Sure Mamadou seen. Ain't mattering to us, our kindness ain't depend in this. Armies different, all is honor. Deserving, this be all that Mamadou known.'

My brain be twenty-odd directions, but I say, 'Is simple lies. Susannah ain't deserve this.'

He flinch like he been stung. 'Nay, truth. She ain't.'

I wait for more dispute from him, but he staring long. A minute pass while we both sorry kept, look past each other. I flick some ash into my shirten pocket.

At last he rouse himself and say, 'Can ask a cigarette from you? Mine all been packen.'

I find the cigarettes, say clumsy, 'Sorry for my mouth. Ain't strong to talk about this trouble.'

'Sure. Ain't strong myself this day.' He light his cigarette with eyes on me, unquiet. 'Been arguing all night, to start my moron children leaving. Some still keep behind. First Library ain't coming for no reasons.'

Be a breath before I comprehend. Then I say miserable, 'Nay, how? Thought you all leaving. Pasha said.'

'We mostly leave.' El Mayor shrug defensive. 'Most two dozen staying.'

'So tell them that they leave. You El Mayor. Can boss them this.'

'I trying, bell, be sure. I worn my voice with arguments. But they believe what they prefer. Already got one runner missing. Fool gone hid himself.'

'But they Christings coming, ya? You told them on the roos?'

El Mayor shrug. 'I told and told. But John, he terrify from life. Ain't want to hear no changes.'

'Damn! They got no house to use. How they will even stay?'

'Stay here. The mill.' El Mayor grimace sorry.

I frown at him a moment longer, then my spirit tire. I sit back to the bed. 'When we leaving? Or . . . you ain't told me this already?'

'Leave tomorrow,' El Mayor say soft, like couraging an enfant. 'My children scrambling now to pack. All downstairs look like hurricanes.'

'My Sengles ready. They all coming, if I got to tie them.'

'Bone. Be gratty company.'

I check to him for sarcasms, but his brown eyes be only sorry. I force a smile and find my wrap of cigarettes. Fish another. Thought go past my mind that I be smoking now like Pasha, two by two. Then my heart change peculiar. Mind flash on the stank of gunshots, stank of growing blood. And I see how Pasha look to Mamadou, check he dead.

This sight repeat in me. Roo look, and look away like nothing. His face be hollow white. Roo say, 'He also?' and he shoot Karim like simple task.

But it been for myself. Ain't wrong. Been war, been for my life.

I light my cigarette and say uncertain, 'One thing this evil day produce. Pasha, how he risk himself. Be sure, he faithful something.'

Then I surprise, how El Mayor go dark. He flinch away, contain his face like he get some bad taste.

'Been rescue me,' I say. 'Sure he . . . kill some children. Ain't think he done this, if it ain't been needful.' I stop on this and feel an after-breath of booze inside my mouth.

'Been defense,' say El Mayor in rough voice.

'Ya, defense.'

'What he said.'

I grit against my memory. Recall the feather in the simper house, shot without no cause. But I say with forcen lightness, 'What you got toward Pasha Roo? You fools had some argument?'

'Nay. We fine as . . . yo, we townie, ain't been argument.'

'So what it is?'

El Mayor sit forward nerviose, unsettle his whitish cat. She leap away indignant, flash her tail.

Then El Mayor look by to me. 'Yesterday, you got my note? Been said, about the proofs.'

'Ho, right. He shown you proofs about the roos? What this been?'

'Was photographs. You know this object?'

'Sure. Is sleeper loot, a picture looking like real life.'

'Nay. Be took from life.'

'Any a picture took from life.'

Now exasperate, go into explanations. Be like his bossing self when he do so, is seriose and plain. Still it take me time to comprehend, yo then I ain't believe. Cannot see how this exist, in any normal world.

At last I say, 'Can be. Will trust this, so you quit explaining. But how these photographs convince you nothing?'

He look by frowning. 'Been photographs of wars before. Things in these wars.'

'Wars? You got these photographs?'

'Nay, he keep them.'

'Foo, so how they been?'

El Mayor frown like difficult feeling. 'Been two sorts. First sort, they give to every roo. Show these to children for impression. Been planes and war machines, all thousand roos with rifle guns.'

'What he saying, right. But how this anger you with Pasha?'

'Nay, been the other sort. These photographs his own. From his own life.' El Mayor look to me, some bitter meaning in his face.

'Ho, you meaning Pasha got a . . . camera? What you saying?'

El Mayor shake his head. 'Had one, sometime. But it ain't this.'

'So what it is?'

'Pasha's photographs shown killings.' He look at me. Can see he hope for understanding in my face.

'Nay.' I huff my breath. 'Roo making photographs while children killing all about? Ain't to believe.'

El Mayor grit his mouth. 'Nay, been made after. Shown the dead.' He wedge his hands between his thighs, look complicate and tired. 'One photograph shown a street. Roos walking down this street, dead children all around like unwant trash. Other photograph, been a photograph . . . some littles dead, and hounds been eating them. One, shown living children with their noses cut away. It be a punishment they do. You comprehend, these photographs was made by Pasha self. He said.'

My mind stop back from this. My trust in photographs go weak. 'These been the photographs? This – cut-off noses.'

'Been other pictures, sure, of only people that he known. But these of killings, been a dozen like.'

Then I breathe relief. 'Can be, he lying that he made them. Found these pictures somewhere, showing things . . . some feary things that been.'

'Ice Cream, nay.'

'Ain't know him like I do. The child a liar born. Be sure, he find these photographs. He only want to fear you.'

El Mayor sit up, be almost anger that he show. 'One shown your Pasha. He sworn me not to say. But sure, ain't worry me to break this promise. Roo been standing by a murdern little, got one foot upon. Little can be eight years old. Neck cut most through.'

I shake my head. 'Can be, this only look like Pasha. Roos–'

'Seen his teeth. The roo been grinning. Grinning, damn. Is truth.'

I shake my head again, but I be thinking of the simper house. The fourteen boy that Pasha shot, no reason.

I say, 'You only frighten. Yo, some other roo can have these teeth. Any a child lose teeth.'

'Ice Cream, ain't got to trust him like you do. Pasha frighten me, yo sho, or I ain't think to leave. Must show these photographs to all my Firsts before no child agree. Will frighten any person, what these been.'

'But why he keep no pictures like? If they been his. Be only blames.' Now my voice be like it beg some help. Hands gone in aching fists.

'I ask him this.' El Mayor's voice come thick. 'He said, "It be my life." He got no other life. Said this himself.'

Now El Mayor reach by and take my hand. Press my bruisen fingers, and he say, 'When he come in carrying you . . . first, I thought he tore you up himself. Like a jumbo cat that carry in a bird.'

'Foo, Pasha got no vicious in him. Ain't like . . . sure, he know a gun. He know a gun, is truth.'

'Can be that he changen now. A person change sometimes. But I ain't trust him, all it is.'

'I ain't change.' My mind skit to Karim. 'Ain't like no mally changes.'

'Shoo. Be saying, he better now. If he change.'

'But I ain't want to change.' My voice come foolish, but I cannot stop. 'Be difference in our life, I know. Myself, I going to stay myself.'

El Mayor smile at this, and loose my hand. 'Foo, you change into my love pony, come the day.'

I laugh surprise at this familiar talk. 'Sure, when you change from a goat. Goat with pony . . . nay.'

We both laugh, a bouncy feeling leant against this bed. Then I sit forward nervy. Reach for cigarettes, then I remind, I be already smoking. A minute pass, then I look by at El Mayor.

He watching on me strange feroce. Frown and say, 'When you come in . . . I seen you hurt. Ain't never felt a thing like that.'

'Foo, was scratches mostly.'

'I ain't known.'

I make dismissing face. But he say hard, 'I love you painful, Ice Cream. Ain't deny me this.'

Then we looking at each other, while my heart be dark and sorry. Be noticing how his eyes set wide apart. A horsen face he got. But it have a handsome sense, is right like all his rangy body. Every girlish child be raw and weak for El Mayor.

He reach and put his fingers to my wrist. The tips touch light. 'I know it ain't no time for this. But can be, we get no other time.'

'Sure,' I say uncertain.

'Ice, you stay with me tonight?'

'Yo sho, must stay if Sengles stay.'

'Goddamn, you know what I be asking.'

Then he lean to me, his lips touch careful at my cheek. Hand gentle on my nape and rest my head into his chest. I breathe there nerviose. Been thinking weak, is right. Been always right. Even Driver wish this for me. Be no better love to find.

But all thought of love end with my hand on Mamadou's chest. Slip helpless in his dying blood.

Sudden, I pull away. El Mayor flinch back startling.

'Will think,' I say in frighten voice. 'But Sengles waiting on me now. I got to be below.'

He breathe out harsh. 'Ain't pushing you to this. Was only asking.'

'I worry for my Sengles, truth. Will think, but . . . be all tasks.'

'Sure. Got tasks to do myself.'

A longer moment, he gaze on me, his face a cheaten hurt. Then he stand up clumsy. Pull his robe around himself, and say in careful voice, 'You think. I be here from middy night.'

'Will think.'

'Room 124. Any Lowell bring you here.'

Want to say I been here any times, but this catch in my heart. 'From middy night. Yo sho.'

He start to the door. But when he reach it, he look back. Ya, his face show that this look feel like a shaming weakness.

I say, strange with want, 'Be gratty. Gratty for your help.'

His face grit up in sudden anger. But he shake his head, say light, 'No help too great for my love pony.'

Then he go out the door, his footsteps hasten to their hush.

28

THE PAPA SICKNESS

I find my Sengles in the Weave Room. This be a grandy hall, two minutes' walking end to end. Place fill with looms, these be machines is making cloth from new. Most is rusty left, be sleeper artifice from old and past. Some bone to use, though never a child make yarn enough to feed them well.

Time I arrive, my Sengles all ferocious at my missing self. The littles run to beg at me; my jones call angry questions. Now leaving Massa seriose, their tempers all gone fickle. Noise be hostilities and frights and grumps.

Jonah say, is Vember month, and sure we going to freeze, without no townie evacs to inhabit. Marlboro mention nasty that if Crow been sergeant, we ain't left. All be vex at Lowells, who took their knives in confiscation. 'Yo they pack their loot,' say Keepers in disgust. 'Ain't worth to rob.' Mouse and Foxen drawing swears in lipstick on the wall, while Shiny Eleven Angels sit by helping with suggestions.

Driver ain't be here. Was brought apart, up in a sleeproom. All I can learn about him be: our good child's pistol ain't been took, and this be stank injustice. Yo Pasha Roo ain't by, nor any a child know where he gone. Worst news, my Asha Badmouth took in birth. Be howling in a sickroom, turning out her baby enfant. Ain't like to think how these two going to travel any length.

Ain't strong to tell my violent day, nor this be fit for littles' hearing.

Say only, been a skirmish to the Armies. I show my petty wounds and let Baboucar touch my swollen lip. Say, 'This trouble gone. Been only chicken problems, like they is.'

Soon my jones go off, to booze or gossip in their custom pairs. But still the littles clamber to me, needy. Maple Two begin a play where he call out my name. When I answer, he say 'Nay!' and laugh. Story Four tell how her maginary animose, the Pickle Beaver, been a Lowell once. He own a bath with science fish: one been chocolate, one been red. Best Creature Five wedge different objects in between my naked toes. Aim to fill each space, and cavil when I let a spoon fall out. Yo ABC come jumping on myself as I be cladding shoes, while different mutts charge at her, bark excitement.

This day, the ferment grateful to my sense. Be life joyeuse, their selfish noise. Every two that weep, be gladness to me that they weep for nothing. My head remember that it hurt, but I unmind this detail. Nor I want to feel my tired self, nor anything of me.

Been most two hours before I try to leave. This begin a panic altercation. Maple Two scream at me desperate, 'You stay now! You stay now!' The bigger enfants grab me stubborn, hurting all my bruises. Only when Mari's Ghost come to the door with Asha's enfant born, they all depart in curiose stampede.

Then I go simple free. Take a chunk of ham from Patagonia pocket – Keepers' gift – and ABC snag this and pelt away before I look. And I walk out to day, squint eyes against its sudden bright.

At the bricky gate, I ask the cryer to find Driver Sengle. This spark a seethe of runners, chasing–yelling through the mill. Waiting, I look out where the sun go settle into Lowell City. It seem to boat away in orange light. A flock of birds go wheeling in this orange, black and small. Go round like gnats, like sparks, then they all swept down into vanishing. The bricky city rest beneath.

Then I magine how we walk out through this broken city. Leave our duresse, and find some woods where memory be clean. I magine our horses snorting under loads, the song of feet. Feel my heart accomplish to that sun, they swoopen birds. My injure body hunger for this walk, like it be rest.

Then behind, a voice call sharpish, 'Companiera!'

Be First Runner by the door, impatience in her small respect. I stand up from my place.

'Come to,' she call. 'Be hasty time.'

First Runner lead me brisk, can feel she run before her nerves. We rabbit down a hall; skirt by the diner, jabbery now with clashing trays and hundred talks. Go up the hinder stairs, and dash two floors in one long breath. Then at the second landing place, she stop, so quick I stumble in halting.

She touch the stairy door. 'Be leftward by. Room 243.'

'243. Yo sho.'

But she still stand in obstacle. Her manner gone uncertain.

'What be, my ten?' I force a smile.

'Driver. Going to say.'

'What going to say?'

'Got the pharmacy sickness.' She sketch eyes down nerviose. 'He sleeping now.'

My heart stop back. 'Pharmacy sickness?'

'Drunk too much papa, you know how.'

I swallow. 'Nay, ain't know this.'

'Do so, sometimes. Been help by First Physician, but he ain't talk yet.'

This meaning dizzy in my head. 'Ain't talk? How sick he be?'

'They call physician for him in bone time. Ain't fear, how he may seem.'

'Physician with him?'

'She gone now, left someone by. They took his papa now. Is safer like.'

I look at her through shady pain. 'Gratty. Respect your help. Sure . . . you leave with us tomorrow?'

Feel worse than I expect when bright First Runner shake her head.

'Foo, you staying by the mill?'

'Nay,' she say low-kept. 'I staying in the city, by.'

'The city? Lowell City?'

'Ya, someone got to keep a watch, what coming here. I hide in all they buildings. Be any situation at the mill, word go to El Mayor.'

'Situation how?'

'If they kilt,' she say like basic facts. 'I still be left to tell.'

I cannot think no courtesy. I say flat, 'You ten.'

She shake her head, frown seriose. 'Be Army get, can hide correct. Yo, if worse become, my brother help me.'

'Brother with the Armies?'

'Ya, Malik.'

Malik be grown fourteen, a boy I often fight in war. I try to think what sort he be, but all my mind be scattern dumb. At last, I only say, 'Bell couragesse.'

'Ain't got no courage.' She nod at the stairy door. 'Room 243. I got to go, be chore. Keep lucky in your journey.'

'Keep lucky you,' I say, but she already turning by. Her feet go twenty–forty down the stairs.

When she gone, my fear return. Take a moment's breathing dread before I open the door. Its weight resist my hands, feel like I hold with mousen paws. My mind repeating: *Ain't fear, how he seem. He ain't talk yet.*

Carpet gape at me. Be lights and doors. I walk into this silence.

243 stand open. All my sorrow draw me on. Be like every step go downward into cold. Then I be at the door.

Driver lain with back to me. Is most like normal sleep, ain't nothing harm in his appearance. Heapen covers on his rangy length. Head show its usual hair. Can hear his hasping breath, slow in its rest.

My heart ease down. Ain't nothing. Too much papa, all it is. Be easy done, the coughing pester so. He sleep it by.

Careful, I step in, my eye gone wary on his body shape. See how skinny he becoming, but this grief accustom. Only when I look upon his face, I feel uncanny. Ain't look like Driver. Can guess him in this face, but ain't the face I know.

Then something inkle in corner-eye. I startle back, my heart beat false.

In a folden chair behind the door, sit Pasha Roo.

Ain't know what fright I get. First is blackness in my chest, then it be only Pasha. Be normal with his owlen looks, his furry hair be muss.

I swallow at my fear and whisper, 'He ain't dying?'

Pasha shake his head, make face like this been foolish question. Stand and gesture by. I slip outside the door, be walking stumbly with my nerves. Pasha come, he close the door behind.

A moment, we stand in this nothing place. Look one to one.

Then I say nervy, 'Why you here?'

'Was me who find him.' Pasha shrug. 'Been seeking you, gone to the room they say. But you ain't there. In hall, was Driver lying.'

'Lying in the hall?'

'Lie, ain't wake. I call, and children come. Make him . . . bring from stomach?'

'Puke, can comprehend.'

'Ya. Breathe better then. He talking some, is better.'

'What he said?'

Can see, Pasha ain't expect this question. Answer pass unpleasant in his eyes, then he say stiff, 'Ain't much.'

'Nay, what he said?'

'Ice, he sick.'

'Yo why he come up here? He look for me? Damn, what he said?'

Pasha flinch, frown to the carpet. 'He . . . asking us to leave him. Leave him die.' Then he glance back nervy, check my face.

'So.' I clench my hands upon their hurt. 'You saying, this been meant. He want to kill himself, you saying?'

'Ice, he ain't think bone. Was pharmacy.'

'Nay, papa never make you . . . why he want to kill himself?'

'Ain't reasons.'

I hiss low, 'Damn, what he said? Say truth. Can know your fibbing, I will know.'

Pasha tense all through himself. Say slow, 'I ask him if he want you.'

I flinch, look to the door. 'And he ain't want to see me.'

'Ice, he sick.'

'Shee that, what he said?'

'Say you . . . make him dead. So you can do this. Move the town.'

I take a painful breath. 'I make him dead. When everything I do be for himself.'

'He been almost sleep. Ain't sense.'

I look to Pasha's face. Again his whiteness seem like sorrow, is like his blood turn pale from grief. But through his owlen face, I see the NewKing. Feel the gunfire in my fear, again-again, like beating. Pasha shoot and shoot, until the hut smell wet with blood. Pasha look away, face white and nothing. Say, *He also?*

Then all the madness of this day go freak. I say, outside all sense, 'Be strange enough, you found him. How this been? You doing something to him?'

Pasha flinch, look down. Get a frown like consternation.

'Go thinking,' I say. 'Think on all your work. Be well.' Tears want to start, but I rub at my eyes feroce. Swollen eye hurt vicious, and I swear.

Pasha say, 'Ice Cream?'

'My Driver . . . ain't believe he say this. Nor he kill himself. Is yours.'

I turn blind to the wall. Can know, I talking madness, but my heart believe this madness. Never my brother kill himself. Is Pasha's always lies. Yo, El Mayor been said, *Ain't got to trust him like you do.* Roo killing littles, El Mayor been said.

Then into this blindness, Pasha speak low.

'Can comprehend. You tell me hate, if you got need. Nor you ain't do mally nothing. At their camp, been me.'

Then everything be dizzy lost. I lean back on the door.

Pasha say, 'I ain't hurt Driver. You know this?'

I shrug at my feeling. 'Ya. I know.'

'Papa change his thinking. Sure I know. Done this myself.'

'Done yourself.'

'Gero, like this papa. Try this.'

I let my hand ease to my mouth. Look at Pasha now, and try to wonder. Think of his foot upon a murdern little. Hounds eating enfants. Gero.

'Been physicians there,' say Pasha low. 'And my soldats, ain't let me die.'

I say cold, 'Should let you.'

This catch him funny somehow. Roo grin up and muttern, 'Truth.'

When I see his teeth, my feeling come precaire. I say in strange high voice, 'Your Deema. Why he burn this house?'

Pasha sigh, his mouth go tired. 'Ain't guess. Can be, he ain't know littles there. He fool, is foolish work.'

'Sure he known.'

'Why he will know?'

'You told me roos kill littles, ya. Was lies?'

He nay his hand. 'This happen in a yeary war. When danger been, for time. Been stories, burning also. But in this time, with Deema, why?'

'Burning?' I say sharp. 'What been these stories?'

'Been story. Some our children, fire a house. Shoot littles when they running out. Been this story.'

'You done this?'

He take breath, surprise. His hands square into fists.

'You done this? Damn, you answer.'

His eyes seek at me, like he try to comprehend. 'Nay. Ain't done this.'

'What you done?'

He stare on me, ain't thinking in his face.

I say, 'How you killing littles? What you done?'

'Ice Cream?' His eyes show grief like light.

Shame come in me, coursing chill, as blood run from a wound. But I only say, 'You go. Get out. Ain't want you here.'

He nod quick and turn. Go clumsy to the stairy door, push outside like he flee. Can hear his feet uneven on the stairs.

I turn slow and press my aching face against the door. Take a mally minute before I open and go inside.

Driver lain just like he been. His hasping breath go by.

I crouch down to the floor. Get on hands and knees, press one hand hard against my bruisen mouth, and weep like any hound. Weep for my brother, and his ruin face and ruin heart. Weep how Pasha save my life, and kill and kill and kill. How he turn feary from my hate. Weep for small Karim, who love my Crow; and weep for Crow gone to the camp of rape, to hell and filth. Mamadou lie beneath, blood on his chest. I weep until I cannot breathe, my hair be wet, all on the floor be wet.

And I crush the sound behind my hand. Driver sleep on in his separate dark.

Be tears, and be the end of tears. Soon my crying fail. Then I sit alone, and all this grief be only damp and aching. Driver breathing on, his unwant life go through himself.

Then I lay by him on the bed. Ain't mind if he be woken so, nor I care for his laws. I hug careless to his body – body that feel strange, is only bones and sleeping weight. But he never wake, he never shift against my holding. Sleep gentle in my arms, and my heart settle to his warm.

When I last look up, that orange light still showing in the window. Yo they birds go wheeling, speckling black, above the city. I think again how we go, leading horses, bearing enfants – march our stubborn trespass into winter. First day we reach the farther edge of what we ever known. Go past the raiding places of the Armies, past all fables heard.

Yo at the end I see, like gem mysteriose, this cure. In my mind, it be an emerald, lying in a rooish hand. Be the greenish color I see, when I close eyes against this light. And I see again the city, its streets of broken glass, its upheld rooms of rats and silence. City of our final leaving, and our first adventure.

29

OF STOLEN CHILDREN

I waken to my name, and look up nervy in besweaten skin. Night be in its blackness. From the window, only come the skeiny light of Lowell's outdoor lamps. Ain't no one by, nor Driver stir. Ain't figure if my name was spoken real, or been in dreams.

My brother lain like sleeping water, loose. Arm rest above the covers, and his hand itself look easy. I touch his shoulder careful, and his breath pause like a question. I hold my breath along. Sigh gratty when he breathe again.

Then I hear the cryers' dim bewail. 'Ice Cream Sengle to the bricky gate! Ice Cream Sengle! Bricky gate!'

I mouth a swear and get up to the door.

Hall be empty, ya the mill is silent with the tardy hour. It be the nothing voice of brick and carpet, like no outside hush. As I go, my thinking stray in guesses, who require myself. First, be thought of middy night. Some guilt beware, is El Mayor, complain that I ain't fill his bed. But he ain't going to call no fickle girl to bricky gate.

Then a wish remember Crow. Now Karim be dead, ain't necessary he remain by Armies. But every conscience know, Crow never come. Is lost to hatred.

Last I decide it must be Sengles. Likely be, they start a loud predicament. Lowells exasperate and rid my unschool children to the yard.

But when I come outside, be still. Only a mockingbird give ugly voice into the vacant dark. Moon grown paunchy, blear in cloud. Stood most at middy height.

I come out on the moon concree. Behind the gate, a tall horse stamp its hoof. A child stand shadowy by. Gate open set, and two guards be before, their rifles idle held.

Guards is First and Second Library, tired in waking. Can see the burning noses of their cigarettes move jiggy, sketching orange flights. As I walk up, First Library call, 'Girl only ask for you. Ain't want to come inside without.' Her voice sound pologetic, she commiserate my woken sleep.

I walk toward, watch how this shadow child appear. She wear a leather jacket, legs show naked to the thigh. Hair wrap up in cloth, and she stand barefoot on the pathen dirt. Got cheekbone face, with big plum lips. She ain't speak out, but when I come up close, can see she watch on me.

Ain't recognize this girl for nothing. In the moonish blear, is shy feroce.

I say, 'Salue, my stranger. What you need?'

She tug at her hair-cloth. Say up scary, 'Brung this horse. For trade.'

Her voice bruise in my memory. Be the simper from the Armies, girl who given me her knife. And it remind, how I been call the simpers from the camp. Ain't seen this girl inside the house, but sure she heard this call.

Now she come, I got all dread against. Be like I cry out in a nightmare, invite its spooks into my day. But I square my heart and say, 'Be welcome. Sure you come with me.'

When she step forward, all her shape be fear. Flinch when the horse step close, is like a six who never ride before. She lead him on a halter, and I wonder if she walken all this way on naked feet.

When she get close, she say, 'Horse was stolen, this be right?'

'Ain't need no horse. You bring yourself, my simper.'

'Yo, I be stolen also.' She set her mouth, defiant frighten.

Truth, Lowells ain't take stolen loot. Be people living on their trade, ain't like no disagreements. But I say firm, 'They laws be by. Nor theft got shame among my people. Sengles' help be yours, you keep by us.'

'Ain't ask no help for help,' she say in pitchy voice. 'Got trade.'

'Yo sho.' I nod to First Library. 'My First, will take this horse for me? Can speak to El Mayor tomorrow.' I give her meaning look, ain't want no squabbles. But she nod and smile.

Then Second Library start to close the gate. The simper tense and stare at this, and when the gate lock to, she close her eyes and mouth a word.

'Ain't hold you here,' I say. 'Can leave, if this become your wish.'

She look round sharp at me. 'Nay. Going to stay.'

I smile back nervy. 'Bone. Come by inside.'

Got no knowledge where to take her. So I lead her to the diner, empty in this nightish hour. This be a grandy tilen room. Got booth tables fixen to the wall, with sofas to. Yo be other various tables, set with wooden chairs. On the wall is all their rostas, wiper boards writ up with task.

Most times, this be a pigly stew. Mess faster than it clean. But this nighting hour, the diner washen plain as silence. Only on the sofas, heren there, be cats asleep.

As she come in, the simper laugh. Muttern something to herself, sound most like fisher Panish. Then she say in happy nerves, 'They eating here?'

'Yo sho. The diner be.'

I start the lights. As they flash on, the simper catch her breath. Cats look up riling from their sofas.

I say, 'Be lectric light. Ain't risky none.'

'I know. Be sure I know.' She stretch one hand up toward the lights, like she will feel their heat. Now it notice, from her shoulder, swing a pinkish sack. Is cloth, and got a face embroider. Most this face be worn away. One eye be only dangle threads. Smiling mouth half gone.

'I grown in a place, been most like this,' she say.

'Before they took you?'

'Yo sho, lectric place. Been finer. But is lights like this. Whole city like.'

Most every simper say she from a wonder town of all richesse. Brag how her people going to come and war for her with brave explosions. But these science children never appear. So I ain't heed this much. I only say, soft as I know, 'Can come and sit. You safe by us.'

I go to a table, sit myself in wooden chair. Then the simper laugh again. Come to her chair unnerven, seem to question how it use. But before I can explain, she sit and smile around. Smile pinch down queery, like she bite her joy.

Yo, in this showing light, can see her face be scarren every way. Eyes blackish prettieuse, but got one eyelid skew and thick. Her nose been broken sometime, take a gentle corner in its length. Along her skin entire, be nicks and lumps.

And on one cheek, it be two blacker spots. Can think, they scars alike. But from all days I watch on Driver's skin, I know them straight. Be posies.

I look down nervy at the table. Got smears of soap upon, some small custodian ain't wipe it proper. My hand inspect this surface, and I say, 'What be your name?'

She scoff breath. 'Foo, I be a simper. Use no name.'

'Must call you something, sure.'

'Call?' She pooch her lips uncaring. 'Who I be, they call me Hak's girl.'

'Hak's girl? OldKing Hak's?'

'This be myself. Thought you may know.'

'Ain't Sengles knowing much of Armies.'

Her eyes change in some puzzling, like she magine how this be. Then she laugh nerviose. 'Ain't know much. Can see this right. Heed, you know how simper girls be took?'

'Sure.' I shrug unliking. 'Bound and took.'

'Nay, what doing after.'

Must be, I look finicky, for she give her scary laugh. 'Ain't mean *they* doings, sure this be . . . Shee, they rapes. Shee.' Then her face go twisten. Tears come up, she rub them as they come. Get a stubborn look in this, like these tears be put on her.

I say low, 'Ain't got to tell me nothing. Be no need.'

'Nay, story be wolfen. You like this.' She look friendly through her tears. Like she offer a gift, hope it can please.

I swallow at my unwant. 'Yo sho.'

'How it being, so. Myself been took by Hak and Bardo. Hak ain't been King or nothing then, a feather like another. Sure they ruin me well, ain't any mystery how Hak be.'

'Can guess.'

'Nay, you ain't guess.' She laugh up harsh, rub at her teary eye. 'You think a million times and never guess. What they do first, they break my leg, so I ain't flee nowhere. Then all they feathers trying me. I lose two teeth in this, been choking blood. And they all laughing, glad. No sho, you guessing how this be.'

'Sure,' I say weak. 'Ain't know.'

Then she recollect herself. Sniff nose and say, in lower voice, 'Ya, when this finish, how they do. Taken girl be sobbing well. Mostly will be bleeding, but ain't no child bear this prettieuse. Then the NewKing come. Ain't show himself before, no sho. He give them plenty time.

'So, NewKing going to the feathers, "How you hurt this child, this poory girl?" Go chase them off. And he bring her to his hut, he give her any care. Pet her. Clean her wounds.'

I shiver, stare some loathen feeling. A memory pass of Mamadou, how he daub me with booze. *Clean your hurts. Is what we use.*

Simper say on, 'Yo he talk, "You feary, child? Ain't fear no more, I keep you safe." Girl, she ain't know nothing. Feel this be the only child she trust. So he tend her there, and when she heal . . . how you thinking? What she do?'

'She stay?' My voice come dry.

'Ain't leave for nothing.' Simper laugh hard, grimace her face. 'Sugar, they simpers never leave. Seen when you call them out? "You free! Can go to Lowell mill!" No sho, they leave. Ain't never be in life.'

She give her thin-kept smile. And here it realize, she hide her teeth. My stomach gripe again. 'This been with yourself? This . . . cleaning wounds?'

'Ho, my story. Right.' Her scars all work in smiling. 'So, in my time, been NewKing Sayd. He take me to his hut, but I ain't talking. How I been, no sho. And he go on his "Where you hurting, treasure? Now you safe." Try to pet my head. Myself . . .' Her face grit up in sudden hate. 'I push him in the fire.'

A moment pass. She pinch her mouth, scorn past me at this memory.

I say low, 'Was vally done.'

'I be from other people.' She wave her hand around. 'People like this here. Never was handled by no male before. Cannot like no handling.

'So yo, continue like this, me and Sayd. He try some times, then he tell Hak, "You like this bitch? She yours." I ain't fight no less with Hak, but this ain't worry Hak. Yo, how he using me, I ain't been prettieuse to any another. Been nothing good to see.'

She laugh hard, grimace her face. Reach in her jacket pocket, get a cigarette. Light her match with one hand. As she suck this cigarette, she look at me with bliss content. Like all her hopes accomplish.

I look down to her pinkish sack, set floppy on the table. Now I see, along its cloth is written words in filler pen. Ink wash out mostly, lines is pale. Words go in twos, and every pair been written by a different hand. Nor these words ain't recognize.

Then it comprehend, is names. Was written on her bag in friendship. And slow, it follow in my mind, these been from children in her home. Must be, she keep the bag through all this time.

Then all my misery be, how this been years. I try to think what years it be since Sayd been NewKing of the Armies, but my mind go flat and tired.

Sack written: Tino Alvarez. Maidali Guzman. Camilo Araujo. Cari Guzman. Ink washen grayish light.

At last I say, 'This why you given me your knife?'

'Sure be so.' She look at me, eyes prideful. 'Ain't had this chance before. But you be worthy well.'

'Shoo, how you know my worth?'

'How I ain't know? A simper going to know all talk. Know pox on all these Lowell companieros. Foo, you think there be a male in Massa woods ain't visit simpers? You think!'

I frown discomfort. 'Sure, cannot be all boys do this.'

'Ain't it?' she say unconcern.

'Nay, cannot be every child. Ain't every male the same.'

'Foo, ain't distress. Truth, some Christings never come, is finicky. "Go with harlots," be their talk.'

'And some Sengles, sure.'

'Can be. Ain't necessary I know all names of Sengles.'

Something trouble in her then. She get up to her feet, hug jacket round herself like chills. Smile nervy at me, then she cross by to a redhead cat. Stoop, touch soft between his ears. He wake and sniff up drowsy.

Then she look back, shaming in her eyes. 'Been talking ugliness. Can feel this. Hope I said no harm.'

'Ain't harm.'

'Had only Hak to talk with, mostly. Feel I ain't know how to be.'

'Ain't got to be no way. Yo, this be by. We going to leave this place. Ain't be no Armies in this story.'

'Can hope.' Her mouth fret close. 'But . . . you ain't worry if I say?'

'Say?' I force a smile. 'Ain't knowing what it be. But sure, you tell.'

She frown back sorry to the cat. 'Hak say they got to kill you. For Karim and Mika kilt. Mamadou *telling* how it been your roo, but Hak ain't want to hear. Go rile the others, sure he do.'

My mind struggle, try to fix this into sense. 'How . . . Mamadou told?'

'That Deema roo can die, be gratty. No one weep for him. But ya Karim and Mika! Hak never care for them before, but now they be his boys. "She kilt my boys," and all his noise. Mamadou been the one was hurt. He ain't got nothing at you.'

'Mamadou ain't been kilt?'

'Ho, I see. You thought he kilt? Nay, been torn up some. He broke his shoulder bone behind.' She touch herself, close at her collarbone, show where this bullet strike.

I say blind, 'I been expect, a person shot must die.'

'Foo, can live. Some children shot three times, can live.'

I try think how this can be, but nothing remember in my mind. Been blood on him, Karim crouch by. I touch this blood myself, but never wonder if he live. Ain't hope.

I sit back, stare my struggling thought. Mamadou come back in my mind, alive. But now he be the NewKing of the simper's tales, of laughing rape.

On a rosta board across, can see where someone writ up large, AIN'T PACK BOOKS. PACK FOR NEEDS. Some other child writ under this, NEEDS: CIGARETTES, BOOZE. Word 'booze' bother at me, recall the Army camp its stank. Mamadou hold my hand so gentle, clean my injuries. How he done with every slave. And Deema rape Susannah by, like Mamadou done all years. Ya, in time of NewKing Sayd, he been a feather like another. When they rape this girl, he been among. So been his life. And I always known – but I refuse to know for selfishness. Dream stupidities of love, and never care beyond.

By the rosta board, a clock be hung. First, I stare through it, gnaw my guilts. But slow, a question bother in me. Can almost laugh when I find that I wonder: yo what time it be?

Ain't cleverish for reading clocks, but this be simple news. Both arms is pointing twelve. Then I shock peculiar, pondering this perfect time. Be like an answer spoken. I look to Hak's girl like she going to comprehend, can share.

She waken from her thought, frown up. 'You fretting something? Expect, Hak never chase you. Be his braggeries.'

'Nay, ain't fretting.' I stand to my feet. 'Should only go. Be tardy.'

Simper startle, budge her cat. He squirm free and brandish tail. 'Sure, you go,' she say unhappy.

'Can put you with my Sengles, if you like.'

'Nay.' She raise her hand, most like she guard from me. 'Be better here. Only . . . ain't think these Lowells rid me?'

'Nay, I go bespeak their El Mayor. Can rest, you safe.'

'Safe.' She nod uncertain.

'They Armies gone, is surely gone.' My voice come hard. 'We leave this place.'

She nod again, consideration frowning in her brow. Then she turn back to the cat and say, 'You keep the horse. Ain't Lowell's.'

Simper smiling dreamy, stroking on the cat, as I go out.

30

BY MIDDY NIGHT

My Sengles sleeping hushen when I look into the Weave Room. Pasha there, lain on a sleepen bag, with Keepers curlen to. Hounds is gone. Can guess a Lowell cat been in this history. Ain't nothing here to keep me, I go on.

On the stairy landing, I stop by the big back windows. Look down on the tumble bridge, the fussing light on river's back. Ain't know how this change, but I come gratty in my temper. Feel like every difficult evil solving into right.

Mamadou living, but I swear my heart forget his love. Behind the simper's tale, this love be filth. Be detestations. Get even angry wish that he been dead. Been grief, but clean to feel.

But always been this better choice. Must only walk some carpet distance, step into a soften room. And in my heart perverse, I crave this choice, like war its wild forgetting.

In the window, my face show, is ghosten in reflection. Face delicate made, its swollen injuries look pitieuse. Girlish child with skinny collarbone – be small in size and feeding, but her eyes be good feroce.

Ain't myself that I been known. Ain't the feary chit that look at me from Hate You's mirror. This be the Sengle sergeant. Child who dare her life in war. Do murdering crime, but got no cowardesse. A proven knife.

I lean forward to the glass. Touch my lips to my ghost lips. Think of every wish, and give this wish into my hurt reflection. Send it to all gods I know – of Armies and of Christings, and the Allah god our greats believe, before he leave them in Two Towns.

Then I walk on, with ravish shyness starting in my flesh. Go through the stairy door, and carpet self feel like it draw me onward, want my life. Come to the door of 124, and these gold letters shine at me. Be bright with some witch meaning. Is like I see them in a distant memory, when I know what come behind.

I take the doory handle and I open.

El Mayor sat on his bed, in his same silken robe and jeans. He startle tense as I come in – and it remind, they knocking on a door in Lowell mill. Ain't just walk in personal rooms.

Then my certainty be by. My mind gone stupid white.

I say halten, 'Got some business.'

El Mayor grit his jaw and nod. Watch narrow while I close the door behind. I think inside myself: *Open the door, ya, can be nothing. Close the door, this be decision.* And it close, and I turn by again. Feel hot across my face.

He watch on me, unspeaking. Light be only from one lamp, ain't tell how his expression be. I pull my Patagonia off, get chills where my shirt light besweaten. Cannot look at El Mayor, but sure I feel his eyes as I go put my jacket on a chair.

When I turn, his face be cold bekept. He say, 'What business?'

'A simper come from Army camp.' My voice rise harsh with nerves. 'Be in the diner now. I ask that she can stay. Be on my Sengles.'

'Can stay. This be all?'

I look at him all kinds of helpless. It inkle in my mind, he ask me here for only mockery. To prove that I be weak for him. Can be, his flirting been some empty jokes, from its beginning.

I feel the shame before. But I say, 'Be middy night.'

'Middy night?'

'So you asken me. Say you be here from middy night.'

His eyes narrow. Then he stand up to his feet like panic.

Sudden, he be grinning. Grin like this be bursting at him, happy bigger than his face.

'Damn,' he say, and shake his head. 'Why you talk of business? Turn me any ways with this.'

'Been business,' I say, grinning back. 'Ain't false.'

'I never hope you come. Been sulking here.'

'Said I will think.'

Then we smiling quiet. He bite his lip and shake his head, like this news ain't comprehend. Yo his watching eyes feel in my skin.

He say, 'Ain't think no more. This thinking past, we right?'

I nod somehow. My smile go soft.

'I got to chase you? Or you coming here?'

Be but two steps to go, but I cross this distance fearing. Feel like I miss somehow, do some mistake. But I come easy to. He pull me gentle to himself.

Is mostly like our normal meeting, how our bodies touch. Like I should kick his shin, push at his face. But now I put hands soft to him. One hand slip in his robe, find where the hairs be on his chest. Where be only skin. My heart beat scary, like I balance on some risky place.

He stroke light against my back. 'You touching me, goddamn.'

I laugh in teary wise. 'I touch you any times.'

'Ain't been touching, this been clawing, bell.' He stroke up to my head, and gentle it against his chest. Can feel his sigh. 'Been walking dead with love for you. I guess you known.'

'Shoo, ain't took this seriose.'

He lift my chin to look at him. 'You be here seriose? You going to run from me again?'

'Ain't going to run.' My voice come breathless.

He touch his finger gentle on my lip. 'You all cut like that. Feel like I going to hurt you.'

But he bend down and kiss me deep. I let my head weigh back against his hand, my body weak like water. Then all our time come back in me – his kisses that I fought in panic, left in strange regret. Now I release beyond this fear, put arms around him needy. Be kissing desperate while my skin go bright and dark with want.

It go careless then. Be hungry meant, as right as war. He take me against him hard. I cry inside my throat. Hold him into all my bruises, then be pulling at his roben tie without no sensible thought. His robe go by. My shirt catch on my face as it come off. Then he rid all my clothes while I laugh breathless high, ain't think to help. He pull me and we go onto the bed, and mad against each other. He muttering, 'Any Christ, you sweet,' and kiss me everywhere can reach.

Then we be facen face again, my leg curl over him. He shift me round until he lie upon. Feel his hardness press against my thigh, I catch my breath. He smile down soft with need. Eyes show a hounden love, ain't like himself.

He kiss me on my lips, my cheek. Say gruff with want, 'Ice Cream. You done this thing before?'

I laugh thin. 'And you? You done this thing before?'

'Been asking you a question, mouthy.'

'Sure I done. I ain't a twelve.'

'Ain't feel like I can stop. But I stop somehow, if you ain't want this.'

'Foo questions. I be here.'

'Yo sho, I going to do this now. Ain't frighten.'

'You be frighten?'

'Hush.'

Sex a science El Mayor know deep. This secret known to every jones and foaly child in Massa woods. I heard from twenty girlish mouths – until this news be boring. Yo I swear he never use myself. Ain't care to be the hundredth story of his goat prowess.

But prowess do what it can do. And on this night, it be my last reliance from my pain.

Lowell bed itself be strange bonesse. Sheets touch like fresh milk taste. Yo his hands be like he speak some mystery language to my

216

skin. Feel scary fine – like falling from a tree, and falling on for hours so. Landing in a bed with sheets like milk. Someone kissing at your neck and saying nonsense kindness.

Times, my heart be distances. Body feel its joy, but I be separate in some height precaire. Thoughts crawl in, like unwant ants – of what be real, and what be false, and how my Mamadou been. But other times, I see his face, and ease in thankfulness. It be himself, my goat familiar. While he be inside me, I been thought a thousand times of love, and love, and everything forgot. I scorn my heart aloof, nor ever a person see this heart.

Ya, when sex be tired, we talk of everything somehow: the simper come; my Driver's sickness; who will stay at Lowell mill. Most and long, we talk about the destinations of our journey. What El Mayor decide, we going to Connecticut its west. Place be clean of roos, how Pasha figure. This dabbit into arguments about the posy cure, and who should chase to Washington – if Lowells smarter for this task, or if my warry Sengles best. Each discount the other, but this dispute end in more unraveling time of sex and crying speech without no words.

Once, he asken, 'When you known you going to come to me?'

I got no answer here. Can say, *I always known*. Be some way truthful, but ain't answer nothing. Can say, *Decide this when I known the truth on Mamadou*. But I ain't wish to tell of Mamadou our histories this night.

I say, 'I never known this right. Can do some acts, then learn behind you going to do them. You know how.'

'Nay, I ain't know. Be some psychology of scratchers. I always know what I will do.'

'Foo psychology. Sound like some disease.'

'Can be disease, when it get into scratcher heads.' He mingle his fingers in my braids. 'Ain't guess, why you kept back from me.'

I ain't react, I stroke his arm. Fret my heart in quiet.

'Ice Cream?' His voice come careful. 'Ain't never think I feel this. But, you need me to be loyal, I be loyal.'

'Nay, you ain't!' I laugh surprise. 'Be like a hound who promise he ain't bother squirrels. Next squirrel come, the hound be gone.'

'Can and will.'

'Find out how. You always know what you will do!' I laugh again.

'Thought this been considerations to you.'

I puzzle at this a minute, try to find it in myself. 'Nay, been only fooling, this. What you got for me, you ain't go feel for no one else. Feeling be particular, can guess.'

'I be jalouse as any brawling imbecile. Cost me nights, worrying who you think upon. Who get your love.'

Mamadou pass my mind like chills. I say discomfort, 'Shoo, I ain't so goatish like yourself.'

Here I kiss him, but his kiss distract. He pull away. 'Ain't know if I like to do you so. Other girls . . . be shame for you somehow.'

'Who going to know? Ain't even know we been together.'

'They going to know we been together. How they ain't?'

'Who telling them?'

His frown go dark. 'Ain't going to be the last time, this. I set myself on fire, you do me so.'

'Nay, nay. I only think, we keep this.'

'Be secrets, what you saying?' Now El Mayor go narrow on me, like he smelling rats.

This bring me into conscience. Somehow, been natural to me, amours cannot be daily talk. My love been always warry crimes, kept in some separate night. But ain't no harm to talk on El Mayor. He be the world's respect.

Only, I ain't want this talk. Feel finicky in every nerve. Can do with El Mayor, but cannot name it like a fact. Cannot.

Then El Mayor say rough, 'You got no other secret males?'

For luck, I laugh surprise. Say without thought, 'Got any dozen. Keep half your Lowells under silence vows.'

'Can answer questions also.' El Mayor make a tighten smile. 'Be asking yes or nay.'

'Nay,' I say with narrow truth. 'I got no males. Got zero. Jalouse my pony, if you need. I always love her most.'

He laugh relief and pounce me, then somehow this turn to kissing. Like magic tricks, my contradictions hush. I ease into my skin. Ain't got the spirit for no more, we sore in every part. Yo we try, and end in sleep, curl up like animoses. Waken kissing more.

And then somehow, the birds be singing their bad news of morning.

Ain't lighten yet. Be darkness morning when I get up tired. Put on my clothes like they be punishment. When I be clothen, El Mayor come fold me in his arms. Hold me against his naked self, give one more kiss on my raw mouth.

Then I say clumsy, 'So we doing this. Evacuation.'

'Quest.' He cosset at my ear. 'Ain't disrespect our quest.'

'Quest sound like a thing grown on your skin. Disgusting somehow.'

'Adventure, ya. Gone sotten with you worse. Ain't cure for nothing.'

I smile careful. 'Got this sickness also. Know I do.'

Then I feel my duty coming like cold daylight, draw me on. I step away reluctant. Feel scary walking to the door. Is like he be a needful fact I panic to forget. Yo, as I open, he call soft, 'I love you vicious, Ice Cream Star.'

I stop with hand along the doory side and say, 'I love you also.'

Then, as I turn away, I terrify sudden to my words. Come down the hall with coward step and think: *Ain't lies entire. Yo, it be done. Must love him, all it is.*

31

OUR LAST DEPARTURE

When I get down to the Weave Room, all my children woken ugly. Must boss each enfant into clothes, and chase the jones to fetch our meal – ain't nothing done without my yells. Half my children doing nothing but they thieve from Lowells. Scramble out, and come back with a useless glove or tato. I get no thinking peace, and soon my night with El Mayor become a distance where some good thing been.

When my tasks be rid, I go up to the second flight to Driver. This trip be risky circumstance – the stairs become an avalanche of Lowells bearing loads. Each step is dodging, shoving, swears. Through this, can hear the cryers' wail begin, and go on larming. Seem every Lowell callen to some place.

My head be tired without no sleep, and I come through the stairy door before my dread remind. Then I hold my step. The hallway gape its mally memories. All the number doors remember like a waiting curse.

First Physician be by door 234, talking in. When she see me, she turn startling. Come down the hall like she confront some trouble.

'What be?' I say in whisper voice, unnerve. 'My Driver woken?'

'Ya. Woken well.' She stop before me, smile discomfort. Hand go to her lip, it dabbit on the posy mark.

I take my breath. 'I come to see him. You know how.'

'Be sorry.' Her smile go stiff. 'He ain't want to see you now.'

'Nay? When he can see me?'

Here she put her hand upon my shoulder. Take all my sense to keep myself from hitting this hand away.

'Companiera,' she say low, 'he shame.'

'Ain't need to shame. I love him any way, is foolish.'

'Yo he know.'

'He can ride? We leaving, but we stay this—'

'Yes, he ride. This passen well.'

I swallow at my guilt. Look past her shoulder with some stifling feeling. 'Want to see him, damn.'

Then, from Driver's open door, I hear a girlish voice. Is laughing, rise up pitchy in excitement. My skin go peculiar cold.

Be the simper's voice. Is Hak's girl, in my Driver's room.

I step back. Brush First Physician's hand away without no thought. 'Sure,' I say confuse. 'What he want. Ever he want.'

'Companiera, got to comprehend. Been hard to him.'

I look at her, but ain't see nothing. All my heeding be for Hak's girl. She talking low, like she tell confidences. Then behind, I hear my Driver laugh.

I shake my head, say forcen bright, 'Bone. You cry me up, ever he want to see me. I be by.'

I walk away, can hardly open the stairy door. Hit my shoulder in the doorside, stumble footless out. Halfway down the stairs, must sit and breathe myself back into semblance. Begin to feel how I ain't slept. My mind be straying, thinking of some road where Driver ride by me. We fox about and laugh together, like we always done before. Then it realize, we ain't. He always tell me disapprovals. How I must get enfants for the town. How I be selfish wrong, ain't got no sense. How I make him dead.

I press my fists into my eyes. Go thinking how my Driver parley times with OldKing Hak. Can be, he known this simper there. He never spoken of her, but ain't everything is telling news. Driver lawful like no superstition, never he do with simpers. Truth, it been my duty that I fetch this simper from the diner. Put her somewhere out of trouble. Where she keep away.

Then weak behind my misery, I startle to my name. *Ice Cream Sengle to the easter gate. Ice Cream Sengle . . .*

I swear and leap up to my feet. Cut through the building, dodging runners, begging my heart that it be Driver. He heard I being by, sent to the gate somehow to call me. Know this be senseless, but I run, I cannot stop my hope.

I come out easter door, and meet the Christing cattle at the gate. Must wait while all these cows progress in stilten motion in. My unrest sweat go icy in the breeze. Final cow go switching tail along, and Lowell Second Stabler last with Tophet's fatty mule.

Only when they by, I notice Pasha.

He stand outside upon the path, a rifle slung against his back. Wear a rooish jacket, gray-and-green. One trembling moment, I feel he invite me out to war.

Then I be walking to, zip Patagonia to my neck. Wear my shoulders clumsy, how I feel. Cryer by the gate look at me mally for my tardiness. Ain't pause to this, I go outside with winter sadness in my face.

Past the walls, can see that Pasha got his roo pack on the ground. A second rifle lain atop. Its black length be familiar nightmares.

'Salue,' say Pasha soft.

'Salue yourself. Got your loot.'

'Thought Lowells take, if you ain't by.'

Then I look to his birchen face, like it will tell me fortunes. Tell how these guns will use, what murder be in these bell goods. But he turn his face away. Bend down and take the second rifle. Lift it graciose and easy in his grandy fist.

He reach it toward myself. Face complicating, but he say no word. Only hold this blackness gift and bite his lip.

I say unliking, 'Shoo, ain't need that. Got my pistol.'

'Nay, you need. Is better.'

A minute, we look one to one. My heart be big and ugly then. The Vember wind cut numb upon my face.

I say, in choken voice, 'Better for murder, what you mean.'

Then can see, his thoughts hurt in him. 'Yes,' he say low. 'You shoot with pistol, they shoot back. With this – ain't likely can. Be safer.'

'Deer ain't shooting back.'

'Deer?'

'We flee these roos for what? Ain't plan to kill no goddamn children. My use for guns be meat.'

He loose the gun down tired. A moment, I expect he take it back. But he say, 'Said you will heed me.'

'Heed you? When I said this?'

'If we go to get the cure. Said you obey my telling.'

I frown past him to the city, like I going to find some reason. It look cold bekept this morning hour. Be a parking building there, before the easter gate. Shape all of grandy windows, but these windows got no glass, is air. Behind, the buildings all got broken eyes. Some shattern down their sides, stand miserable in their lost brick. Holes show their inside rooms, grown strange with moss.

Then I magine Washington like this, a city of absent ruin. The cure there, guarding by some thousand roos. How Driver wait behind.

At last, I swallow my dislike. 'You promise, ya? We get this cure?'

'If you obeying.' Pasha nod.

I laugh sour. 'Foo, start with that, I doing every errand you can think. Caught some tricky manners, you.'

But we both smiling now. I feel relief, ain't know from where.

Then he reach the gun again – ya, this gesture loving somehow. Is like he move to settle a blanket round my chilly shoulders.

I take it careful. Hands soothe to the rifle's weight, its metal cold like honesty. I sigh out in feeling. Can feel without no thought, its make be right.

I say with weak conviction, 'Ain't need this yet. To Washington, be weeks.'

'Can see roos before.' His voice come low and shy like mine. 'Ya, is other children.'

'Children like ourself? Ain't fearing them.'

When I look back to his face, he smiling. Eyes be gratty soft. 'Must teach you how it use.'

'Expect you press the trigger, nay? Ain't mysteries.'

'Is matters teach.'

Then a shiver grip in me. 'Hold. What gun this be?'

He frown to it. 'It be Kalash.'

'Kalash?'

'What they call. Kalash their sort.'

'But, this ain't the gun that—'

'Ho, you meaning . . . nay, I keep.' He touch the gun he wearing. 'Mine.'

'Bone.' I sigh again and hold the gun against me clumsy. Look to the pack left on the ground. 'Guess these other pistols . . . they be useful. Deer, I meaning.'

'Yes.' He stoop down for the pack, gone easier through his grandy self. 'Be gratty, Ice.'

'Foo, who you got to thank, I wonder?' I laugh my nervy breath.

'Nay.' He rear the pack upon and stand up to his height. 'Is bone.'

Last, before we turn inside, I fumble up the rifle's strap. I say its name in mind, *Kalash*, and slip it over my thin shoulders. Its weight rest to me good, feel strong. Is like a promise there – a carrying oath that I do any evils, but my brother save.

My next hour spent in Lowell Storage, scratching in their ammonition. A hundred diggers push around, and be some nasty squabbles, when they question what I robbing there. Yo, when my bullets gathern, John of Christ come in, with teary thanks for all the Tophets' rescue. His face unshape with bruise, got bandage nose like wrennish beak. Onto this hurting mess, he leak his eyes. The Lowells gather curiose, and soon they all respecting me with hero talk, while I embarrass like a turtle naked from its shell.

Then I must visit all the Christings in their Lowell partment. Here wives yappit nonsense, how their Jesus help me in the fire – the littles said they seen Him there, with shining head and blooden hands.

My courtesy tiring now, and I say only long annoyance, how they morons stay in Massa. Insist they think again; insist the cure and every hopeful fact. But all they comprehending be, this come from Pasha's mouth. Any word of roos be 'lies of Satan' to their mind. Yo, while this fray continue, hurt Susannah watching silent. She still in godclothes, grime and torn. Her braids undone in shagginess. Ya, her eyes beweepen. Look like bruises in her gentle face.

Before I leave, I talk to her apart. 'John, he ain't got sense to count his feet,' I say. 'Must tell him.' Try every argument I can, and even give suggestion that she come alone, with her own enfants. But she watch her sorrow eyes, and say at last, 'Be Christ His will. Hope you remember us.'

From this discontent, I go by hasty. Trudge my load of bullets through a dodging scram of Lowells; gather my Sengles with alarming yells. Be counting heads and telling orders, when the cryers speak.

They call from every side and ring the walls. Call every leaving child to easter gate. And as they yell, their looning screaming settle into unison. Soon they speaking in one beat, like all the mill sing vally. And through the mill, a cry come back, of children scream excitement. Yo my Sengles shout till ain't no hearing. I laugh crazy into this. Bend and heft my gun Kalash, sling up her strap like ready habit. Pasha catch my glance and smile somehow, with fuzzy eyes.

Be scrambling then to ready all. Must wrangle all my children to the yard; catch enfants into carry packs and horsen carriers. Our new Army horse, of Hak's girl's stealing, cheer my greedy littles. They spend entertaining minutes, give him goofen Army names like

Frighten Imbeciles and Dare-to-Hide. Ending be, is callen Piglet somehow, though he monster tall.

Every matter hurry, yet it take ten times the work of drill. Through around, is Lowells running in the same haste madness. Every second, be more children, till ain't room to swing an arm.

Then, tall among, my Driver come. Walk normal, like ain't nothing been. He shaven fresh, look shining bone. Wear his blue Carhartt jacket. I shout to him and grin unthinking, point him to this Piglet horse. Yo, he smile at me. Mount without cavil, leaping well. Then my heart change high in strength. Ain't even mind when I see Hak's girl straggle behind, eyes to my brother. I wave to her, she make her pinchen smile.

Lowell mill give hundred and ninety children, Sengles thirty-seven. Yo these hundreds and our beasts be many for the yard. Some wait behind in shoving groups, go tiptoe to see where we leave. I hold Money's halter rope, and grip so hard I feel the pulse of heartbeat in my injure hand.

Then Keepers call up laughing, 'Lowells sobbing for their cats. Look by.'

She point to the easter door. There a clutch of Lowell children dabbit, cats in arms. Cats squirm unliking while these children pet them and complain. One cat bolt panicking among the cow legs while a girl skree after, 'Robot! Robot!'

And here the hundreds all turn forward. I turn forward, leap my heart. Can see my El Mayor vault up to easter wall. He stand there vally, yelling couragement. Around, be larm and muttering, bleating sheep. But he call brave above.

Ain't get no conscience what he say. Be rousing speech of maple futures, rivers flown with wine. Be what a child expect, in louder bucketloads. Yo I only know, I watch on him with pounding joy. My heart be graciose and huge and red for him and our adventure. Be madder than no happiness I known.

He finish, jump down from my sight, and I turn grinning to my Sengles. Call, 'We there! We going real!'

They yell back spiriteuse, shove at each other in excite. Then we wait another prickling minute while these hundreds shift. Step and step, we walk out to the gate. Come on the bridge, and there the city wait. The bricky ruin of my dreaming hope, its sky be blue as wonderful. Walk on to bigger day, like all my wishes stepping to their life.

THROUGH BANDON WOODS

Vember 1–28

32

OUR JOURNEY: VEMBER 1–26

Days that come been clean bonesse. We keep to 495, a highway broad as any field. Got a twin highway the same, these two companion faithful. Together, they go stretch and snake across all unkept distance, till they find our new Connecticut.

All this way be forest. Ain't scarcely notice when the Massa woods be left, and yonder start. A hummock seem familiar in your eye; then it come queery that the individual trees be strangers. Some places, both roads vanish, eaten by the growing wild. Look like the highway dive beneath a cliff of skinny trees. Will see a roadsign stood peculiar in a flock of birch; a lonely patch of road remaining stubborn like a mushroom. Then, without no visible cause, the highway start again, with only nibbling bush around its edge.

First week of journey, we see children sometimes by the road. These always fleeing terrify, like we be deadly ghosts. Yo, at one town, the jones come out with guns and heavy clubs. Only words they give be threats, if we ain't leave direct. Come to comprehend, these be the raiding places of the Armies. All they known of strangers been their children robben in the night.

But as we stalk the deeper west, the only houses be old evacs. Then oaks and beasts and sun be all our friendship.

Most the Lowell children painful to this outside life. Will grumble on their bedless sleep, their blisters and their dirtiness. Get backward moods, where all be climbing trees to scout First Runner. Magine how she come to tell them nothing mally been, they can return to their warm rooms.

But for my Sengles, journey be familiar bosky stars. Hammocks slung in rustle trees, the morning fire and meat. Wash in a brook ain't got no name, and come at dawning to the bluish number highway. These mornings, walking never seem like work. Weather mostly chill and dry, get only brightness sweat. We follow our shadows to the west; a still hawk scout above. Walk out long and long to night, that come to meet us with its sunset. And sleep, and wake again with noisy hundreds to our company.

Soon our march of every child be townie in my eyes. First ahead, go Lowell stablers, driving the horses–cattle forward in their snorting hundreds. Wherever a hill rise up before, can see these brownish beasts drab up to fill the roaden shine. El Mayor and his close children – First Electric, First Contractor – always walking last. Their horsen sledge of wine make up the lazy rear of our procession. Sengles mingle forward–backward, bothering and thieving. My littles' clothes be soon a circus pigliness of thefts, and be a pride to them, that they wear nothing of their own.

Hours go in walking thought. Be like a time of flu, when nothing tasky can accomplish. Spend afternoons in worry on the Lowells–Christings left behind; then I dream forward to Connecticut its unknown woods. And times, I wander lost in dreams of Mamadou the NewKing. Guess if he still keep by roos, and if he can survive. But this release, and all my frets release and comb out into sense. Come into this present world, where is only sun and road. Trees shushing slow with their last leaf.

All these journey days, my Sengles hunt, try their new guns in practice. Yo, in my chase, I use my rooish rifle, good Kalash. Gun be heavy carrying, and kick unsteady when she shoot. But she looking far with good attention. Got three settings: one bullet, three bullets, and all bullets splashing wild. Three-bullet shooting good for deer. No deer ain't fleeing after. Yo, Pasha never let me leave the camp without this weapon. Roo always think some children by the road will kill us for our goods. When I say it ain't no children here, he answer dark, 'Yo where they gone?' – like all the children here been kilt by worser children. While we slinging hammocks at night, roo often stalk the woods around, in scout for these road people. Ware his rifle to the forest's birden peacefulness.

These evenings be a vasty camp of swayback tents and hammocks. Get a dozen fires lit, until the woods become a scatter of slipping lights and shadows. Every night, be Lowells singing gospies by the fire. First Gardener play bow-guitar, while girls sing high and wisty.

And, most aster nights, when songs be by, when Sengles gone in sleep, I creep soft from my hammock. Pick my footsteps cautieuse, creep to the dark outside all people. I stalk to the tent of El Mayor.

This love be fickle in its joy. Be nights we parley in amour until the darkness morning. Will drowse and kiss and whisper in his scramble bed of blankets, and the cricket woods cry glad around our sex. Talk then be mostly gladness swearing, and they maple flatteries is foolish to repeat.

But moren more, our conversations bicker into strife.

First fight be my insistence that we keep our love in secret. Never my heart accept that every Lowell–Sengle know. Truth is, my love be sulky beasts. Will vanish, then come back alive, then turn to mean dislike. Ever I magine telling every child, it feel like shameful lies. In walking hours, I often think of leaving him for honesty – but when I see him in his tent, I change in weak regret. Will only beg for secrecy again, with pale excuses.

El Mayor resent this awful. He crave to wake with me in arms, to name Ice Cream in happy boast. And he start in jalousie, what ears I keep this secret from. For this, he asking tireless, who done love with me before. Will name all children he can think – Jermaine and Popsicle and Crow; ya any Lowell who show eyes to me, or give me friendly gift. Sometimes, from drowsing quietness, he say in sudden pain, 'Nay, who?'

Answer is Mamadou and Mamadou, crime that love its darkness. And something inkle to me, El Mayor ain't going to bear this news.

Yo in sneaking thought, I wishing on the NewKing still. Ever I scold my nonsense heart, it beat its same direction. Be even times my skin resenting El Mayor for only this, that he ain't Mamadou and cannot be and never be.

So from the drowsy end of love, I often slip in need away. In sudden change, ain't want him grabbing me, requiring me with questions. Leave El Mayor with jalousie and come back to his hurt.

Our other fight be on my plan to go to Washington.

How it is, the Lowells never trust me with the cure's importance. I be a girl fifteen, a Sengle ignorant, and all it is. So they plan to go themself – all their older males, and El Mayor in leadership. Ain't fret them nothing, when my Pasha say they all be murdern. Nor they ask his help. They can find Washington with maps, is all their project need.

Truth, been gratty to me, if they take me in their company. But El Mayor's insistence be, that I keep safe behind. This give me contradictory moods, and I start thinking reasons why the Lowells sure to perish.

I chew all this to scraps with El Mayor, any a night.

'Some fightless diggers,' I will say. 'What you doing there? You lay some carpet for these roos?'

'And you? Look at yourself. You small as foals. Is like a ten.'

'Shoo, I be with Pasha safe.'

'You trust that yellow cannibal? He lie more than he speak. Goddamn, ain't *let* you go with him.'

And so we skirmish long and long – who be foolish worse, and who preventing who from going. How roos be risky for a female, but be safe for males; or safe for warry Sengles, but will kill a Lowell quick as sneezing. How Pasha self ain't be no kitten, sensible to trust.

Times, these nighten conversations mingle in my tired day. I start to think like El Mayor, doubt Pasha's every kindness. Get memories of Army camp, the feather that he kilt for nothing. Ya, worst and fresh in conscience be his photographs of war.

I seen all these photographs now, except the one of Pasha self – object he ain't never mention, nor I brave to ask. Even without this, they be nefasty ornaments.

Is some where roos walk past dead children like they nothing bushes; or stand in laughing talk with some child torn in pieces at their feet. Be children without noses, ya, which never figure in my eyes – keep thinking that the picture torn somehow on its thin cloth. And be one photograph of only cut-off hands, a bloody dozen. Look like uncanny spiders, heap in sunlight on young grass.

Is calmer pictures, show their helicopter planes and long-nose tanks; show a city burning, hazy in enormous smoke. But even when these photographs show only lazing roos, one roo will hold a weirdo rifle, bigger than no normal gun. Pasha's explanations of these weapons be unhappy hearing. Yo he name the roos, and mostly add to this: 'He dead.'

Photograph that linger with me worst be of an inside room. Can see this been a lucky place, with tilen floors and window glass. Walls painten perfect blue. Got a sofa made of shining leather.

On the sofa lie two girlish jones, look like they dress for church. Both is bloody dead. A tennish boy lie dead the same, beside them on the floor. Wall scribble in their blood. Is bloody pools and drops upon the tiles.

Among this horror stand a yellow roo. He point a pistol to his own head, like to shoot himself. But he grinning, is some joke that happen in this camera moment.

Every time I see it, I keep staring minutes at this picture. Feel like something that happen to me in another life.

All Pasha say, this killing was mistake. Roo be Seryozha, was a yeary friend he had in soldat days. This Seryozha living, best he know.

When I ask him what mistake this been, and if he worry for it, Pasha only say, 'Be war. Is normal.'

And truth, what Pasha tell me of his histories be a shorter list. Can learn, he joining to soldats when he been fourteen years. Can learn the places where he war – some dozen fights in Africa, with city names that ain't pronounce; Venezuela, place of spotten panthers, where he learning Panish; Yevropa – rooish word for Europe – where roos leave in bad defeat.

But he never tell particulars of his selfen life. Ask if he miss his townie home, he say he ain't remember this. Ask who his mother been, he say, 'A girl.' Will tell peculiarities sometimes of his Russian Federation – on their driving cars, and how they buy their goods with money paper. But he name no person of his life, ain't mention no event.

Ask how he live for sixteen years of war, my Pasha answer nothings. Mostly be, 'Ain't kilt.' Ya, once it been, 'Ain't live, the others die.' Will name the places where he fight, but ain't say what he doing there. Always be, 'Is war,' and shrugging. Only thing a child can tell, is something make him want to smoke.

One time I ask him, 'What you done so foul, I cannot hear?' He smoke in silence then, think separate in his furry head. At last, he say, 'I told some lies.' When I repeat my question stubborn, he say, 'You want to hear my lies?'

But worse beyond no other silence be his manners on the cure. Vember passing long, and still he tell no plan for Washington. Will only say, 'Be thinking.' No complaint can get another answer. He thinking and he thinking, but he never tell these thoughts.

Our journey lasting its third week before this strife conclude. Be on a morning when I go for deer and Pasha follow after. He say he like to hunt again – but from his worry looks, can know he got some word to say. So I agree with beggar hope.

This day, the morning risen thick. Snow waiting heavy in the clouds, the light be shabby gray. We stalking through some wither fern, scarce past the campen noise, when Pasha speak behind.

'Ice? On Washington.'

I flinch immediate to him. Find him standing clumsy somehow, fidget hands upon his gun. And he say soft, 'How, if I go alone?'

First, I ain't comprehend. Say dumb, 'Alone without myself?'

He shrug. 'Be most a week, two weeks. Can get cure easier so.'

Then I narrow on him careful. Yo, like I expect, his bluish gaze gone stupid blank.

'Shee.' I huff my breath. 'You clear as nothing. Got your lying face.'

'How? Ain't lie.'

'Be easier, right. Because you never go to roos. You go sleep in some evac and come back with sorry explanations. If you coming back.'

'Bone,' he say with stubborn mouth. 'I take some Lowell. What can do.'

'Lowell?'

'Take some male. Be better.'

I stop on this and narrow eyes. 'You mean, this Lowell watch you there.'

'I done without. But you ain't trust.'

'Is clever thought,' I say unpleasant. 'Which Lowell you prefer to kill?'

To this, he frown disgusting, drop his gun loose on its strap. 'Kill no one.'

'So, this Lowell coming back? I guess.'

'Come back if I come back.'

'So you ain't coming back? Gratty for telling.'

For a breath, we stare against each other in our different upsets. The snow begun around, in seldom flakes like pointy air.

Then he say hard, 'You ain't safe with me. More than Lowell.'

'Ho, because I female?' I huff an angry laugh. 'Ain't try this, Pasha.'

'Yes. Is truth.'

'Damn, you terrifying. How I live by you these weeks? Heed, you bring me, or I go alone. I go without yourself! Ain't waiting on your goddamn nonsense!'

Pasha raise a fist in temper. Yo, quick without no thought, I spit on it. The roo flinch back and grab his gun. I grab my gun.

We both hold, unnerve. Roo clutch his rifle against himself, face pinking in distress. A snowflake drift between us, tumbling. Then he swallow strange, his hands go softer on his gun. Then he say underbreath, 'Ain't kill no Lowells. I never thought this.'

And he turn himself away. Sit down into the messy ferns. Crouch to his gun, like curling to an injury its hurt.

I stare a moment to his furry head. Then I crouch by, say hot, 'You heed, this nonsense finish now. I taking Money south tomorrow. I learn whatever you hide, can die without no painful curiosity.'

'Nay, Ice.'

'Yes, Ice! Be watching Driver die. Your moron lies and "I be thinking". Cannot bear this!'

Can hear him breathing fast, his body clench in hot reaction. Then he say low, 'You think, they keep the cure in camp? Where it can steal?'

'Ain't going to know. You never told.'

'It be in boats. Far in water.'

First, I only get a dumb relief, he telling facts. Then this news settle in me. 'They grandy boats you speaking of? Is there?'

'Ya, is there.'

'But . . . ain't impossible, we steal this. Swim somehow?'

He reach to a fern and tear some fronds away, crush these in hand. 'Nay. Be nothing worth. These boats, ain't get inside from swimming.'

I grip Kalash. 'And if I fight for roos? You fight for them. Live fifteen years in this.'

'Is differences.'

'Is lies.'

He turn to me. Fist tense around the fern, his eyes be shaming misery. 'Ice Cream. You be a girl.'

'You saying, going to be like Army camp. Something like.'

A hopeless pain go through his face. 'You ain't live long there. Yourself, be nothing you can live.'

'I live . . . I can live. But you saying, ain't no use.' Can feel my sorrow, hard behind my eyes. 'They take me on no boat, ain't going to be. Is right?'

His face relieve. 'You comprehend. Ain't use.'

'So we dying anyhow. You saying, all this been for nothing?'

He drop his crushen fern, look down. Then his voice come whispern, feary. 'Nay. I thought a plan.'

I catch on this. 'Plan with myself?'

'Ya.' He shrug annoying. 'You ain't heed, so.'

I find my cigarettes and take one out. Light it gratty, feeling aftersorrows in my heart. Then suspicion bite in me. 'Hold – can know this plan?'

He laugh some choken way. 'Can know.'

'Yo tell. Can tell me now?'

'What I think,' he say in careful voice, 'you come with me like wife.'

'Ho, roos keep wives like Christings?'

'Ain't like Christings,' Pasha say unhappy. 'Some soldats keep girls.'

'Yo sho. They going to do.'

'They comprehend this. I ask for cure, for you. For favors, or can pay. Physicians take pay sometime.'

'Sure.' I sigh my smoke out glad. 'I thought of this myself.'

I glance at him, and find him clenchen down around his gun. Face turn away, but still can see, the child embarrass mean.

'Foo.' I laugh. 'You touchy something. Ain't fret myself if roos believe we wive. This why you kept it all these weeks?'

'Nay, ain't this.'

'So why? Ain't science plans. Can think of this before a month.'

He shrug misliking. 'Cannot be always by you there.'

'Your risks again, I guess.'

'Yes. Ain't jokes.'

'Foo, is raping problems.' I laugh nervy. 'What you meaning.'

'Someone hurt you, ain't know how it be.' He shake his head resenting.

'They rape me, how it be. Ain't mysteries.'

'Nay,' he say harsh. 'Ain't know how I be.'

This notion stop me queery. Remind how Pasha done at Army camp. Yo, he hunch to his gun again. Hand tearing ferns, and drop them by.

'Better we living, Pasha,' I say soft. 'Sure I known. Some Deema rape me, be my mally luck. It need no acts from you.'

'Ain't easy like you think.'

'So it be crafty. How you got to do.'

'Ya.' Then Pasha look toward me, like he check some fact. Think a moment, and grit unhappy. 'Nay, I think some way. Be some soldats can trust.'

'Bony to hear.' I laugh, and Pasha make uncertain smile.

'Is truth,' he say. 'Some soldats bone.'

'Sure I believe. Is only funny.'

I shake my head, look to the farther woods. Can see the seldom snow against the sun, like tiny dust. I try to think some circumstance where I will kill for Pasha. Sure, if it been his life, ain't questions. Think arguments to tell him this, but all my thoughts be puttering moths. I suck my cigarette.

At last I say, discomfort, 'I never thanken you. How you come for me at Army camp.'

He laugh soft. 'Is truth.'

'Felt two contradictions in this. How . . . they people shot. Ain't thought to thank.'

'Is normal, ya. You only be a small.'

When I look, he lighting up a cigarette. Smile show on his face. I say, 'Can insult how you like. I going to love you for this real.'

His face go soft embarrass, but he keep eyes on his hands. Say quiet, 'Ya. I going to love you also.'

33

THE SIMPER, OF HER PEOPLE

Day behind this argument, we pass into Connecticut. Ain't no line to show – must figure this from roadsigns, where they left. Now be petty days before we reach our safer home. Ya, woods continue solitary bell. Be even questions sometimes, why we never roam before, like this been pleasure escapades.

Myself, be readying my fear to go to Washington. Now it being real, all apprehensions change in me. My walking hours become long maginations of my rape. How Pasha kilt in my protection; what resulting after. Roos cut off my nose, my hands. Hounds eat my dying flesh. I start to figure days till January, wish it being farther. These days can be my only life.

Ya, be times, I get a sneaking wish to never go. My weakness think, no child can change all problems of this evil world. Go to roos, be moron suicides, like Pasha ever sworn.

But my contradictions fail to nothing when I see my brother.

These days of tired wandering, Driver sicken past no comfort. His hands be thick with posy sores. His cough be raw and long. He skinny in his clothes, and now he lose his careful dignity. Will ride a cart among all enfants, drowsing in the middy day.

Yo, his heart be bitter. He dead-among – must walk unseen through Sengles like a starving ghost. Sure, Lowells talk to any, ain't respect this definition. But Driver narrow and contrary to their every friendship. And to myself, his manners most like hatred. Any a careless thing I say, he hear it vain or selfish. Avoid me how he can, and when he ain't, his face be cold dislike.

The only talking he befriend be with the simper, Hak's girl. Seem she always by him, laughing nervy, make her pinchen smile. Ain't a week gone by before she sleeping in his hammock. Be times, he sit her on his Piglet horse, teach her to ride. Then her scar face be enfant seriose. Her hand go in forgetting to the horse's mane, stroke wondering. When Driver touch to shift her leg, her eyes be desperate sweet. Then any blindness see, she gone in love.

In manners, the simper be a strange and worry animal. Flirt with some male, then she look angry murder as he go. Wear a Lowell workshirt deep unbutton, showing most her breasts; yo any boy go look, she grasp this shirt together feary. Every change be fickle: is skitty and rude and shy and hard.

I never get the bravery to ask how she know Driver. Prefer my own excuses over truths I cannot fix. But at last I learn this sideways from another history.

Been our first Connecticut night. I gone to Driver to tell about my loves with El Mayor. Be my first trial to say this secret, for El Mayor his hurting pride.

So, after evening meal, I follow my brother to his hammock. Begin in hopeful nerves.

'Was thinking, ya, of El Mayor. How you always say, we can pair well. You mind this saying? Been feeling, it be sense to choose this. Now is better sense.'

Driver been readying his sleeping goods, but now he frown to me. 'Sense?'

'How you said, our Sengles be too few. Ain't keep without no help.'

'So you trade yourself for gifts?' He narrow on me cold.

'Foo, ain't like this.'

'How it is?'

'You always say, he love me well. Ain't remember to you?'

A doubt show in his eyes. 'Ain't thought I driven you to this. I know I ain't been thinking well, sometime.'

'Nay, you only saying, it be politics to do.'

'Politics.' He scoff his breath and reach by to a branch. Crack off a skinny twig, then twist it in his fingers, thinking. My eyes go skitty to his hand, watch for the posy sores.

At last he say, 'Ridiculous enough, you get an enfant belly now. But ain't need El Mayor in this.'

'Yo, he ain't right with you?'

'Child go with every girl he see. Can make your politics without that.'

I take my breath unsteady. 'Ain't necessary is politics.'

'Ain't bone politics,' he say, and make his bitter smile. 'But it be like yourself, these days.'

'What this going to mean?'

'It mean, you ain't gain nothing from this. El Mayor will use you gratty. But this never change your wealth. He got more pride than this, to pay for love.'

Then some misery freak in me. I spit out blind, 'Truth, El Mayor ain't go with simpers none. Is better sort.'

Driver's face go stiff. 'Forget this, Ice. You put this notion by.'

'Nay,' I say desperate, like I catch at something slipping from my hands. 'You ain't listen. How we even talking so? You blame me always.'

'Can be some failures in me, sure.' He turn sharp to his hammock. 'But you name them without me.'

'Driver, ain't meant nothing. I done worser things than ever you done.'

He rub his palm against his brow. Say cold and soft, 'I know.'

Then the world go weak in me. I want to ask him what he know. I want to pologize and beg. But I only step away and mutter some by-salue that come out griping.

I go to the bosky darkness, seeing nothing real. See Mamadou the NewKing over me in angry love. Karim in all his blood, and every stank deed of my life. And in my darkness heart, I see the simper smirk her pinchen mouth, her mouth full of all ugliness. Her mouth that Driver heed.

I go in painful mind to seek, and find her where I most expect. She dabbit by the Sengle fire, is lurking like she fear some insult. Truth, my littles do her petty evils, been occasion. Toss her shoes into a brook, or tell her Armies looking for her. My brats jalouse on any stranger pairing with a Sengle jones.

As I walk to, she look up wisty in her blackish eyes. But when she know myself, she brighten gratty.

'Ho, girl,' I say. 'Can talk apart?'

'Be sure.' She haste to fetch her sack, and come behind with eagering step.

I lead her to our walking highway, private at this nightish hour. Road be like a valley of sky between the forest's detail life. Where we come out, a roadsign lean: SPEED LIMIT 65. In woods across, is horses tethern, and one blackish pony look up to us curiose. Munching sprig hang from his mouth.

I sit in the middy road, and she sit to me, smiling. She wear old jeans of Asha Badmouth, patch on both their knees. Look glad attention, like a hound who wait to do his trick.

'Bone,' I say discomfort. 'Only got one question to you.'

'Heeding,' she say, and touch her ear.

'I only wondern, ya. You spoke to Driver of me somehow?'

Her smile weaken puzzling. 'Nothing you ain't like to hear. Be all bonesse I got for you, ain't mysteries in this.'

'But you told some knowledge? Ain't got to be a thing is mally.'

'What sort knowledge?'

I look up at that watching pony. He still gazing, switch his tail. I want to drive away his stare, but he look brainless on.

I say, 'From Army camp.'

Mention Army camp, her face change inward. She shake head reluctant.

'All it is,' I say, 'when I been hurt there. By they feathers? You callen me the NewKing's Sengle. Always wondern to this.'

'Shoo, I known you gone to him.' She pooch her lips, look cautieuse.

I catch my breath. 'And you told Driver?'

'Ain't guess I done. He never known?'

'Nay, been something . . . hurt him if he learn.'

'Ho, I see. He going to think, been harm in this.' Her plum lips gather to this thought. 'You like, I tell him how there ain't no harm.'

'Ain't got to learn I been there,' I say hasty. 'Best be so.'

Then her frighten telligence be sharp. 'I keep this. Never fear me.'

I sigh. 'Gratty, truth.'

'Easy favors.' She laugh happy. 'Saying nothing ain't no work.'

'Ya.' I brush my hand along the road, pick up a straying pebble. 'But only wondering . . . how you known I gone to Mamadou?'

'Shoo, how you think?' She grimace sly. 'The NewKing told all ears.'

I startle nasty. 'Shee, he told?'

'Told, the fool he be. Then feathers bother him all right, how he go bring them cooties. Sengle love disease.' She laugh harsh and cover her mouth.

'Love disease? He said we doing love?'

'Nay, ain't fret.' She shoo her hand. 'He got no tempers for a lie.'

Word 'lie' come fresh in my relief. I notice my hand be crushing painful on its pebble. Loose it down. 'So what he told?'

'Mostly said you got some fight with him. Bringing it to the camp like some big jones will do. But – how he said – you be a skinny girl, is some ridiculous. Some terrify virgin lose her sense. It been . . .' She hold and bite her lip. 'Is how they talking, ya.'

I breathe through my frightening nerves. 'Ya, I gone to fight. Been once.'

245

'And then he want you queen.' She pooch her lips like preciation. 'Foo, sister, if you seen they brawls! A Sengle queen, you
magine!'

'Feathers want no Sengle queen?'

'They fearing murder wars, it been. But all they going to say, your
Sengles stank beneath no pride. Call Mamadou a wolf who do with
chickens.'

'Ho!' I laugh peculiar. 'Who be chickens? They the chickens.'

'But you guess, why Mamadou wanting you?' Her eyes grow
sharp with mischief. 'What he saying, Christwives all been using
backwards-forwards by some digger. Or they twelve. He want no
twelve. Yourself – be bell, and grown fifteen, and virgin.' She laugh
high. 'You heed? A virgin, what he want!'

This take me in bad surprise. Almost, I say I be no virgin.
Mamadou known this best of any, months before he want me queen.
Been work he do himself.

But I catch in sense. I only look back to the pony, want some
witness to this rat injustice. Yo, he drowsing now, eyes shut. Lean
sleepy to a tree.

'Truth, Driver told me,' I say low. 'How Armies think to take me.'

In my corner-eye, her hand stir on the road, touch there like
thought. Fingers spiderish in moon. 'Yo sho, I warn him self. How
Driver known.'

'You known him then?' I say in careful voice. 'At Army camp?'

'He never mention this?' Her face go hurt, but then she nod like
thinking. 'Sure, ain't going to mention. See this right.'

'Nay, why he ain't mention?' I take shorter breath. 'Been something wrong?'

'Now, ain't wrong.' She shrug. 'They times, he kept his sickness
quiet. Why he come to OldKing Hak.'

'Hak?'

'Hak selling papa. Child who want it secret, go to him.' She
look to me, face shy in memory. 'Any a child ain't want to talk to
Hak so much. But Driver stop with me sometimes, we talking.

Like two friends will talk. I *going* to warn him how they think to steal you.'

A moment, I only stare and breathe. Then I look down easing to my hands. 'Been right.'

'Then Driver never come to camp again. Gone sour on Armies, sure. But I gain him back. You seeing, sugar? All be evens. Give good, or you give evil, it come back to you again.'

I nod, gone staring at the grainy road. 'Be evens, ya.'

Then the simper touch my arm. I flinch at this but smile up hard.

'Ho, I got some Lowell wine in here.' She heft her pinkish sack. 'You like some wine?'

'Sure.' My shoulders ease. 'Wine I can use.'

She fetch out a corken brock. Is sleeper glass, with sticker glue still bleary on its sides. She uncork the brock and take a drink. Hand it to me.

In this, it notice that her pinkish sack turn round. Show the side she always keep close-held against her belly. Got no written names on this. But in the full moonlight, can see where broidery been yank out rough. A word sketch there in holes. SOLEDAD.

When I look up, she watching on me sweet. I point to the sack. 'Soledad?'

She flinch, look hasty to it. 'Ya, Soledad. Been my name, sometime.'

'Ain't want this name no more?'

'I give it up.'

'Always want to call you by a name. Ain't like to call you simper.'

'Can call me Soledad, you like.' She touch the sack, frown at her unpicken name. 'Driver call me this sometimes. Been stubborn to this, but I easier now.'

'Foo, ain't need to bide they Armies' filthen rules. You gone from them.'

'Nay, I rid this name before. Ain't lost it to no feathers.' She look up seriose. 'When I gone to be Maria.'

*

247

Maria she explain to me before, for any lengths. Be a matter of her people – children living in a city grandiose in wealth. Got every science there. Is lectric lights and tower buildings; photographs and working cars. Had a cat she call Bigote, drank his water from a glass.

Simper's town been Christings – though she disrespect this name. How she explain, our Massa Christings be in fallen creeds. 'Sleeper faith,' she calling this, and say the sleeper faith be wrong, though how this prove I never learn. Right faith call 'catolico'. Prettieuse word enough, can be a wolfen name for enfant.

Catolicos believing two-stick Christ. Get all this Bible story with its water-walking and generose fish. How Jesus born to Mary who been virgin. Papa Joseph stand by whistling, got no sex to do.

Their Mary call Maria, and catolico Maria go from unfuck birth to all adventures. Since this been sleeper times, when Jesus grown to size, she living still. Then she become Christ's queen and bride. Still they do no sex, is more like animoses here.

When Jesus dying murdern, his ghost go into Maria. Survive in her, so god remain, available to children. And when she die, the spirit move into some new Maria. This repeat in every history. Maria die and be reborn, is usual nonsense gods will do.

In the simper's people, the living Maria rule the town. This a person child. Ain't special nothing. Maria walk on feet and eating food and making shee. But they believe god live in her. They do some church accomplish this, with godly clothes and blessing wine. When this finish, she know wisdom, be unblemish right.

Can tell without no wondering these be diggers. Senseless as a moth.

I say, 'Ho, you try to be Maria? Kept this quiet some. But why you leave your town for this?'

'Gone to find a Jesus.' She gaze along the road, bright thinking. 'How Maria be known.'

'Easy found, you bear him pregnant. Once you learn this trick, is done.'

'Foo!' She laugh up sudden, push my knee with shooing hand. 'Ain't looking for no enfant, crazy.'

'You get a finish Jesus somewhere?'

'Sure. Take your apostles, go to yonder miles and seek.'

'What these opossums useful for?'

'Opossum! You know vally well it ain't opossums!' She laugh breathless, press her fist up to her mouth. Then she say, like she bait my mischief, 'If you become Maria, your apostles going to rule the burrows.'

'Burrows being what? Opposums living in these burrows?'

'Known you going to say that!'

'Foo, burrows ain't no name to me.'

Her smile go shy. 'The town be grandy, ya. It rule in parts. These parts is callen burrows. Apostles rule the burrows, ya Maria ruling over all.'

'So apostles going with Maria, out to catch a Jesus. How you going to know this Jesus?'

She shrug and look down at the road. 'Jesus ya be white.'

'How he white?' I say, though sure I guess.

'White like roos. They skin, you know how.' She frown at me, ware some insult. 'Jesus white.'

Truth be, I embarrass, that any child believing this. Get some stupid animals, but never a fish will worship roos. But I polite her, 'Ya, can see. Scarce beast, and vally to take.'

'Scarce, is truth,' she answer gratty. 'And sure you know, he only representing Jesus so. Ain't exactly him. Nor he represent until he do the sacrament. Then he give his spirit for Maria. Only be Jesus for this sacrament.'

'So any whitish child can serve this need?'

'If they grown and male. Yo, roos be always this.' She smile hopeful. 'See how this be fitting? White and grown and male.'

'Ain't you steal our Pasha. Is Keepers' roo, she definite to this.'

Expect she laugh, but Simper-Soledad frown hard.

'No sho,' I say unliking. 'You got wants for Pasha?'

'Nay. Is only, Maria being . . . like yourself. Be virgin.' She get her Armies look, mouth grit. 'Look at my face, you knowing I ain't this.'

Here my sympathy gripe. I take my pebble up again, turn it nervy in my fingers. 'Ain't know from scars. Can get scars any way.'

'Ya. But I ain't this. Been going to find my Jesus, when I was took. Took by Hak and Bardo, you know how.'

'Right.' I grip the pebble hard into my palm.

'Apostles sleeping.' She laugh thin. 'Opossums play dead then.'

'Shoo, you admit, this story sad as rain. How they done you.'

She shrug, eyes hard in distances. 'Only been thinking, how Hak dying now. He can be dead, this time.'

'Ya,' I say encouraging. 'Be evens, how you said. He getting what he give.'

'Ain't evens, nay. He only sick. Ain't nothing like he done to me. And Bardo. All they feathers.' Her face clench like pain. 'But why they got to be like that? Ain't want to hate them anyhow.'

'Going to hate,' I say confuse. 'But now they rid. They gone.'

'Ya.' She nod distracting. Turn her face by, pulling at a braid. Then she lift her sack in clumsy hands. 'Be Driver waiting me. If you . . .'

'Be right.' I nod unthinking. 'Should go sleep. Is tardy hour.'

Simper cork and pack her brock. Rise with conscious gesture, like she flee before my friendship change. Yo, as I stand, she mouth some unvoice by-salue and haste away.

34

OF DANGER ITS ARRIVAL

Be the following night our journey turning desperate strange.

Day been easy innocence. Sky clean with sunlight, and we coming to a stretch of better road. Even got patches somewhere in the holes. Our cars ride easy. Only the roo get superstitions – be these patches, must be evil roading people by. At middy meal, he come to me with some wrap paper in his hand. It be a brownish scrap, got BIMBO writ in wash-out blue.

'Ya,' I say. 'I seen these papers by. And so?'

He give me disapproval look. 'Is new.'

'Foo, how is new? Look how it fading, been through any a rain.'

'Be paper. Rotting quick.'

'So, newness be that it exist?'

He grimace to the woods, like he can smell they lurking children.

'Sure,' I say. 'Be roading people here who wrap some objects. Prove they want to kill us. Be all any people want.'

'Ain't funny.'

'Been waiting years to murder us particular. Happy day for them.'

'Need a guard,' he say annoying.

'We walking here with guns. Ain't notice?'

'Nay, by night. Camp need a guard.'

'So you guard. I sleeping nights myself.'

Roo crush this paper in his hand, and go off with disgruntle face.

Still, when we walk again, I got some careful nerves myself. Keep scouting to the roaden margins, seeking for no evidence. But be no farther trash nor trace. Even the road look misbegot again, its patches old as silence. Patches needing patches self.

And the sun dim forward, fallen west. Camp be made with normal bother; early night be simple. I sneak apart to El Mayor, and even sleep some time with him, how I begun to do these nights. Learn to wake before the morning even think of dawn.

So it been cat hours, when I sneak from his tent in carefulness, that trouble find myself.

El Mayor keep his tent apart, some walk into unpeople woods. Nor no one wonder at this habit. Lowells expect, will be some secret traffic to his bed. Same reason, my departure from his tent be chancy done. Anyone see me in this place, my tale be known entire.

So I creep slow, with watchful eye for any waking Lowells. But I scarce begun when ABC come barking from the woods.

She jump up and tag her forepaws happy to my chest. When I push her off, she prance around and settle in woofing stance. Bark a loudness conversation, sending woofs in ten directions. Even her tail wag at a noisy bush.

I try shooing her, for all the useless this will be. She only sit and interest happy in my shooing hands. I go and grab her mouth shut, while she wriggle consternations. Yo, here it notice, ABC wear something round her neck.

It be a reddish ribbon, tie there close. My first thought be, was done by our Tequila. Decorate my hound, the same she do to any patient creature. Then I see something on this ribbon. Orange object, piercen through, it cling there like a bauble.

It be a leaf, is curlen tight. Autumn color, but still got younger softness. And something chill in memory. Leaf curl like Crow and me done, when we written secrets so. Yo even in the forest dark, can see the markings on its skin. My every conscience know, is Crow his writing.

But ain't no Crow in this. Crow been left some weeks behind. All Armies left.

I tear the leaf away. Let ABC go loose, and she run bucketing off into the trees.

Then I stand up feary, head to the road for its good moon. My legs be going clumsy, and some part of me still hear my noise, be conscious of the sleeping tents. But be no waking noises as I step out to the light. Unroll the leaf in watery light.

Pen gone through the leaf in places, ink been spotting dry. Is tiny wavers where the pen skip over leafen veins. But its words read plain.

WE HERE. THE NEWKING COME FOR YOU.

My skin go cold. Stand in the silent moon, and I stare blind at these dim letters.

First, I struggle to believe the Armies here, in our far woods. Feel like ABC must run the distance back to Massa. But slow, I figure this. They ride on horses, got no enfants by. Be most four days to ride. Only it seem peculiar, they still keep their tired evils – that any a child still care for queens and raids, when all our life be gone.

Come a stupid wish, I can ignore this warning still. Be took to Mamadou his love, and any other futures die. Only I cannot and cannot – be the cure, my Sengles' need.

Then I conceive the Armies in their raiding camp behind. Hammocks like our own, the same low fire built with reluctant wood. Their capture nets and ropes. NewKing Mamadou in his anger. Crow there, still caring for myself somehow, in darkness of his moods.

My ABC been always sweet for Crow. Must be she sniff him out. He use this chance, sneak separate from the feathers, write this leaf in warning. But sure they cannot steal me. Be two hundred children round myself. Yo, I got Kalash. They feathers come, I shoot them, quick as swatting.

But in my nether mind, a spooking memory be dark. How Soledad said, *Hak say they got to kill you. For Karim and Mika.* No hundred children, nor Kalash, can save me from one sneaky gunshot.

Then I hear a step behind. I wheel, grab to Kalash. Shadow rise, and I round to it vicious.

Before I know, I point Kalash at Pasha, swallowing fear.

He flinch back. 'Ice. Is me.'

'Foo! Creep up on people, damn.' I loose Kalash down to my waist. Leaf crush up, sweaten in my fingers.

'Bony done.' He gesture at my gun.

'Lucky you ain't shot, come creeping like that.'

'I learn now.' He laugh soft.

Almost, I slip the leaf into my pocket. In this instant, it seem like a secret must be hid. But then my reason sharpen. 'Pasha. Got some trouble.'

'What trouble?'

'They Armies here. You magine this, they come for me.'

Then I explain this matter. Flatten the leaf for him to see. He only glance upon, and he go startling, swearing rooish. Grab my sleeve, and pull me toward the woods.

I laughing underbreath as I go after. Muttern, 'Foo your panics. Worser rabbits.'

He shush me angry, push me toward a tree. Turn back with gun in hands. Can see his face gone misery now. Is like his worries concentrate into one bitter taste.

Pasha whispern low, 'Where they will be?'

'Anywhere.' I shrug. 'If they be even scouting me tonight.'

'How many they will be?'

'Can be only three, for raiding. Most they bringing be twelve boys.'

'Is all got guns?'

'Sure. Got Deema's guns and three they own. What they have.'

He make disgusting face. 'Mally.'

'Shoo, ain't think the NewKing shoot me.'

'Fool.' Pasha shake his head. 'Ain't think. You only know, when you be shot.'

This take unliking in my skin. I settle against this tree, look round. We come into the Lowells' tents here, scattern populous and close. Camp be full of sleeping night, ain't feel like danger anyhow. But I know from my own sneaking, be no craft to come up unawares around the camp. Be any shadows where an Army can be lurking with a gun. Wait for my showing head.

Then Pasha whispern, 'Is certain, they come for you only?'

I fidget my hand along the leaf. 'He going to say if it be war. Can write it so. Is different acts.'

'If be roos also?'

'He writing this,' I say in better confidence. 'Crow leave no Sengles to the roos.'

Pasha nod unliking. Seem he seek his mind for other fears.

I slip the leaf into my pocket. 'All it is, I find a tent to hide. Be most an hour to morning.'

'Nay. Can shoot you in a tent.'

'Ain't going to know I be there.'

'Know if they watch. Need walls to hide.'

I start to cavil that it be no walls for any miles. But then my conscience pause. 'A ditch, can be.'

'Ditch?'

'Ya, be a brook. Will be some places there. Hide in its banks.'

He take a deeper breath, his face ease better. 'Can be bone.'

I turn by, and Pasha come beside. He waring round like any strangeness, aim his gun at shadows. This catch in me, and I keep rifle sharp in hands, glare at the trees. But nothing stirring. Only movement be a Lowell ten, smoking by his tent, who look surprises at us as we pass.

Brook go shallow through the camp, must follow it beyond. Here we find a corner where the brook dug in around a boulder. Got a maple on the other bank whose roots be risen tall, create a natural hide. Brook thin with autumn, got some inches dry around. Can hunker well. Pasha wave me in. He stay above, still scouting.

I go crouch to the rock. Shift till I find a place that fit my back. Keep Kalash bright on my knee, watch for places where a prowling Army can approach. But truth, they got to know where I be hid, or else they pass by blind. Yo even if they track us here, I going to see them first. I settle in my confidence. Feel almost warry that I think of this solution to myself.

Then some minutes pass before I comprehend, is boring. Brook smell froggy, got a weighing dampness in its air. Rock be cornery at my back. I whisper up, 'Shoo, come down here. Is lonely.'

Pasha's rustling stop. He whisper, 'Hush.'

'They glad to shoot you also. Know this.'

'Need a guard on camp,' he whisper back in angry voice. 'Must wake some children.'

'Blablabla. You coming down?'

'Be they roading people also.'

'And be bears. Or lightning strike you. Owl of misery.'

I feel in my pocket, check my cigarettes. Is only two. Decide, I smoke the first when I begin to feel the cold. Soon as I decide this, I be cold. Then a fly come niggling round my face, seem to consider if it want to dive into my eye. Magine the hour ahead, I start to think of shooting with some friendliness.

Then Pasha whisper, 'I think, ain't no one.'

Almost I laugh. 'You coming down?'

'Come for parley.'

He stalk down careful, ware his gun. Ya, when he hunker by, his size so cumbering big, he block my moon. Now can only see the sky, mark out in cobweb branch above, the squiggling light along the brook.

Then he say cautieuse, 'Ice Cream?'

'Ya. I here.'

'Armies making camp, can be?'

'Be likely. Night be mostly gone. Can all be sleeping now.'

He shift restless, tense his rifle. I look to him, but only see the furry light around his hair. Gun silhouette against the brook light.

And he say, 'Be bone, I go to shoot them?'

'Damn.' I spit into the brook. 'Is ugly notions, roo.'

'Must do. I thinking.'

'Yo, Crow be with them.'

His darkness shape go sorry to the brook. 'Crow. Ain't thought.'

'Go to shoot them, damn. Why you always think of killing?'

'For reason here.'

'Reason, foo.'

'Can know Crow's face. I kill they others only.'

'Ain't you listen nothing? Can be twelve children there. You kill them all?'

He ain't answer this, but sure I hear his stubborn in the dark. He take his rifle up again. All his shape be waiting force.

'Heed,' I say. 'We go and parley with them. All it is.'

'Parley make them leave?'

'Ain't going to know until we try.'

'I know. Is soldat work. I know.'

'Soldat work, goddamn. This why you kill that feather, at Army camp?'

'What feather?'

'Feather in the simper house. Some fourteen boy. I always think of this.'

'He got a gun.' His voice come angry dull.

'He ain't. Got nothing like.'

'Can mistake. Can happen so. Is normal.'

'So soldat work mean, kill for nothing?'

His stillness feel like anger. I watch past him at the water, but all my nerves be in his cold respect. My heart peculiar close.

At last, he answer low, 'Mean, keep living. Keep your people living.'

'Kill any another child?'

Expect, he going to cavil this, but he say simple, 'Yes.'

I take my breath. 'Some bad cowardesse.'

'I living. You be living.'

'So, you be a bone soldat.'

Pasha's shape go lower. Fingers come in bald moonlight, feeling in the dirt. He scrabble a pebble out and take this in his whitish fingers.

I say, 'You sad as losing, roo. Every word you say.'

He sigh and toss his pebble. It clop in water, courteose small, send rings of moon along the brook skin.

I say, 'Shee, they Armies likely only take me anyhow. Ain't murdering much. They rather rape.'

Pasha shake his head in gloom dislike. Can see, he prude this rape, like males will do.

Now mischief catch in me. 'Can be best, they take me. I learn what happen to the children left in Massa. Guess I escape, sometime. Worser wear, but still can talk.'

Pasha say unhappy, 'I ain't let them take you.'

'You ain't want to know what been in Massa?'

'Nay,' he say flat. 'Got no want.'

He chuck another pebble in the brook. It slap there angry, lift a splash.

'Been only fooling with you. Shee.' I sit back to the bank. Its cold touch through my jacket, send a tinge into my spine. I get my cigarettes out and count them over. Put them back.

Then Pasha say resenting low, 'Mamadou ain't your friend.'

I shrug, surprise. 'Sure I know this.'

'You tell me once, you got some love with him.'

'Be other memories. Is done.'

'So, why you protect him?'

'Protecting no one. Shee, no wolf kill all those children. Ain't for love, is person feeling.'

Can feel his unbelief. His hands shift nervy on his gun.

'Goddamn,' I say, 'you got to know, I be with El Mayor these days. No Mamadou in this story. Done.'

Then hotness brighten in my face. Feel like swears inside, ain't know how Pasha always get my secrets. I duck my head and touch my lips to Kalash's friendly cold.

Pasha say cautieuse, 'You be with El Mayor, like doing love?'

'What else you think?' I laugh into my gun.

'I ain't known this.'

'Ain't going to know. We kept this quiet to ourself.'

Can hear him shift behind, like he discomfort. I look back. He holding on his gun precarious now, like it be careful goods. When he catch me looking, his face change. He say, like he excuse, 'Be bone child. El Mayor.'

'He worthy, truth.' I sit up. 'Infantize me sometimes, but he bone.'

Then Pasha say unliking, 'How, if you go pregnant?'

'Foo, must be pregnant, sometime.'

Expect he going to mention fears again, our needful journeys. But he say, 'You young for this.'

'Ho, you dreaming fantasies.' I huff a laugh. 'Be almost old. Ain't like to get no enfant when I be sixteen or seventeen. They never going to know me. I can die before they talking words.'

This hush him well. I watch the squirming water light, taken in worry dreams. Truth, I got no haste for enfants. Can see myself, all bellyish trudging, going to roos for robbing work. Must hope, I find the cure before I grow no heavy baby. But I got no sign of pregnant. Is always hope I got a molly belly, never get no life.

Then clear into the night, we hear a voice, come harsh in skree. We hand up our guns. Some time, we only listen scary. Hear every detail of the passing water, how its moods repeat. Then the voice come close and long. Is Keepers' squall, go peaking terrify in the quiet woods.

Fast as thinking, I leap up. Ya, Pasha rear behind, we running, crashing, up the closer bank. As we come, can hear more voices yelling, various in distance. And I know, these voices be of Sengles. Yell my name in fright.

First we see be Hate You. She dash up anxy and call back, 'She here! Ice Cream be here!' Then Keepers run to, wild, with hammock hair and teary face. She barrel to me, crying, 'Where you been? Was roos? Nay, where you been?'

'Been no roos.' I cosset at Keepers' head. 'Ain't nothing like.'

Keepers slap my arm. 'Nay, you been gone!'

Then Jonah sprint in from the road, with million terrors in his face. 'Jermaine still looking. Someone got to tell him.'

'So tell him,' I say riling. 'You all worrying for what?'

'You lost!' say Keepers.

'Foo, ain't lost! Been only by the brook.'

Then Jonah say in trembling voice, 'The simper be by you?'

My heart misgive. Can see how Jonah's tears begin, his brow knit feary.

'Nay,' I say. 'She gone?'

'Ya, and Piglet gone,' say Jonah. 'Army horse, he missing.'

Hate You say, 'Our good child found them gone. And you was gone.' Her face be set in fear confusion, like she wake in fright.

'Be only Piglet gone?' I say. 'The other horses left to us?'

Hate You nod. 'They left.'

I try to think how Soledad can take this horse herself. But she got no reason that she leave in secret from my brother.

Then Pasha say behind, 'Armies. Been no guard.'

'Sure I know!' I say. 'Been my mistake, you right. Think forward.'

'Armies?' Hate You say. She blink hard, like she try to focus this.

'Got word from Crow, they here,' I say in misery. 'Come tonight. How long the simper gone?'

'Ain't know.' She look skitty to the trees. 'Our good child only woken.'

I breathe and try to find my thought. Leaf said, THE NEWKING COME FOR YOU. Cannot be meant for no one else. But Crow care for no simper. Ain't figure he will, she Army goods by every definition. And be sure, the Armies steal her back. Seen my stupidities, I ain't think this sooner.

Then Hate You say uncertain, 'Now they got her, Armies leave, you think?'

'Nay.' I breathe out harsh. 'They wait for me.'

'Why they waiting you?' say Jonah.

'Ain't your problems,' I say short. 'They here, we still can get her.'

Hate You say confusen, 'Get her?'

'Get her?' Jonah parrot. 'How we get the simper? She be theirs.'

'We getting her,' I say frustrating. 'Be no arguments, you heed?'

They stare reluctant faces back. Jonah wipe a tear away, eyes bright with sickness look.

'Yo heed,' I say in lower voice. 'Me–Pasha going now, scout where the Armies be.' I look to Pasha. 'We be right?'

He frown uncertainties, but I say harder, 'Yo we right. Hate You, go and wake they Lowells. Any jones who got a gun. See they ready when we come back.'

Here Keepers say in fright joyeuse, 'Be murder war. They Armies perish.'

'Damn!' I say. 'Ain't be no murder, nor this be your parley, small.'

Jonah pinch his mouth, touch to the pistol at his pocket. 'I got to come? Must fight the Armies?'

I sigh frustration. 'Nay, ain't got to come. But tell Jermaine. Now move yourself! Go on!'

They catch a second, gape at me, like they will beg for different orders. Then Hate You yelp and go. And Jonah swear, go running terrify like he flee his death.

I turn, touch Pasha's shoulder, and start off. He come behind. But when we gone past hearing distance, Pasha catch my arm. I wheel to him, my fear gone angry. 'What? Yo what you need?'

'Ain't got to come.' His hand grip in my arm.

'Nay, what you saying?'

'You, ain't got to come.'

'I coming. Nor it be no needless killing. Heed my word.'

'Ice, this ain't your work.'

'I coming, get no fool mistakes. I coming.'

His face grit hard. 'Nay. We both stay here, if you be so.'

'How? If I be so?'

'Needless killing.'

261

'Shee, we only scouting now.'

His hand close painful on me. 'They can see us.'

'So they seeing. And?'

'Ice, why they come? They come for you.' His bluish eyes gone bright with need.

I shake my head. Catch breath and try to figure. 'So, they see us, we can fire in air. They running, like they done at Army camp.'

'Ain't think this. Or they never run.'

'Damn, how my thinking be in this?'

'Must shoot.'

'Been said! I going to shoot.'

'Nay, must shoot someone. Must . . .' Can see him struggle with his words. My body be a white impatience. Pasha say, 'I shoot first. They run, is bone. But cannot trust this. Ain't going to shoot someone, you staying here.'

I shake my head, can feel my sweat begin. 'Nay, if–'

'Ice, I ain't take you to be kilt!'

Then his bluish anger find my heart. Something weaken in me, was like a choice that vanish there. I say, 'Be bone. I shoot.'

He loose my arm. I start to turn, but he grab to Kalash. Find her safety switch, and fix the setting to three-bullet. He say, 'When you shoot, must aim again.'

'Yo I know! Been hunting every years!'

He free Kalash and say, 'Is right. Like hunting. Think like this.'

Now dawn be starting in the east. We stalk into its gray suspicion. Trees lean over their first shadows, and the dampen leaves go docile soft beneath our feet. Light be enough to find the prints of Piglet's hooves, but dim for hiding. Is perfect for our task, but all this weigh unwanting in my nerves.

Keep thinking restless, Pasha got no moods to only scout. He go to murder simple, if they see us or they ain't. But truth, can see no other end. Armies never give their simpers, ain't their honor so. We leaving Soledad, or must be war. Is Pasha right.

Try telling myself some worser stories of their Army rapes. How they done Soledad. Can be, they rape her now, is like themself. Fix this in mind, and I decide again to do this, shoot a child. Decide again. But behind, I see how Pasha aim on green Karim. Remember how the feather in the simper house jerk back and wheel. Fall through his falling blood.

And we going through the woods. Ain't nothing. No unplace sound, no smell of smoke. Is only time. Pasha moving dreamen slow, his rifle conscious in his hands. Yo I feel like madness, slow beside. Once, a squirrel badge up by our feet, and we both jump like chickens. Come back to sense with rifles pointing wild. Then we go back to stalking. Ain't even feel no smile at this. I only hear our telling noise and swear inside myself.

And time go into time, until it feel like a forever task. Must wonder if we pass the Armies somehow. If they heard us, and they stalking to, around. Yo, all this weaken and return to green Karim again. How I will aim, and shoot, and someone wheel into a flash of blood. If it be Mamadou. Be Crow. How someone turn and shoot on me.

Then I smell smoke. I stalk on for some steps, ain't trust my feeling. Pasha walking on, ain't notice. I squint forward scary. Ain't see no motion yet, I start to wave my hand to Pasha.

Yo as I wave, I hear a rumbling sound come from my other side. Is like horizon thunder, but it grow and it continue. Come slow mysteriose, a constant grinding that rise from behind, and stay as one big blowing note. But ain't no storm. No thunder: sky look perfect clear around. And then it passing forward big. Pass us again, again, in waves. Ahead, it jitter and change and hush. I hold in unmeaning fear, like panics in a nightmare, where the dread ain't got no self. Is only knowledge with no thing to name.

And Pasha standing still. His rifle weaken in his hands. Roo be looking big-eyed into nothing. The smell of smoke remain in this, like comfort I can hold to. Is smoke. Is Armies, something that I known.

Then a gunshot deafen loud. As I startle, come more gunshots, pounding into everywhere. We both gone flailing to the ground. I fall clumsy, belly down. Be scrabbling hard in panic, like I need some lower ground beneath. Gunshots kicking all my sense, be like a hundred guns at once. Pass a gasping madness before I find my hold upon Kalash. Look up squinting, almost blind. Eyes themself be fearing. Gunshots go in bursts, knock all my courage twenty ways.

But when I look up, Pasha kneeling. I stare at him unknowing, and he wave me angry up. Only then, I feel how nothing changen in the air. Shots ain't come at us, be somewhere else – and then they stop. Stop like nothing been. Hear voices shouting somewhere. Be too far to comprehend.

First moment, I ain't brave to move. Feel like any part I show will be shot into pieces. Then I grit my jaw, I creep one leg to rising pose. Yell swears in my head, and grip Kalash as I get to my feet.

I feel the nothing in my flesh. How the air stand calm around, ain't nothing killing me. Voices dimmer in the woods beyond. A horsen neigh.

Pasha be standing in some staring terror. Rifle to his shoulder, but he got no aiming face. And I shoulder up Kalash. Go forward quick, ware angry in the trees. I stalk into my terror. Hear Pasha hasten noisy after, but I got no care for this. I only feel the smell of smoke. A rustling through the trees. Where those shots been.

Then in the woods before, my eye catch a moving shape. I startle jolten. Rifle falter as I start to duck. Then it recognize. A horse. It move at shouting distance, shape confusing in the trees. I ware my gun again, my finger slipping sweaty on the trigger. Watch feroce until it feel like I must see through these trees. See everything I need. But I only see the horsen shape in shifting parts of brown.

Now Pasha stalking past. I go along, my rifle moving awkward to my walking. And we come toward this horse, and see the trees and see the horse. Be this and then there be some quiet smoke. Another horse beyond.

We stop in thinner woods, among a dozen nervy horses. A fire be burning low. Is various trash around, and no one there.

Now our paths confuse. We turning, seeking, aim guns every way. One moment, I turn round and touch my shoulder at a horse's nose. It snort and back away, and when I look, I know the NewKing's buckskin stallion, Beg-No-Pity. Is like a memory jump out from my head.

Then Pasha call to me. I want to shout at him to hush. But I come along, see where he waring on the ground. My rifle loosen in my aching arms.

On the ground, lain curlen, be the feather red Malik. His cardinal feathers crush along the earth, and blood lie red behind. Blood gone particular on the fallen leaves, confuse their different shapes. Now it remember senseless, he First Runner's brother born. Remember how I fight him once, and he start giggling foolish when I clout him in the eye with mud.

I whisper dumb, 'He dead?'

Pasha crouch beside. Expect, he going to touch Malik, but he reach down where a pistol fallen from the feather's hand. Grab this hasty, rise again. Shove the pistol in a pocket and say in undervoice, 'He dead.'

'How you know?'

Pasha ignore this. He looking round, a frown set deep. Then his eyes sharpen. He shoulder up his rifle, go in crouch against a tree. And I hear voices come again. I almost swear. I want to run. But I take my rifle up. And I be turning, watching for whatever I must fear, when Pasha swear beside.

I start to see the motion gathering – something strange that come from all the woods – when Pasha grab my rifle. Yank it down. Panic freak in me. I grip Kalash in watery hands, but Pasha pull it by again, and move in sudden certainty to stand in front of me.

First I see be rifles. And for some moment, this be all I know. Is rifles going to shoot me. Trembling starting in my knees. Then Pasha free Kalash and drop his rifle sudden to the dirt. Lift hands up clear above his head.

And some dozen strangers come in, walking through the trees. Is boyish children, jones I never seen before. All is wearing brownish jackets, and all is pointing rifles. My mind go too clear. Can hear each step, can hear how other children come behind me. And in front of me, I see my Pasha's back, held stiff and painful. How his hands be shaking where he hold them in the air. A curl of brownish seed caught in his hair, and some motive in me want to catch it out. I rid this thought, and in some inkling dread, I drop Kalash. She fall and thud like any object, but my heart react. I crave and crave to grab her back. Be like I cannot breathe without. Hands be trembling same as Pasha's, I grip them into sweaten fists. Sweat draw a sharp line down my back.

A stranger shout some angry words. Cannot comprehend, I feel my mind gone deaf somehow. Roo's shoulders ease a breathen touch. He call back. But I ain't comprehend this neither, is like some madness wasten me.

Stranger talk again, and Pasha answer. Cannot see this talking child, is hid by Pasha's shoulder. But it start to comprehend, is words like fisher Panish. Ain't my brain is wrong. Is unknown words. Somehow this feel like a promise, how this can come good again. And I fasten on these words. Try to find some meaning, but nothing recognize.

Pasha say another word, sound almost like a warning. Then his right hand ease gradual to his pocket. He pull out the pistol of Malik with only fingers. Lift slow, gun hanging limp, and drop it to the ground beside. Then he say, in strain and furiose voice, 'Ice Cream. Leave your rifle.'

'I done,' I say. 'Is done.'

He crane his head somehow, look to Kalash beside my feet. Then his shoulders ease. He call more Panish, and a child come jogging, crouch by us. Child's elbow hit my leg as he gather our guns, and he grin scary to me. Say something and laugh at himself. Then he step back and lose among the others. Here I feel a nakedness. All my body want Kalash. I turn around, and at my back, it be more children standing.

In this, it start to comprehend, there be some forty children. Forty boyish children with forty rifles in forty brownish coats, their hair cut close the same. Is like a weirdo dream. Come uncanny, how their faces various, they move each in different sense.

Then, behind, a girlish voice cry glad and furiose. All these rifle children turn, be like a wind go through. They laughing as they step apart. One and one, the rifles turn from us, they loosen sideways.

And through this sudden path come Soledad.

35

THE ROADING PEOPLE

She wear a brownish jacket like the others, over her same jeans. Jeans of Asha Badmouth, patch on both their knees with darker cloth. Simper come grinning huge, walk like her feet themself be breathless. Cry a Panish word, and all the rifle children laugh.

Then she spread her arms. For a breath bizarre, she stand and stretch like joy outside herself. Her pitchy voice come up, 'Ice Cream!'

Pasha shift before me, turn to look into my face. See his eyes, is like he dead and walking. Like no person there.

I say to him in breaking voice, 'Is Soledad.' Then it remember, he ain't know her name. I shrug and step around him as the simper dash to me, she grab me ardent to herself. Her body feeling small and helpful. I begin to cry at this, I say, 'Goddamn, what happening?'

She say in laughter, 'Be my people. We got you now, you bone. You right.'

She turn her head and call more Panish, bold. Rifle children walk toward, and I grip her in blind uncourage as they come close. Now they at touching distance all around.

Soledad ease back from me, is smiling all her eyes. 'Ain't got to worry now. We take you.'

I shake my head, feel stupid in my wits. 'Ain't want no taking.'

'Nay, be bone. Ain't nothing mally.'

Then I notice children grabbing Pasha. Cold go through my

stomach. They pulling at his arms behind, fix some metal joins upon. Take me a stumbling second before I understand this object. Word come to me, *handcuffs*, be a sleeper artifact. But cannot remember why it use – if it be only science rope, or do some hurt beyond.

They pull Pasha forward, and I cry out lowish in my throat as he be took from me. But Soledad keep one arm around my shoulders, shush me in soft repetition. *Be bone, you good, ain't fear.*

And we walking through the woods, with rifle children crowding round. Some talk to Soledad, and she keep saying, 'See, see.' Give her pitchy laugh and grip my shoulders close in sympathy. I saying, 'Nay, what be with Pasha?' but she only say her *bone* and *good* and *never fear me.* I want to break and flee, but I got Pasha in my terror. Keep my eyes toward him where he led. His hands seem normal, handcuffs make no blood. His head kept low.

We come to the road, that patchen road of yesterday. Upon this road, now stand real cars. Ain't rusten, got full tires upon. Be a sort, got something like a carten shape in back. They gaud in paint, got reddish bluish stripes along their flanks. On one stripe, be writ in white: DEFENSA, C. DE LAS MARIAS. I stare at this unknowing.

Here be some discussion. Soledad release my shoulders, start to argue in. A tallish child come to, he answer her with tired anger. She go mad to this, be pointing back at me and yelling.

Can see Pasha on the other side of all these talking children, stood with thinking misery in his face. One child hold his elbow, another point a rifle on him. He watch on me like I be something past.

Then Soledad turn to me, is looking like her feelings injure. Say in her argue voice, 'Fools thinking, you jump out. Been telling them, you ain't some imbecile, jump from a driving car.'

Here first it comprehending to me right, these cars is working. I shake my head in freshen panic. 'Nay. Where you be taking us?'

'We only going to a town is by. Can trust me, Ice. I keep you well.'

'Nay,' I say breathless. 'Got to get back to my Sengles. Yo Pasha, why he bound like that?'

This she ignore, she give her pinchen smile. 'Be bone. Me and my Carlos sit by you. You seeing, this be right.'

Trip in these cars be like an aching fever. I be took in carten back, with Soledad and five big rifle children. Pasha brought apart, nor I ain't see him all this journey. The car jerk into motion mostly like a normal cart. But then it gain to speed until it be like falling sideways. Feel like an endless scream somehow, I gripping anywhere I can. Ya, it leap awful from each bump, while roar be fearing in your ears. Trees go past so quick, is like they dropping sudden from a height. Rob hasty from your eyes, and wind hit vicious all directions.

Rifle children all sit careless to the sides, ya Soledad laugh, while I fight off a puken feeling. All my need be for my Sengles. Feel like a baby small, ain't got no knowledge to rely. Trees sprinten past. The unknown faces grin, shout words that got no sense. Yo, in this, I notice all the rifle children's hands is writ upon. Got spidery pictures on their hands, dimmish green and black. Is only drawings, but I feel some monstrous in this, some hell meaning.

Only help, I look at my own hands. Same hands as ever been. I fix upon their scars from Army camp, still showing dark and light. These be my actual life, was real. This happen to myself. I still be Ice Cream Star, ain't going to alter anyhow. And the road grind under, shivering in my teeth. Wind beat my braids against my face.

Only when I hear some scatter shouts, I look up scary. See our Massa camp slip past, all children dodging from the road. Some standing by to stare. I scramble quick, leap to the side, but someone kick my feet from under. I be caught in arms, pull down. I kick and fight, but only get some laughter, shouts around. Soledad be crying, 'Damn, you done it! Ain't believe!' Then I settle weak. Be sitting against this stranger jones, who keep me huggen to. Can only see, above the car back, how some Massas running after, struggling on the road, but it be like they running backwards. They only shrink, and when the highway turn, they wipen gone.

Then my tears come and I forget. Ain't even try for nothing. The carren wind dry these tears stiff against my cheeks. My arms still caught by this big jones, I cannot rub my face. Feel this other helplessness as my nose go thick.

At last, the car turn by and slow. Go on an earthen road, can feel its softer hold beneath. We slowing more, car jerk us backen forth, and stop. Noise sigh and hush.

Stranger jones let go my arms. I pull sharp from him like I rid an insult. Now I feel some hope again. Camp ain't likely be too far. All this can explain. I get Pasha, parley for our freedom. These people Soledad's, she love me well. Still can be right.

Someone pull the carten back out flat. Soledad stand to her feet, go graciose along the carten floor and leap out to the dirt. Turn back grinning, saying, 'Almost home, some wonder this.'

I stand up to my feet. This big jones waring round me with his hands, like I may fall. I walk along the carten bed, feel its weight shift underneath. Jump to dirt, my feet come gratty on its friendly stillness. Here be rifle people moving all around, fetch goods from cars. They go in tasky certainty, but every child stare on me as he pass.

Place be a normal evac. Can see, ain't no one living here. These rifle people using this, how Sengles use an evac sometimes as a camping place. Got some low unroofen houses, straggle along a broken road. Closest be a Citgo store, its yardroof burnt and broken. Citgo got its major window bust out, open to the air. Inside, is rifle children talking, nosing toward some papers on a table. All this got haunten looks in dawnlight, gray in ghosty wise.

Then I hold my step. Along the Citgo side, on concree ground, be eight Armies. They kneeling in a row, backs to the wall. All got their arms behind, can figure that they bound like Pasha. Most show signs of beating; bloody lips and fatten eyes. A rifle child ware by them, skinny jones in greenish cap.

271

Farthest Army to the right be slumpen forward to the ground. Is dead. His head be crusten blood, and blood smear high upon the wall behind. Blood spread beneath his face, look like a reddish blanket lain for comfort.

Before him crouch First Runner. Ain't in this row, her arms be free. Got her hands flat to the dirt, is crying onto these. Her face be cut in petty nicks. It freckle with red hurt. And I recall Malik, dead at their camp. Her brother born.

I find Crow with my eyes. Find Mamadou in this row, his right arm bandage to his side. Fear start before I know, this ain't new injuries. Be Pasha's gunshot. And still, this ain't feel real to me. Cannot believe is them. Yo, all they Armies stare on me with thoughtless fixity.

Through this, my heart be catching false. Think any ways this can be right. My face feel wrong with sweat.

Then Soledad come back. Stand full in my sight, and put her hands on both my shoulders. She look mostly like herself, a panic child with needing eyes. But be a nasty brightness to this. Is like she swallow too much joy, and now it hurt inside.

'You bone?' she say in her sweet pitchy voice. Close, can smell her boozen breath.

'Nay.' I try to shift, look past her shoulder. 'What this be?'

She tug my shoulders. 'Heed on me. We going to do this.'

'What happening with they Armies?'

'Foo, ain't nothing.' She laugh breathless.

'You going to free them, ya?'

Soledad pooch her lips. 'Child, this ain't yours. You heed me now.'

I swallow, but my swallow go wrong somehow. I cough weak against this, swallow again. 'I heed. But you will free them?'

'Ain't fret. Ain't got to fear me.'

'Ain't fearing you, goddamn. Got better fears.'

'You got no fears, I saying. Heed.' She narrow seriose. Her fingers tighten in my shoulders. 'How you found your Pasha Roo?'

'Ain't found him. He been by me all this time. We gone for you.'

'Nay, shoo. When Sengles found him first.'

'Found him . . .' I try to see behind her again, she catch my shoulders fast. Eyes look some jitter feeling. Be like joy and panic in one mood.

She say in teaching voice, 'How you found him. Who been by you then?'

'Ya, Driver find him. In an evac that we burnt, roo come out running. Ain't no news in this.'

Soledad nod, stroke on my shoulder. 'Bone. Was Driver there. What other children been?'

'Ain't know,' I say. But then it start to answer in my mind. Be comfort to recall this day, is sweet in townie distance. 'Ho, been Keepers by. Asha Badmouth and Jermaine. And myself, is all was there.'

'Is four.' Hands on my shoulders soften. 'Sugar, you doing bone. You cool. Now I going to leave you think. You needing twelve, you mind this? Twelve.'

'Ain't been no twelve. Damn, they going to kill they Armies?'

Her face go tense. 'That ain't your trouble.'

'Why that feather kilt? They Armies taken you again?'

'Nay, we take them,' she say, smiling queery. 'This time, they be took.'

'How, for yourself? For how they done you?'

'Ho, should be forgot? Been nothing?' Soledad laugh high and frighten, sans no smile.

I shrug against her pinching hands. 'Can leave them. Sure they . . . now you safe.'

'Cannot help this,' she say breathless. 'Heed to me, you worry for yourself. You going to think of twelve.'

'Who these twelve? Ain't getting nothing of this.'

'Be your apostles.' She smile false. 'Opossums. How you say.' Then she lean to me, confiding. 'Sure I know, ain't been twelve children there. Is politics. Be something you can do for me. We right?'

I start to cavil, I got no opossums. Got no want for these. But I look on her madden eyes, her smile gone tense into her scars. And I breathe in well. 'I think.'

'Bone. I going to leave you here with Carlos.' She speak sharpish past my shoulder. That same big jones who catch me in the car come by. Say some unknown courtesy and aim his rifle toward my chest, as Soledad skit hasty off.

I muttern low and empty, 'Right, you threaten to kill me. Bone.' Look around until I find my Pasha. He kneeling like the Armies, by a dusty car. My spirit seize. I turn to Carlos, say, 'They going to hurt the roo?'

He smile back meaningless. Is like he sorry for my broken words. Be a twentyish male with friendly eyes, is Christing handsome. I check down at his hand, scribble in greenish spiders and long guns. Ware back on the Armies.

Now it waken in my mind, how Soledad talk of Jesuses. Sure, be why she stealing Pasha. Want to rule her people somehow. But she said, was clear to this, she cannot be Maria.

Then it realize cold, she talk of *my* opossums. *My* apostles. I be choosing twelve. This fool Maria be myself.

All this go frozen in my head, while I stare on the kneeling Armies. They looking past, lost interest in me. Can comprehend, I cannot help them. Got no use.

Ya, Soledad come back. Come to Carlos, grab his arm, and make like she will swing upon. He laugh and touch her head. Say some loving Panish, and she go on toes to kiss his cheek. He turn away, go off with rifle balance in one hand.

Then Soledad back smiling in my face. 'You thought?' I smell her boozen breath again, sharp like the stank of fear.

'This be something . . . like you say about Maria?'

'There you be.' She laugh up bright. 'You got some quicker brains, you thinking.'

'Yo apostles, how this working? What this going to mean?'

'Be your people. Like you choose your selfish town. Ya, Carlos been apostle to myself, in time.'

'Your people ain't hurt these apostles?'

'How they hurting them?' She shake her head. 'You heed my word, you and apostles better than no luck. You cherry.'

'Right.'

'Hurt them,' she muttern underbreath. Shake her head admiring, like she preciate a joke. 'Last they ever do, hurt no apostles.'

Look at her madness eyes, and behind I see the green-cap jones who guard the Armies, small in detail. Cap push back on his head, his hair show fuzzy brown. I take my breath and say, 'Is Crow been by.'

'Crow?' Soledad's face change nerviose.

'When we find Pasha. Crow been by.'

She look mistrust. 'Yo sho, he been your Sengle. See this.'

Then some anger brighten in me. 'Ya, and Mamadou been by.'

'Cannot be.' Soledad's eyes gone cold. 'Ain't right.'

'I saying, Mamadou been.'

Her face set tight, her scars stand in my eyes. 'You need some trusting people. Ain't be right.'

'I giving twelve.'

'What you trying?'

'Give you twelve. Is all I do. Yo First Runner been, she by.'

Soledad shrug angry. 'She be bone. What you like.'

I try to see the Armies again. But Soledad dodge in my vision, raise her hand into. 'Ain't try this, Ice. You going to need this choice. Ain't games.'

'Ain't games to me.' My mouth feel dry and sick. 'Why you doing this? Is madness.'

'Nay. You going to comprehend.'

'What becoming to my Sengles, there in camp? They free?'

'Yo, I see them right. Can trust me, got no harm to them. Lowells, all they children bone.'

'Pasha safe?'

'Pasha, foo. He precieuse to us, be sure.' Then her eyes look tired upon me. Smile gone beggarish, is like her earlier self come through.

'Need some time for this, goddamn.'

She twist her mouth and shrug. 'They do your papers now. Is sticky on these matters.'

'Papers?'

'Ya, the papers. Got to fix this now.'

I bite my lip and cough somehow into my mouth. Try to think. Look to Pasha, where he sit against the car. Someone given him a cigarette, he smoke this with no hands. Talk around it, and the cigarette dip and jerk with motion.

Then it frighten in me sudden, this be real. Ain't going back to camp. Be some future to me I ain't recognize.

I say nervy, 'These apostles ruling, how you said? They do jones work?'

'There you thinking. Yes, they is. You need them well, ain't going to choose no Mamadou.'

I shake my head, grit to my need. 'Ya, El Mayor been there.'

'Right, now you figure better. El Mayor.'

'This make eight.'

'Eight.' She huff her breath. 'Eight with Mamadou. You stubborn something. Think who you going to work with, treasure. Need no sentiments in this.'

'Nay, Mamadou been there. Yo Hate You, and . . . ain't know.'

'Best they be males,' she say. 'Eighteens or like, you easier set.'

'Bone, take First Electric. Ya, and First Contractor. Right.'

'Sugar, you done. Be well.' She smile and leave her hands from me.

'Nay, this eleven.'

'And be myself.' She frown simple, like she teaching facts. 'Truth, you going to need me real. Someone who will know.'

Then greed fix in her eyes. Can feel, this be the matter's heart. She cannot be Maria, so she want to be apostle, for whatever worth this be. I want to say it angry – how she steal us for her selfishness. But I swallow my unliking. 'Sure, you good. I value this.'

She look behind, can see she think of leaving. I say quick, 'But how you making me Maria? Cannot be.'

'How it is.' She wave back to her Carlos, waiting by the Citgo. 'Got to stand your proof before. But you be good.'

'Be good? Be some insanities. Ain't know your people nothing. Nor I want this.'

'Sure you thinking so.'

'And if I ain't? Can we go back?'

She call some Panish over shoulder. Hold up one finger. Then she looking back at me, her face show glad relief. 'You found a Jesus, Ice. Ain't be no other definition.'

'Pasha ain't no Jesus,' I say flat. 'Be things, but he ain't that.'

Soledad laugh, and shake her head. 'Told you, Ice. He representing this. Know he ain't Jesus.'

'Damn, answer me. If I reject this?'

She look by, distract. 'Ain't going to be.'

A new jones biggen up from nowhere. Shift his rifle to useful posture, stand unwanten close. Then Soledad be gone, is passen with her skitty haste. The new jones say some courtesy and grin, spread out his fattish face.

I grimace and turn my head to watch how Soledad walk in the Citgo. Children there all ware to her, is sudden conversation. Then they bend back to the spreaden papers. Inkle in me, be my papers. Whatever definition this be.

Then I look back to the Armies. Recognize another feather, be their old Hamid. Is twenty years, been start his coughing posies. Other feathers I only seen in war, ain't known their names. Then it remember how me–Pasha gone to murder these same children. I grimace my unliking, look to Pasha. He sat back to the car, scratch his face against his shoulder. Be only one guard on him now, child standing bored with lazy gun.

I say to my own fat-face guard, 'I going to see my child.' I point to Pasha by the car.

Guard frown. Nod at Pasha questioning.

'Yes. Right.' I nod some twenty times, like this will help his knowledge. Then I start off careful. Fat-face follow curiose.

Pasha see me coming, he raise eyebrows. Face grow sarcasty looks as I crouch by. The fat-face jones stand smiling friendly. Hold his rifle upon, like this be favors that he do for us.

Pasha say, 'The simper safe.'

We both laugh our nerves, like this ridiculous as any humor. Then he say, 'Roading people,' and we laugh this laugh again.

I say, 'Yo sho, I listen to you soon. I going to learn this wisdom.'

'We finish,' Pasha say. 'Ain't no soon for us.'

'Ain't lost your misery. Bone to hear.'

He shrug. 'Got cigarettes. In pocket.' He nod his head toward.

'Ho, you in my ruling now. Cannot smoke without.'

'I trust.'

I find his cigarettes while Pasha smiling up to fat-face. Say some Panish words, and fat-face grimace. Point his rifle sharper.

I say, 'What you told him?'

'Say you robbing me. Is joke, he got no humor.'

'Guess he ain't.' I take a cigarette myself, put one to Pasha's lips. Light my zippo for us. Pasha breathe his cigarette hungry, squint against the rising smoke.

I say, 'I got some news.'

He look a question, breathing smoke.

'They ain't want to kill you.'

He mumble past his cigarette, 'Gratty to them.'

'Hold, you got to hear the reason.'

'Reason?'

'You be Jesus Christ.'

He shrug. 'Ain't comprehend.'

'Nor myself. They stupid as a hat.'

Be hot to tell my gripes on Soledad, require his thoughts. But then Pasha ware behind me. Bite his cigarette.

I look back. By the Citgo, where the Armies kneeling, come out

Soledad. Her big Carlos waiting by, show a petty pistol. He hold this careless into Mamadou's face. Talk angry down.

Around, can see the rifle children rouse. Some go off in haste, while others linger with all staring eyes.

I stand up sharp. Be thinking desperate how I shout, claim my apostle. What I going to try. But then Mamadou stand. He look uncaring past the pistol, past this Carlos, to myself. Carlos shove him somehow, and the NewKing smile and turn. Pass into the Citgo room.

This perform again with Crow, while I be breathing in my sweat. Crow never look to me, he walk by hasty. Then the green-cap jones take small First Runner by the arm. She stand up duteous, still be staring to her sorrow nothing. Green-cap go in the Citgo with her, close the door behind.

Then Carlos reach to Soledad. She catch hard on his hand and put her head against his shoulder. Now can see, she weeping bad. Got a bottle in one hand, she turn her head to drink from this. Go sobbing back.

Carlos pet her head, he talking to her seriose. Feathers watch up, like this be some teaching done for them. They watch how Soledad stand back from Carlos, shake her fattish braids. Look round herself into the clouden day. Low and busten houses looking murky in this light.

Then she take Carlos' pistol. Gun silver prettieuse. Is like a jewlerie, like candy. And Soledad stand hunchen, looking at this shiny gun. Her pitchy voice rise up. Come strange with distance, changing in the wind. But can hear, is sad complaint.

Then, second's thought, she point and shoot a feather in his knee. Only when he scream, I shut my eyes. The scream wail out, catch with breath, wail again. Another shot come loud. The scream go weaken into sobbing.

She shoot again. She shoot again. Every shot repeat in me, screams panic in my blood. Be thinking how I yell into this, but I ain't got words. Confuse with Panish and these strangers, got no starting thought. Then all the screaming hush, the shooting halt. I look up dizzy.

Two feathers to the left be lying dead. Their blood grow on the concree ground.

Next feather in the row be old Hamid. He talking low, his eyes on Soledad. Talk constant, smiling, while she put more bullets in the gun. Hamid's face spatter bloody from the murdern child beside. And Soledad be crying still, her shoulders tremble as she work. Carlos keep one hand upon her back. Ain't he nor Soledad be heeding to the begging feather.

She point again, her mouth grit like she frustrate. Shoot Hamid in his talking mouth. He knock back to the wall, a struggle passen through his arms. Then he slide down sideways, leave a ragged smear of blood behind.

Ain't think to close my eyes again. I watch while Soledad aim on a fourth, who break and jump into her, running panic off. Is shot down by some unseen rifle easy, before he take five steps. Child go to his knees, like he tire sudden. He lie himself polite onto the road, while his blood come out in generose wash. Then he shiver and rest with mouth yawn open.

Last feather sitting hunchen, eyes is shut. Soledad wipe at her face with her pistol hand. Face wetten awful, all her body sob. She speak to Carlos, and he nod. He take the pistol, touch her shoulder. Then she turn and stumble to the feather murdern in the road. Kneel by his feet and close her face into her arms.

And Carlos crouch beside the shut-eye child. Talk in quiet voice. Seem he explaining, though can guess is Panish, feather cannot heed. Feather begin to shake his head. Speak from his closen eyes, cringe blind.

I step forward now, is like I wake. I call up, 'Soledad?' Then my fat-face jones take hold across me, talking in a rush. All his grinning pass, he talking like he beg some help. I panic, scratching at his arm, but he hold to. Pasha call my name behind, and all this be like nothing happening while big Carlos point his pistol down with angry joy.

He shoot the feather in his gut. I weaken dull. Watch stupid while the boy curl on his side. Is ducking his head to see his hurt. Carlos now return to talking, and it almost hope, he done. Feather going to live somehow. Like Mamadou from his wound, can live.

Carlos look back to Soledad. Then he turn sudden and kick all his weight into the feather's gut. This bring a birden screech, and Carlos kick and kick again, until it come like wonderful when he go shoot the feather dead.

I ease back, heart struggling in my chest. Then it notice, in the Citgo window, be a scramble fight. It realize, this fight been on some time, and then I see like natural facts, is Mamadou. He war his one good arm against some struggling children. I nod to myself, is right. And I push free from the fat-face jones. Sit down careful. Find my cigarette almost finish. Suck its last breath and throw it by.

Look back to Pasha, he be whiter white. His face show beaden sweat.

'They ain't going to hurt you,' I say frighten. 'Ain't be.'

He shake his head. Blink where sweat gone dripping in his eye.

'Nay,' I say, 'we living yet. I be soldat for you, you good. You good.'

He make some fever smile. 'You my soldat.'

'Nay, they ain't going to hurt you.' I look around for Soledad, but she still crouchen in the road. Her hand be forward in the feather's blood. My eyes flinch back from this, I say more desperate, 'Truth. I got word, Pasha.'

He lick up at his sweat. Face settle into misery again, he staring at the blooden Citgo wall. The feathers lying various dead. And he say quiet, 'You ain't know, Ice. You ain't know.'

36

TO MARIAS

Our farther hour be hurtless fear. Two rifle children come with angry faces, unloose Pasha's handcuffs. Then Pasha–me be put into a car. Ain't like the carten car before, this one be closen with glass windows. Seats be fat and soft.

Once the doors be shut, this car become a simple trap. Doors got no opening handles to, nor pushing budge them any. Ya, between the front and backward seats is screen with netty wire. Can see how this been staplen in the roof, the seaten back. I tug thoughtless at these staples, sans no strong intention. Is only bellious mood without no hope.

In the forward seat, drive Carlos, Soledad beside. Ain't talking, both is sorrow dull. Soledad got her window open. Lie her head onto this windy space. When I call to her, she only nay her hand. Ain't stir to look. Ya, this hand still red on all its fingertips with blood.

And we go on the number highway. Car drive almost easy, like it skating on a floor. First minutes, Pasha–me talk low, is counseling together. He calmer somewhat, heed me well about this Jesus nonsense. But he add his misery: 'Know how this Jesus story finish.'

Soon we drift to separate glooms. I stare sideways in the window, and the trees become a fuzzy storm, all losing hasty back. In this, a snow begin, and Soledad raise her window up. Car remain in closen heat, while this snow float its millions on the other world outside.

Then it be hours and nothing. We fly sorry through the snow. Around be forest, whitening on its arms, like all our walking woods. Yo, sometimes a farm appear – fields looking scrappish after harvest, cows in sleepy hunch. My heart go strange to see this life, beyond all worlds beknown. Notice carren vehicles by, and I begin to guess, these farms belong to Soledad's mally people. Then be dizzy feeling, how we flying every miles of distance, and all land be theirs.

Once we pass a broken city. Got tower buildings higher than no Lowell edifice, but ain't a child to see. Some buildings lost their walls. Can see the inside partments in their grid; or be only a skeleton of metal, tall into the sky. Cars be turtlen on their roofs, streets choke with color trash. Be like a goliath wind torn up its every part. Snow puzzle above this havoc like it seeking help to this.

And the city pass behind, we meet the snowing woods again. Is coming middy day, the world stand on its narrow shadows. I try to think, how El Mayor be driven so, to be apostle. Can hope he be joyeuse, riding in an actual car. Then I worry on Driver so, my Sengles, as the snow depart, a perilous sun come to the day.

We start to come to blocking gates. These is clumsy artifacts, set across the road. Got one space, is big enough to fit a normal car. Above this space be always writ: PROHIBIDO EL PASO SIN LICENCIA. This got a rifle guard who stand beside in bitty house. At each gate, Carlos fix his window down and show some card. Rifle guard inspect this, say some courtesy and we go on.

This repeat some dozen times. In this, we come to evac country. These evacs various in suffering. Some places be all broken roofs that float upon a wash of junk. Others is healthy towns, with houses painten fresh and standing fences. One place show a sleeper flag that tumble its stripy flank in wind. Below, a sign be written: DOLL'S AMERICAN CONVENIENCE. Smoke rising somewhere, join its whiteness to the snowing air.

Last gate, be thirty rifle children. They gather to the car, and

Carlos get out calling happy. Then these children all be shoving, gaping eyes at me and Pasha. All faces nose toward the window. I feel unliking sick. 'Damn,' I say. 'Herding strangers everywhere. No person going to live.'

Here Soledad look back. 'Ain't think like this. They glad to you.' Face show her joy precaire again.

I make an ugly mouth into the window, but the children laugh. I grin back before I think. One boy make a sign with skewen fingers. I try this for myself, then some five children bending to the window, make skew-finger signs. All laughing pleasure, and this start to mingle in my feeling. 'Sure,' I say, 'they can be bone. Ain't going to prejudice.'

'I prejudice for you,' say Pasha, and Soledad laugh birdish from the front. She say, 'You narrow, you.'

Then Carlos get back in the car. We drive through the gate, and Soledad sit up bright. Say back, 'Can see, Marias there.' She point the forward window.

I put my face up to the netty wire. Ahead, there be a spiky nonsense on the near horizon. Is like the working part of a machine, all different grays and stalks. Stand like weirdo teeth against the lighter gray of sky. Take me time to guess, these teeth be edifices. Then I sit back, dizzy. Try to wonder at their size, but all confuse in distance. At last I say, 'Goddamn, ain't real.'

'Ciudad de las Marias,' Soledad say in scary pride.

I say, 'It look like some New York.'

'Been that,' say Soledad. 'In time before. Now is Marias.'

Pasha staring for himself, his face a mix of want and dislike. When he see me looking, he shrug nerviose. 'New York. I know this.'

'Bone, we all is knowing this.' Sudden, I feel anxy light. I say to Soledad, 'You bringing El Mayor this way, yo sho?'

'He be behind.' She heeding to the city with mouth open, like she want to eat it.

'El Mayor go love this,' I say. 'Be his lifen fantasy.'

'Is right,' say Soledad. 'He right.'

*

We skirt along some gristy river, floating with all brownish trash. Road here be wallen in with metal ruin, wreck concree. This pass in sudden breath, and we be in the city self.

Now buildings block us either side. Most got windows blind with wood, but some be living bright with glass. All stand close to the road, it be like driving down a housen hallway. Along, be children, walking careless at the roaden margin. Some be rifle people, but is also boys in churching suits, and girls in heely shoes and dress.

Be signs in every place, yo all these signs is sleeper old. Most words is garble: Dolphin Fish Plaza, 99 and UP. Can guess at Fabco Shoes and Kennedy Fried Chicken. But cannot tell what Blimpie Subs will be, nor Custom Image Apparel. I try reading signs to Pasha, but he make discourage face. Turn moody to his window.

In this, I get a fear bizarre, how they make me Maria here. Ain't even normal towns. Be towers fabulous, and thousand children. No dirtfoot scratcher ruling here, is gaga in itself. Ya, I feel like sudden falling, how my Sengles far from me. I grip against the door. Push stupid, like it going to free somehow. But my sweaten palm slip helpless.

Then we come beside an open place with healthy trees and grass. I fix on this. Get frantic hope, this city ending now. We come back into woods. Yo, all been jokes. Been anything but real.

But now, I see the city grow ahead in worser heights. It plummet strange into the sky, ain't even spy the buildings' heads. Ya, the car go slower. Turn and come up by an edifice white and grandiose. Got twenty rows of windows, and all windows fresh with glass. A dozen rifle children waiting to its steps, beneath a canopy with golden jewlerie upon.

Car stop and ease its voice. Then the stillness feel uncanny. I wish awful that we driving on somewhere. Drive back.

But the rifle children all trot toward with interesting face. Soledad say breathless, 'Yo we here. The Ministerio be.'

'Here,' say Pasha dull. He rub his face and look to me.

'No sho.' I look out scary.

Soledad open up her door, step out and stretch her arms. Then she open Pasha's door. Say happy, 'Come, we here.'

He go out, I shove along. Step out careful, like I feel the ground may still be moving. Rifle guards shift back, create a path toward the steps. Ain't aim on us, but every hand be conscious on its gun.

Yo, Soledad start up the carpet steps, wave us behind. I follow careful, Pasha by. We walk between these guns, and Soledad go open a glassen door. Then we step inside, and all the rifles left behind. Be like a noise depart and leave us in relieving hush.

Inside of this building be like something cut from ice and sugar. Be grandy as an evac warehouse, but all luxury clean. Got some hanging lights is like goliath dandelions of glass. Curtains be gold color, and rangen in some frozen perfectesse. The floor gleam white, the walls gleam white. Ain't any a speck nor mark of use.

In the roomen center, be a statue made in blackish stone. Show a girlish child, is swathen like she wearing Army godclothes. She sit with knees apart, and across her lap, a naked man be lain. He straggle sick. Girl look down with interest, like she think of eating him.

By this statue, stand five children. All wear dresses, though they boys. The dresses black the same, their skirts be longish to the floor. One child wear a red cravat, tie nett around his waist. Its end drain simple to his knee. Yo, all these children look up as we come. Their mouths false into smiles.

Soledad walk to the redwaist child with eagering step. Crouch graciose and kiss his hand. Then she polite them all. Her shoulders cringing, all herself be like a pologetic hound. Blackdress children smiling to her voice, while they inspect me careful. Ain't even notice Pasha much, their need be on Ice Cream Unworthy. Feel they think to eat me, like the statue girl. They scout my meat.

Some minutes, Soledad speak to the redwaist child. Her voice come telligent attention, like she giving news. Among her Panish noise, appear some words like *Sengle, Massa, Lowell mill*. These pass like flashing birds, and then she Panish on the same. Yo, all this time, the rifle guards be staring through the glass behind. Somehow, is like they growing there. Their bad attention weigh my nerves.

Then sudden, the redwaist child speak sharp. Soledad hush, and crouch herself. All the blackdress children touch their palms together, like an unsound clap. They turn from her and wander by.

She come hasty to us, all her body bright with joy. Say, 'This been Pedro, apostle of Inúd burrow. All be right, you going to see. Now, Ice, you come, we got to parley.'

I look to Pasha, but Soledad say quick, 'Nay, Pasha going separate.'

'Foo separate,' I say. 'Pasha going to know whatever I know.'

'Ain't secrets,' she say hasty. 'Be your questioning. Is needful so. They keep him well, ain't nothing harm. Must be.'

'If you saying, got no choice, then say this.'

She make a nervy grimace. 'Is right. I only hoping, be without no ugliness.'

'No choice,' say Pasha low. 'Is normal.'

I start to cavil, but Pasha nay his hand. He grimace back toward the door – the rifle children stood outside. Yo, as I looking, Soledad yell up some Panish to them. Door open, and they stamping in. Then Soledad grip my arm. Only see a flashing glimpse, how Pasha watching misery, guards gathern to him silent weird, as she draw me away.

We go through some window doors into a jumbo room. Here the ceiling all is glass, shape graciose with broidery metal. Walls be butterish in color. Got some prettieuse stalks in honey stone up to the roof.

At a bureau by the farther wall, stand two tennish children. Their heads is shaven to the shine. Wear dresses like the others, but these be brown. Both look to me with biggen eyes, then turn back guilty to the bureau.

Center to this room, a longish table wait. Be gleaming wood, and to this table, any chairs is set. They all the same, with seats of golden cloth.

Soledad bring me to the table's end, the sergeant place can be. Tap on its chair, and I sit down discourage. Feel conscience for my journey grime, how I be the only dirt. Soledad pull a chair herself and sit. In this showing light, her cheekbone face look raw bewept.

'Guess your people found you,' I say thin.

She smile pologetic. 'Nay, I finding them. Known them from their trash, gone looking. Took all hours of hunt. Ain't mostly slept.'

'Nor myself. We thought you taken by they Armies. Pasha and me come out for you.'

'Nay, I gone through the Armies.' She laugh nervy. 'On this horse. They come yelling, but I gallop on. They never known was me, can guess.'

'They learning this.' My voice gone rough. I put my palms down to my jeans.

'Can leave that,' Soledad say, breathless low. 'We got no time.'

'Nay, how my Sengles going to be? And Driver? You never thinking this? They terrify, and–'

'Shoo, your Sengles bringing here. All bringing here.'

'You take us all?' My voice break high. 'Ain't to believe. Goddamn, cannot!'

'Nay, heed!' Her eyes go panic. 'Got to do this questioning right, or you ain't safe. Ain't they be safe.'

'Is prettieuse, ain't safe! Been safe before your insect deeds.'

'Ice, all it been,' she say in beggar voice. 'Found my people, then I saying natural, you got a Jesus. *Going* to say. They seeking such, all years. Yo, the old Maria dying. Someone got to rule the city.' Her face go sharper, like she proven point, cannot be argument.

I scoff breath. 'So be Maria self. Ain't – nay, nor Pasha in this. Shee your goddamn people.'

'Ice, ain't heeding! Got to heed. You ain't do right, you dying here!'

'I dying why? Ain't be no sense!'

'Trying to tell!' Her voice go high in nerves. 'You losing time!'

My heart kick backward in my chest. I touch the knee hole on my jeans. Find a straggling thread, and wind this thread around a finger tense. 'Ya, say your words. I heed.'

She clutch her hands together on the table. 'Apostles going to talk to you. Ask questions of yourself.'

'What apostles? Ain't be mine?'

'Nay, sure. The old apostles. Is like a test, if you be bone Maria. I learn this, when I want to be Maria, in time before.'

Want to say, I ain't be bone Maria. All is madness. But I look on her blooden hand again and sigh my breath. 'They ask me questions. So?'

'Ya, I tell how you must answer.'

'Ain't going to answer truth?' I grimace, feel tired in my mouth.

'Nay, be matters . . . complicate.'

'Sure, I be a Sengle. Lying ain't no work to me.'

'Be bone.' She smile encouraging. 'Ya, most major that they ask, is war. How you feel to wars.'

'You got some war?'

She wave a hand, like ridding this needless question. 'What you saying – war be evil, but is sometimes needful. Evil, but is sometimes needful.'

I look at the browndress tens. They writing something on some cards. 'Ain't an answer, ya?'

'Right, you seeing. Cannot answer. They going to try and make you answer. All you say: War be evil, but is sometimes needful.'

I sigh. 'War, be evil work. But is sometimes needful.'

'Bone.' She breathe out rough. 'Second matter. Be anything you ain't comprehend, say: Must discuss this with the church. Ain't answer nothing, say the church discuss this.'

'Must discuss this with the church.'

'Next matter. They marrying here in twos. Ain't get no Christing flocks of wives. One wife, one male. Like ducks. You see this?'

'Marry like ducks. Two children only.'

'Keep this clear. And tell them Sengles doing so.'

'Foo, Sengles do no marrying.'

'Ice, told you. Cannot–'

'Bone, we marry honest. Be no fickle people, Sengles.' Here, I laugh in nerves, but Soledad look harsh severe.

'Also, preventing enfants be an evil.'

'So sex be always bone?'

'Nay, shee.' She startle fresh at this. 'Be only bone when children marry. Evil if they ain't. Learn this well.'

'But when they marry, must do sex?'

'Ain't this.' She smile unhappy. 'There be a science for preventing enfants. Science they got. Is evil.'

'How this science work?'

She make a ridding gesture. 'Only must know, is always evil.'

Ain't comprehend for nothing, but I nod. Look skitty at the window doors. The blackdress children multiply there. Now it be a flickering wall of black behind the glass. 'How it be, if I ain't question well? Can leave?'

'You question well. Ain't fearing this.'

'Nay, what will be? You answer.'

'Ice, ain't stand your proof, this meaning you be . . .' She pause, her scar face work in thought. 'Is like taboo. You be a false Maria. Mean, you evil.'

'So I be evil. Got good company in this.'

'Nay, then you die.' She smile into her scars. 'When your proof become, you die.'

I feel tired anger coming through my fear. 'I got no wants to be Maria, simper. Tell them now.'

'Nay.' She hold her hand up anxy. 'You die the same for this.'

'For what? Damn, ain't no sense.'

'Ice, you found a Jesus. Be Maria, or be false Maria. Ain't no other thing.'

'So I be false. You telling them.'

'Nay, false Maria need to die. Been said!'

'Is normal,' I say in disgust. 'You be some ugly goods, this people. Why you brought us here? Ain't need to put me in this murder.'

She take her breath. 'Ain't going to be. You heed me, all be bone.'

'I heeding. Got no choice, is normal. Pasha right in all.'

My mind feel skiddy. Try to think, what answers she been given.

I wind my finger in my jeans thread, thinking back until is plain. Then I say, 'Go on, I heed.'

'These be your major questions. Comprehend?'

'Be decision, whether I comprehend. Must discuss this with the church. All I know, we must get enfants, no preventing this. And must marry a duck, no other way.'

'Ain't–'

'I know. Was joke.'

'Bone. Be other matter.' Her eyes skew nervy to the glassen doors. 'Pasha.'

I swear underbreath. 'Here it be. Pasha right. Goddamn.'

She grit her jaw, can see she thinking desperate. 'Get your questioning, they going to ask you on him. Truth, can keep him.'

'Keep?'

'Can keep him by. But this disapprove. Only one Maria kept her Jesus, and was every trouble. Most times . . . is done like in the Christing story. Jesus die.'

My heart narrow harsh. 'My Pasha do no trouble. Give him cigarettes, he easy.'

'Nay, be problems. Maria and Jesus both is god.'

I want to scoff, how any child believe that I be god. That any snot-nose child be god. But I only say, 'We god together. Be no problems.'

Unhappy growing in her face, most like she going to cry. 'They ain't approve this. Can fail your proof for this alone. Then Pasha kilt with you. Ain't be no help.'

'But it been done before?'

'Ice Cream. Be problems without this.'

'I asking, be some chance?'

'Ya.' She pinch her mouth. 'They desperate well, or you ain't been in question.'

'Desperate, right. Relief to know, they ain't be imbeciles entire.'

'Nay, ain't imbeciles none.' She look grim, like this be mally news.

A minute, we sit in angry quiet. I watch upon the browndress tens. They working fretful, like they fear us. Duck their heads and whispern. In this, it notice, these be girlish children, shaven females. Surprise misgive in me, and I scarce be listening when Soledad speak.

'Ice Cream. Pasha be a sleeper.' Her voice come slow precaire.

I frown to her. Feel something queery in this, like the shaven girls. 'Sleeper, shee. He be a moron roo.'

'You friending with him, sure I know. But sleepers, they ain't be like us.'

'What difference this will make? You ain't like me, neither. Will say, this sleeper try to save yourself this morning. This same day.'

'Nay, they sleepers all be slavers. In Time Before, they slavers. Every history. Ain't like us.'

I say loud, 'And how they also Jesus, wonder this.'

'Be more in this than you can know! You think before . . .' She swallow back her noise and say low, 'Think.'

'Nay,' I say cold. 'You think how this sleeper gone to save you. This morning, gone and risk himself.'

'Ain't listening right.'

'Yo heed. They kill my Sengles also? Kill all Massa children, for some moron superstition?'

'Nay,' she say in sobben voice. 'But, Ice, it–'

'All I need to hear. We done.'

'Ice, ain't for myself. Is needful.' Then she flinch, ware to the window doors. 'You think. I got to leave you now. Goddamn, was other matters.' She skit to her feet. Give me one final seeking look, and smile her pinchen way. Then she go to the window doors. Open them with careful softness, and she slip away.

I sit back weak. Be longing for my good Kalash, my Pasha. Can wish I sleeping better yesternight. Feel white inside my head. Try thinking of these answers, but now Soledad be gone, they seem insanities no child believe.

Then a browndress ten come toward. Got jutting ears, show out peculiar with her shaven head. She look skitty to myself, then start around the table. Set cards down, one to each seat. Check at a paper as she go. I stand up jittery and go behind. Cards going so: *Juan de Quinta, Felipe de Metropolitano, Simón Zelote de Loisaida.* Come to one that say *Pedro de Inúd,* and I get a kindling notion. First part be an apostle's name, can guess. The other be their burrow. Girl finish with the cards and dabbit by, spy curiose at me.

'Sister,' I say, 'you need that paper?'

She startle like it been the table self that spoken words. A moment, I think she cannot comprehend. Talk Panish like the rest.

But she lower eyes and muttern, 'No.'

'Be gratty, I can have it.'

She look at it doubting. 'You want this?'

'Got these names, I guess? Is names?'

She nod slow. In this, it notice, her shaven head got drawings on. Is like the drawings on the rifle children's hands. Blue particular on her head, shape like spiken flowers. Even her jutting ears got petty lines.

She bolden herself and reach the paper to me, smiling bashful. Like I expect, it got the table drawn, with each name set in place. At table's head, be writ, *Maria Postulante.*

The ten say whispern, 'You go for Maria?'

I take unliking breath. 'Ya, guess I do.'

She smile again, scratch at her shiny head. Look at the other ten with priding eyes. Other ten look back, is jalousie in her pet face. This a tallish child, is catten prettieuse, even in baldness.

I wave the paper, say, 'My tens, you knowing how these names pronounce?'

Eary Ten get mazing smile. 'You don't know the apostles' names?'

'She just came here,' Catten Ten say bossy. 'Why she going to know?'

Eary Ten pert up her eyes. Begin to sing a melody. The other join with laughing face. A moment pass before I comprehend, this be a memory song. Give all apostles' names in easy quickness. Then I watch the paper, heeding, try to match these names and words.

Get them to start again–again, until their rivaling be, how quick they sing. Their birden voices confuse together, break in giggling.

Then sudden, they both startle. Hush and ware the window doors. Rifle children moving there, be voices risen loud. Tens turn jumpy, run toward a farther door of simple wood. They fluster out, without no by-salue. The door shut hard.

Cannot react nor think, before the window doors come wide. I skit into my chair and shove the paper to my knees.

37

MY QUESTIONING FOR MARIA

A black parade of redwaist children come in, one and one. They looking at me various – smiling, boring, curiose – but all this brew into my nerves. Be mostly boys of bigger size. Is only one a female, and she loafen fat, grown in richesse. Most wear black dresses, but be one in brownish rifle garb. Yo, the last is wearing jeans and button shirt like any person. This jeans child be gazen bell, is Sengle tarry with long eyes.

I check the paper, haste to find their names as they take chairs. Across from me, at table's end, be Pedro de Inúd – child Soledad been speaking to before. Sixteenish boy beside him smiling puppyish, like he cheer my courage. His blackdress got some stains along its front, like he been eating soup. Name, Juan de Quínta.

Apostle speaking first be handsome slim, got beard is shapen ornamental. Ain't Panish that he talk but sleeper English, knot in definitions. Can guess is greeting speeches, but these words go jumbling quick. I check the paper for his name: Felipe de Metropolitano. Ya, he finish on an easy saying: 'And please, be honest with us. It's really best, for your own sake.'

I narrow at this bearden boy, can smell some threat in this. But I only say, 'Be thanks, Felipe. Sure, I answer truth.'

This bring some petty consternation. First I wondern, if I said his name correct. Tens is chancy people, cannot know what jokes they play. But then it comprehend, they ain't know I got their names writ. Think to explain, but then they start their questions.

This work be suffering beyond mosquitoes. Ain't never felt no personal shyness, but here it inkle how a shy child feel. Times, I speak too long, and feel they boring while I stumble words. Then is times, I saying only 'Yes', and they look cheaten. They ask in sleeper English, but talk Panish between themself. Yo, once, all questioning stop, while two apostles argue Panish furiose, but I ain't guess its reason. Soon sweat coursing down my sides in tickle bothers. Throat be dry beyond, and every smile feel false and strange.

Begin to know, is friends and enemies in this apostle twelve. Pedro de Inúd ask questions that is sneaking helps. Yo, can guess that Soledad told him news of me before. He ask if I be leader in my people; can say yes to this. Then he ask how many children living in the Massa woods. Ain't mention Sengles particular, so it come out like I lead four hundred children, powerful grown. He talk clear and slow, ya every question hinting to its answer. 'I hope your people are Christians?' 'We believe religion must be the basis of the law. Would you agree?' Even when I understand no word, can know these answers yes.

Worst enemy be crafty-beard Felipe. Look friendly in his smile, but every question be a trap. Child smart as twenty heads; my victories all be steps to new defeat. Be like fighting Mamadou in war. Yo, any word I speak, Felipe saying he ain't understand. Say this kindly, like he sorry for my stupid mouth. Result be, I must answer simple words, sound like an imbecile two.

Some apostles never speak. They only stare my face and pick their cuffs in boring fidget. Strangest be the child in rifle clothing, name Simón Zelote. His eyes fix to nothing, lost to any world around. Once, I glance on him and see, he sob his breath. Wipe tears. Others ignoring this, like it be normal expectations. And soon his grief seem natural to myself. Feel like it be his task to weep the truth of this discussion, while we others speak our courtesy lies.

Be friendly Pedro who ask on war. Feel foolish when I say this 'evil, but is sometimes needful' speech. But can see how Pedro look relief. Then Felipe push for honest answers, and be entertainment, the dozen ways I say this nothing. Soon be gobblegook: 'War be awfulness, but when the circumstances needful, going to need this awfulness, but . . .' Felipe self look dull to this. He lose his fight in boredom.

His be the questions on preventing enfants. He give me any tricky cases: if a girl been rapen; if she rapen by her brother; if she rapen, and is dying sick. I cannot guess, how they prevent this enfant, when the rape be done. But I ain't pause to wonder. I only say, is always evil, like my Soledad insist. Yo, I be strict on duckish marriage, feel a Driver lawfulness in disapproving all exceptions. Almost become a liking game, to slip Felipe's traps. See how he smile and smile, and suffer his heart malicieuse.

Be other questions, if I using pharmacies, what sex I done. I guess these answers well, can know all Christings will be pudy miseries. Is nay and nay, I never nothing, spent my life with hands in pockets. Ya, times, I ask them definitions, and they begin to rival, explaining what some pharmacy be. Then is plain to see that they all try these evil pharmacies themself. Yo in this, the prettieuse jeans child – Santiago be his name – give me a cigarette, is gratty took.

First trouble become, when someone ask: 'What's your stand on homosexuality? Do you agree it should be punished?'

I know this *homosexuality*'s meaning – every ten learn sleeper words for sex. Ya, I gone braver now, and my heart catch on Crow. Can see him in the powerline road, his sweating desperation. So I say foolish, 'Nay, ain't need to punish this.'

Here even Pedro startle. All look disliking at me, and Felipe smiling greedy. He say, 'You don't believe it should be discouraged?'

I shrug. 'Discourage how you like.'

'But not punished?' He touch his fingertips together, looking soft at me.

Some stubbornness catch my heart. 'No sho, it be their personal trouble. How you going to punish them?'

Young Juan saying anxy, 'In our church, we punish this with prison. It's not perfect, but–'

'It's God's law,' say Pedro. He fix me with a knifen stare.

Here Felipe speak in Panish, and they wrangle nonsense words. Then I remind correct, this ain't no argument, it be my life.

When the Panish finish, Pedro rub his eyes in tired discourage. He say, 'So how would you discourage this?'

'Must discuss this with the church,' I say unvoice. 'Is reasoning here.'

Felipe frustrate well. 'We want *your* opinion. We already know what we think.'

'Never had no homosexuality in my people,' I lie cold. 'Is city manners, I expect. The church discuss this best.'

Then me–Felipe badger words until the others start objecting. I come from this struggle with sweaten palms. All the lights become a streaken glare.

Quick upon this, come a weirdo question from a posy child – Bartolomeo de Morrisania in my paper. Got reddish sores all on his lips, look painful as he talk. This bother in my mind as he speak his confusing words. Be Panish in their wrong pronouncing.

I say, 'I don't understand. Could you repeat that, please?' Is what Felipe mostly saying, now I got this nice.

He say slow, 'It is, you are going to use the clause, senyora?'

'Clause? What be this clause?'

Pedro say, with meaning look, 'If you use the clause, the apostles we have now stay in their places.'

Then every child be waring on me but the rifle apostle, Simón Zelote. He gaze his teary eyes the same.

I say, 'What being with my own apostles?'

'They would be in an advisory role,' say Pedro. He glare painful at me, like he force his thought into my head.

'Advisory meaning . . .'

Pedro say slow, 'They would still have an apostle's privileges. It's a very rich life, to be frank. But they wouldn't have our responsibilities.

The clause allows you to keep the experience of the apostles we have now. It means we can continue our work.'

Here, first time, the prettieuse jeans child Santiago speak up lazy. 'Because we're so fucking wonderful.'

Most apostles look impatient to this, though young Juan laugh.

Then my mind come clear. Apostles ask to keep their power. Ain't no science to guess what they prefer.

I say firm, 'Be sure, I use the clause. You staying by.'

Around the table, faces ease. Feel water-hearten with relief myself. Now first I comprehend, why someone want me for Maria. Ain't going to boss them nothing. Got no brains to this, they ruling free.

But here, as if he spite my joy, Felipe say, 'I've got just one more question. About your Jesus.'

My courage stop in middy course. 'Ho, you meaning Pasha.'

He smile patient. 'Pasha, if you want. I heard a rumor–'

Here everything break down in Panish. Children shouting rage, all hands go flying in their gestures. Young Juan risen to his feet, like he prepare to clobber Felipe. They yell and point their fingers while I sweat.

Then, sudden as it start, it finish. Juan sit back down and tug his blackdress straight with bellious yank.

'To go on,' Felipe say, like nothing been, 'I'm concerned as to whether you're going to complete the sacrament.'

'Sacrament?' I grit my jaw, already feel some unlike guess.

'The sacrament of the redemption,' Pedro say, with meaning eyes, 'You understand, Christ dies for our sins. It's a cornerstone of our belief.'

Felipe say on, pleasant, 'The sacrament requires the candidate – you – to give Jesus the spear, as described in scripture.'

'Give Jesus the spear?' I say.

Here bell Santiago strike a thumb into his chest, make dying face. Felipe closer to me, never see this demonstration. He say, 'It would be your part to complete the sacrament. By giving the–'

'Stabbing Jesus in the heart,' say Santiago with disgust impatience.

Felipe frown to this, but then he nod. 'I think that's clear.'

I want to go in explanations, how Pasha save my life. Ever they think of sleepers, slavers, ain't be Pasha anyhow. Nor we got ambitions to their city. All we want be life.

But I only say, in choken voice, 'Nay. I ain't do this.'

'Okay.' Felipe smile, sit back with one hand flat against his chest.

'You understand–' say Pedro.

'I understand,' I say. 'Ain't do this. You keeping Pasha with me, or you . . . you ain't.' My hand go nervy to my waist, Kalash's empty place. I sit back perilous to my chair.

Now all be grim bekept. Only prettieuse Santiago smile some wisty wise. When he see me watching, he nod slightish. I frown, want no approval from these roaches anymore.

'I think we're finished,' Pedro say. 'Do you have any questions?'

Question be, how they will kill me. But I say in furiose coldness, 'Nay. We finish right.'

They stand to their feet. Muttern some courtesies, then they go hasty to the window doors. Can see they all be eager to discuss my awfulness apart. Only Pedro keep his chair a minute, stare at me with sickness. The tearful rifle-clothe apostle, Simón Zelote, stop by him. Ask something Panish. Pedro look up and nod sad. Simón Zelote call out toward the wooden door, where my tens left before.

Door come open, but it ain't the tens who coming out. Be four other browndress people, males with shaven heads. Is eighteens, best I see, and bigly. It brighten in my nerves, they kill me now. These callen to my murder.

My heart go wrong with fear. Ain't want this death. Start thinking how I crawl beneath the table, find some chance to flee. I think of hides and dodges, skinny chances. Bullets that can miss.

But through my fright, it notice, browndress males is smiling courtesy. I put my palms upon the table edge, feel sweaten there. Last apostles leaving now, go through the window doors and pet them shut.

Browndress males nod to me pigeonish. One with fatly cheeks step forward. He touch his palms together in that silent clap they do, and all his fingernails be carven to the same clean shape. His face be shiny like a china cup.

'Senyora, many welcomes. I'm Ermano Anselm. I'm here to be your guide, which is my very great pleasure, of course.'

I loose the table, feel a limpish coldness in my hands. 'Ain't fail my proof?'

'Oh, no.' His eyes get mischief look. 'The proof will be tomorrow. Your fun is only starting.'

All I comprehend from this, I ain't be kilt until tomorrow. I match his smile with rinsen feeling. 'Bone, tomorrow. Yo what your name be? Sorry, I ain't heed.'

'Anselm.' Then he sweep his hand toward the other browndress jones. 'And these handsome gentlemen are Ermano Pablo, Ermano Benedicto and Ermano Miguel.'

I nod foolish at these brown ermanos. Feel some kinly warming to them, children who ain't kill myself.

'These brothers don't speak English. Not a word.' Anselm make sorry mouth, but his eyes gleaming impish. 'So in a sense, it's just you and me. We're – I'm – here to take you to your medical exam. With a tiny detour along the way.'

Medical can comprehend, yo detour be no name to me. But I only say, 'I got to come with you, is right?'

'Is right,' he parrot helpful. 'Got to come.'

They lead me to the wooden door. Come in a hall with carven falalas and dandelion lights. Stop before some silver doors without no handles to. A Panish ermano poke a button in the wall. One door split open, and its parts go vanish in the walls.

I try not to show impression. Look careless, like these vanishing doors is common to myself. Yo, the room behind be tiny. I go in duteous, but it scarcely fitting all us five. They turn around and face back to the door like they will leave again. Ain't sense for nothing, but I turn along. Wait for instructions.

Vanish door shut up again. Ermano poke another button. Then

the floor shift sneaky underneath. I catch the wall. Pass some dizzying fear before I know, this room float upward. Then I get superstitions, how this room push through a solid building.

Anselm see my face, but only shrug. 'This is a divine miracle called an elevator. We're all very jaded with such marvels here.' He speak in Panish, and the other ermanos laugh and nod. Then Anselm say to me, 'Yes, we're agreed. We're jaded.'

'How this meaning? Jaded.' I force my hand loose from the wall, bring it shaky down.

'Oh, it's a very insulting word. Really, we ermanos are a very self-hating group, especially certain brothers – brothers of an unmentionable type. Pablo here is one notorious one, though he would be the last to admit it. And we don't have your courage, but we're not so lost that we don't appreciate it. Do you understand that?'

'Nay, be sorry.'

'Yes, I didn't think you would. But I hope you last long enough among us to get it. Retrospectively.'

The elevator make a pinking noise and halt. I spook again, touch to the wall. Silver door split open.

Known we moving, but still it come uncanny that this hall be different. Be no falalas, is plain. Yo the wall before is writ: MUSEO DE LA RESIDENCIA.

I go hasty out, ain't like this elevator nothing. Panish ermanos drift behind. We all come in a jumbo room with glassen walls. Behind this glass be cases, is like windows of some evac stores. Anselm lead me on, past various weirdo objects in these cases – science instruments and jewleries and strange guitars – to a line of dresses worn on plastic mankins.

Be some twenty–thirty dresses, going in a spacen line. All be white and skirten huge, all complicate with lace. They frothy long, look most like standing waterfalls. The mankins' plastic heads each wear a nebuleuse white curtain to. Yo all these dresses got some spattering stains, in frighten red.

I pause, look down this whitish reddish row. Anselm come beside, look courteose in expectation. He touch his fingers to the glass. 'This little one is Maria Vigesima's. She was found by our soldiers, living with a Jesus alone in the middle of the forest. Very romantic, don't you think? She was only ten years old when she stood her proof. So she was in her plenitude for nine years, our longest serving Maria.'

This garble in my sense. I look to Anselm with some worry need. 'Is blood?'

'Holy blood, senyora. Sangre de Cristo.' He look curiose to me. 'They'll be fitting out one of these for you, about now. A clean one, of course.'

I take my breath, think of the spear. 'For this proof, can guess?'

'Strictly speaking, it's for the sacraments. The proof comes after.'

'What be this mally proof, then?'

'Well.' His eyes go kind in thought. 'You'll be in a very beautiful church. You have the sacraments, and then the very charming apostles you've just met will come out, wearing very beautiful robes. Each apostle will give you a cup of wine to drink. Theoretically, it's Christ's blood, but it's going to taste a lot like wine.'

'Theoretically? How this mean?'

'It's wine.'

'Then what be?'

'No, that's all. Did I mention the cups are very beautiful? They are.'

'Drink twelve cups of wine. Be proof how drunken I can be?'

'Well, there isn't much wine in each cup.' Anselm pooch his lips. 'But it's enough to kill you, if someone thinks you're a false Maria.'

I narrow on this notion, look back to the dress. Blood gone brownish in the nooks of lace. 'Need only one from all these twelve?'

'Yes, it can be just one, I'm afraid.'

'Be a vote, can see.'

'Oh, no. If you're a false Maria, it's God who strikes you through His blood. The apostles are only His instruments. Or that's what people here believe.'

'Fools never heard of poison?'

'That's a terrible thing to say. I'm going to pretend I didn't hear that.'

When I look, he smiling at me with some mischief kindness. I feel jittery bad. Be sour to lose my life this way, ain't nothing of myself. Is like a frog caught in a fishing net, drown without sense.

I say, 'If I ain't drink?'

'Their dresses aren't here. But yes, it has occasionally happened. So, if you don't drink, you're treated as a false Maria just the same. The crucial difference is that you're still alive when your body is burned.'

'Shee, you burning peoples?'

'Before my time.' Anselm make finicky mouth. 'Let's keep it that way, please.'

I start walking slow, look superstitious at these guilty dresses. Some got only speckling at the bottom, or a wipen mark. Yo, some is splashen full. As I go, they getting older. Reddish color fading various, and the lace gone smutten yellow. I think how all these girls pass proof. Twelve cups been yes for them, feel like some risky luck.

Then I come to one unblooden clean. I hold, inspect it careful.

Anselm come behind, he tap one fingernail to the glass. 'Maria Condenada. Our Lady of the Living Jesus.'

'Ho,' I say, remembering. 'Girl who keep her Jesus by?'

'Yes, like you.' Anselm smile pologetic. 'I'm sorry, I couldn't help overhearing, because I was listening at the door.'

'Sure, I do the same, if there be doors to listen. But how she been, this girl?'

'Well, not great.' He sketch an X upon the glass. 'She killed a lot of people. Or her Jesus did, it isn't clear. To give an example, all of her apostles were murdered, which left a bad taste. In the end, she was killed by her own guard.' He give me gentle look, coy in his eyes. 'Officially, this all happened because she was a false Maria, wed to Antichrist. In fact, some people object to the inclusion of her gown here, but it's all history. And he who does not remember history, after all, is doomed to repeat it.' Then he pooch his lips. 'Less officially, she was having sex with Jesus.'

Take me a moment, while I sift they mystery definitions. Then I say shy, 'This ain't allow?'

'Senyora, Maria is a virgin. Virgin Mother, Virgin Bride, Virgin Widow. Virgin virgin.'

'Got this,' I say nervy. 'Child unfuck.'

He laugh up bright. 'You got this. Good, I hope so. Anyway, my educated guess is that there was another side to this story. There are feelings about white people here. You could call it superstition, or you might just say it's prejudice. Anyhow, it's been a long and thorny history.'

'But they Jesus, you believing that.'

'Oh, our citizens will worship Jesus dead on the cross, no question. But if some living, breathing white man tries to tell them what to do – well, it was a very unpleasant war. They do say civil wars are the worst.'

I look again upon the unblood dress. See where a fly got in this case, is looping scarum round. It stop in itsy focus on the mankin shoulder.

I put my fingers to the glass, notice a sketch of blood on my own knuckle, hurt in gathering wood. Been two nights before, in making camp beside the highway. I grit to this remembering, come like rain morose in me.

Fly skit up, replace itself onto a reddish dress along.

'Anselm,' I say soft, 'it be no way, they leave me free? Ain't care to be Maria none. I mostly wish to go from here.'

'Don't say that to people, senyora. And no, you can't just leave.' He tap the glass beside my hand. When I look to him, his face gone tense. 'Now, please pay attention. There are a lot of arguments going on right now about you. And when I leave you, I'm going to go and argue myself – that they ain't kill you, just so you understand. But you'd make my life much easier if you'd just say, "Yes, I'll complete the sacrament." Jesus will die for our sins again, and everyone will be happy.

'Honestly, if you want a white boy living in your rooms, I don't think it would be the end of the world. Some people would be upset, but it's wonderful gossip. It would spread joy among the common folk. However, I won't be pouring your wine.

'It's not too late, if that's what you think. Tell me now: "Yes, Anselm, I'll complete the sacrament. Now I understand." I'll go and pass it on, and all your worries will be over.'

I look past him to a blooden dress. Its skirts be furrish, where the blood gone moldy. 'But be some chance without this?'

'What if I say there isn't? There is no chance, senyora, do this or else you are going to die.'

I swallow rough. 'My people – children who been with me. They be hurt?'

Can see his eyes gleam like temptation. But this pass in wisty look. 'Not really, senyora. But you'll die, you will certainly die. Isn't that enough?'

'Die or murder, what you saying.'

'If you fail your proof, Jesus dies anyway. Do you understand that?'

I nod, lost in darkness feeling. When Soledad been warning this, ain't felt like truth. Now it come real. A poison cup I drink. Or I be took to burn in agonies. Be tomorrow, at a definite hour. This day be my whole life.

And now, my coward self begin its weaseling. Pasha self will comprehend, they kill him neverless. Yo, if I be dead, ain't trust that no one fetch the posy cure. Driver dying certain. And fear repeat: roo die the same, is only sense.

But then my heart skeer wrong. I see how Pasha watch my treachery, as I raise this spear. How I will stab, his suffering cry. How I turn, wet in his blood, from his unliving body. His blood hang here in ever witness.

And I know, this ain't myself. I be only Ice Cream Star, a bird of hotness, fool for tears. This act ain't mine, can never be in life. Ain't strong for treachery.

Soon as I decide this, all my conscience come back clear. It realize, I never get the cure without the roo. Driver ain't in this. It only be myself I waste.

I say soft, 'Death ain't no argument to me. Can die for this, be right.'

Anselm take his breath. When I look, he got some complicating sadness in his eyes. 'I thought you were just ignorant. But now you're making me wonder if you're actually in love.'

'For Pasha? Nay, ain't this.' I turn from the line of dresses, look where the Panish ermanos standing. They whisper with bald heads together, scalps drawn various with flowers. I smile strange, feel how I never learn these drawings' meaning. Ain't no time. And the glassen hall be painful in its actual self. Is here. Is all things join to my last life.

Anselm say, wisty slow, 'You're sure you understand?'

I shrug. 'Kill Pasha, or I die. I understand enough.'

'You're a very dangerous person, senyora. You're making me have feelings.' His brow furrow up. 'Oh, well. Let's not despair just yet. With the right support, there's always hope. Where there's money, you know, there's hope.' He perk then, his attention shift. 'Perhaps we'd better go. The doctors will be wondering where we are.'

He wave the Panish ermanos to, turn to the elevator wall. I give one parting look at all the dresses, their red cowardesse. Go with shaky brightness in my legs.

38

OF MEDICALS

We take another elevator trip, come to a different hall. Is grayish paint and grayish tiles. Got pue of bleaching wash. Come along this hall, and my mood changen to a joy precaire. Begun to love this single day jalouse, my living body. Feel even happy, these ermanos got no danger self. Their life seem endless sweet, and already it be strange to me I ever been the same, can live uncounten days.

And Anselm pause before a door, gray painten like the rest. Open this door to brighter light. He nod me past. I go with dreaming fear. Yo I feel this fear like bliss – be mine, is life bonesse.

Here be two girlish children never met. From their shaven heads, all drawn upon, guess they ermanas. But they clothen different. Is almost like a rifle garment, but in bluish cloth. Anselm come behind, and speak some Panish to these medical strangers.

They talking, while I breathe the bleachen air, look at the room. Is bureau cabinets built along the walls, with petty signs in Panish. All be nett with curiose objects, jars and standing artifacts. Middy to the room, a table be, is covern with thin paper. Ain't no chairs to this, and now my mind begin to wonder what we do. What they expect. I scout the room for some escape, but be no windows here. Be nothing.

Anselm explaining to the blue ermanas, sketch in the air with hands. They nod in sympathy, then they all look toward myself.

Anselm say to me, 'Okay. I'll be outside. This shouldn't take too long, and then you're finished for today. The doctors just need to know if you've eaten anything since this morning.'

'Eat?' I think to this, ain't hardly recollect this day at first. Must go through every part before I say, 'Ain't eaten nothing.'

'Good, that's helpful. Though I can't see what they'd do about it, if you had. Oh, well, not our problem.' He turn back to the blue ermanas, speak some petty words. They both nod smiling, look approval.

Then Anselm go, wave one hand fluttery over shoulder.

How they do this medical, be scary fascinations. First I must change to an uncraft dress, ain't got no zip nor buttons. Ermana use some tuben object that attaching to her ears, press its cold end to my chest. Must breathe, and breathe again. Then some fatty bracelet going on my arm and puff up tight. Injection needle using backward – make its tiny hurt into my arm, then it pull blood into some cup. This cup taken out, and it replacing with another cup, which fill with blood the same. Be some queery feeling, watch my blood go splashen out. Feel I should fear, but I only admire its perfect red. Wonder if all children be so red, or if this meaning something. Then I must go to toilet room, piss in a plastic jar. Be finicky worst, how this jar feeling warm when I be done.

Then the small ermana take all these blood and piss jars, covern tight. Go out in tasky mood. Now I must lie down. The tall ermana probing me with fingers. I try to bear this courteose, though it be miliations. She touch me like she testing fruit. In this, her face join seriose.

Last work, she put her palm flat on my stomach, pressing fast. Reach between my thighs. Push tensen fingers into myself inside. This be some ugly misery. Is like a petty rape. Almost, I start to fight this treatment, when my mind stop cold. Remember Anselm's words: *Maria is a virgin. Virgin Mother, Virgin Bride, Virgin Widow. Virgin virgin.*

Now panic join in me. Feel these probing fingers and I wonder if this notice. Try figuring if it help to lie – say it been accidents, ain't sex. Want to beg her, they ain't kill me now, will leave me to my proof. Keep my last day, is all I want.

And the fingers ease from me. As she stand back, I see her face gone grim. She turn away. I try to see her face again, but she go hasty by. Pass out the door.

I sit up, breathing strange. Try to tell myself, ain't been no hope. But all my loving mood be gone. Behind the door, come risen voices. Some argument be forward, and can feel, they arguing my life. I want to listen to the door, but sure will all be Panish. My life decide in mystery words. I cross arms to myself, is panic scorching in my mind. Try to think escapes, but these all baffle in the rifle children round this edifice. The elevator. Start thinking nonsense, how I crawl into a cabinet. Kill them with injection needle, stab their throat. Somehow I can.

Then the door come open hard. Fear catch in me when I see, it be the Panish ermanos. I stand to my feet, be saying, 'What? What you need?' But they ain't heed, they rush and catch me simple by my arms. Then my sense be gone, I fight in terrify scramble, kicking feet.

Ain't knowledge in this minute. I kick the papern table hard and then my leg be caught. Is twisten. I kick my other leg, and this blow finish sound, but then this foot be caught, and I get a freaken sorrow when I see is Anselm. He hold my foot with grit frustration, muttering words. I yell blind, 'Yo leave me! Leave me free! Goddamn, ain't done you nothing!'

Through this, Anselm speak in scolden voice. 'It's going to be all right. We're going to be – all – right.' And I be on this papern table, held again. Some madness fear in me, that they go rape me. I tear my arms, hard as I can, and loose one hand a second. Bring this scratching by, and catch a blue ermana's face. She wheel back screechen. But my hand be caught again before I even make a fist.

I start to say, 'My proof tomorrow. Got to leave me for this,' and Anselm talking through, 'Just calm yourself, we're going to be all right. Please trust me.'

Then the tallish blue ermana be above. She got injection needle,

smaller than the one before. I stare to this like it will give me knowledge. Then my arm be held in steely pain while she come bending
close. Slip this needle in my fearing skin. Press the injection and I
know, even before the blackness start its closing, I be done.

I try to say, 'You leave my Sengles, they ain't hurt for this,' but
these words drown into darkness. And I still hear their voices talking
in relief, relief malicieuse, as all my struggling empty into death.

39

THE NIGHT BEYOND OUR LIFE

Wake from your death, can think, you will surprise. Can be, you guess this be some ghosten afterworld. Rise with unconfidence, take time convincing life be real. Then can expect, you tearful gratty, holler for your joy.

But I only waken slow, in usual laziness. First worden thought be, 'Ho, I living.' I still be half in dream, about some cows I got to steal. Only way to steal these cows be to convince with lies, but they frustrating cows ain't comprehend my English speech.

Through these dreams, I feel myself lain on a springy bed. Ain't wearing normal clothes, my arms be bare. Cows drift back into forgetting, and I start remembering the city, all its glassen lights. Even in sleep, I ain't forgot this be my final day, and now I feel some gratty luxury, that life remain. My body real, is feeling warm and tired.

Then it notice that some bigger person hold me from behind. Arm be loose around me, and their body resting to my back. Yo, is covering blankets – holding person lain upon these blankets. Cautieuse, I open eyes.

It be a princen sleeproom. Got furniture with every gaud and falala richesse. Fantasky rug and furnitures; painten pictures on the wall; brocks of swanly flowers. I be lain in a jumbo bed, with blankets broidern silver. Ain't no one I can see. Even the stranger arm be hid in blankets. I keep careful still. I only lie considering a picture on the wall, show Jesus bloody on his sticks. Feel some defiance to this Jesus, left to die by coward Maria. But the golden frame be wolfen, carven thick with leaves.

Yo, as I attend this, it notice that my belly pinch. Be uncanny wrong, an almost pain, an almost hunger. Only then, I worry clear who holding me. I shift in natural fear, and I be loosen. Grandy arm flee by, is rummage commotion in the springy bed. I rise up panicking, catch for balance with a clumsy hand.

Behind be Pasha, staring his frosten eyes. We tense at each other, wild in startle.

Then he ease. Lips soften to a smile. 'Ice. You bone?'

'We ain't escape?'

'Nay. We here.'

I spy a window behind him, and my heart go small when I see it be dark. 'Damn, is night?'

'Ya, is night. You sleeping long.'

'Goddamn, ain't got to sleep.'

I feel that griping pinch again. Touch my hand down to my belly, seeking for its hurt. Flesh be healthy normal, got no injury can tell. Yo between my legs, be something thicken. Is like a serviette for bleeding times. I touch this superstitious. Wonder if this bleeding can begin, while they been probing me.

Pasha waring on me, got his rooish worry face. He say, 'You bone? You want some water?'

'Water, sure. You right.'

He get up, go to a bureau and fetch a china brock. Pour water in a shope of carven glass. While he doing this, I pull the blankets by, look down myself. Almost expect to find some strangeness, but is me the same. Be wearing whitish silk, a nighting dress long to my knees.

Then Pasha bring the shope and I drink thirsty. In this, I tense my belly, try to find its injure place. Ain't like no hurt I felt before. Is like they add some part to me, and this new part ain't fitting right. I finish the shope and set it on the bed.

Pasha stood by with crossen arms. Got his same rooish clothes, though he took off his pocket jacket. Whitish tee look almost clean, but pants got mud to shin height. His blue eyes feroce with thought.

I say, 'Where we be? Is still their – what it be?'

'Ministerio, ya. Room above.'

'How I come here?'

Pasha make discomfort face. 'Children here, ermanos, bring you.'

Take a second before this word *ermanos* recognize. Then Anselm come disgusting in my memory. 'Ermanos, right. You talk to them? Swear, they doing something to me. I feel queery.'

Pasha look guilty at the floor. 'We got wine. You want some wine?'

'Damn, answer questions. Sure I want some wine, but answer questions.'

'I talk to them, yes.' He turn by nerviose, go to a skinny-leggen table. Fetch a bottle, already been half drunk.

'They told you any knowledge?'

Pasha lift the wine, drink greedy. Then he come with sad respect and reach the bottle to me. I keep eyes on him while I drink. Wine be smooth and sour. I ease the bottle down and hold its cool against my pinching belly.

Pasha sit down on the bed, rubbing at his face. I start to think some better question, when he look up miserable and say, 'Ice. You was pregnant.'

I ware on him precarious. 'Pregnant? Like with enfant?'

'Ya, they say. Say to tell you.'

I press the bottle harder to my belly. 'I be pregnant.'

'Nay.' He grimace, look down to the floor. 'Ain't pregnant now. They end this.'

'End this? Nay, how they can – how they even known?'

'Can know.'

'Nay, how they know? Was nothing . . . I ain't known.'

He shrug miserable. 'Is ways.'

I lift the bottle to drink, and feel that pinching like a loneliness. Drink hasty, press the bottle to my belly again. Behind, some thought about preventing enfants come to me. Evil science. 'Yo what they do? They kill . . . what they do?'

'Ain't like an enfant,' Pasha say low. 'Only be beginning.'

'Be dead inside me?'

'Nay, is gone.'

'They take it? Mean, it living somehow?'

Pasha flinch. 'Nay, Ice. Ain't–'

'Sure. See this.' Hurt thicken in my chest. I go drink from the bottle, its last wine come seldom in my mouth. Bite on this taste and wonder how my baby with El Mayor will be. It been an enfant of my arms, can see it grow to three or four. El Mayor gone stupid prideful, if he known. If it live.

'They say to tell you,' Pasha's voice come low. 'I ain't want. But they say, important that you know.'

I look to him lonesome. 'Sure it be important. Nor you keep this. Cannot keep things from me, Pasha.'

'Ya. Be sorry, Ice.'

His face grit in shame. And now I feel the heavy night, the indoor silence like a darkness. It whispern: *You die also, soon. Dead mother of a murdern enfant.*

Then my heart crave to my Sengles, how I never see them more. To Driver, his frustrating eyes whenever I talk risky. But never I see these eyes again, I never see him more. Nor I seeing El Mayor – is like all children die to me. Death be a final loneliness.

Or can be only Pasha die.

I look to Pasha, and notice some chapping redness on his lip. Then my grief rise huge.

'Damn,' I say low desperate. 'I go think of this some other day. If it be other days. They put this filthy pain on me, I got no time.'

He grimace to the floor. 'I know.'

'Right.' I sigh my breath. 'They told about this proof?'

'Told me much, enough.'

'Much enough. I heard this also.' I look scary round. 'Goddamn, they got a guard? Be any way we leave this place?'

315

He make his sorry grimace, shake his head. Pick at the blanket for a moment, then he look to me. Eyes pale like grief. 'Ice? Ermanos told how you must kill me.'

I say quick, 'Ain't killing you.'

He frown unliking, start to speak, but I say, 'Nay. Ain't start this.'

He start to speak, and I say, 'Cannot hear this shee again. Cannot.'

He start, and I say, 'Pasha, damn!'

Then he shake his head and smile. Point toward the bottle.

I look to the bottle, puzzling. 'Ho, you want some wine?'

Pasha nod. Make drinking motion.

I laugh, nosy sounding from my grief. 'Nay, it finish. Sorry, I ain't thinking.'

'I can talk?'

'Talk, so you ain't say – what you know.'

'I show you trick. You bone to walk?'

'Guess I do.' I reach my feet toward the floor. Get some complaining nip inside, but I feel only riling to this. I stand and find my balance.

Pasha get up to his feet. I follow behind him to a door, is carven over with starry shapes. This open to another room enorme, with goldish fatty chairs and sofas. Floor be darkness wood, with grandy rug, pattern in wheeling flowers. Painten picture on the wall show a sleeper girl who touch her belly like myself.

Pasha go to a table with a plastic artifact upon. He lift the upward instrument of this. Stretch out a curly line. Roo put this instrument to his cheek and poke a button on the body. Can hear some buzzing. This repeat some times. Then it hush, and from the instrument come a tiny voice.

I startle well. Pasha give his mistooth grin, begin to talk in Panish. Plastic instrument answer small, and Pasha speaking back. Then he leave it down. Instrument sit back in its perch.

'Be some invention,' I say superstitious. 'Phoner, it be this?'

'Tel-e-fone,' he say in roo pronouncing.

'Ya telephone. First Electric's cat been namen so. Is brainy goods.'

'Trick ain't finish,' Pasha say. 'You see.'

I frown to the telephone. Be naive in looks, white plastic with silver apprehensions on its face. Ain't stirring none. I go and sit myself upon a sofa. Keep attention to this telephone, what it may do.

Then come a staggern knock. I flinch hard.

Pasha go easy to a door. Open, and a brown ermano look in nerviose. Ware on Pasha and talk some whispern Panish. Pasha speaking back, and the ermano reach a bottle. Roo take this helpful, raise it up to me like victory. 'Want any other? Food?'

'Sure,' I say in falter mood. 'Can want some food.'

'What you want?'

'Meat? Whatever they going to give.'

Pasha speak some Panish. Ermano asking back with nervy frown. The roo say, 'Carnay, carnay.' Ermano laugh, he look at me particular warm. Then Pasha say some quick politeness, shut the door again.

'Going to be some minutes,' Pasha say to me. 'It got to make.'

'Cherry trick. Think they bring us rifles?'

He laugh soft. 'You ask.' Then he go to a fatty chair, fetch a corkrew from its seat. Begin to worm this at the bottle. I watch his jumbo self, his birchen and morose respect. Remember how he holding me in sleep, and get uncanny sadness. And I think, we being like preventen enfants somehow – how we caught inside this night that never have a living day. Our only life be in this night. My only people be himself.

Then Pasha change his grip, and yank. Cork's plop startle in my nerves. Roo come forward, holding out the bottle.

I take it careful in both hands and say, 'Ain't kill you, all it is. We die, can die together. Yo can be, is hell. We journey there in company.'

Pasha make a face. 'Ain't heaven?'

'Heaven be for Christings. Any little knowing this.' I sketch division with my hand. 'We Sengles go to hell.'

'I be Christing. Born to.'

'Foo, you be a murdering roo. You come to hell with me.' I heft the bottle, drink a swallow. Lick the aftertightness from my mouth

and say, 'Know what you going to say in hell? You say, "Is normal."
What you say.'

He go sit himself upon the sofa's other part. Reach down, pick
nerviose at crusten mud on his pant sleeve.

I say, '"Tock vote. We burn forever, normal." What you say.'

'Can be,' he say unheeding. 'Ice. You talking to them much?
Ermanos?'

'Much enough,' I say. 'More than I wanting.'

'They tell their politics? Of war?'

'War be evil, but is sometimes needful, all I learn. Can guess all
killing needful to these insects.'

'Ice Cream, you be hurting?'

'Nay.' I make a face. 'What news you heard? Is something help
us live?'

'What it is.' He look up tense. 'Got plan, if you become Maria.'

'Ain't much if. Goddamn, I need no ifs. I need some plan to live.'

Pasha look frustration. He reach and take the bottle from me.
Raise and drink his hungry way, then rest the bottle down on his
long thigh. Something in this actual leg remind: is Pasha dying also.

I take a ragged breath. 'Be sorry. What you saying? Wars or like?'

'I think a better plan,' say Pasha. 'How you get this cure.'

His farther explanations all be Mariano histories. He learn this information while I still been gone to sense. This been eight hours of
nothing, and he trying what he can – do flatteries to ermanos, and
ask every nosing question, till they rid him for mistrust. Pasha add
some telligence he known from roos, and find a plan. But sure, I
cannot see at first, how any cure be in these facts.

It starting with their Jesus whites. When the city been young, the
Nighted States still had some whitish children. Ain't even roos, was
sleepers who surviving WAKS somehow. These hide in lonely forests,
fear all children for disease. If they see no blackish face, they flee,
or fight like seven nightmares.

Then every girl who want to be Maria must depart in hunt. Choose her apostle twelve, and they roam perilous to find a Christ and capture him alive. Return like heroes, ya she rule the city for her vally deed.

But, as time depart, the richer Marianos start to cheat. Ever a whitish male be found – whatever person snaring him – they buying him for wealth. Rich people keep these whites in capture till the old Maria sicken. Then they choose what girl they like, and kit her with a ready Christ.

So years continue, and these forest whites exterminate to zero. But, in lucky help, the roos begin to send soldats. These first soldats come to the Nighted States for spying work. Look round, and they steal children, question them for informations. This been the truth about our Massa people stolen, in years before.

But in Mariano lands, roos be like walking money. Any be seen, a thousand greedy children come in hunt. Roo capture to be Jesus, and he murder, all it is. No spy escape with life.

How this mattering to us, the roos ain't know Marias much. To them, it mostly be a blankness where their children die. For this reason, now they leave Marias City harmless, while they raid Washington and Massa, either side.

Other facts my Pasha learn be on the Mariano wars.

In years before, Marias city fight a hundred miles of distance. Gain towns into their ruling, like they picking easy fruit. Northward, this be farms that feed the city meat and grain. South, is their obedient cities, Fort Dix, Penn and Ballmer. Their arrogance start to hope, they win the Nighted States entire. Make it catolico, for God's joy.

But their last wars been shameful lost. These been against the city Quantico, in farther south. The Quantico people call marines, and these marines is smart in violence. In two wars, they kilt the Marianos into shreds.

Most Marianos finish now with war. Was burnt and learnt. But be one wealthy burrow, Inúd, is always hot to fight. Inúds ain't hear no coward reasons. All their love be fray.

Soledad ya be Inúd. Anselm–Pedro be – all children helping me is from this burrow. If I become Maria, I be theirs for politics. Then the Inúds expect a war on Quantico, to heal their pride.

Pasha tell all this, and look at me with owl importance.

I scoff breath. 'Foo, all I learn, you townie with ermanos. Heard their every life.'

'Be my work so.' Pasha shrug. 'Friending. Find some use.'

'Nay, be saying, how no cure be in this?'

Then the door knock sharp. Pasha make a shushing gesture as he rise to open.

Brown ermano push a wheelie table in, spread thick with smelling meal. Child muttern Panish courtesy, go out again with nervy haste.

Me-Pasha never fed from yesternight. Meal stop our talk. We eat standing, hush with greed. Get some fatty meat, is deery somewhat, but be soften dull. To this is tatoes and some bony greens and breaden cakes. I eat like brainless hound, most bite my fingers in my rush. In this, the pinching sorrow in my belly soften, feel like heat. And I get some pleasure grief, how all this mystery be strange – the easy meal, the goldish chairs, the shining floor of oak. Picture girl who look out sorrowing bell, touch on her stolen enfant.

When my hunger fill, I go sit to a table by the window. Gaze into its glass, while Pasha eating undiscourage. First I watch my reflection. Ain't mirror clear, all I can notice be the whitish garment, catch on my shoulders with thin ribbons. Face be wisty shadows.

Then I see, beyond into the night, is nothing there. Be grayish dark, but ain't no trees nor buildings. Ain't no ground. Is nothing, like we bury in grayish earth.

I put my face close to the window with some starting fear. Here I find some ground below, sky distance from myself. We caught up in the air like circling hawk. I grip the chair, unnerve. Stare down, and I begin to recognize trees. Be mousen size below. Among, be thousand itsy movements. First I think of insects, but soon it realize, be people. Their faraway deep come dizzy to my flesh, like falling in tender fright.

Then Pasha come, stand to the table. Look down to me sorrowing, while I watch him in reflection. Through him show this bosky floor of life, careening far.

I say nerviose, 'So how this bring us cure? Ain't said.'

He nod scouty. Go off to a shelf and fetch a paper.

Paper be a map of Nighted States. It look like sleeper maps; show the country green with brownish scarring, town names writ in black. But, look more careful, New York City gone, instead is *C. de las Marias*. Below, is names from Pasha's story: *Fort Dix, Penn, Quantico*. Farther south, be some peculiar names like *Disney World* and *Drown*. All the west and all the middy part be blank of towns.

Pasha let me scout the map a minute. When I look up questioning, he put his finger to Quantico. But he say, 'Washington.'

'Washington?'

'Yes. Marianos call this Quantico. Be same as Washington city.'

'Shee.' I frown in closer, skeering somehow in my heart. 'You saying, roos fight Quanticos next? This meaning, roos will lose?'

'Ain't that.'

'Foo, admit these Quanticos can win.' I sit back disappointing. 'You only being contradictory.'

'Nay, Quanticos ain't win.' Pasha smile. '*You* can win.'

I distract to Pasha's hand, tensen on the map. Notice how it cover in gentle hair, is yellow strewn. Got a deepish scar across the back, sort made from burning injury. 'If we live, you saying, you want to make war on your roos?'

'Yes,' say Pasha in impressing voice. 'Two cities fight. If Marianos fight by Quanticos, can win against the roos.'

'Ho, Marianos do this? Quantico be their enemy, ya.'

'You be Maria then.' He make impatient face. 'Can figure this. Roos ain't come till January. Be all time to do.'

I frown to the map. 'I thought we never can beat your roos.'

'Can here. Roos bring only enough of soldats, guns, for Washington. You join, they ain't expect. Is chance you win.'

'Chance? You saying, we can lose?'

'Yes.' Pasha wave his hand dismissing. 'But if you losing, still can parley. Can get cure from this.'

'Parley? Roos will parley?'

'Yes. In war, is parleys. For . . . trade prisoners. Be different parleys.'

'Trade prisoners for cure. See this.' I narrow on his face, considering. 'But if we lose, Marias City all be taken, ya?'

He make obvious face. 'You fleeing then. Take cure and flee.'

I laugh surprise. 'Foo, you got colder morals. Thought your roos was worser death.'

'Can win also.' Pasha shrug, get foolish smile himself.

'Marias children ain't no wonderful themself. Choice of awfuls, can see this.'

Then we smiling to. I look at Pasha with good townie feeling. Seek his chappen lip, but it ain't showing in this light. His beard begun to grow in these two nights, cheeks look doggish. Face soften in relief, his bigness arms is loose and spent.

Then my conscience whisper soft, *Stab Jesus in the heart.*

I shiver and sit back. Say low, 'Can figure this tomorrow. If it be tomorrow. Got only hours, ain't spend it all on futures we ain't see.'

His eyes go uncertain. Look to the map, and touch a finger wisty onto Quantico.

I say, 'Wish we can go outside somehow. Hate this indoors, feel like I breathing my own breath.'

A moment he sit closen on his thought. Then he rouse himself, look up. 'Be an outside room.'

'Foo, how no room can be outside? Is contradictions.'

'Nay, I show.'

Pasha stand up nervy. Go to some longish curtains, pull them open to glass doors. Through, can see a dimmish porch. Doily sort of metal chairs with flattish pillows to.

I feel some disappointments. Had a yearning for the woods. Wish it been some elevator, can step to forest from this room. But I make preciating face. 'Is right.'

'Be cold for this,' say Pasha low. 'I telephone you coat.'

'Ya,' I say, with forcen lightness. 'Ask for Patagonia. They roaches robbing me.'

Pass some waiting minutes before the ermanos bring my coat. We try to make some gladder conversation, memories that been. But every talk stray into death. Soon we guessing if it be no afterworld to see. Even hell come liking to our fear, but neither can believe.

I tell him how our Popsicle return from death one time. Say he seen a hell, where he met all the dead he ever known. Dead live in this hell like normal. They told him that the fire accustom, and when they hunt a turkey, it be ready cooked. Pasha laughing to this silly, when the knock come at the door.

Coat ain't Patagonia. Be a bushy furren item, white and longness to the floor. But I settle to this, will not spend my final time frustrating. Clad it on, and we go out into the friendly cold.

Porch ain't glorieuse for nothing, but got healthy air. I step to the raily edge, my bare feet chilling glad. Lean out, spying for the trees, and Pasha lean beside. Forest still be tiny strange, but look more real without the glass. Branches blowing, is restless with good life.

Then come a cry below, and all the bosky darkness stirring forward – like someone tip the ground toward us, and all loose objects sliding to the edge. Be the children of these woods, come running toward the Ministerio. They sift through trees and crowd against some obstacle line I cannot see. Hundred voices raise and join into a storming larm. Yo, all these children lift their arms, reach toward us from their plummet depths.

I flinch from the railing feary. Pasha muttern rooish, wave me back. We prowl to hidden space. Breathe scary while the skree discourage slow, like sinking from its weight. Soon it only be one voice. Can hear how this child weaken hoarse and palter into silence. Only then we ease and settle in the doily chairs.

Clouds part above, and show a blanket of good stars. We both fix on this, and I expect our usual silence, but somehow I start to talk. First be talking sad of Driver, how I learn his sickness on the day that we found Pasha self. How I swearing Pasha ain't a roo, for his protection. We both remember, talking, how I took his gun away. Talk about Karim, and how he die for nothing wrong – and we agree all murder be for nothing. Ain't no reason worth a death. But we contradict this for the death of Deema Roo, and then we argue if we be deserving our soon death. Argue if we dying real, or if we save somehow. And we agree this death be funny, if it ain't been us. Jesus self will laugh.

And Pasha tell me of his wars, and how he done all worst things you can do, more times than he remember, when he been dumb with pharmacies and murderous with fears, and then he need to just forget. He tell me stories of this, but he ask me that I never tell, if we both live beyond. I promise honesty to this, and so I never done. Then he say about the times he try to kill himself, but always he was found and made to live. Ya, he argue, like I known he will, that I can kill him also. Ain't need him for the cure now – and it be like killing Deema, justice for his evil life. And I say again that I ain't kill him, and Pasha say he thought I maybe changing, if I known his crimes – but any blindness known was something like, and I say nothing to this. Then Pasha take my hand, and I cry somewhat, but he never seeing in the dark. And we sit in hunting silence, smoke with our free hands, and coldness settle feroce on our bare faces, as the dawn begin to sneak its faintness into this black city crawling with unknowing children, and our mouths begin to taste of terrify and animosen love. Until the sun be risen dull, and knocking come, our death come knock impatient in the room. Yo we ignore this hatred detail – until they come for us without no pity, soldiers and ermanos, talking disapproval, talking meaningless and pulling me, and I loose Pasha's hand, and he look shame as I be led away, and I call back that I will find him. Ever hell be big, will find him there. And if it ain't no hell, it been a bony night, was bone as any, and if we live, yo if we live.

40

OF PROOFING

This death morning spent in grooming. Be exasperation, how I live these final hours with strangers tugging at my hair and pinning cloth against my frighten skin. Everything is fingers. Start to flinch whenever I feel a touch.

Two girls who pester most be callen Altagracia and Mercedes. They nasty prettieuse, chub females with all paints upon. Both is skunking with perfume, and all their helping children skunk. Is only Altagracia–Mercedes speaking English any, and it be Panish in its sort, pronounce in noses and confusions. But they keep pronouncing on, with scarcely taken breath.

Mostly they talk grooming yappit, until I hating my own ears, be angry that no child be born with ears. And while their voices pippet round, is always fear within. Any comfort I can think, I terrify the same, and my mind slip to needless maginations. I think of snake Felipe, apostle of Metropolitano. How he will smile like honey as he hand his murder cup. How this poison act, if it be painful. If I refuse to drink, how I be draggen out to burn. How it can be, that Ice Cream ain't existing anywhere. Will be no me to know that I ain't there.

And I must stand and raise my arms. Murder dresses clad on me, and strip away, flung off like grandy swans. Mercedes work with pins around my waist. Then must lean back with hair in faucet water, feeling devil miseries.

In this, I think to draw their talk to something that distract. So I ask if Marianos ever can bear with whitish children. Be dreaming how I save my Pasha, and he live among. So I ask, if be some white with kindly manners, how this been.

Then Altagracia make some pittering talk, how whites be Satan's get, was made in person shape for our confusion. In their old America, whites had a bad religion where they worship paper money. Was mally churches callen banks, deciding all their laws. These whites live like diseases, all was homosexual selfish. Good black children was kept as slaves, or capture into gloomy prisons. She keep on with this blablabla, while she pluck at my face, until it be a nagging madness.

At last I speak up breathless, say, 'Your people ain't no differences. You worse. Be farts that blame the cheese.'

She startle back. 'Senyora?'

I hush myself. Can guess that I look peevish as a boring mule. Only I muttern, 'Get your own white people, kill them gratty. Pasha mine. Is townie children.'

'I not kill anyone, senyora.'

'Nay, you ain't kill no one. I feed you to him first. Be right.' Here I begin to cry, and Altagracia–Mercedes cluck around me like two picking hens. Pat my face with serviettes and stroke me till I swat them.

When they finish me, I wear a dress like all the others. Top be covern in some pearls, the bottom feathery big. Hair braid with diamond jewleries, and Altagracia fix a band of pearlen beads atop, with straggling gauzen cloth loose down my back. Clip diamonds painful to my ears, string diamonds cold around my throat.

Then Altagracia say she teach me through the sacraments. She take me to a grandy room, is empty of no furnitures. Here we go through any witless actions. I must say 'See' for 'Yes', and kneel and handle golden rings. This be the wedding sacrament. Then she giving me a wooden object like a boaten oar. I hold this embarrass, till she say, 'When the wedding over, apostle Pedro give the spear.' Then I throw it angry to the floor, gone hot through all my skin. Altagracia cry, with scary looks, 'I must to teach both ways. Is not my choice, senyora.'

So I stand trembling while she take the oar up in her hands. Show me how this murder done, explaining spears their use, like any fifteen child ain't know. And here my coward heart begin to muttern its temptations. Truth, I cannot cause no wars to Washington if I be dead. Pasha only be one life – I win this cure, and every children save. Ya, Pasha thirty years, is like he living twice already. And I see Driver's face in mind, his eyes gone furiose with pain. For all the murders Pasha done, one life. Roo ask for this himself.

And Altagracia tell how I must find my place, and use my weight. How I must force this spear until he die. Then all my body feel this thrusting blow. My muscles gather bright. Is even pride, how I be strong. Can do this work correct.

'When he dead, you kneel,' say Altagracia. 'On the blood, is good. Spear clean with dress. You try, senyora?'

To this, I cannot bear no more. Say hoarsen furiose, 'I seen. Now show the other way.'

So we do this action, I repeat its queery words, and go until we come to drinking cups. Then I be weak from every fear, and ask if I can have some wine. Or booze be better. But this ain't allow.

They pick at me some more, and tell me cigarettes ain't allow, and seeing Pasha ain't allow, and pick at me. Try to pull me to a mirror, but I lie nasty that, among my people, mirrors ain't allow. They take this with surprisen admiration. Yo, now ermanos gather in. Some rifle children coming, wearing different clothes, is reddish color, but their guns the same. All glance nerviose to me, ain't nod or greet or nothing. Altagracia pull me to a middy place among these children. Give me last instructions, pick my hair a final time.

Then we all walking down some broaden stairs, go lower lower, any wearing time, until I feel they take me clear to hell. Wish I dying so without no proof indignity. But we come into the room of dandelion lights, the statue of the girlish cannibal. Walk out to the bluish street. And gathern to the streeten edge is all the normal people of Marias City, the littles and the jones, with dirty coats and needing faces, roaring in their thousand voice. All madden as I come along, is pointing fingers, grinning strange, and we walk through their skree that swell against the buildings' rocky flanks. On the street be scattern flowers, whitish petals shivering and drifting in the wind. My ankles feel like angry water, but I walk correct. Concentrate upon the cutting bother of the heely shoes, and go with feary upright step, longing that I been a rifle child, ain't got this pinching dress and freezing arms and death and death.

Rifles halt before an edifice savage in bellesse. Is towers and like-nesses and curls, and all been carven out of stone. Ain't believe in gods before, but cannot see how any person children make this edifice. A different fear become in me, that this real god exist. But my heart insist its hatred to any god who kill my Pasha for some fool performance, and I get some better valor, walking small into this vasty place.

Inside, be worse bellesse. A music come from loften height, some moaning instrument. Be thousand people sitting in benches, wearing churching clothes. All about is carven – flowers and curls and stony children. Be tall painten windows showing long-nose sleepers acting scenes. Forward is a stage with golden canopy upon. On steps before this, apostle Pedro standing. Wear a silvern dress, wash shiny to the floor.

Beneath the canopy be Pasha. He bounden to a stony cross with both his arms. Ain't hanging, but he stand upon a granite step, feet bound the same. Look like normal rope they use, done up in fisher knots. He wearing brownish pants, is simple made, but all his chest be bare.

See him there, my heart go black. It rage without no mind. I try to look away, but my eyes need to him. Will see and see.

And I walk forward. Yo the rifle children fall behind, stay guarding by the doors. Be thinking how I run, if I can make them shoot me somehow. Be the death I will prefer, but still be chance no cup will poison. If I do this killing, be good chance. And I go forward, remembering these gaga sacraments. Feel the sweat bright on my face. Pasha watch me come with dazen eyes. Pedro step aside.

I go and stand to Pasha, heart gone scrambling. Be almost blind without no thought, I only see one detail. Neat on his chest, there be a blooden mark. Show where my spear should go, is cut into his whiten skin. One shivering breath, it freak in me, they stabben him already. Kill him with some knife, left me no choice. But then my mind clear cold, can see this cut be scarcely bleeding. And it notice, roo got any scars along his chest – long nicks and dimples, purple and white. I get another madness, how he live beyond these every wounds. Sure, he surviving any stab I do.

Then Pasha swallow at his throat. I look up to his frosten eyes. They terrify in strangeness, like he fear me now, too late.

Yo we stare together, two small terrors in this giant room. Behind us, children watching from their benches, and the rifles watching, as the moaning song close to its finish. All come silent.

I crouch down to my knees. Gather the skirt around myself. Look up to Pasha again, and mouth his name, but he be looking by. His bluish fright gone to the watching room.

Then apostle Pedro come toward me, stepping careful. I watch to his face, and feel all hatred I can find. Hate his melancholy looks, I hate his gracile hands. Silvern cloth got broidery upon, in complicating flowers, and I hate these flowers, all my bitter living hate him.

He speak. Be Panish, chanten long, his voice be like complaining water. Yo he coming to a pause. And I remember, and say, 'See.'

Then he put his hand soft to my head, and speak again. I be almost longing to his gentle touch, his haten touch. He pause again, and I say, 'See.' Rise to my feet, with trembling gone all through me. Hold out a trembling hand. Pedro catch it still. He fit a ring onto my finger.

Ring be carven gold, fit loose. I want to shake it free – but I close fingers on it. Nor I brave to look at Pasha. I stare frighten into nothing.

Speech begin again, and now a blackdress child come up, is carrying an actual spear.

Spear ain't prettieuse like every object here, is plain for use. Shaft be oaken, blade is longer than no knife. Its edges perfect sharp. Any girlish arm can kill with this. My hands guess how this hold, what force it take.

Then Pedro take the spear, step graciose to me, and hold it out. I take it with some sudden greed, and hold it well in both my hands. Pedro's face change warm. His eyes skit up to Pasha, wanting. Suffer how he want. I stare on Pedro, and my breath come faster, hands grip well.

Be only a lurking moment that I look to Pedro's throat. See how this throat can stab. My arms join, brighten in their hate.

Yo when I look to Pedro's eyes, he seen. He frozen blank, got superstitions in his pressen mouth. I be gratty for this alone. I hand the spear back smiling and say clear, 'No puedo. No.'

Pedro take the spear with wisty blinking of his eyes. My arms go trembling down again, while behind, is muttering in the benches, children sighing somehow. I look back to Pasha. He still ware on me with frighten blankness. Rain-color eyes look almost white.

Pedro step away, and with no feeling sense, I go to knees again, work at my Pasha's bounden feet. Behind, the children muttern, and I feel hotness in my face. Begin to hurry, fear that someone stop me. I stand to work his handen knots, and feel my Pasha's frighten breath, hot at my nape. Rope chafe my fingers, and my belly pinching deep again as I free his last knots. Pasha never look to me. He only step down, stumble on bare feet. Stop with some different fright, and I turn perilous.

Apostles stand behind. All wearing garb like Pedro's, washing silvern to the floor. Cups is gold, with reddish stones. A moment, I expect that Pasha fight through these, we run. But nothing be. We stand the same, and when I look at him, he stare to nothing. One hand press his chesten wound.

Then I tell myself, *I drink some wine. All I must do. If it be death, this dying do itself. I only drink.* And the apostles all step forward, as the music start again, its moaning wind and voice.

First apostle coming be Simón Zelote, tearful soldier. Hold his cup out, and his handsome jawbone face show nothing. I reach and take the cup. When he release, its weight surprise my hands. It take some strength to hold this, and I look defiance to the gold, the darken wash within. Ain't look like wine, is almost black. But I raise it, tense with spite. Gold chill my lips, I tip it clumsy. Then it taste too sweet for wine. Be squinting at this wrongness. All my throat join to reject it, but I swallow harsh. Wait for the pain, the wasting feeling. What it be.

Simon Zelote reach his hand. I be blind in wondering as he grasp the cup. My hands come loose away, and nothing been. I stand the same. I look, alive, up to the next apostle. Got better courage, and be comfort that I ain't recognize his face. Be some apostle who never asken questions, got no care. Wine be the same, a sweetish gulp and nothing. He take the cup, and I be feeling gratitudes when I see the next apostle be Juan, young child who favor me. I drink his wine with almost greed, gladden in its safety. Then come posy Bartolomeo, child who ask about the clause. Feel worse to this, been something maudy in him, but I take his wine, drink hard. I almost drop this cup. He must catch it hasty from my loosing hand.

Then my fears begin to waste, be tired of this fright. I only force my strength to meet these coming faces, take their cups and drink, and drink again. Be wishing only for the end. Be gratty now to die, ain't bear to agony more in fear. And it go on, some unlikely stretching time, repeating and repeating. Music moan, disturbing in my ears. The crowd stare cold. I begin to notice the apostles' expressions, who be nervy, who be calm. Girlish apostle frown at me so hard, she rumple her chin. Yo, prettieuse Santiago wink, like this be littlish game. Only after I drink his cup, I guess he want to reassure. Was hinting, this ain't poison. I look after him in wish, long to his sympathy. Then I look back and see Felipe.

Child looking maladies of fright. Face be bright with sweat, jaw clench. Hands grip knuckly to the cup. Is like he try to crush it gone.

And I know, in evil calm, be now. I look back to the rifle children at the farther door, but got no strength to think of running. It wonder how they doing, if I yell that this be poison. Spill it like an accident. Behind, be thought of burning – and how, when I be draggen out, all children see my cowardesse.

Then I reach to the cup from simple habit. Felipe flinch, but ease himself and leave it to my hands. I take its sickening weight, and glance around the watching children, how they waring on this sight. Be like they know, they spitely curiose. Then all my fear be gone. Is only the metal weight in my two hands, the dream bellesse around. Felipe's face be cringing dread, and I feel scorn against this weakness.

I raise the cup in simple strength. Find the cold edge with my lips.

Taste duller than the other wine, but I swallow without thought. And I look back to weak Felipe, thinking how he watch me die. My mind say, *Now I die, see what it be. If it be anything.* I look to the painten windows, the complicating reds and blues of drown sunlight, wait for this mystery. My heart beat skitty, like a hand-caught bird his frighten heart.

But nothing be. I breathe, and feel my scary hands tight on the cup. Nothing be. Felipe watching to me, never move to take the cup. Look only changing fear. Yo, my own fear start again. Keep waiting for the pain, until is hope and panic and every struggling need inside myself. Then sudden, Felipe reaching out, his face gone sick. I give the cup to him with almost guilt. He look inside, check that I drank.

Then his eyes widen to me. Grown shiny now with tears. He whisper something helpless, be a prayer or beggary.

And he turn and stagger by, a silvery change in my blur sight. I stand empty-hand and sick. Feel dizzy through my body, like it poison with its life.

Then Pedro coming last, is looking tired in relief. He hand his cup like normal guesting. This I drink thankful for its wine. Wish there been more. And Pedro take his cup and I be cold with sweat and living weak. Some madness smile come on my face. Pedro make a two-stick sign into the air before me. Speak some louder words, and all the people in the benches say up, sudden and bold, 'Amen.'

And Pasha take my hand in his cold sweaten hand, and we walk back. Go between these benches, all the children standing to their feet. Guards gather to us at the door, but no one touching us. No tardy poison work in me. It be no harm.

So we walk out to the street, its sunlight and its ravish voice. Walk into the shouting city, city that I rule.

41

OF ANSELM WEASEL

Scarce remember how we starting back, get only scraps of knowledge. My elbow caught by Pedro, he whispern gratulations in my ear. Then he gone. We in the road, among the redcoat guards, the thousand strangers screaming wild against the gray and sunlit buildings. Pasha by me looking ghosty weird. Somewhere we stopping, caught, where children run into the road before. Get some skirmish there, and all red soldiers gather to me–Pasha, ware their guns around.

One turn to me and call above the noise, 'They clear soon. No have frighten.'

Comprehend this poory, but I say, 'I be Maria now?'

Child look like he scary from no answer, but he nod.

My heart clear sweet. I say, 'My brother, can I get that rifle?'

He startle in his eyes. Be a skinny male, look mostly fifteen like myself. And he look troubling round, like someone rescue him from this confusion. Then he try, 'No need. We rifle for you.'

'Want your rifle,' I say. 'Damn, I asking this.'

Ain't expect result, but he go meek. Reach his gun. I take its weight, its loving coldness. Try to nod my friendship to him, but he turn away. Then I look to Pasha with some pride, but he watch forward at the altercation. So I hold the rifle different ways in privy joy. Ain't right as my Kalash, but still is bold in heaviness. Its trigger loop fit to my finger sweet.

Then the skirmish clearing, we walk on. I hold the rifle to my waist, walk glad in weapon bravery. When we catch again into some fool commotion, I crouch down. Reach beneath my fluffet skirt, unhook my heely shoes. Twist these off, and sigh joyeuse. Crouching there, the yells be dull among all standing bodies. I catch a trodden flower in my hand, and remember how I going to live. Ain't be my last flower, and I laugh toward the dirty street and feel my bony rifle and my flower and my life.

In this gratty moment, I dream how I can escape. But Sengles catch in mind – must wait until they bringing safe. And, strange behind this, come a ravish memory of our war. Truth, we want this city and its thousands. They fight for the cure. Then all my blood exhilarate, is like careening light within.

I look up dizzy and find Pasha narrowing on me. He shout through the noise, 'They give you gun?'

'Nay, I ruling here,' I shout. 'Take what I like.'

'Give me.'

I stand up glad on naked feet and hand the rifle easy. Then my loot be by. We moving forward, Pasha got my rifle at his other side. Keep it ready, like he done in all our Massa journey. Redcoat guards squint at the roo disliking, muttern Panish. But I ain't minding this. Ain't even scarcely miss my gun. I watch on Pasha, how his naked chest look chickenish in the cold, and feel some vasty love. Love the frosten air and love my bare feet on the gritten road, yo this whole moron city shout my love in millions, ring the sky.

When we come to the Ministerio steps, guards start to filter back, and all relief be thankful. I hitch my dress and scramble up the steps like eight joyeuse. Pasha running after, gun caught easy like he do. Another range of guards be there, they open doors to us, and then we be inside, like falling in a bed of silence. No one even there. My feet come smooth onto the tilen floor.

Then I grab Pasha's arm. He turn to me, his face uncanny soft. I say, 'We living, roo. You even guess that this can happen?'

'Yes.'

I laugh up wild and grab him round his chest. Crush him hard, and he begin to laugh, a beagling sound. He arm me round and heft me in the air, until I kick his leg. Then he loose me, and I stand with hands up to his shoulders, saying, 'Shoo, I save your life. We fair now, one for one.'

Pasha laugh and touch my cheek, his face go drunk with feeling. Eyes be lit and starry, grin confuse with my same love.

Then behind, a glassen door come open. I look round, still grinning, feeling happy to all children made. But then I see, is Anselm.

Only in this moment, I recall my robben enfant. Pasha stiffen hostile by. As Anselm come up smiling, I touch conscious to my belly. All my various temperaments gone dizzying, joy and rage and grief.

'Santa Maria,' Anselm say, and stoop himself somehow.

I grit my breath and say, 'Should call me Ice Cream like a person.'

Anselm straighten up, touch fingers to his hearten chest. 'A first point of etiquette. When people greet Maria, they expect to kiss her ring. That's the routine.'

'Ain't interesting what you expect. Yo, where my Sengles be?'

'Your people, yes.' Anselm make mischief smile. 'Your apostles are in your rooms, although they've scattered into hiding. They don't seem to like each other much.'

'Yo sho, they hide. You capture them with guns, what else they done? And where my other Sengles?'

'Everyone you want will come. Please trust that, santa reina. Now I was wondering – it's very selfish of me, but I was hoping I could speak to you alone. Is that possible?'

'Ain't going to kill us now?'

'Oh, no.' He shake his head like this be some ridiculous.

I look to Pasha, who be heeding narrow. 'You bone here, Pasha? Going to parley.'

Pasha make sour face. 'Want rifle?'

'No,' say Anselm quick. 'That really won't be necessary. Maria?'

'Yo, we can talk. Ain't guess you going to like this talk.'

'That's very kind. I think we can find a private space, if you'll just follow me.'

He lead me to the elevator hall, is talking boringness about my rooms. How this be the top three floors of this whole Ministerio. I sharing these with my apostles, ya and Jesus bringing there. These floors be callen the iglesia, and he go in blablabla about their wonder furnitures. Soon my mind distract to thinking how I going to fear this Anselm. Be dreaming how I bring him to my rooms, and all apostles beat him, when he say, 'Maria. Are you listening?'

'Nay, ain't listening. What you need?'

He hold up a scrap of metal. Narrow on this well, I recognize its use. A key.

'You use this key to call your elevator,' Anselm say. 'The other elevators won't go to your floors. It's to ensure your privacy.'

I reach for the key, but he draw back his hand. 'No, santa reina. This is mine. I'll have yours sent up later.'

He plug this key into a golden plate upon the wall. Elevator swallow its doors. I go in reluctant, still be chewing on my angers. This elevator bigger than the other, almost roomen size. Got velvet walls and hanging pictures. Anselm step in and poke a button. Doors knit up, the elevator start to drift above.

I take my breath. 'Yo heed. I got–'

'No, wait.' Anselm hold hand up sharp. 'First, I need to congratulate you. Your proof went well, didn't it?'

'Sure, be alive. Can see this.'

'Yes, it was lucky, wasn't it? Now hold on.' Anselm turn and poke another button. Elevator shudder and stop. I look to the doors expecting that they open, but is nothing. Be unfriendly silent in this closen place, feel like a deafness.

'So.' Anselm smile back to me. 'I was interested in your impressions. For instance – were there any moments when you felt nervous?'

'Nervous. Nerviose, I guess? Been nervous since I met you people.'

'I'm sorry to hear that. But you didn't feel uncertain about one apostle in particular?'

'How you meaning?'

'I'm meaning that Felipe seemed very – nerviose. To me.'

I frown on him closer. 'You was there?'

'Front-row seat, senyora. I am the director of the Ministerio, naturally I was there.'

'Yo sho, Felipe mostly ruin his pants with fear. If he got pants.'

'Yes, and I think he was surprised at the outcome, don't you?'

'What you saying? Damn.'

'Well, Felipe seemed very confident that God was going to strike you.' He frown like he consider this question. 'Perhaps it was religious conviction.'

'You saying, he thought his cup been poison.'

'If you want to put it that way.' Anselm make a blissen smile. 'I, however, wasn't surprised at all. Why do you think that is?'

I make a face. 'You pour this wine?'

'Oh, no, senyora. They do that themselves, of course.'

'Foo, you going to tell me or you ain't. Boring, these confusions.'

Anselm look politeness to this. Seem he expect that I will ask again, but I go stare beyond. Pull on my pearlen headband. Start to find the pins is holding this, and tug them out.

At last, he sigh and say, 'Well, like most impossible things, it was a matter of money.'

I shrug, tug out another pin. 'You paying this Felipe?'

'Oh, no. We paid a gentleman who provides poisons.'

My hand pause in my hair. 'Someone who providing poisons?'

'Yes, senyora. A gentleman who's very far away right now – and very rich. After all, Felipe paid him also. Now, you may know that some poisons are completely tasteless and odorless. Some are also harmless. This one was the poison we call water.'

Now Anselm gaze on me with bright congratulation smile. I magine how Felipe buying poison – what he think. But be a jar of normal water. He pour this, trembling, in his wine. Go scary to my murder.

Can feel, is vally mischief, but my eyes got only hatred. Yo it notice behind Anselm on the wall, a painten picture hang. Show a girl with armen enfant. Both got gold circles drawn around their heads, and the baby reach up thoughtful to his mother's face.

'In a case like this,' say Anselm, 'we usually say "Thank you".'

I say cold, 'You save myself, is gratty. But you kill my enfant.'

The happy vanish from his face. He knit his hands together, eyes gone tight. 'Of course. I shouldn't have forgotten.'

'Forgotten? You forget your killing easy.'

'No.' His voice come thin. 'I forgot that you don't understand.'

'I understand enough. You–'

'No, I'm sorry. You really don't.'

Then we glaring one to one. His chubben face be gathern in some mally telligence. Notice to me how his beardskin gone in stubble, this passen night. Shaven head be grown the same, confuse the spidery drawings there like dirt.

'Please listen,' he say cold. 'I'll make this short, and hopefully we will never have to mention it again. There are many, many things you can do as Maria. Having a baby is not one of them. Let me repeat: you cannot have a baby. I saved your life not once but twice yesterday. Now, an ordinary person would say, "Thank you, Anselm. Thank you for saving my life, not once but twice." But you are Maria, so whatever you do is right – it's the will of God, and I do not question it.

'Now, I know that you are a virgin, and you will stay a virgin, because you are Maria. Therefore you could never be pregnant again. That cannot happen. And because I feel very strongly that it cannot happen, I had the doctors make sure it cannot happen – at considerable risk to myself. Now, an ordinary person might say, "Thank you, Anselm. I can see you've done me an incredible favor." And I hope someday when you understand this better, I will hear that thanks from you.

'The reason you will thank me is that, even after you stand your proof, there is one thing that can make you a false Maria. If you are not a virgin. So please don't give anyone the idea that you aren't a virgin. A false Maria must be killed, and we would all like to relax now. I hope you agree.

'Regrettably, a few people know about this incident. Someday, one of them may talk. If that day comes, I will deny it. It will be my word against theirs, and I will win that contest. Unless – I hope you're listening now – unless I change my mind about you.'

'Nay.' I shake my head, unnerve. 'They doctors doing what?'

Anselm sigh out heavy. 'It's a tiny piece of metal. In a day or two, you won't even feel it.'

'Metal?' I startle cold. Touch to the cloth against my belly. 'Inside myself?'

'It won't do you any harm. It's very small.'

I grip the lacen cloth. Look scary to the picture, enfant reaching to his mother. Get a troubling feeling, if these golden circles mean they dead. 'Cannot get no enfants?'

'That's what I'm telling you.'

'But can this fix?'

'It can. But it won't.'

I shake my head again. 'Nay, why you want to ruin me so?'

'I just told you. Senyora, were you listening?'

'Yo I know. You saying.' I try to figure reasons, but all my mind be on this artifact. Little piece of metal, some unperson thing inside. Yo if we leave this place, is done. Never I going to fix, ain't even Lowells know this stranger science.

Anselm say, soft in my thought, 'You won't appreciate this, but we risked a great deal ourselves by doing this. It's a very serious crime here.'

I take a ragged breath. 'Preventing enfants, right. Seriose crime you do to me, first day I come.'

'I promise, this is not how we usually welcome visitors to Marias.'

'And now you know I got this thing, you kill me any time you like. What you saying.'

'I'm sorry. I wish I trusted you to make your own decisions. But I don't.'

'Damn, what you even want from me?'

'I want this city to be run responsibly. You can't do it. You don't know anything. You cannot make the decisions you need to make. And, as of this moment, you are – in name – the ultimate power here.' He make a narrow smile. 'Another problem that's been solved. Thank you, Anselm.'

'Foo, it need no threats. You want to give me help, I heed.'

'That's funny. I seem to remember you didn't listen to my last piece of advice.'

'On Pasha?' I scoff breath. 'Is differences. This been a life.'

'Maria,' he say soft, 'there are four hundred thousand people living in the lands you govern. And if you last with us, you'll see some of those lives lost, through decisions we have to make. Your Russian boyfriend is only a detail from my point of view. I'm sorry.'

Take me thinking time to even comprehend this speech. Then I want to cavil – say I never care to rule this city – but my conscience stray to Quantico, and every hope be rotten.

I look back sorry at that enfant picture, and Anselm frown. He turn and look himself. Huff breath and say, 'Well, that's unfortunate.' Then he reach and poke a button. The elevator shift again.

I feel some sick relief. 'We finish, ya? Can see my children?'

'Soon.' Anselm sigh. 'But you have a ceremony first. It's the signing of the clause, to reinstate our glorious apostles. So – if it's not too rude to ask – I do hope you can write?'

42

THE PARLEY FOR MY WAR

Ceremony be in trono room, a hall enorme. Got ceiling painten rich with blue and clouds and flying enfants. Be flower trees in silver jars, make rows along the tallish walls. Between this, all the floor be empty – dapple tile and nothing. Only is one goliath chair, of carven gold and gems.

This be Maria's trono, where I sit in tall discomfort. Apostles kneel below, still in their silvern garb of proof. Robes wash on the tiles around, look like they spilt somehow. Ya, Anselm spilt along, in duller brown.

They start by chanting unison, a Panish prayer of endlessness. Through this, I feel a lonely conscience, how my children wait above in my iglesia rooms – Driver and El Mayor; my Keepers Eight in noise familiar. All my hurt insist toward them, as the Panish moan, the painten enfants flirt their wings above.

I distract the time by finding snake Felipe with my eyes. Want to feel my fear again, like touching a wound to check its pain. But he seem small unconfident, knelt in his silvern wash. Then I seek Simón Zelote – the child in soldier clothes who weep terrific at my questioning. Look and look, but cannot find, until I doubt my wits. But when I count their numbers, be eleven. He ain't there.

Ain't time to wonder this, when Pedro rise up from their line. He carry a slice of whitish papers. Silver pen be lain across. Come toward me, prayering still, and stoop himself as he come close. When I take the papers, the apostles all stand up and hush.

All this signing be, must write my name. Ain't my Ice Cream name, is now 'Maria XXVII, SR de la C. de las Marias'. Name be printen in the signing place, need only copy this. Yo, Anselm said I must make show of reading. This be drill. So I page through with scarce attention, fidgeting the pen – until I spy the line on war.

It read: 'The apostles above named have the power to declare war and to decide the military strategy of Ciudad de las Marias, independently from any other person or body.'

Here I put the pen down sharp. Read the line again-again, until its meaning clear. Then I scout through all the pages, look for other talk of war. Can feel the time prolong, feel the apostles' scalding eyes, while I frown through all longhead words. Ya, be no other mention. Is only this – all war be theirs.

When I look back to them, apostles tired in frustration. Anselm fixing on me mally. Threats watch from his eyes.

'I write my name,' I say, 'then it be done? Your powers keep?'

Anselm say in voice like poison honey, 'That is the point.'

'Then nay. Is something I must ask before.'

A groaning sigh go through them all. Even Pedro grit his face, clutch silver dress in both his hands.

'Please, santa reina,' Anselm say. 'I think you have our full attention.'

I start the parley for my war with tactic carefulness. First, I say how roos maraud in Massa now, steal every child. Tell every evidence I know: the radio speech, the photographs, the guns that Pasha–Deema bring. And I explain the cure its promise – how roos live to seventy years, like sleepers of the past.

Can see from Anselm's eyes that he already heard this news. Pedro look the same, and be some others, though their names forgot. Must figure Soledad told them every fact, this passen night. But snake Felipe stare at me in daze, like all his blood be mysteries. Bright superstitions woken in his eyes.

Yo, when I tell the plan for war with Quantico, they all change tempers. Faces grit misliking. They start frowning each to each. Feel in myself, how Quantico been their yeary enemy. Is like I begging Sengles that they fight for Armies, old in hatred. I hear my voice come beggarish, and I haste to my end. 'So I require a war from you. Must fight the roos from Nighted States and take their useful cure. Hope you agreeing this, for all our lives.'

Be a breath of achen silence. A drop of sweat go anting from my armpit, tickle down.

Then come a barking laugh from Santiago – prettieuse child who worn jeans to my questioning. He say, 'You want us to fight *for* Quantico?'

'Yes.' I hold my face correct. 'How it result, I do.'

'That's hilarious.' He look around. 'Who wants to tell the Marines?'

'Thank you.' Anselm make a narrow smile. 'Would anyone else like to comment?'

Here puppyish Juan speak up, with shyness face. 'But, santa reina, there's no proof. It's only something Jesus told you.'

'No sho.' I scoff my breath. 'Seen other roos. Ya, been the photographs.'

'But, senyora,' Anselm say in helpful voice, 'about the cure, it's only him. And that is the main point.'

'Nay, been the radio speech. Roos offering cure, was said direct.'

Anselm raise a finger. 'And I forget – why didn't you take this generous offer?'

'Was lies,' I say impatient. 'They only wanting us for use.'

'And you knew this how?'

'Ya, Jesus told us. So?'

'Jesus.' Anselm draw a circle in air with finger. 'We are back where we started.'

Now Pedro say, in caring voice, 'Please try to understand, senyora. You're asking us to give our army to Quantico – to our enemies.' He spread his hands like helplessness. 'We can't risk the city's safety

345

on the basis of one stranger's story. Jesus's, of course. I don't mean yours.'

'And the whites aren't coming here,' say Juan. 'If they attack Quantico, that's good for us.'

'Nay, be the cure,' I say annoying. 'Why we need to fight.'

'But please,' Anselm say in, with looks of friendly understanding. 'We can address this to everyone's satisfaction. We'll just send someone east – to your Massa, santa reina.'

A moment, the apostles only frown at him, confusing. Then most their faces ease.

'Send someone to Massa?' I say unbalance. 'How this help?'

Anselm gesture like simplesse. 'It should be easy to find proof. If everything you say is true, we'll find a war in progress.'

'But you find no cure,' I say. 'This going to be in Quantico only.'

'But senyora,' Juan say, his puppy face bright seriose, 'we'd find white men to question. That's what Anselm's thinking. Isn't it?'

'Yes.' Anselm smile to me. 'We'll capture some. It's what we do.'

'That's good,' say Pedro. 'If they all tell the same story, it would give me much more confidence. And if everything else checks out.'

I shake my head. 'Why you ain't go to Quantico direct? When January come, be any thousand roos to ask.'

'Wait,' say Anselm. 'To be clear – right now, there are no roos in Quantico?'

I shoo my hand. 'Been said. Ain't there till January month.'

Anselm nod. 'So if we go to Quantico now, we'll only find . . . Marines. And I don't think they'll be very happy to see us.'

Around the room, be preciating laugh. Bell Santiago muttern, 'It would be pretty funny, till they shot you.'

I say frustrating, 'Shee, can tell them why. Must warn them anyhow.'

'When we're certain, yes.' Anselm knit his hands together. 'But for now, the only way to be certain is to send a party to Massa. If they find this army of white men, if they capture some for questioning – it's a different situation. I hope that's clear?'

Here I notice snake Felipe narrowing on Anselm hard. Now it

come queery to me, Felipe ain't spoken all this time. Child been all mouth the day before.

I take courage up and say, 'Felipe, what you thinking?'

He startle, look down to the floor. Even his silver dress look flustern, like disturbing water. 'I think . . . I'm not sure what this search is for.'

'Weren't you listening?' Anselm say unpleasant. 'I did just explain it twice.'

I say, 'So you believe, Felipe?'

He shrug annoying. 'I don't know.'

'That's what the search is for,' say Anselm. 'So that we can know.'

Felipe look to Anselm cold. 'I'd like to hear who's going, at least.'

Young Juan say up quick, 'I'll go. I'd like to go.'

'So Juan is going?' Felipe say, his eyes still hard on Anselm.

'And Juan will take his guard, I expect,' say Anselm. 'That's twenty men?'

Juan nod with warry looks. 'Twenty-two.'

'And perhaps we could have the penal company?' Anselm smile sharp to Felipe.

Felipe startle, frown his mouth. Before he answer, prettieuse Santiago break in rude, 'The penal company? Why not send real soldiers? Just ask Simón.'

Anselm flinch to this, say thin, 'I'd rather not disturb Simón Zelote right now. So, Felipe?'

'I get it,' Felipe say with some unliking. 'You can have them.'

'So, Juan, his guard, the penal company – that's eighty, altogether.' Anselm look to me. 'Is that acceptable to you, senyora?'

Now my blood be bad with doubts. Ain't comprehending much, but sure can feel, they plan all this before. Most likely be, when Soledad told her story, they begin to plan. Anselm and his friendly apostles figure through the night, decide this search for evidence.

Ain't see how this be differences – can think for hours or think for minutes, still they want their proof. Nor they agree to war without.

But mistrust be loud, is like a stank in every thought. Ya, when I looking to Felipe, all his face morose with hate. He stare on Anselm like he watch some poison insect, wish he got a shoe to crush it.

'Yo, what this penal company be?' I say. 'If they ain't soldiers, what they be?'

'They *are* soldiers,' Pedro say assuring.

'They're criminals.' Santiago laugh. 'They get out of prison to fight in wartime.'

Anselm say, 'The penal company we have now already fought in our last war. So they aren't fresh from prison, senyora. Really, they're like any other soldiers.'

'Traditionally, they're sent to dangerous duties,' Pedro say. 'And this – if you're correct, senyora – is certainly dangerous.'

I doubt around this, but can see no wrong. Sure, what I known of Mariano crimes, these penals can be bone as any.

'Is well enough,' I say at last. 'But I will like to go myself.'

They all get puzzling eyes. Juan say uncertain, 'Go yourself?'

'I go to Massa,' I say clear. 'Can help to find these roos.'

This bring a storm of every nay. It be *unthinkable* and *crazy*. Even Felipe say it be impossible for danger – is funny, when he only try to kill me hours before.

At last, I yell into their noise, 'Bone! But I will send some child my own! Or I ain't sign no clause, can be forgot!'

They hush with various disturbance. Ya, can notice, most these children look to Anselm seeking help.

First moment, Anselm spite his eyes. Pluck his brownish dress like clothes themself be an exasperation. But soon his face go mild again. Can see, he find a better thought.

'That's actually a good idea,' he say. 'Your people know the region. Send whoever you like, senyora. It's nice that you want to participate. And now that that's all settled, can we get back to our original purpose?'

He look suggesting to the clausen papers on my knees. Then all apostles perk themself, like hounds who smell their meal.

I stare a moment, lost in doubts. Think how it can be, if I demand the war begin, before I sign their mally clause. But if these fool apostles do their search, they learn the cure be real. Then sure, all other plans be by. They need this cure like any person. Ever they be reptiles, ain't no reptile glad to die.

Murder dress feel sticky now, is itching on my sweaten back. Yo, the windless silence ache. Everything be tight and wrong. But I take the pen in feeble hand, fish out the signing page. And I look down, seek my new name.

43

SIMÓN AND THE MARIA GONE

Ain't heed how the apostles leave. Their stoopings pass in corner-eye, their Panish mutters pass. Light flutter in the glassen door as it come open–shut.

Then only Anselm stand below my chair, the clause glad in his hand.

'I must congratulate you,' he say. 'That was genuinely exciting.'

Some time, I only trace my finger on the chairy arm. Got shape of golden pigeon that sink claws into a golden heart. Eyes be bluish gems, stare no expression to the lectric light.

At last, I look to Anselm tired. 'How long this hunt for roos can take?'

'Not long. Ten days, perhaps. They can take trucks out to where the road ends. And then they'll pick up horses.'

'Shoo, ain't known you keeping horses. Seen no horses there.'

'But *your* horses are there.' Anselm make his mischief smile. 'I'm sorry, senyora, it wasn't possible to bring them back so quickly. And as you see, it was lucky, after all.'

'Lucky,' I say short, 'if you ain't plan this all before.'

'Oh, are we being honest now? That's nice.' He stretch with catly satisfaction. 'Senyora, may I sit? It's not correct form, but I'm actually tired after that.'

'Sure can sit. You want this chair?'

He laugh soft. 'Oh, no. Far too symbolic.'

He settle frogleg on the tilen floor without no circumstance. Set the papers on his knees, start shuffling through with gratty smile. Truth, I get relief myself, now all apostles gone. After all their strangeness, Anselm feeling mostly like a friend.

I say, 'Can ask you something, Anselm?'

'You have a voice, and I have ears.' He fish out my signing page and laugh. 'Oh, look. Your handwriting. Oh, no.'

'Heed, where Simón Zelote been?'

He set the papers down. Look to the flying children on the ceiling, mourning eyes, like they commiserate his always problems. 'Well, she notices things,' he say in underbreath. 'She isn't stupid.'

'Going to notice. And when you said you ain't disturb Simón Zelote. What this been?'

'Well, Simón is our ranking general. So if we sent regular soldiers on this search, we'd have to ask him. And *that* would disturb him.'

'Then how the penals be Felipe's, if they soldiers also?'

'The prison is in his burrow – it's really a bureaucratic detail, santa reina. Not interesting.'

'But why Simón Zelote ain't been here?'

Anselm sigh. 'Okay. But this will be your final lesson of the day. I am really tired beyond words. So, perhaps you noticed Simón crying yesterday?'

'Sure.' I shrug. 'Was weeping like a messy two. Be weirdo generals.'

'This is something you can probably understand. Maria often has a favorite apostle. We call this a Joseph. Does that suggest anything to you?'

'Nay. Be nothing helpful.'

'I think we're past the point of mincing words. Simón was the lover of the last Maria. Repeat that wherever you like, it makes no difference now. Which is a great relief.'

Almost, I ask if this Maria got device preventing enfants. If Anselm rule her so, with maudy threats. But now my anger tired.

'So she sicken bad.' I shrug. 'Why he going to sorrow.'

'It's more than that. You see, when there's a new Maria, the former Maria doesn't just leave her place. She gracefully departs from life.' He flutter his hand toward the cloudy ceiling.

'Depart from life. She kill herself?'

'Thank you. You understand.'

'Nay, why she doing this?'

'Well, usually for religious reasons. We don't like to have two living gods. In fact, we dislike it so much, her suicide isn't always strictly voluntary. But in this special case – although very few people know this – Maria died three days ago.'

Still be puzzling on this *voluntary*, when his last words come plain. 'She dead?'

'Yes. That's something you should *not* repeat. There must always be a Maria – every second of every day. If Maria is dead, there is no god. And worse, there is no government.' Anselm narrow eyes. 'Of course, Felipe wanted to go on pretending the last Maria was still alive. He didn't want a real god, unless he had chosen her himself.

'But happily, that's behind us now. Tonight, you'll hear the bells ringing to announce her death – and there the crisis ends.'

Be worrying this when something inkle doubtful in my mind. Is from what Pasha saying yesternight, about the Jesus whites. How rich people buying them, to keep until Maria sicken. Then they choose some girl obedient, give her Christ to use.

But now they got no roos in storage. If Anselm kill myself, can be no proof, and no Maria new. I pick around this, working thoughts, while Anselm square the clause in hands. Stand weary to his feet.

Then my mind focus sudden. I break into precarious laugh. 'Goddamn! You catching Christs in Massa! What you needing there. Yo weasel!'

He give unshaming smile. 'Well, I suppose we will, senyora.'

'All Pedro's shee, goddamn! They even questioning these roos?'

'Of course, the questioning is real. We have two reasons for the search. At least two.'

'But then you choose a new Maria, ya? And I depart from life.'

'Not at all, santa reina. We often keep these Christs for years. And I don't want to kill you at all. I think it would give me bad dreams.' He make regretful smile. 'Still, we need the option.'

Then he regard me curiose while I regard him back. I try to read some meaning in his face, but be no use. Feel like I stare into a light and only hurt my eyes.

At last he say, 'Now, before I go, I have a question of my own. Just something I've been wondering as we talked. That baby of yours – I don't suppose it was Jesus's?'

This startle through my tired nerves. 'No sho, it ain't.'

He nod with comfort smile. 'Then, santa reina, I have a request. On this search, please send the boyfriend. The father, whoever it is. The situation with the last Maria, with Simón – it wasn't ideal.'

'Foo, ain't your trouble, who I send.' A superstition creep my skin.

He nay his finger, smiling sweet. 'Everything is my trouble. So you'll send the father, please. Now, do enjoy the rest of your day. The guards will see you into your elevator. I'm sorry, I will get you that key.'

Then he cross to the door with easy gladness in his motion. Door swing brightening and release its light.

44

MY WORST APOSTLE MET

In the elevator, I lean nervy to the wall, guess how my iglesia rooms will be. If my children hide there still, and how I bear to see the NewKing. How I bear Soledad. If Pasha be there yet, and if he learning any telligence.

Doors open soft, and I step out. Be dandelion lights and ruggen hallways, hush in all directions. Painten sleepers look sad from their frames like they beg freedom self. Yo soon, I recognize this place. Is where me–Pasha spent our yesternight in feary wait. This be the hall where I been draggen out, its quiet light the same.

First door I seeing be the sleeproom, where I woken with the roo. Is parten on a dull unlight. I go to scout inside.

On the grandiose bed, El Mayor lain, sleeping loose. Wear clothes is mostly normal, churching suit with whiten shirt. First Runner curlen by his feet in Marias finery gown – a fall of washen pink, look queery on this child austere.

Then my spirit catch in teeth. I hold in perilous thought.

El Mayor been obvious choices for the Massa search. I send him, I be sending my best eyes. Child smart as books.

But sure, if Anselm want to rid him, El Mayor be rid entire. Could ask him neverless, with proper warning of his risk – but when I think of doing this, my heart go false. Cannot. Nor I be brave to tell him on the enfant, how it murdern. Gone vally to my death, but I be weak to say no hurt.

I step back superstitious from this door. Go on, with sad excuses in my mind.

I come next to the sofa room, without no clear intention. Room empty of no people, but its doors be open to the outside porch. A knifen breeze come in. Yo, through the glassen doors, can see a child outside, is bigly made.

He show in profile, and the glitter sun confuse his face. But his hair be croppen like a Sengle's, rough correct. I step to the doorway gratty, drawing breath for Driver's name.

Then he startle to me, and is Crow.

He wearing Mariano clothes – a churching suit of perfect black – but all his skin look tired from weather. Eyes be red like hurt. Yo, he wear the marks of godscars in his cheeks, still purplish raw. And I recall Karim. How his hands guard to his face, want desperate to save himself. I see Crow's godscars like an injury left by this bad killing.

Almost, I turn away. But Crow's hurt eyes catch to my guilt. And I step out to the fearing cold. Watch Crow's deep-known face, the unchin jaw and lashy eyes. And Crow be watching with no comfort, stare like I be no one.

I say soft, 'Salue, my Crow.'

'Salue.' He duck his head in nerves.

'Be sorry for your feathers,' I say weaker. 'How . . . they shot.'

He shrug like this be stupid mentions. 'You save me, I guess.'

'Ya, and I be gratty for that leaf you sent. Your warning.'

He grit closer now. His face look mostly like denials, like he going to say it been no leaf. But he say, 'Ain't guess you want no warning.'

'How I ain't?'

'Thought you come to Mamadou yourself.'

Go guilty in my heart, but I say quick, 'Nay, why I go to him?'

Crow laugh undervoice. 'You be his queen. Ain't remember to you?'

355

'He keeping that?'

'Yo sho, he keep it.' Crow laugh pitchy, rub his mouth. 'Got some resentment, I ain't know.'

'Ain't chase us all that way for this, I hope.'

Crow's laughter pass like it ain't been. He look back to the raily edge. 'Nay. Ain't for this.'

I follow his eyes out to the tower buildings, a jaggen crowd of gray. By sunlight, can see they ill bekept. Windows mostly gone, is moss along their stain concree.

I say unhappy, 'Mamadou told they others, how I be his queen? Told Driver?'

To this, Crow's eyes disgust. 'Nay, he ain't talking much, himself. Can keep your prettieuse lies.'

'Lies? Nay, what this going to mean?'

'Be all you caring for, that Ice Cream keep in admiration.'

I startle ugly. 'What this be? Nay, how you always be so vicious?'

'Only be saying how you do. Is how you be, but you ain't never seeing, Ice Cream God.'

'God? You lost your final brains?'

'You god here, what I heard. Heard all this story. How you save the roo.'

'Truth, ain't kill him. And I save yourself. And so?'

Crow turn outrage eyes to me. 'How he precieuse? He killing us. He kill us glad.'

I take a ragged breath. 'Karim, you meaning?'

'Yo sho.' His face go twisten. 'I kill your roo. Want only chances.'

'Roo come to save my life at Army camp. Ain't been–'

'And what you come there for? Shee, save your life! No person murder you!'

'I been there for the Christings, damn! And Deema trying – nay, you wrong. You wrong.'

'But why Karim must die for this?' Crow raise a sudden fist. 'Roo kilt him why?'

'Ain't Pasha–' Then I catch my voice. Brace in the freezing wind, and Crow's eyes fix on me, is agonies. And it realize, he ain't know I ask for Karim his death. Know nothing.

I say, with falseness burning in my chest, 'Pasha, he had no time to think. Was seconds.'

'But why the roo be living still?' Crow's voice break high. 'Why he ain't dead?'

'Damn, he ain't known! He seen me hurt, and shoot. Ain't be his blame!'

Crow stare through a breath of rage. Then he say rough, 'Ain't going to kill your roo, ain't fear. Keep all your filthen males, you safe.'

'My males? Goddamn–'

'I wish I never send that leaf! Shee for yourself! You poison!'

'And what that leaf been even for? If they ain't come to steal me?'

'Mamadou going to steal you! Shee!'

'You said, the Armies ain't been there for me. You only said!'

Crow open his mouth, but bite down on his words. He look back to the city. 'We coming . . . ain't for that. But Mamadou thinking, if he get you, you will speak for him.'

'Speak for him?'

'Ya. Be yourself, he thought they others heed.'

'What I will speak?'

Crow frown, his eyes gone blank. Raise one hand toward his face, like seeking to take some troubling thought away from there. Say with scarcely breath, 'Ask them to war.'

'War?'

Crow start to speak, but then his face go wrong. He breathe out hard.

A coldness inkle in my heart. 'To roos? He warring to the roos?'

Crow nod and gesture with one hand, like waving at some knowledge. Eyes spark in sudden tears.

'Crow, what been? Why – what the roos done?'

'We the only people left,' Crow say in strangle voice. 'What they done. Roos kill them all.'

Then he begin his story, on this lofty edge of nothing, where dead towers watch their broken eyes. Wind suffer in my flesh and beat my braids against my naked shoulders, while Crow tell the final memories from our Massa woods.

45

THE ROOS IN MASSA WOODS

'That Deema told what going to be.' So Crow begin his tale. 'Always been telling, if we hurt him, roos kill us with every torture. He *love* to tell us stories, what they do. So, how he dead . . . ain't nothing change to eyes. But every person known.

'What Mamadou want, we hide. Ain't wait in camp like easy bait. But half they feathers never heed. OldKing Hak, ya any person close to him, ain't heed. How they saying, Mamadou turn coward since he shot. They choose a different NewKing, call him digger, worm, all that.

'Can know, they people dead. They all be dead.'

Been seven feathers, ya and Crow, who leave with Mamadou. Go with vindictions from their people, go with only carrying goods, and stash themself into an evac in the wrecks of Lowell City. Building be six floors of decay walls and unglass windows. Been left by even mice and birds, its only life be rot. In this unlucky home, they make a camp with sheepskin rugs. Set their carven gods around, and blacken the mouldy ceilings with the fire of sacrifice.

Then all they do, they scout for roos. Go seek the woods, the broken city; haunt the ash of Tophet gone. Creep superstitious by Lowell mill, that lost its noisy hundreds. Lectricity dark, its turbines hush – but on the walls be always dozen children waring out with guns. Worst strangeness, these be often Christwives. Yo, how the feathers learn, these wives will shoot at any moving life.

Crow tell me: 'We been in this evac, I ain't know. Two weeks. Nay, I ain't knowing days. Time it finish, all they feathers do, they booze and fight. Beat myself, you know that. And Mamadou healing, but he changen. Ain't want no one talking to him. Always staring like he hate. But how it been, you only seen him, and you known he going to live. Who stay by him, can live.

'Yo, all that hunting that we do, we never seen the roos. Seen nothing till the plane.'

Time the plane appear, been middy meal. The NewKing's feathers sitting to a corny stew. They telling dreams, like Armies do, and gray Yusuf make joking prophecies from these stories. Day risen clean, the buildings all be fuzzy bright with sun.

First knowledge been a deafen scouring. It grow impossible, be loud like nothing that belong in life. Noise tremble in the walls, ring in their skulls, buzz wrong in flesh. Feathers go sprinting to the windows, screaming fear unheard. Expect to see the sky torn end to end, a hell of lightnings. But all been blue and simple, while the noise grow past no bearing. Be like some invisible monster crush the world entire.

When they spy the rooish plane, it seem a petty detail. Ain't even move its wings. Is still. Fly like an object thrown, and cannot feel how all the noise come from its posing tininess.

It go as quick as bats, and score the blue with whitish smoke. And it come around, bring its goliath noise again. When it fly toward the Armies, they all duck, go flailing down. But when the sound retreat, they rise. Lean out again with showing courage. Musa fire his pistol at it, but be stupid helplessness, like shooting at a cloud.

Then in the farther city, rise a trembling light against the day. A deeper thunder follow, shuddering in the planken floor. Yo, when the plane pass round again, can notice petty sheddings falling underneath its body, like it drop its shee below. Brightness waken from this shee, that thunder loosen out. And they understand, is bombs. Stuff from fable histories, is happening now in sight.

Ya, as they comprehend, the plane turn off, like losing interest. Some time its noise go weaker, before the hush close sudden in.

On the bland horizon, is left a leaning trunk of smoke. Keep sturdy white, and spread its haze into the morning clear. Ain't no sound from this. Can only hear the normal flies that bother their forgotten meal.

'So all they fools talk big, you know how. Want to join the roos again, like they each getting planes from this. Sure, no one going to say they frighten. Bombs been *wolfen*. *Cool*. The other feathers left in camp, *they* frighten. Shee they going to talk.

'Then Mamadou tell them to go scout. Wish you seen, how they change. They pissing terrify. Run off, but I ain't guess they scouting much. Hiding, be more like.

'Yo, Mamadou send me separate with Malik to find the bombing place. Ain't lying – if Malik ain't been, I gone to hide myself. Keep thinking, bomb been poison. Ain't want to breathe.

'So anyone known, this been the mill. There in the city, ain't be nothing else. So we gone there.'

Been twenty minutes walking, and they pass this in a boding silence. Both be walking jittery, checking to the sky for planes. Yo, as they come, the air go thick. Be stinging dust that blow about, must squint to almost blindness. It got a teasing warm that fickle and vanish in the wind. A weirdo pue begin, is teary sharp like onion smell, as they come to the mill canal.

The mill be gone. Where it risen tall and large, is smoke and empty sky.

This goneness take them both in spooking. Be a moment, Crow decide this ain't the place, they stray somewhere. But the water recognize, glut with dust and rubble as it be. Ya, in changes of the breeze, Crow see a piece of house wall left, a set of broken windows. In one, is curtains moving, dabble across the jaggen shapes of glass.

Fire freak bright among. In the water, be mounds of brick, with splinter wood stuck out in points. By one of these, a yellow shirten shape float in the cloudy water. Crow cannot tell if this be someone drown or only empty clothes.

Beyond this, cannot see no people. Be no crying voice. Can only hear the trampling noise of fire, its crackle. Their own short breath.

Without no word, they start to skirt the mill upwind. Come past a city building that been hit, its upper part collapse. Here the air be dull with smoke, must pull shirts over mouths. Then, along the mill side, can see the wreck of easter gate. Its bridge be broken off halfway, precarious in air.

On this bridgen edge stand small First Runner. Her face be sparkling blood.

Malik see his sister, and he yell. Go sprinting, leaping wreckage. Come to the gate and scramble up its ruin. Some bricks kick out from underfoot, and he slip clumsy as First Runner turn and run to him. He catch her in his arms, and as he lift her, she begin to wail. Crow stop below and stare up with no notion what he do. Is only scary from this wail. He want to run away and never learn no farther knowledge.

Then Malik turn back, skid down an avalanche of brick. As he release First Runner down, Crow see the scarlet glittering spread across her cheek. Is blood and glass. All her clothes be wet and various red with blood and brick dust.

Then she start telling, loud and strange, be people in this ruin. They all was screaming. She try to swim across, but it be burning still. Been too hot. Water itself been hot. She talk on, garbling, how it been some roos, she watch these from a window by. Been fifty roos, ain't guess how many. Lowell guards fire shots at them, been shooting backen forth. But these roos run off, is gone. Then come the plane, the bombs, she been thrown down.

And she begin again to say, how people be in there. Must help them, but it still be burning. She say these contradictions, until Crow shout at her in nerves. Then First Runner hush, touch to her bloody face in puzzle. Ain't seem to even notice when Malik grip to her hand.

Malik say soft, 'They kilt, my sister.'

'I know,' First Runner say with fixen stare. 'We got to help them.'

But when they turn away, First Runner come without no cavil. Start to pick glass from her face as they pass to the normal day, where all the buildings whole and stupid-looking with their blank unhurt.

When they come back to their evac, it be no one there. Malik clean down First Runner's cuts, using his knife to pick some deeper splinters from her skin. She hold careful without tears. Only shut her eyes sometimes, take breath. Ya, Crow gone standing to the window, watch the smoke from Lowell mill, when steps sound on the stairs.

Mamadou come in alone. Is wrapping his arm back to himself, been washing it below. His face be tired from pain, and he look to First Runner cold with no surprise.

Malik explain, this be his sister. Say how the mill be gone, and he repeat First Runner's sayings, how she seen the roos, been shooting. How they all was screaming. Crow add nervy in, 'It been no voices when we come.'

Mamadou finish with his arm and pin the bandage to. Say easy, 'I remember her.'

Then he kneel down by First Runner. She sit dazen, trace her fingers through a sheepskin rug. And Mamadou ask her quiet, if she been keeping watch for El Mayor. She nod to this, but never look. Stare on her working fingers.

'Sure you meant to follow them,' the NewKing say like logic.

She glance toward Malik, look back at Mamadou with blank mistrust.

Mamadou say soft, 'Yo, where they gone?'

Here the other feathers run up noisy on the stairs. Come in with all their talk, kick round their goods, seek for some booze. But soon they hush, come staring at First Runner and the NewKing, where they matching stubborn looks.

'Where they gone?' say Mamadou.

First Runner say with sudden hatred, 'Cannot tell you. Got instructions.' Her blooden face gone in its sweat, hand gripping in the sheepskin fur. Malik stand tense behind, look feary from the NewKing to his sister. Ya, all the feathers watching, from wherever they fetch up.

'Nay, you going to tell,' say Mamadou, like he giving news.

'Is threats?' she say in breathless voice. 'This do you nothing. Cannot tell.'

'Ain't threats. I known you from an enfant, how I know. Guess I remember you better than you remember me.'

She frown to the sheepskin, grit her mouth. 'You ain't know me.'

But Mamadou stand away, uncaring. And he tell the feathers that they leaving Massa woods, will follow after the people gone.

Crow tell me: 'Sure, he got some plan. Been planning every days for this. But how he never saying what it be . . . ain't plans we going to like.

'But all they feathers *run* to do his word. Ain't think for nothing. Pack their goods, and talking like . . . like every Massa *townie* now. Like Lowells going to *want* themself. Ain't even wonder how we going to find they other Massas. Mamadou said, and all it is.

'But sure, I gone with them. Ain't staying there alone, no sho.'

Where the NewKing lead them first, been to the Armies' horsen field. Was dusking, and they scout into the woods with nervy dread. Been days since no one seen the other Armies. Cannot guess their moods. Ya, anyone expect, the horses guarding in these risky days. Or can be, those Armies gone. Be roos who wait in ambush.

But they find the horses normal, tether to dragging logs. No child be by, no threat. They mount, and Mamadou lead them down the path to Army camp. All wonder why he take them to this risk, but no one brave to ask. So they follow through these woods they know, into the dusty grass, the huts still standing where they been, and past where Yas and Bardo lie unmoving in their blood. Past Peter Christing-born, and startle a fox is chewing Peter's guts. Ride past a gut-shot hound, is staring blind into the sky, and Mamadou rein his horse before the simper house. He unmount clumsy with his one good arm.

Been only Crow and Musa gone with Mamadou into the house. And, like they known it going to be, all people kilt inside. Musa go hunting through the bodies, find his enfant Faisal. Crouch and chase the green flies from his face and cry some strangle noise. Can hear another feather puking miseries outside.

Mamadou watch on this with face besweaten. He skinny from his sickness, and his face look skullish dread. He look like he belong to this hell unworld. Can see he known what he will find; he seen this in his hatred dreams, these days. And he stand there with his starving looks, the king of these red children. King of flies and murder.

Crow go out again, ain't want to bear this. Come and take his horse's reins from Malik, who stand bewept and strange. Ya, First Runner sit her horse beweepen. She say to Crow, 'Be Gosha dead?' He know no Gosha, but he say, 'They dead.'

Then Mamadou come out. He walk straight to First Runner and polite her with her Lowell name. Is speaking soft, though his face still besweaten, eyes feroce. He say, 'Can fight roos with a hundred, but I cannot fight with eight. I know you gone to Lowells, but you be our child. You strong. Now tell me where they others gone. We going to make this right.'

And in these farther days, following on the highway in our chase, all feathers come into belief, they bring war to the roos. Nights, they burning sacrifice to Shango god, and swear this war. Journey been terrify and strange, was watching for roos with every step. They watch the sky their enemy, wake to each sound in nighten woods.

Ya, they live among their ghosts of feathers and of slaves, until they feeling like a troop of dead, bound in revenge for their own killing.

And when Marias soldiers took them, Yusuf object in voice. Yell frustration how they must be free, they going to war. He keep on swearing though these strangers never comprehend. But Crow been glad in capture, feel they save from their insanity – until they taken to that Citgo wall, and Yusuf yelling weak annoyance, and some boy shoot Yusuf cold.

Then it going like I know – Crow and Mamadou kept apart, the other feathers shot and shot. Nat Mass Armies finish in easy minutes. And all this night behind, Crow think, if Pasha never kilt Karim, Karim come to this wall, will die the same. And Crow only wonder, how no child surviving ever – how he live no sixteen years, when every day can be a gun, a moment's anger. Live these years, and still remain, unwanten, like a punishment. Crow condemn to stay in this world, naked from no covering earth, this world where no good child belong.

46

THE GUNROOM TALK

So Crow tell his story, standing on this porch above the murmuring city of Marias, while the Vember cold grip in my flesh. When he finish, we look east, like we can see the Massa woods from here. Like it will come back to our wishing, how it ever been. And, senseless, I remember a day when Crow and me and Hate You gone for bait worms in a brook by Tophet. How we watch the Christings' grandy house and plan to steal some cider. Hate You creep toward the barn in bravery, but a mule bray loud, and she come scrambling back in tears. When we was sixes, new to life.

Then, in darkness of my feeling, I remind Susannah's face, the day we left from Lowell mill. Her eyes still scary from her rape; her soft bellesse been like a showing wound. And all the Christing littles by – enfants that I save from fire, to live for petty weeks. To scream and die in different fires.

A wolfen sadness chill me. I look at Crow and feel a freezing in my bones like heartbreak.

Crow grip his hands in fists. Frown to them like he wonder at their life, that they can feel and move. Then he loose his hands, say low, 'He want to talk to you. The NewKing.'

'Nay, why?' I take a narrow breath.

'I ain't know.' Crow shrug resenting. 'Ever he want.'

'He wanting me to speak for war somehow? To children here?'

'Ain't wondering this. Shee his wars.' Crow squint back to the city. Can see his old hostilities begin, his shoulders tense.

I look to the farther sky. Be thinking sorry, be no sense to see the NewKing now. Got better troubles than himself – my war, the search to Massa woods. But here a notion pinch.

Be on the search to Massa, how I fearing to send El Mayor. But who must go, be Mamadou. Is obvious like eyesight. Be dangers natural to himself; be wars he want himself. And it be like a grief I always known, and struggle to forget.

Then Crow say, low into my thought, 'I going now. Guess I find Driver.'

This name distract my feeling. I look to Crow in quick relief – expect somehow, I go with him. We sit by Driver for some easy time, all maladies apart.

But Crow ain't even look to me. Turn hasty to the door.

I take a breath jalouse and say, 'You know he callen dead? Our – our good child be?'

Crow catch on this. Look back to me, hate brilliant in his eyes. 'Shee, I ain't Sengle now. Can leave your rules. Be dead myself.'

Then he stalk off into the gleam iglesia. Pass a door, and in a second's breath, he lost entire. Even his footsteps vanish, swallow in all rugs and walls. Leave only a mally wish, a misery where he always gone.

A minute behind, I go myself. Come through the sofa room and feel some fear to be alone. Be thinking of my Pasha's tales of crimes he done. How these crimes been real sometime. Was done to children like the Christings, like the simpers and their enfants.

Pasha been right that I should kill him. Crow be right, was selfishness that I ain't want my Pasha dead. And I should die for green Karim. Yo, the feather slavers – how Soledad shooting them, was sunlight justice. But Soledad should die for this, been murder neverless. And I cannot see how any child can be forgiven. I try to think of people who hurt no one, but cannot see them different. Circumstances be, they find the evil that they do.

In the hall, I find the tennish ermana with the jutting ears. She got a filler pen in hand, is drawing on her fingernails. When she see me, she startle back. Muttern *santa reina*, and slip the pen into some pocket in her browndress clothes.

'Salue,' I say. 'You needing something?'

She nod with confusen look. 'I wait for you. Brought your key.'

'Key for . . . elevator, ya?'

'Elevator.' She flash a gaptooth smile, hold out the key. Her fingernails got hearten shapes upon, in shaky blue. I take the key, warm from her palm.

Then she say whispern, 'Santa reina, downstairs wanted me to say . . . we English for you.'

'English?'

'Was always spaniels Maria, it's everybody says you're different. See, you know what spaniels is?'

This baffle in my sorry nerves. I only shake my head.

'Spaniel, that means Spanish. Rich. Apostles, they's all spaniels. But most people here, we're English. Working people is. The spaniels, they don't want no English Maria. Braw, no. But we're for you, they . . . the kitchen people and downstairs, they told me I should say. I'm sorry if it's wrong.'

'Nay, be no wrong. Ain't comprehending much, but you be bone.'

'Comprehend? Oh, sorry, cause I'm Loisaida people, so I talk so bad. I'm sorry.' She hang back, smiling anxy, clutching hands into her dress.

Then I get a different thought. Say low in courtesy, 'What be your name, my ten?'

She scratch her forehead, shy. 'Tamara.'

'Bone, Tamara. Can do some help for me?'

'Yes, santa reina. Course.'

'Be gratty. You know Mamadou? Apostle so.'

'No, please. Don't know.'

'Be a bigly jones, scar cheeks. Got his arm bound up.' I cock my arm against myself.

To this, her eyes go frighten. I say, 'You know him, right. He be here?'

She shake her head unready. 'Santa reina, please. He left.'

I startle. 'How, he gone?'

'Gone outside.' She point the windows. 'Next house, the firing range there.'

'Next house? Foo, they allowing him outside?'

'Course.' She shrug like obvious questions. 'Do what he likes. He's an apostle. But, I should bring you?'

A moment, I only clutch the key in my besweaten hand. Then I say in narrow breath, 'Be gratty, Tamara. Guess this can be right.'

Where she take me, be some walk along the outer street. Four redcoat guards come worrying along, and I distract my nerves by asking them their names. They pronounce these with delighting shyness. Yo I notice – what I scarcely heeding in my early fears – two sky towers, taller than no heights I ever seen. These got no normal walls. Is made entire of darkish windows. Glass be mostly shattern, and it look like their tremendous skin been eaten rough by moths.

House where Mamadou gone be like a smaller Ministerio. Is flights of whitish stone, with carvings fancifying its big door. On its lower floors, the windows gone and blind. Replace with brick. Coppery letters on its front read: *Cuartel de la Defensa, Brigada Municipal del Barrio Quinta*.

We come into a grandy room, got nothing in itself but doors. Is muffle banging in the walls, like someone hammer nails. Some browncoat soldiers there be smoking, leaning careless to a wall. When they see myself, they straighten frightening. Tamara call some Panish, and one soldier skit toward a door.

When he opening this door, the hammering come ferocious loud. Be guns. I think in sudden fright, they shooting Mamadou there. But when I check Tamara's face, she got exciting smile. Skree breathless through the larm, 'He's there, senyora. You can see.'

Then my comprehending quit. Cannot guess what morons hunt with guns inside some house. May be rats they kill, but no considerate child chase these with bullets. Ain't surprises they lose all their windows.

Soldier by the door go yell. In second's change, the gunfire hush. Then come any-number soldiers from the open door. All stare on me with biggen eyes and muttern *santa reinas*. Point rifles to the ceiling as they gather to the wall.

At last, the soldier by the door call Panish back to us.

Tamara turn to me. 'Senyora, can apostle Mamadou keep his gun? Man's asking.'

'Shoo, he got a gun?'

'Course.' She get amusing grin. 'Here's the firing range. But he can keep it?'

'Sure, can keep it,' I say wondering.

'Then good.' Tamara stoop her courtesy. 'He's there.'

Gunroom be untold in length, and empty of no furnitures. Floor littern with spent bullet shells, look strawly in their scatter. On the farther wall, be grandy paper drawings hung – pictures of children, sketchen plain, and all been shot some dozen times. In other circumstance, can laugh, what nasty fool invent this game. But in the middle room is Mamadou.

He wearing his same clothes from Massa woods, jeans and unwritten tee. They dirty with their use, and loose upon his thinner body. Right arm unbound, but still he got a bandage thick beneath his shirt. Pistol held in this right hand. Hand smart as ever been, although his arm hold careful, stiff. Yo, even in his injury, in grimness of his children lost, he bell like hungry night.

Ain't neither of us say no greeting. I only turn and close the door, heart snatching in my chest. Think how I be his queen – and how I lain, confuse, while Pasha shoot him. How I approve the killing of Karim, and if he heard or known. Yo, as the door come shut, my belly pinch, sharp like a hating word. And it realize cold, this murdern baby can be his. Enfant can be Mamadou's get, from the killing morning of roo Deema, of Karim.

When I turn back from the door, he got his pistol in his belt. Hand touching on his bandage, but his face be cold the same.

'NewKing,' I say, 'I got an ask.'

He narrow mouth but say no word. His eyes drift to my naked shoulders. Study there, and thinking gather in his tired eyes.

I say on hasty, 'How it is. This city in my ruling now. So, how I decide, we going to war upon the roos.'

His face shift slightish to this, like he taste its meaning in his mouth. He say low, 'Been easy done.'

'Ain't done,' I say annoying. 'Why I being here.'

'Heard no ask.' He look back to my face.

'Yo, how it is.' I take a breath. 'The children here ain't trust the cure without no evidence. Nor they will fight unless it be. So they send a search to Massa. Catch some roos for questioning.'

His eyes light into mockery. 'They trust some roos before yourself?'

'Be my roo they ain't believe. Guess they ask various roos, be different. Or they plan to torture them. Ain't know their vicious thoughts. I only want to ask, if you will go.'

Then all telligence vanish from his eyes. Is only blackness grief.

My heart make smaller fist. Can feel, I been a fool, I ain't expect this. What Massa being now, no person strong to see again.

I say, 'Ain't got to go. Can send–'

'I do it.'

We watch each other careful then. He got hazard looks, like he may break in sudden rage. Yo, I can feel my body's blood, its knowing.

I swallow at my achen throat. 'Ain't answer yet. Be other matters.'

'I do it. Be no questions.'

'Damn, ain't heard.'

His hand move sharp down to the gun, like he will shoot me for annoyance. But he only say, 'So tell your matters.'

'What it is. Can be, they want to kill you.'

Then his body ease. He laugh in underbreath. 'I knowing this.' He shake his head, like wondering how no child miss obvious facts. Look to my dress again, and say like carelessness, 'I do it. But I can like to bring some child my own.'

'Guess they allowing this,' I say uncertain. 'You bring Crow?'

'Crow, can be.' He shrug. 'First Runner, who I mostly want.'

First, I think this be some joke. Ain't bringing smallish girls for his protection, be no sense. But Mamadou waiting simple, like this been some sane requirement.

'Shee,' I say. 'Been worse enough, they Lowells left her there. How every fool use tens for their war business, ain't believe.'

He shake his head. 'You ask her.'

'Child be ten. Ain't bringing her to that.'

'Got reasons.'

'Reasons how?'

'Nay, Sengle.' Mamadou smile insulting. 'Ask her.'

Now I exasperate for truth. I frown past him toward the drawings – outline pictures with no face, torn various with holes. The Citgo murders flash in mind, First Runner weeping in the dirt. How she duck her scabben face, stare empty to her hands.

Then my anger weaken to a bitter pointlessness. Can guess, whatever arrogance he believe, First Runner never go. Nor El Mayor approve. Be squabbling over fantasies.

'Will ask her,' I say softer, gazing still upon the drawings. 'Ya, be one other matter. The Marianos question roos in Massa, how I said. And they going keep some roos. Want Christs to make a new Maria.'

'Nay,' he say in voice like sudden knife. 'They ain't do this.'

When I look to him, his eyes be dangerous black again. I say tense, 'Ain't yours to worry.'

'They kill you if they doing this.' His voice disgust. 'Ain't heard?'

'Sure I heard. Heard all communications, how they kill me. But what be important, they can have some other plan. If they only catching Christs, be bone. But–'

'Going to do what I will do. Need no instructions, girlish.'

A moment, we be only glaring on each other, hate and nerves. Then Mamadou shake his head again. Walk sudden to the door.

I take frustrating breath, think how I chase him past all staring guards. But when he reach the door, he only fidget at the handle. A petty click result. A lock.

Click be uncanny in my nerves. Already I know, but I say stubborn, while he walking back, 'Nay, heed. They think I sent you there to kill their Christs, be only grief. Ain't sense to–'

When he reach to me, I scare through all my blood. But he only take my ear in hand like casual nothing. Pull its diamond earring free. Consider it with eyes, then slip this diamond in his pocket. My skin still startle from his hand, ain't comprehend how it be gone.

'I do your expeditions,' he say. 'Nor it be no new Maria. They fight our war, then I will take you out of this. What going to be.'

'Nay, NewKing. Ain't–'

'But when is done – you mine. You comprehending this?'

I touch thoughtless to my ear. Say rough, 'Nay, ain't about that.'

Then, before I can expect, he reach and catch my braids. Raise his other hand, and form it round my throat like choking. I feel my blood beat frightening in his hand. He feel my headlong blood.

Can see his face exhilarate and need. Feel how his kiss will be, and how we struggle on the floor, our knifen-fist of loving war. Yo, tears come vicious to my eyes. Be like a death somehow, be like my love itself go weep.

I snatch his hand out of my hair. Twist free with gasping heart, and say, 'Cannot.'

A moment, all his body disbelieve. He move to grab me rough. But then he hold himself, shift back. See me again in hard surprise.

And – what I never seen before – the NewKing hurt for me. He love but cannot, like a normal child who bleed his want. Yo, even this be arrogance in him, be cold and grandiose. Is like a blackness sky that hurt with lightning.

He step back in stiff respect. Say cold, 'Is bone, Maria.' Turn like carelessness, stalk to the door without no backward look. Open to a room of startling faces, and he gone.

47

LAST TALKS OF THIS ENORMOUS DAY

Tamara trail me back with curiose looks, but I ain't got no talk. She leave me by my elevator, and I go up alone. Stare empty at the painting there – white mother smiling foolish while her enfant reach his pinkish hand. Gold rings for death around their heads.

And I come out to my rooms without no expectation fear. Be figuring only if First Runner sleeping still, if I must wake her. How I ask on Massa, and lead her into safe refusal. How El Mayor will help.

Yo, as I walk into the shadow hall, be Driver coming toward.

He wear some Mariano clothes – shirt of fashion white, black pants. This stranger garb show all his skinniness like new surprise. Neck be shrunken in its collar, sleeves hang empty-looking. Ain't the brother that I known – child who can break a table with simple hands, child solid as a fact – and in my first distress, I want to hide like he be nightmares.

But when he see me, he go easy. Eyes relieve and smile. All his monthen bitterness gone, like this been dirt that rinse away.

'Been looking for you,' Driver say.

I smile uncertain. 'You gratty met.'

Then his eyes sketch to my dress, his smile break into laugh. 'Foo, sister. Guess they fix your grooming. You look like one of these.' He reach and stir the glassy dangles on a dandelion light.

My heart light irresponsible. 'Dress precieuse yourself.'

He make a face of joke disgust. Find a tabbet on the wall and switch the dandelion on. It light up stupid brilliant, and we both go laugh again.

Driver shake his head, still grinning. 'You mind, when you was six, you get some hatred to all clothes? Must sit on you to dress you.'

'Ain't remember.' I smile foolish. 'Remember how you make me wash.'

'I only try this once. Still got a scar.' He touch his wrist.

'That scar been warry cuts. You lying air.'

'Been Ice Cream teeth, it been.'

'Shoo, they sitting on me also. Dress been force, you know that right.'

To this, a weakness trouble in his eyes. He frown to the rug. 'The children here . . . they leave you now? You safe?'

'Ho, guess you heard about their proof?'

He start to nod, but break in coughing. Put fist to his mouth and say between, 'Ermano – told us. But – they leave you now?'

My heart go tight again. Remind all Anselm's threats, the Christs they bringing back from Massa. A moment, I even want to beg protection, like a frighten six.

But I say, 'Yo sho. I be Maria now, be past no harm.'

He sigh, and bring another cough. Touch his throat annoying. 'Ya, they told us yesternight. Ain't slept for much.'

'Never thought they tell you, shoo. Be sorry that you worry.'

'Need no sorries.' Driver get his sergeant face, a strict considering. 'I ain't weeping if they kilt the roo, myself. But how you done, be proud. You vally.'

'Foo vally. Stubborn, all it is.'

This he leave in disregard. Frown seriose and say, 'But, Ice, ain't want you risking so again. Was thinking yesternight.'

'How again? Been said, is done.'

'Nay, sister. What it is . . .' He cross his arms, get difficult looks. 'Ain't necessary you go to roos. Should stop you weeks before.'

'Foo, how?' I say, surprise. 'Ain't going to stop me.'

He shake his head. 'Yesternight, been thinking. Was my own selfishness, I never stop you. Fearing for myself.' His voice go harsh to this, most like he going to cough again. But he only grit his mouth. Thumb find a posy on his finger, fidget at its redden sore.

Then I comprehend his moods. Child spent the night in waiting for my death, and thinking every guilt. Now his hatred be forgot – like how my every gripe at Driver vanish like uncaring things, the day I learn his sickness.

'Shoo, brother,' I say soft. 'All this be by, ain't be no subjects. We warring for the cure now. City going to fight these roos.'

Then I explain the plan entire – from Pasha's news of Quantico to my apostle parley. Only, I give this history some changes for his comfort. I tell about the search to Massa, but never mention Christs, or doubts about the apostles' right intentions. And I say easy certainties, that we defeat the roos – how they surprising helpless by our thousand–thousand guns.

As my tale continue, Driver's eyes flash with peculiar feeling. He smile, but bite his lip and frown again. Look almost shame. Keep rubbing at his throat, like he will soothe its natural fear. All these changes sting my guilt – but I keep talking glad, my voice ring strong.

At last, he smile correct. Say soft, 'This grandy city war for us. They roos be sorrier.'

'Truth,' I say with falsen lightness. 'Be some sorry roos.'

'Roos coming January, ya?'

'January. Be only a month to wait.'

Driver shake his head and look up smiling to the dandelion light. 'A month. Ain't to believe.'

I watch him now with misery grown. Be comprehending, I must tell these lies to all my Sengles. Can only Pasha know the truth. Ya, Soledad be townie here – will learn all facts without myself. Must beg that she ain't telling Driver, for no circumstance.

To this, a better notion come. I say, 'Ho, Soledad be by?'

In second's change, his face go harsh. 'Nay, why?'

'Only to ask her on this place.' I shrug. 'Politics, you know how.'

'She gone.' He set his jaw. 'I told her I ain't want her by.'

'Ya?' I say feeble. 'Where she gone?'

'Gone where they tolerating murder.'

Now his face be only hatred. Is like our journey weeks, when he been vicious on myself.

I clench my hands. 'But, brother . . . it been reasons why she kilt they feathers.'

'Been reasons she will kill our Crow? She going to shoot him, if you ain't been by.'

His eyes hate into mine, and I say weak, 'Can be. You right.'

'And she must risk yourself? Know why she doing this? To be apostle. Rich without no work.'

I shrug nervy. 'Ain't been only this. How she believe–'

'Got her religions, sure. But I can live by her?' He clench his hands, then flinch. Frown angry at his posy fingers.

Now my heart be simple hurt. Politics be forgot; yo, any angry vengeance gone. I only feel how Soledad love my brother, all our journey weeks. And without her, he been alone. No Sengle hear his voice. Will be alone in sickness, days to come, in this abnormal place.

But I say, sad past no help, 'Ain't want to live by her myself.'

Driver ease his hands, his eyes gone sensitive with pain. 'Ya, need no more talk. She gone. Gone to her people somewhere.' He cough again, and all his face look shaming hurt. He cough again.

'You bone?' I say unhappy. 'Sure, must be physicians here.'

He swallow at his throat. 'I only need some rest. Ain't slept.'

'It be a sleeproom by. Was El Mayor there, but–'

'Nay, I got a room below. Be bone.'

Then we standing clumsy, caught in opposites and wants. I glance down to my precieuse dress, my hands in clean unhurt. Muttern soft, 'Be bone, yo sho.'

He nod. 'Sleep better now I seen you.'

'Sure,' I say. 'You only keep yourself. We all be right.'

When Driver gone, I walk straight to the sleeproom. Door still parten, El Mayor–First Runner where they was. I stare on them a longer moment, knowing I should wake them. Convince First Runner from no Massa search. But at last I close the door behind myself with careful softness.

Be tricky work to cross this jumbo bed. I ware on El Mayor–First Runner, how their sleeping change. El Mayor lain with back to me, scarce move with breath. But when I soften down to him, his body startle gentle. I touch my arm around, and his hand fumble to my wrist and pull me to. I form myself against him and he settle into sleep again.

Then I lie to him quiet. He breathe against me, and be relief, how our two bodies know each other. Is like a pharmacy that hush and soften in my blood. Some while, I worry on my Sengle littles, how they bringing here. Fret on the search and Mamadou, on Driver's sickly looks. But soon, this misery weigh me into sleep. Fall into struggling dreams, and wake sometimes and grip to El Mayor more needy. And sleep again and every sadden kindness be in this; is like I dream into a heaven for all children waste with grief.

Yo, in the farther hours, I wake startling to a noise. Be a pounding note, repeating dull outside the nighten windows. Sound go on persisting, until it inkle in my mind: is bells. Ring for Maria gone, the lover of sad Simón Zelote. Cry her death to every knowledge.

Then First Runner's voice come by my feet. 'Ice Cream? You waking?'

I shift my head to see her. She half risen, looking fright. Her scabben cheek be swollen somewhat, and her left eye open squinty.

She whisper, 'What it be?'

'Is only churching music,' I say whispern. 'Bells they ring.'

'Ain't them? The roos?'

'Nay, nothing harm us here. We good.'

But she still look her scary eyes. I take my arm from El Mayor and reach. 'Shoo, you come here. It need no fearing.'

She crawl to, cringing low, like she expect these bells crash in the windows. Come to my arms and duck in tight. I go whispering, 'Be no roos, be nothing mally here, be safe.' Then I hush and only let her hear my quiet breathing, until her breath come slow the same.

At last, she look up to me, shaming gentle in her eyes. 'Ain't sleep with no one since I been a little.'

'Can share one night. Ain't mean you little none.'

'Nay, I know. Person going to frighten for a while behind this, Mamadou say.'

I swallow at this name, but say assuring, 'Sure they do. He right.'

Then her face tense, like she distrust. She touch her scabben cheek. 'You know what been in Massa?'

'Ya, I know.'

'You know.' Her eyes relieve. 'And you ain't feary.'

'Sure. You keep by me.'

'Nay,' she say pickety. 'I only think, ain't necessary children fear from this. You ain't. The NewKing ain't.'

I bide a minute in my thought, feel how her smallness breathe. Then I say cautieuse, 'The NewKing never fearing much, no sho. Is even going back to Massa.'

Expect, she scare again, but her bruise face be only puzzles. 'Nay. Why he ain't told me?'

'Decide this while you sleeping, compa. He going to catch some roos. He never fearing them, can see.'

'Can go with him? He said?'

I tense misgiving. Feel the bells continue and I try my mind for help. Yo First Runner watch in need. Look tiny in her injury, in pinkish Mariano dress with lacy flowers on its neck.

'El Mayor will want you here,' I say at last. 'Can need you, compa.'

'Nay, Lowell gone,' she say like facts. 'You ask the NewKing if I come?'

'My ten, you want to hunt the roos? You shivering here from only bells.'

'Be his to choose,' she say with peeving mouth. 'He going to want me.'

'Ain't think he want you safe?'

'Be safer by the NewKing. Safe as wolves, how Mamadou say. He said he want to leave me?'

Then her eyes beg all their feeling. She start to pick her scabben cheek with fingernail, in nervy fidget. Ya, can see her face grow in betrayals, painful dark.

'Leave your hurt, you do infections.' I touch her picking finger. 'Now I going to tell you truth. The NewKing ask for you particular.'

'He ask for me?' Her hand go still, her face clear in relief.

'But he ain't need you, ya. Child big in years, can keep himself.'

'He ask for me. Yo, see?'

Before I can object again, she nest her head down to my shoulder. Can feel, she find her happy endings, want no onward tale.

Some time, I stroke her shoulder, think vindictions on the NewKing. Bells ring on, sound like they calling *fool, fool, fool*.

Then, above the sofa, I notice the picture of crossen Jesus – picture I seen yesternight, when we been waiting for our proof. Is painten brownish-reddish, with a blackness sky behind. Jesus agony in his blood and loosen down with pity face. Is like he wanting admiration for his feebleness.

I feel the paining of the bells, and think, *Nay, death be easy, coward.* And I close my eyes exhausting, holding to First Runner soft. Be gratty we survive our proof. We live into our war.

OF GODDING IN MARIAS

Vember 29–Cember 25

48

FIRST GODDING DAYS:
VEMBER 28–CEMBER 10

Be the following night the search depart for Massa woods. Mamadou, Crow and small First Runner all go in its company. Search leave by careful dark, nor any person see its shy departure. How Anselm wish, this business of the roos keep secret now. Ain't want all Marianos hounding off to seek the cure.

I ain't see Mamadou again before they leave, nor I see Crow. My only news be from First Runner, who come for departure thanks. She tell, with duty face, how they been keeping an hour with penal soldiers in guardroom below. Ya, half the penals drink themself to puking in this petty time.

She say this plain in facts, then add, 'The NewKing telephone this booze. Apostle privilege.'

'For friending?' I say. 'Or he drink himself?'

She get a lurking in her eye, like she consider secrets. But she answer slow, 'Juan given him no rifle. Some penal trade him rifle.'

'Foo, they sell their guns for booze?'

She shake her head correct. 'For diamond. But none will trade, till they been drunk.'

This talk leave me in better tempers. Think how he took this diamond from my ear without explaining word, and trust he bring

First Runner also for some secret cause. But once they gone, is only silent wondering to feel.

Then days come after days, and every day the same in fearing wish. Be nights in my iglesia rooms, where Sengles soon be living, with their piggery and skirmish. Ya, all hours of tired sunlight given to my godding work.

Each morning start with church for me and Pasha Unluck Christ. Must groom beyond no human looks, walk out with redcoat guards. Come to San Patricio, the edifice of our proof. Here we sit in porchen seats aloft, with brown ermanos round. Children in the benchen seats below gawp at us greedy. Then hours drag through the morning, with their marches to and by, and singing. Pedro come out to the stage, talk Panish in impressing voice, and someone sing again, and march, while every boredom die inside.

First churchen miseries, me and Pasha sitting mostly like we dead. Feel they staring eyes, and Pasha listen all attention. Tell me afterward what Panish things been said about ourself. But come a day, my Pasha smoke a cigarette, and no one cavil. Then one day I bring Kalash, and spend this time in fool experiments, if I can lift her barrel with my toes. Behind this, we both smoking constant; drawing pictures of Pedro in the Bible book its margins; sleeping with face in arms upon the rail. Yo, I always bring Kalash, however Anselm scorn this practice. Gun become a panic want, like when littles got a favorite toy or shirt they always hold.

Church ending after miseries entire, can think, it will be night. But ain't yet middy day, as we go footless sleepy to our rooms. Now Pasha get some rest from trouble. His days be playing carden games with soldiers of our guard. Yo, he grown ambitions, that he doing sex with Altagracia, so he chase her sometimes, though she only give him nays and noise. He be a whitish demon to her attitudes, unfit to touch.

Myself, my after day be in receptions. This meaning that I capture to the trono room its golden chair, with Anselm by in watch. Then a march of different strangers coming with their grumbles. Their water stanking with disease; their roof be made of holes; their burrow hospital be wild with insects. My part be to heed, do god behaviours, write my name. Is Anselm who give answers, while I hush for ignorance.

Be days before it notice, Anselm follow some visitors to the door. Shake hands in parting, then he put his hand into a pocket. Pocket fatten through the day. When I interest in this practice, he explain unshaming, children bribe him money to help their need. Ask if he do their will, and Anselm say, 'I try, senyora. But I'm afraid it's not always possible to be honest in this work.'

Apostles coming to reception also, with all signing papers. These gone friendly to me now. Will tell exciting gossips, bring me gifts of jewlerie. But Felipe never come; he only send some underchild with papers and respects. And from Simón Zelote, be no whisper.

For these receptions, Anselm teaching me Maria manners. I learn to speak in queenly voice, remarkable and kind. Move graciose and slow; be slow and graciose in temper. Cannot sit frogleg in chairs. Nor I can scratch, nor spit, nor smoke except in hidden privacy.

Some ways, I stubborn to no change. Cannot remember forks, and always start to eat my meal with hands, disgusting in taboo. Ya, my speech keep all its rough ungrammar. In sleek Maria voice, will call an apostle 'farting mouth'. Is what the Marianos call my ghetto sensibility.

In lazy hour behind receptions, Anselm also teach me basics on Marias City – how money papers work, and how they punish children for their laws. Most importance be, how children here got Panish–English sorts.

The Panish be the rich. Is callen 'spaniels' for dislike. They live in perfect homes with water toilets and lectricity. Wear every luxury of clothes, nor these be evac loot – all making new by tired workers. Yo, the English live in evac partments, rotten to describe; unwindow places where the shee collect in nasty buckets. They wearing rags and plastic bags, and eating water soup.

Of Panish, only be two burrows: Inúd and Metropolitano. All apostles be from these two wealthy burrows of the north. Inúds be soldier people, loving war above all pleasure. Ya, the Metros be like Lowells, prideful for their trading wealth.

I be Inúd Maria, from the chances of my capture. So it be natural to think, Inúds will like me well. But all they spaniels be the same in hatred for myself. My living Jesus hurt their faith; my manners hurt their snobbery. Nor they forgive my speech – some spaniels learn English for its use, but all disgust its ordinary noise. Be sorry their apostles never murder me, and all it is.

But for liken reasons, the poory English love me well. Little they known about our Sengles, but they know we ain't been rich. Ya, I speaking English, and my ghetto habits cheer their pride. Soon they gone in rumors how I help them into better power. They learn my rightful name, and call me Ice Cream Star sometimes for love.

Above all children be my Anselm. Nor his power ain't through laws. How he tell me once, 'I am your representative, santa reina. That is my only role.' But from his yeary sneaking, he own every child important, like some minnows in a jar.

This craft begin with simple money. Most apostles, ya ermanos, fatten on his mally wealth. Is other children weak in scandals – be homosexuals, or use pharmacies, or they rid their enfants. Anselm learning every dirt, and turn it to obedience. If any decent child be left, they lonely in their goodness. Try rebellion, and they lose employments, or be rid to prison. Yo, all Anselm's minnows only smile to this injustice.

Only exception that I learn be Felipe de Metropolitano. I asking once how Anselm rule Felipe, and he say, 'I don't. He is my last frontier, and I really think the case is hopeless. I do hate honest people, they really have no place in politics.'

'Foo honest,' I say. 'He only try to kill me for his selfishness.'

'Yes, and Felipe seems remarkably shaken by that incident.' Anselm make a malice smile. 'I've heard he's actually praying. So I'm told.'

'Shoo, ain't every child pray here?'

'Yes.' Anselm make meaning face. 'But Felipe is praying in private. In an apostle, santa reina, that's a symptom of mental breakdown.'

Time these lessons finish, it be always graying night. I elevator to my rooms, where ABC be waiting. Her barking celebrations bring my Sengle littles out in skree. Then I must heed all enfant news: who bitten who, who wetting pants, what Panish swears they learn. Often, they start a tackling game, and never leave me free till my white dress be mostly footprints.

My brats accustom to our palace life without no circumstance. Each morning bring some brave disaster: they clog the toilets with their socks; break sofas with their jumping games; throw pillows out the window at ermanos walking by. Days, when I be gone, guards take them to the woods below. Here they join in wars with children of the orfanato homes, where Mariano littles live apart from jones in noisy herds. Nights, they sleep on floors and anywheres, in blanket nests – beds be disgusting to their scratcher morals.

These nights, when all my littles sleep, I spend discussing war with Pasha. Will sit with maps of Quantico, and Pasha guess our battles, pointing where our soldiers going to meet. Explain artilleries and trenches; bombs of burning and of choking. Tell how the roos got disadvantage, since they war to steal our children – cannot murder us entire, or all their blood be waste.

He also tell me how to parley with the roos for cure. This parley being needful, how the cure be kept in boats apart. Even if we kill every roo soldat, these boats departing safe. But on these boats, be any hundred cures in ready storage.

Best luck, we beat the roos entire, and trap their every soldiers. Only let them leave in boats when they give all their cure. But if the rooish army flee, can trade them prisoners we caught – and Pasha say encouraging, we start this any time. First roo we catch, we trade. Save Driver before we even start to win.

Yo, in any venture we can think, is work of parleys. For this need, my Pasha teach me rooish seriose. We often dabbit time in church so – whisper joking ear to ear, or roo our petty gripes. And in the thickening night, we roo for hours in the sofa room. Make commentaries on our day, while Keepers roo in echo.

When these occupations weaken drowsy, I go to my sleeproom. Bed always crowd with littles, smelly ABC among. Yo, Pasha sleep in sofa room beside, with my Kalash – he never lose suspicions that we murder in the night. Be times, I wake and find him peering in my door with owlen worry. He whisper 'Ice, you bone?' and smile embarrass to my teasing answers. But truth, I always sleeping better when my Pasha been.

And I sleep and wake to this, until it be a life like any, ordinary from its use. First days, been even vally somewhat. Excite the city's bigness, ya my godness, how our war can win. But even in this innocent time, it been one poison detail: the despairs of El Mayor.

His gripes begun on our first day of Mariano life – behind the night I slept with him in arms, First Runner by. I woken in this bed alone, and live my day without regrets. Done my first church and first receptions, conscious only for myself. Return to find my Sengles come, and bring their tantrums into peace. At last, I standing lonely on the outside porch of my iglesia. Watch my townie stars and try to recollect my feelings. Then El Mayor appear and close the glassen door behind.

Child look besleepen messy. His churching suit all muddle in its shape, his hair be flat and skew. Worst be his pinchen face. Is like a picture drawn of how he suffer his murdern children, ya the wreck of Lowell mill.

Before I think no words, he say, 'Ice, why you slept with me?'

Take me a breath to comprehend. Then I say, 'Thought you liking this.'

'But – Ice, you knowing how it is? These people kill you if we do so.'

I shrug nerviose. 'Been only sleeping, with all clothes.'

He take a shivern breath. 'Ice, ain't like robbing eggs. Is death.' His voice catch thin and he look anxy to the glassen doors. Say lower, 'Yo, how we going to leave this place? Be any miles of guns to pass. The roos and then these madden children. Why this got to be?'

'But heed,' I say, low cautieuse. 'I thought . . . we stay some time. Place can be useful to ourself.'

He cross his arms, clutch to himself like freezing. Ain't look at me, he only clench, frown awful to the floor. 'Nay, you want to stay? Because you ruling here?'

'Shee, ain't for that! What Pasha thought, we war upon these roos. Got this whole city now, be chance we getting all their cure.'

He give a snorting breath. 'Pasha.'

'Heed, be a city in Washington. We join with them against the roos. Be two cities fighting, Pasha say we winning so.'

'Ain't care what Pasha say.' Now he look up with grieven rage. 'I need to leave this place. War can be years.'

'Ain't going to be no years.' I say, surprise. 'How it be years?'

'Is war, they lasting years. Guess Pasha never saying this?'

'I know, I know, but this be petty wars. It only be one place.'

'Ice, I cannot wait no years nor months. I be eighteen. You get this cure some years behind, I never live to . . . Ice, you never think of this? Of me?'

'Sure I think of you. Of Driver also. Why I want this war.'

Then all himself seize vicious. 'Nay, you want this war because *your roo told you to want.*'

Now I be only staring to his face, sans thought nor breath. Porch come familiar now, and in my corner-eye a doily chair seem townie like a friend. The sofa room shine warm behind the glass, and be familiar. Is El Mayor gone strange, with twisten face and churching suit. And he narrow on my dress, say harsh, 'Heard how you marry with him.'

First, this ain't even comprehend. Then I shake my head, say dull, 'Ain't marrying real.'

'And you want to die for him? This ain't been real?'

Here my patience lose its grip. 'Should kill him? Sure I dare my life. Think I ain't done the same for any Sengle? For yourself?'

'Ain't try this. Think I cannot see?'

'What? You seeing what?'

'You never want to tell me of your loves before myself. I figuring why.'

I laugh in stagger breath. 'Now I be doing sex with roos? You ain't believe this self.'

'Yes, I believe. What else I can believe? You dying for him why?'

'Heed, this be Ice Cream Star, I going to do some bellicose nonsense. I be a fool to die. But I ain't false to you. Ain't false with any roo nor beast nor person. Damn, ain't been!'

Can see he catch on this. His painful face go soft, want to trust.

'Shoo.' I shake my head. 'Come hold me. No one even there to see ya, the last Maria, she done sex, and no one bother.'

Can see his body tempt, his eyes be yearning in their shame. But he reach to the door. 'You ain't the last Maria. You my Ice Cream. If you kilt for me . . . been worse enough, my children dead at Lowell. Be too much.' And he slip out, go fleeing hasty to the farther rooms.

Behind this, he be wrong to life and difficult to friendship. His children kilt be like a blame he wear, a hatred to himself. Some days entire, he only sit in bed and gloom at reveries. Talk to him of war, his only answers be despair. Will say in choken voice, 'I fight them. Got no wants to live myself. But you wasting misery to plan. Ain't be no goddamn plans.' Ya, with every word, he looking painful through his skin entire.

His Lowells keeping in a neighbor edifice, call the Bergdorf Goodman. They settle easy to this change – disapprove the building

392

for its lack of perfect baths, but love the city's smart richesse. But El Mayor soon quit to visit. Some Lowell always asking mean, why he left any child at Massa; say everyone been living still, if El Mayor insist they come. Be brats who even spit at El Mayor for their resentment.

In this malaise, his jalousie to me grow past no sense. Be mostly Pasha he suspect, but also be Jermaine and Anselm, any living male. Worst evolution, he start questioning children on my loves. He even bother Driver on this, and he quiz my small Tamara. Soon any blindness guess that he got histories with me himself. But El Mayor cannot resist his mouth. Must ask and ask.

This bring me into tempers for my selfen loneliness. Gratty to his fears, I be Maria Virgin, gone from flesh. Never can feel his hands, nor any person's wanting hands. And all this feary time, my body grieve its missing life. Be all my days indoors, I never freezing in the difficult air. Ever I stretch my arms, be Anselm chiding me for rudeness. Life got no dirt nor washing rain; no love nor pounding war. Be like the world feel nothing for myself.

Yo, come a day, me–Pasha coming back from church, and Pasha walk before me sleepy in the Ministerio hall. Then some wildness catch in me. I leap upon him from behind, in murder dress and heely shoes. Kick his ankle loose and topple him back upon myself. We land thudden, Pasha crushing me painful at my ribs. First he only brace, surprise. But I reach up to his face, and catch a finger in his nose, my favorite nastiness from Army wars. Then he tear and hit me honest angry with his elbow. I grab his hair, jab him in armpit, but we both start laughing silly, tumblen like we be. Look up, and all our guards be staring terrify, ain't know who they must help or fight.

Then Pasha pulling free, he go on hands and knees beside me. All his furry hair dishevel. He say, laughing breathless, 'Fighting like a girl. Pull hair.'

'What you think I being, foolish? Fight more, this girl go teach you cowardesse.'

Then I punch him smart into the eye, but he cannot quit laughing. He say gaspen, 'Useless. Got no arm.'

'Foo, you asking me to hurt you real?'

Then Pasha shake his head, complain injustice. Say he cannot hit me, I be hurt. Our soldiers start to laugh themself – be our funny manners of barbarian, can see. Pasha rise up to his feet, and I get up with perilous grinning, feel some starting life.

He say, gone seriosen shy, 'Want to fight, you need some learning. Cannot fight like that.'

'Ho, you bragging air. You fight so special, how you lose they teeth?'

He make a face. 'Nay. I teach you. Seriose, you miserable.'

So we start our fighting games, that become a Mariano gossip for dismaying morals. Can comprehend, Maria and Jesus boxing, be ungodly sights. One moron padre tell us we must pray against temptation. More practical ermanos tell us explanations, how this seem. Even my Tamara Ten go nerviose. Tell me privy it will harm my brains.

But our vally guards will find us fighting mats and so. Bring us to the Ministerio ballroom, when night be gone in quiet. There we scrap joyeuse, and Pasha teach me pranks of war, with killing grips and gouges that be useful even against the roos. Truth, cannot war angry much. Pasha twice my weighing size. He knock me into dreams, if he ain't careful. But we sometimes come to church with vally bruises, neverless.

One night, this fighting broil into an honest argument. We resting from our scraps, akimbo on a fighting mat. Pasha sitting frogleg while I lain with spraddle arms. Both wearing soldier clothes for ease; my murder dress be waiting on a doily chair beside. Ya, Pasha got a cigarette – roo cannot live an hour without this comfort in his mouth. Guards smoke also, by the farther wall, in muttern conversation.

And Pasha say from nothing, 'Ice? When war begin . . . you leaving here?'

When I look to him, he got peculiar cautions in his face.

'How?' I say. 'To Quantico?'

'Nay, Quantico,' he say misliking. 'Woods somewhere. Apart.'

I rummage myself up to sit. Ain't nervy yet, be only puzzling, what he want to mean. Ya, Pasha watch with sharp attention, like he heeding some event, beware its wrong result.

I say, 'What woods? Foo, how you meaning?'

'Is better,' he say cautieuse, 'when war begin, you hide apart. Can take all Sengles, what you should.'

'Shoo, been coward gods. I make this war, then hide myself?'

'Be normal that Maria hide. I talk to guards on this.'

'To guards? Foo nosy. Need no guards' opinions, what I do.'

Pasha pinch his mouth, look to the guards in differences of thought. I look to them myself, see how they smoke in boring mood. Guard Lopez tell some braggeries, while the others grim their face.

And Pasha say low-voice, 'If we lose, roos come here. To Marias.'

I look to him annoying. 'Need no losing talk, goddamn.'

He nay his hand. 'You need. Must think.'

'So they come here, and every child be kilt, while I hide cowardly? You bitten by the evil insect, roo. Ain't to believe.'

'Help nothing, if you kilt.'

'Nay, is your old attitudes. Must check ten ways before I sneeze. Nor we losing, roo. You keep this straight.'

Then his voice come sharp in riling. 'Is only demonstrations, how you brave. Ain't useful nothing. But you must do . . . do foolishness. Must always die.'

'Foo, must always die. Ain't even plan to lose. They dooms be yours.'

'Yes, can lose.' His mouth grit bitter. 'Yes.'

Then I get up in quick disgust. 'Lose and lose! Ain't needing this. You plain depressing, all you be.'

Pasha be on his feet in angry instant. I raise my wary fists, expect our skirmish start again. But he stand only furiose, hands clenchen at his sides. Say hoarse, 'I helping you, before. I help you?'

I narrow on his grieven eyes. 'Sure you done. You help.'

'Help your Sengles. Help . . . at Army camp.'

'You save my life. I know.'

'This . . . be what I ask. That you hide. Be for myself.'

Then his eyes yearn to my face, can see them thinking every story. The dandelion lights shine dim like underwater sun, and Pasha look uncanny white. Yo, his need catch in me. Feel how I love himself the same. Even a guilt begin, that I ain't thought how he keep safe.

'Bone,' I say reluctant. 'If we lose. But you hide also, Pasha.'

He give a longer sigh. Smile funny, like he feel stupidity. Then, without changing face, he swipe and swat me unawares. Yo, I laugh angry, dodge around. Punch short into his guard, and we go scrapping again like nothing been. Chase and jab and yell frustrations till our mally nerves forgot.

49

OF SPYING VARIOUS

When two weeks be gone, and ain't no news from Massa woods, I lose impatience with my pointlessness. Be the tenth of Cember, roos expect in January, and still I cannot trust the Marianos' plans. Apostles swear they glad to war – they only wait for proof. But every day come evidences of their wrong intention.

First, they insist we cannot tell the city on the roos. About the cure, can comprehend, is reasons for this quietness. Once it be known, all desperate people run to roos direct. But be no harm if people warn about the rooish armies.

I argue this to Anselm, ya apostles, till my voice be old. But they insist that Marianos scare hysterical from this news. Be riots terrible. The city wreck to crumbs by looting. Is even problems, how we ever bring our soldiers into war – they going to terrify idiotic, that their enemy pale.

'You don't understand how whites are regarded here,' Pedro say in teaching voice. 'In our Bible, they're described as hell's offspring, a race of giant scorpions. If people thought there were thousands of white men headed for the city, it would be chaos.'

'So Jesus be a scorpion god?' I say. 'Be white himself.'

Pedro make a pickety face. 'No, Jesus was God incarnate. He was only sent as a white man to give whites a chance to turn back to

God. But they killed Him, as we know. And since that time, the whites are damned. They are demons, santa reina.'

'Your people killing Jesus, time-again. You also demons?'

'Perhaps you should read the Bible,' say Pedro shortish. 'But *we* will decide when and how to tell the city. You don't know what you're dealing with.'

Truth, I be ignorant as feet. But can know, my Pasha never treating like no giant scorpion. Be plenty Marianos who dislike him for his weirdo color; is even fools who think his touch be poison. But no one doing riots when he enter rooms. Ain't be.

I try a small experiment, with kitchen people of downstairs. Sneak to them by darkness morning, when they chopping–washing foods. Stand in their grease abode – with queery conscience for my diamond looks – and tell them every information on the rooish army.

These workers all be English poor, and first they only dumbfound that Maria visit their dirty selves. But when they comprehend, they do no chaos, nor they panic. Only frown discomfort each to each.

At last, one girl say shy, 'Why don't everyone know about that, senyora?'

'Apostles want it secret,' I say. 'Got all stupid reasonings. Yo Anselm, he the worst.'

Hear Anselm's name, and all these children terrify out of sense. Go begging, I ain't tell him that they even heard this news. Say how they losing jobs for this. Can even be, they rid to jail. Yo, as I leave, I hear a girl say, sour in undervoice, 'Why's she want to tell people things that get them hurt? I just don't know.'

Next doubts beginning by my guards. Before a week be gone, these children be like townie friends. Pasha spend most daylight hours in their smoky company; ya, my girl fourteens be broiling into love amours with them. From our first days, they known about the roos, against all secrecy. Live among all Sengles, and they hear abundant word. Best Anselm can ever do, he frighten them for knowing.

Now, as our second week prolong, they talk some cautieuse surprise, how no one start war preparations. Weapon factories make no extra bullets; soldiers sitting lazy. Any war before, it been all hasty work to this.

One day, walking to church, my closest guards explain all reasons known. These be Julio, Metro child who love me with his eyes, and Bean, a chubly English, rude in ways. Pasha walk ahead with different guards of his new friendship. Can hear them noising Panish, while our talk go careful soft.

Bean begin. 'What I think, they're afraid to make a lot of guns right now. Do that, and people will think they're planning to fight the Marines again.'

'Foo,' I say. 'Who want to fight Marines? You only losing twice.'

'Inúds, that's all.' Bean shrug. 'They never give that up. Half the city already thinks we're attacking Quantico this spring. Cause – excuse me, santa reina – *you're* an Inúd Maria. How people see it.'

'That war, nobody want,' say Julio. 'Metros also, we don't want.'

Bean huff breath. 'Yeah, really. You'd have a rebellion on your hands. Start off trying to fight Marines, you'd end up fighting the English here.'

'But ain't no war like that,' I say annoying. 'We fight *for* Marines.'

Bean nod. 'I'm only saying what people will think. They don't know nothing about your war. So you go making a lot of guns, there's going to be craziness. Guaranteed.'

Here guard Lopez straggle back from Pasha's group of talkers. Can see, he overhearing, now he come to fix our notions. Lopez be Inúd himself, and always loud with townie pride. For this, he be a hatred object to all other guards. He wear a scarf with eagle picture – flag of their Inúd – and this scarf always robbing, and is found again in guardroom toilet.

Now Lopez say confident, 'Senyora, it is nonsense. There is enough of weapons. Why no one makes more.'

'Enough?' say Bean disgusting. 'What I heard, we're already short on bullets. Get a war, we're finished in a couple of hours. Unless you want to fight with sticks.'

'What *you* heard.' Lopez smile superior. 'And you heard Inúds are afraid from English. But we like to fight your English. It is easy like target practice.'

'Point is, nobody's fighting,' Bean say cold. 'There isn't any bullets to do it.'

Here Julio nay his hand to Bean, and tap one ear with meaning look.

Lopez see this, and say huffish, 'I am not a spy.'

'Oh, you're not?' Bean laugh nasty. 'Sure, you're not. That's funny.'

Lopez scorn his face and say, 'Senyora, I am sorry. I don't continue for respect to you.'

Then he haste back to Pasha, stalking like an insult cat.

Bean muttern, 'Guess Anselm's paying Lopez money for his gorgeous looks.'

'Yes,' say Julio cold. 'For that, and spy.'

Last worries come from Sengles. From our first days, I asken all my jones to scratch for helpful news. They mostly fail in uselessness. Jonah discover naked dancing shows in Chelesí, and he forget all other life. Villa do her usual filth with every living male. In Loisaida burrow, Hate You lose her shoes to gunpoint robbers. Behind this bad adventure, she be cowardly to outdoors.

But Asha Badmouth and Jermaine go spy like natural rats. They visit Santiago in his palace Residencia; then they go shooting cans with English scratchers in a field of garbage. One night entire, they boozing at a soldier barracks of Inúd, and Asha return with soldiers' names writ uppen-down her legs. Yo, every place, they asking–sniffing for all gossip known.

Most they hear be tales fantastic. Get fables on myself, how I do sex with Jesus, or with Pedro, or with some mystery child name Tony whose existence be a question. Be worser talk on Pasha, how he eating insects at all meals, or babies – anything but food. Also be whispers, showing that some gossip leak about the cure, although this story always suffern some peculiar change. Strangest version be, that roo meat cure all maladies. Eat Jesus's body and you live forever. My sixes heed this seriose, and soon they picking Pasha's hairs from furniture to swallow.

But be one story all my guards approve for simple truth. Is on Simón Zelote de Loisaida, sad apostle. How rumor tell, Simón ain't only be the general of armies. In last Maria's time, he rule the city mostly by himself. Other apostles been some nothings, living scary to his will. Even Anselm stick in second place.

First, this cheer me wonderful. Can hope, Simón become my friend against all Anselm's threats. He doing with the last Maria; never he be indignant that I going pregnant once. Ya, he must hate Anselm, how this weasel rob his power.

But, before I start no plan, a worser rumor come. This tell that Anselm kilt Simón Zelote for some politics. He keep this careful quiet. Simón be popular in the army's love.

This be a time when Anselm and myself be most like friends. All my reception hours, we exasperate at fools together, and when they go, we ease in scabby jokes. I got my trono chair, but he must stand his aching feet. So when receptions finish, Anselm splay himself upon the floor. Ya, become my careless habit that I lie longside. Sometimes in this, he stretch against the floor in catly luxury. Rest cheek to its stone – and I will stretch and rest cheek to the stone in thoughtless kinliness.

So, in this question of Simón, I go ask Anselm straight. And he agree the tales about Simón Zelote his old power. Tell all disgusting memories of the horrible this been. 'He would summon us to his house in Loisaida, all hours of the day and night, to issue his instructions. Often from his bed – and sometimes, Maria was *in* the bed. But no matter what he did, Simón was beloved.'

How Anselm explain, Simón be Metro; his Maria been Inúd. So every spaniel glad to them. Ya, the English give Simón respect as vally general. 'The worst thing about a war, senyora, is that it produces war heroes.'

But when I ask about Simón his murder, Anselm only laugh. 'Now he's dead? How thrilling. I wonder if anyone's told Simón?'

'You saying it ain't true?'

'It ain't true, and Simón ain't dead, and the word is *isn't*.'

'Then why he disappearing, if he loving power so?'

'But he didn't disappear, senyora. His Maria died, and he lost his support in Inúd, and with it went his power. And one of those losses – I won't guess which – struck him down with terrible grief. But I'm sorry to say, it didn't kill him.'

I bring this story back, and Asha Badmouth say annoying, 'How you even ask that rodent? Sure he going to lie. Heed my word, Simón be dead as bacon.'

All this leave me in suspicions past no toleration. Yo, two weeks be gone, and never a budge been taken toward my war. So now I go in personal hunt to find a friend important – anyone who know secret pox, and ain't in Anselm's ruling.

First want be for Simón Zelote, if he living anyhow. So one night when no one watch, I go with Julio–Bean to Loisaida. But we can only meet Simón's own guards outside his door. Nor these Loisaidas will agree to take no message. They say, Simón depressing since his old Maria die; dislike all politics for his resentments to the living world. We roam around the house, but all we seeing be shut curtains. Come back frustrating tired, to Asha Badmouth's jeer of 'Dead as bacon'.

Next I seek Soledad, but this sad child be lost entire. What my Sengles heard, she live by Pedro in Inúd. Yo, when I ask Pedro, he swear ignorance to this – but his eyes false. I send Jermaine and Asha scouting there, but be no help. Pedro's Residencia got all guards with mally temperaments. Ain't want no Sengles setting foot, nor they admitting they know Soledad's name. My children watch some days, but see no trace her face. She gone like breath.

In final desperation, I think on poisoner Felipe. Ever he try to kill myself, he hating Anselm right. Yo, now it seem peculiar, he ain't coming to receptions. Is like Simón Zelote – but Felipe living to all eyes. Every morning, he give noisy sermons in their Metro church.

I ain't try to go myself. Cannot want Anselm knowing. Felipe be his worst mistrust. So I think a foxery, how I send El Mayor. Child need good distraction, and he love politics like food. Nor no spy beware him, how he droop pathetic all these days.

First I asking, El Mayor give only nays and miseries. He cannot, and ain't want to, ya be moron enterprise. When I insist, he asking vicious, why is mine to choose. Talk stank on Sengles, and fifteens, and gods who cannot use a fork.

But when I coming back from church next morning, he be gone. Hate You say he left to Metropolitano for my task, and Asha Badmouth add, 'He looking prettieuse. Clean as a dish.'

When El Mayor return, is tardy night. He stomp in glad bedrunken, shining face like he infatuate. Tell laughing stories of Felipe's brainy talk, his snobben wife, his Metropolitano Residencia that be palaces beyond. How they got a boy to serve their food who wearing whitish gloves. Give demonstrations, how he talk to them in sleeper English, sounding like peculiar books.

I ask him cautieuse, 'You starting anything of politics?'

'Foo, bell,' he say. 'I had a cat, I naming it Felipe's Secrets. Yo it changing names before it learn to answer. Fact be truth.'

Behind this, most his days be there; yo, all his talk be stories, how he win Felipe to his love. No time be gone before he sleeping at Felipe's Residencia, get his selfen room. These nights ain't pleasure for myself. I known his goating habits. But cannot cavil, when he only doing my requests.

First news he bring, Felipe got psychologies on myself. Ever Maria come in mention, Felipe hush like sudden hurt. When El Mayor go ask on this, Felipe get a pickety face, like it be ghetto questions. Say, 'Religion shouldn't be a subject for casual conversation.' No asking get a different answer. Be a closen door.

403

But soon Felipe starting his own questions, how I be to know. If I be nice or evil; be like normal or be strange. Now El Mayor get entertainments, lying on my holy self. Explain my hatred to all sex; how I save deer from cruel hunters. Say how I weep sometimes, when children only mention violence. Ya, Felipe heed this seriose, and only look for more.

One night, when they both gone in wine, Felipe start his own insanities about my perfectesse. Say any child who seen myself must know, god living in me real. I be compassionate and pure, cannot kill even roos.

Through this, El Mayor be mostly choking not to laugh. At last, he ain't resist his mouth. Say in sleeper wise, 'It's strange you tried to kill her then.'

Felipe startle awful. 'You – she knows?'

'Sure, she knows that,' El Mayor say. 'Nor she doesn't blame you, brother.'

This ruin Felipe's face entire. He go in boozen tears and start to gabble all his murder tale. Say how he try this poisoning, for selfish politics. But God defeat his evil, though God must use Anselm's hand. Best El Mayor can comprehend, Felipe knowing this been tricks. But he still believe this been a miracle somehow – as if no basic child can fool himself, is supernatural strange.

Yo, now Felipe do all godly sorriness for this unmurder. Go days without feeding, give free money to needy beggars. And he praying to Maria god, that she forgive his crime. This Maria be myself, but ain't myself – all skewball notions. But why he never coming to receptions, been for guilt. He shame himself before his human god.

'I lost my faith in the last Maria's time,' Felipe say. 'I don't think anyone could know that woman, and still believe. But when I gave Maria – our Maria – the wine, I realized. As soon as I saw her face, I *knew*. But it was too late then.'

El Mayor get pities now. Say soft, 'It's not too late. She's living, see that.'

'No,' Felipe say with tragedy looks. 'I mean, it's too late for me.'

Behind this sad exposure, El Mayor go bold in questions. Ask on the search, the war, and even say I sent him for this cause. But now Felipe lose his drunken face. Go scary quiet. At last he only say, 'Please tell her she doesn't have to be afraid. As long as I'm here, she's safe.'

In this, another week gone by. Is Cember 21, and still from Massa be no whisper. Search been gone some twenty days, is twice our expectations. And now my sleeping nights become all terrors, how the search destroy. Keep waking from nightmares where the searchers capture in a burning house. I trying to save them, but I got no hands, roos cut them off. Or it be Money burning, trotting normal like this fire ain't notice, and all her burden be the NewKing, dead. And I wake in fright, and cannot sleep again. And cannot sleep. Nightmares leak their panic into morning, and in church I sometimes hold to Pasha's hand. Only then I sleeping fearless, head down to the wooden rail.

Times, in my waking nights, I go to sit by Driver's bed. Be foaly in uncertainties, I yearn toward my brother. Yo, he soften to me now, his bitterness forgot. Will call me fondly names like *treasure sister* and *potato*, like he done in better years.

But all this time he weaken. He sleeping in the middy noon, gone into pharmacy time. His posies grown to sores, and every movement be a wincing hurt. Yo, all his talk be sickness. Ain't even try to fool me that he got no other life. He give his coughing speech and gasp it back – and all be of physicians' sayings, or of pills the Marianos give for pain. His breathing be a weary labor, and can see that Driver frustrate sometimes, wish this task been rid.

Once I try to sleep by him, from clinging lonesomeness. But I ain't sleep for nothing, only listen how he stir in pain. Think how the cure come slow across the ocean, and rage to swim out to these boats, with gun between my teeth. Fret through the night at all my feeble helplessness.

Now I start telling Anselm, we must send to Quantico for parleys.

Must start our war without no extra proof, it cannot wait. But he only heed me like a hound that yap in dull annoyance. The only change I win, the weapons factories start their tardy work, creating bullet-guns. But even here, is problems. How my guards warn, this bring the city perilous in gossip. Every fool believe we going to fight the Quantico Marines.

Come a day, it be a marching manifestation in the streets. Some thousand children yell their hatred to this unexisting war. And soldiers grabbing people from, bring them to prison in their blood. Next morning, when I walk to church, is children kneeling by the road. Say nothing, but they wearing black in token of their grief.

Day of manifestations bring some mystery joy to Anselm. In sudden change, his manners smile. Go laughing–joking through the day. Yo, all apostles happier kept. They grin in meeting, and their eyes share in some glad conspiracy.

This bring me into scary moods, what trickeries be forward. My Sengles know no telligence; nor El Mayor heard nothing strange. Yo, questioning Anselm be no use. He say his nothing and nothing else, and smile to my frustration.

Next day, these complications bring me–Anselm into open strife. Been in our privy hour behind receptions. We lain together on the floor, our habit from more friendly time. Yo, I ask what we do, if no one coming back from Massa.

In days before, this question going to bring his snapping-turtle face. But now he answer light, 'Let's think. We send another search? No, let's wait peacefully for death.' He gesture to the painten ceiling. 'Heaven will receive us.'

'Shee,' I say annoying. 'Least we do, we tell the city. They all in pointless frights about Marines.'

Anselm taken with a yawn. He rid this slow and say in sleepy voice, 'Yes, they're halfway to insurrection. So you believe it would help to say we're actually planning to fight white demons – who may not exist?'

'Roos exist, goddamn. Kilt half my children with their stank existence.'

'Senyora, I'm pointing out that nobody will believe it.'

'Believe it, if we tell them right. If apostles telling, they believe.'

'Because our apostles are known for their perfect honesty. I understand.'

I sit up frustrating. 'People going to learn it be the truth. Ya, cannot be no worse. Go on like this, it be rebellion total.'

Anselm shut eyes like simple peace. 'And if there is rebellion total, we will squash that rebellion totally. It won't be the first time, sadly.'

'Kill your own people, for some misbelief? Been prettieuse.'

'Yes, regrettable. But if we didn't, there would be rebellions every month. We've had that also.'

'Foo, you trying to fret me now. Ain't even mean this awfulness.'

To this, he only nay his finger. Look like he mostly sleep, his body loose in its long dress. And he muttern from shut eyes, 'War is evil, but is sometimes needful.'

At first, I still believe he only pesting me. I even consider tickling him, how he lain unbewares. But then a nasty inkling come. Why they making extra guns, it ain't to fight no roos; ain't even been to please myself. These guns prepare against rebellion. They made to kill our selfen people.

Almost, I rid this thought. Remind, the guns begun this strife. No person thinking to rebel, until the guns been made. But cannot lose my doubt. It stick and stick like evil smell.

I look on Anselm, where he lain in his same peacefulness. I say, 'You do this filth, it be without myself. Know this.'

'You're joining the rebellion?' Anselm open curiose eyes. 'Brave girl. But shouldn't you check with Felipe first? I know you place such reliance on his advice.'

'Ain't seen Felipe since the clausen signing,' I say stiff. 'Be no Felipe in this story.'

'That's nice to hear. I like to hear nice things.'

Our eyes meet in some bad comprehending. Then Anselm sit up

and arrange his dress around his knees. Fold his hands and say like simple task, 'About your baby.'

I scoff breath. 'Shee, known your threats. They old.'

He say on unheeding, 'At this moment, two people know about that incident. Pedro and myself.'

'And physicians know.' I shrug annoying. 'So?'

'No, actually, there are only two people.' He look to me with teaching face, wait for my understanding.

My gut go cold. 'You saying, they dead? You murdern they physicians?'

Anselm flutter his hand toward the cloudy ceiling. 'Yes, sad. But getting back to the point. Pedro does *not* know about your advances to Felipe. And I'd advise you to keep any thoughts about rebellion from him also. I actually like you, santa reina. I would miss you if you were gone. Pedro . . .' Anselm make a sour mouth. 'He isn't so enamored.'

This fight been Cember 23, when my Maria life seem like it been a year of winters. Must walk to church and sit in meetings, sign my name to papers. I scarce remember how the earth can feel to naked feet. My body start to feel unclad without Maria dress; sometimes I startle that my Sengles ain't stoop down to greet me. I terrify for the search, I fight my voice for war, think madness plans – yo these despairs come normal now. I scarce expect no other life.

But it been only one more day when all this misery shatter. Ya, my Maria life go shattering, lost into the past.

50

OF VANISH PEOPLE THEIR
APPEARANCE

This ending start on Nochebuena – night before their Navidad, the birthing day of Jesus baby. All the city be in tinsel ornaments and sprucen rings, and half our guards–ermanos gone to festival in their homes. But my Maria work been long the same. Send me to my iglesia rooms with sad and skinny moods.

Then I be in the sofa room, lain flat in silken underdress. Got church at middy night for Nochebuena pookery; I rest my pinchen skin before the worser grooming this will need. Keepers on the floor beside. She got a bitty plastic cow, is trying to saw its head off with a meat knife. Pasha telephoning cocktails, our new habit in this time.

Through this, Jermaine be reading the Marias Bible out to us. Be mostly like the Christings' book, but got some scandal differences. Jermaine been Christing born – his early brains been pickled in their nonsense – and now he angering how the Marias Noah take extra children in his boat, a whitish pair without no morals. God want to drown all whites and leave the world to Noah's blackish get. But Noah foolish in his pity. Cannot leave all whites to die, whatever stank they be.

Seem funny to myself, and I be laughing when El Mayor come in the door.

I saying, 'God some helpless mouse, cannot just kill these roos? Squitch with fingers, they be done.'

'He strike them at His will,' Jermaine say seriose. 'But you ain't seeing–'

'Ice,' say El Mayor with nervy looks, 'can talk to you apart?'

I sit up hazy, smiling to him.

Pasha cover telephone with hand and say to El Mayor, 'Want some cocktail?'

El Mayor look cold to this. 'Nay, I need no cocktail. Ice Cream?'

'Yo sho.' I get up hasty. Be mostly fearing, been some trouble down to Metropolitano.

He say nothing till we gone into the sleeproom by. Then – how he never done these weeks – he close the door behind.

My heart unbalance, guessing he invite me into love. But when he turn, his face be all resenting misery.

And El Mayor say, 'Why you got to show yourself like that?'

'How you meaning?'

'Wearing unders.' He swallow at his throat. 'You know.'

'Ain't unders. Yo who thinking what I wear? Be later hours.'

'He thinking. Roo be thinking, sure is right.'

Then I comprehend. Injustice flash into my nerves. 'You ask me here for this? I thought this nonsense been forgot.'

He get a look I recognize from jalousies before, like all his mind be burning red. 'Ain't forgot by every child who tell your dirt in Metro.'

'Now it be gossips?' I say hot. 'And how I even do no filth? Got a dozen children watching, ever I pick my nose.'

'Ain't mine to know.' He grit his mouth. 'In Metro–'

'Metro, shee! And sure, you brave to mention Metro, where you keeping every nights. Guess what you do there.'

This catch into silence. We look bitter, one to one. And El Mayor say cold, 'Be only doing what you done yourself.'

Take a staring breath before I comprehend his meaning. Then the room go small somehow. I say, 'Nay, truth, you got some girl?'

He flinch, look to the floor. 'Why I cannot?'

'But you . . . you done this real? Ain't only saying for some punishment?'

'Punishment for what? What you done?'

'I done nothing! Shee you know! You only guilty for yourself!' My voice break high, ya I be shivering, crossing arms against myself.

Then something falter in his face. He narrow on me in painful thought. I take a choken breath, feel weightless somehow with my awful. Confusen mind keep saying, ain't no reason I should hurt. He fleeing me all weeks, we finish. Nor I love him right – but to this thought, my heart go skeering red.

Then El Mayor say softer, 'Ain't mean nothing, what this been.'

I scoff a teary laugh. 'You told this girl that she be nothing?'

'Ice, nay. Ain't no girl. Was girls. You know how.'

This saying jeer inside my head. *Ain't no girl. Was girls.* Cannot see how it be worse, but all my body strange with cold. 'Should expect. How you be.'

He shake his head, his eyes gone wisty shame. 'Ain't even come to say that. Had some news. It all come wrong somehow.' He look down to my dress, and all his face be feeling misery.

'News?'

'I seen you there . . . be like I lose my memory.'

'Shoo, what news you got? Can leave this. Want to leave this now.'

He gaze at my dress a longer moment, like he finish some thought. Then he look up and say, 'Think I seen Mamadou.'

First, this ain't comprehend. Is like he saying it in Massa – he seen Mamadou in the woods. I even tense in worry that his jalousies found their right object. But then my mind come bright. I say with catching breath, 'Yo, where?'

'In Metro, in some hinder street. Child been in soldier clothes, alone. But can swear it been himself.'

'Ain't spoken to him?'

'He skit away before I call. Felipe been with me, I ain't want to chase.'

'Goddamn, should chase.'

'I know. Was . . . sure I know.'

I force my painful mind to think. 'You figure he fled from Massa alone? He hiding?'

El Mayor grimace his unknowing. 'You heard nothing here?'

'Nay, been normal boredom. Navidad and so.'

'Can be some soldier, only look like Mamadou. But I can swear, it been himself.'

I grimace into thought. Cannot see any reason Mamadou come back alone. Even if they try to kill him, he ain't never fled – been impossible for pride. A moment, I consider if he murdern all these children – sixty penals, twenty guards and Juan. Return with only Crow–First Runner and slip into hiding.

Then El Mayor say soft into my thought, 'I got to go. Felipe wait for me in Metro. For Nochebuena meal, you comprehend. Ain't be no other reasons.'

I flinch, look up uncertain. 'Sure.'

'Ain't want no girl before you, Ice. You knowing this?'

'Yo sho,' I say in difficult voice. 'Can guess.'

'Love you worse than broken legs. Ain't brave to risk you, all it is. I even think of this, I lose my wants.'

'So they be lost.' I force a smile.

'Nay, shoo.'

He reach out to my shoulder. Touch it careful soft, like he be touching to a wound. Yo, I confuse in sorriness. Now Mamadou woken to my heart, can want no other hands.

But El Mayor freeze in a sudden conscience. Look back to the door.

Yo, as if his fear call it to life, a knocking come there hard.

El Mayor startle back. I flinch myself, call up in nervy voice, 'Yo what?'

'Senyora? Can come in?' Be the voice of my guard Julio, shy behind the door.

I look distress to El Mayor. Already he stalken far from me, frown guilty to the wall. I say fretful, 'Sure, come in. Be here.'

Julio open quick. Glance to my underdress, then look away with careful face. 'Senyora, is from Simón Zelote. He want to see you now.'

Bean peek past his shoulder. 'He sent a car. It's down there, if you want to go.'

'Simón Zelote?' I say footless. 'How . . . he saying what he need?'

'They don't say what.' Julio shrug. 'Ask for you, to Loisaida. Is too late?'

Bean muttern, 'Seven's not late. She's got four hours till church.'

'Loisaida, foo,' I say unready. 'Why he ain't come himself?'

'How he does,' say Julio.

'Bossy,' Bean agree. 'He even sent his guards to bring you.'

'Guards?' I say misliking. 'You be sure they even his?'

'They're his.' Bean nod with knowledge looks. 'They was here a lot, when we had the last Maria. Same routine.'

I look back to El Mayor, who still be frozen in dismays. Now I be fretting if this can connect to Mamadou. If all the search return with him, be there in Loisaida. But ain't no reason they gone to Simón. They should come here.

Yo, dark in memory, come Asha Badmouth's *Dead as bacon*. Guards be Simón's – but any a child can send them with an easy lie. And if Simón be dead, these guards ain't here for no good task. Yo, Anselm's threats repeat in mind. Can magine how I go to meet a ghost, and die in secret night.

But I say in hoarsen voice, 'Ya, can tell them that they wait. I only need some clothes.'

51

BY SIMÓN ZELOTE

Simón Zelote's car be large in elegance. In its back seat, can stretch my legs out long, breathe only leathern smell. The guards and driver all be Metros, clean in soldier clothes. Try asking what Simón want, but they comprehend no English word. At last, I sit back nerviose and stare the passing streets.

Loisaida be the neighbor burrow to the south. Place be a wilder dereliction, and its children poor. Got crime in every sort, and starving, every bad unhappiness. Ya, most barracks there, to keep the soldiers' misbehaviors where it be no worth to harm.

Come across their border, and the road be sudden rough. Car joggle like a trotting horse. Buildings all got cloudy plastic covering the window holes, and hills of trash beside their doors. Upon this trash, the snow be clean, but all around be trample filth. Most thing I notice, be some littles by an orfanato, chasing pigeons. They wearing blankets, stead of coats, and plastic bags on their sock feet.

Residencia where we come be drear concree, sans no bellesse. But here the windows all be whole, the road be swept and nice. Wear Mariano flags along the front, flap sad in Cember wind. Yo, as I come out of the car, a redcoat guard step from the door. Call clear polite, 'Senyora, please to follow. Simón is waiting.'

The way be simple halls without no pictures, nor no softening rugs. Come to the office door, and it be plain as nothing. Wear no sign. Yo, as I take the doory handle, a last reluctance grip in me. I magine this ain't Simón. Be traps. Is Anselm's soldiers there. I open with chilling expectation, squinting from mislike.

But be an office room like any. Ya, Simón be there, familiar in his soldier clothes. Stand to his feet with Panish courtesy.

Simón a child of middling height, with handsome looks of houndish sort. Bear himself peculiar straight, like all his muscles fix with hardness. Now he look tired rough, his face be scurfy with unsleep. Can see his age upon – is twentyish in heaviness.

Ya, I go fascinating to the drawings on his hands. How I know now, these showing ranks of soldiers, and the wars they fought. Simón's be everycolor stars and numbers, meeting crafty. Thicker on each hand, an L for Loisaida writ in black.

The office self be picky clean. Smell be piney wash; his desken papers fix in perfect stacks. A pistol on his desk be shining jolie like an ornament. Wall got photo of the last Maria – long-face girl in finery clothes like mine, but black for widowing.

Once we sat, Simón Zelote dabbit time with pale excuses. Say how he thought, is best we meeting here, be better privacy. He sorry to ask me here on Nochebuena, but is urgent. Talk various shee that children saying, when they dread what they must say.

Through this, I waiting weak. His tired face look no good news. Mamadou in my fear, and I be watching him with hawken need. I even begin to dread, Simón will take me into prison now; the searchers brought a Christ, and all my usefulness be by.

But when he creep onto his meaning, pigeon up to it with words – first actual sense he saying be, 'Maria, are we planning a war against Quantico?'

Almost, I laugh relief. 'No sho, we ain't. Be nothing like.'

'I'm glad to hear that, senyora.' He nod, his eyes still glooming. 'But if that's true, I've got to ask myself why we're making a ton of new artillery. And I also wonder why Anselm's telling me different.'

I startle. 'Anselm? He said we got war to Quantico?'

'No, he's Anselm.' Simón smile sour. 'The man didn't tell me anything. But when I asked him, I couldn't get an answer. Instead, he started asking what I know about their current preparedness.'

Here I remind, Simón Zelote ain't been at the clausen signing. Never he heard my tale about the cure, the rooish armies. And then he disappear from sight, been sulking in his home. But sure, he be apostle, ya is general of armies. Ain't sense that no one told him on the roos.

I think to tell him, but my nerves be wrong. Ain't guess why he kept ignorant. Nor I want to step in Anselm's tangles unbewares.

I say cautieuse, 'It be no war on Quantico, truth.'

Simón sigh tired, his eyes still brooding in their disbelief. 'Santa reina, how about this: I'll tell you what I *would* tell you if you were planning this war – even though I know you aren't. Can we do that?'

'Ya. Be nothing wrong.'

'Good.' His face go easier. 'So, there's one main idea I want you to leave with. You cannot take Quantico.'

I shrug. 'Sure, known we losing twice.'

'It's not just that. There is no way. I know that sounds extreme, but hear me out.' He smile, look friendlier now. Unknit his hands and rest them down. 'So, I'm guessing Anselm told you about the place. They're not as rich as we are, and their population's a fraction of ours. Sounds like a good proposition, right? That's what we thought when we first went there.

'But there's just one problem. They only have a hundred thousand people. But they have three million land mines.'

Must be, I look stupid blank. Simón ask careful, 'Do you know what that is? A land mine?'

'Sure I know. But any million? How they making this?'

He grimace humor. 'Senyora, Quantico doesn't produce much. Their buildings are falling apart, and there isn't a working car in the place. Pretty much all they make is armaments, and they've been at it a very long time. That city's been attacked by all its neighbors for hundreds of miles around, for decades. And they haven't lost an inch of ground. The neighbors – they're all gone.'

I think of roos attacking there, and start to feel some warmness for these Quanticos. 'So where these land mines be? It be some circle round the city?'

'Good question.' He smile encouraging. 'I'll give you a quick idea. Take a block like this one. Mostly four-story apartment buildings. No special targets, nothing industrial. So in that block, they'll have maybe two hundred land mines. You have to walk a maze to get through that street, and that maze is completely invisible. Try going into a building, same thing. Land mines, booby traps. You duck inside, chances are the room explodes. Or it fills with poison gas, that's another favorite toy.'

He sit forward, mostly like he gladden to this evil news.

'What else you get, every block is going to have at least one barricade. You're not taking any vehicle into Quantico. Barricades are mostly made of old cars, patched up with concrete. But they leave some gaps, so they'll be shooting at you through those holes.

'And they also like to decorate their barricades, for the entertainment of guests, with dead bodies. Since nobody's attacked them for a couple of years, that's probably going to be skeletons. But if you fight them for any length of time, it'll start to be people you recognize. And you do *not* attempt to retrieve those bodies, because they're booby-trapped.

'Windows above, you get your machine guns, light artillery. They'll have grenades, including some cute incendiary grenades that basically burn you alive. And the Marines live beside their weapons, not just when they're at war, but all their lives. You do not catch them off guard. So if you thought you could find the land mines, and dig them out, and crawl over the barricades, and actually go somewhere – you're doing that under heavy fire from all directions.

'And this is how their kids grow up. From the time they can walk, they learn *where* to walk, or else they don't grow up. And those kids fight. Here, we'll send someone into battle when they're fourteen years old. So that's humane, that's the right thing to do. They don't even think about that. The only thing they care about, as far as I can tell, is their holy city.'

Now Simón sit back, eyes set on me with expectation. Catch a pen from off the desk and start to click its nose in–out.

Been listening with ten attentions, seek to memorize these details. At last, I nod. 'Holy city. This be Quantico self?'

'Well, yes and no.' Simón put by his pen. 'So, if you've looked at maps, you probably know the Mall.'

'Nay, ain't know this.'

'Well, you don't need to, because you're never going to see it. Basically, it's where the old government buildings are, from the United States. That's what they call Washington – the Mall – and it's what they're sworn to protect.' He smile grim. 'According to them, everything there's exactly as it was before the plague. So when they're not manufacturing land mines, they're polishing the piano in the old President's drawing room.

'In case you aren't getting the point, they're dangerously insane, and the form their insanity takes is that you cannot take Quantico. And you wouldn't want to, unless you were as crazy as they are.'

Only when he pause, and sit back in his chair with some release, I feel my risen joy. I breathe in good content a minute, looking out the window at a partment building set across. Got broken windows with some clothes hung drying on their jaggen edges. I magine Marines with rifles there, aim on a troop of sorry roos.

When I look back, Simón be frowning puzzlement at my glad eyes.

I say, 'Artillery cannot clear these mines?'

He grit impatient. 'Some. But say it did. Then you're looking at destroying every inch of the street. Some people think that can work. They're mostly people who weren't there last time.'

'But what – yo heed. Be only thinking, if you got some planes?'

Now Simón look queery, like he guess if this be jokes. Say flat, 'You don't.'

'Nay, but if. Is theoretical.'

'Fine, santa reina. I'm only speculating, but as far as I can see, you've got the same basic problem. You can win Quantico, if you can completely and totally destroy it. So theoretically, you could flatten the entire place from the air, and then take possession of the smoking rubble.'

Here I begin to grin, ain't keep my feeling for no sense. Think how I telling Pasha. He sure to find some negative, but I see no badness for myself. Be only usual questions, why no person tell me this before.

Simón smile back, some careful wise. 'Did I say something funny?'

'Nay, is only wolfen. They Marines, be feary peoples.'

'Wolfen, right. My boys have started saying that.' He narrow on me curiose, eyes gone to wary kindness. 'Have I been making a fool of myself? You really never wanted to attack Quantico?'

'Ya, I said. Got no wants.'

Here Simón begin to ponder in his bony eyes. Think on our new artillery, or on Anselm's sneaky hints. Can see, he puzzling different, but he still ain't get no comfort.

Then I lose all defenses. 'Truth, I want no war on Quantico. I only need their help.'

I told my news of rooish war and pharmacy any times. Can think, I seen all possible reactions to this story. But Simón's be strange beyond.

First I mention roos, Simón surprise like any a child. But after this, he only go depressing and depressing. Even when I tell about the cure, he gloom the same. Ya, within this grief, a fury harden in his eyes. He clutch his pen in hand like he will break it for his hatred. Time I telling on the search, he ugly with distress.

I end my tale with scary conscience. 'Sure is mally, how they never told you. Cannot figure this.'

Then Simón sit back. Drop the pen loose on his desk. 'That's no surprise. The rest – I don't know where to start.'

'I know it be unlikely tales. Is why they send a search.'

He hold up his hand. 'Senyora, let me help you. The apostles believe you about the cure. They have no doubt that there's a cure. What they told you – that is not what's happening.'

I take sharp breath. 'Nay, how you meaning?'

'We've known about the cure for years. The Russian army – all of it. Our last eight Christs were Russian. I've personally heard these stories five times. I've seen the kind of photographs you're talking about. I've even seen a Russian helicopter that crashed down by the coast.

'Sure, most people don't know. They never get anywhere near these Christs. But Anselm, your apostles? They've been planning against this day for years. The *only* thing we didn't know was when the Russian army would come.'

I be mostly trembling now. I clutch into my dressen skirt to hold myself correct. 'Then why they sent no search?'

'Because it's not a search.'

'Nay, what it is?'

'Think about it. We can't fight these Russians, that's pretty obvious. So what are our choices? What do you think a man like Pedro sees in this?'

'Pedro?' I seek in my mind. 'Seem goodly sort enough.'

'Pedro is the most self-interested person I've ever known in my life. Okay, I'll save you time. Pedro wants the cure for himself. And he'll trade the city for it, everyone here. That's what that search is. They're sending Juan to make a deal with the Russians.'

'Deal?' My voice come false. 'To sell our children to the roos?'

'That's right.' His mouth disgust. 'That's not what they'll tell people, of course. They'll promise everyone the cure – if they just do what they're told.'

A coldness settle on me. 'But the cure be only for . . . Pedro?'

'Pedro, the other apostles. Anselm. A few dozen people close to them. Most of those people don't know it yet, but they're the chosen. The rest – they're livestock.'

Here his voice break weak. He make a loathing face, look to the picture on his wall – the old Maria in her blackish finery. 'I'm sorry, santa reina. This is the wrong way to tell you this.'

'Ain't mattering ways.' I cross my arms against my chills. 'But how you know? Their . . . deal and so.'

'Senyora, it's the plan. Same plan they always had, for when the Russians came. And you understand, the penal company aren't coming back from that little outing. They're a first gift.'

Now Mamadou come in mind. Flash in my heart joyeuse that he escape, be here alive. But then I think of Crow, First Runner – and every thousand children, in this city of my helpless ruling. How they sold in ignorance.

'I'm sorry,' Simón say through my thought. 'I would have liked to fight your war, for what it's worth. It was a smart idea.'

I look to him distracting. 'So you ain't agree their plans?'

'No, I did not.' Simón say thick. 'I'm a soldier, santa reina. I die for my city, my city doesn't die for me.'

'But why you vanish all these weeks?' My voice catch high. 'Why you ain't been? If I known sooner, we can stop them.'

Simón stand up like sudden impatience. Turn to a soldier coat hung by and fetch it from its hook. Start cladding it on, while he say flat, 'I was told to vanish, santa reina. The deal was, I keep out of politics, and they don't kill me.'

Now my dread gone heavy. Want to only sleep somewhere, forget I ever hope for life.

'It's funny,' Simón say on, 'I told Anselm I was glad to be out of it, and it was true. I'm sick of it all. But when I heard the talk about Quantico . . . I guess you never get over some things.'

'They ridding you for this, I guess. So you ain't mess their plans.'

'Yeah. And I thought they just hated me.' He laugh short and look back to his old Maria picture. Gaze in suffering thought a moment, face gone tired beyond. Then he turn like sad decision.

Take the pistol from his desk. Lodge it in a holder on his belt, and frown to me. 'You should go now, santa reina. They'll already know you're here, so you don't have a lot of time. Pedro will be at the barracks of Inúd by now, getting troops out after us. So what you need to do – find Anselm. Tell him what I said, and say you're on their side. It's the only side. Do that, and you could live for another fifty years.'

I take empty breath. 'Nay, it be done? You trying nothing?'

'Me?' He laugh sour. 'No, I'm an idiot. I'll try to get to my soldiers, and I'll probably be dead inside an hour. But you should just try to live through this, senyora. It isn't your fight.'

52

OF FIRST REBELLIONS

Ride back from Loisaida be a worser desperation. I stare the broken streets, the littles racing in the trash, and think how it will be, when roos arrive. How, in church, apostles tell the rooish lies in ready voice. Children go obedient for the cure – and slave to wars afar. If any person try resistance, Anselm got all guns to use. These preparations done and done.

And if I heed Simón, I be there also, faithful to their lies. Can hope they give me cure for Driver – be small price for my obedience. Is even chance, all Sengles save, to live uncounten years.

But every other child go perish in the rooish wars. Only be enfants left, that roos will bandon for their uselessness – some hundred thousand enfants, that the city already poor to feed. These starving long, without no help.

And I stare into the passing streets, and breed in rage.

The car stop to the Ministerio. I come out to its hush of Navidad and empty night. Only be my feet to hear, gone crunching in the harden snow. Come up the steps, and in the entrance hall, the dandelions brighten lonely, seem to shine with cold.

Here I pause and heed to nothing. I think, and grasp precaire, and always find new desperations – how soldiers of Inúd already coming, in their violent hundreds; how Sengles caught among, and be too many to hide, too weak to flee. How I be small and ignorant, in a world apostles rule all years.

But soon I see my single choice. It be a hope without myself, a chance beyond my life.

And I grit at my unwant. I turn into my fear. Stalk to the wooden door that open to the underfloors of work.

These worker stairs is narrow plain. Must hike my skirt and lift its heavy tail across my arm; step cautieuse in heely shoes. I come into the unlit hall below and pass the kitchen self, where children clattering–talking still, cook Navidad feasts in preparation. Glass in its door be smeary wet, they show like struggling ghosts. Yo I go onward, loosing down my skirts, toward the guardroom's noise.

This be a room of humble use. Walls brown from yeary cigarettes; the carpet thin as Vember grass. This night of festival season, all the working guards be there. Also be kitchen girls in grease attire, sit drinking restful wine. Ya, Tamara Ten be by, and Pasha big among.

Their larm be laughing shout, in personal English of their burrows. Be tossing darts and carden games. Some hunkern to a flop-ear puppy, say admirations while he chew ferocious at a shoe. One guard wrestle a kitchen girl upon a lopside sofa, while she laugh, 'Your knee! Jo, mano!'

When they notice me, this noise go out like quenchen flame. Guard leap off the kitchen girl, and she sit up with panic eyes. Even Pasha look alarm, put down his shope of wine.

I get sorry inklings self, how this fiesta ruin. A moment, I magine how I leave them in their happy ignorance. Choose safety, and seek Anselm for confessions, how Simón expect. Yo, this cowardesse feel right; like every world desire this cowardesse, and call it wisdom.

But I say in faltering voice, 'My children, need your help. Truth, I got no one else to trust.'

They stare back uncomprehending. Can see how Pasha's eyes misgive. A kitchen girl look scary to a guard, then bite her lip.

'What it is,' I say on stronger, 'be asking that you go tonight, tell every child about the roos. You seek the barracks first – tell any soldiers you can find. Most importance be, how roos steal children for their wars.'

They all look frightening to each other. A girl say in confusing voice, 'Get prison, what we get from that. That's stuff I didn't even like to know.'

'Is prison for tell secrets,' Julio say.

Bean scoff nervy. '*Military* secrets, what they're calling that. We was told what happens if we tell that story. Lots of details.'

'Ain't fearing this,' I say up louder. 'Soon it be no prisons left. What I learn tonight – it ain't no search they do in Massa. They going there to sell you to the roos. Apostles want the cure themself – and only for themself. All other people here be sold like meat.'

Then begin impatient time of questions, ya and scary cavils. I must explain the falsen search three times; explain three times, how good Simón been kept in ignorance. And I explain again–again what they can do in help. How they must go to every barracks. Tell the soldiers there and call them out to brave resistance.

Through this, their mood begin to quicken. Fury grow, infecting through them all in righteousness. When any child talk scary, the others badger him with scorn. Is only Pasha silent, face gone whiter while the noise increase.

Ya, sudden in this ferment, Tamara Ten ask in exciting voice, 'Senyora, does the penals know?' Around, the talk go hushing, while I narrow on her eary face.

I say, 'Ain't guess they known before. But now they caught by roos themself.'

'No, but they's in Loisaida.' Tamara make a priding smile. 'I just heard tonight, but they was there two days at least. Down in the projects, where they are.'

The kitchen girl say in, 'I heard that. In the Reese, what people said.'

'The Reese?' I say confusing.

'They's projects,' say Tamara. 'In the Loisaida River.'

'Goddamn, they here?' I say, 'Is anyone spoken to they penals?'

'They's hiding, why it's there.' Tamara shrug. 'Course you can't speak to them.'

'Reese, it's in the floods there. Half in water,' say the kitchen girl. She put a hand up to her waist to show.

'Yeah,' Bean say, 'criminals hide out there. It's nasty work to get them. It's a tall old building, you know, and you're in a boat . . . if they got guns, bye bye.'

I bite on my nerves a minute. Try to figure how this meaning, that the penals all escape. But can find no sense.

At last, I only say, 'The penals ain't our problems. Nor we can stand all hours discussing. Now, you go. Be losing time.'

Then Pasha speak up, sudden harsh. 'Nay. Anselm's people come for you. If be no guards–'

'That's right,' a girl say frighten. 'That could happen.'

'Yes, they come for me!' I say annoying. 'Nor no few guards can help. They kill you also, any child who know. Now go! I keep myself. Ain't want no child remaining! Go!'

They scatter then like sudden fire. Guards snatching rifles from all corners, duck to fetch their coats. Girls rush with frighten step. Tamara push behind, is giggling high with littlish nerves.

This noisy minute pass outside and dwindle up the stairs. Leave only smoky trails from cigarettes in silent air; the puppy in a corner, licking at a carpet stain. Ya, be Pasha grim.

Then the bandon quiet hurt my nerves. Feel like nothing been. And in the hush, can hear Simón his certainty, his tired despair: *I'll probably be dead inside an hour. You should just try to live through this.*

And Pasha say, 'Come, Ice. We leaving.'

'Cannot,' I say thoughtless. 'Must be here.'

'Must?' His voice catch angry. 'You need to die?'

When I look, his body grown with rage, his face be empty white.

'Guards,' Pasha say. 'You knowing, some be spies?'

I shrug. 'Yo sho, be some.'

'You known? And where they gone, they telling Anselm. Soon be soldiers here.'

I take a scary breath, touch to the sweat along my throat. 'Soldiers already coming. Spies ain't matter.'

Then, without no farther word, he come and grab my arm. Start to the door, be dragging me behind with stagger feet.

I slap at him in angry nerves. 'You quit! We leave, and then they take my Sengles? We hide while they all kilt? Goddamn, you quit!' I tug his fingers loose, pull free and stumble against a table.

He frown savage, bluish eyes be like an angry blindness. 'Why they killing Sengles? Ain't no sense.'

'Pasha, think! Do this so I come back. Anselm keep my children, and if I ain't return–'

'Nay.' Pasha make disgusting face. 'You magining. They never think this.'

'Yes, they think! I knowing Anselm! Be the first he think.'

'So Sengles hiding after.'

'Pasha, I got no moods to fight! I want to see my Driver, before they come. You can flee. Ya, go! Wish you been safe.'

He grit to this, say stubborn, 'Nay, ain't leave you.'

'There, you see? You see?'

We stare at each other for a second, breathing scary. Then his owlen face go soft. 'How I can hide? Be obvious white. But if you only rid they clothes–'

'Yo deaf! You heeding me? I going to see my brother now. Go to the Lowells there! They going to know some place to hide. You go!'

He only shake his head, and I turn flinging to the hall. Trip stumbling on the stairs, and climb their second part with hands and feet. Keep expecting he will chase me, almost be a need. But I come to the top, and be no sound behind. And I go on.

★

In my iglesia rooms, be still, with heavy mood of sleep. I creep by littles, curlen in their makeshifts under chairs. Pass a tray of cocktails left undrunk, gone pale with melten ice. My heart beat in my throat, and I keep heeding by each window for the larm of cars, of soldier voice.

Come to Driver's sleeproom, and I slip inside like hunting, careful for my rustle skirt. Be thinking how I leave him sleeping. Cannot tell him nothing, only be to kiss his face.

But as I start across the darken room, his voice come soft: 'Ice Cream?'

I catch in awful grief. 'Ya, you can sleep. Was only–'

A lamp come bright beside the bed, with Driver's hand upon. He squint to me, say in his scratching voice, 'You bone?'

'Yo sho.' I force a smile. 'Been drinking below. For Navidad, you know how.'

'Navidad, be right.' He smile. 'Physician said. She left for this.'

'Can sit by you a minute? Ain't need to talk.'

'Be sure. Ain't seen no one today.' He flinch and cough his throat. Take breath behind, then smile again.

I come, sit to the bedfoot. Look nervy to the yellowing lamp, the jar of pills that shine its glass. The covers rumple and confuse their broidery of stars; his arm lain dark across. Some paper tissues crumplen, white and delicate like flowers. This scene reflect soft in the window, with the moon behind-among. Yo, I hold this moment in my need. How the room be gentle quiet, only be his breath to hear. How my brother live, and I be living. That this be our life.

In this, I go remember, when I been a foaly six, my Driver tell me that the moon be made of salt. Said it be some moon rains, when the salt come to the Earth. What salt be, is crumbs of tiny moon. For years, he never admit that this been fables. Ya when I cry, he say I be a moon for salty rain. But he never crying nothing. Earth child, what he be.

I want to remind him this somehow, chuff him for his old lies.

Tease him, how I always done, that he lose these prankish moods when he becoming sergeant. But it suffer in my mind. Can know now, why a sergeant lose his happy foolishness. Ain't nothing for himself, and now I see – what I ain't guess before – Driver never gladden to this work. Been always worries, and our Sengles always fewer, hungry grown. The happy year he made in ruling, he given us his last good life.

Then Driver say into my thought, 'Ain't fearing it no more.'

I look to him unready. When I comprehend, I shake my head. 'Ain't need to fear. We bring the cure. You only keep yourself.'

'Nay.' He take a heavy breath. 'Be tired.'

'Shoo, I only woken you. Why you tired.'

'Nay. Been only thinking, is gratty you can have this cure.' He make a weary smile. 'Give you time to get some enfants. How you shy from this, I ain't know.'

'Be why I need you living, brother,' I say forcen light. 'Myself ain't making extra Stars. You get them for us both.'

As I saying this, I hear a carren roar in distance. It grow and complicate, be dozen cars approaching loud. Now I still watch Driver's face, but I be heeding to the night. A grief hysterical in my chest, but I will feel no grief.

Driver say, 'Be sorry, Ice. Been trying how I can.'

'I know,' I say distracting. 'Truth, you keeping bone. You strong.'

To this, his eyes go cheaten. He reach his hand to me. I take it, careful for its sores. Then it surprise in me, how Driver's hand feel solid warm. It be a living hand, can heal.

He say, 'Mean something to me, how you try . . . the cure. It ain't your blame.'

Be gathering to answer when a shock of gunfire come below. I startle to my feet, and Driver loose my hand in quick surprise. Then he frown toward the window, like resenting this intrusion.

'Is Navidad,' I say in skinny voice. 'Why it be guns. They shoot at the sky in their fiesta times, what Anselm told me.'

'Shoot at the sky.' Driver shake his head. 'Be waste.'

'Truth, they morons mostly. Yo, I got to be below.' I try to bring a smile, but all my face feel strange and false.

Driver's eyes go disappointing. 'Ain't meant to grieve you, sister.'

'Shoo, I come back,' I lie, with guilty miseries in my gut. 'Ain't grieving me. Got work, but I come back. You only keep yourself.'

53

NOCHEBUENA ITS FIRST MURDERS

Leave him, I be dead alive myself. Think of the windows by, if I can flee from their uncanny height. Magine how I hide beneath some bed, while soldiers kicking through. I feel how I must go. Face any guns, so they keep from my Sengles.

I step inside the elevator, lean back to the wall. Doors close solid, and I close my eyes against my fear. Hear my breath come quick and angry, feel my final time departing as the elevator sink. Think how Driver hold my hand, and been like something lasting, safe to love. How I will never see him die, be safe from this forever. And the elevator gather underfoot. I frighten up.

Doors come open to the empty hall. Only a moth be flickering at a dandelion light above. Can hear male voices from the entrance hall, in Panish talk. Ya be strangers, all these voices strange.

I go out precarious, clutching hands into my skirt. Ankles be unstrong with fright, must concentrate to walk correct. And as I come out to the hall, all soldiers round on me.

Be mostly fifty soldiers there. I balk my step, feel like my blood depart in flying dizziness. Need to run, to crouch behind some object, but I hold. I only make a throaten yelp as they all turn their guns.

A dozen soldiers run toward. Bigly child with stubble face get to me first. He grinning like some hate insanity. Aim his rifle in shooting posture, straight into my eyes.

A second, I be dead in mind. My body terrify to nothing, like it turn to absent water. Above this, I be thinking, *Nay, must be some way to live.* Then the child loose down his rifle, laugh in gloating voice. Another soldier grab my arm.

Be a sickness moment when I know them for Inúds. Can see it from their mustache face, their looks of wealthy feeding. Yo, they mostly wearing scarves of eagle flag like Lopez. Be Pedro's men. Know this, and I wince eyes from them. Is like their looks be poison self.

Only then I notice Pasha by the doors, with soldiers round. I lose my panic then, twist my arm free. Say high, 'Ain't need that.'

Inúds raise up their guns. But when I walk toward Pasha, they only follow, waring rifles.

I go to him with every madness noisy in my head. Feel everything be right, once I can only be by Pasha. They kill us, but I lose my terror. Death be safe in comfort – and I walk to him on feet like cotton, feet without no blood. Yo, Pasha watch me come like I be everything he fearing worst. Got marks of beating on his face – blood in his corner-mouth and reddish scuffing on his temple. His eyes be senseless bright.

When I get near, he reach to me. Then I go smiling terrify, and take his hand in mine. Some child say annoying Panish, but they never hinder.

And I say to Pasha, in my slow rooish, *Why you ain't hid? Should hide.*

First he stare on me unheeding, trancen with his grief. Then he say, *How I can hide?*

Go to Lowells. How we said.

His hand tense in mine. *Without yourself? Lowells never take me.*

Sure they done.

They risk themself for me?

I look to his bluish eyes, and this go desolate through my

blood. Forget my rooish, and I whisper, 'Be sorry. I ain't thought.'

Then his eyes soften weak. He muttern, 'Nay. Ain't never left you, truth.'

Now come some Panish shouts behind. Our closer soldiers push at Pasha, point us to the doors. Another soldier open, and the wind come freezing in. Pasha loose my hand, and we go through, all soldiers shoving round. Come out to honest cold. The Cember wind grip in my flesh.

On the upper step, Inúds all halt in gathering. Me–Pasha caught among. Some child nose his gun into my arm, most like he seek attention. But when I look to him, he staring pointless at my breasts. I cross my arms. Dread risen stiff and bright along my sweaten nape.

Then a groaning start along the street. Is cars in haste approach – and for a breath insane, I think these cars be help. Be friendly soldiers, callen by my guards or be Simón somehow, with Loisaidas for our rescue.

But Inúds look toward the noise like normal expectations. Ya, three cars come driving in. All blue the same, with Barrio de Inúd writ on their paint. They slow up to the step.

Two soldiers trot down to the first car. Open its hinder door, and in its seat, can see a child in shadow. Their hands go in to catch him, and he move like cringing, skree complaint. But they grabbing at his arms, they haul and struggle him out. He fall on knees in snow, and be a roo.

Roo be barefoot, and even in darkness light, can see these feet be wrong. Is purplish, and they swollen big like shoes. As the soldiers drag him to the steps, he keep on handsen-knees. Strain anyhow to hold these feet above the hurting ground. While he fight, he looking wild around for any help. Yo, his eyes find Pasha. He rear and scream his voice in beggary.

Pasha only stare to this. The other roo start struggling, screaming, catching at the steps. A soldier point a gun into his face, and he flinch back annoying. Cry in peevish voice, *Brother! What they want with me?*

Now Pasha seem to wake. Gather himself in breath and yell, *Fight how you can! They kill you!*

A soldier beside us turn his rifle. Swing it rough and club my Pasha in the head with its thick stock. Pasha hunch, grab to his head with nuisance face. The other roo swear high.

Soldiers by the other roo now grab him by the arms. Go dragging him up the steps on knees and belly. He fight backward with his weight. Can hear his yelping breath. Yo, Pasha watch, one hand still touching to his injure head. Ain't show no feeling, he only stare attentions. But when the soldiers drag the roo into the Ministerio doors, Pasha's face go soft in hurt. He look to me and say, 'Now they can kill you.'

It take a puzzle breath before I comprehend his meaning. Then I laugh surprising, weak. 'Ya, be a Christ. Can see.'

Pasha make impatient face and look back to the cars. I want to say some vally joke, how they be morons neverless. Kill every person here, and still they fuss to make a new Maria. But cannot think no words to this. Is only skew insanities, how God survive when we all kilt. How any person worship gods, when gods ain't even brave to die.

Then sudden, the soldiers shove us forward. The clubbing soldier point his rifle close to Pasha's head, so it keep nosing in his hair as we go down the steps. They bring us to the roo's car, and Pasha duck inside before they ask. His whole body be disgust now, like he hate this imbecile work. I creep in behind, and scare peculiar when the seat be warm. Look back, flinching to a touch, and find a fifteenish soldier tucking my long skirt inside. He startle back with pology face. Say whispern, 'Lo siento.' Another hand go slam the door.

Car got a wiren barrier between the forward and the hinder seats. Nor it got no inside handles. Be like the car that brought us to Marias first. A simple trap.

As I notice this, the driver open up his door. Stand out from the car, and walk back toward the cars behind.

Then Pasha touch my arm. Say whispern, 'Ice, can need your diamonds.'

'Ho, think the driver trade for this?'

He shake his head with obvious face and gesture to the car's back window. 'Can break.'

I sigh preciation. Work the jewlerie hasty open, pull it tugging from my throat. Then Pasha wrap the diamond string against his knuckles. Put this diamond fist in pocket, then look back to me. 'Can be, we jump out while they drive.'

I nod and reach down to my feet. Pasha watch this doubtful until I unhook my first heely shoe, show it to him.

'Hurt you,' he say soft. 'Bare feet.'

'Be Sengle feet. They tough.'

Then he stiffen somehow, staring to the window over me. I look up scary, and find Anselm standing by the car.

He talking Panish with our driver. Got a carboard cup in hand, and as I watch, he sip from this. Look jittery, and his other hand keep rubbing at his shaven head. His pointy eyes glance to me and pass on, while he still talking.

At last, the driver nod. Come climb back in the car, clap his door shut.

Then Anselm turn, look to me straight. Through the dirty window, his chub face be tired resenting. He call, voice dim behind the glass, 'I wanted to save you, santa reina. I was trying.'

Then all my terrors break in rage. I scream, 'Ain't want your saving, filth! How many people need to die so your unwanten life continue? Nobody want you living! You an unwant cockroach! Cockroach!'

While I be yelling, Anselm turn himself with tensen body. Walk to the car behind and climb inside. Slam its door loud.

Then I sit back in breathing misery. Pasha got his worry face. Ya, the driver laughing to himself, look at me in his mirror. I call to him in trembling voice, 'Ho, where you taking us?'

The driver only lose his smile. Reach forward and he start the car. I scoff, bend down to rid my other shoe. Yo, as I get it free, the car hitch forward. I sit up, look back scary where the Ministerio swerve away. Its lights pass off behind and start to lose behind the parque trees.

Among these trees, I see, in sudden tininess, Tamara. Is walking seriose, alone beneath the bosky shadows. My heart go strange to this. I look back to my Pasha, where he sitting tense.

He whispern, 'Going northward. Metro, can be.'

'Prison there.' I whispern. 'Where they killing us, can guess.'

'Ya,' Pasha say distracten. He raise a shushing finger, look back to the following cars. I look back self, and spy my Anselm in the car behind. He in the forward seat, but got his body twisten back. Is arguing something, wave one arm. His cup held stiff apart. Then we pass beneath a light, and everything erase in glare.

Pasha bring out his diamond fist. He muttern rooish, *We go in the woods. Can hide, then see.*

I nod and turn to brace myself. Look anxy to the passing street, how it slip fast behind.

Then the driver shout. The car pitch violent, squealing noise. Quick as punching, Pasha–me thrown into the wiren barrier. My breath chuck out, and I fling back again into the bouncy seat. Pasha fall on my wrist somehow, and I gasp rough with pain.

Car rock back, and all be still. I lain half on the seat, can only see my Pasha waring. His mouth be dripping blood again.

Then the gunshots start.

I cringe down. Yell Pasha's name, ain't got no knowledge why. He duck, then rise again. Punch heavy to the backward window. His fist skeer off, ain't even make much sound. But he gather and punch again. The window changen crazy. It hold a second, webben white, then fall in shatters down. I squinch my eyes as glass wash tickling down my face. The gunfire risen sharp, like loud complaint against this wreck.

I look back panicking, blinking glass, and find the wiren barrier got a glossy wet upon. Is red in streetlight, it be blood. Got time to

436

only notice the driver's skewen head, his face be wrong, then Pasha pull me back. He yelling, 'Ice! You follow! Now!'

'Ya, I know!' I say in brainless fury. 'Yes!'

Then he go barging all his force back through the shattern window. I take a scary breath and climb out after, clumsy in my skirts. Lace catch somewhere as I land my hand down on some spearing glass. Yo, I keep scrambling on its sticking pain, I tear my skirt, be free. A soldier running past, and as he look to me, a gunshot louden. He snag in air, pitch forward.

And I pitch forward, knowing awful, this been someone shot. I slip down from the car's hind end, land soft on Pasha's back. He grab me rough, be hissing rooish. Push me, until I comprehend and crawl beneath the carren belly.

Expect he follow, but he leap away. His shadow vanish. I lie into the slushen grit, behind a wheel its scaly flank. My breath come fast in bursts, I peer out to the glistening street. Be craving to know what guns these be, to spy some face I know. That Julio–Bean be there. Simón.

First, all I seeing be the soldier shot. He curling, still alive, around his hurt. Seize and stretch and seize, like worm that struggle on a hook. A gunshot ring against the car, and all its metal wince. I flatten myself harder, fist my hand unthinking on that glass. Pain recognize in distance, but then some feet go running past, and it be Pasha's churching shoes. I creep forward, till my face press to the rubber wheel its dirt. Try seeing where he gone. The snowy wheel be wet against my cheek.

Then a body fling down on the road. Is Anselm, scrabbling on his back. Feet seem tanglen in his long brown skirts, his throat be blood. His face be inches from my face, and in this brainless second, I take breath to call to him that he crawl under with myself. But then a soldier's feet run in. One boot come down on Anselm's chest, ya Anselm grab its ankle weak. A rifle nose slip into sight, and shoot in Anselm's face three times. Blood fly warm into my eyes, wet chunks hit stinging at my brow. Be squinting blind against, is only unbelief in me. My mind keep saying loud that this ain't been.

Then someone grab my foot. I kick in panic, yelping breath. And Pasha yell behind, 'Come! Ice!'

I scrape around in panic, bang my shoulders to the carren belly. Skirt lace catch again and rip again with gratty ease. I fling into the scary open, where my Pasha wait in crouch. Got rifle now, and both his hands is dark, is red. He wave forward, and I leap with him, run quick on hurting pebbles. Be steep exhilaration now to run, to flee like I been needing. But Pasha pull me sudden back. I come stumbling, swearing. He push me at an open car door.

I yank resisting, but he force me harder, yelling rooish. I dive in, swearing madness, and he push in big behind. Slam up the door, grab me again. I struggle thoughtless as he force me to the carren floor. Flatten himself above me, and the car begin to move.

First moments of this journey, I be only trembling, breathing tears. Ain't even sob correct. Only be a shivering through myself, and breathing out in wet. Keep rubbing at my face, think how these tears wash Anselm's blood away. I find some glass left on my cheek, and flick it from me panicking, like it be a piece of death on me. In my mind, I see how Anselm lain. How he grab the soldier's boot like beggary. The gun come down. It flash and flash. Be trying to think of justice, how he taking us to kill. But nothing righten in my mind. Any evils Anselm done, they been enough. Ain't want more evils. I only crave the hour before, when no killings been.

At last, I notice Pasha stroking on my shoulder. I open eyes. See the floor its dust, a flatten cigarette end there. My diamond braid hang by. Still got a speck of glass among the hair, shine brighter than its gems.

Then Pasha say low, 'Ice, you hurt?'

Take a breath, and I surprise when my voice come like normal. 'Nay. You hurt?'

'Nay. Ain't need to frighten now. We bone.'

'Ain't frighten.' I swallow at my throat, say weak, 'You crushing me.'

He ease his weight away, push up to lie along the seat. I turn myself, look wary up. Car got one shattern window. Glass remain in jags, crush into sparkle toward its hole. From here, the wind come mean on my wet face. I clutch against myself and say in whisper, 'Who they be?'

'Ain't know,' say Pasha.

This catch me funny somehow. I laugh, and only then get conscience that I still be weeping. Rub at my face and say, 'Goddamn. Been wolfen, that. Been wolfen?'

'Nay.' Pasha touch my shoulder again. 'Sure you ain't hurt?'

'Yo, my hand.' I open up my palm. Shard of glass be obvious big, and I go pick it out unthinking. Then sudden blood wash down my wrist. I laugh up thin, while Pasha swearing. He grab my hand and wrap it quick into my dressen skirt. Pull the lacy fabric tight, and close my hand upon.

Then a voice come from the forward seat, 'You two all right back there?'

I shift to sitting. In the forward seat, it be two children. The first a Ministerio driver that I known, our Pepi. The other child a stranger, chub-face jones in soldier garb.

Pepi sketch his eyes back, say in anxy voice, 'You got the message?'

'Message?' I say hoarse. 'Nay, what you meaning?'

The stranger child laugh harsh. 'Figures. Ricky's an idiot.'

Pepi nod toward him. 'This is Taco. It's my brother.'

'Ho, Taco,' I say stupid. 'Like the meal.'

Pepi–Taco laugh, but Pasha say impatient through, 'Where we go?'

Taco stiffen at this. Look back disliking on my Pasha. 'Just making sure we lost those Inúds. Then we're going to Metro.'

'Nay, we in Metro now,' I say.

Taco bring his face to better courtesy. 'Miss Maria, we just got to shake off anybody who's following us. Don't want them to know where you're going. That'd be a whole other mess.'

'But I want no Metro,' I say. 'What we wanting there?'

Pepi say, with sorry grimace, 'Take you to Felipe.'

'Felipe?' I say footless. 'Apostle Felipe?'

'Yeah, that's the one.' Taco get a careful face. 'So, Miss Maria, here's the thing. Felipe wants you to show up at his church. It's Nochebuena mass, so everybody in Metro's there.'

'Ain't safe,' say Pasha.

'Oh, really?' Taco squint at him. 'I didn't know that, thanks. Now I'm suddenly scared for the first time.'

Pepi say in worry voice, 'You don't afraid, senyora?'

'Afraid?' I clutch my injure hand. 'Nay, of Felipe.'

'It's really just getting there,' Taco say. 'The bad guys don't know Felipe's left the team. So, you get in the church, you're good. You got Felipe's guards, you should be safe. And we'll just disappear, so once you get inside–'

'But hold,' I say. 'You saying, Felipe sent you? This be his?'

Taco biggen eyes. 'You think Felipe done this? Serious?'

'Then who?' My voice come peevish. 'Who you be?'

For answer, Taco put his hand up, show its scribblen back. Black among the soldier drawings be a fatten P.

I frown, think through all burrow names. Taco wait with mischief pleasure – like we play at riddles, and he choose his question well. At last, my wits come clear. 'Goddamn, you penals? What it is?'

'Yeah,' say Taco. 'Guys back there who saved you. Penals. Remember that.'

'Shee,' I say, 'but how you known to come? My people told?'

'Miss Maria,' Taco say, 'we didn't know a goddamn thing. We thought we was picking you up from the sidewalk, peaceful. And I cannot believe Ricky didn't give you the message. That's some limp behavior.'

Pepi say with nervy laugh, 'When we come, is soldiers every-where. We don't know anything. We must get other men, so quick.'

I shake my head. 'But how Felipe be in this?'

Taco shrug. 'Do we know? We don't know. Mamadou said to bring you to Felipe, so that's what we're doing.'

'Mamadou?' I say footless. 'Nay, was Mamadou sent you there?'

'Yeah, you're in Mamadou's war.' Taco grin. 'I'm sorry, Miss Maria. That's what's happening.'

I sit back, staring foolish. Now the car, its darkness wind, feel like peculiar sleeps. Taco go lean down, can see him fishing up a bottle. Uncap the bottle and he drink, and all these shadow motions be a disbelief to me. Only the cold seem real, the forward seats close to my nose.

Then Taco squint eyes back to Pasha. 'Mister Jesus, can you be a second gun for me? Just lying there . . . I mean, no offence, but she's the one who's got to live. That's what we're doing.'

54

THE SEARCH TO MASSA WOODS

For longer time, we going nowhere. Pasha–Taco keep their windows down, ware out with guns. I shiver and clutch my hand onto its blood, press back to Pasha's warm. Car swing us to its weight in turning, rile its engine louden-soft, and Taco's voice continue through the wind like comfort dream. He telling the story, how the search transpire in Massa woods.

The searchers been Juan's guard of twenty men, with sixty penals. Ya, been Mamadou–Crow–First Runner, quiet kept from all. Bossing been apostle Juan. This child be a young sixteen, face still got looks of baby chubness. Most every penal–guard look huge beside his ungrown self. 'So, how that always goes,' say Taco. 'Juan's just got to show how tough he is. Kid's never been near a gunfight, so don't *nobody* tell him nothing. But basically, Miss Maria, that's the definition of an officer.'

First night been easy journeys. Drive to Citgo camp took petty hours; our Massa horses there. Only been some trepidations when they choosing ponies. Marianos mostly never sat a horse before. Of all they children, only Juan be cleverish to ride.

Juan take the NewKing's personal stallion, Beg-No-Pity. Choose this grandy horse for show, and suffer his bucking tempers. Mamadou–Crow take Army beasts; First Runner take my Money, kickety mare who dislike strangers. The others find some Lowell horses, slow to any bother. Ya, it take some sweating work before they make these animals move.

Beyond these normal mishaps, been no trouble their first days. Was only on their third night out, no histories begin. This been a petty incident about the NewKing's rifle, that he buying with my eary diamond.

From first beginnings, the child who sold this object get regrets. But his greed ain't tolerate to trade the diamond back. Instead, he sneak around the NewKing, robbery in mind. But how it is, my Mamadou bewaring murders on this trip. Even in sleep, he leave Crow watching or First Runner. One always waking while the others rest.

This bring the penal – Sticks in naming – into bad frustrations. So, on this second night, Sticks wait until First Runner's watch. Tackle her from behind and rob the rifle from her unsize hands. Then he stalk careless off. How he think, be any fight, his townie penals join with him.

First Runner stubborn as a rock, and all her mind be honor. Ain't even comprehend no person do this wormliness. So she dog this penal's heels, explain his fault with loud complaint. When Sticks only swearing back, her noise increase to yell. Soon every child be woken, griping, ya the NewKing first among.

Can think, the NewKing risen angry to this stealing problem. But he laugh like the others, how First Runner read this jumbo soldier lessons on his cowardesse. When Sticks swat a hand at her, she dodge, but never quit her scold. Soon be children shouting that he give the rifle back. Ain't no one sleep without.

Taco tell us: 'I think Sticks might have just done it. But Mamadou decides to make an issue. He gets up and says, "I fight you for it." So, we all knew Mamadou had the broken shoulder, so people's saying, "You can't fight with all that." But Mamadou won't let it go. And Sticks, he comes out ready. So that's what they done.'

Sticks be burglar people. All his boxing been with stubborn

443

windows. Yo, Mamadou scrapping every day of life, how Armies do. So this fight be quick and done. Soon Sticks be flubbering in the dirt with blooden nose and gasping breath. Mamadou kneel upon and rob my eary diamond from his pocket, fling it in yonder woods. Sticks spend the farther night in hunting for this small richesse.

After this, the penals hold the NewKing in regard. Nor they lose respects when Crow explain what Nat Mass Armies been. To them, the simpers be like sexy fantasies. Ya, tales about the feathers kilt – by roos, by Soledad – become their tragedy entertainments. They prize myself in admiration, that I save the NewKing; yo the NewKing be like sacred heroes, that Maria save him. All be mysteries of drama, better than no boring life.

Fifth day of this search, the expedition catch two roos. These fled the rooish army themself, behind some crime they done. Yo, they relieve to hear the Marianos talking Panish. Like Pasha, this be languages they learnt in earlier war. Juan and his closer guards go question them apart. They be an hour away, then Juan return with pleasing smile.

One capture roo, guards shoot direct. Ain't hide this for no decency. The other roo, they hold and break his feet, to keep him from escape. Smash them with a rifle stock, while he scream and beg his life. Then they lift him, sobbing, feeble kept, to ride behind a guard.

How Taco say, this cruelty start a time of evil moods. All hours, can hear the roo his groans. When he must climb down, land on his feet, he scream like baby agony. And now Juan take a sideward road, without no explanations. Road be thin and overgrown, is mostly lost to trees. Yo, thick along its length be bandon towns.

'That road was terrifying, serious,' Taco say. 'It was just empty houses, and you could see that people'd been living there. Yeah, you could *smell* it. Cause we'd come through a patch of houses and, my god. You try breathing through your mouth, and you could *taste* it. Just dead bodies. The penals was all praying, and these are not religious people. And when you saw a body – sometimes they'd left them hung in a tree – at first, they'd look like they were moving, you know? But it was just all maggots. And that Russian crying and screaming. And all the time, he keeps saying in Spanish, *No, we're going to the Russians here. Why are we going to them?* You know, he still prefers *us*. So, you start to think about that.'

At first, the penals see no necessary wrong, to go toward Russians. All known, they hunting roos to question. Only, they argue backen-forth, if two roos been enough. Their most suspicion be, Juan got no brains for warry task, and lead them pointless into danger.

But Mamadou born to evil ways. Worst guess will be his first belief. Yo he known Deema; known what roos expect from helpful children. Start working in his mind, and ask Juan's guards some sneaky questions. Then it take no thinking hours before he compre-hend. He tell his conclusions to the penals in his confidence, with certainty of pride.

At first, they shoo his notions. But their progress through dead towns prolong a day, another day. Soon no evil seem peculiar to belief. The corpsen pue keep sickening in their breath, the Russian's wailing scrape their nerves. Camping at night, no child can sleep, go jittering up at every sound. Yo, Mamadou say and he repeat, *Juan bring us to the Russians now. We be his first payment.*

Second night of this, they come to woods beyond no houses. Is dusk, but ain't no child got moods to camp. They dread the forward path, and dread the woods immediate around; dread the road behind with all its bones and horror stank. Yo, as the sun go quenching into blackness, they hear voices.

First, they only halt their horses, irresponsible with fear. Even Juan stare terryifying round and aim his gun at shadows. But slow, they start to hear correct – these voices be of enfant children. Is littles, squeaking harmless, somewhere in the forward dark.

Then Juan trot on forward. The others follow, laugh relief. Be magining some healthy place, some company from fear.

Through the inky trees, the town be normal in its looks. Houses all sit close together, streets be trodden grass. But, as they ride in, a scream come up. All petty shadows scatter, vanish like some panic mice. The houses slam, the woods go crunching with all desperate feet. Time they come out to the clear, be only the houses with their unlit windows, dumb in silent woods.

Juan go yell, in Panish ya in English, promise friendship. This only bring a daring skree, 'We got guns! Go away!' Penals–guards try calling also, swearing various to faith. But be no farther word. Only can see a rifle pointing from a neary window.

Taco tell us: 'So, Mamadou says he'll send First Runner, and everyone else should back off. He just says this, like he's in charge. But nobody's got any better ideas. And yeah, she goes, doesn't even say anything. Knocks at a door. And they let her in, and it's like five minutes later, all these little kids come out. There was just little kids, that's all it was there. Nobody over ten years old.'

Been most five hundred enfants in this clutch of twenty buildings. All be from the murdern towns beside that evil road.

Some was left by all their older children without violence. How this been, a roo appear, tell promises about the cure. Roo say it be one day of walking to their wonder hospital, where every jones can heal. But no littles can accompany. Place be risky for their health. So the older children leave, with only carrying enfants taken. Nor no whisper coming back. These children gone and gone.

Worser stories start alike. A roo appear with promises, but children slow to trust. His promises becoming threats, and when this ain't succeed, the roo depart. Return a week behind, with hundred others, wearing guns.

Times they only herding jones together, shoot no child. But where too many people hide, they murdering for demonstrations. Will take whoever come obedient; then they hunting through the woods with hounds, kill who they find.

Ya, been one town where every child been murdern, small and big. Only one petty six survive, who hidden sneaky in a woodpile. Stay in this darkness, terrify, while shooting–screaming pass and dwindle. Come out to a world of dead, all staring, crawling strange with ants.

Now, ain't no older child remain. In all these woods, is only brats. By fews and fews, they gather here, for comfort in their numbers. Ya, these weeks, the winter worsen into cold starvation. Now they eating moths and bark, whatever seeming most like food. Already some smaller enfants die from want.

These tales bring the Marianos into awful sentiments. Soon they given most their food away, forgot their practical minds. They sleep that night on floors, with littles cuddling to their warm. How Taco say, most penals–guards got enfants of their own. Can do some vicious manners, but they weakly for a baby.

Yo, every child expecting certain, now their journey find its end. Will bring these enfants back in rescue. Obvious be simple. With-without no cure, the city need to rid these Russians. It even be insistences, they kill their captive roo.

But in the morning, Juan say they must ride on. Enfants ain't their care, they must continue with the search.

'Now, if we *don't* do what he says, we can't go home. That's the thing. It's a disobeying orders thing, I don't know if you know that. And it's weird. That point, we all believed – the penals done – what Mamadou said, how they'd sell us to the Russians. But we all started down the road again. It's habitual or some shit, I don't know.

'So I don't know how far that would have gone. If we would have done something. Cause then Mamadou starts to come to us, and says he's going to take Juan out. And we were, okay, that wasn't no problem. That was good. And he says, when he does it, we should go back to the town. He'll meet us there.

'Well, we started hanging back right off. Cause we didn't know

447

what the guards were thinking. Nobody's happy, but what are they thinking? It could have been a whole firefight.'

How Mamadou rid Juan safe, been neater foxeries. He take a piney stick. Peel it particular to hurt. Then, in their normal progress, he trot up behind where Juan ride Beg-No-Pity. Raise arm and land this stick with force in Beg-No-Pity's tender parts.

Horse hit out like bullet furiose, Juan clinging on. Ya Mamadou gallop after. Guards startle footless, take some time to even know their eyes. At last, they go pursuing, but they all be stupid riders. Only lose themself in trees, their horses sluggish to no chase.

Penals never wait. They turn back to the enfant town. After a minute's ride, they hear some gunshots from the hinder woods. Get to the town at their slow trot, and Mamadou be there already. He riding Beg-No-Pity, and he raise Juan's rifle in his hand. Pass this off to Sticks while all the others laughing wild relief.

And Mamadou say, 'Whoever fear rebellion, go and find they guards. Ain't need you. But whoever want to make this right, you come with me.'

From this moment, he been telling orders to them all. He leave some children back to bring the enfants to Marias, ya First Runner stay in trust. Others ride home quick. Infest the projects in the flood. Been there eight days, done every spying work, prepare their secret war. Now, how Taco boast, they take the city, rid these wrong apostles. Then they go to wolfen combat, kill all Russians born. Be histories to write about their missions wonderful. 'Seriously, what we're doing here? Who else ever done that? I'll tell you – no one done anything like it, Miss Maria. What I'm saying.'

55

THE METRO SPEECH

While this news continue, my hand quit its nuisance bleeding. Taco reach us back his booze, and Pasha clean my face with this, rub with his inside sleeve. He find a cut above my eye, and I try to gladden, how I maybe get a bragging scar. But, ever Taco rest his voice, I see my Anselm in the dirt. The rifle nose come down. His dying blood hit on my face. Then I push back toward Pasha's knees, gone shivering awful through myself. Once Pasha lean down and arm me round. We huddle in the dark, my head press into his warm throat, while shadows slipping over us, the cold wind ache its voice.

Taco's story finish, and I be lying half in sleep, skirt wrap around my freezing arms, when the car come slow and stop. I open eyes to friendly lectric lights, good nighten softness.

Pasha say, 'We here, Ice.' He put his palm down to my forehead, like he check my fever.

'Ya, I bone. Is Metro?'

'Should be okay here,' Taco say. 'Unless you go in and Felipe's dead all over the place. That'd be a bad sign.'

We all laugh scary to this. I sit up, rubbing at my head. Feel like it going to ache, but it be only weighten wrong. Pasha open the carren door, and I crawl out behind him, feeling bruises stiff down my left side. Step out on snow concree that ache into my naked feet.

Pasha slam the door, and our good car go driving off in roar. I look back startling, feel some cheaten nerves that Pepi–Taco gone. Then Pasha touch my arm reminding. I come hasty on my painful feet toward the churchen steps.

At the doors, there be three Metros watching for us, perfect in their wealthy clothes. They do stooping reverence as I come. A fourteen girl in blackish furry coat hold out a cup to me. Say Panish, touch her chest. Male beside her say, 'For warm, senyora.'

I take the cup. Is gratty hot in my stiff fingers. I think of poison, but I drink it neverless. Is heaten wine. Pasha fussing at my skirt, brush something from its cloth. Stand up again with worry eyes. I hand the cup back to this girl and whisper, 'Gracias.'

Then we pass into the softer cold of this big church.

Be lit with thousand candles, set in spidery metal tachments on the ceiling and the walls. Even with this, the church be gentle with good brown darkness. Seats be full, ya children standing thick behind–around. All be in everycolor finery gowns and churching suits, and when they see me, they all kneel. Look like wildflower grass that flatten in wind. Yo, from this thousand, come a sigh. Is like the church itself moan wishful. Can hear a girlish sob among, and mutters of *Maria, Maria*.

Felipe waiting in the forward church. He shaven off his crafty beard, and he gaze naked on me, eyes religiosen weak. Silver robe hang like a mood of passion, fit his love. He beckon hand to me.

Pasha stay back by the door. Ya, I step lonesome through the hall, go forward conscious on bare feet. Skirt brush against the Metros, who still bow their heads unseeing. My sleepiness be gone, and now I feel myself a dirty fear. Can smell the blood on me again; the booze where Pasha try to clean it. Any Maria grace forgot. Be walking like a tired scratcher, come back sick from war.

As I come close, Felipe kneel. I know this ritual now, and I reach out my unhurt hand. He take it, kiss its ring, and rise up easy to his feet. Eyes shine like heavens, and he muttern soft, 'Tell them, santa reina. About the cure, the Russians.'

'You ain't told?' I whisper weak.

He shake his head with worship looks. 'Don't worry. I'll translate for you.'

Then he turn to the kneeling crowd, rise somehow in his height. Cry up, and his voice sound heroic big, he ring the hall. Is Panish, wrong to comprehend, and I be only thinking desperate, feeling for my needful words. Yo, too soon, he turn to me. His eyes be shining expectations. I take a scary breath and face the crowd.

Speech begin from nothing – Massa woods its happy quiet, finding Pasha in the burning house. I tell about the cure, tell every evidence that drive us to our journey. Gather in passion as I tell about the clausen signing; how I ask apostles for a war against the roos. Yo, my voice come ragged when I tell the search its treachery. How Simón kept ignorant; how Anselm come to kill myself for only knowing what they do.

Ya, turn and turn, Felipe repeat in Panish, like a songly answer. Our voices echo, thin and full, the candles change their light.

Last, I say feroce in need, 'Can know it be a wrongness to you, that I be Maria. But no one sell my people to their death. Ain't going to be. And ever I be a stranger, I ain't leave you from the cure. You all will live, or I ain't live. I fight by you to my last blood.'

While Felipe repeating this, I gaze out to the spaniels. Their faces now be wondering stark. Is like they witness some impossible change – a moon that speak, a sky that part to show a face. Yo, I feel my heart again. Feel how I come on tired feet from Massa with this message. And in their scary faces, these rich worshipers be like myself; like all bad children callen to a goodness past all hope.

In sudden change, Felipe hush. Raise both his arms like victory.

Then all these Metros leap up to their feet, yell heart's approval. Shout come exploding huge, then break in differences of voice. Be weeping, ya and laughter. People hug each other wild. Can see some mothers pull their enfants up to stand on stumble feet.

Ya, Felipe gazing at me footless, ravish lost. His face besweaten bright. His eyes be tears. Here I remind uncomfortable, this child

451

believe that I be god. Magine how he say some prayer insane, and I must answer.

But when he speak, he only say, 'I've got a car waiting, santa reina. We decided it was safest that you come to my house.'

56

FELIPE HIS RELIGIONS

Felipe's Residencia be a palace huge in white simplesse. Got garden trees around, and lights of Navidad along its brow; is sprucen decorations to its pillars. This night, be any dozen guards around the outside wall. They touch their hats as we pass by. Ya, while we coming up the steps, we hear the guns of our young war, a battering in distance. Shots thicken to a cicada trill of noise, then switch in hush.

Pasha walking by me, and I catch onto his sleeve. A moment, he only watch on me, is like he love my face. Then he say hoarsen, 'Ice, we safe here.'

I shake my head, let go his arm. Been feeling how these warry murders mine, I ask them into life. But I got no words for this. I only look unhappy to Felipe. He halten tense before us, his silver dress swing into stillness. Say low exhilarate, 'You know, all Loisaida's come out for us? Simón Zelote's with us, he's got five hundred men out fighting. And all the southern barracks – I heard you sent your guards to raise them, senyora?'

'Ya,' I say distracting. 'Guess I done.'

Felipe shake his head like wondering miracles. 'It's really happening.'

Then clack footsteps sound behind the door. A light flash on inside, and tall Felipe shrink somehow. Flinch as the door come open.

*

This problem be Felipe's wife. Girl be prettieuse as heavens, clad in lily garments complicating pink with lace. Is showing pregnant, and even her pooch belly seem an ornament. Ain't help but wonder if my El Mayor done love with her.

She lead us in with showing manners. Kiss my ring, do stooping courtesies to Pasha Jesus. Say we must call her by her name, Carola, like this be a gift. She take us to their tree of Navidad, explain its ornaments – and all these be some flatteries on Maria and her Christ.

But in this, her smile discomfort. Ever she look at Pasha, all her face go stiff like tasting mud. Keep skitting eyes toward Felipe, like she ask some needy question. Can guess without no words, she wish we never coming here.

When all emptinesses done, she take Felipe by his hand. Say something low in Panish that make Pasha frown his eyes. Then she–Felipe bicker soft, their voices habit bitter. Once, Felipe grimace to me, but this bring Carola worse. Her voice choke up on threatening tears.

At last, Felipe woof up loud, make stopping gesture with both hands. Carola take her breath, step back. Heely shoe clack loud, is like a stubborn last objection. But she force decency to her face. Say to Pasha thin, 'My husband wants talk with our lady still. Please, you come with me, I find you a room for sleep. You want some meal?'

'Sí, gracias,' say Pasha shy.

Carola beckon her hand and turn with sour glance at Felipe. Roo grimace to me in by-salue. I muttern, 'Save me food.'

The room Felipe bring me to be prettieuse bizarre. Walls cover entire by jumbo pictures, showing sleeper children easing in a parque woods. They romp on swings and hug each other in some puffety clothes. Room be lacy green with painten trees.

As we come in, Felipe pause. Unbutton his silver robe, and sling it careless on a chair. Beneath, he wear a fashion suit, elegant in blackness. He tug this straight, sit on a sofa. I sit by with curiose mood. Be woken from my tired, like war bring its own feary morning.

'Santa reina,' he say soft, 'I know this has been a difficult day. But I've been wanting to talk to you so badly.'

'Could talk.' I shrug. 'It been receptions.'

'But what I have to say to you . . .' He cross his arms against himself, eyes shining. 'And now I don't know how to start.'

'Shoo, you talking bone.'

'It's just, I've been praying to you so long. It's just strange.'

I flinch queery. 'Sure, your faith.'

'Oh, I know you don't believe that. El Mayor told me.' Felipe smile. 'I've figured out how it must be. Really *only* a true Maria would deny she was a true Maria. If you felt that you were acting for God, you would be eaten up by pride. It would corrupt you. So paradoxically, the fact that you don't know is a proof that you're genuine.'

'Foo,' I say discomfort. 'I been God, I going to notice.'

'No, it's the spirit that's in you, that I can see and you can't – that's the gift. It's obvious – only not to you. That's the essence of your purity.'

Feel some worse discourage. Be like arguing with glue. But I try, 'Your other Marias, they denying this?'

'That's different.' He make painful face. 'Our other Marias were completely ordinary people. But the whole process was corrupt. The last Maria had two abortions, I don't know if you know.'

I fidget nervy at my skirt. Find the patch of blood from my cut hand, gone stiff along the lace. Then I say low, 'You known the other apostles' plans? About the search in Massa?'

He flinch, look guilty to the floor. Nod with stricken face.

'Yo, why you never told me?' I say. 'If I being God and so.'

'Anselm told us that you knew.' His voice come rough. 'Of course, I see it now.'

'Nay, I sent El Mayor to ask you. Why I asking, if I known?'

'But El Mayor . . .' Felipe look up nervy. 'I didn't trust him. The way he appeared and wanted to be my friend . . . I thought he might be Anselm's spy. And anyway, Mamadou came right after that. Did you get the message from Ricky?'

'Been no message, shee. Ain't even got no Ricky there.'

'No, he's mine. He's . . .' Felipe catch his voice, look miserable back to the windows. 'Of course, you're right. I should have seen. But you have to understand, it's how we are here. It's like we're all asleep. We grow up, we fall asleep, and then the horrors that scared us before – we're doing them. We're the monsters in the nightmare.' Now tears grown in his eyes. His knitten hands be clenching hard. 'It took you to wake me, Maria.'

The gunfire sound again, come louder. I ware to this with almost love, how it be solid real. Start wishing I been by this fight, free from these talk insanities.

When I look back, Felipe's face be bright in need. He say, 'Did you know that this is all in prophecy? The cure, the Russians – it's all foretold in the Bible.'

'Foo, Bible got no roos. Nor it got no posies neither. WAKS, whatever you calling it. Ain't be.'

'No, listen. In the book of the Apocalypse, it's there. In the time of WAKS, Satan's brood – the whites – were cast into the abyss. But in the last days, Satan returns, leading the armies of the unrighteous. You see? That's the Russian army, now. And after their defeat, the children of God who remain – they live forever.' He look seeking in my face. 'They live forever, Maria. It's the cure, that's what it means.'

When Felipe argue, be a beary force of certainty. Ever he talk nonsense, get a weak suspicion that he right. So I only cavil, 'Ain't be no forever cure. Pasha definite to this. Can live seventy years or so. Seem like forever to us, but it will end.'

Felipe shake his head. 'Many Bible passages have to be interpreted metaphorically. Yes, it seems like forever to us. And so the Bible says: "forever". It's written in poetic language, there are hundreds of instances like that.'

'So how we win this war? The Bible telling that?'

'That passage is short,' he say with knowing gladness. 'When Satan's armies come, they surround the city of America – obviously Quantico–Washington. And then God sends a fire from heaven to destroy Satan's armies. You see how it all corresponds? The fire from heaven – that's our army.'

Here my patience ruin entire. Known these metaphorical tales. Metaphorical mean, the story be stupidity beyond. So they pretend it meaning something else, whatever they like most.

'Easy miracles for God. We do them while He sitting lazy.'

Felipe smile. 'Yes, El Mayor thinks it's funny, too. And don't worry. No one expects you to come to the war. You'll stay here. If necessary, we'll evacuate you to the north.'

This catch me unbewares. I crush my blooden lace into my fist. 'Shoo, meant no insult to our war. Be certain that I come. Should be out fighting now myself.'

He startle bad. 'No, santa reina. That's – of course you can't.'

Another bullet sound, close in the night. We both stir, glance to the window. It reflect its same untelling glamour, curtains furl around.

Felipe look back to me, smiling tense. 'The most important thing you can do is to keep safe. No one would want you to put yourself in danger. You're the city's soul.'

'And the city warring now. Be natural I going to war.'

'No,' he say, in straining voice. 'I could never let you risk yourself.'

'Ain't let me,' I say thin. 'You keep me here in Metro. Ever I want.'

'Metro? Is that it?' He shake his head with easing smile. 'But you'll be restored to the Ministerio, as soon as it's safe. And did you know that Anselm's dead?'

'Ya,' I say in sour voice. 'I known.'

'So it won't be like it was before. You'll be restored to your proper place.'

Now he gone gazing at a painten picture on the wall. Show a boyish child in weirdo suit of shiny blue. Child kneel by a girlish

457

sleeper, hug his arms around her waist. I watch along and magine myself back in the Ministerio. Life be papers and receptions, always in some skyless room. Yo, be some Metro ermano, give instructions in my Anselm's place. And so they keep me ever, till they murder me in fresh caprice.

At last, I sigh my misery out. 'Felipe? You know, where be El Mayor?'

Felipe frown. 'Why? He's upstairs.'

'In this house?' I rouse in hope. 'He knowing I be here?'

'I think so. But he's been there sulking, ever since Mamadou came, so I'm not sure.'

'Ho, Mamadou come here tonight?'

'A few hours ago. He came in the middle of dinner.' Felipe smile like funny stories. 'He appeared in the dining room, and just started telling me what to do. El Mayor actually dropped his fork.'

I smile discomfort. 'Sure, he will surprise. But he ain't sulk for that?'

'No.' Felipe shrug. 'I think it was something Mamadou told him.'

'Something – nay, what Mamadou said?'

'I don't know. Before Mamadou left, they talked alone for a couple of minutes. And then El Mayor came back and asked to stay. That's all I know.'

'El Mayor ain't said why?'

'I did ask.' Felipe laugh. 'My guess? He's being a little childish because he was left out of all the conspiring. He was obviously upset, but he insisted there was nothing wrong.'

I grit into unhappy thought. Truth, El Mayor ain't preciate that Mamadou boss this war. But that ain't give him sulks. I try other possibilities – that Mamadou said some insult, or had mally news of Lowells – but these fitting poory also.

Can only be one answer, what this conversation been.

I swallow at my nerves, say soft, 'Where Mamadou being now?'

'I don't know exactly.' Felipe narrow eyes in thought. 'By now, he could be back in Loisaida. He's got a sort of headquarters in the projects. It's the Reese, a building in the flooded–'

'Ya, heard this. And El Mayor . . . can see him now? He waking?'

Felipe make discomfort face. 'It's probably not a good time. When he heard you were coming here, he specifically said he didn't want to see you.'

'Ain't want to see me. Right.'

Felipe smile indulgent. 'Anyhow, it would have to wait until tomorrow. He's not alone tonight.'

57

TO LOISAIDA BY OUR WARRY NIGHT

Behind this, I beg weariness. Felipe plead me to some food, but I lie that I got no hunger. My best wish be loneliness and sleep. So he lead me up some stairs of whitish stone to his wife's sleeproom.

Ain't tell me it be hers, at first. Only, when I notice heely shoes left by the bed, I ask. Then I got no words to argue. Ain't like to rob Carola's bed, but I be wild beyond no patience. All myself be like a waiting scream.

When he gone, I sit down on the bed, collect my problems. Fret on Driver, all my Sengles, left in chances of this war. Guess on the fray in reckless night, and if it can accomplish. Worry how Pedro still alive, can tell about my murdern enfant. Then mad Felipe change his love like blinking. Join in burning me, for insults to religion.

Through this, I keep distracting to the room where El Mayor be with some girl. These walls be catching his familiar sounds, his breathen flatteries. And likely, he know I be here. Take this naked girl against him, and his mind be vengeance.

What Mamadou told El Mayor, must be the history of our loves. Truth, soon as they two talk alone, can know this secret find its mouth. All it need, one mentioning myself, and both will change behaviors. Then El Mayor begin suspicions. Nor the NewKing slow for hints. Will guess I done with El Mayor, insulting to his wolfen heart.

And, first in all this yeary day, I think of Mamadou right.

I stare into my bloody heart, and see a clean ungiving love. Been what we done, a truth beyond all painfulness. Our last spring before these hells, we torn each other out of life. And his scorning furies find me, even in this city's hundred thousands, in its thronging soldiers, ya in havoc war.

Then my desperations join into one red decision.

I stand up from the bed and strip the diamonds from my ears, my wrists. Toss them to the bed, and spit behind. Unhook the murder dress and let it drop in heavy slump. Still the room be warm to my bare sweat.

Be thinking every twisty plan, but my first hope come right. Sleeproom got two closets and these all be rich with clothes. Is like an evac in a dream, where every marvel loot be whole. I find some blackie jeans, knit sweater. Pull on some socks with greedy love, goods I ain't had these weeks. Scratch a jacket coat, is thick for winter, light for task. Last I find some shoes that mostly fit – zip boots without no heels. These I keep in hand, and I go listen to the door.

Be only muffle voices, closen far into some room. Ya, when I open careful, hall be black. Is only a line of light below one door. From there, can hear Carola–Felipe, arguing unhappy dim.

My hand be cramping sweaty on the boots as I creep down the stairs. Come in the empty size of the Residencia frontroom, gray in snowlight. Only movement be some shadows troubling at the windows, branches tugging in unheard wind. Tree of Navidad stand lonely, like a hostage from these trees.

As I crouch to put on shoes, more gunshots come outside. I pause and try to feel their danger. Remind Felipe's arguments about my necessary life. But I still be Ice Cream Star, last of the Sengle sergeants. Be kin to warry plight and forests. Got no careful heart, nor I will live beyond my pride.

And I cross simple to the door. The locks undo in one loud second.

Door open into grandy winter. Steps got fraily snow upon, is thin as paper tissue. Be witchen quiet, cat hours of our war. The only life be guards, stood on a scrabble of footprints by the open gate. These look up questioning to me.

As I come to them, I duck my head, put one hand bashful to my face. Say in my best sleeper English, 'I was visiting El Mayor. I go home now.'

Then I haste past, cold freshening in my breath. Guards watch without no cavil. Only when I reach the street, one call, 'Senyorita! You want a car?'

'No,' I call back nervy. 'Need no car.'

'Is dangerous tonight,' he say in disapproval voice.

I nay my hand and go on hasty. Feel their eyes until I come into the Avenida. Turn there, and I be hid behind the buildings by the parque. Then I go on in stride, my body thankful like it weep its capture. Night be like a self I walk into, my good belief.

First blocks, ain't no people by. When I come near Quinta borders, I sprint some way from passion, skidding careless in the snow, and only hold up when I see the Ministerio. Got its usual vanity looks, the windows golden lit. But in its yard be trucks of the Defensa. Soldiers crowd the steps, ain't tell if they be ours or enemies. I look to the iglesia's height, scout for my Sengles left, but only see its same bright windows. Hear no fight. So I turn eastward from this risk, go toward the evac street of Madison.

This farther walk through empty Quinta be a glory rest. I stretch my legs in horsen stride, and all my body wake joyeuse. Even the seldom bullets bring my heart big in my chest. Between the towers show the stars of every night enorme, and sometimes come the glitter sound of breaking glass, like starry voice. In one passing street, I see a band of scouting soldiers. They startle to me, raise their guns, is like a fluttering clutch of birds. But when they see me better, they ease. Got eyes for only risk, and they give no attention as I pass.

Then be minutes walking south before I see no other children. These coming few, and all be raggity boys. Some stealth by alone, some going loud in swagger groups. But all got bags of heavy goods. One child push a wheelen cart, fill with all clothes and instruments; a tall lamp nod its head atop. Begin to comprehend, they thieving loot, in chance of war.

One clutch of boys stare after me, call filthy invitations. But even this be pleasure, how it ain't no guards protecting me. Any terror can be mine. Here first I remind my Pasha, miss him in my joy. Be conscience, how I left him with no word in their unliking palace. But be late for this regret. I only swear myself to fetch him, soon as I get means.

My heart relieve again when I come in the pue of Loisaida streets, their trash and stanking life. Ya, here be every people noisy. Is street-fires set in barrels, with all children gathern round; vendedoras selling cakes or salty fish from tables. One orfanato home got all its scarum littles in the road. They play some snowball game, fight crafty among the heapen trash. Wear plastic coats with their home number, 224 E. 10th, writ scrawly on the back. This mind me of the enfants left in Massa by the penals – how they travel slow afoot, First Runner in attendance. Must wonder who be ruling in the city when they come.

After this, it be a quiet stretch with only inside life – voices in the blanket windows, shivering lights where there be fires. And here, a raggity sixteen boy begin to follow after me. Ever I turn to look, he make a face of unconcern. Stop by, pretend he checking something in his jacket pocket. But when I go, he follow. Is there and there and never rid.

I swallow my impatience. Hurry my step toward some gathern people – a vendedora of pepitas, with a straggle of littles by. These be skinbone eights with shaven heads, talk Loisaida foul. Words be mostly 'shit' and 'braw', with hooting laughter, swiping fists. Fourteenish vendedora heed them nothing. She only fret her fingers through her moppen hair, sing underbreath.

As I come toward, she look up hushing, hopeful for a sale. She check my clothes, speak out some greeting Panish.

'Senyora,' I say nervy, 'can tell me where the projects be?'

She ease disappointing. 'Projects? Which you after?'

'They projects in the water, ya. The Reese.'

She check my clothes again with queery frown. 'You looking for someone there?'

'I got to go there, all it is.'

'You go straight down.' She point. 'When you hit the water, you'll see. But it's not worth it, whatever it is.'

'Nay, I know some people there, be right.'

She pinch her mouth in disapproval. Muttern some comment on my brains and turn her face away.

Yo, when I look back for that sixteen boy, he gone from sight. First I relieve. But then it realize, he can be watching me from hiding. Once I choose my path, he sneak behind.

I head down, feeling jittery. Haste through a block of darkness, and I come into a mess of children, gathern in a street fiesta. They cooking meat on streeten ovens, standing plate in hand. Girl on a step play bow-guitar. Some males sing boozen loud. Remind to me it be their Navidad, is normal joy around.

Behind this be another quiet. Hear laughter from the higher windows, but they show no light. I keep to the middle street, clear from all hides among the trash. Be waring into darkness, strain my ears at every sound.

Yo, as I reach the cross-street, come a skitter of feet behind. I wheel toward a flailing shadow that grab my coat and yank. I skid on ice, catch to an arm. It knock away, and something kick my feet from underneath. I scrape heels, hit jarring on my back, as someone jump upon me. Sit a heavy dig into my gut. Only then I see him – the sixteen boy, face twist in panic. And a flashing shape, a knife, come big toward my face.

He say strangling low, 'You make a noise, I kill you.'

Knife press sharp against my throat. His face be straining furiose, while I breathe stiff against his weight. A hand start seeking round my body, push into my pockets. Knife shift thin against my neck. Draw a stinging line of fear.

He swear against the nothing that I got. Unzip my coat and seek beneath. Dig rough into my jeans. Yo, in this, his face begin to change. Hand slip beneath my sweater. Face sluggen into need, his fingers close ugly on my breast.

Then I take ragged breath, say quick, 'I got a ring. Is gold.'

He look to me dull, already distant in his want. I raise my hand up sharp, show him the gold ring from my proof.

His fingers fasten harder on my breast, then slack reluctant. He say impatient rough, 'You take it off.'

I bring my hands together slow. His eyes turn to this gesture, as I breathe and brace my strength. Think of Army wars I known, of knives and bigger children; Pasha's tricks of rooish fight. And I break sudden. Hit his knife away with all my force. Ya, with my other hand, I punch my thumb into his eye.

He make a strangle yell as I twist wild to shove him by. But his knife find me. Hit straight to my chest. It catch my collarbone, and its point dig, burn through the skin and by. I bring my fist up lucky, meet his forward weight with knuckles in his unguard throat.

He skitter back on knees. Make strangle cry, as I come to my feet, kick solid in his nose. Then he fall back, and I chase quick. Kick at his knifen hand. Knife fling away, go skittering noise and flashing in the street. He scramble after, but I kick his jaw in flying hatred. Then I only see a flash of him with blooden face, eyes shut and tearing, as I break running, dodging ice.

I spy the knifen gleam. Skit to, and snatch it by its blade. Then I be only fleeing, running hard with gaspen breath. Tardy fright be mad in me, how this been stupid lucky. Feel the burning where the knife caught in my upper chest, gone softer with its blood as I sprint on.

I only quit when I come to the water. Stop by its icen margin, panting wild. Hand grip the knifen blade, my fingers gone unfeeling with the cold. I breathe myself back into semblance, while I scout for risk. The only people be two eightish littles by an unglass store.

One carry a moppen handle. Swing this against a dead streetlight. Make a ringing sound that carry high across the empty night.

I unclutch the knife. Find petty cuts into my palm where I been gripping careless. I touch my collarbone, check at the brightness hurt of blood. Is only pain, ain't damage much. The cut be thin across the bone. Ya, Carola's sweater ruin right.

I shove the knife in my coat pocket. Look to the water, while half my conscience heed for sound behind.

A fringe of ice lie flat upon the street, crust white with snow. Beyond, the water empty black. And in this tarry water, dull like tired maginations, a building greaten huge into the sky. Ain't showing fires, is dark. Is like a blackness hole in starry night. And now it reach my stupid mind, it be no means to get there. Be freezing river between.

I stand, grinning consternations, staring at this obvious water. Projects in the water, said this like I got some notion. Ain't never wonder to me how you swimming to this place. Sure, be a clever hiding. But it ruin Ice Cream Moron's night into catastrophes.

Almost be thinking how I straggle back. Be any robber child, can fight with better luck, got my own knife. But then, in tiny distance, I spot a child stood by the water. He staring, nothing-doing, and my habit feel a recognition. Be a guard. I sigh away my panics, start toward.

As I come, can see he ain't a soldier by his garb. Wear wool hat and double coats, but still he stamp against the cold. Behind him, drifting loose on darkness water, be a boaten shape. Is small and look dishevel right; even in weak moon, can see it lose its scrubby paint. Look like a story of sinking, but I watch on it with every love.

Child see me walking toward him, and he straighten, toss his cigarette. Eyes notice my nice clothes with disrespect.

'Yo, brother,' I say polite. 'How I can get that boat? Be for the Reese?'

He shake his head, laugh nasty. 'Where the hell you from, girl? You don't get that boat.'

'Then how I getting to the Reese?'

'You don't. Where you from?'

I look to him, the boat, with sick unliking. Touch my knifen hilt, but all my braver feeling gone. Start magining how I dive in water, swim toward some open window. If this Cember water kill me, or be only miserable.

Then he speak careless through my thought. 'I tell you what. You want to go to Reese?'

'Been asking.' I look to him sharp.

'Give me a hundred dollars.' He grin.

'Foo, I got no money, brother.'

'You got *no* money? Pretty girl like you, I don't believe that.'

'Your belief ain't going to change my pockets.'

He grin again and shake his head. 'No money. That's a shame.'

I look frustrating to the boat. Magine jumping, but sure he fight. I end in water neverless. Start to guess, how I must wait till Mamadou passing by. How sorry-tail I going to feel for hours in this place.

Then some feeble brains wake in me. I say, 'You work for Mamadou?'

'Well, that's a question. Thanks for asking, I don't think I'll answer that.'

'Heed, he going to want to see me.'

'Really?' He shake his head like pity. 'Girl, you're not as interesting as you think.'

'He want to see me, truth. Can ask him.'

'So what's your name?'

I catch reluctant. Glance to the boat with sad discourage.

'Don't know your name and got no money. You in one pitiful way.'

'Damn,' I say riling. 'You want my name, be Ice Cream Star. You tell him that.'

'Oh, yeah?' He raise eyebrows. 'There's a lot of Ice Creams in the streets these days. I'll tell you something, he is most of all not interested in that. Go sell it somewhere that they want it. Seriously.'

Take me a breath to comprehend. Then I laugh up sharp. 'Girls use my name for selling love? You people sick as something, shee. You sick as rat disease.'

Now he get a trouble face. Say hard, 'You crazy, girl?'

'Nay, you ignorant, be our problems. Cannot know what you been told.'

'You're saying you're Maria? That's what you're saying?'

'How it be, my brother.'

He scout uncertain to my clothes, my face. Muttern, 'Accent that you got.'

'Yo right. Known Mamadou, you know this accent. What it be, you guess?'

He narrow eyes. 'Serious, you aren't who you say, you coming out in pieces. This isn't no night for games.'

'I know what night it be, more than you know. Now get that boat.'

58

THE ROOFEN CONVERSATION

Boy oaring for us both. I only sit in wetness, smoke the cigarette he given me. Boat draw a tail of moon behind, quivering restless on the black. Ya, when we come into the building's shadow, all be blindness dark. Is only the reaching splash of oars, the tarry pue of river wet. Near the building wall, its size feel heavy in the air. Then we float past the corner and the moon light on its brick. Show where a line of greenish moss rise furry above the water's shine. Yo, from a lower window, be a knotten rope hung down.

Boy ain't come with me. He only tell me how I go. Climb in the window, then be twelve floors of stairs. The NewKing's people at the top.

This be no special craft. Scut up the rope, come down inside to scrabble noise of scaring rats. The steps be pissen miserable, ain't only stank but sting your eyes. Is sticky underfoot. At every floor, be some bust window, and its light show clops of trash, a tiny haste of roaches. But as I go, I feel some foolish happy, how I done this wildness. Touch my cut chest and laugh through breathlessness that I be here.

At the stairy top, a soldier child lean to the final door. Be stood above all light, show only as a living darkness. His rifle watch me sharp as I come up.

As I pass the moonlight from the last bust window, he flinch hard. Loose down his gun and say, 'You're kidding.'

I stand breathing rough, touch careless to my diamond braids. Behind the door, can hear some laughing voice. Girl say a shooing word, a boyish voice go yell return. Then the girl be talking longer. The other voices hush.

At last, I get some breath and say, 'It be Maria here.'

'Yeah, it's Taco here. I don't believe it. All that work.'

I laugh thin. 'Taco, right. Our people took the Ministerio?'

'Who's asking? Yes. Why are you here?'

'My people in the Ministerio, they ain't hurt?'

'They're fine. They stayed where they was told.'

'Need no speeches, brother. Let me by.'

Can see him shake his hatten head, a troubling in the dark. Then he reach back to the door. It drift away to smoky light.

In the room behind, the windows cover up with boards. The light be only scattern candles, stuck to every flatness. Air blurry with undrifting smoke. Stank be of beer and feet. Got a dampness warm, like sweaten heat grown under blankets.

Be some ten children, sat on lopside chairs and wooden boxes. All gather round a science instrument, is glowing faint with heat. Be mostly penals, drinking Sirena beers, their jackets open sloppy. Even in this muddle light, some recognize myself. They startle, biggen eyes. Go whispering each to each till every boy stare curiose.

Ya, be one girl, in boyish undershirt and loose blue pants. Sit straight as grass. Got flatten nose, but still is prettieuse goods. A daisy face, how Sengles say. She look up friendly, then turn to the tallish jones beside her. Shove his shoulder and laugh.

Take a second before I know this jones be Mamadou. This be the second he look to me with fear.

Then he come standing to his feet, and be himself in scorn bellesse. He wear a soldier jacket. Hair cut close, got stubble beard grown on his face. And everything in him be right to me, as ever was. Is like the world remember its evil goodness.

His children look to him, to me. Fascinate like littles spying curiose

470

on jones affairs. Only the girl sit easy like she been. Scratch at her neck and frown.

Mamadou say low, 'Got blood on you.'

I shrug. The cut pull stiff. 'Sure, some fool stab me. Want my ring.'

Penals all go flinch. Look to my chest, the ring.

'Ain't bleeding much,' I say defensive. 'Ya, he sorrier now.'

A queery restlessness pass through. Now the girl be smiling curiose while all the others frown.

Mamadou shake his head. 'Come by, Maria. We best talk on the roof.'

Be a ladder to the roof from the bepissen stairway. Come out, you standing on some street material, open to the sky. Low concree wall around be cresten white with lumpy snow. Below, the river draw its blackness past, slow under coursing moon. Ya, the city by – its bandon towers standing with a gentle dust of light around their feet.

I come up first, go breathing to the stars in curving night. Then Mamadou climb out. Rise graciose with easy strength. Walk to me, and before I can expect, he take me by the shoulders. Grip there hard feroce. Then we looking one to one, with all familiar war.

'Hope you ain't lost me Metro,' he say quiet.

I scorn my eyes. 'This why you given me to Felipe? Be some pay for him?'

'Given you to no one.' His hands take deeper in my shoulders. 'Put you where you need to be.'

'I needing that? No sho. I done my prisonment, it finish.'

Mamadou shake his head. Loose one shoulder, and feel along my collarbone, find the sweater's tear. Then he go unzip my coat, while I grit hot despair. Yo is other mysteries, how his face good in my eyes. Is like a meal of wanting.

'Ain't going back there,' I say weak. 'Felipe mad as rotten eggs.'

Mamadou only watch my chest. Tug and unstick the sweater from its blood, a jarring hurt. He pull it by, seek for my wound.

471

'And heed, I going to fight this war. I going to goddamn Quantico, ain't keeping like a goddamn hen. Shee, leave that.' I catch Mamadou's hand.

He look impatient to me, while I grip his wrist. His fingers still touch light on my bare skin.

'So you go to Quantico,' he say. 'Who said you ain't?'

'Felipe, ain't you hearing?'

Mamadou grimace. 'Ever Felipe say, got no significance.'

'You ate a book? Significance? What sleeper words they feeding you?'

A moment we be staring at each other, cold farouche. Then he twist his hand free. Reach and pull me hard against him. His other hand catch in my braids, and we be kissing wild in need.

Kiss be a feary knowledge, where the world of coldness fly around us. All the blackness city and the stars grow huge and they be nothing. His hands stroke over me, reminding. Tell me quiet honesties beyond no words that pride can say. And my body brighten with insistence, love him burning good. I touch his face, his neck, and hold to his right strength with all damnations in my fearing blood.

Then, in moment's change, we both remember where we be. I pull back soft like taken breath. Mamadou ease his arms. He sigh and rest his lips down to my throat.

'There you be,' he say low. 'What it is.'

I form my hands along his back. Can hear the river's voice again, like every pestering that ain't this love, that cannot hush. Feel my heart beat small to him. I want him perilous for one final breath. Then I see the city dark behind, and shiver from his warm.

He loose back and scout my face. His eyes be glad feroce, is like a victory he see. Ya, I tense. Say soft resenting, 'What you said to El Mayor?'

Sudden, he rid me from his arms. Step back, disgusting in his face. 'El Mayor? Shee El Mayor.'

'Ain't got to say it then.' I hug myself, feel sorry bitten. 'Who going to lose you Metro, be yourself. Go to El Mayor with that, be lucky Felipe ain't hear all they histories that same night.'

'Gone to him with nothing.' He shake his head, like marveling my stupidity. 'Digger want to weep his problems. Ain't asking for this pleasure, sure.'

'Love problems?' I scoff breath.

'Sort of problems he can have.'

'So you share alike.'

Mamadou squint his face, like he defending from some mally smell. 'Interest me, when his love been starting. Thought it may interest him, what other loves you had this day.'

Take a breath, before this figure. Then memory come ugly, when I first done sex with El Mayor. Night of that day of murders in Army camp. Same day I tangle last with Mamadou in our fear amours.

I force my careless voice. 'Who counting hours? Was children kilt this day. Found what be insignificant.'

'He going to cry for what be insignificant, ain't my trouble.'

'So you rid him from me? Easy notions.'

Mamadou insult in his eyes. Grit like he bear down on pain. 'Sengle, you mine.'

I take an empty breath. It come a trembling sadness out of nowhere. 'How? I be your queen or so?'

'You mine. All it is.'

'Law be, I ain't your queen no more. I left. Must be a simper.'

'We past laws now. This be reality.'

'Reality.' I force a laugh. 'Was in that book you ate.'

He shake his head in some disgust. 'You need to eat that book.'

Then we staring evil to each other. Both be breathing rough. I think to spit, to punch his face. But every notion pass in nerves, and Mamadou still stare his cold belief into my eyes.

'Ice Cream Star,' he say, 'you never caring for that digger. Same day. What this going to mean?'

I pooch my lips. 'You ain't make much impression. What it mean.'

'Learn this, fool. I ain't him.'

'Ya, I notice this. And so?'

'You want to ruin some digger's feelings, be yours. I got no feelings you can ruin.'

'Got no feelings, right. You made of cheese.'

'Ain't his sort of feelings. Nor you stupid to miss this fact.'

'Fool and stupid coming brave from Mamadou Cannot Read.'

'Same day. Be paltry, girl. Ain't never like that digger myself, but nobody deserve that. Next time you want to tell me insults, talk.'

'I write a note. Somebody read it to you.'

His eyes widen to this. Then he laugh. Shake his head and laugh into my face like easy pleasure.

'I been with him months,' I say. 'Was all about yourself, I guess. Every person living just for you. Ya, I be yours. Been yours these months.'

'Goddamn. Ain't Sengles allow to tell the truth?'

'I guess that girl below, she also yours?'

Mamadou startle eyes. 'Patricia?'

I get uncertain feeling, but I hold my scorning looks. 'Girl got a name? Where be your Army morals?'

He bite his lip and grin, his anger gone in admiration. 'Ice Cream Star.'

'Ya, I also got a name. Known this.'

Mamadou laugh short. His shoulders ease, he look back to the city's blacken heights. Ya, my anger weaken sudden. I follow his gaze and find the moon, its paring shape particular white. Can hear the guns again, so far, their clatter weaken in changing winds. And I love the NewKing, like exhaustion of bellesse. Be stars, and be himself, in lonesome stretching of my heart.

A burden cloud touch on the moony edge, begin to hush its light. Moonlight swallow, and the city's towers lose their shape. Dark settle against my eyes. Then we be watching into blackness.

I say soft, 'Was vally, what you done. They penals.'

A thick explosion rise in distance, lose into the wind. Can hear my breath, the stirring river. I look to Mamadou, but he be only a shadow in a blackness.

'Can comprehend,' I say on thinner, 'why you putting me in Metro. Only, ain't been needful.'

He sigh out some tired thought. 'Ya, can be bone you come. Can use you here.'

I swallow, say braver, 'Think we keep the Ministerio?'

'We keep it. Problems with Inúd.'

'Guess we ain't fight the roos without Inúds. Soldier people.'

Be a troubling in the dark as he turn toward me. I tense, expect his hands. But he only say, 'They come to us. Come to Maria, how it be.'

'Ain't no right Maria to them.'

'Face them how you done, Inúds respect that. Bravery.'

I cross my arms low on my ribs. Hug deep into myself and say, 'NewKing. Be something you should know.'

Then my heart flinch queery. I square my hands in fists, hold painful into my cut palms. And I say soft, 'When we come here. I been pregnant.'

Can hear him breathing in the dark, but he ain't speak. Be his breathing and my frighten breathing through the grandy cold.

'They kill it,' I say whispern. 'Anselm's people. Ain't know how, some surgeries they do. They give me pharmacy, I ain't known. Now Pedro sure to tell this story. Threat they always make, so they can burn me for a false Maria.'

I hear his breath, gone harsh like mine into this blinden nowhere. A tear slip down my cheek, and I hold, shivering. Expect, he mention El Mayor. Say insults on this baby, got from father unbeknown.

But when he speak, he only say, in thicken voice, 'You hurt?'

'Hurt?' I swallow, try to think. 'Nay, been weeks before. Ain't hurt.'

'Bone. You ain't hurt.'

Can hear him shift again, and then his hand touch to my arm. I ease to this, my tears come looser. 'Told you sooner, if I known you doing this. But only Pedro know, now Anselm gone.'

'Pedro,' Mamadou say in almost whisper. 'And the simper known.'

A moment, I cannot remember who this simper be. Then I say low, 'Nay, she ain't . . . be Pedro who will tell. She vanish anyhow.'

Mamadou's hand go gentle to my cheek. It say his angry love – *you mine, no morning come before your enemies die* – while Mamadou say quiet, 'Patricia fix that cut for you. Ain't guess I coming back tonight. Best you stay in my room, no one messing with you there.'

'Sure.' I swallow at my tears.

'Will send for you when it be right.'

Then his hand be gone. His shadow retreat with crunching footsteps. Only, as he come up to the stairy hatch, he pause his step. Look back in untelling darkness. Then he bend hasty and be gone.

I stand a longer minute, faltering in my tired courage. Be thinking, *Sure, he kill whoever it need. Is war we do.* But still it pinch in misery that Pedro dying for my ask. Like I murder Karim with one small word.

And the cloud slow from the moon. Light give back its silver grief. Empty towers sharpen, like a goliath monument of loss; a burial yard of giants left upon the fearing world.

59

OF QUANTICO ITS WARS

When I come down to the smoky room, the penals gone. Be only the Patricia girl, sat on the floor to clean a pistol. She stand up quick when I come in, this half-gun in her hand, and her long body fine like prettieuse rifle. Then it remember nasty, Mamadou never saying she ain't his.

'Sorry for all negligence before.' She smile, correct in friendship. 'Didden know who you was, ma'am.'

'Need no special manners,' I say shortish. 'Ain't those times.'

'Well, thass very kind of you to say, ma'am. Very kind.'

I look by to the room. Floor be beery cans and bootprints, cigarettes and tramplen clothes. It seem a home of usual things, too shabby for no harm. But in my corner-eye, Patricia smile, reminding like a sting.

I say unliking, 'Mamadou said, you fix my cut.'

'Well, certainly be happy to, ma'am.' She nod like gratty news. 'Idden going to be like your doctors, though, should warn you.'

'Ain't science none. Be skin hurt, mostly.'

'Thass fine. It'll be an honor, ma'am.'

She go off to a grandy pack, set in a darker corner. Pick through, and she talk friendly nothings, how she keep her things together in this den of bandits. Tell stories of their thieveries, while I watch her slender arms unhappy. Ain't heeding sense until she say, 'Of course I mean no disrespect to your soldiers, ma'am. But things is facts.'

'Ho.' I narrow to her. 'So you ain't a penal self?'

'Wadden no shame, ma'am, if I was. But no.' She stand up with a metal case in hand. 'Like you say, we all past formalities, so I'll introduce myself. I'm Captain Patricia Mason, ma'am, United States Marine Corps.'

I take a startling breath. 'How, you from Quantico?'

'Yes, ma'am.' She grin. 'Here two days now, enjoying Mister Mamadou's hospitality here.'

'Goddamn, how he fetch you? Someone got into Quantico?'

'Well, I unnerstand the boys he sent had some experience. They was smugglers, make a story short.'

'Wolfen.' I shake my head, admiring. 'So, you being here, it mean your people trust us? About the roos?'

'Well, sorry to say, Mister Mamadou's boys did get a mosquito's welcome. But it don't need trust now, ma'am. The Russians are there, they're live in color.'

This chill through all my pleasure. 'There? The Russians be in Quantico?'

'Not in, ma'am.' She frown light. 'We all sticky on that little distinction.'

'Ho, cannot get in. Your land mines.'

'Yes, ma'am,' Patricia say with mischief grin. 'Quantico welcome mat. Now, maybe I should look at that cut, if you feel comfortable. Truth to tell, my folks all believed you Marianos was soft. Easy life, you know. But it's a pleasure to meet a leader that do close combat right. A natural pleasure.'

Wound seem nothing feary, but Patricia say it wanting stitches. She offer that she go and threaten the drunks downstairs for booze, but I reject this help. Be my vanity now to show no weakness. So I sit on a box with *Licencia Agricola 62 – TOMATES* on its shabben flank; Patricia perch beside. Then I hold reluctant, gritting against her needle's hurt, while she explain the Russian war at Quantico.

Quantico be three parts: District, Arlington and Washington.

District be a city of ruin. All streets got ugly barricades, and every window show a gun. Arlington be forest, with only fewer living homes. Got trenches dug instead of roads, and land mines scatter like bad acorns.

Between these go a grandy river, full of ruin bridges. Along this river, be the secret city Washington. Here be President's house and old museum palaces. Ya, be Arlington Cemetery, where all ancient soldiers bury, when it been America.

Roos invade at Arlington. Yo, can guess, they known about the land mines from some spies before. Before they setting foot, they bomb a path of ruin through the forest. Smash the land mines best they can, to clear a road that lead across to Washington itself. Road be made, the roos come in. Bring more artillery trucks and tanks than sorrow ever known. But still be land mines somewhere. Soon their tanks begin exploding, block the road for all behind.

Ya, Marines be waiting. Begin all shooting backen forth. And how it is, the smart Marines be free in all directions. They still know where the land mines be, can use all crafty hidings. Roos must use the path they made, without no covering safety. Yo, this road lead only backward.

So soon the roos depart. Quanticos plant new land mines hasty, while the planes begin to come. Game start again from zero.

Roos do invasion trial four times, then bore from this unhappiness. Now all their visiting be planes. These spread poison gas and burning, every scaring awfulness. The Quantico enfants now be living underground, in concree tunnels.

Yo, along their bombs, roos dropping papers overhead. These invite the Quanticos to surrender. Tell the roos' demands.

'All they're asking,' Patricia say sarcasty, 'is half of our grown Marines. Marines fighting for the enemy, would you believe.'

'Right.' I flinch as she tug needle angry through my skin. 'Ya, then they take the other half Marines, without no asking.'

'Thass the truth, there.' She pause her hand, a plastic thread strung curly from it to my throat. 'You see the position now. We all die together before that happens. Hoping you can make a difference to this outlook, ma'am. I do hope.'

'How their bombing road be useful?' I say, watching on her needle. 'They wanting children only, why they head to Washington self?'

She grimace as she pinch my skin together, aim her needle. 'Well, all's we know, they left Washington alone so far. She's pristine. So how it looks to us, ma'am, they want to take Washington intact.'

'Nay, why?'

'Well, it idden no land mines there in Washington. Thass a thing. But I think it mostly is, they know what it means to us. Thass our heart, ma'am.'

'Ho, they wanting it to trade. If Washington be whole, they trade this for your soldiers.' See Patricia's frown, and I add quick, 'If they can take it. Guess they never can, no sho.'

'Well, the truth being,' she say, nosing down to tie a stitch, 'if they wadden afraid to bleed, they could maybe do it. Been on the radio back to Washington, and Arlington's looking pretty effed. But we've been trying to let them know that would be a supremely dumb idea. They do *not* want to set their nasty little white feet in Washington, no.' She take a scissor, clip my plastic thread. 'And thass your last stitch, I'm sure you are not sorry to hear.'

'Gratty.' I sit back, breathing better. 'But how you mean, they ain't want Washington?'

Patricia snip her scissor shut. 'Ma'am, our laws are crystal on that point. Foreign power takes the city, thass an Article 57. And I'm sorry to say, nobody walks away from that.'

'Article 57?'

'Suicide Article, in our founding charter. You see, we have three nuclear devices. Don't sound like much, but it'll take out the city and most everything around it. Yes, ma'am, the day a foreign army enters Washington, we hold a little rematch in hell.'

60

LAST MEETING OF THIS NIGHT

Be Patricia Quantico who take me to the NewKing's room. Way be through a hallway where the light be only cobweb moon, come faint from parten doors. Ain't heaten, and the Cember cold feel like a death in indoor stillness. To the end, we come into a darkness closen as a fist. I follow her soft footpats, find a doorside with my hand. Then she strike a match, and reddish shapes fit sudden in their place. She light a candle on the floor. Say her longer courtesies of Marine, and go off with dark looks, still warring Russians in her mind.

Room got only a mattress bed with blankets neat bekept. Window boarden blind. One wall be thick with hanging objects, and I recognize the NewKing's leathern jacket from Army days. I go to it with sneaking wish, listening uneasy that Patricia ain't return. Hold it to my face, but its good smell gone dim with freezing. I breathe this disappointment, then I put the jacket hasty back. Crawl into the bed, and I pull blankets overhead.

I think two lives of misery in this hiding. Go from the Quantico nuclears to Pasha left in Metro to my asking Pedro's murder. My mind distract to Mamadou's kiss, and I be whispering curses to my own cold hands. And Anselm's voice say flat, *I wanted to save you, santa reina.* He stalk away while I skree hate, and then he fallen in the street. His last blood hit my face. And I want a cigarette, and curl my knees up, shivering queery. Last, the Massa enfants wander sleepy through my mind – five hundred littles in the hungry snow – and I be thinking, half in dream, we got to hunt them food, when the door fly open.

Candle flame skit out. A boyish voice swear underbreath. Booten feet come toward, and I pull down my blanket hasty. Peek my hot face to the winter room.

Crow's voice say, 'NewKing, you sleeping?'

First I only hold, surprise. Then some perversity wake in me. I say careless, 'Think he gone.'

'Shee.' Crow laugh unsteady. Be a wait of fumbling, then he scrape a match alight. Squint funny past it to myself. Is wearing clothes of penal, with a rifle slung low at his waist.

I tense, prepare my sarcasms. But Crow grin, say in laughing voice, 'Ice Cream? I thought you been in Metro.'

I narrow on him wary. 'Left. Can see that.'

Then he bend careless, light the candle. Shake his head, still grinning. 'We been at the Ministerio. Damn, that Asha Badmouth never change. She see me, first words from herself be, "Foo, you ugly in that brown." Was shooting all downstairs, yo I been mostly pissing terrify. Come up, think how I find them dead. But they all eating nuts, sat on the floor. And Asha, "you ugly in that brown".' He laugh, stretch out his arms.

'Ya, she discouraging somewhat.' Smile begin reluctant in my face.

'Shee, this building made of ice. How they rats survive? Skinny fur they got, think they all dying frozen.' He look to me friendly, hugging chillen to himself. 'Can get under with you? Truth, I freezing here.'

I catch on plain surprise. 'Can, if you want.'

He slip his rifle off, and scramble to. Be clumsiness while he come in, the blankets flying, lose their warm. Crow laugh anxy, shoving. At last, the blankets tuck, his shoulder settle cold against me.

Then be peculiar feeling, Crow beside me, like all foaly years. Even how he bigger grown, his elbow shape still fit my arm. My heart gone weirdo sweet, but I keep wanting to object, he hate myself.

'Gratty, damn,' he say. 'Foo, guess we going back there. Now you here.'

I shrug against him nervy. 'To the Ministerio? Why?'

'Put you back in ruling place.'

'Ruling?' I laugh thin. 'Ain't ruling much.'

'Nay.' Crow shake his head. 'It be symbolic, what the NewKing say. So children see we win. Then they all join with us.'

A moment, I feel plain resistance. But Crow nestle to me, shivering, and my contradictions fade. Truth, I ain't complaining if they bring me to my Sengles.

'So,' I say, 'it been your penals took the Ministerio?'

'And Simón, his soldiers there.' Crow get his grin again. 'Foo Loisaidas, they insane. I been screaming when it all begun. Ain't seen the air for bullets.'

'Sengles ain't been hurt?'

'Nay, no one shooting there, upstairs. Ain't no one there to fight. All we done, we clean out they Inúds. And kill the roo.'

I seize with awful heart. Then I comprehend, say jittery, 'Roo with broken feet? This roo?'

'Been the only roo they bring from Massa. Mamadou kilt Juan before they get no others. How it been–'

'Nay, I know.' I take a better breath. 'Know this.'

When I look, Crow frowning on me skeptical. I try to make my face correct, but only see this sorry roo. How he crawling from the car, his feet all purple wrong.

Then I cannot help my mouth. 'Ain't need to kill him, ya.'

Crow scoff breath. 'What that Simón said. "Keep the Jesus, he be useful."'

'Shoo, useful. Child ain't got no goddamn feet. Ain't harming peoples so.'

Crow wave dismissing hand. 'Is politics, what Mamadou say. So no one make a new Maria.'

'So Mamadou shooting him?'

'Nay, some penal doing this.' Crow get admiring smile. 'The

483

NewKing, he fought where they fighting back. Foo, he run out of bullets once, and this Inúd come at him, shooting. Mamadou, he come straight back at the man and grab his gun. Same gun that shooting at him! Inúd surprise so much, he trip his feet, and Mamadou shoot him straight. Child vally, damn.'

I narrow sideways to him. 'Thought you ain't like Mamadou.'

To this, Crow hush. Frown soft, like trying to remember distances. 'Sure, then,' he say uncertain. 'Ain't like no one then. Hate everything for being.'

Can feel him start to bob his toe in nerviose habit. Want to kick him, make him quit, but I still be shy from this. I shift away, say cautieuse, 'Hate me for being, I guess.'

'Yourself?' He give an anxy laugh. 'Ain't mysteries why I hating you. Thought every person seen.'

'I ain't, sure.'

I look to him and find his eyes unhappy on myself. He swallow, say in clumsy voice, 'How you was.'

'How I was?' My voice break strange. 'Ain't been so nasty then.'

'Nasty, shee.' Crow look away. 'Lucky, what you been. Every person loving you, best genius ever made. Yo, how Driver favor you, it give me other malice. Shoo, when he given you that horse, remember to you?'

'Horse been from El Mayor. Driver only let me keep her.'

'El Mayor.' Crow grimace. 'Right. All males be one big ball of want for Ice Cream Perfectesse. Myself . . .' He catch his voice. Crow's foot keep bouncing nerviose, while his face pinch resenting.

I want to cavil, Crow's life been no awful differences. Had all I had, except this pony. No person force him gunpoint to be skew. But when I look to him, his unchin face be its own argument. Froggen looks be poory luck enough for seven lives.

'Been harder years for you,' I try. 'Fourteen and so.'

'Shee right. Fourteen.' Crow huff his breath. 'Fifteen, was worser anything. But been my foolishness, that I expect the world be fair to me. How Mamadou say, you only got what justice you can make.'

This crush my pity whole. Ain't comprehend how Mamadou's sayings turn to no religion. I kick Crow's niggling foot and say sarcasty, 'So he making justice?'

Crow's foot halt. He tense beside me. 'Sure he do. You ain't dead, is you?'

'Only be thinking, maybe you make his sayings to a book. Be a chapter all on slaving.'

'He been an Army, how he going to do? Children change into their circumstance.'

'Guess Mamadou saying this?'

'Whoever saying it, be truth. I changen.'

Crow flinch clear from me, and we grit at each other sideways. But, as I think our yeary hatreds wake, Crow ease his face. Smile to some funny thought.

'Sure, you got other feelings,' he say. 'Like how Mamadou be about yourself.'

'Nay, what you saying?'

'Saying, it be familiar shee, you stanking on him in his bed.'

I start to cavil, this ain't what he think. But Crow begin to laugh – his bravo laugh, big like his singing. Then it come funny to myself, how I been sniffing at the NewKing's coat, but cannot hear him praise.

I laugh along with heaten face, and Crow shove teasing at me. He say, 'Goddamn, I wish you seen him when he got to say "Maria". Look like he swallow a whole potato. His face gone all–' Crow try to make this face, but cannot change his laughing mouth.

'Guess he hating me this time,' I say with moron smile.

'Hate you? Mamadou glad to hate you, once he use you seven years.'

'Foo. It need that filth?'

He squeal a worser laugh. 'Right, you a virgin. Pudy for no sex.'

Then Crow go telling humor tales about my virgin self. How

penals asking Crow on me, and he must lie about my purity. '"Oh, nay, she innocent right." I get a nosebleed, how I choke my laughter. And Mamadou gleering at me, like he eat my head if I say wrong . . . Ya once, this penal Donx come telling stank on you and Pasha. Mamadou gone as green as paint. Go pounding down the stairs, can hear him down there shooting rats. And Donx say, all confusing, "Didn't think Mamadou was religious." Shee, it mostly kill me. Swear, the rats was laughing while they shot . . . And when we plan your rescue, some child tell Taco, "Watch yourself. She going to be afraid with penals. Don't say no bad language."'

Here, Crow lose his final brains. Laugh till he bringing tears. He see that I quit laughing, and go leap on me and tickle my armpits. Become a squallen fight, both yelling, giggling twenty–forty. I only rid him when I find my knife and ware it at his face.

After this, we slump in bed, go talking townie memories. Is nothings of our robbery tricks, and scraps we had in tennish age; winters in the Tophet barn, and wars we fought among their hay. Be the conversation that I always wish to have with Crow, all years he keeping spiteful. But now every remembrance wisty, how this life be gone. Ya, be sadder hearing, when he talk about Karim their love. He mention this in shy half-sayings, watching careful to my face. Then I begin to weep my shame. Ain't brave to tell confessions – it be no forgiveness in this crime – but my eyes keep dripping sorry.

Crow say soft, 'Should tell you sooner. Ain't trust no person in they times.'

'Nay, you was right,' I say. 'I been some fool to judge. You right.'

And we gone in dreaming sorrows, smoking Mamadou's cigarettes by the candle's final gasping light, when footsteps come loud down the hall, and voices rough joyeuse.

Be Taco and a band of scrabble penals, calling me back to rule.

61

THIS MORNING ITS BONESSE AND EVIL

Is fourish darkness when our car start toward the Ministerio. Who come be Taco–Crow, ya Donx. This be a long and skinbone child, look like he made of elbows. We take a car that been 'donation' from apostle Pedro. This meaning that the penals rob it from his dispatch yard.

As we pass through Loisaida, streets be empty strange. Is only seldom cats and rats, all scuttling hasty in the cold. Yo, worse in my discomfort be the city's warless silence. Ain't notice when the gunfire quit, but now its missing voice be awful. Feel like the city kill itself entire, leave only stone and sky.

And we pass from Loisaida's ruin onto cleanly road. Come up Madison, where the stores all lost their windowglass. Some goods spill messy in the street, but most be gone to thieves. Donx drive slower here, keep squinting forward at the road. Only noise be our car's groan. It grow and wash out small in echoes from the closer buildings. Somewhere be lights of Navidad, shine heedless to the warry mess. And no one there and no one. Now ain't even rats to see.

Then, in the forward darkness, rise a boiling thrill of voice. Ring strange among the towers, cannot tell if it be rage or gladness. Seem like it raining from above, and shiver in the air. Be thousand children yelling, breathless long like cricket voice.

Donx stamp the brakes in fear reaction, slow the car to creeping. Crow swear, go crouching low. I start guessing brainless, how our soldiers give up shooting. Solve this fight with shouting argument.

Donx say low, 'It's not guns, anyway.'

'Ain't mean we got to drive into it, damn,' Crow say. 'Best we turn back.'

'No,' Taco say. 'I want to see.'

I ware up, frightening now. 'If it ain't fighting, what it is?'

Donx stop the car, half to the crossway. 'Look there. There they are.'

In the forward street, can see a mass of thicker dark. Is moving toward us slow and various like drifting smoke. Be a crowd of children, shifting gradual down the street. Can hear, the voices come from there; can guess its shifting shadows. Yo, as they come into the crossway, and moon lighten them, can see they all be walking backwards. They watching to the farther crowd, in ignorance to us.

Thick among be soldiers, but is also brown ermanos. Even be some orfanato littles in their number coats. Some thirteen girls be stood in nighting dress, with blankets round their shoulders. These strain on tiptoes, scouting past the other children's heads. Then one girl notice our carlights. Squint to us, and shout some word. Then all the thirteen girls turn round, wave like inviting us to festival.

Yo, through the ferment come a horsen neigh, particular like music. I sit up, waring breathless. When it whinny up again, my heart go weirdo bright. Then I be fumbling for the doory handle, running from the car. Crow shout behind, but I go sprinting heedless. Come to the mass of children as they break apart, shift toward the roadside. First, I think they recognize me – give Maria room. But then I see the littles coming slow along the street. People all be stepping back to let these enfants pass.

Be any hundred littles there, in dirty clothes of moth appearance. Their coats stuff fat with paper; heads be mostly lost in scarf. Got packs upon their back, so each look like a shamble bear of cloth. Bigger tens be pushing wheeler-carts with nests of baby twos, who skree appalling to the crowd. And down the street, as far as eyesight, be more littles come the same. All dragging in exhaustion – but soon it realize, they also slow because they eating food. Yo, as I watch, a Mariano girl come from a house with bread in hands. She pass this to a scruffety eight, and soon the bread be torn in pieces, stuffing in all enfants' mouths.

Then, tall among this littlish mob, I spy my pony Money. Her spotten flanks be queer like maginations in this muzzy light. Before I think, I yell my voice. Then she spark feet, come barging glad. First Runner small astride – is yanking at the reins, while Money scare all littles from her path. They skeltering in all directions, like a splashing wake. Then Money nosing in my face while I reach to First Runner, laughing breath, my blood spectacular with joy.

First Runner cry in high frustration, 'Leave my mare! She biting peoples!'

I call brainless. 'You ain't hurt? You bone?'

Now she recognize my voice. Go startle, gape her mouth.

'You bone?' I cry again.

'Ice Cream?' she say in breaking voice. 'You all alive? And Mamadou?'

'We bone! All be the same!'

'Then why–' She look to the littles, who be pausing back, uncertain. An eight yell something to her, but she wave a nay ferocious, frown to me. 'Truth? You ain't lying?'

'Swear my head, they bone!'

She cry perilous mean, 'Why no one come? Been walking days, and no one come. We starving there!'

'My ten, we never known!'

'But – El Mayor be bone? Ain't lie!'

'Ain't lying! Bring these to the Ministerio! Be all rooms there empty.'

Now she recollect her pride. Snuff nose, and say in pickety voice, 'Thought this ourself. But where it be?'

'Can follow our car! We going now!'

As I turn to point, Crow be there, crashing to me huge. He grab my collar scruff and yell, 'Damn, what you doing? What you thinking? What?'

'Shee!' I yell back hot. 'These be the littles come from Massa! Ain't you see?'

'Ain't only littles here! Is every people! Damn, come back!'

He start to haul me by my collar, while my Money startle. Pick her feet, neigh warm and smelly in our face. I laugh and call back to First Runner, 'Mind, you chase our car!'

Then I turn, go jogging back with Crow, while he still swearing mean. But by our car, now be some dozen soldiers, gather to Taco–Donx. Crow balk, throw out an arm to stop me.

'Crow, it's good,' call Donx in boring voice. 'They're ours, it's cool.'

Then Taco saying something low. All soldiers startle awful. Go stoop a hasty courtesy to me, while Taco grin his face.

'Come on,' call Taco. 'You got to hear this. Jimmy, tell the story.' He nod toward a bigly soldier with a bandage hand.

Jimmy look up shy. 'Yeah, I was only saying, it's over.'

'No, the story.' Taco shove his shoulder, grin to us. 'Jimmy was with Simón's boys uptown. They was shooting it out with Inúds from barracks there, when all those kids come through.'

'Yeah.' Jimmy make a nervy smile. 'We was in the park up there, just killing each other, you know. And suddenly, a thousand little kids walk smack out into the middle.'

'And it all *stopped*,' say Taco.

'So it start again, now they all past,' say Crow.

'No, mano.' Taco flap his hand dismissing. 'Think. What do they do, those Massa kids, whenever they see grown people?'

'Ask for food,' Donx offer.

Taco point to Donx and nod. 'And then it's a conversation, what it was. One second, people's shooting each other. The next second, it's a mess of kids. And those kids go up to Inúds, to anyone. They don't know the difference. Beg for food, and the next thing, they're telling their whole sad story. Well, our enemy, they got real confused. Jimmy, tell them.'

'Yeah, the best part,' Jimmy say. 'Then, Simón, he jumps up on a car and gives a speech. Somebody shoots at the man, he doesn't even shut up. Simón, you know.'

'That's what he's like,' say Donx.

Jimmy nod. 'So he tells them how the apostles was planning to sell us all . . . you know. The whole thing.'

'And you realize,' say Taco, 'these guys all fought with him before. He's the goddamn general.'

'That was it, senyora.' Jimmy smile. 'The enemy, they just listened. Like they all come there to hear a speech. And then they marched off after him like ducks. Barracks of Inúd, who these guys were. The faithful.'

'The *last* of the faithful,' Donx say.

'People, it's over.' Taco draw a finger across his throat. 'We won.'

Then only be two blocks to drive, but it take careful minutes. Always be some littles, wandern stupid in the road; be soldiers climbing on the car joyeuse. Yo, in this petty time, I start to feel my tired body. Cut palms begin to itch; my stabben chest feel sorry hurt. But all these pains be gratty now, feel heavy like a gift. Keep thinking how I go see Driver. Sleep by him in company. Can tell him how we get the cure in petty days, all problems done. Say this, then we both sleep like heaven.

And we stop to the Ministerio steps. They litter spectacular with glass from gunshot doors and windows. We step out in a throng of soldiers who skit back, gasp blessing words. I drowse afoot as I go up. Look back for Crow, but he be bickering still with Taco in the street. They mix into the thousand littles coming slow like clouds. I go on toward the entrance hall, where dandelions still be lit – yo, now their dangles stir from wind invading through the broken windows. Come to the door, duck through its missing glass.

In middy hall, it be a clutch of my own redcoat guards. I start toward them, grinning mouth, but they all look away. Their manners be severe, like they uneasy for some problem. I hold my step, considering sudden if some guard been kilt for me.

Then Julio step from them hasty. His reddish coat unbutton sloppy, face gone panic bright.

I say confusing, 'Julio, you bone? They never catch you?'

'Senyora,' he say hoarsen. 'Is your brother.'

My sleepiness go weak with fear. 'Nay, Driver? What it be?'

'Hospital, he go.' Julio look frighten to the door. 'Hour past.'

'Nay, what been?'

'His sickness. Bleed inside, they say. Take him for help.'

A moment, I cannot take breath. My heart fill all my chest. Then I gasp somehow, 'Can be, my car still there. We–'

'Yes, senyora. I stop them, yes.'

Julio run out the door. A moment, I be only frozen, staring into nothing. Want to shout some argument, how hard it been, ain't justice. Then terror rise, and I go run. Come out on the steps, and dodge through littles coming up. Be this careful movement, and be the blackish sky tremendous overhead, its dull, uncolor moon. As I see the car, with Julio waving by, a red distress, my terror bite into me worse. Be like no feeling that I known. Is like a killing sickness. I catch my hand up to my throat and go on with this terrify evil breaking in my heart.

Quinta hospital be the home where this white terror live. Come in a bleary whitish hall, and Julio shout his Panish at an enfermera there. She scramble to find papers. Mutter panicking, while I grip fingers sweaty in my pockets. Then we go down halls with rubber smell of pharmacies and illness. Be blue medicals scrambling past us, like a pulling wind; be tear-face children leaning to the walls. Our enfermera talking feary Panish, until I ask in fright, 'What she saying? Driver worse?'

Girl hush at this, look down with shamen eyes. 'No,' Julio say hasty, 'she say, is sorry, they busy from the war. Too many sick here.'

As he say this, we come to the elevator hall. Here stand two medical children with a rolling bed between. A fifteen boy in soldier clothes lain there, got redden bandages to his throat. He breathing scary fast, stare at the medical boy beside, who muttern over–over, 'Tranquilo, tranquilo.' Our enfermera start explaining to them, waving hands. Then the medicals stare to me, stoop courtesies with muttern prayer.

Ya, the injure soldier make a face of beggary. Struggle a hand toward me, make a breathen noise without no voice. His body straining while the medicals hush him nerviose.

Julio say soft, 'He want a blessing, senyora. Is scare.'

I nod without no mind. Step toward him, and he ease back, tears beginning in his eyes.

I say what Panish prayer I remember, voice dim from its fear. Injure child watch on my face with hungry hope, eyes gentling. When I finish, a medical whisper, 'Gracias, bendita reina.' I look to her, and she be weeping – a scary fourteen with lips blooden from their winter chapping.

Then the elevator open, and the soldier shut his eyes. Face clench back to its hurt.

Two twelvish girls come staggering from the elevator, sobbing awful. One be wailing, 'No, if he's not here – they said. He got to be here.' The other hushing her, look shame to us as they push by.

Then we all shove in this elevator, be no moron courtesies. Ya, all its floor be footprint blood. I shut my eyes to this, my terror sharper. Pray to the nothing I believe that all these children save. Pray this war forgive, or that I die for any guilt. If any person die, it be myself. Ain't Driver die for this.

Injure soldier and his medicals leave on second floor. Ya, we go upward to the fifth. In this petty time of waiting, our enfermera talk again. I look staring to her, but now I only think of bleeding inside. How this happen. How any person stop this, once it be. And

Julio say, unmeaning in my fear, 'She say, these floors be only for sarcoma. Good help they give. You not worry, is good.'

Take me a breathing minute before I remind, sarcoma meaning posies. Then my mind start babbiting Panish – *sarcoma, tranquilo, bendita reina, gracias* – in some reaching madness.

Elevator open to another hall, is white the same. The enfermera go up to a door across, stop quick. She whisper another endless fear, and Julio say to me, 'Is here, can go. Only, you are quiet for him. He need sleep.'

I breathe out, try to relieve. But my heart stuck in that terror. Be like the world become a brainless light, deep in my eyes. I reach to the doory handle with this terror sprinting past and past.

Inside, is dimmer light. Driver there in gentle darkness, lain into a bed with rails beside. I close the door behind and feel its petty noise in all my blood. Then I go terrify to my brother.

Bed be clean as enfant snow. His sore hand bandage white. With the heapen blankets, his body showing healthy size, and even his shut eyes look happy, like they drowse in good content. But he be dead.

Cannot tell how I know. But when I look into his face, my whole self scream that he be dead. I reach my shaking hand up to his nose and feel for breath. Touch to his neck, feel for no heartbeat. And my mind be running fright, how Driver breathing loud these weeks. Ain't be no quiet in his life. He dead, is dead.

Come a moment lost while everything shrink hard in me. I sit heavy to the floor. Feel like I going to die myself, my heart be like some crushen mouse. In my mind, I say to Driver, *Brother, no one seen you dead but me. You can come back, nobody ever know.* Clench eyes shut and make a prayer to my nothing god – whatever god it be, whatever ghost can hear this prayer. Yo, can almost feel a listening there – a misten sympathy, like darkness sunlight in shut eyes. I reach out to this feeling, beg and beg with gritten teeth.

But this spirit hear me with a sad refusal in itself. All my magination cannot make it answer yes.

And I open eyes on Driver's stillness, cold the same. My fear turn somehow, and I comprehend, it ain't been terror. Been grief too big to know. I whisper, 'Damn, I love you worse, my brother. How this got to be?'

At last, I take a corner of his sheet and wipe my eyes. Look to the door. Be like I never seen a door before, its shape look some ridiculous. Wonder how doors be even useful. Why no person making doors, when it be children dying. And I stand up weaken, feeling sore in all my body. Bend to Driver, and kiss him on his forehead – cool and dry and gone – and kiss him again, and stand up frightening, how I never kiss him another time. But I make myself turn to the door. Come out, and Julio leaning to the wall, face blank in weariness. Enfermera by, is looking at her fingernails. They both startle up, grit into worry at my sight.

I say soft, 'Julio, he dead.'

'Dead?' He look confusing to me.

'Ya, he dead, my soldier.' I swallow on this saying, taste a bitter something in my throat.

Julio narrow to me, clutch his hands up into fists. Glance frighten down the hall and whisper, 'Your Sengles are there. Was wait by him.'

'They ain't know he dead?'

He make a gentle grimace. 'No, senyora.'

I breathe out long. 'My Pasha ain't here? Jesus?'

'No, senyora. Don't know where is Jesus.'

I nod weak, feel some unknowing love for Julio, how he helping. But then a bitter hurt seize in me. I say hoarsen, 'Julio. How many floors it be here, for sarcoma?'

He look uncertain. Turn to the frighten enfermera, ask low. She frown with seeking eyes to me. Say careful, 'Senyora, eight.'

'Eight floors. Right, you see this?' I say rough. 'Why this war been. We going to end this now. Goddamn this, cannot be.'

Then I turn unthinking, start to walk back where we come. Julio follow, saying, 'Senyora, you don't want Sengles? Is good, people help.'

'Nay.' I pause my step. 'Ain't nothing help.'

Then my tears come blinding, and he lead me by my arm. I stumble in the elevator, thinking of that moon rain. Salt that last forever, grief that live beyond all life.

62

OF NAVIDAD ITS FINAL GRIEFS

Be one more meeting in this evil morning of our victory. I ride back seeing only tears, hands clutching in their cuts. And when I step out to the Ministerio, El Mayor be there.

He waiting on the steps, and when he see me, all his body change. He start toward, then halt uncertain. Raise a gloven hand.

First, he look good familiar, and my heart reach to him in its pain. But as I coming to the steps, I reach down for my skirt, how I will lift it climbing stairs. When it ain't there, I shock peculiar. Remind Carola's clothes and all disorders of these hours. How Mamadou tell El Mayor our loving histories. How Felipe say, with shaming smile, *He's not alone tonight.*

Then I see El Mayor again – his bitter mouth, his hard respect. And I know, I cannot even tell him on my Driver. Ain't brave to say this news to his unlove.

With this, my hurt be by. Is like I step out of my awful heart. And I walk up the steps without no conscience, why my legs be weak. Why I must wipe my face. Come to El Mayor and I say plain, 'Salue.'

He nod. 'Come from Felipe. Business, ya.'

'Can tell me quick? Should sleep.'

El Mayor's eyes hurt fresh at this. A moment, I expect he going to start in accusations. Yo, all my body sicken sudden. Be only breathing, concentrating how I keeping on my feet.

But he collect himself, say stiff, 'What it be, the Quantico girl come to Felipe. Now our rebellion done, Marines want you at Quantico. Negotiations, what she said.'

I shrug without no mind. 'When I will go?'

'To middy day. Felipe send a car.'

'Foo.' I make a weaken laugh. 'Felipe send me there?'

El Mayor frown. 'Felipe want to go for you, but Quanticos ain't want him. Ask for yourself, and that Simón. How Simón be general, can see. But for yourself . . .'

'Right, why they wanting me? They ain't believe Marias gods.'

'Ain't know. But it be only talks. Can think, you coming back tonight.'

'Be bone. I going, sure.'

Then, from nothing, we both catch into precarious silence. He narrow to the steps, the glass and ice in trails of glittern blue. Yo, I stare empty at himself. He dressing fine, like all these days – coat smooth like pony's flank, boots perfect in their leather shine. But his face be hurt precaire. Look like he live ten years in hell, and come back younger somehow, foaly for no difficult life.

At last, I say, 'My Pasha here?'

A moment, El Mayor stare on, unheeding. Then he say, 'Nay. He at Felipe's, talking with that Marine girl. War informations, you know how.'

'He ain't resenting how I left him?'

To this, El Mayor frown, like he figuring something ugly in his mind. Then he say rough, 'Sure he resenting. Cannot do like that.'

'Do how?'

'Using people.' El Mayor squint his face. 'And then they rid. Forgot like nothing.'

'Nay, I – ain't like that.'

Now El Mayor look hard to me. 'People here, they want to kill him now. Guess you ain't heard? This morning, been a crowd out by Felipe's, calling for his murder.'

I swallow at my fear, say rough, 'No sho. Why anyone kill Pasha?'

'He Russian. Ain't a bony day to be a Russian here, no sho. Felipe's own guards want to kill him. Ya, that Carola want to give him to them. Fear her life.'

'But they ain't–'

'Nay.' El Mayor pooch his lips, most like this be a disappointment. 'But Felipe had his work to rid them. Nor it help, that you been gone.'

I nod stupid. 'Been wrong to leave him, sure.'

El Mayor smile like bitter jokes. 'Ya, first they find you gone, roo swearing Anselm's people took you. Say you never left him without force. Then this morning, Mamadou come and said you gone to him. Roo suffer this, be sure.'

A moment, our eyes meet precaire. I say, 'Nay, Pasha blame me, truth? Ain't be . . . from yourself?'

For a risky moment, El Mayor's face fill with rage intentions. But he grit mouth against. Put hands in pockets and say cold, 'Ain't want to know why Mamadou come?'

I shake my head. 'Be tired. Can like–'

'Was bringing news. Who he murder.'

We both tense to this heavy word. Can feel my terror start again – the whitish evil growing big – and I say quick, 'Yo sho, been war.'

'Been murder,' El Mayor say cold. 'What Mamadou done, he gone up to Inúd, their Residencia. Bring some Quinta soldiers, say he got a message for Pedro. No one known him there, he go in straight. Shoot Pedro, and they shooting Pedro's guards. Then he find Soledad.'

I flinch. 'How, Soledad?'

'She living there. She gone there when you rid her.'

'Ain't rid her. It–'

'Yo, ever it been. She there. And Mamadou seek her through all rooms. You comprehend, this killing ain't been chance. He saying this.'

Now my mind go vicious black. Remind the roof at Reese. How I told Mamadou of the threats to kill me for unvirgin god. How he say, *And the simper known.*

Then El Mayor take ragged breath, say like his final strength, 'I know she kilt his feathers. He an Army, need his vengeance. But–'

'Nay,' I say without no breath. 'You wrong. He killing her for me.'

'For you?' El Mayor grit his face. 'Be vally mad, ain't for yourself.'

I shake my head, a blank exhaustion gone through all my blood. 'Kilt her . . . sure I ask him. I ain't name her, but . . .'

'Ain't name her, but you ask him? Ain't no sense.'

I think without no mind, *Been for my safety, El Mayor. Mamadou thought she telling how I done with him at Army camp. But Soledad never even known. I lying to her, and she trust me like an easy fool.*

Be standing now with tears gone helpless on my face. I say thin through my achen throat, 'Cannot explain. Been something she known . . . he thought she known. But ain't been his.'

Now El Mayor's face weak in ruth. 'Ice, nay. He doing this, ain't yours.'

'You wrong.' I clutch myself, gone shivering. Now can smell my stank of fear, is sharp like nasty pine. 'Yo, I should sleep. But tell them I will go to Quantico. Be bone.'

'Nay, heed. I know I said some nonsense, all these weeks. But truth, you blind to trust. This secret male of yours – it been the NewKing? How this even been? And Pasha, he your friend? Ice, you ain't seeing what you need.'

'Ya,' I say rough. 'Should sleep now, truth.'

'Ice. You watch yourself.' His eyes fix to me, sad uncertain. 'Whatever been between us . . . cannot want you hurt.'

I say quick with aching voice, 'Be gratty, but should sleep.' Then I turn sudden, dash up skittery on the icen steps. Can hear him call behind, and I run faster, gasping breath. Duck through the broken door, and look back frightening through its jags of glass. El Mayor stood footless. He got one hand out, reaching toward, like he càn catch me still.

Then something in me know, I never seeing him again. Feel Quantico's distance, and the warry deaths around us both. How he eighteen. How children dying real. Ain't only fears, is real.

My heart stab hard, and I call foolish, 'Ever it been, I love you! Ain't never quit to love you, never!' Then I turn again, go hasty like I flee my words.

Yo, as I reach the elevator, I hear his voice, small like a thought: 'I love you also! Ice? Ain't risk yourself! Ain't need to risk yourself!'

My farther day be lost to me. At the iglesia, I go stumbling wild to Driver's bed. Weep into gratty sleep – and wake again to Keepers talking something, sitting on my waist. Hate You come and lift her off, but I say, 'Nay, she good. Ain't like to be alone. Ain't leave me.' Someone try to tell me Driver dead, and I turn harsh away. Curl stupid to my pillow, ain't got the bravery to say I know. Then through my sleep, be Sengles whispering by, sat on the floor. Sometimes I wake and talk some nonsense sadness that I ain't remember. Hold to Asha Badmouth's hand or take a cigarette from Jermaine. And always be some children weeping, with the sorrow that I know.

Ya, they keep me company in dreams. Be reveries of snakes who taking Driver off to live with them, of caverns where he trap in ice – and always be a Sengle in my dream who whisper help. Once, I wake to find Crow sleeping by, curl on the covers, face beweepen like the rest. Then I dream into a burial yard where Crow be saying, 'Driver living underground. Come back, once they explode the city.' Then I look and see, this burial yard stretch past all long horizons. And Crow show me a greenish gem, which be a magic weapon, kill all roos. I say, 'But Pasha be a roo.' Crow say, 'Is right, you got to choose,' and I wake panicking in tears. ABC stand up, put her wet nose against my nose, and Keepers look up from the sofa saying, 'You ain't going to die, now you be sergeant?' Then I wake from this, and Keepers sleeping on the floor, my ABC be gone, and I ain't know if the question been a dream or real.

At last, I wake alone. Clock be eleven, and my task remember. I rise in brainless weakness, wash myself before I start to think. Clad a murder dress and diamonds. Go sit weary to the mirror, but forget to look. And I smoke two cigarettes, sat blind before this mirror.

Think how I parley to the Quanticos, while Driver dead. And Driver dead.

In this, my Sengles start to gather again, ask scary questions. I rouse my wits, go call them round. Try to explain my leaving, but my smalls object in voice. Mustafa Five begin a game, where he announce I coming back tonight. I say, 'Can be tomorrow,' and he shout, 'Tonight!' and it go on, till all my scratchers yell 'Tonight!' together with exciting rage. In this, Keepers go and bring Kalash, huge on her shoulders. I say with weaken laugh, 'For killing roos,' and she say strict, 'Only must kill them if they mally. Or shoot they feet, be better.'

Then it be clocken twelve. I clad my furren coat, and Jermaine go down the elevator with me. Kiss my cheek in by-salue, and I go out the door, guard Julio following with my journey case. Be two trucks, then be my car, a grandy sort with bigger wheels for riding on rough ground. Got some child driving I ain't know. Ya, in the car's back seat be Pasha.

Roo look grim and unbeslept. One lip still swelling from our violent yesternight, is lopside red. When I shove in beside him, angling Kalash sidelong, he flinch away. Grit like anger, look down to his hands.

We ain't say nothing. I close the door, the driver say some Panish courtesy, that I repeat without no mind. Then we driving, and this motion take me in accustom tiredness. Be like my warry night continue, but I feel how Driver been in it somewhere, and now he ain't. Ya, the chill feel like this absence, how the windows bloom their cold. And Pasha by, in strange unsympathy, while we drive away from every other child I love.

Riding down through Loisaida, we sit in this porcupine silence. I lean my forehead to the window, feeling wrong with painful life. Watch dumb how Loisaida pass, its shamble homes and trash. Feel Pasha watching by, but got no bravery to look at him. I think to speak, but all I got to say be *Driver dead*. Yo, now my grief begin to gather teary. I think away from it, bite hard into my lip. But they nuisance tears come on, until my breath hitch up and gasp. Then I be only leaning to the window, sobbing in shamen misery.

'Ice?' say Pasha cautieuse.

I wave a shooing hand. Rub eyes and swallow feroce, but nothing help. At last I say, between two sobs, 'Why you be here?'

'Ice, ain't got to cry.'

'Yes, I got to cry. Why you be here?'

'Quanticos ask.'

'Yo why you got to be like that?'

'Ain't being . . . Ice? You cry for this?'

I take a ragged breath and turn my ruin face to him. He look almost tears himself, is clutching scary fists.

Here the driver ask some worry Panish. Pasha answer soft, then say to me, 'You needing something? Driver ask.'

I shake my head, mind gone in awfuls, how this be a driver. How the city full of drivers, like this word been chosen for my pain. And this grief dabbit to its end, while Pasha frown his apprehensions.

At last, he say in hoarsen voice, 'Ain't mean to be no way. Was sad myself, Ice. All it be.'

'How you been sad?'

'Sad.' He make a face. 'How I being.'

'Been wrong to leave you. Sure I know. But I been only stupid, Pasha. Ya, I got nothing left to grieve with. Be finish, be too much.' Tears start again in this, while Pasha watch with strange attention. Is like he work some problem while I rub my messy nose. I wipe my snotten hand off on the seat, and Anselm's voice say in my head, *That really is disgusting, santa reina. New heights.*

Then Pasha say into my thought, 'Ice, I going back. Why I be sad.'

'Back how?' I keep eyes toward my knees. 'You ain't go to Quantico?'

'Nay, heed . . . Ice?'

I take a ragged breath and nerve myself. Look back to Pasha

503

where he sitting tense with shamen eyes. He got one hand upon my coat, clutch in its fur unhappy.

'Heed,' say Pasha careful. 'Quanticos got capture roos. Patricia going to put me with them. When they trade prisoners, I go back.'

'To roos?' I scoff a disbelieving breath. 'Marines ain't rid you there. Ain't theirs to rid.'

'Nay.' He make a painful frown. 'I ask. They promise this for my help.'

Now I stare at him with only fright. 'What help? Nay, what you saying?'

'Help. Give informations. Yesternight, I do already.'

'But – you go back real? Ain't for some tricks?'

'Go back.' He shrug. 'I stay by roos.'

'Nay, you cannot. Why? Why you even saying this? Cannot.' My whitish terror back, hard in my chest.

'Ice, ain't right I being here.'

'Ain't right? Ain't say that. Why it ain't?'

'Seen, when you left from Metro. Ain't right.'

'Nay, I need you,' I say breathless. 'How this happening? Now you going to leave me? For . . . been for they fools who want to kill you? Because I leave you there?'

He look down to his fisten hands. 'Ain't nothing that you done. I only want this. Cannot stay here.'

I think desperate, but cannot find sense. He go back to his roos – the murdering children who he hate. Left him in Metro for one night, and this be his insanities. Ain't even justice he decide this, I ain't known this going to be. Never left him for one second, if I guessing this. And I seek in memories, why Pasha want to leave me so. Seek, and feel this terror blind against my searching thought.

At last, I say in feary breath, 'What El Mayor think – he always think you wanting me for love. Ain't this somehow?'

Pasha tense, frown to his hands. Face start to show his pink embarrass.

My heart beat jags, but I say on, 'It be no sense. You love a person, why you going to– shee, this driver comprehending?'

'Nay.' Pasha smile, look sidelong to me. 'Quanticos want no English driver. Hear secrets.'

'Bone. Nor I want this, right.' I swallow weak, say softer, 'Pasha, if you needing this, I do . . . ever you need. Should know. But why we ain't continue like we been? Ain't see how this be awful so. A month, can go on for a month. I only need some help.'

He clench against this. 'Nay, ain't so simple. Be nothing you will comprehend.'

'How?' I laugh up weak. 'It be some rooish feeling we ain't get?'

'Can be.'

'Shoo, been a joke. What feeling? Seem like you be a mammal, mostly.'

A long time, Pasha hush, but I can feel his answer gathering. We come up on the bridge, and the sweep of battern Marias City widen everywhere around. Car rise among its hundred towers, jag and windowless, and we break into sky, with only steely webs of bridge above. Be children working at the edge, and they all turn to watch. Pasha put his hand up to them, smiling weak, then rub his eyes. We come out over sparkling water, bridge posts blurring past, and he look back to me in his blue grief.

'Ain't told you, Ice,' he say. 'I had a daughter.'

63

PASHA ROO HIS WARS

Pasha get his daughter in an African place call Lagos. Be a city for boats, set scattern to the sparkling ocean. Time Pasha come, the roos been ruling this for twenty years of peace. Keep soldiers there to hold the city, but got no killing war to do.

He been eighteen self, young by their rooish definitions. Been soldat four years, but he ain't scarcely use his gun. Only fighting that he seen was in the European wars, and this been careless battles. His roos kept mostly safe, and blackish Europeans been no person children to him. He felt their deaths like hunting sorrow – going to pity, but can sleep without no bad reminders. Nor he try no gero yet. Still was glad with foolish life.

Ain't posies left in Lagos, gratty to the rooish cure. So the girl who bear his daughter been some twenty-four years. Already got one walking enfant. With this son, she selling corny cakes around the rooish camp. Girl be a backward something like my Hate You, shy bespoken. Pasha friending with her, ya his townie soldats friend with her. Name be Ekuah, but they call her Kusha, rooify her name.

What Pasha say, he been some prettieuse goods at eighteen years. So, how it begin, this Kusha love him with her eyes. Say nothing, but she start to gift him food and trinket goods. Will hold his hand in rooish greeting, and her scary eyes go unpredictable at this touch.

Soldats be ungentle mouths, and soon they teasing Kusha ugly.

Ask if she using Pasha yet, and swear they do her better. Warn her about his rooish love diseases and his unsize parts. Ya, Pasha start defending her. This bring her into worser love, and ain't no waiting time before he lose his seldom morals. Got no love for her himself, but this be hanging fruit.

Is histories of soldat, and all his use of her be fickle. He visit in itchy moods, and scratch, and leave without no care. His talk to her be all excuses, and he watching other girls while she cling frighten to his arm. Yo, when she go pregnant, first he only blame her carelessness. Enfant be no interests to a male, how Pasha ever thought. Only be a natural litter soldats leave behind.

But soon an inkling pain begin. When roos make greasy jokes upon his fathering, Pasha suffer queery. He start to notice enfants – ya, these mostly being beggars, asking by the rooish camp. Nor he can ignore, that many of these got rooish looks. Be soldat get, from girls of Lagos, took for rape or money. See these enfants' misery, and soon Pasha sleeping guilty. Watch Kusha's belly like she grow some judgment on himself.

But when his enfant born, these contradictions be forgot. First he see his daughter Femi, was like he recognize this creature from prediction dreams. In second's thought, he know all certainties of her important wonder. Then he ain't care how no one mock. He only live to help this enfant. His heart become a happy pain, and every other world be a surrounding to this love.

This Femi grown six months, when Pasha's roos call into war. Be in farther Africa, where children fighting bellicose to rid the roos entire. First battles be no circumstance. Roos kill some bellious children, and come back to Lagos dirty, booze their wretchen nerves away. But the Africans' fury grow. More children joining in rebellion, until the deeper country be a stew of thousand wars.

Wars lengthen into years, and worsen into ugly cruelties. Worst fights been in nefasty jungles, ripe with all infecting sickness. Is poison snakes and giant ticks and spiders, every nightmare creature.

Yo, is times they war in thirsty desert, lost without no goods. Here is rains of burning sand, like breathing broken glass. Be places God made in His days of hatred.

Now Pasha's warry crimes begin, in hells of always killing. Be towns where roos kill every person various, for angry sport; be towns they blinden every child, and leave them to their slower death. Ya Africans do liken tortures, and leave these frightening dead by rooish camps. Pasha's townie soldats mostly kilt. He sent among some new soldats, and they be kilt the same. Pasha see so many deaths, he feel familiar with a body's guts more than its clean outside. Come time, is only one soldat of his close people still alive, Seryozha who been fighting with him from their first beginnings.

And in this terror, all soldats use any pharmacies they find. Drink booze and they drink anything that smelling half like booze. Pasha start with gero, dust that can besleep all fear, make any conscience dumb. So these be drunken horrors, a sleepen blundering through screams and bombs and mutilation dead.

In injury or for relief, soldats be sent to Lagos. Pasha come there any dozen times in these bad years. To him, this city be a home, a shamble heaven safe in peace. And there, he always seeing Kusha quieteuse and Femi.

This baby born with normal skin and hair, but Pasha's bluish eyes. Look like she seeing something wonderful blue. Is gentle shy, ain't got no fight. Love her brother and her mother; ya all other people be a frightening problem to her. And she love Pasha simple. Will tell him hours of nonsense tales; draw pictures on his whitish arms; sleep riding on his shoulders. She always begging, he live with them. Ain't want to comprehend there can be reasons that he leave. Yo, he love her with a stupid madness. All his hours of freedom be by her, or buying gifts to her. He bring Kusha's family to a better part-ment, feed them all. Buy a camera and fill his pockets with his Femi's photographs. Believe these keep him safe in war.

Now, in his wars, he fighting to survive for her protection. Care only that he live, and Pasha hate these children who will kill him, leave his daughter to the world alone. He breed some fever longings, that he murder every person living, only to keep his Femi in this safer loneliness.

Be eight years of these African wars, and Pasha changing evil. Gone vicious to the new soldats, ain't bear their bragging innocence. Is shrunken skinny, lose his teeth from accidents and hungers. Ya, gero be like air to him, his need for waking–sleeping. For gero's sake, he townie with all children who got pharmacies. Physicians be his favorite joy. These, with his soldat Seryozha, be his only friend-ship.

Other Russians joke on him, but give his evils some respect. Is warry changes, known and known. And every gossip tell, in battle, Pasha trusty certain. Will fight like seven rabies, save these people he disgusting at. They call him Vampire, and they leave him to his angry misery.

How this finish worse, Lagos self break in rebellion.

Been Pasha's normal barracks night, of gero and unfriendly silence. He gone in pharmacy sleep, and dream blind through the first explosions. Only know of anything, when he drag from his bed to fight. Then he grab his pack and gun. Go out in wild confusions where his soldat gang be joining. He thinking first, they taking to some sudden war beyond. Mostly frustrate how his pack fill wrong, with every peaceful object. Got cooking grain and camera, but ain't warry gear enough.

But then a close explosion come, shake bad familiar in the earth. All soldats laugh or swear, call speculations where it been. Pasha hear the gunfire rise behind and comprehend. War be here. His Femi be among these bombs alone.

Then he ain't even sneak. He break in run without no care. Push through soldats, like every child will comprehend where he must be. Ain't hear if no one yell, ain't heed. Dodge through the gathering trucks, and he sprint breathless to the havoc streets.

Worst slowness of this journey be its danger. Pasha been soldat too long to risk no stupid death. Ya, this night be every desperate child out in some hunt. Some be only thieving, but is also angry rifle bands, gone seeking roos to punish. Nor he dare to start no gunfight, how he be alone. Must creep by hinder streets, must duck from every moving life.

Be twice, he caught into some hide, while battles deafen close outside. Then he fish out his gero, how he craving since his woken sleep. First time, he risen stronger from this. Go with clarity bright, and even gladden to the risky dark. But when he catching next, is houry time, inside some pen of goats. Only is bullets maddening outside–above, the squeal of beasts. Then he finish all his gero out of hate frustration. Hunch in a dream of screaming goats, and farther screams of men; the stank of warry fire, that always find some poison thing to burn.

Time he leave, his mind be smoky as the ruin town. Then he wander lost and lost. Ain't find no place he recognize, and times, he ain't believing this be Lagos. Drift in memories of awful cities where he war, when every world destroy to figments, and his people all be dead.

Pasha scarcely notice when he find his way again. Only is following streets toward his heart, without no thought betook. But it be clear and vicious to him, how the war die into quiet. Guns choke into hush, and only can hear the seldom cry, the frighten voice, of their results. Then Pasha run without no mind. Be thinking terrify, he miss the war. Ain't killing who he need, and Femi left.

So he run through smelling smoke; run past the dead, lain skew and red. Sometimes, by these, be children weeping; sometimes, children rob their pockets. Once, some gunshots follow him, but Pasha lost his mind for risk. Be flaming cars somewhere, and buildings, and these be only brighten ornaments to his one fear.

When he come to Kusha's place, the edifice be whole unhurt. Is even lights in windows, voices muffle in the upper floors. Door open normal like a dream. Kusha's partment be on bottom floor, and he hold stiff with clamoring heart to see a light below her door. Hear someone walking there, and he go yelling, gratty wild.

But when the door come open, it be his soldat Seryozha. Child step out to the hall and close the door behind himself. Pasha try pushing past him, but Seryozha hold and block him stubborn. Yell till Pasha heed.

First Seryozha explain some pointlessness – how he come behind the fighting, seeking Pasha self. Tell news of battle while Pasha stare, gone trembling through his flesh. He got no courage left to ask, and only watch Seryozha's face in terrifying need.

He ain't remember how Seryozha say that Femi dead. What he remember be what he ain't seen, the killing self. For years behind, this strange unmemory come to him at thoughtless moments – the knife, her choking scream, and blood that always frighten him again.

Been in the early night, before the fighting even start. Some Africans come for Kusha in a vengeance demonstration, what become to girls who go with roos. They drag her to the street for rape, be yelling filthy mockeries. Femi running after, while Kusha scream at her to hide. But the enfant chase until she trip akimbo in the street. Then some worser child catch up this Femi, see her bluish eyes. All finish in a moment's rage.

When Pasha's memory return, Seryozha stand against the door. Got sickness face, and Pasha struggle to remember why. Is like they standing there for hours, and Pasha seek his mind, confusing, how he can save Femi. Remember again that she be dead, like he forgotten this a thousand times, and keep remembering unwanten.

And Seryozha say, like offering comfort, Kusha still alive. Rapists frighten at Femi's murder, leave her mother there unhurt. Now Kusha be inside. Is with her sister and her son.

Pasha only repeat, *They leave her.*

Seryozha say, *They leave her, yes. Ain't done her nothing, brother.*

*

What happen next be strange again. He know he fighting with Seryozha, though he ain't know why, nor he remember how this struggle end. Ain't remember how he coming in and seeing Kusha. But he remember shooting her. Been certain in his fever mind that Femi kilt for Kusha's dirt, her shamelessness. He even glad as she fall down in blood, relieve to rid this evil. And he shoot Kusha's sister, Kusha's son, without no thought. Shoot them like a natural thing – like someone throw a ball to you, and your hand rise to catch.

Then some time, he roaming in the partment, raging blind. Break a window with his fist and laugh hilarious at his blooden hand. Kick at the murdern son, then break in tears when his Seryozha cavil. Try to hit Seryozha, but he got no strength. Can scarcely breathe. This seem funny also, and he laugh until Seryozha laughing, wrestling him to peace.

Next memory be, he sitting on a sofa by Kusha's blooden body. Is weeping while Seryozha talk some useless noise above. All he knowing, Femi gone. Her body taken to the church, and Pasha cannot comprehend how no one do this cruelty. And he weep there in Seryozha's noise for countless time. Be like he fall forever, ya forever, in a single hour.

But at last, the gero weaken. Leave him in this actual room, the bodies splay and still. Then, in some loathing need, he get his camera from his pack. Make the photograph I seen: Seryozha before these murdern children, holding a pistol to his own head, grinning desperation.

Time Pasha tell me this, we be in bosky country, past no houses. Both is crying somewhat, smoking tireless with the windows open. We got the furren coat across ourselves, but still be shivering. And we hush some time, watch out the windows at the woods – the icen branches glittery to the clouds, a fuzzy sun. A winging crow stop on the snow and fold into a blacken stitch. Be the bellesse of all my younger days, but now it seem like maginations. Life now be wars in broken cities. All my futures be like Pasha's pasts.

At last I say, low in my voice, 'This when you try to kill yourself?'

Pasha shrug like obvious questions. 'Yes. Was right.'

'But you ain't meant this murder. Be something . . . like it happen to you, ya?'

He shake his head, eyes tired beyond. 'Ain't want excuses. I only explaining how I been with you. Was Femi somehow. Keep thinking like you Femi, if she grown.'

'I be like her?'

'Nay.' He smile funny. 'Been only something that I need. Thought I can keep you safe.'

'Done this. You save me, fact be simple. Yo, how this make you go to roos?'

He take a suffering breath. 'Ice, comprehend. Ain't right I being here.'

'Nay. By roos, ain't right. Think what you only telling.'

'I be a roo. What I be.'

'Foo, how this mattering any? Been a roo this time, ain't matter nothing.'

'Matter,' he say painful. 'What I seeing yesternight.'

'Nay. Be only notions, Pasha.'

His eyes fix to me seriose. 'Marianos hate myself. You never see this? How they talk?'

'Nay, ain't every person so. You friending with they guards. They never caring how you be a roo.'

He shake his head. 'If I ain't friend, they kill me sometime. Why I friend.'

'Foo, you magining dooms. They never done.'

'Yes, and kill you also,' he say in rougher voice. 'Like Femi.'

'Shee. Marianos kill me, can be. But ain't for this.'

He shake his head. 'If you been at Felipe's yesternight—'

'Then I protect you better. All that been.'

'Ice, you ain't know.' He grit like pain. 'Seen this before, in Africa. They hurt you also.'

'Nay, they ain't even hurt yourself,' I say with choking breath. 'Felipe keep you.'

'This been one time. It be again.'

'So we can leave this fool Marias. Do this war, then we skit to some woods. Think Keepers hate you? Any Sengle?'

He take breath to cavil more. But then he only fret his mouth, look past me to the window. 'I be older, also. Ain't natural I be there. Cannot explain.'

Here I frustrate, how I got no knowledge I can argue. Never been no thirty years myself. Try to think how it will be, to always be with eights. But it never feeling so with him. We talk like animoses always. Risk our life together, plan our war. All be no sense.

Then he say soft, 'You still get cure for Driver. Now, ain't need myself.'

I flinch. Clutch hand into the coaten fur, my throat gone tight. 'Nay, Pasha. Driver dead. My brother dying yesterday.'

He startle up, look his blue grief to me. Be a moment that we linger in this closer misery, while the snowy rumples of the land be always huge around. Then his eyes pass into shame. He whisper, 'Be sorry, Ice.'

'Ain't need your goddamn sorry!' I break out in sobben voice. 'Need you to stay. Ain't want to live myself, you all be . . . you all gone. Cannot do this anymore!'

'Ice?'

'Ain't know what I even doing now. The cure, these wars. Why this all been? Be begging, Pasha.'

He reach out then with helpless ruth. I take his hand, cling hard and say, 'Ain't let you leave. You mine, you hear this?'

He laugh rough. 'Your roo. Like Keepers.'

'Nay, you be my person. You like my other self. Ain't right you leave. You got to feel this, Pasha.'

'I feel this. I love you, Ice. But–'

'Nay. I love you also. Damn, you leaving nowhere. Will not let you.'

I grip tight to his hand. Be thinking madness, how I keep this hand. Ain't loose it for no circumstance, give him no freedom for escape. Already begin to worry how I sleep, to think of handcuffs, when he say in unbreath hurt, 'Will think.'

A gray relief run through me. I say weak, 'I chase you to these roos, you do no foolishness. I will.'

He make a face. 'Be sorry for Driver. Sorry I ain't been.'

'I look for you. Thought you must be there somehow.'

'Be there, if I known.'

Then we fall, in sad exhaustions, to our hunting silence. Keep holding hands in thoughtlessness, and stare out at the farming yards of Jersey, their houses few and far. Yo, as we stare, the houses thicken. Become a broken city, scarren black by ancient fires. Its ruins decorate with perfect snow. One street become a brook, grown pale with ice. Ain't no showing people. Can only see a lonely deer gone nosing in an evac yard. Yo, all this winter got a ghost unbeing from our warm inside.

Be scouting in this wealth of evacs, magining their loot, when something bother in my mind. I look back to Pasha. Find him watching on me sorry. His hand change in my hand, and we both smile.

'Ho,' I say, 'you hearing on their nuclears at Quantico?'

To this, he grimace like bad taste. Before I can react, he rid his hand from mine, stretch out his fingers.

I watch this hand with superstitions, crave to snatch it back. 'Yo,' I say nerviose, 'they wrong to you?'

He shake his head disgusting. 'Be no nuclears.'

'Patricia never told you? Got three nuclears there. They losing, Marines explode the city.'

'Ya, she told. Is lie.'

'Foo, lie.' I laugh. 'How you will know?'

'Is obvious.' He shrug annoying.

'You ain't even been in Quantico. How it can be obvious?'

Then Pasha start in explanations, how these nuclears cannot be. Best I comprehend, this need some weirdo metals no one have. Must make these metals special, and this need expensive miracles. Nor it be any chance, Marines keep nuclears from the older past. These never last in health. Be only poison garbage now.

'Think she known, is lies,' say Pasha at last. 'They lie to fear the roos. Lie to you also, so you tell the same.'

'Roos even hear these tales, I wonder?'

'Hear from prisoners, yes. But ain't believe.' He nay his hand. 'Been nuclears using in Russia, real. We know what this be.'

I think on this a minute, watching on his owlen face. He frowning into nowhere, like he still resent this nuclear lie. Gnaw fretful at his swollen lip.

'Is better,' I say uncertain. 'If we lose, still can escape somehow. Ain't everyone explode.'

Pasha lose his griping face. Get delicate looks and reach back for my hand. I give it hasty. Get a shiver at his friendly warm.

'Ice,' he say soft impressing, 'you ain't stay in Quantico?'

'Stay?' I shake my head confusing. 'Now? Why I will stay?'

'Nor you staying in Marias? You go hide in forest, how we said?'

I laugh uncertain. 'Nay, you saying this. I never said this.'

'Said.' He press my hand until I feel its yester cuts. 'You mind, we fight one day? Said then.'

'So, was lies. Ever I said.' I look nervy out the window. The bosky country start again. Be unleaf forest where the pines among look fat like bears.

'Now Driver gone . . .' He take a difficult breath. 'Ice, you heeding?'

'Nay, ain't heeding. Cannot hide. You know I never done this.'

'No person blaming, if you hide. Felipe–'

'Be insane. Is mad as flies. Ain't need his fool opinions.'

When I look to Pasha again, his face be strict in misery. He swallow hard and say, 'If roos come to Marias . . . cannot be safe.'

I say in almost shyness, 'Nay, be safer, if you only stay. Think all we done, and I be bone. You be my lucky shadow.'

Pasha try to free his hand again, but I cling fast. He startle, then begin to smile. 'Will think.'

64

BY QUANTICO

We talk ourself into exhausting sleep before the car arrive. Both dozing, topplen clumsy to our windows, when we fetch to stillness. I waken to a camp of tents, all green the same, set neat in rows. Behind–around be forest trees, with evac stores among. Can see, these trees grown up to bigness through some older city.

Around our car, be watching soldiers, dress in dapple clothes. First I see this garb, I think of roos and sit up frightening. But these be blackish children, normal made – Marines of Quantico.

Pasha turn to me with drowsen eyes. 'Think we walking now.'

'Yo right.' I look unnerve around. See where Simón climb from his truck, and I take up my coat.

We step out our different sides. Come in the air of Cember, silvery cold with playing wind, and clap our doors shut with one sound. Around, it be the shushing woods, the bigger sky of life. Sting bright on my cold eyes. Ya, Marines watch curiosity on me, on Pasha Roo.

Simón walk to in dull exhaustion. Say short politeness, then he only stand and rub his eyes. Remember now, he fighting our rebellion yesternight.

Ya, from a forward truck, Patricia climb out, stretching glad. Come striding to us, breathing misty puffs as she approach.

'Ma'am, sirs,' she say. 'We're picking up a couple folks here. Purposes of getting you to Washington with life and limb.'

Patricia wave three twelves to us – two boys and a girl. These say friendly courtesies, but all be strange to comprehend. Got slur pronouncing, like a hound that try at human speech. The girl say last, 'If yaw loosen sight of us, keep tight. Idden wort yaw life a guess at a singular step.' She saying this three ways before we start to understand, we ain't to move without a Quantico by, to show our safer footing.

Then Patricia form us in a line, a Quantico between each stranger. We go off so, Patricia leading. Shoes already start to fret me as we cross the last safe ground.

First land-mine paths be forest. We pick around the trees in crafty loops, though ain't no risk to see. Be even squirrels dashing careless. Land mines show nothing to the eye, nor it be no exploding squirrels. Must wonder if these mines be like the nuclears, fables for belief.

We duck into an evac store, go down stairs to a basement room. Its one wall got a blasten hole, lead clear into the dirty ground. This be the starting tunnel of the underlands of Quantico. Marines pause here and turn on handlights. Shine these forward as we step nervy.

Be an earthen burrow with wood supports along the walls. Lead downward through a chill of neary dark. Go ducking here, then we step out into a cold enorme. Ain't see much in the skittering lights. Is only scant expressions of flashing water, a metal rail, concree. Be one unhappy step in water that seize cold into my shoe. Then we walking normal on loose pebbles.

Quanticos keep pausing here, say, 'Watcher step.' Flash their lamp upon some obstacle – a chunky rock, a snaggle of wire – that show like an important ghost in this white spot of light. Last *watcher step* be when we come upon a grandy table object, blocking our forward path. Here we must climb up, myself the clumsiest in heavy fur. On this table, the Quanticos scatter, wander from their finicky line. Patricia call up, 'Now the gennlemen will give us a ride into Foggy

Bottom, yaw be glad to know. Sit wherever you like, it don't matter. This cart here's all safe.'

Then I see in the various lights, the boyish twelves crawl down beside. Seat into some steel devices, fasten along this table. Come slow to my mind, is weirdo bicycles. Be a cart we standing on, these bicycles pull this.

Patricia come beside me, say, 'Go on and sit. All due respect, those shoes have got to hurt.'

'Foo,' I say superstitious. 'They twelves can move all this?'

'Don't you wonder, ma'am,' the girlish twelve say at my elbow. 'One dies, we got a hunnert more.'

Be some laughter in the dark, and slurren backtalk I ain't get. I sit myself obedient. Pasha's face flash in a passing light as he sit by. Then all these lights extinguish, and the cart creak forward, hitching gentle. Find a breeze, then it coast on.

Cart be longer time in journey, and Pasha start in talking to the girlish twelve – Sharice in naming. In the dark, we all heed soft. Is like an entertainment that they doing for our boredom.

So Pasha say, 'You living in District or in Arlington?'

'Living, sir? Well, thass depending.'

'Depending?'

'Sir, I think yaw thinking of my position. Thass in the District. Position in the old German Embassy there. But, not bragging but, I did ready some street in Arlington myself.'

'Ain't been staying in tunnels?'

'No, sir, thass for baby children. Lessen we get an air raid. Then we go. Yoller going to see it, at Foggy Bottom where we disembark there. Thass my home shelter there, sir.'

This pass to conversation on these air raids. Sharice explain the warning siren, and the twelves all do an imitation of its howl, echoing queery in the blackness. She tell how they do pack-and-duck – a drill for running to tunnels – in one minute twenty. And times, they go out during raids, to put out fires from bombs. When Pasha ask her if she fearing then, she laugh her scorn.

'Who you asking *that*? Guessing you don't know much about Marines.'

While her voice go on, we start to see a gentle light before. First it be a yellow muzziness, feel like a blur mistake. But slow, it sharpen into details. Can see the concree walls, the snaky brightness of the rails we ride on, opening to this light.

Far off, a child call out a muddle word. Patricia answer loud. Then we slow into this lighten place, and be a dozen soldiers waring from a shelf above. As we stop beside, can see these all be petty eights. They all give hand-salues, and stand back tasky seriose.

We climb up to their concree shelf. Be long like inside street. Floor be covern with some thousand mattresses, particular in rows. Ya each mattress tucken, perfect square, with greenish blanket. Look like a decoration to the floor.

Here Patricia halt us, say in loud instruction voice, 'Going up top now. So please do keep in mind, there is some chance we get an air raid while we're walking. You hear that siren, you *do not run*. Keep in line, keep your eyes on that person in front, and we go back orderly. Very small chance they hit us. But if you run yourself along that street, you *will* be instant dog food. So hoping you keep that thought foremost.'

She form us back into our line, and we go off again. Be stairs, a rubble floor, and stairs. Come outside, and be surprise that day be waiting normal. Got a fisher sky that promise rain without no storm. Sun be a whiter nudge in hazy cloud.

City beneath this sky be every sort of leering ugliness. Both sides is bricky buildings, seven floors, and all their face be harm. Some walls be torn away, and rooms be showing black within. Is edifices scabben burnt, and places shaggy with dead moss. Windows be a gross confuse of boards and rust barbwire. Here and there among, can see the poking noses of guns, but cannot see no person face behind.

Street self got no roaden skin. Instead, is various trash. This be set in careful patterns – squares and lines and circles, made of pebbles or broken brick or planks. Ya one nearer patch be bones, and outline all in skulls.

From a bar set high across the road, be three big roadsigns hung. First is English, and it read:

HOW TO SURRENDER
Stop where you are. We can see you.
Put both hands in the air to indicate your intention.
Slowly remove all weapons and drop them in front of you.
Step over them and put both hands on top of your head.
Wait for directions.

This be painten black on yellow, faden with long weather. Next sign be Panish, and the last be rooish, fresh in brighter color. Another sign below, set on a pole like normal streetsign, read: Block I-23 NW – 544 Confirmed Kills. Number on this sign been painten out and rewrit, over–over, is showing lumpy fat.

Patricia look back pologetic. 'Hope yall excuse the decor. Unnerstanding, I do hope, we get very few invited guests here. Had our share of the other kind, excusing present company.'

Simón Zelote say behind me tired, 'It's fine.'

Only then I realize, some skulls here be from Marianos. This fasten in my mind as we go forward in our zagging line between land mines unseen.

Be a minute's walk before we come to our first barricade. I been dreaming sorry, and ain't notice till we be upon. Barricade be two layers of rusten cars, with various junk among – brick and bicycles and wood. Patricia call back sharp, 'Like to ask our guests to wait and only climb with instructions. It's a little persnickety here.'

Then she leap up squirrel quick. Pause light above, stood on the rusten belly of an upturn car. I glance where she gone, and see a skeleton hand thrust out beneath all cars, splay on the road. Beside it, sans no useful sense, be various boots, stood like they wait for feet.

Then Pasha climb up slow, Patricia pointing where each foot must go. They pass out of sight, and my Quantico twelve skip up. I watch his steps and go the same, while he frown worrying at my skewen weight, the dragging coat behind. Come thankful to the ground and he say fretting, 'Worry about those shoes, ma'am.'

I shrug discourage. 'Guess they boots ain't for that.'

'What boots? The boots . . .' Child catch my meaning and glance back peculiar. 'No, they're from dead folks, ma'am. You won't like that.'

Pasha frown, but when he see me looking, he smile foolish. I catch mischieviose, call low, 'Ain't finicky when they kilt them.' Roo make a face, nay slightish with one hand. Then the others join behind, and we shift on again.

'Shoo, most my clothing always been from people who was dead.'

He look flustering to Patricia, who say, 'Thass the worst, ma'am, you'll be fine.'

Ain't much farther that we go. Pass two more HOW TO SURRENDER signs, and various posten warnings: 'Do Not Enter: Certain Death', 'Trespassers Will Be Burned Alive'. On one wall, be painten big in letters worn with age: WELCOME TO QUANTICO – ROACHES GET IN, BUT THEY CAN'T GET OUT. Ya, always be the faceless rifles poking out above. One follow us with its black eye, and Patricia call up strict, 'You know better than that, I do hope.' Then it be funny how this rifle get a hangdog look.

Be only one more barricade, and I take this barefoot. Is easy going so, though I must tread on bones with naked feet. Come down a final street, with usual burns, rust wire and misery skulls. But forward, it change to perfect grass, still green in Cember month. Ya, all the grassen blades be short the same. Is laken in its smooth. Come up to this with easing breath, and when Patricia step out on its healthiness, she move aside. Wave us forward, saying, 'Okay, you can move freely here. I'm sure thass like to be a relief. Now, where you see this grass, you're in Washington. You can walk like home. But *do not* venture into the maze there without one of us. You keep that difference foremost, please. Sergeants, thank you, and you can now rejoin your positions. Seen some paramount work today, and I hope you three will appreciate this historical memory.'

Before they leave, these twelves all come up separate to Pasha–me–Simón. Shake hands and thank us for the opportunity to serve. Then they sprint off, zagging careless back through wreckage streets.

We continue along the grass, while Patricia explain our privilege, that we get to see their White House. Come past some trees, and soon we find this edifice grandiose. Patricia talk on in friendly boomery, naming Presidents who been here, like these be bragging definitions any person know. Here Simón Zelote cavil, how black children all been slaves and prisoners of these mally Presidents. Then be entertainment, how Patricia choke polite. 'Sir, as you say it,' she say thin, 'must be a measure of truth. But I hope we all agree to disagree today.'

We head up to a shorter mansion, callen West Wing by Patricia. She say our parley there, in Situation Room. We enter in a hall morose, and halt before a normal door. Patricia give some whispern hints of our behavior, skitty grown. Take Kalash from me, in strictness to their parley manners. Then, with forcen smile, she open the door.

65

THE SITUATION ROOM

Parley room be drab, and got no windows. All its light be false. Be a longish table, and three children to the farther end, all twentyish in size. They all come to their feet respectful, ya all wear the same – blue soldier clothes with whitey belt.

Patricia doing introductions, hasty in her voice. Child at the enden place be leader, callen Commandant. He taken with his posies, got all crusting sores along his brow. Next be the general ruling Arlington – tallish stick with prettieuse mustache callen Hatter Diaz. Last be a girlish general, Verna Mitchell, lead their telligence work. This be a child with biting face, hair braiden back so tight it give her head a snaken look.

When this courtesy done, Patricia rid herself away. We sit with heavy scrape of chairs. But before no parley start, Simón start speeching on their older wars, and how all wrongs forgot. Yo, he mention every wrong the Quanticos ever done, in saying how they be forgot.

When Simón exhaust his speech, the Commandant say nice, 'Well, we certainly do appreciate that, General. Hoping we keep that spirit. But getting straight to it, we all like to know what conditions you placing on your help.'

I say quick, before Simón can start again, 'We want the cure. Be glad to rid they Russians, but we mostly want their pharmacies.'

Hatter general make a friendly smile that perk his mustache. 'Well, thass okay, if they got anything. You know, ma'am, wooden be no surprises if it wadden even true.'

'Yeah, their miracle cure,' say Verna Snakehead. 'Our opinion, it's a ruse. Russians started out here offering us that medicine – with one small condition of total surrender. Well, I'm *still* waiting for a reason to believe it's there.'

'Ain't your worries,' I say shortish. 'We know it be there.'

Verna scorn her lip. 'Well, I'd thank you *not* to go saying that to my Marines. Get our kids believing that, you can kiss morale goodbye. Get people deserting to the enemy – which I do believe was the Russians' whole idea.'

'Now, wait,' say Hatter. 'Assuming it's there, which I guess the lady's got her reasons. Still, there's the problem, how you get it. Situation now, we hadden got in their camp, except as prisoners. But saying that changes, saying we even win. Well, they all likely to pack their bags and go. Why it's no guarantees, being honest with the lady.'

'Maybe the gennleman could comment on that.' The Commandant nod to Pasha.

Pasha get bewaring face. Say slow, 'Cure be on boats.'

'Well, thass it,' Hatter say exciting. 'Boats, they're way off down the coast. And they never come anywhere close to shore, we all been watching that. Even getting a shot in, I don't see a way.'

'Ya.' Pasha nod impatient. 'Cannot take boats. But Russians trade for prisoners. What we plan.'

Verna huff infuriating. 'There's a fine idea, I'm sure. Begging your pardon, but we trade our prisoners for prisoners. While there's one Marine kept in captivity, that's what we do. Trade prisoners for some potion you'd be a fool to drink? Well, thass a great idea – if you're a Russian.'

'General Mitchell,' say the Commandant, 'asking you to remember where you are.'

'Sir,' she answer cold, 'I'm hoping you don't listen to this with any credulity. I do hope.'

'Well, there's trades and trades,' say Hatter with impatient smile. 'That Russian colonel you got, Verna, he's worth something to them. Supposing we all winning, you ask anything you want for him.'

'Not guaranteeing he survives the duration.' Verna scorn her mouth. 'But if he do, yall certainly can trade him for magic beans – when my people are all back home.'

The Commandant say sharp, 'You're forgetting circumstances, Generals. We don't win this war, we're losing *all* our people, without exception. So, in the interests of concluding this alliance, interests of winning this war, I want to personally promise our guests, we will cooperate in any reasonable means to get this medicine. Thass including use of future prisoners, if thass what the situation calls for. And, Generals, I do expect you abide by that.'

Hatter–Verna heed all this with looks of stiffen conscience. Then both muttern, 'Sir, yes, sir,' and give each other mally eyes.

The Commandant cough in his hand and turn with tired smile to me. 'Now, we certainly do appreciate you coming, in what's an hour of need. But I'm hoping it won't be any surprise, we got a request our own.'

'Request?' I say unready. 'Shoo, we going to help your war.'

'Now, ma'am, if you hear me out. So, unnerstanding you believe in the medicine, thass a thing we knew and expected. But what alarms us there, it gives the enemy a place to drive a wedge. They get nervous, they just offer you medicine – if you all join up with them. Then we got two armies at our gates, and whatever intelligence that we shared, necessarily shared . . .'

'Concern being, you change sides.' Verna narrow eyes at Pasha. 'Particularly seeing you got your Russian sympathies, preexisting.'

'Excusing the general's frankness,' say the Commandant. 'There it is.'

'That won't happen,' Simón Zelote say with insult face. 'If you knew anything about our city's history, you'd know that.'

'Well, sir,' the Commandant say, 'thass very reassuring to hear.

But my request is for the lady here. Ma'am, all we're asking is that you'd stay with us for the duration of the war. You'd be a very honored guest in the White House here, that's my own home.'

Hatter smile to me with sweeten eyes. 'See, ma'am, you staying here, we don't believe your folks will abandon you. It's a pledge of faith, how we see it.'

Before I think no answer, Pasha say, 'Cannot.'

Marines all flinch then, look to him in various dislike.

'Sir?' the Commandant say short.

'You asking, she stay here?' say Pasha. 'Maria stay herself?'

Simón Zelote add in stiff, 'You're proposing to keep Maria hostage.'

'Well, hostage, thass a word,' say Hatter, touching his mustache nerviose.

'It's options we could have, if there's that trust,' the Commandant say. 'Hostage, that sounds nasty, but you think about our position. Can't plan much, if we expect that information goes to the enemy.'

'It's maps, it's anything,' Verna say. 'Use of that tunnel you seen. Cause those tunnels' whereabouts, that cannot fall into enemy hands. Thass an area where I'm already unhappy.'

'Maria cannot stay here,' Pasha say, eyes furiose on me.

'Ma'am?' The Commandant nod to me. 'We could have your thoughts, we all be thankful.'

Then every child fix eyes to me, their faces grim in overlight.

First, my thoughts be easy yes. It always been my expectation, I war here myself. But how Marines be gleering on me, something trouble in my gut. Remind that I be here alone, without my Sengle children. Remind the land of skulls and bombs around.

'Nay,' I say nerviose. 'You thinking wrong. We help your fighting, then you asking asks. Is backward somehow.'

The Commandant take slower breath. 'Well, ma'am, I'm hoping you give it thought. It's a thing we really appreciate.'

'Cannot,' say Pasha straight to me. 'Cannot.'

I frown to him unhappy. Yo, when I see his white disquiet, I remember sudden, how he going back to roos. Said he will think, but never sworn he stay. All been some arguments.

Then a mally conscience whisper: *If I stay in Quantico, he never leave me here alone. Must stay for my protection.* This thought go scary and it pass, leave shivers in my blood.

'If I ain't?' I say unsteady. 'We still fighting, with–without.'

The Commandant cough and swallow at his throat. Say in thicker voice, 'Well, you seen our streets, ma'am. Your troops can't help so much, if they can't set foot. Thass only a first example.'

Simón Zelote look back to me feroce. 'Maria, there's no necessity for our troops to enter the city. We can attack the Russians from the rear. We can attack supply lines.'

'I'm sorry to disagree there.' Hatter give a shortish laugh. 'Supply lines, you're talking helicopters. So, good luck with that. And I was thinking myself, your boys come in on the rear. But if–'

'Excuse me,' Verna say in harsh. 'If we're discussing tactics, I'd like to ask that the Russian gennleman leave.'

This catch my temper, and I say, 'Shee, better you leave yourself.'

'Now, I wonder what your interest is, ma'am,' Verna say with skinny eyes. 'Why you want the gennleman to hear all this, I certainly wonder.'

'Oh, Verna, learn a different tune,' say Hatter sudden sharp. 'We wadden discussing tactics. Hardly got to any discussing at all. Personally, I'm here to win a war. If I wanted a catfight, I'd get cats.'

Verna give him ugly looks. 'General Diaz, thanks for your maturity. But if we're talking disposition of troops, I think we better do it without a Russian representative. If thass catfights, fine.'

'Now, hold on,' say the Commandant. 'Is that acceptable to the lady?'

All faces turn to me again. Even Simón give me some hinting look.

'Nay, he helping us these weeks,' I say unnerve. 'Ain't needful.'

The Commandant begin to speak, but cough into his starting word. Swallow and say breathless quick, 'Excuse my saying, General

Mitchell does have a point. Thanking the gennleman for his help, but it's getting into an area that wadden anticipated . . . hope you all can see.'

As he saying this, I feel it clear. Truth, Pasha being Russian self. Is natural suspicions.

But when I try to think agreement, something narrow in my chest. Get superstition feeling, Pasha go to roos if he leave now. He take among all Quanticos, beyond my watching eyes, and lost. How Driver lost, while I been gone.

When I look at Pasha, he lost his rage. Stare to me weak. And in my mind, that mally whisper come again, insisting.

I say, lost in fear, 'I stay here. If it be a help, I stay in Quantico. Be right.'

Pasha sit back sharp, while Hatter say in voice of big relief, 'Well, now, thass something! Ma'am, and I'd say, thass brave of you, I was going to say that.'

'Yes,' say Verna softer. 'That is a help.'

'Makes it a different picture,' the Commandant say with easing grin. 'I do thank you, ma'am, and we'll try to make your stay very pleasant. We certainly will.'

Here Pasha stand up sudden from his chair. All startle back. The Commandant say footless, 'Sir? You all right there?'

'Can go,' he say in absent voice.

'Nay, Pasha,' I say. 'We ain't said–'

'Well, thank you also.' Verna stand up ready. 'I certainly appreciate that too.'

Pasha push his chair back clumsy. Verna pass along, she open the door with quick impatience. Pasha start behind, then hold. Step back to me and bend down hasty. Kiss me on the forehead. Then he turn and he be gone. Door shut against my frightening look.

This kiss stay wrong in me. Ain't Pasha manners that he do no kissing, ain't himself. Ya, in my wrong feeling, the Commandant begin to cough again – a longer trail of coughs with fretten swallows in between. I grit sharp, look to his posy face with struggling heart.

Simón Zelote start to talk now, how my safety can assure. 'You'll need to make us comfortable, if we're going to work together . . . regular communications and some means . . .' and he say on, while Verna coming back, without my Pasha. And someone answer shortish, and someone answer glad, and all be voices. I try to heed correct, but then the Commandant cough again, and my mind deafen in unsense. I only see the harshen light, their faces looking skully ill.

I see Hatter frowning worry at the Commandant before grief swallow me entire. Room become a smaller darkness. Feel weakly cold, like all my blood be tears. Be gripping in my dress – their voices babbiting around me – swearing my heart that Pasha cannot leave. He know that Driver gone. He going to know I need himself.

Then this confuse to Driver dying lonely in his bed. How he pologizing that I try so hard, and still he die. All times I dare myself, all sweating work, a city's ruling – and still I cannot save one life. And this new war will spend its blood, and Driver still be dead.

Ya, my mind recall a rhyme I known in littlish years. Be about a boy was lost, and every creature work to find him. Birds fly seeking, and the foxes sniff, and moles dig underground. Even the sun go look for him, and water hunt in all its brooks. But he never found, and every part end with the rhyme:

> These are the creatures that live in the world,
> And these are the things they done.
> Uppity busy, and everywheres,
> But Mannity still be gone.
> Mannity still be gone.

Through this, I hear Simón say low, 'Maria?'

Look up, and all the generals frown on me. The Commandant say, 'Ma'am, do that sound possible to you?'

When I take my breath, feel like it cut into my chest. 'Sorry,' I say. 'I be tired. If Pasha–'

Then I sob out hard. My tears come helpless, and I skit both hands up to my face.

Can hear in shamen awfulness, how every child be saying 'Ma'am? Ma'am?' Someone touch my arm, ask something, but I cannot think. And they standing up. All noising with their slurren courtesies. Close through this, Simón say low, 'Please understand, Maria's brother died yesterday.'

I look to him, surprise. Be like I ain't remember any other child know this. Then it be some comfort, how his eyes be sharp feroce. Look like he ready to attack no child who tell me wrong.

But they give sorries courteose. Hatter reach a cloth to me, and even Verna saying they never guess, and be good courage that I come. I use the cloth to wipe my face, say choken, 'Nay, be right. Can need a cigarette, all it need.'

Hatter's voice come near beside, 'Now, ma'am. We can carry on without you until tomorrow, the very least. There's Mister Zelote here. I think you've done everything anybody can ask.'

The Commandant say kindly low, 'Ma'am, I think we can all use time to gather thoughts. Maybe I show you to your room, you can rest. And anything else you need, you just speak up.'

Ain't comprehend this well, but I say, 'Ya, be gratty right.'

'Thass fine,' the Commandant say. 'We've all lost people, everyone here. You're among friends, ma'am, forgetting all politics. I hope you appreciate that.'

This bring my tears again, and I say thoughtless, 'Sure. Be gratty, brother.'

Then be a strange walk to the White House self, all generals fluttering round. Must concentrate on seeing where I walk through always tears. We come into a hall of whitish luxury, ride an elevator, yo all be sobbing and confusions. At last, we stop beside a door. Here Simón and everyone be gone. Is only the Commandant. He say pleasant, 'This is the Queen's Bedroom, ma'am, what they call it. Thinking it be appropriate.'

I say soft, 'Where Pasha be? My . . . Russian child.'

'Ma'am, thought you knew. He's talking to some of our folks now. And then, at his request, he's going back to his own people. Thass the arrangement that we made.'

My mind go struggling feary. 'Nay. He change in this.'

'Ma'am?'

'He promise, ya. He got to be with me.'

The Commandant look discomfort. 'Ma'am, I'll certainly ask him. Can't exactly have him in the White House here, but . . . well, you leave that to me.'

I shake my head. Look past him like my Pasha going to be there. 'I cannot stay alone here. Sure he know.'

'Hoping you won't feel alone with us, ma'am. But I'll ask him, you don't worry at all.'

'Ya, send him here. I need him.' I say this peevish like a little, then I go inside. The Commandant stick in the doorway, explaining how is empty here, tell pologies on his missing staff. 'Everybody's fighting now. So things got a little dusty, but I'm hoping you can see it's no disrespect.' He linger in this till I lose my strength, sit on the bed. Say rough, 'Be thanks. But send me Pasha.' He make this promise again, and go at last. Close the door onto a petty sound, is like a final cough.

Some time, I stare into my blindness, heeding for my Pasha's step. Keep swearing he must come. Cannot be Driver gone and Pasha both. But all the house be dumb. Be dead. At last, I curl onto my side, gone weak from useless wish. Hug my knees and wait my misery into nothing sleep.

66

OF ROOISH PRISONERS

I wake again in nighten closeness. Only a gentle yellow lamp be lit beside the bed. Gone sweaty in my dress and coat, and I sit weak confusen while my every griefs remember.

In this, the room begin to notice. All be ickety pink. The walls and rugs and every other object pinking various. Pink and pink, like sitting in a mouth. Only unpink object be my blackish journey case, brought from Marias with all packen clothes. Some child must carry it here while I been sleeping. Now it seem queer familiar. Is like an actual object that appear inside a dream.

For longer time, I only sitting, restless in despair. Think how I can ask to leave, pick through the land-mine streets again. Beg a car, can get back to my Sengles by the morning. But then a notion hold my mind.

Pasha still be here. Is somewhere in the city, with Russian prisoners waiting trade. Can even be, he never meant to leave. Verna took him, and he gone obedient to help our parley. Only must fetch him out again, and he remain with me.

I go to the door and open hasty. Call up, 'Ho? Be someone by?'

Answer be silence, dumb as ice. I breathe my courage up again and step out to the hall.

Their elevator work like ours. I ride it down and wander lost through luxury rooms, all fade with dust. Keep calling, but my voice be only a strange intrusion in the deafness. Get superstitions, every person kilt while I been sleeping long.

At last, I find an outer door. Then it be relief to step into the good outside. The air be living with bright wind, the sky as huge as feeling. Is darken trees before, all shushing happy with their leafen voice. Cold seize into my face, my eyes. But ain't no child to ask. Be no one there and no one there.

I stalk across the grass, come through a spacen line of trees. Can spy a bigger field beyond, still clean with no explosion patterns. A tickle of movement there come hopeful. I haste my step toward, pass through a clutch of heavy pines. Here I halt in staring.

Center of this field an artifact rise, white gigantesque. Is tallish like sky towers, but ain't shapen like no building. Be skinny long with pointen top, and got no windows all its height. Look like goliath stake, craften out of moon. Around it, be a ring of poles with flags of old America. Look tiny there, their stripen rags twitch pitieuse in wind. To every side, the grassen field go widening out to milen distance.

First my nerves wonder if this be a nuclear weapon that they keep. Guess how its poison kill the trees around, leave only grass. Yo, as I stare, a child come striding. Follow around this flaggen circle, holding a rifle loose.

I speed my step toward him, breathing funny with my spookery. He still be tiny in his yonder when he pause in noticing. Straighten up and ware his gun.

I halt, yell up, 'Salue! It be Maria, from the north.'

Child hitch his rifle wary. Beckon to me with his hand.

Last walking be a long impatience. Face numb and sting with Cember wind. Ya, always be that artifact, moon weapon in my eyes. It grow overhead, while the ring of flags seem always small the same. But truth, these flagposts be four times the height of the watching child.

At last I come to talking distance. Can see the soldier's troubling face in moonlight, how he tense his gun. Frown at my furs, my diamond head – can see he worry in duty, I be beasts beyond his knowing. I guess him at fifteen, and all my spirit be a thankfulness. At last, be someone by. Can ask.

'Hello, ma'am?' he call. 'You all right there?'

'Sure, be right.'

'Guessing you do have a pass? Didden catch what you was yelling.'

'Know no pass. Been saying, I be Maria. From the north.'

'Oh.' Uncertainty go down himself, a pology in his body. 'Do beg your pardon, ma'am. We was told, but I didden expect to see you here. Hoping you aren't lost?'

'Nay. My brother, what be this building for?'

He look to it, puzzling. 'Well, thass the Washington Monument. It's for . . . I don't know how to tell you. Memory, I suppose.'

'Ain't a weapon?'

He grin up sweet. 'Oh, no, ma'am. Lessen it falls on us, the old boy's harmless as a sock.'

I look unhappy to this monument, try to feel it harmless. But closer, it be only worse unnatural in its white.

'Dang,' the soldier say beside. 'Thought you was a ghost, first saw you. Thass funny about the monument, you thought that. Hope you don't mind me saying.'

I look back at his friendly smile. See where he growing scrabbity beard, still seldom on his cheeks. 'Brother,' I say nervy, 'you know where they keep the prisoners? Russian children, what I meaning.'

'Well.' His face ease seriose. 'They're the other side. But these aren't children, ma'am. They're fully grown, for certain.'

'Other side?'

'I'll walk you. Guess it idden any harm you seeing.'

He set out at lagging pace, while I keep by impatient. And as we walk around these flags, the child say nerviose confusions – how this look irregular, but be telligence reasons, what they do. 'If the Russians know these boys are there, they're thinking twice about where they bomb. Plus, we want to get these boys talking. Don't know what information's there.'

'Ain't talking?'

'No, the Russians who's cooperative, they're not down here shivering. They were at barracks, if they hadn't been traded home. These folks have got to earn that soft bed.'

As he saying this, I spy a shape by farther flagpost. Seem a heap of clothy trash, like I seen in Loisaida sometimes, frozen to a wall. Come walking, and can see another, another. Then it tweak in sense, is people bound against these poles. Ya, all be slumpen queery, like they fallen there from beating.

I stalk angry forward, while the boy call out his frighten, 'Ma'am?' Be only thinking, I free Pasha now. This nonsense finish right.

Only be six children here, bound against six flagposts. Sit curlen to themself, arms caught behind. All wear dapple suits, and nest their faces in their collars, ducking from the windy cold. Still, can see in second's glance that Pasha ain't among. Most is darker furry, and the yellow roos be smaller than my Pasha, most like normal children. Come to the end and I look forward to the empty flagposts, helpless lorn that he ain't here.

Soldier fetch up to me, say breathless, 'Now, ma'am. Please don't go running off like that. I'm responsible here, what happens.'

'At barracks, you saying, the others be?'

'If anyone's left, they're there. Thought, you come here, it must be these you want.'

I look back scary to this row. Now it realize strange that these be Pasha's natural people. All furren like a hound, their faces squarish made, pink in this cold. Been talking all these weeks of roos and Russians, known was thousands like. But it never realize correct, they all be looking so.

Come staring at the nearest child. Got weirdo hair, ain't yellow but is white. Ya, like the others, he sit heedless dull. Ain't look to us.

I say thin, 'Where barracks be?'

'Truth is, ma'am,' the soldier say behind, 'I think those guys is gone from barracks.'

'Nay, how you meaning?'

'They done an exchange tonight. Pretty sure it was everyone who's not here.'

'Tonight?' A knowing misery rise into my throat. 'Is done?'

'Well, it's getting on to midnight now. Best I know, they gone at eight. And it's a short walk, when nobody's shooting at you.'

A moment, I get screaming feeling. Want to grab this child and shake him. Make him find they generals, and insist they fetch my Pasha back. Can threaten we ain't help their war. We join with Russians, they be sorrier.

But this fever pass and leave me weak with nonsense feeling. Stare brainless to the monument, its goliath flank of moon. Feel somehow, it be evidence – should know when I first seen it, Pasha gone.

The soldier say behind, 'I'm juss hoping our own people's come back. I got to be out here, or I'd know better, ma'am.'

My eyes stray to the white-fur roo again. A wind gust sharp, and he clench through his body. White hair blown and blown.

I sigh my breath. 'Need hats.'

'Hats?' The soldier follow my gaze. 'Well, I guess thass not for me to say.'

'Ya, gloves. They losing fingers so.'

'Thass their own choice, ma'am. Like I said.'

'Nay, how long they keeping here?'

'See, it's five days, and they won't help us at all.'

'Five days.' I take a nervy breath. 'They dying so. Is Cember month.'

'Don't think they'll die. But they do, it's themselves to thank,' he say stubborn. 'Barracks is nice.'

'Foo.' I shake my head. Go toward this whitish roo and hunker. Soldier dabbit nerviose behind.

I scout the roo's face best I can, how he ducking in his collar. Skin be strange like Deema's, though his face ain't uggety much. Is only wrinklen fine, and chap from cold. Ya, can see his ear been hurt. Mark redden black with scab.

For a perilous breath, I only know that he ain't Pasha. Seem worse injustice, how he be a roo, but still ain't Pasha. Like he only be this different roo for spite, for selfishness. And in this moment, I remind the murders in the Massa woods. Can know why someone leave him freezing. Beat his ears, do any hurt.

But this pass like chills. It be a child who clench and suffer. And I try their rooish salue, how Pasha teaching me. 'Privyet.'

A moment, he ain't stir. But then the child's white head come up reluctant from his collar. Now can see, his mouth be bruisen fat, like punching injury. Hurt move like speech, but ain't no sound. He frown and swallow slow.

I roo to him, *What be with you?* But this bring only more bad swallowing. A humor look come in his eyes, and he duck back into his collar. Shut his eyes again.

I stand up shaking somehow. Look to the soldier child where he be frowning disapprovals.

'Ma'am,' he say, 'I don't think you ought to be doing that. It's interfering in an ongoing program, see.'

'Why he cannot talk?'

'I wouldn't be in a position. Please.' His eyes turn blaming to the whitish roo. 'Ma'am, he's probably only thirsty.'

'Thirsty how? Ain't talk for this?'

'Well, I'm guessing,' he say shortish. 'Said to you, I am not in a position.'

'Look like you got two hands. Ain't water nowhere?'

'Ma'am, I'm going to ask you to leave the area. Please, you can talk to my commanding officer about this in the morning. Colonel Rocher, he'll be here at eight.'

I look back at this row of huddlen roos, my guts reacting hard. The monument enorme stand over like a god of cold. And I turn without no words, go stalking past the slumpen roos, the flags that stutter on the wind.

It seem like ten forevers before I reach the White House door. Then I go hunting, quick with rage. Will open a door, grope to its light. Switch on a sudden room of golden ornaments and fatty chairs. Scout quick, then I stalk on. Seek only water in this dry richesse.

At last I open to the cookroom – steely place with metal cabinets covering every wall. Ya, be a sink with faucets. I scratch around the cabinets till I find a jumbo brock, is glassen sort with useful handle. Faucets working right, and I start filling it with colder water. Then I figure better, change for hot.

While this brock fill slow, I go through droars and find a scissor. Fit this in my pocket. And I be breathing gratty, watching the water rising in the brock, when the skree begin.

Be deafen loud. Is like it shrieking huge inside my head. I jump, grip to a table, as the skree go shriller high and hold this shrillness for unbearing lengths. Wail down and rise again, and here at last it recognize. Is warning sirens, how the Quantico twelves sung in the tunnels.

I feel my different sweat of fear, a shivering in my coaten warm. Magine planes and bombs, and my bad nerves be raw, be white.

But I take the brock and hug its heaten weight against my chest. Grit my fear as I go stubborn out.

On the frosten grass, scream fill the air as thick as drowning rain. The cold join to my fright, and I hunch to the brock its warm. All I can think be that old rhyme: *These are the creatures that live in the world, and these are the things they done.* Repeat this like a superstition while I stalk this milen grass. And I be hurrying tense, a sweating detail on the huge blank field, when the explosions come.

Be like neary thunder, trembling loud. It hit again, again, and shudder awful through the ground. Ring in my guts. Soon I be trotting clumsy, water splashing on my coaten arms. I argue to myself, roos never bombing Washington itself. But cannot rid my body fear. Be hunching terrify while these explosions pounding all directions, flash the dull horizon.

Be almost to the monument before I see, the soldier gone. Then cowardesse insist that roos be bombing here. He known and fled. But I force my footsteps onward. Come where the flags be easen loose and limp, despite all battering noise. The roos be woken now. Tense various, like they guard from different blows. They watch the flashing sky.

One and one, they startle as I come. Look after me with open mouth, as I go without reason to this last white roo. He sitting sharper now, and from his swollen eyes, he look to me with courteose surprise. Is like I be some older friend who visit without expectation.

I kneel to him, feel glad to crouch myself below the noise. No rooish word for drink remember. I only raise the brock. Arms tremble, and a neary explosion shiver the earth beneath my knee. Ya, the roo frown doubtful, like he consider what new punishment this be.

But when I touch it to his mouth, his eyes catch telligence. Then he drink greedy, shutting eyes. Spill some slightish dabble down his chin, and he lick after this. I give him to drink again, and now another roo be shouting, dim into the ever siren. I rise up, heave the brock against my chest. Be breathing hard in nerves and wishing I can hear this breath.

Become a straining task, this ever lifting, ever care. Some roos speak, but any word be mysteries in the noise. The air begin to stank of smoke. Times the sky shock grayish, fickle to orange, then be black the same. Ya, once a clutch of planes tear over and deafen the sirens self. And I keep on, lean toward another whitish face. Tip this aching weight up to a mouth is straining open, feary that it miss its chance. Yo, all they faces be like mistaken tries at Pasha's face.

Next task be worse, of tearing up my coat. Ain't no scissors made for cutting fur. Must figure a means to stab into this, rip and scissor and force. Nor I can do this with coat on. Must sit freezing on its tail, work with shivering arms. But at last I cut away a raggity length of sleeve. Carry this to my white-head roo, who watch now curiose. I roo to him, *hands, hands,* and show him how he use this fur. To this, he laugh. When I reach the fur back to his hand, his fingers flinch, but cannot catch. They dumb from cold. Must form his hands inside myself. Hold them in my hands until they warm to better use. Then his body clench at the returning feeling, sweat his pain. But I rise away, ain't got no time for sympathies.

And this continue till my mind stray foolish. Be gratty to the bombs that they continue well, give time to work. Wish the sirens quit, and wish these roos quit saying things I cannot hear. Cold take until my selfen hands go stupid, hurt like naked bone. Be breathing smoke sometimes. The sky gone smutten, lose its stars. World burning while I freeze; I shiver bombs and shiver cold.

Ya, in this ever pain, I realize these be prisoners. Be what we trade for cure. Been reasons that they cannot die. Almost, I wish the guard come back, can tell him this with righteous face. But underneath, I know like shame, I save them neverless. Ain't brave to kill. Ain't brave for war, ain't brave.

Then sudden, the noise wail down. The sirens droop their screaming into hush. Explosions gone, and in the quiet left, can hear the rooish gabble. They talking each to each, in louder voices from their deafness. When I give the final child his fur, he roo in dazen curiosity, *What you be?* Be tired for foreign answers, and I only roo, *Ain't know.*

Then I go walking backen forth. Tuck hands in armpits and stalk quick to wake my warmer blood. So I be pacing, shivering, when that fifteen guard come striding back.

I stop in my footsteps, tense. His face knit in worry, and when he come up near, he say, 'You was out here through the raid, ma'am?'

'Sure, can see.'

'They was looking for you. They–' He catch his voice. Notice the furry scraps, the brock left empty. 'Oh. I see you been busy here. Thass . . . I don't think that was right to do, ma'am.'

Then I take breath, and he take breath, and we begin to argue.

Skirmish over these fur scraps go on till whisker morning. Guard argue, then he find a child of better rank to argue. And this go on through ranks and hours, while roos watch on joyeuse. Ever an officer leave in rage, they call up cheers together – though I tell them, in my stumble rooish, this be mally help. Ya, between this bother, I keep skitting to the White House. Take covers from the beds and bring these back with stubborn fury. Wrap the roos from head to foot.

In this last work, I start to roo to them with better luck. When I tell them what Maria be, they gladden entertaining. One child seem ready to believe that I be godly mother. Another offer filthy that he give me better Jesus. All start to call me Masha, and they get some curiosity, how New York fighting now. I say friendly, 'Yes, all cities here fight now. You Russians finish.' They answer back with laughing insult – and we interrupt again by some new angry Quantico.

Last come the Commandant himself. He start in sadder disapprovals, how they all been seeking me. Was fearing I run to the land mines, skitty from all bombs. He bring a coat – a grayish object, sizen for a bigly male. Settle this around me fussing, and he beckon me some steps apart, to talk in privacy.

He say, 'We all was thinking, ma'am . . . not going to say we stop our interrogations. These boys stay right here. But if you want to bring them water, basic needs – well, it's possible we accept that. We'd only ask, you put that to some use. Thing is, you got a good start here. It's every chance, these boys will trust you. So if you could get them talking, ask some questions we provide you with . . .'

'Ho, be spying?'

He make stubborn face. 'Can't always have perfect honesty in a war. I know your religion maybe tell you thass a sin–'

'Foo sin.' I laugh up soft. 'Sure I do spying. Be no problems.'

'Well, thass fine.' His face ease softer. 'And any information you get, we all be thankful. But our main priority there. I know Patricia told you about our nuclear program. Now, the problem we got, the Russians are determined to find that out the hard way.'

'They ain't believe.' I nod unthinking.

'Yeah, thass it. Now, these are all men of higher rank here. Why they're assets. So, expecting they do go home sometime . . .

it's paramount they go back with the right information. The Russians have got to know, there is no victory here. There's no good ending.'

I think to ask if nuclears be fables, or is real. But I got no strength for more disturbances this hour. So I only say, 'Be right. I try.'

'Well, I am grateful, ma'am. Hoping you appreciate that we all want to make this work.' The Commandant sigh, frown to the roos, like he guess what I see in them. A moment, his face be only sad in worrying. Then he flinch hard. 'Ma'am – you took those blankets from the White House?'

I shrug. 'Ain't known no other place to rob.'

'Rob,' he say in thinner voice. 'Thass nice.'

'Need hats. What they need most.'

Roos watch back with nerviose disliking in their eyes. Look sorry in their shamble wrappings, various with flowers or stripes. Can see they worry, why I ain't fight with this newer child. Be thinking how I say in rooish, *I ain't bandon you*, when the Commandant say grim, 'Goddamnit, I'm standing here, and the Russians are coming into Arlington again. That's what that bombing was. This – well, this could work. But it wadden a thing we appreciate much, and you are not very popular with my people this morning. Now, I expect you to return those blankets where you found them, and anything else you *robbed*. And I'll ask you to show more maturity, from now on. I hope thass clear!'

Then he turn sharp and stalk away. Unhelpful roos call out a cheer of mockery to his back.

THE WAR AT QUANTICO

Cember 26–January 6

67

MY WAR BEGIN

Time be fickle objects, and perverse to any wish. A glad week vanish as it born. Ya, a misery hour will stick and grow, and cannot rid. So, when I counting after, my time in Quantico been eleven days. But when it live, it seeming years of loneliness.

My Sengles keep in far Marias, safe from any roos. Been my own wish, but still I miss them worse than fear expect. Always I forget that they ain't by, expect them in my want. Will save treats for my greedy eights; remember rooish words for Keepers; will think, when night be darkening, my children wait for me. Cannot learn they gone. Pain never lose its first surprise.

Yo, be frustrations, how my Mariano soldiers ain't arrive. Always be in conscience that the NewKing coming with – but days go past, and they still marching slow and slow by hidden roads. Get fantasies where the NewKing ridden fast ahead of every troops; step in my White House room like natural rights, and lock the door behind. Then it seem impossibilities, that he ain't here. Each petty day seem like a wrong eternity.

And I watch the flash of bombs and think of Pasha by the roos. Must suffer on his treachery; guess how he kill my selfen people, like his mally tales. But cannot magine this correct – like ever when I attempt to know his crimes, my mind be blank and strange. Will start with blame, but always end with my same loneliness.

*

My most relief be small participations in the war. For this, I must insist like ten damnations. Quanticos want me in no risk – but I ain't grown to be some pamper queen, use feet for only holding shoes. So, after houry threats and brawls, they give me runner task of bearing messages to Arlington.

For this work, they teaching me to walk the land-mine maze. Truth, this need no genius brains. All is patterns that repeat. Sawdust circles safe to walk around their farther edge, but must cross all squares of bones direct, however you be finicky. I also learn to walk the tunnels underground, in craft of blindness. Stalk sidelong to a rail, and kick with foot to check its distance. Times, I even run – will sprint my heart to reckless nothing, till I tire or trip my feet. And at last, I climb out to the bluish wildness of the day. Breathe and blink the sun joyeuse, before I must climb down again into the dirty trenches.

Arlington trenches be a maze cut deep in rooten earth. Some be shallow, wreathe with old barb wire and barricading trash. But most got walls high overhead. These using for all peaceful life. Get chairs somewhere and eating tables; beds with cleanly sheets beneath a roof of slanting tarp. But, ever their condition be, all trenches stanking unbelievable of rotting meat. Ain't no trench where no one kilt, nor every scrap can bury nett. When this corpsen stank be fresh, it be particular as a word. The Quanticos burn smelling wood to rid this evil breath. But it be there and always there. Stick in your hair, your clothes, and soon all smells be bad reminders.

First week, my task be safe as any life. This be a time when roos do only bombing from the air. My only fight be ducking into tunnels, coming out again. Wear soldier uniform, but never clad its pinching helmet. Bring Kalash for only her respect.

But when I been in Quantico six days, roos learn the land-mine patterns. They catch some talking prisoner, and every secret told. Then they teach soldats to do this stalking in some hasty lessons, and one day of sunlit frost, they make attack enorme.

*

Hour they come, I been in Buckethead trenches, far from any tunnel. Been seeking a difficult captain here, while every smaller Quantico make scabby eyes at me. These children hate all Marianos for our history wars; say courtesies if they must, but cannot make their faces smile. At last, I found a helpful thirteen boy. Been heeding his directions, standing by an eating tent, when roos announce their visit with grenades.

Accustom now to goodly bombs that shiver all the ground, and I ain't comprehend at first. See smoke in farther trenches; hear a banging, thick and dull. Ya, my thirteen boy scream nonsense words and crouch to handsen knees. Eating tent go flapping wild with children scrambling out, and all the land around break deafening with guns.

Yo, while I stand in puzzle, a grenade come chucketing past. Sock to the tenten roof, and slide. Look like a fatly beetle, ain't nothing frightening to see. But every child go diving vicious, and – for stupid luck – they knock me down.

Feel the explosion as some stinging dirt, a shock in ears. And then I jumping to my feet – in unison of every child – and scramble with them to a farther trench, no thought betook. Got Kalash in hands, but holding wrong. Is loose and skew. Sneeze the dusty air, and follow brainless.

Then be time of running, falling on stomachs, scrambling up and running. The gunfire shift to left, to right, is big and small like changing moods. From yells, I start to know, we heading forward to the Sooner trench, but ain't know why. I guess no reasons.

Ya, we come to a shallow place, and see the land above. Strange in innocent daylight, be all hundred bigly roos upon, go running– crawling like we be. Most is small in distance – seem like toys of magination, flailing shadowy in the sun. But be two children close and huge. Was crawling to the trench ahead, but now they heel back to us, shoot direct.

Then, without thinking sense, I shoot – yo every child be shooting wild. Ain't aiming, only shoot, like slapping a stinging wasp in panic.

Be a longer second before I know, Kalash got safety on. Ain't rid no bullet. And I fall hasty, claw her switch with weirdo fingers, strange to use. Find her three-bullet setting, and relieve. And see a Quantico child lain on his face, his neck torn through. Blood be moving, kicking from his wound. A girl crouch by him, rise again with blooden hands and awful face. Shout high and vicious, 'Eddie's dead!'

Then my body hunch in dirt, is stubborn to no change. Bullets pass overhead, like skinny wind. Marines crouch, leap to shoot again, and crouch.

Ain't know how I decide. But I leap up and shoot feroce. Fall down again and swear my moron brains, that I ain't aim. Ain't look. Leap up again, and no one there. Then all Marines be running again. I run. Come to the Sooner corner, and the gunfire louden vicious. A child in front go staggering down.

All Marines jump to the wall before I guess to fear. Ain't think until the bullets come at me. Then I see the grandy child who shoot, stood in the trench before, and point my gun in hate. Shoot right. And shoot again at nothing. Been only one roo there. He down, is sitting bloody, drop his gun.

The smart Marines know this somehow, and all go plungen forward. Sprint around–upon this gunshot child. Someone shoot him again, is yelling curses, then he run away. I be left one second that remain, is like a silence.

Shot child be black. Ain't rooish nothing. I seize cold – then see behind, his clothes be roo. Is theirs. It be a slave who fight for them.

In this second, I see his eyes concentrate feroce. Is like he studying his death, look out for any small escape. Then his face lose its thought. Without no visible change, is brainless things.

And I see my Quanticos far ahead, and I go run.

This battle last for awful time, but be no other blood I seen. We shoot at farther roos, and cannot hit, and duck again. Then be a time we lose somewhere, in trenches no one recognize. Ever we try, the gunfire always shrinking into distance. Ya, somewhere in this time, a twelvish girl turn to me, saying mean, 'Who in goddamn hell are you?' When this fact discover, they all giggling high to tears. Girl bow to me in mockery, but an older boy go shove her. Say with laughing voice, 'She got a kill, you idiot. What you got?'

When we find the battle again, is done. All children slacking rifles, talking various in nerves. Yo, General Hatter there. Yell orders at anyone he see. And be peculiar to myself, he look the same as in the Situation Room – foxen child with prettieuse mustache, perfect in his clothes. Stand like easy afternoons, and shout like pleasure, like a song he sing to feel his voice.

He yell me back to Pentagon tunnel. I leave through familiar dark, sweat chilling on my skin entire. Get to the White House, and I wash myself for longer time. Keep thinking awful, can be Pasha that I shot. Ain't even look before I shoot. This thought come back and back, and every time, it be relief that this ain't been. Is only when I clothe again, be walking out to feed my roos, I mind the dying child himself. Then I sit down in the frosten grass and weep my eyes.

Yo, as I cry there stupid, feeling nothing but my gripping throat, two Quanticos go past. One say to the other nervy, 'Wow. Whass wrong with *her*?'

The other say low-voice, 'Oh, thass the New York girl. I think her brother died.'

68

OF ROOS THEIR COMPANY

Behind this fight, I be forbid to venture outside Washington. How Patricia say, 'You get your head blown off, and we all enter a world of crazy.' So my new task be digging trenches new for Washington's last defense, in safety of the rear.

Chore be at Arlington Cemetery – a field of hundred thousand burial slabs, in whitish lines like crops. This be the final ground that roos must pass to enter Washington, and all Marines be grim, that trenches needful in this backward place. We dig shallow, above the holes old soldiers bury in. Yo, always be some jokes, how we preparing bunkbed graves. A child say to me once, 'As many folks dead here as we got living. Kinda puts perspective.'

Between ourself and Arlington's battles stand the cemetery hill. On its crest be Arlington House – a grandy pillar mansion watching downward like a moon. Ya, is something in this house that never settle in my eyes. Ain't white, is only pale uncolor. Look like rooish skin. Groom perfect, but ain't use. It be museum, keeping dead with all its ancient furnitures. Often behind it rise the smoke and rattling jolts of war, and in my mind, I feel it like a staring enemy. Get mally dreams where Pasha living there among all roos – but be an evil Pasha, coming at me violent with red hands.

These days be work and fear and work again, without no kindly word. Marines ain't glad to strangers. Even my digging crew dislike my help. Ya, worse be fights with generals about the rooish cure. Verna still swear it ain't exist; ya, Hatter say, 'Not asking how I can live a hundred years, when people's shooting at me.' When I remind their promise to trade prisoners, they grim their mouths. Then the Commandant will mention how my soldiers ain't fought yet – they still march southward, slow and slow. 'So your side of the deal remains to be seen.' And Verna add, she glad to trade my roos – once I convince them Marines got nuclears. 'Achieve that, there's some chance the Russians leave, and we don't all die here. If thass a thing you even think about, I don't know.' Ya, when I tell my selfen doubts on nuclears, they rile like wasps – but never offer proof that they be real.

In truth, my only friendship be in my sad company of roos. Be enemies, but they always glad to me. Theirs be my only smiles. Yo, in nights by them, there been bellesse that sing into my mind; a witchery of grieving stars that Washington was for me.

Mall be a milen field of grass with princen mansions to its edge. In this guerra season, it mostly bandon from no life. Can stand in starry wind aloft a pillar edifice, look out on only empty palaces and ornamenting trees. War be a sometimes deafening of bombs and needling sirens. Plane rip overhead, or stuttering light go in the farther sky – but I stand harmless, like this all be dreaming maginations.

These nights, I sleeping by the roos, now that their guard be gone to fight. Ain't do this, and some bitter Marine come pour cold water on them, kick them in the face – any viciousness they dare. So I scratch a hammock from storage, sling this on two flagposts. Sleep there in coat and sleepen bag, restless with the sometimes bombs and always muttering of roos.

Be curiosity, how these roos is like and unlike Pasha. How they compare, no roo can answer any question normal. Ask where his town be, roo say, 'The moon,' or give a town name made of swears. Ask what they eat in Russia, they eat dirt, and dirt be healthier than no food – why crops grow in it. Ya, while this roo be talking, his neighbor roo will mutter sorry, 'Lies, lies.' But he give no better sense, got only other lies.

Any spying dabbit hopeless in this swamp of fables. Can ask on war, or on their freezing toes – they answer foolishness, and gladden if I smile. Yo, ever I mention nuclears, the roos go laughing simple. Try every gambit, but it fail embarrassing. Once I forcing actual tears, say weepen, 'Wish it being jokes. Can die in this myself.' But all I gain, they rival to comfort me that it be jokes; Marines got no more nuclears than they got wings to fly.

First roo from the left be yellow Vitya, mouse of spooking. Every bombing, Vitya sob and twist against his pole – yet he suffer beatings from Marines in courage silence. Next be Kirill Filth, whose only talk be sexy feats he done, and like to do with me. His favorite game be to insist he got a pain between his legs, and ask me that I check it. Another evil mouth be my Bashir, but his unpleasantries be hatreds on the other roos. Is cowards all, gross with unwash. Got no right morals in their brains that wreck with love diseases. He always explain, he ain't no proper Russian, is Kavkazky peoples – vally children who behaving decent like no roo.

Two roos vanish after my first night. If they talk obedient, or they kilt, I never learn. They leave a space where I sit sometimes, leaning to a flagpost. This be between Bashir Hate Everyone and my white-hair Polkovnik, child who be my closest problem in these nights of clamoring war.

I learn his three-part name – Mikhail Arkadievich Razin – and I call him this sometimes to try its tangles in my mouth. But in my mind, he always be Polkovnik, rooish word for colonel. Ya, even when we speaking English, he call me Korolyeva – roo for queen. We say these names in mockery, and they grow their selfen meaning in our hours of strange unfriendship. Polkovnik be Polkovnik, Korolyeva be Korolyeva – and in my mind, these two still struggle, through all times and darkness, on a field of grass, backs to a tower monument of grief, while angry wars of evil and bonesse burn in the sky around.

Polkovnik Razin be an upright child, sit proper as a hawk. Got most no lips to see, his reddish face be sharp in all its parts. In sunlight, hair be grayer than is white, and eyes be normal brown. These eyes be ponds of sentiment – sympathy and love joyeuse. But always his sharp mouth be harsh in plans.

He never waste his breath to lie. Ask a question he ain't like, and he keep only silence, disappointing in his eyes. Then he ask something of myself, like demonstration how these questions meant to be. First times he do this, Bashir go roo, 'Ain't need to talk to him.' Ya, when I answer the question, Bashir roo disapproving, 'Mistake to talk.'

I ain't tell Razin nothing on the fighting, nor he ask to this. Ours be chatterie of nothings – hounds and blizzards, fatly meals we had in better time. Ya, Polkovnik be a hunter, and we share some vally tactics from our wars on deer. And most, he always ask about my personal day, my moods. Talk sympathy, and blame Marines for their unkindness to myself.

Can guess without Bashir, Polkovnik got no honest love for me. Ever we friendly grown, can always smell his own intentions. For this mistrust, I keep my privy informations silent. Ain't speak of Sengle town, nor any child important to my love. Ain't mention that I known no roo before. Talk like I always living in Marias, without love nor hatred; like I first discover problems when I come to Quantico. But he the only Russian speaking English fit for conversation. So our talks become my lonely habit.

First time he fish a secret from me, be the day I first do digging work in Arlington. I come besweaten muddy, wearing soldier garb, to feed the roos. Must hunker to give them their corn crackers – only food the Quanticos will allow to prisoners. Then roos got contradictory moods. Vitya complaining of his sores; Kirill keep trying to suck my fingers. Bashir must tell me seven times how Kirill ain't need feeding. Be wasteful, since Bashir will only kill him, once they free. 'Ain't need to feed this person, Masha. Listen to your friend, ain't needful.' He name Kirill insult definitions I ain't comprehend, while I be sat with cracker in my hand, in dumb exhaustion.

Come last to Polkovnik Razin, who watch clever in his humor. He say nothing while I feed him, only give me looks of mockery thanks. Is like this feeding be a joke we doing for some fool's belief.

But when the crackers finish, and I buffing off my palms from crumbs, he say, 'My Korolyeva, why such dirty clothes?'

I say shortish, 'Come from working.'

'Wrong,' he say ready. 'Beautiful girl must be in diamonds, pretty dresses. Should not work.'

'Need no mally diamonds,' I say, rising tired away.

'No, I explain. Come, come talk.'

Then my heart catch wistful. Be sad from hating eyes, is craving to this easiness. So I settle by him, fetch a cigarette in gratty rest.

First he go in explanations, how bell females precieuse. Be unlasting flowers, but ain't nothing on the Earth so good. God made diamonds, silk, for only marvels like myself. But truth – he add in sorrow – my bellesse be lonely circumstance. Males be always wanting from me. Ya from girls, be envy.

This envy word be Razin's favorite joy. All children envy me, and I be blind that I ain't notice. He like to say the rooish word – *zaveest* – and sigh, like he regret these evils. I heed polite, but know, these Quanticos zaveesting nothing. Theirs be simple hate.

Now he continue, pondering, 'And difficult to be Korolyeva, lonely.'

'Nay,' I say unthinking. 'Is lonely when it ain't no closer people.'

'Closer? Who be closer to you, Korolyeva? Who you miss?'

Feel how he brighten, like a hound that get a scrap and look for more. But I be in tired wits. Say thoughtless, 'Got a brother.'

'Older brother?'

I fret my shoulders. 'Sure.'

'And he fights now. I understand. Why you always worry.'

Relieve in me somehow, he guess this wrong. 'Sure you right, Polkovnik,' I say friendly. 'Worry bad.'

He shake his head. 'But is not necessary, Korolyeva. Listen, most injuries are nothing. Go home, rest. Is nothing. And many never injure. Look, I am fifty-two years. How many wars I was, I do not know.'

It soften in me, this can be real kindness. I think of Mamadou, and guess he be the sort that never injure. And when I look to my Polkovnik, his eyes be normal sad.

Then he say, 'How he is, this brother?'

'How brothers be.' I shrug.

'But it is different, I think, without a father. A mother. You see?'

'Nay, how is different?'

This dabbit into longer talks. He telling how, in Russia, brothers rival for their parents' love. Yo I ask questions, how it be to have these living parents, when you grown fifteen. This lazy on some pleasant time, while evening darken to the moon, begin to grow its first white stars.

But as we come to yawning hour, Polkovnik say like sudden thought, 'Your brother now, he talks to you?'

Then my suspicion wake. 'Got no means to talk. He done it, if he can.'

'No, always are means, my Korolyeva,' he say like surprise. 'Have radios here?'

'Ain't your problems, what we got. He got no means, and all it is.'

'You defend him, yes. But he should talk to you. No, I am not sure I like this brother enough for you.'

I heed this quiet, smoking, looking at my townie stars. Then I say, in colder voice, 'Best we ain't speak of him.'

He sigh low. 'You don't trust. Of course, you are smart to doubt. But I only like you. And not only beautiful girls are lonely. Sometimes, old unbeautiful men are lonely also.'

★

Behind this, Polkovnik Razin always ask if I heard from my brother. Make face of disapproving sorrow, when I say I ain't. Yo, I begin to notice, all his talks be pities somehow. Pity my risk, my loneliness; pity that I be short for life. He even giving pities, how the Russians do this cruel war – say he be soldat and cannot choose, but still is sorry. In this, he mention Europe, older enemy of Russians. 'This war, they will say it is a crime, but still they do not help you. Yes, it is a bad world, Korolyeva. It is a bad world to be weak.'

And once he say, like helpful notion, I should work for roos. 'It is good for Russians that some Americans speak for them, you know. And you are Korolyeva, important person. They will make very beautiful life for you.' When I give scorn to this proposal, he get pity eyes again. 'I am sorry it is insulting. Of course, you will never do this. You are a good person, but it is now unlucky.'

How it come worse, he learning pox on me in his interrogations.

My other roos be mostly left to rot in easy misery, but Polkovnik Razin dragging off to question every day. From these conversations, he return with ugly bruises. Yo, as the war grow in unluck, Marines try worser cruelties. Soon he come with fingers broken; fingertips lost all their nails. Can notice he sit skew, breathe shallow, from hurts beneath his clothes. When I ask on this, he answer jokes. 'They exercise their arms on me, good for their health.' Or, 'It is age. Do not grow old, Korolyeva, you see it is ugly.'

From this, Quanticos learn exactly nothing. How Patricia tell, the Polkovnik stubborn in unconsequence. Ask him warry questions, and he say, 'You like to fish?' Then come some torture cruelty, and he come gasping up and say, 'I am never lucky to fish, me.'

They hate him worse for this. Be only dreaming when they murder him to a respecting silence. Still, is times Marines distract. Yappit on fishing for some minutes before they gather hatred. And somewhere in this talk, he catching gossips on myself.

This conversation come the day my Marianos start their war. They gathern at last in easter woods, behind the roo positions. The night before their first attack, I travel through the tunnels to speak to them in couragement.

This be a speech of their goliath deeds that every years remember. Tell how all children, ya myself, be praying for their life feroce. I wear Maria dress and speak impressive in my reina voice – stood on a trucken rear, with fidgeting pines and oaks around, the vally stars in bright attendance. Keep watching, but in all these thousands, cannot find Mamadou nor Crow. Be only shadows–shadows, blurry in the forest night; an everywhere that say 'Amen', and stand with sudden leap of darkness.

This night, my sleep be on a bicycle cart, returning through the tunnels. Keep waking to the tunnel thumping strange from bombs above; the speckle sound of crumbles falling in the wettish blackness. Come out and straggle to the monument with hopes to sleep some more – but sky be dawning bright as I sit heavy to my flagpost. Then Polkovnik Razin call out soft, 'Korolyeva. Come, please. Talk to me.'

I sigh exhausting. 'Already hear you better than I want.'

'No,' he say in injury voice. 'It is personal matter. Please.'

I look to him reluctant. In this morning light, can see results of all his questionings. Face be bruise and blood, is swollen weird on its left side. Even his ears be colorn wrong. Look like he painten in cosmetic by a pranking little. But he look to me with his same eyes of loving friendship.

I get up, frustrating in my ruth. Sit frogleg by. The wind be sharp, and we both wearing furry soldier hats. Remember to me queery, how I putting his hat on like mine.

He narrow on me kind. 'I want to say I am sorry, Korolyeva. They told about your brother dying.'

Almost, I stand again. But I be tired for demonstrations. 'Can leave this,' I say hoarse. 'Ain't need your sorries anyhow.'

'No, please listen. It is this. My brother died when I was sixteen, also.'

I narrow to him cautieuse. His hounden eyes gone tired in sorrow. Even his unlips be sad, look most like human mouth.

'Your brother,' I say soft.

'He was older, also. It is a terrible thing, Korolyeva. It is something, you know, that I still hurt.'

Then he begin to tell the story of his brother's killing. Go into rooish as he talk, like he lose conscience of his speech. Is something about a cat his brother keep, a boat, then all confusions. His eyes be far in memory. Times, he smile his hurting mouth, like greeting to this past.

Last he say, in careful English, 'It was my first death.' He turn his loving eyes to me, seek comprehending in my face.

At this moment, Bashir call sudden, 'Lies!'

I startle, ya Polkovnik's face change wonderful in hatred. But he only muttern, 'Fool.' Look to me like he expect agreement.

I say stiff, 'Be sorry. Cannot want to talk on this.'

'You said.' He frown, think on my face. 'You are somehow cold. I understand. My brother could not save. It is different.'

'Different, I ain't know.'

'Yes. For you, it is more bitter. If your brother was with us, we save him.'

'Shee. Roos never going to help him,' I say harsh. 'Nor I ain't love you for this fact.'

He nod. 'Too late. If it was not these foolish wars, perhaps.'

Now I clench my hands, begin to stand up to my feet.

'It is a hard death,' he say on. 'I am sorry you must see this.'

I narrow on his ruin face. 'I guess your death be also hard.'

His eyes light with natural pleasure. Face break in a smile. 'Good, Korolyeva. Yes, they will kill me. Why we cannot say this? But, before my death, I hope you will still talk to me sometimes. And perhaps you cry a little when I am dead? Yes, you will cry together – you and Pasha.'

Almost, I ask how he know Pasha's name. Why Pasha cry for him, how he know anything of Pasha. But my better sense return. I turn and stalk away, all furies kniving in my heart.

69

OF BATTLE VARIOUS

This morning when my Marianos join be our best hope. My soldiers coming in surprise against the rooish rear, while Quanticos attack the front. How all armies mix together, the rooish planes ain't useful much. Can bomb themself mistaken. And sure they never prepare against the numbers that we bring.

Every child be in this fight. I even go myself to hold a trench in Arlington Cemetery, with petty eights and injure soldiers. Ain't expect no fighting there, but Quanticos want a last protection, if roos break toward the deeper city.

These trenchen hours be nerves and nothing. In this backward place, we get no news. The only word be gunfire. I lurk in mud with my Kalash, agony my freezing toes. Times, my attention tire, and I watch idle at an antler beetle, crawling woozy in the dirt. Ease my nerves by reading burial stones of these old dead. My hiding stone say only BENNETT, but be stones beyond with various informations – mystery names of places gone, like Arizona and Wisconsin; prettieuse ranks like Purple Heart.

Then I drift back to fear, heed to the guns like I can read their voice. Mamadou, Crow, my friendly guards – each shot I hear can be their murder. Arlington House stare from the hill, and always my nonsense heart insist, this edifice be evil. Is like a mally warning from a future where we all be gone.

Yo, as the hours go long, my mind stray back to the Polkovnik. Worry to myself, what he can mean, that Pasha cry for him. Want to believe, was only lies. Traps, like all his brother talk. Try to decide, I never go to feed the roos tonight. They hunger for one day, be nothing I ain't done myself. But my misery know, I going to go. I going to ask.

And children around me talk, and hush in heeding, and talk again. Once a girl call back in panic, 'They're coming! I can see!' Then we all snap ready. Grit a panic time, where every rustling leaf become stampeding Russians. At last, a child shoot into nothing, and others join along, create a wave of feary noise. But this pass to quiet again, and we guess slow, all been mistake. Then is queery disappointment, how this terror cheat away. Leave us stood the same, with foolish smiles, sweat chilling on our necks.

To dusk, the gunfire hush. Is only smoke remaining, hazing thinner in the purplen sky. Then children gripe impatient, how this silence tell us nothing. Ain't know if we win or die entire. All be gone in argument, if we should send a scout, when a raggity troop appear on hill above.

See their uniforms of Marine, and all the eights go larming glad. Some leap from trenches, start to run exciting toward these friends. But as these soldiers straggle closer, can see they carry injure children. And they become a thicker swarm – dozen and dozen pairs, each with a blooden load between. When they come to hearing, they yell angry for our help. Ease their burdens to the ground, and run back up the hill.

Hurt soldiers carry on a sort of hammock, slung on poles. With this weight, it be a weary journey to the hospital, across the bridge at Washington. Most our carriers be eights, and it become a straining progress of some hundred scattern littles, with load of screams and beggary. I carry with an injure girl, got bandages around her chest that redden slow with this long effort. She muttern once, confiding, 'That broken rib keeps shifting, ow. But it idden kilt me if I'm still complaining, right?'

First child we carry got a bandage wrap around his hips. Ever a step misgive, he gasp. Is sweating greedy in the cold. Soon he only begging that we put him down, ain't hear no reasons. When we come to the hospital and set him on the floor, he keep on asking that we put him down, as we turn sad away.

We go back for another, and meet a wave of limping soldiers, coming back with lesser hurts. These call informations to us, but each tale be different. We winning bone, or losing awful, or no person going to know. Only certainty they agree, Marines been dying generose. 'It's a lot of blood,' one say, with feary laugh. 'Don't got many more days like that, I don't think.'

We carry two more children, as the darkness clearing into stars. First be a girl with blooden chest, skree agonies when we lift her. She grip her arms against her sides, tears running from her scary eyes. Halfway on the bridge, she settle to a sudden calm, and when we reach the hospital's lights, I realize she dead, with tears still bright upon her cheeks.

Last injure soldier got a shatter foot, and sob this journey through. Say angry, 'Yeah, it's only a foot. Got two. I got another foot, I know that.' Then he go telling ugly stories, children that been kilt. At last, the girl I carry with say, 'I don't want to hear that, please. I leave you right here on this bridge, I will.' Then he go hush, smile to me pologetic through his tears.

This final trip, I staggering tired. First time since my trip from Massa, I feel Kalash her weight, wish I can rid her. And it come ever stranger, how we creep across the river like a different river of moaning pain; how the full-grown moon stare down unblinking on our struggle. Some time I weep without no thought. Grieve these screaming–muttering children; grieve my Marianos that ain't got no warmer hospital. Magine how Crow or Mamadou carry so, and if they scream. If they be silent, close to death.

When this work finish, I go to my White House room to wash. Then in the bathing water, I break sobbing for Crow and Mamadou – although it feel like mally luck to weep, before I know they hurt.

Then I ain't want my soldier clothes. They burden with this night of screams, like all their dirt be blood. So I put on Maria dress. Clad soldier boots and coat to this and – like I known I will – I head out to the monument. Fetch prisoners their sorry meal.

Russians waiting like they ever been, in hurting boredom. As I come to Vitya, I even feel a gratty peace to this. Yo, it seem some ridiculous, I ever fearing no Polkovnik. Whatever he say on Pasha, it ain't guns. Ain't harm me anyhow.

Vitya–Kirill quiet, and I do this work with habit ease. Time I coming to Bashir, I yawning to my task. He hush moody like the rest. Take his water and crackers with an inward heedlessness. Only when I stand to leave, he roo up sudden, 'Masha, wait.'

When I pause, he struggle to stand, his handcuffs scraping on the flagpost. Blanket fall clumsy at his feet. This be a child with hawken face, is mostly nose and blackish eyebrows. Feel queery, he now tall above me, with his looks farouche.

He roo in almost whisper, 'Want to thank you.'

'Need no thanks,' I say confusen.

'Nay. Want you to know, I preciate this. Can be, ain't other chance to say.'

A moment, I think foolish that he know some secrets of the war. That roos be here tomorrow, kill us all into one heap. I say, with nervy laugh, 'Foo, how it be no other chance?'

'Mikhail Arkadievich.' He nod toward my white Polkovnik. 'Come back from questioning with word. They trade us back tonight.'

I catch a startle breath. 'Back to Russians?'

'Yes. We going back.' Then Bashir nod again, toward where I see in farther dimness, my Polkovnik lift his head. 'Except for him. They kill him, send his body back. They tell him this.'

First moment, I feel only angry. They trading prisoners, should be for the cure. Ya, they should tell myself. Nor they murder my Polkovnik, sans no ask. He mine. But soon my rage become a weakness in my tired nerves. Truth, Quanticos do how they like. Ain't going to heed me nothing.

I say soft, 'But what they trade for?'

'Ain't know. Ever they think they want.'

'So you free.' I smile unhappy. 'Can kill Kirill now.'

'Masha,' he say darker, like he disapprove my joking, 'you go back to New York now. Be many Kirills in this army, you comprehend? Be bad here, when we come.'

'Foo. Ain't necessary you win this war.'

'Nay, you must go. You go.'

I look by to my white Polkovnik. Bashir's eyes follow my sorry gaze, and he catch breath impatient.

'I only want to thank you,' he say shortish. 'I thank you, since these vermin ain't.' Then he shift down his post again, sit frowning to the grass. I wrap his blanket thoughtless to him, while he keep stiff in anger, like he now resent this help.

I go on, hugging the brock of water close, my spirit strange. Polkovnik watch me coming with his looks of loving mischief. Ya, like he always do, he take his drink and food before he speak. Ain't want to be himself until this humble task be by.

Then he say in quiet voice, 'Bashir, he told you?'

'Sure.'

Polkovnik nod. Frown past me, scout into some narrow thought. I stand away, gone thinking how I argue for his life. Be magining some trade I do – what petty use I still can give – when his voice come curiose, 'Korolyeva – I can see your dress?'

I look to him, surprise. In this moonlight, all his cuts look black like clinging dirt. One eye swollen blind. His beard got burns into its whitish scrabble. And he say softer, 'Please, you take off the coat a minute. Show me.'

Come pudy somewhat, but my natural vanity rise against. So I unbutton this coat and pull it off onto one arm. Watch careless to him, while the cold seize feary in my skin. Ya, he look with preciation in his one good eye.

Then he say brighter, 'Yes, you are beautiful. Pasha is very lucky.'

'Shee.' I scrabble to put my coat on. 'How you even knowing Pasha? Shee you always talk.'

'I am his officer once.' Polkovnik smile his hounden eyes. 'But Pasha Toporov everyone knows. He is a little famous, I think. Now, please, it is right we talk. Please sit.'

I sit without no cavil. Even feel joyeuse to skirmish, like this be a pleasure I been waiting for all hours. Fish a cigarette from my coat while he love eyes at me.

'So, my Korolyeva,' he say. 'Pasha Toporov and you. Tell me.'

I shrug. 'Nay, what they told yourself?'

'He is your husband. In your religion, he is Jesus.' He smile thin. 'It's funny to me, you understand.'

'Sure. Been funny to us also.'

'Yes, you aren't from there. I heard.' He raise eyebrows curiose. 'You took Toporov there with you?'

I light my cigarette with showing carelessness. 'Took from where? I guess you heard this also.'

'They said Massachusetts. Yes?'

'Sure,' I say. 'We catch him there, ya been another Russian we kilt.'

'Yes.' He smile some knowing mischief. 'You didn't like him so much?'

'Ain't like no Russians in Massa.'

He laugh. 'But Pasha Toporov, this you like.'

'Shee, ain't necessary I kill all children I ain't like. See Kirill living there.'

'Of course, Korolyeva. But no one kills Pasha Toporov.'

Can feel his poison start to come. I draw some smoke and hold it hungry, looking to the winter grass, its shab and mudden baldness. Get a chilly memory of the injure soldiers on the bridge.

'Vampire,' say the Polkovnik soft. 'What we call him.'

I shrug unliking. 'Ya, he told this.'

'Of course, he tells his wife. Secrets of the bed.'

'Foo. Can be, they told you Maria do no sex. Ain't normal wives.'

He laugh bright at this, say something rooish I ain't comprehend. I frown to him, and he take breath. 'I'm sorry, Korolyeva. It's only difficult to believe. The man I knew, he wasn't so respecting.'

'Pasha got other girls he doing with. Ain't mysteries this.'

'But he left you pure. I understand.'

'This be your talk? I want some filth, got Kirill.'

'No, listen.' He shake his head, eyes easing soft. 'I die in the morning. It is no reason I keep secrets now. And I think you need advice, since Toporov is going to live. The vampire always lives.'

Want to give him nay, but this word *secrets* catch into my need. I swallow soft and say, 'Sure, be advice. Ain't caviling this.'

Polkovnik nod like courtesy. 'So, first, it is a question. Your city, it fights here for nothing. It is a difficult problem for me, I cannot understand. But when I learn Toporov is there, it is now very easy. So I ask you, Korolyeva, it is Toporov gives this plan?'

I sour my face. 'Heard no advice.'

'You don't like to discuss.' He smile. 'But please, I tell you, the Russians are very happy with this plan. It is difficult to take a city, you know. Very difficult war like this. So Toporov thinks, he brings what the Russians want. The soldiers only. Your soldiers come to open land, they catch very easy here. Also it does not need two wars, it saves much work. And then your city is left. No soldiers there, we walk in like our home. It is wonderful like gift.'

'But my soldiers rid your Russians,' I say thin. 'Forgotten this.'

'It is brave to say, Korolyeva. Only, it is sad to be not true. But I will tell Toporov's story. It is very necessary for you, I think.' He sit back to his pole with face of easy satisfaction. 'First, he is from Volgograd. Perhaps he told you?'

'Sure,' I lie. 'He told.'

'But Volgograd says nothing to you?'

'Been to no Russia, nay.'

'We start with history lesson, so.' Polkovnik nod with smilen eyes. 'History, my Korolyeva. Our Russia fought two wars with Europe. The second war was foolish and small. It is not important for us.

But the first was serious war. We thought then, we take Europe. It is not a big army there. But rich. It is wonderful war, everyone is thinking.

'For few months, we win. The Europeans are afraid. They threaten they will fight with nuclear missiles. But we did not believe, because we win very well, and it is no nuclear missiles. We believe they cannot reach us with this, if they have. It is not so easy to do.

'So they make demonstration. They bomb three cities. Chelyabinsk, Tula, Volgograd. It is not large cities, you see, it is more compassionate. Only two hundred thousand people die.' He give his pleasuring smile, make all his injuries seem like harmless paint. 'You understand nuclear bombs? I think, Marines don't understand this much.'

'Know somewhat.'

'So you will know. These cities are gone. Toporov was fourteen. This day, he is in the forest alone. Walk on a small river, it is hills both sides. All this – fire, wind – pass over him. Parents, every person he knew, they are killed.'

I stare on at the grass, show no impression. Only a coldness shiver in my breath.

'Toporov, he has nothing,' Polkovnik say in easy voice. 'So he goes in the army. Good. It is what a boy will do. And he is intelligent boy, works hard. He does better school of military. Everything right, he does this.

'Then he goes to Africa, eight years. You understand – the war here, it is unpleasant. What Africa was, you don't imagine. Some battles, a thousand soldiers go, it is five come back. And many die very badly. A Russian is taken by Africans, it will be many hours to die. What we find, it does not look like a person. And sometimes, was no food, no good water. So it was common, Africans and Russians eat each other. Our soldiers hunt for food – it is animals, or it is people, the same. It was a joke we had, when a soldier dies and goes to hell, he does not notice. Eight years so – but the vampire lives.

'Then he comes to fight for me in Venezuela. First, it is very good. Not like Africa. We are only taking people to work for us.

Help them from their sickness, feed them. But, Korolyeva, I don't know why it is so, our workers are never grateful. Some weeks, some months, and they always try to kill us.

'My men there, was two hundred twenty soldiers. Who is alive now – four. Three, we leave in a plane. We think Toporov is dead like others. We come back two months after, an army we bring. We find the vampire fat and whole, at our old camp. He has a hundred Venezuelans there, they call him "Papa". They are feeding him, give him girls. They are dead now also.

'And now I learn he comes to New York, where we lose every man we send. But the vampire lives. Always, the vampire lives. How you think he does this, Korolyeva?'

Here he begin to go in stories of all Pasha's crimes. These mostly be familiar – what Pasha telling me himself. But the tales be different in this hearing. I got the injure Marines fresh in my memory. Feel how the children kilt by Pasha scream the same, die in their terror. Polkovnik talk on cold, and the world become a vasty darkness, an ever night of weeping children, while the moon watch down its one cold eye.

At last, the Polkovnik say, 'But I am boring you. I will not tell the other stories, they are alike. And this is old to you, I see. Of course he told his wife.'

'Sure,' I say. 'He killing people. Be soldat, is what he do.'

'Soldat?' Polkovnik laughing almost happy at this word. 'Korolyeva, this person is an officer of spetsnaz.'

I shrug. Look back at my Bashir, who lean against his post, stare empty. Can wish he say his angry rejections now.

'I see,' Polkovnik say in humor. 'This also tells nothing to you. So I will help you. For Toporov, spetsnaz means, his work is to lie to people like you. You do what he says, it is useful. When you do not, it is something wrong, he can kill you very easily. This is his education to do.

'He is very good at this work, people trust him very much. I will tell you my belief for why. People meet Toporov, they see the sad young boy from Volgograd. He has lost his parents, he is very sad and it is pitiable. But this finishes badly, I am sorry. These people always die, because the man Toporov is something other.

'Now you are sad, your husband is going back to Russians. I am dying, so I tell you for a gift – he never left the Russians. What he did with you, it is work. When he is Jesus, he does this for Russians. Talks love to you, for Russians. And if it is good for Russians, he kills you and all your people in one night. And sleeps well after. Who your Jesus is.'

I heed this with a creeping in my blood. Is certain, Pasha always lie. And when he change his stories, say, 'Now this be truth,' I go believe. Ya, first chance that become, he skit to Russians. Rid me with no word. And in this inkling cold, I doubt my war from its beginnings. Been Pasha's plan, Polkovnik right. Bring all my children to this hell, and never I mistrust, how Pasha be a Russian self.

Then all suspicions drop into a vasty loneliness. Magine how Pasha been fourteen. Step from this river ditch to see the world gone into nothing. An everywhere of fire, an everywhere of blowing dust. His people become a burning smut; his town blow in the sky as pointless dirt. Yo cannot watch this fire forever. Cannot only feel this fear. Come time, he must decide, where he will go. Walk away somehow, and be a vampire, wrong for life – so I despair, and watch the Polkovnik's ruin face, his sorrow eyes.

'But he gone back,' I say at last, peculiar hoarse. 'Ain't need these stories.'

'You need.' Polkovnik nod. 'Soon Russians take the city.'

'Or they ain't.'

'No, it will be. You know. So, here is advice. Don't trust Toporov that he keeps you safe. My Russians take a city, it isn't good for girls. You understand. And if Toporov finds you – you learn what he is some harder way.'

I huff my breath. 'You saying Pasha kill me? Why?'

Polkovnik sigh. 'I'm sorry, what I must say is ugly. Maybe he kills you, when he finishes. Many soldiers do so. Toporov only is the worst. You understand?'

'Rape?' I laugh mishearten. 'I hunt alone with him all weeks. Sleep in a room together. He want to rape me, need no monthen wait.'

'You fed him? You protected him? Yes, I think. But now, you have very little to give him. One thing.'

'Nay, you disgusting, all it is. Like talking to a pig disease.'

This he ignore. He shake his head, say soft, 'Of course, I protect you myself, if I am there. It is my pleasure to do. And I am colonel, it is my power. You know, I am not a perfect man, but I am not Toporov.'

Then my whole blood chill in relief. I laugh out good. 'Tell every pox on Pasha, so I save your life. It needing this!'

'Yes, Korolyeva.' He smile easy. 'It interests us both that I am living then. It does.'

'Interest me nothing, child. Ain't fearing Russians much.'

'You are so foolish? I don't think.'

'Ain't need you nor Toporov Pasha. I ain't be here, tomorrow day. I go back to Marias.'

Be lying for simple rudeness, but as I speak, it tempt in mind. Will go back. Sleep my misery with my Sengles, telephone cocktails. All this awful be forgot.

He nod like he expecting this. 'Good. This is much safer. But you notice, I am asking for my life. So I give you other reason. When this war finishes, if we are both living, I give you medicine.'

I still be dreaming on Marias. Take a painful minute before I comprehend his meaning.

Then my heart go agony red. I look by to the moon, lorn in stupidity.

Polkovnik Razin say unheeding, 'It stops your disease, you understand. I can send you medicine for – what I think – ten people.'

'Nay,' I say lost. 'My city be hundred thousands. Come there with ten cures, what this will be?'

'It is what I can give. You see, I don't lie to you. And again, it is my pleasure to do.'

I try to think objections, but my heart run to my Sengles, El Mayor. Ya Mamadou seventeen, can sicken any month. Nor I want Polkovnik Razin dead. Is easy trades.

But my mind grip sudden dark. Realize again, the Quanticos kill whoever they dislike. Can beg, but cannot force them. Be no help.

For a longer minute, I think desperations to this problem. How I cut his handcuffs. Rob the key, wherever it kept. But every plan be old. Consider all this already, any time the Quanticos hurt him worse. Cannot and cannot.

'Nay, brother,' I say low. 'Will ask. But they ain't going to heed.'

Been gazing past him to the monument, and when I look again, the Polkovnik's face be different strange. First that I seen, his cuts and bruises look like they belong to him. Can see all weeks he living so, in aching cold and torture. How he despair his life these days. How I been his one chance.

I say low in ruth, 'Why you ain't told them what they need?'

'You are an idiot, all the same.' He narrow on me tired. 'Dear idiot, I told them what I know, when I first was taken. But it wasn't what they need. It was the truth. So this must continue until I help them, or I die. But there is no help for them. There are not even happy lies, lies they can believe. There is no help.'

A wind kick up, and draw a sounding flutter through the flags. We both tense while this noise pass like soft gunfire. Then the wind die sudden. Can feel its silence in the grassen distances around.

I say soft, 'Ya, see this.'

'Good. Please, no more idiot questions. Instead, I ask a favor.'

'Favor?'

'It is not bad, Korolyeva. I really think you will not offend.' His eyes light in some humor. 'I only wish, you touch my face.'

I startle into smiling. Ya, he smile back. The creases deepen in his cheeks, his swollen lips go skew. 'Yes, I am a person,' he say mischieviose. 'It embarrasses you, of course. A person is always an embarrassment.'

I shake my head. 'Ain't that. Is only queery.'

We regard each other for a moment, smiling strange. Then I take my hand out of my pocket. Pause in sudden worry, he can bite this hand somehow. But he be still. Look to my face with quiet expectation. And I reach out careful, touch my palm against his cheek.

His face be cold in this dark winter, rough with scrabble beard. Ain't even feel like skin, is all a harshness. But he lean gentle to my palm. Half shut his eyes, take breath in deep. Then slow, his eyes grow tears.

I almost startle my hand away. But I hold. Watch how these eyes weep actual water. How he swallow his throat and grit his mouth against his tears.

Then he turn his face quick, kiss against my palm. Lean back away. Say hoarsen, 'Thank you, Korolyeva.'

I put my hand back in my pocket. It feel peculiar there, is like he left some gift into my palm. 'Yo, what your crimes been?' I say soft. 'Known all Pasha's awfulness before.'

His tearen eyes catch humor. 'No, please. I am still hoping you will cry for me.'

'Foo, ain't worry that. I cry for any moron thing. It be no flatteries, but I going to cry.'

He laugh. 'I also. You can see. But I thank your cheap tears, still. And I tell you more. I trade you favor for your touch. Perhaps they will not kill me. It can be only threats, you know. If we are both living tomorrow, I give your medicine.'

'Bone, be trade,' I say in reckless mood. 'If we both living, I come get this medicine.'

'Yes, come. I will show you our beautiful camp. And I give you medicine for all the world. Then you work for us, it is no more problems. We eat good suppers together, good conversation. Perhaps we are going to beach.'

Be readying some nonsense answer, when a notion wake. Is something of my Pasha Vampire, standing from his ditch to see the

574

nuclear dust and fire. How Europeans send this bomb. Thought come like jokes at first, but sharpen to a vally foxerie.

'But it is serious,' he say on. 'I give you what I can. It is a little problem to do. But how I am looking, I can ask many things. I am a wounded hero.'

Then my lying mind be ready. I make sorry eyes. 'Be gratty for your wish. But truth, it be no chance to live.'

'No.' He make a chiding face. 'I am being happy now.'

'Nay, heed. Can be, Marines ain't kill you now. But it be other problems.'

'What problems? Not to die, I do not mind other problems.'

I look back to the monument and swallow nerviose. 'Sure you know, your Russians ain't the only people with all science.'

His face puzzle slightish. 'It is a big world, yes. But how is this important now?'

I shrug. 'You know. Is Europe.'

'Korolyeva,' he say in pity voice, 'I think this is Toporov's lies. This is the Europeans will save you? They come from sky like heroes? No, I know this lie.'

'Foo, what they say–' I catch my voice. Make face of caution nerves.

'Who says?' His voice come soft polite.

I keep frowning, thinking hasty, how this got to sound. But, before I start, he say, 'Europe is a nice place. Rich, safe – it is wonderful place. But they have no interest in you. You think, because their skin is black, they care for you? You are again an idiot.'

I shrug. 'Can be, they never care for us. But they hate you enough.'

'Korolyeva, I am tired for riddles. There are Europeans?'

'Sure, they in Marias now.' I fish another cigarette, light this with showing nerves.

Polkovnik laugh up sudden, 'You are saying, they give you help already? Korolyeva, you are a bad liar.'

'Nay, Polkovnik,' I say sarcasty. 'Quanticos been making nuclear weapons all themself.' I suck my cigarette and spit out smoke, heed to his heavy silence. Then I go on, with sounding anger, 'Sure, Europeans want this quiet. But I ain't caring for their secrets now, no sho. Be late for this.'

When I look to him, his face be strange in pondering. He say, 'I understand. You let me live, and I tell my people Europeans gave you nuclear bombs. What Marines threaten, it is always true. So we must run away, or it is nuclear bomb. I understand?'

'Ya, tell. Be gratty that you live. But I ain't guess your morons heed. Must die before they trust.'

He narrow on me with some pleasure in his beaten face. Eyes lost their loving stickiness, is clear with interesting mind.

At last, his face break into humor. 'Korolyeva, I will tell you the most true thing. I am not interested if your story is lies. It is a good story, and I will tell it. And also, I will send you medicine. A girl like you must live.'

'Must interest you,' I say nervy, 'if you all be kilt.'

'My interest is not necessary, please. It is our rules to tell such stories. It is intelligence, you know. And this – someone will listen. Yes, it is a very wonderful story.'

I narrow on his ruin face, but cannot feel no certainty. Try thinking how I better my lie. But what I known of Europe, nuclears, mostly be an ignorance.

At last, I only say, 'If it come wrong, I cry for you. Swear this.'

'No, you will not have to cry.' He smile into my eyes a moment, then nod toward the White House. 'Now you will go and ask my life, I think. Before it is late.'

70

OF OUR LAST DESPERATIONS

I find the generals where I most expect, in Commandant's West Wing office. Be grandy room of eggen shape with yellow-stripen walls. Got two standing flags – one stripy flag for old America, and reddish sort for their Marines. In middy room, two sofas face each other, long in yellow cloth.

Now, to these sofas, Commandant–Hatter–Verna sprawling loose. They dirty in exhaustion. Wear sweaten undershirts and muddy dapple pants, sock feet. Be Patricia also, sitting sloppy on the floor. She got one arm in stiffen cast, and one pants leg roll up to show a chubby bandage on her shin.

Room stank of feet and booze, and they all fisher drunk, with woozy eyes. Floor be a scatter of boots and guns and bottles. By Patricia be a crutch, akimbo over muddle coats. Strangest be to see their Verna Snakehead lying on a sofa, one leg spraddlen on its back.

When I come in, they startle wary. But when they see me clear, they change again and break in laughter. Hatter clout the Commandant on his shoulder, say, 'You cheated somehow. We all know you cheat.' The Commandant swat tardy at his hand, be laughing silly.

Patricia get her breath and call to me, 'Ma'am, sorry. We had a little bet when you was coming. And if – what you wearing.' Then she catch ridiculous again, grin while she say, 'Don't know why it's funny, ma'am. I don't.'

'She's no ma'am anymore,' say Hatter. 'She's a – whatever Russian ma'am is.'

'She's a Russian's fuckdog, like us all,' say Verna, choking laughter.

'Mouth, yow. Thass disgusting.' Hatter slap at Verna's foot.

Patricia grimace pologetic. 'Don't need to mind what we all saying, ma'am. We're experiencing despair, see.'

'Yeah, you got to despair,' say Hatter. 'Or you got to leave.'

I scout around their faces, wondering. 'Damn, you drunk as something.'

'*Razor* sharp eye on that girl,' Hatter say. 'Need some kind of certificate, that.'

'Foo,' I say, 'I only come to ask – you trading back they prisoners?'

They all go groaning various. Be a flutter of hands, grab for their booze. Verna muttern, 'Fuck your prisoners. Jesus Fuckdog Christ.'

'You can leave that language, please.' The Commandant nod toward me. 'Lady wants to know what's happening.'

'Okay!' Hatter stand up to his feet and brandish his bottle round. 'Commandant is always right, so I want to tell the lady the war news – finishing with her Russian prisoners, who is so dear to all our hearts. So, first triumph, we only lost *most* of Arlington. Didden lose every inch at once. We're specially proud of that. Second triumph, we lost most of our artillery – now thass key for morale if you wanted to die. Meanwhile, we reaped so many enemy casualties, it is irregardless they killed more of us. Saying, three times more?'

'Oh, shut up,' Verna say.

'I hear four times. Four times more. You see your typical Marine of the new age there.' He point his bottle to Patricia. 'Half-cast, half-man. And your people fought real bravely, ma'am, for about ten minutes. Up until they remembered how to run, they fought like lions. But, the good news is, this is the good news. We get to give the Russians back their prisoners, without getting any of ours.' He make a puken face, sit down. 'Thass where I started drinking, there. That conversation with the Russian general. I needed some disinfectant post that.'

'Shoo,' I say. 'So what you trade for?'

'We're taking the little kids out,' say Patricia flat. 'Get a ceasefire up till midnight, and we get the kids out safe. Your folks are taking them in up north. Necessary precautions.'

'Expecting you go also, ma'am.' The Commandant turn sad eyes to me. 'Iss a good long walk in those tunnels, but anybody show you. Go whenever you like.'

I nod uncertain. 'Can be right. But heed, I had a notion. What it is, I guess it ain't no nuclear weapons? Truth?'

Here all look to the Commandant. He be swallowing booze, break into coughing as we watch. Swallow hard at this and rub impatient at his throat. 'No, ma'am,' he say hoarse. 'There certainly is not.'

'Wouldn't help much, if they was,' Patricia say. 'Be incinerating ourselves about now.'

'Nay, is right,' I say. 'Been fear you need.'

'Yeah, that didn't all occur,' say Hatter. 'The fear part.'

I nod. 'Think I can bring this fear.'

I start to tell them hasty what I learn of Europeans. How I fit this to their nuclear lie for the Polkovnik's ears. Generals heed me frowning, strain to figure through their booze. But soon they nodding, warmer kept.

When I finish, the Commandant say, 'You're certain he believed you, ma'am?'

'Ain't swearing that. But he will tell. It give them doubt, the least it do.'

'They'll wonder why we hadden blown them up already,' say Patricia.

'Well, that was always the thing,' say the Commandant. 'There's possible reasons, if they think.'

'Grabbing at straws,' say Verna thin. 'If they believe that, I don't know.'

'It's an okay straw,' Hatter say. 'If you didden have any other straws. It's a straw.'

'No, this is hopeful a little bit,' the Commandant say. 'Looks right, that we're getting the kids out. That's the right appearance. And any little dent in their morale, even if it's just that.'

'And the lizard colonel lives,' say Verna. 'Thank you, New York.'

'Now, I'm giving this a yes. Thass all.' The Commandant look to Patricia. 'So, Captain, if you let the boys know what they're doing.'

'Sir, yes, sir.' Patricia reach her crutch, go hoisting clumsy to her feet. Then she look back to me. 'And ma'am, if I could have a private word? It's not anything, it's just something.'

I follow her down the hall, back to the night its brittle cold. A snow beginning now, in heavy flakes that come down straight like aiming. Patricia stop beneath the jutting roof and ease her crutch. A minute, we only stand in silence. Worry to the night, the snow that fill the air with gentle lines.

Then Patricia sigh. Turn to me with conscience face. 'What I wanted to say, ma'am. Verna didden want to tell you this – but the Commandant figures you got a right. So, avoiding all unpleasantness . . . thought I better talk to you alone.'

'Can see.'

'So, the little kids leaving, the Russians and everybody knows about that. But – unless your trick works, ma'am, which I certainly hope – everybody else is going, too.'

'Foo.' I take an icen breath. 'All your Marines go flee?'

'Well, it's a couple battalions staying. By Fort Myer, Arlington Cemetery. They'll do what they can, but thass one big distraction. The rest of us, we'll be in the tunnels. Going out to the end of the line, at Glenmont.'

'Glenmont. Be the north?'

'Yeah. Verna figures that exit's safe. No indication they know that's there. It's not what anybody wanted, you know that.'

'Truth, I never thought you leave.'

Patricia nod unhappy. 'Well, it's not the end of the story, ma'am. When everyone's on their way, our boys here set fire to the arms depots. Got fire breaks around the Mall. Engineers are saying that Washington all be safe. But anything outside . . . well, it's a lot of explosive in those streets.'

'Ho, you burning District.' I laugh thin. 'Be spite to them?'

'Something like that.' Patricia shrug. 'Thing is, it's our people the Russians want. So we burn any supplies. Hole up in the woods, see who's willing to starve the longest. Guessing that be us.'

She say this warry, but is something weakening in her eye. I nod slow in pondering, look back to the snowing night. Try to believe the roos discourage so, ain't coming north in vengeance. In this, the cure remember, like a wisty desolation – remind when I expecting cure for every child. When victory been this.

'Ma'am?' Patricia touch my shoulder.

I startle to her. 'Ya, is clever. Sure, they roos depart.'

'Well, thank you, ma'am. But what I wanted to say, it's about your Mamadou.' I flinch, and she add hasty, 'Don't worry now, he's fine.'

'Bone.' I sigh unsteady. 'So what it be?'

'What's going on, your other people's leaving. But Hatter wanted some extra soldiers for the operation tonight. So, what I unnerstood, any job like that, your people send the penals.'

I shiver somewhat, dig my hands in pockets. 'Simón deciding this?'

'Yeah.' Patricia make a face. 'Thass what I thought. It do have a taste.'

'Taste?'

'Thing is, Simón's a fine general. He can do it.' She pooch her lips. 'But, mind telling you, I think that Mamadou's a genius.'

'Genius?' I laugh nerviose. 'What genius meaning in your people?'

'Oh, you don't think? Okay, lady, but your little stick-fight in New York was sharp. Some creativity there. On the part of Mister Mamadou, every time, what I saw. Put him in that Simón's place, you seen something today. Why Simón wants him in the firing line, you want my opinion. Eliminate the competition. I know that game.'

'Right.' I frown back to the field. Snow gathering now, is like the grass fill slow with gentle light. Yo, can only feel how children going to show against its whiteness.

Patricia touch my shoulder soft. 'I'm sorry, ma'am. I'm only talking. Mamadou'll be just fine. That type's bulletproof, you know that.'

'Ya.' I force a smile. 'Genius and so.'

'I guess you got something on with him? What I was thinking.'

I look to her careful. 'Something on. This meaning love?'

'Yeah. Don't want to assume on gossip. But those penal boys, they talk.'

'Been something like.' I shrug embarrass. 'Most been forgotten with this war.'

'Forgotten?' Patricia grin. 'Well, you're casual. Don't think I'd forget that boy so much.'

Cannot think anything to this. I only get a heaten face. Frown to the snowing night and wish into its blackish whitish stillness.

Patricia say beside, 'I had a little case for him myself. But I couldn't ever see it being anything real. Idden only that he never looked at me – thass facts, in case you're worrying. But all that man ever talk about was war. He idden going to sit and hold your hand, I'm saying. Guess he's like you – "forgotten with this war". I like that.'

I look back to her, breathing better. 'Ya, war be first. Is honor so.'

'Honor, thass his word, all right.' She make an innocent face. 'So, I guess you wouldn't be innerested where he is now? I guess not.'

'How you meaning?'

'Well, they're up at Fort Myer. That ceasefire's on till midnight.' Patricia pooch her lips. 'And now . . . well, it idden but eight o'clock.'

'Ho,' I say dumb. 'Can see him.'

'Well, you didden hear it from me, ma'am. Cause this here, the Commandant is *not* on board.' She fish into her jacket pocket. 'But, just so happens, I drawn you a map.'

71

FORT MYER, BY THE NEWKING

Must wait then through Patricia's warnings, how I must return. 'Midnight, that means midnight. Didden want to be your cause of death.' Must skit back to my White House room and change to soldier garb, sling my Kalash for decency of war. Then I go running through the streets, in careful dance of land mines. Duck in Farragut shelter and I sprint between all littles' beds, left nett in straight geometry – like they expect to fear the roos with their sheets' perfectesse.

Yo, in the longer darkness that go underneath the river, I find the terrors waiting in my heart. Can feel, no one expect these soldiers left in Arlington will live. They sacrifice, so all the others flee without no harm. Mamadou give to roos like bait – all his bellesse, his wolfen courage. And Crow, who scarcely known no joy. They rid like nothing worth.

This mix into the greater horror of our war's defeat. The Quanticos flee to woods, but sure they capture neverless. Marias taken quick behind. Whoever ain't be kilt, will slave to wars of cannibals and tortures. And all our littles left without no help, in starving winter. My Sengle enfants left, to fight for scraps, to hunt with unschool hands.

Yo, Pasha convince me to this war. Told every careful explanation how we can defeat the roos. But now I seen this war in life, I seen our petty rifles warring with the rooish tanks and planes. It never been no hope. Roo got to know this, plain as eyesight. He live by Russian armies sixteen years.

And in the eyeless dark, Toporov Vampire coming real. He stare from every blackness, be like shadows of the nothing there. I walk through nightmares where Toporov killing Sengles for their meat. He stand on a murdern eight and grin – and this dead eight be Keepers.

Climb outside at last, and I be wrong besweaten, gasping thin. Must pause into the sanity of night, breathe to my townie stars. Then my heart come back again, my bravery return.

Come out by Pentagon exit, where the land lie flat, is bare of trees. The snow quit now, but done its harm. Land gleam white, and every stick show obvious by staring moon.

Ain't want to walk the land-mine patterns, how they all confuse in snow. So I take the overpass road, that ride aloft a bridge of highway. One side, be the cliffy shape of Pentagon its ruins. This night, smoke rising from its yard, where soldiers tent for rest. Lift delicate white, and change itself in thinking complications – like this be a camp of ghosts that wandern innen-out of clouds. Yo, on farther hill, can see the peak of Arlington House. It only be a house, with normal pillars and triangle roof. But its pale looks still chill in me. Is like an evil fact that I be slow to comprehend.

Behind this sight, I run on quick. Want no more mally thoughts. Ya, be relief when I step to a housen porch at last.

This Myer house be bricky edifice, sizen like a Christing home. Expect it be some bossy child to meet me, but its halls be empty. Can only hear the woof of soldier talk beyond–above. I go toward this voice to ask – but then I see, each door here got a name writ on in charcoal. Is sleeprooms, give particular to each soldier who need rest.

NewKing's door be easy found. It be the third inside. I pause before this door, gone shy with all distracting feelings. Think of knocking, but I never knock on doors before. Scarce believe that any a child do this in actual life. At last, I bite down on my courage. Open the door in quick unthought.

Mamadou lain asleep. Be on a springy bed, the blankets pull up to his ear. Can hear his breath go deep and slow. Room seem like it sleep along; his hanging goods seem like some grayish objects in his dream. And it inkle strange in me, I never seen him sleep before. Ain't seem like Mamadou, that he sleep. My mind keep thinking this unsense as I close up the door behind. Crouch down, undo my boots. Unclad my coat and leave it to the floor.

Then I catch in different nerves, that he ain't going to want me here. Child need rest. Is war to do. Stare at my coat, think how I still can leave. But cannot move myself. At last I look by to the NewKing's face, like he will sympathy.

His eyes be open. Ya, they show a waiting fear – the same quick fear he shown when I come to him at the Reese. Expect, like any time before, he settle into scorn. But his face go only cautieuse. And when he speak, he say, rough from his sleep, 'Door got a bolt.'

I go and fix the bolt without no word. Take off all my clothes in shivering haste. And when I come to him, can feel we both be frightening like no cowards. I even muttern foolish, 'Damn, be cold,' and press against him like it be his warmth I seek.

Then, in this hour stolen from the war, our love be worse beyond. We cling together with no words, until our scary silence be another nakedness. Is loving with no fight, is helpless. Every touch be words insane – and be the only truthful words I known. Be like a perfect name. Bed make its noise, and someone laugh outside – but no outside seem real. He in myself, without no difference, and this be my life.

And it be by. Our fear be by, and we lie simple in our bodies. He hold my face in his long hand. I hold his hand against my face.

Then I say soft, 'I fought in trenches there, one day. Been nothing feary.'

Mamadou lying like he been, but I can feel his breathing sharpen. In rooms above, be footsteps now, and sounds of draggen loads.

I say, 'Got my rifle also.'

Mamadou kiss my brow then, start to pull me closer to. I stiffen from him. Say up short, 'Be saying, I can fight by you.'

His laugh come warm against my ear. 'Girl, you Maria.'

'Ain't been Maria when – nay, be some nonsense words. Maria.'

'Who you fighting by, be penals.'

'Ya, be penals. So?'

'They ain't accepting this. Maria fight by them?'

I loose my breath. 'Yo right.'

Out in the night, some male be talking now, in voice of cold instruction. Ain't hear particular words until some hundred children answer unison, 'Sir, yes, sir!'

I say weak, 'Ain't any means we fight by Quanticos? They ain't care.'

'Think that, you ignorant to fight.'

'Nay, I know. Was only . . . sure, I know.'

Then Mamadou put his hand across my eyes. I grab up at his fingers, but he catch this hand. Can feel him laughing soft against me, and I say, 'Yo fool. What you want?'

'You fearing for me, Ice Cream Star?'

'And so?'

'Fear for myself.'

He put lips to my throat, say quiet, 'We fight an hour, most it be. Ain't even got to hold no ground. Fight till we lose, then leave across that bridge. All it is.'

'Ain't what Patricia said.'

'I ain't plan to die tonight. Ever Patricia said.'

Be a minute then, he kiss my mouth. I lose in darker thoughts, ain't even heed this kiss its pleasure. Be mapping his battle in my mind. Fight at Fort Myer, then they must retreat through Arlington Cemetery. Cross the bridge to Washington itself, then find a tunnel to flee.

I see the cemetery clear in memory. Trenches I dug myself; the gravestones that be extra hidings. But be the naked bridge.

At last, I pull away. 'Yo, do me this. I meet you at the bridge. On Washington side, ain't asking that I fight.'

He shake his head. 'Nay, Sengle.'

'Shee, ain't no harm to you. I know they tunnels like my hand. I bring your penals safe from there.'

'Nay. Got an ask myself.'

I grit impatient. Steel myself against his normal vanities. But he say only tired, 'Need you to take First Runner out.'

Then all my nerves break into laugh. I sit up, pulling blankets. Ya, the NewKing catch this foolishness and start to wrestle, push me down. I shove my knee into his stomach, laughing breathless. 'Nay, you bring her here? You mad as netten fish, you mad.'

He laugh back to me. 'Ain't bring her, shee. Child sneak behind.'

I hold, still clutching his arm in wrestling pose. 'Foo, come sneaking?'

'How she is.' He shake his head. 'Got a horse, she ride.'

'Damn, she brought my Money here?'

'Horse in the woods there, sure.'

'Goddamn.' Then we only smiling close. Thought come to me that we got only minutes, then is death to face. But I ain't want this thought. I rid it silent from my mind.

'Ho,' I say at last. 'How you known you need her on that Massa search? For they enfants. Always wondern this.'

Now he get defensive looks. 'Ain't known. How I known?'

'Yo, why you bring her then?'

First, I expect he never answer. Will give some talk on mouthy females, got no brains to hush.

But he say low-voice and rough, 'She been my only person, why. Others all been dead.'

This catch me in surprise. 'Of Armies?'

'How it is.'

A moment, I be only puzzling, watching on his face. Think to

587

mention Crow – but Crow ain't Army right. Be Sengle. Yo, of anything, I never guess this been some freak of sorrow. But sure, if only Keepers been alive of all my people, I ain't leave her from my sight.

I put my hand up to his cheek. He flinch, but allow this gentleness.

And I say soft, 'Thought I been yours.'

Expect he mock, but he look to me seriose and glad. 'Ya,' he say quiet. 'And be yourself.'

72

THE FLIGHT FROM ARLINGTON

Be some sorry time while we both dress, he gather up his kit. He checking magazines and fix them in convenient pockets. I keep hush – ain't want him to distract from carefulness. But penals start to noise outside, ain't worrying this question. Try the door against the bolt, knock rude.

Yo, when I stepping from this room, they startle like no mice. Take a thinking minute before they know me. Stoop their courtesy. Then every child look to the NewKing shy in gratulation. Mouths working strange, how they attempt to eat their foolish grins.

Mamadou ignore these shows. Go yelling most like Hatter done, the day I fight at Buckethead. Soon be penals running out and in and all directions. Even Crow go by. He stumble at my sight, then call a feary salue and scatter out. Mamadou never look to me, but keep one hand upon my elbow. Hold jalouse like love – but then he loose me with no difference. Yell instructions while I miss his hand.

Yo, before I guess, the NewKing stalking to the outside field. Give one backward look, too quick for no expression seen. Then can only hear his voice, go good feroce into the night.

I still be gazing footless when First Runner appear, led by a bigger penal I ain't know. She lost her neatly looks in these hard weeks, is skinny and unwash. Her face bewept and furiose.

Penal stoop his courtesy to me, say muttern Panish. Then he tell

First Runner, 'Look at that. Maria's here to take you. Look at that.'

First Runner narrow to me resenting. Say in stuffy voice, 'Been with the NewKing?'

'Sure,' I say. 'He said I take you, child.'

'He slept?'

This touch me sharp. But I lie, 'He resting bone, yo sho.'

Penal loose her hand. First Runner come to me in duty manner. But her eyes keep peevish and when she come up close, she muttern, 'Ain't want you.'

Penal shake his head and give me pology smile. 'Senyora, you best go. She don't know how to walk the streets, so you got to allow for that.'

'Foo. How she got in here?'

He make a face. 'Marines.'

'They bring her?'

'Yeah, she's a smart kid.' He look to her. 'You told them a couple of lies, didn't you?'

'Ain't lies,' First Runner say. 'Thought he will want me.'

'You see him by,' I say. 'When he come back.'

Then she only nod, face closen to its private hurt.

How she ain't know the maze, we head to Pentagon tunnel by the trenches. First minutes, these be crowden wild. Be dodging backward–forward through Marines who swear impatient; edging past artillery guns and heapen ammonitions. But soon we go beyond these preparations into lonely place. Walk in the trenchen darkness, and be like we treading underwater in some nighten river, see the light suspending soft above. First Runner go ahead – I keep her in sight, against no last escapes. Ya, she walk stooping, in betrayals of her smallish heart.

My dooms of earlier night be by. Now I be lost in fantasies, of how my lie on nuclears work. The Russians leaving now, without no harm. The war be done. Moon show middy night – this ain't exact, but cannot be much less – and been no incident. Yo, as we walking farther, every sound be gone but our own feet. Silence be uncanny in its sweetness, like a singing note.

I imagine how the roos depart. Ya, Polkovnik sending me the cure, like promise word. Cures be only ten, but if we living every years, be chances to discover more. We find some way to Europe. Buy this cure by bellious Africans. Can even be a gift from better roos.

I live beyond, and Mamadou live beyond. We flee Marias City. Ya, how Armies gone, no child think mally to our love. He get a baby with me – belly device be gone somehow, I getting enfants every year like seasons. We live, can see these enfants grow. Will be like Russian parents, caring for their every want.

And I watch First Runner small and vally, how she pace the night. Magine her our enfant grown, and luck her in my mind.

We come beneath Pike overpass, gone in its blacker shadows, when First Runner halt her step. Look perilous to me, then turn her eyes back to the night.

'Roos be there?' she say.

She looking north, and without thought, I shake my head, point to the west. She round to this, say scary, 'Near?'

Truth, ain't know how close they lurk, what ground we lost this day. But I say like confidence, 'Ain't near. Can be a mile.'

'We leave before they come?'

'Shoo,' I say in forcen cheer. 'I thought you come to war, my ten.'

Then she lose her face entire. Break in sobbing tears and say, 'Other time, he want me. I ain't known. Ain't need to rid me like that.'

I put hands on her small shoulders, start in calming talk. Say how I prefer to fight myself, but been no help. How any child respect her bravery. Ya, and Mamadou do. But be instructions also. Sure she know.

Through this, I heed the quiet night. Feel how the time go long, and nothing be.

Last I say, 'He love you like himself. You be his people, child.'

She snuff her nose. 'I know.'

'I going to bring you safe. Why he given you to me. He never done, if it ain't right.'

Then she nod reluctant. Rub her nose and look back to the west. Yo, as I look along, a heavy beat sound toward the river. We both flinch back. A blink behind, it shiver underfoot.

It beat again, and beat. The sky flash gentle, weirden blue. This flash repeat in trembling, then it fickle everywhere, while gunfire jitter and spread its noise across the broad horizon.

'What it is?' First Runner say in breaking voice.

'Shee, we late. Keep forward. Go!'

Her enfant manners pass like blinking. She break in run, yo I run gratty on her sprinting heels. We flee simple from the war.

The beating–jittering grow, and now the ripping skree of planes begin. Sky keep shivering wrong. Yo, as we pass the Pentagon, a light dart angry in its ruins. Flash and spit there. Loose a huff of blackish smoke above.

Then everywhere ahead, be flashing, pounding, gusting dirt. My ears be screaming, and the wind keep hitting hot and wrong. First Runner lose her sprint. Jump to a wall and hold there, crouching strange. I hunker to her, touch her shoulder. She hit my hand away, turn yelling, as the overpass explode behind.

We both knock scattering to the ground. Air shove wrong in my lungs, my ears, can feel it press at my shut eyes. Dirt sting my face, and I go sneeze. Then I be blinking, scrambling free. First Runner there, is whole. Stare panic to me, while dirt still spatter down on her shock face.

I yell, *Come on!*, but hear no voice, hear nothing. Ears be dumb. Nor First Runner heard. I grab her hand in brainless fright. Pull her to her feet, and stagger on into the flashing silence. Be thinking only of the tunnel. We getting underground, and all be right. Can still be right.

But when we come to our next turn, the trench be full with rubble earth. Ahead, the tunnel gone. A scrap of Pentagon sit huge upon its missing place. Sky be bleary above with dust. Moon glown peculiar red.

And all I know, next tunnel we can reach be to the west. Roos will hold the trenches there. Ain't safe to use these now. Must crawl between, on open ground.

My ears be full with weirdo ringing. Hear bombs again, but only as weaker thumps, like littlish foot. To this, the earth be shaking restless, like it dance its nerves. First Runner tugging at my arm, ain't comprehend why we ain't run.

I yell, big as I can, 'We got to crawl above! You heed?'

She say something back, deaf in my hearing. I shake my head and move her hand. Fasten this to my leg. Hold till she take the pants cloth in her grip. Her eyes stare terrify at nothing, but when I start to crawl onto the rubble, she come right. Clutch to my pants and pick her way.

Then the pounding only lengthen through all helpless minutes. Be crawling knees and elbows, bellying down to close explosions. Can feel First Runner yanking on my leg in terrify jolt. Air thicken with sprawling dust, with smoke; moon vanish in this pall. Come to the land-mine patterns, and be miseries to find their shape. Must squint through tears, eyes stinging. And come a new explosion, and it flash, ring sickening through my guts. Keep thinking it must quit, ain't bombs enough. But it keep on, while I pick at the ground, clear snow with numbing fingers. Scout the land for walking roos. Scout for my right direction.

At last, through clogging smoke, can see a blacker cliff that rise ahead. It be the Henry Overpass. Cannot see who lurk beneath. But beyond its danger, land be thick with standing evacs. Is trees to hide and bushes, every wonderful object for our help. Then be three minutes' walking to the tunnel. Be no distance.

Once this relief become, I realize we crept beyond the bombs. Sky only flash behind in distance. This hit me with elation like a pain. Ain't even think of life, I only madden that we can leave this place. Be somewhere without terror. And I crawl faster, feeling a strength, how everything be done correct. First Runner's hand still clutch my leg. We living, can be right.

Come to the overpass along its side, in scrabble bush. Yo, as we near its opening, I halt. Check to First Runner. Her face be panics, she stare blank. Try gesture explanations, how she stay while I go forward. But she only clench, eyes tearing. At last, I push her from me. Hold her down until she keep there. She weeping, trembling through herself. Yo, then I recognize, we stoppen on a patch of bones. She cringing all her arms, lie on these bones but hate to touch.

Ain't time to worry this. I crawl ahead. Check backward and she still be there, a hand press to her face. And I go careful on, try to beware my noise without no ears. Come sideward to the overpass tunnel, cautieuse in shadow.

And when I come along its concree side, peer in the spreading tunnel, be three rooish soldiers there.

They watch the flashing sky, like this be festival display. Smoke cigarettes, and talk beyond my deafness. Laugh their mouths.

First instant, I grip to Kalash. My nerves be mad to shoot, to rid them. But I hold myself. Feel down Kalash with sweating hand. Check her switch. I crave her every-bullet setting – will shoot them any hundred times. But I only got one magazine, can be no waste. I put her to three-bullet, bring her slow and slow to her right pose. Creep, elbowing, until I peer direct into this tunnel. Roos show clear against the farther light, and I rest my gun solid on a scrap of broken road. They never notice, never look. All their attention be the farther trenches, ya the bombing sky.

I find my aim. Breathe short with terror, feel the earth that chill my belly. Yo, as I stare, one roo step by, reach to his pants. Undo these with particular motions. Turn himself to piss.

Then my heart leap queery. I sight upon a different soldier, who ware outward, gun in hands. Before I can think anything, I shoot.

First child be hit and hit and hit – Kalash's sweet three bullets. I gasp exhilarate as the roo beside him wheel. His gun stare all directions. I shoot again. Miss awful, and he turn straight to my rifle flash. Shoot when I also shoot. And he be hit, go cringing. Lift his gun again, and I feel how my voice cry out in anger. But before I shoot again, he fall. Slip from the light.

And be a second when I only want the final roo to vanish. Cannot bear no more, cannot. But he turn from pissing pose and grab his rifle also. Pants gone clumsy round his legs, but he shooting toward. Is panicking–shooting, pitching huffs in earth around my face.

It take four tries to down this roo. Be a hopeless always, while his bullets seek me, blast the dirt. I miss and miss again. He ducking to the wall, lose out of sight. I shoot the air. Be breathing rage that he ain't die. Must die, he need to know.

When at last I hit him, all my brains be gone in rage. I stagger to my feet. Run stupid to they roos – and one come sitting, clench his gun. I shoot him again, in chest, in face. Go round to shoot another roo again. Ain't trust they dead. But all my bullets gone. I standing helpless, terrify, in my sweat.

Roos be still. The sky flash silent, framen in the overpass. Smoke drift black across the wester sky.

Be an evil second when I cannot think. All plans be nothing. A roo lain with no face, his yellow hair still whole. Is Pasha. But it ain't. It ain't. And cannot hold for this, ain't time.

Then my mind come back like pain returning to a frozen hand.

I duck to a blooden roo. Seek his clothes until I find a rifle magazine. Try this to Kalash, and it be right. I seek his pockets more. Find another, then I need to turn away to puke. But nothing come, ain't eaten. I only choke my gut, and spit, and hate this wasten time.

When I got three magazines, I stalk back where the overpass be open into violent sky. Ain't see First Runner nowhere, but I got no panics left. I only yell my lungs until I see a stirring in pattern snow. Eye find her there as she raise up her head.

I wave her to. Wave again–again, while she still stare and cringe her arms. At last, she start to crawl – when I remember, she ain't know her path. Be land mines still.

Yo, First Runner jump up sudden. She sprinting toward with all her legs, while I scream desperate that she stop. Wave arms. Then I recognize the kicks of dirts around, the gunfire.

I never see the bullet strike her. She running, then she flail down hard. Ain't think, I dive to her. I get a clumsy hold, and stagger back. A bullet clip my sleeve, then we be in the tunnel's hiding. Yo, I weaken in relief, when I see she injure in her thigh. Ain't murder wounds, is nothing.

I hoist her better in my arms. She clutching my hair, is lost all sense. But I unmind this, nor I feel her weight. I go sprint through the overpass darkness. Jump unthinking over a roo lain dead, and in the farther night, can see a tower building, sweet with walls.

Building broken on one flank. My boots crunch bright across its ruin. Get to its door, and scramble in with gladness flushing through my blood like water. First Runner pull my hair to agonies, yank my head in angles. But I can almost laugh, how pain be nothing. How we live to feel good pain.

I settle behind a fatly desk and rest First Runner down. Child sobbing, crush both hands up to her mouth, as I tear off my jacket. Wrap its sleeve around her thigh, pull tight. Hold this with knee. First Runner start to fight me, but her hands be weak. Be small. I pin them with my other knee.

All I see to use be laces in First Runner's shoes. So be longer minutes while I pull these, and she fight, and I tie different knots around. At last, it holding right. Cut deep into her flesh, but it ain't bleeding more. Ya, First Runner hush. Is only panting, staring to my face. She watch my face like it the only thing she ain't fear.

I smile. Say in my unheard voice, *You bone, my ten. It be no harm.*

She hitch her breath and nod. When I loose her hands, she rub her dripping nose, still staring to me. I say, *Now be no distance. We be right.*

I lift her across my shoulder, so her head hang down behind my back, legs kicking loose in front. Can feel her gather breath, cry out pain. But I unmind this, be no time. I get her weight correct, and stride back to the awful night.

Next journey be no matter. Road ain't got no trenches, and is thick with helpful trees. Trot to a tree with breathless force, lean to its trunk and rest. Earth trembling softer now, and every jolt be sweet reminder that we leave the war behind. Is even calm enough to feel some vanity that we survive. And we surviving still – dodge to another tree, and vanish to its trunk. Rest and breathe, ain't lose my strength. It all be wolfen done. Can live, and we deserve this life. First Runner holding to my waist, got back her sense. Is smart. Can live.

Come to the tunnel's road with sudden panic, that it close with bombs. But the hole be clear. Is perfect in a patch of naked street. Must only cross this space. Before this final risk, I resting longer to a building side. Watch everything and breathe my strength. Stroke on First Runner's back. A wind begun, and moving branches sketch in corner-eye. Keep flinching to a motion, and it be a waggling arm of pine. Ya, when I try to bring Kalash to aiming pose, is useless sweat. First Runner's legs be there and there.

Yo, I lose my last impatience. Step out perilous to the moon.

And a roo step instant from a building side where he been waring. Raise his gun in aim.

I weaken sudden, lose my breath. Almost drop First Runner, and must grab her. Got no sense to think.

But he ain't shoot. Roo yell out to my deafness. Jerk his rifle.

I take a breath, but feel no air. My legs gone queery, need to sit. Roo jerk his rifle again. Shout his mouth.

And I call rooish, *Got sick enfant here. Ain't shoot.*

Can see, this Russian speech take him in puzzling. He ease his gun. I smile to this, as my mind lose its telligence. Can think no complications, so I only roo, *Be gratty.* I nod to the tunnel's hole.

Then I step forward, concentrate on only walking my weaken legs. Smile foolish, and I muttern roo, *Be gratty, brother. Be gratty.*

Roo be a dark-fur child, most like Bashir. Can be sixteen, is small. Last I see him, he let down his gun. He watch with troubling eyes. And, steppen-step, we sink into the blackness. Lose from sight.

Scarce remember this tunnel walk. Been black, it been exhaustion. Been minutes where I known I cannot walk no more. And I walk on. Then another minute so, another, through an hour. Past Pentagon, the tunnel flooding nasty to my ankles. Know this be mally, but be weak to fear. The water be only another tired weight that drag my feet.

Felt when I begin, I never lasting to the tunnel's end. So I decide on Farragut exit. We come out on the Mall; hope soldiers be retreating from the bridge. If they already gone, I bring First Runner to the White House. Ain't no hope, but it be warm. Is food.

And I step forward and step forward. Try every means to do this easier, but it be the same. Shift First Runner – but then I only frighten how she flopping loose. I touch her bandage, but feel nothing with my frozen hand. Be dark, be deaf. And be no help. Step forward and step forward.

Yo, at Foggy Bottom shelter, where I pause to check, she living. But at Farragut, she be dead.

Ain't comprehend at first. Be resting on the Farragut ledge in its good light, watch gratty to her bandage thigh. It show no extra blood. On a neatly bed beside, a soldier lying dead, but this ain't fear me somehow. His stiff face seem to care as I lean down to small First Runner's face.

Ain't no breath. And when I feel her throat, ain't beat. Be thick and cold.

Then I look down at myself, and find her blood.

I carry her to the White House. Gone stupid in despair, and only remember how a Lowell child bring back from dying once. He drowning in an icen pond, and they go soak him in warm water. He live again, spit out his drown.

Mall be empty, ain't no child. Nor be thousand footprints – we come early somehow, though it seem I struggle through all hours. And I bring her to my room, Queen's Bedroom of this empty mansion. Run a heaten bath. I rest her in this water in her clothes. Talk thoughtless to her stillness. The water pinken slow, and she lie dead.

Then, soggen how she be, I carry her to my bed. Yo, always in my injure mind, I know that Mamadou coming. Remember how he said First Runner been his only person left. How I said, 'Thought I been yours,' and he look to me seriose. And I feel her blood gone cold, gone sticky on my legs, my belly. Cannot meet him so. It be too much.

I tear these clothes away. Wash at the sink with wetten towel, scrubbing hasty at my skin. Be three towels red before I done. Yo, in this, my ears begin to hear. Ring shrill inside, but through this ring, I hear the water's push.

Got no other clothes, so I put on Maria dress. Clad the grandy coat the Commandant given me in better time. Put on heely boots – walk clumsy but they got no blood.

Last before I leave, I go back to First Runner. Lean by her and say soft, 'You good. Ain't nothing harm you more.' Words feel insulting once they said, but cannot think no other words. So I only kiss her brow. Pull blankets on her smallness, cover up her terrify eyes.

Then I sling Kalash again, and go back to the night.

73

OF MY LAST WAR

As I cross the empty mall its snow, I gone in stranger minds. Be thinking blind of Pasha. How we find him in that burning house. He run, and Driver shoot at him. Roo wheel back with his pistol, and I walk up, terrify and bold. I hold his gun nose to my chest. He look at me, besweaten scary, and all children love each other. He let go his gun.

The vampire live.

And then he killing Deema and Karim, shoot Mamadou. But he saving me away, all children love each other. Or he need myself to get him food, the vampire live. And on our journey walk, he want to murder the Armies, but he lose this chance. These Armies must be shot by Soledad, while she weep desperate lost.

The vampire live. I braving poisons for his life. He cannot die. He hold my hand like animoses, every day I been a god – and rid me, when his chance become. All children die who love each other, but the vampire live.

He tell me we can win at Quantico. Promise me the cure.

I come to the bridge, and still its length be empty. Only movement be at Arlington, flashes where bombs strike the land. Explosions sounding far, it almost be a comfort noise. Yo, a smutten mist drift toward, across the river's blackish shine, and I be gripping Kalash like I prepare to fight this distance. Be thinking how Pasha been fourteen, and watch his burning city. How I kill him with this gun he given me. He kill myself. All children love each other when they dead.

I grip Kalash and grip Kalash. Cold deaden in my face, my hands. I watch the flashing hill and my nose run with cold, but I ain't crying. I ain't remember life, I only know this night that cannot be. This sky that kill its earth. And first, it only be a petty strangeness when the soldiers come.

Bridge be a milen length, and they show first as squirming dots, a dirty bothering in my sight. But they running quick, and soon I see them individual. No flashes chase them. Cannot feel they flee from nothing special. They cross this snowen path through air like running be a pleasure game.

Get briefer panic, they be roos. But their disorder fleeing, ya their every looks, show they ours. Yo, then ain't nothing I can do. Must wait, cannot change anything. So I stand helpless, furiose, as the first soldiers come.

Quanticos–Marianos all wear dapple clothes for war. This end of the bridge, they mostly walking, lost their fear. But they spread apart in darkness, cannot see their faces right. So I take off my coat. Bare myself in Maria finery. Stand middy to the bridge, and I stare desperate for my Mamadou. For Crow. For any penal who will tell me word.

Soldiers come in threes and twos. Some talking in a fever haste, some staring grim to nothing. One child pass me weeping, while another soldier yelling to him, threaten a fist into his face. And their numbers ever thicken, until the bridgen height be dark across with struggling children. Yo, now I standing in Maria dress, each person stare. But all be Quanticos with hostile eyes. Be strangers.

One officer come with scary looks, say, 'Ma'am, you need some help?' I ask him hoarse for Mamadou, penals, but he only say, 'You're not going to know until tomorrow, serious. You got to come with us.' But I rid him with some lie about Patricia fetching me. Turn back to watching all wrong faces, rubbing my icen arms.

This waiting lengthen to impossibilities. Every child who pass me, my eyes catching to him hungry, then fall away in cheaten grief. Once a gait, a flashen face, be Mamadou in my eyes, and I call out, run toward. But he turn and be a stranger flinching from my savage looks. Then I go furiose against all penals, how they never come. Try seeking Taco – be luckier to seek a child I wanting less. But the soldiers only clutter my sight with needless faces, until each child seem like a separate insult. Is like each say in passing, *Mamadou dead*.

In this, bombs scarcen fewer. Hush away and leave their bruisen haze unmeaning to the sky. Be only pittering guns, sound harmless in their quietness. And here the coming soldiers start to thin. Be twos and ones. Some carry injure children, slung on backs, or held between two people. Be their familiar cries and mutterings, scarce in growing night. And then the forward bridge be bare of life. Be only one last soldier come alone. He stumble as he pass, look superstitious dread at me. Break to a limping run, and his steps eager to a final hush.

The bridge be empty. Gunfire only be a memory of noise that yearn in mind. Night can hear again, the breeze and river like a rougher silence. On Arlington shore, some trees be burning. Arlington House got a pinkish glare that dull and sharpen in moods of smoke.

I stare, and conscience whisper to me, I must leave. The Russians come. But I stand trembling in the cold, glare furiose at that far hill. My blood be one red wound.

And time bleed into my despair. The bridge be empty dumb, its snow all eaten gray with footprints. I look back to Washington sometimes, but this bring me angry, thinking how I walk here, still with hope.

When the first explosion come nearby, I startle vicious. Turn quick and see a goliath orange bloom of fire and smoke. Only then I comprehend, it be the District burning. This be fires set by Marines. Ya, this explosion growing into roar, all ammonition bursting wild. Feed red into the ashen smoke, that pump into the air like flowing water, sprinkle its blacken flecks. Another explosion burst, bloom huge. Be like a fire monster lift its head, look hungry to the city. Ya, the horizon gleam mysteriose and reddish to the north. Fire rushing like a second river flowing dry and restless toward. The city lose its air in roar, like breathing out its life.

Then it comprehend, I be the only living child in Washington. Others all creep off in darkness. Their city burn behind, and Ice Cream Star remain in careless witness.

When the gunfire come again, I be unheeding in my trance. Accustom to this noise, become like birden voice in woods. Only slow, my conscience wake. Gunfire come from Arlington – and I squint back in worry, scout for Russians on the bridge. But it be clear.

Then my worst madness rise. I gaze along this bandon bridge, and think how Mamadou be a genius. I think, guns be himself, he fighting still. Ain't dead for nothing. Penals do some vally desperations, then they coming here. I grab him in my arms, and be all victories farouche.

Ain't know how long this ravish unsense live. I stand and heed the burning city, the guns beyond the water. Magine how the NewKing come across the bridge, all penals by. Be Crow with mally noise, my Taco. If tunnels burn, can swim the river out. Still can be right.

And this hope live, while fires grow brazen around, the air be sweaten warm. Continue while the gunfire thinning slow, come seldom. Die to nothing.

Arlington be silent. Nor the bridge change in its white unlife. The river pass, and I breathe in the hating stank of smoke, and start to weep. Weep at the uncaring hill, the bridge that will not bring them back. Weep at the muzzy stars, mind gone in thousand hysterias of grief.

And my weeping die – like all my bell and wolfen children – and my heart go clear in pain. Heart fill me like a knife. I wipe my tears on my rough coatsleeve, look toward Arlington's shore. Fire on the hill be gone, and it be only ugly white.

I know, like nightmares I remember, Pasha Vampire there. My white Polkovnik there, with all his powers, with cure that can be mine. Mamadou there, and Crow. Be dead or prisoners on that shore. Yo, the bridge shine in my eyes. Be only death between.

Then I pull on my coat. Stretch arms into its warm and whisper, 'Shee your Russians. Shee you all.' And I spit upon the ground. Swear low at any god that be, and go.

I start across the bridge. I head for Arlington.

Come out from the fire's ardent air, and colder night be gratty. Breath come clean and sharp, is like a truth that hurt inside. I keep Kalash at readiness, be scouting forward for no Russians. But all be silent. Hear only my crunching steps in snow, my short insisting breath.

When I look back to Washington, be only smoke to see. Come up in bunchy trails beside the moon. Cannot see the palaces, but the whitish monument stand clean apart without no hurt. Be like a simple burial stone for this whole murdern city.

Come over the bridgen arch, and still be no one. Here I pause. Take off my coat again, wrap this upon Kalash to hide her. Figure, I come in girlish finery, sans no showing gun, be chance the roos ain't shoot me.

Here, the hill be clearer in my eyes. Can see a monument wall, bash down in places from artillery. A patch of cemetery show small campfires by the rumple trenches. And I see some itsy people, moving in this patchen white.

I creep in to the bridge's stony railing. Its top reach to my chin, must only stoop and I be hid. So I stalk forward, crouching. Scout through the railing sometimes, see how roos be doing various. Their dapple clothes confuse in dapple ground. And, as I come toward the bridge's end, I start to hear their noise – a passing truck, a shouting voice, a muttering that change in wind.

At the bridge's end, be trees. Block all these roos from sight. I straighten here, grab up my skirt. Run to a broken memorial wall, duck in its friendly shadow. Then I take a deeper breath. Feel how my ravish fear bring all my blood into attention. And I step onward, walking easy past this final hiding. Come to a darkness under trees, can see the whiten graves beyond, the stripy looks of snow and earth. Among, be working roos. A shovel rise and strike, and first I think they make new trenches. But, as I come, can see these shovels claw into the higher banks. Scatter their dirt into a trench beside. Then it come natural in mind, what work this going to be. Like we always joking in our trenching work, they bury children. Make a rooish cemetery in the cemetery's skin.

I come up stronger. Grip to Kalash, and find a useful hold beneath the coat. Yo, now can see the hill entire. Be every dozen roos in carrying task, a haste of grandy shadows. Night be patchy larm of voice and crunching feet and digging. Bright among, there be a fire, with roos stood talking round. From their slaggen posture, can guess that all their work be booze.

When the first roo notice me and pause, my heart twist queery. He straighten, point with lazy gun. Child beside him shift and look. Then all the drunken roos ware up their rifles as I come toward, heart watery in my chest. Yo, now I come to my first murdern body, pause my step before.

Be a blackish child in dapple uniform, face down in earth. Legs finish in an unshape darkness, speckling far in snow. Ya, in a trench beside, can see another – sitting curlen with his head thrust back to show no face. Below his brow is jaggen bone and meat, a reddish scrap hung down. Unhurt ear look perfect neat beside. I fetch into stillness. Look up again to find, everywhere along this hill, be Russians watching me.

I loose my hands slow from Kalash. Begin to raise them in the air, skin flaming in the cold. And I step precarious around the child kilt at my feet. Keep eyes to the drunken roos, and gather breath to call.

Ain't time to even fear, when footsteps run to me behind. A yell come stark, then someone catch my arm and pull it vicious. I strike against without no thought, turn wild, and find Bashir.

I stare up to his hawken looks without no mind to use. He shout some rooish in my face, rage breathless. Shout and shout, before I comprehend.

Why you here? Why you here? You cannot be here! Why you here?

I start laughing somehow, and this bring Bashir ferocious. He grip into my shoulder, shake me rough. Begin a grosserie of cursing, where I comprehending only words for *imbecile* and *dead*. And he finish again with *Why you here?* in choken voice.

I touch to his gripping hand. Roo hoarse, 'Need Razin, brother.'

He stare a moment, shattern in his face. Glance back to the roos around the fire, who all be watching interest. Then his mouth twist angry. 'Nay. You dead here. You already dead.'

Feel some impatience, how he talking pointless, and I roo, 'Ain't care, how I be dead. Need Razin.'

Then someone call his name behind. Still holding to my arm, he turn and yell. Some laughing voices answer. Then a clutch of roos walk out from forest shadows, smiling curiose. Be seven, all with hawken face, dark fur. Is queery, how they so alike, ain't telling who be which. Only their beards be various grown. Ya one got fatter gun, wear necklace of long bullets round himself. And it inkle in my mind, these be Bashir's Kavkazky people – his vally children who behaving honest like no roo.

One child with thinner beard say weirdo words, ain't rooish. Then they laugh hilarious. Bashir grit, shake his head. He talk back unhappy in that weirdo speech, but end with *Razin*.

Kavkazky roos show mock impression. One clout Bashir against his head, and start a longer speech of dispute. Another Kavkazky talk in louder, naying his big hand.

As this squabble rise, a yellow roo come staggery from the drunken fire. Call down. Bashir let go my arm. Turn shouting, grab his gun to ready. And all Kavkazky roos go spitting vicious in this second. Yell shrill, and fix their guns to shooting pose.

Yellow child halt surprisen. Shout some quick filth, and turn back, calling peevish to his friends.

Bashir turn furiose to me. 'You see. Now we be kilt for you.'

'Nay, he rid,' I roo unsteady. 'You fear him bone.'

Bashir swear underbreath, while the fat-gun child put hand upon his shoulder. Fat-gun child talk low, like he speak gentle to a spooking mare. Then he clap twice on Bashir his shoulder. Say in rooish, 'Is normal.'

'What be, my brother?' I roo dumb.

Bashir look to me tired. 'What you ask. We taking you to Razin.'

'Bone.' I smile my mouth. 'Be gratty.'

He shake his head, resentment waken in his eyes again. 'What you think he do? What you think?'

Fat-gun Kavkazky roo to me, 'Bashir is guilty, girl. You help him, and now – you see? Very bad.' But he grinning friendly, like he gratulate my crazy wits.

Bashir say, 'Give her to the filth here, be no difference.'

'Nay,' a long-beard Kavkazky cavil. 'Razin, is interesting what he do. These, we know what it is. Not interesting.'

Bashir go muttering nasty to this, while long-beard smile to me joyeuse, put arm around Bashir. And I smile back. Heart revel in its panic, all my body warm like rest.

'Ain't nothing to me, what he do,' I say. 'Be gratty right.'

74

OF THREE DESIRES

Way to Razin be a maze of nightmares. Must step over gutten people, scattern parts of flesh. Times, a ruin body, seem like nothing that can live, scream awful to us as we pass. Kavkazky roos keep all around me, waring to the sides. And every minute be new Russians, come with booze insistence. Some be only curiose. But others coming in belief, Bashir's roos taking me to rape. They offer help with this, nor they be ready to discourage.

With some rapists, Bashir will only mention Razin, and they rid. But often, a hopeful rapist cavil, Razin get me after. Say filthen jokes to this, call insults on Bashir's dark roos. One skewtooth child keep pace with me, go spitting sideward on the blackish dead, and grin to me behind. Soon it be a following band of dozen cockroach Russians. All spew threats and maudy jokes.

Bashir ain't speaking mostly. He walk grit in stormy moods. Yo, must trace between all trenches and must keep together close – be always new attentions. But in some quiet moment, he say sudden that Kirill dead.

I be pausing to step around a murdern soldier's head. Be caught in frighten sickness, and I say distracten, 'You kill him real?'

'Nay.' Bashir give sideward frown, like he impress some meaning. 'Your Razin kill him. But was many kilt.'

'How?' I say. 'Razin killing Russians?'

Fat-gun child begin explaining, but this muddle in rooish definitions, be no use. And my mind be stupid, trying to know that Kirill dead – in all these ruin bodies, Kirill be somewhere. I work to save him all these days, and now he end like nothing. Be a thicker piece of dirt.

Then Bashir say sudden to the fat-gun roo, 'Lies, lies.'

'Razin's lies,' the fat-gun say. 'Is better than no truth. Can kill you.'

Another Kavkazky laugh. 'He ruling now, his lies be truth.'

'Nay, hold,' I say. 'Who ruling?'

'Razin ruling,' say Bashir disgusten. 'The general been kilt.'

I grimace puzzling to him. All Kavkazkies break in laughter.

'Girl,' roo the long-beard child, 'is bad job, general of Russians. Short to live.'

'Our children kilt the general?' I say.

'Yes,' Bashir say cold. 'Think this.'

'Nay.' The long-beard grin to me. 'This been Russian vote. Soldat dislike general. He do mistake, and general rid. So Razin punish Kirill. Punish whoever he mistrust. They shot. Child who do mistake – I think he is healthy.'

'But we forget this now.' The fat-gun nay his hand. 'Is old to talk.'

Then another stanken Russian come with interest to me, pushing, and when this struggle done, Kavkazkies go on in nerven silence. Ya, I be trying for relief, that Razin powerful grown. Ain't going to be no general above, insisting that I murder. But most my fear be on our forward path.

Been climbing ever upward, stitching a path through stones and trenches. And, every turning, Arlington House come larger in my eyes. Is mostly like a normal mansion. Windows plain, and all be clean, like showing innocence. But these humble looks misgive me worse. Be how, in a dream, an object looking ordinary – a shoe, a rock – possess all maudy powers. If it touching you, your soul be rid. Or how a child with normal parts, who eat and smile like any person, will kill, spit on the dead, do laughing rape.

Try thinking how I come to my own death, it be no fear beyond. But cowardesse insist, cannot go here. I even remember Felipe's nonsense talk of Satan's armies. Can feel how Satan living there, in company of his demons. But at last, we come past all the burial stones and fires, and only be this mansion left to see.

Leftward in its yard, there be a row of sprawlen bodies. All be roos, with furry hair. Each blooden at his head, the blood trail prettieuse in snow. Can see how they been kneeling in a line, particular correct. Then their neatness spoil by sloppy death.

Ya, here the rapists ease from us, lose backward in reluctance. Then the Kavkazkies lag behind. Soon only Bashir still stalk by me, despairing in his fury.

House got low steps in front, that lead up to a pillar porch. On these steps, be sat some twenty roos. They easy kept, be drinking–laughing. Got no drunken slobbery – is only loose in pleasure, like they laze behind a grandy meal.

Polkovnik Razin be sat middy to the steps. Face still blooden right, and both hands bandage into whitish mitts. He wear his dapple clothes, how every Russian clad this day, and look no different to the others. But can feel how every child attend him. Yo, as each roo notice me, he check to Razin nerviose. Can see, this be the Polkovnik's house, his line of neatly murders. Be his unworld of rape and screaming dead.

Beside him on the steps be Pasha. Pasha rest one hand on Razin's shoulder, easy in his body. Wear dapple clothes familiar to me from all days in Massa. But he strange to recognize, in all this thousand world of roos. Ya, he look to me with some expression that ain't his. Can be fear, but ain't his fear. And Pasha take his hand from Razin's shoulder, stand up sharp. Polkovnik Razin glance to him, then turn his gentle eyes on me. Is smiling curiose, like I be pleasant expectations.

Bashir step back without no word. Turn down to the better shadows, to the better dead. Ya, I go on, rage gripping hot. My fear be rid. It be Toporov in my heart of blood. I come uncaring through the snow, its grub of cigarettes, red footprints. My eyes keep sharp to Razin. Ain't want Pasha in my sight.

I stop at talking distance. Say in English, 'Come for my trade, Polkovnik.'

An unknown roo ask something low. Razin answer rooish, clear in humor, 'Be Toporov's wife.'

Then roos around be laughing, look to Pasha curiose. Ya, I keep eyes on Razin. Know, if I look to Pasha, my wolfen certainty be lost.

Razin raise a naying hand. Say English through their laughing noise, 'You want your medicine, I understand. But I am sorry, Korolyeva. Of course, I send this to New York.'

As he talk, the other roos hush down. Heed to this English speech with squinting face.

I take a feary breath. 'Gone to my people?'

Polkovnik pooch his nothing lips. 'I am sorry, Korolyeva. The man who takes it . . . How you are not there, I don't trust. He keeps it, I think. It is bad.'

My heart go vicious, helpless, but I hold my face correct. 'Mean, you still owe me somewhat.'

'Of course,' he say with pleasuring eyes. He look up to a brown-head child, say some low explanation. The faces round begin to puzzle. Ya, I see Pasha stir in corner-eye, and flinch my hate.

Razin look back to me polite. 'Ask what you want, Korolyeva. You see I am rich today.'

'Right,' I say. 'Can guess, you got some prisoners?'

Razin's face go thoughtful, like he measuring inside himself. 'It is a good thought, Korolyeva. The least, I owe you four people. It is the right thing, to show we are not ungrateful.'

I grit, be thinking hasty, how I argue for more children. Magine how the penals going to beg, while I choose four. How Mamadou refuse to come, pride stronger than no fear. So it come like nonsense when Razin say, 'But I think, your soldiers are male?'

My breath come short. 'Ya, they boys. My Marianos be.'

He shaking his head before I finish. 'Again, I cannot help you.

Male prisoners, it is why we fight this unpleasant war. No, it will be an impossible thing, so I am sorry.'

I say, before my grief come full, 'So girls left free? Or they all kilt?'

'This, it is something you know.' Razin smile. 'We talked of this.'

Be a moment while I comprehend. Then all the world go blind. Be saying into rage and nothing, 'Your children raping all they female prisoners. What you saying.'

'Of course,' say Razin in my blindness. 'Today it is like that.'

'Yo filth,' I say in choken voice. 'Nay, why you even living? Seen some ugliness, but Russians be like walking puke! How you never kill yourself, be some disgusting mysteries. Maggots, what you is. You–'

'No, Korolyeva,' Polkovnik say up loud. 'Not like this.'

I catch my voice, grit to him with my cold hands shaking on Kalash. My spirit be a weaken thread. Like I already start to die.

He shake his head. 'You must know, the hero gets three desires. You now lost two. I am a very bad person, you noticed this. I also noticed this, so I do not anger. I still give your last desire.'

All roos be fascinating now. They open-mouth in wishing they comprehend. Ya, I glance thoughtless to my Pasha. He watch me with disgusten face. His eyes be thin in anger. Ain't nothing like himself, and for a moment, I think it be some other roo. Then I flinch my eyes away, tears starting in my throat.

'Bone,' I say rough. 'Free they girls.'

Polkovnik sigh. 'Again, it is a bad choice. What happens now, I cannot change. If they live, they soon are free without your help. But now – to stop this, it will be a very bad fight. And my friends here also want to live.' He shake his head like disappointing. 'You waste your three desires. It is a sad story, I think. It ends badly.'

I shrug against my wasting feeling. 'Be no matter. Got no other wish.'

'You want nothing?' He raise eyebrows, smiling. 'No, I can't believe.'

'Ain't going to beg my life,' I say cold. 'Kill me or you ain't, be without this.'

'That is very good, Korolyeva. I think, you are like a wonderful actress.'

He turn by with pleasure eyes, begin explaining low in rooish. Russians heed with curiose looks to me, while I stand pointless. Begin to feel the cold again, and clutch my fingers in my coat.

Polkovnik finish, make sorry gesture. One roo say, *Nay, is sad.* Others laugh and nod, in preciation of this bony sadness. Polkovnik nod, turn back to me.

'My Korolyeva,' he say kindly, 'we are all sorry for your desires. But I think, there is something more you want. This I will give to you, of course. You want to see your husband.'

I keep eyes on Razin cold. Heart be a throng of evils, but I only say, 'I seen him. Got no other wish.'

'But you want to be with husband alone. I am a person, I understand. This I can give you.'

Polkovnik look to Pasha. Ya, my hands go harder to my gun. Begin to guess my last desire be Pasha Traitor's death. But when I look up to his owlen face, I lose in weakness. And now the Polkovnik talk his rooish low. Russians wake in movement, all come gathering quick to me. Their faces bright from entertainment, got no resenting mood. Nor I fight as they take my Kalash. The coat go with, and my belly come sudden freezing as they step away.

Then Pasha come toward. I clench with panic loathing. Look back toward the line of dead, the only children here I want to know.

Pasha take me by the arm without no word. Hand grip deep, is hard. I never look at him. But when he pull me, I go with.

He lead me past these roos – past the Polkovnik who look up with happy brownish eyes – up the steps, into the porchen shadows. He open the mansion's door, and we go in a darken hallway, smelling cold with dust.

Then he fling the door shut hard. Close us in shadow darkness, where the outside noise be helpless dull. My throat gone tight with dread. I twist against his hold unthinking. But he drag me rough along, into an eating room, cold with unlife. Pass on, through one more door, and in this farther room, he leave me free. Shut the door behind, go hasty to a petty sofa. Drag this back against the closen door.

Then he sit upon this sofa, put his face into his hands, and break in sobbing tears.

75

MY FINAL PARLEY

I stand a longer minute, heeding strange in inside darkness. Room be a clutter of every shadow. Is paintings to the walls, but cannot see their pictures right. Various chairs stand round, like people in five different moods. And in two grandy windows show the farther fire of District, a maudy glow that thicken the horizon.

Pasha weep alone, bent on his sofa. Wipe his face with jacket arm, but never look to me. Ya, in my flesh, still be the fright unbalance of his dragging me. I comprehend that I should say some word, child crying so. But I gone stiff with some unknowing feeling.

And slow, his weeping ease, his breath go lighter. Soon he only staring to the floor in hunchen shadow.

Then he say, resenting soft, 'You cold?'

'Sure I be cold.' I fret my shoulders. 'But why you crying? What this be?'

'You come here,' he say angry. 'Should be in Marias. Said to Razin that you going.'

'Gone if – nay, how you telling shoulds?'

His face tense like he going to shout. But he only straighten, pull his rooish jacket off. Reach it to me.

I step toward and take the jacket. Clad it on, with queery sorrow how it stank of Pasha. Smell like our hunting days together, before

I guess that roos can wash. And it be warm from him, its sleeven cuff wet from his tears.

Then I come cautieuse, sit to the sofa. Look to Pasha where he hunchen big, face low in shadow. 'Polkovnik told all stank on you. Know this.'

'I know. He joke on this tonight.'

I take a needy breath. 'So it been lies.'

Be a moment's silence, while he fish a cigarette from his shirt pocket. Match brighten up, and by its flame, can see his painful face. Got dirt along one cheek, with tearen paths run through it white. He skit the match out hard. 'Told you all this before. Ain't lies.'

I flinch annoying. 'Nay, ain't told me. Told me fictions, how you flee the Russians. All your sorry feelings, how you kill yourself. Your daughter.' My voice catch sour. 'Ain't matter nothing, but you lying right.'

'Yes, ain't matter. This been also truth, but it ain't matter. Told you I be mally, but you ain't believe.' He look resenting to me. 'But you believing Razin, why?'

'Shee, I believe the war tonight! Be some thousand children dead around us for your treachery. Should let them kill you in Marias.'

'Yes, you should. I told you this.'

'Nay, damn! Why you told me to war? You known we cannot win. But you be faithful to these maggots, why?'

Then he look to me full. His face be dim in shadows, but can see his eyes particular, suffering their anger. 'Nay. Ain't faithful to them, fool. I done this for yourself.'

'Myself?' I scoff my breath. 'Ain't for myself. I wanting this?'

'I try to get you cure. What you need.'

'And where it is? All children slaven. Dead. It be no cure.'

'Ain't better way.' He grit his mouth like pain. 'All choices mally.'

'How this be better choice than anything? Other choice, they kill us slower?'

'If you trading prisoners, how we said–'

'It been no thousand prisoners here! We losing, ain't remember? Even if Marines agree to trade, been nothing. Dozen cures.'

'*You* can cure,' say Pasha savage thin. 'Yourself. All I try.'

'Myself? This war been for my precieuse self? No sho, it been!'

A moment he stare furiose to me, ain't seem to even breathe. Then he say harsh, 'When it been Driver, you fight for one cure.'

'Without no hope to win, I ain't. Kill any thousand children? Nay.'

But as I say this, doubt misgive. I even get a nonsense thought that Driver still can save, if I agree. Yo, Pasha shaking his head with bitter mouth.

He say, 'And if you ain't war here, roos take Marias neverless. They wait some months, be most. Ain't waiting long. It been no help.'

I catch on this precaire. 'But . . . you can tell me. Why you never said, we got no chance?'

'Ice, think.' His bluish eyes gone stark. 'I say, and you ain't war. You running here alone. To roos.'

'And so? I be one child. You seen outside? It be a world of dead!'

'And now you here! All been for nothing!'

'Shee, ain't even truth! Ain't for myself! You left to roos, first chance. You theirs. Or why you left to them? Nor I want fables on no daughter.'

Pasha flinch from this, look narrowing at a chair across. Suck his cigarette, breathe out a ghosty reach of smoke. Ya, in this smoky breath, all meaning blanken from his eyes.

'Pasha, shee!' I say. 'And now you giving me your moron face? Ain't guess I even leaving here, can learn some sense before I die.'

He tense indignant. 'You ain't dying. And you the moron.'

This catch me funny in my nerves. I laugh while Pasha muttern, 'Why you come here? Moron, laughing. How I going to help you now?'

'Nay, what you caring any, vampire?' I say through my laughter. 'Should be raping me right now.'

Then sudden, he be on his feet. Rouse over me furiose and yell, 'You wanting I should rape you? What you want?'

'Foo, what you saying?'

'Ain't need to call me vampire. Nor you need to talk of rape.'

'Was jokes.'

'Nay, ain't jokes! And you ain't leaving here, is right.' He look sharp to the window. Suck his cigarette bright and spit out smoke. 'Ain't jokes.'

'Foo, Pasha,' I say softer. 'Why you angry so? Ain't meant no wrong.'

'Rape you? I ain't never touch you.'

'Damn, ain't meaning nothing like that.'

He sit down, all insults in his face. Say peevish, 'Truth, you cannot leave. Razin going to want you now.'

This shock peculiar in my nerves. I sit back to the sofa, crossing arms against myself. In the heavy dark, roo look uncanny, like in our first days – face flat, with chill uncolor eyes.

'Razin?' I say hoarse. 'Why he wanting me particular? Got other girls to use.'

'Ain't that,' say Pasha in disgusten voice. 'Can leave that.'

'Then what it be?'

He wave away this question, hunch again with bitter frown. When he suck his cigarette, I notice by its swelling light, his knuckles scuffen bloody. I look by, swallowing, at a painting of a sleeper head. Wait some time of fear while its white face be blurren dark, got no expression I can see. Be thinking how I beg if I can leave here, neverless. Need only to walk across the bridge, wait for they fires to cool.

Then Pasha say, 'You talk to Razin every days, been stupid work. He be a sort, ain't bone he even know you. That he think of you.'

'So he think of me. And so?'

'He think,' say Pasha slow, like he explain to imbeciles, 'and think some use for you. All this night, he seek you. Send soldats to north, if they can catch.'

'But why? All I be asking.'

Pasha shrug resenting. 'He want you to work for roos.'

'Shee, work for roos.' I laugh up tight. 'I help them take Marias? Razin know I never doing so.'

'Ain't for this. Ain't for Marias.'

'Then what it being for? Ain't sense?'

Now Pasha make a difficult face, look to the moonlight windows. I follow his eyes and find the smoke horizon there, gone dull and thick. But soon it realize, the roo ain't looking to the District. He heed the voices in the yard, is waring for no change. To this, my selfen nerves go thin. Think on the filth soldats outside, who chase me every step for rape.

Then Pasha frown toward his hands, say slow, 'Ice, been your lie. How Europeans give you nuclears.'

'Foo, no one believing this.'

'Nay. *We* ain't believe. But someone can believe.'

'Shee, who?'

'Heed. If Europeans give you nuclears, been crime. Be grandy crime. Razin want you to accuse this crime. To Europeans, Russians, every people.' He look to me for comprehending, hopeless in his eyes. 'Will be in Europe. Where you go.'

'Foo, Europe.' I take unbelieving breath. 'Razin take me to some Europe, to only tell this lie?'

Pasha's face go worse. 'And you must tell about the war. Tell, how Russians want.'

'War? Yo, how they want it told?'

His misery work in complications, thinking in his face. 'What Russians say about this war . . . be like the radio speech. You can remember?'

'They helping us with pharmacies.' My voice catch sour. 'For nothing. Cause they caring so.'

'Ya. What you must say. The Russians help, do nothing mally.'

'And they slave our children,' I say hard. 'This be for help?'

'Nay, ain't slave. It be no slaves. Your people fight for roos because they want. For justice.'

'Justice.' I laugh bitter. 'And any fool believing this?'

619

'People there, how they will know? They never seen Marias, Quantico. They never seeing war. Most they believe on war, is lies.' Then he look wishful to my eyes. And it realize, he wanting me to answer yes. Want this vicious, but he never dare to ask direct.

I nod dumb. 'Guess Razin sent us here so you convince me?'

'Nay.'

'How, nay?' I scoff my breath. 'Is what you doing. All you doing.'

'Nay. He known, you ain't agree.'

'So what this be? All be no point.'

Pasha shake his head. Go fish another cigarette. Light with hasty hand, breathe out a dirty veil of smoke.

Then he look to me precaire. Be concentrating wary, like he narrow on a deer with gun. And he say soft, 'I going to tell you truth. You can believe?'

'Ain't know. I going to heed.'

'Razin think you love myself. Love me . . . like a male.'

Here we both flinch in conscience. I want to look away, but I be shy to move somehow. Think pointless of Toporov Vampire, and my heart beat queery, like it want to be some other place.

At last I say, 'And so?'

'What he think, he give us room apart. On boat.'

'Ho, he want to breed us?' I laugh choken. 'What this do?'

'Be so I giving love. I show like I protecting you and . . . this. Be nine days across the ocean. You be alone, except myself. When it finish, he think you obey.'

I take a careful breath. 'But you ain't do this . . . love?'

'Nay,' say Pasha hard. 'I love you honest. Ain't for this.'

I knit my hands together. Feel like tears, my breath come scarce and rough. Magine this room on endless ocean. How Pasha trying love, I be alone from every person known. And Razin wait somehow, the soldats always loud outside.

I say thin, 'I believe.'

Pasha let out a ragged breath. Look down to his cigarette, his big respect be helpless. 'I ain't do Razin's games. But I be asking, so you live. If you ain't agree . . . on boat, this death be mally, Ice. You there with all soldats. How they do. And then be drowning.'

'Can shoot me now.'

Pasha flinch to me. Stare a pause of fright, reach toward my hand. But then he mind himself, pull back.

'Nay, I ain't saying right.' His voice come high like choking tears. 'What be important, if you work for roos, your children safe.'

My heart bite cold. 'Children? Sengles in Marias?'

'Ya, roos go there now. But if you work for roos, they keep your Sengles safe. They all be safe.'

Now need grow in me. Rise mally, like a puking sickness. Start thinking, it be only lies. Be for some Europeans–Russians, strangers to my mind. Ya, they believing garbage like, be their stupidities to thank.

Through this, my need distract to Mamadou. Wonder if I can beg his life somehow, in extra trade. Crave to ask if Pasha know, if Mamadou be dead or prisoners. But already can feel the grief that waiting on this answer.

I say in first attempt, 'Be any way . . . they keep Crow safe? Take him from prisoners?'

Pasha's face catch into fear. 'Nay, Ice. They–'

'Sure, see this.' I take a choken breath. 'But Crow be living? You ain't know?'

'Ya, I seen. He there in prisoners.' Pasha make a forcen smile. 'Got injury, but this be small.'

A noise of rooish laughter rise outside. Gunfire louden there, and Pasha startle. Look to the window angry. Then he look back to me and smile again, his face a dirty fear.

I say weak, 'And prisoners here, they go to Europe also?'

This catch him in some conscience. 'Go . . . they go to Africa. Wars there.'

I nod stupid. Look back to the window. City purpling still, and lower stars be hazy dull. Can see the Washington Monument, look smallish wavery in the smoke, but still be white the same.

'What it be, you guess?' I say. 'Number of children that you took? Some hundreds?'

When I look back to Pasha, he stare to the window self. Fist his blooden hands. 'What Razin think, it be five thousand.'

I make a throaten noise, is almost sobbing. 'Nay, cannot – how they get this? Ain't been no five thousand caught.'

Pasha raise his cigarette and find it dead. Grimace painful and throw it down. Go fishing in his pocket.

Then I comprehend. Ease back to the chillen sofa, shivering in my coat. 'Tunnels, I guess. They catch them there?'

Pasha nod. 'Where most our people being now. At tunnels, or . . . catch Marianos.'

'So how they do this?' I say thin. 'Quanticos never surrender so. Must kill them all. Ain't take them living.'

Pasha scratch up' a match and grimace in its light. Suck his cigarette and say in empty voice, 'Use bombs, is gas. Make children sleep.' He toss the match like ridding this notion by.

'Sure,' I say cold. 'Tunnels bone for this. Was gift.'

'Ya. Was what roos hope.'

'What *you* hope. You hope.'

He look to me with his blank face, but now can know it be no lies. Is shame. Face whitish like a bone.

I say, 'Can notice, you ain't warn the Quanticos this. You ain't.'

He ain't speak, he only shake his head. Hand clutch his cigarette.

'Truth, yours been genius work. Yo, I work bone for you. I working any weeks to kill my children.'

'Nay,' he say thick. 'Ain't like this.'

'Yes, like this! But it be done. Ain't speaking for your cockroach Russians, while every children took to die. Africa – you told me what this be. I goddamn know! Heed, you get reward for this? They pay you something?'

'Nay,' he say in nosy voice. 'Ain't pay.'

'Is rank you get? What they do?'

He look to me awful then. 'Ice, ain't you need to die for this.'

'How I can live? I speak for roos while . . . nay.'

'Ice.' He hitch his breath. 'Who we catch now, ain't like Sengles. These been soldiers.'

'Nay, they been Mamadou!' My voice choke bitter, and I start to cry. 'They been my goddamn people. Ya, First Runner dead. She ten, ain't be no goddamn soldier!'

'They kilt without this, Ice. It—'

'Nay, they ain't! They ain't! Must be some chance that someone live!'

His eyes grow their own tears, his face gone soft in littlish misery. '*You* can live. I trying to save yourself. You fight me why?'

'Ain't want to goddamn live!' I sob out hard. 'I finish living!'

Then he reach sudden toward me, pull me hard into his arms. Yo, I lose in weakness. Hold against him, weeping breathless. He muttering teary, 'Never want you in this. Ain't even want you by me. Any child I know, they ending mally. Nay, why you come here? You been safe.'

'Ain't want no safety. Want to die.'

'Ain't let you die. Ain't let you.'

Then we only hold together, weeping into dark. He stroke my head against his chest, and we cry passion hard, like running into breathlessness. Be like we seeking something with these tears, some hope to feel. Seek in our orphan loves their dead. Seek in a dark bewept. Yo, I feel this been the truth of all our time together. We always been a grief that huddle close against a vicious light. And he bend to me and kiss my hair, in last tendresse of need.

But tears be like all tears, a water that weaken into emptiness. Then only be this room, gone hazy with cigarettes. Be the outside noising of soldats, the always cold. Be ourself, wet-face and clutch together, shy in sudden conscience.

And slow, he loose from me. I sit back, feeling strange and small. Cross arms against my chest, and shiver in his jacket's warm.

Pasha sit back muttering low, 'Ain't let you.' He seek his pocket for cigarettes, hand moving clumsy weak. Ain't find them, and he leave this hopeless. Only stare to the floor with ruin face, tired and spent and white.

And here I know, like worser truth, my Pasha never being false. He caring for no roos. He caring for no town of people. In time, he faithful to his daughter; when she die, his faith die also. Then he find myself. And when he said he want this war to save my life, been simple truth. Yo, if it been needful, he kilt every Mariano with his own hands, so I keep safe. So been our war.

But this war ain't only Pasha's. It been also mine. I known that we can lose. Pasha told me this himself. But I thought to save my brother's life, and cannot hear no doubts. I risk my whole believing city for this single love. And even when Driver gone – is Pasha right, all choices evil. Can leave all children dying of posies; or I kill them in some war.

And my heart suffer, and crave to leave this mally world, and it beat on. Quantico burn red in the window. Rooish laughter rise, be still alive beyond all death.

At last, I take a breath, say dumb, 'Can use a cigarette myself.'

He find his cigarettes in different pocket. Give one to me, light a match, and watch my face particular in its quick light. Yo, when the flame be rid, and I be sucking on this gratty smoke, he say, 'Mamadou ain't dead.'

Take me a second to know these words be real. I narrow on him, still blind somewhat from the matchen flame. 'Nay, you know this certain?'

'Ya. Gone to Marias with your cure.'

My blood flash hot and strange. 'Goddamn. He there? Why you ain't said?'

'Be saying.' Pasha shrug.

I laugh dumb. 'Foo, Razin choosing Mamadou? Been queery choice.'

'Ain't choose,' say Pasha shortish. 'He ain't even know who Mamadou be.'

'How, been luck?'

'Nay. He ask me to choose. Because I know yourself, he ask.' Roo look to his blooden knuckles. 'Thought Mamadou keep you safe.'

I stare joyeuse and weak a minute. The smoky pall of District in the window draw my eye, but cannot feel its misery now. Luck woken in my heart. Can think, is even chance the NewKing give the cure to Sengles. Sure, he got no child his own.

Then a notion stir in mind. Start like a bitter joke – a loathing on this time of evils. But it twist somehow. Grow real and real in quickening thought. Is like a birthing foal that find its feet and rise up as a horse. And when it find its shape, is bell as wonderful.

I say precaire, 'When it be done – I told this lie – what be?'

Pasha flinch, look sharp to me. 'Ice, you heeding? You will do this?'

'Hold.' I ware my cigarette. 'Be asking, I can go back? To Marias?'

His face tense again. 'Roos go there now. Ain't–'

'Shee, answer questions. They will bring me?'

'Can be.' Pasha seek my face. 'If they think you theirs.'

'Europeans, they got cure?'

He get bewaring looks. Say stiff, 'Will cure yourself. Do this.'

'Nay, what I thinking. They will give it somehow?'

Pasha get his worst naying face. He shake his head and shake his head. Ya, when he take good breath, his voice be rage. 'Roos warring in Marias! You heed nothing? Ice!'

'Nay, roos been weaker, if we got the cure ourself. Ya, Europeans got no boats?'

He swear rooish, stand up to his feet.

I say up harder, 'People die for this tonight. To get that goddamn cure. Yo, all my children die without. It be a country dying here.'

'Ain't save countries, Ice!' He turn back furiose. 'Is moron work. Can save a person. Save two people.'

'Nay, you going to help me, roo! It must be something, from all this.'

'Cannot.'

'Goddamn, you help me! Or you watch me die!'

Then he scream harsh and loud, 'Ain't say this! It be cruel! Ain't say this!'

Even the roos outside go hush. Is like the world stop on its feet. Yo, I cringe back in body fear, expect his fists. Heart pounding bright.

But when he only hold in stare, I reach unthinking for his hand. Then his face go weak. He take my hand and muttern, 'Ice, ain't say this more. Ain't say.'

I take a sorry breath. 'But cannot be for nothing, Pasha. All they deaths. And you be bone, I know you be. You know.'

He shake his head, begin to answer – when footsteps thud inside the house. Go shivering tender in the floor, and rooish voice come muttering toward. Pasha freeze with agony face. Noise gather close, and he say low like helplessness, 'Ain't talk to them. I do . . . you only keep with me. Ain't talk.' Then the door kick hard against the sofa, jar my frighten back. And, for the first time, I hear their *vampeer* – rooish word for vampire – callen like a simple name.

Pasha shout back rooish, 'What you need?'

'Be time!' A child roo loud with boozen voice. 'Razin already gone!'

The door push hard again. Some child go laugh and muttern swears. Pasha's hand grip hard on mine, until I feel my hand its every bones. He whispern dumb, 'It all be right. You only keep to me. Ain't talk.'

Yo, as I stand, the sofa shift against my legs. The door come wide.

And then it be all roos. They jabbering, pushing elbows, as we stumble to the vicious night. I still hold Pasha's painful hand, and every world be roos. Guns fearing in my sight, be blacker nothing by the moon. Roos' dirty voice come hot around my ears, their dirty laugh. The dead we stepping over be theirs; the smoke we breathe, the stank of guts.

And we come to a helicopter plane. Its headblades spinning, blurring, so the wind hurt in my eyes. Its roar unbearing loud. We step inside, roos jostling everywhere, I cannot flee their touch. And be this helicopter's inside room, without no seats. Got smell like rifle oil, that changing sudden when the door come shut. Become a soldat pue of sweat, of booze. A smell of sex that sicken in my mind, was rape. Roos flop various to the floor, and all be close. Must sit into their unwant touch. A child start shouting 'Korolyeva!' at me through the blaring noise. Laugh ugly, though I never look.

Then the helicopter skew like losing balance. Fling and fling itself, and fall from earth. Lose into trembling air. I panic breathless, clutch at nothing, my own legs – while roos laze careless. Only lean their balance, like sitting a tricky horse. I think in distant mind, *Ain't nothing. Flying. What it do.* Look up, where be two scuffen windows, round like scary eyes. And as the helicopter tip in air, I see a swipe of broadening road.

Road got some weirdo trucks with rifle noses, pointing various. Thousand children walk behind. They clog and fill the road. All stir together like an awful worm.

The helicopter bounce and all be gone. See only dirty sky. Yo, I keep seeking with my eyes. Crave to see if these be roos, or be my people stolen. I stare the windows, while a stranger hand reach toward my face, and Pasha swat it back. Swat it back. The helicopter tip again, and show a blackness that stretch forever, shivering by thin moon. Is water. And I know impossible, these children lost forever. Every Quantico, and every Mariano. Penals. Crow. They never seen again.

Yo, before I feel this right, my Pasha catch me to himself. Hit wild at some soldat's hand. A child yell up like glad discoveries: *Shto, vampeer vlublyon!* Then roos all laugh to choking, while I comprehend without no mind: *The vampire gone in love.* And Pasha clutch me hard. I scarce can breathe for his hard arm. I push my hand against his chest, but it do nothing. Only feel his shirt besweaten, and when I look to him, his face be dead with hate. I close my eyes.

Then be a never time, before the helicopter falling, easing like this life can end. Can think, we crashing simple. All be rid. But still the rooish yells continue. The room chuff down, chuff light, and find its feet. Its closeness open. Helicopter roar come deafening big. Is cleanly wind again, and when I open eyes, my Pasha staring at me close. Hair stick to his face with sweat.

Roos scramble out, rid wonderful away. Yo, Pasha take my hand again, stand to his feet. I come shaky after him, and only when we steppen out, I feel the ground be wrong. Be weirding, lifting under-foot.

Take a minute of brainless fear before I know, it be a boat. We standing on its roof, that pose unsteady on enormous water. Air breathe wet, feel big and wrong. Floor change again, and I clutch Pasha's hand. Feel our sweat. Soldats stalk behind–around, and the helicopter breathe down. Its noisy wind come deaf; a different wind cut sleetish at my face. And in this wind that feel like icy nakedness, soldats still noising past, my Pasha say hoarse in my ear, 'If you do Razin's ask, I help. What you ask. I help.'

I flinch, touch to his arm. Already his sleeve be damp from rainy wind. 'The cure? But you ain't lying?'

'You got to heed me. You will heed?'

'I heed you always,' I say choken. 'How we do this war. We killing everyone.'

'Ice, be asking.'

'Nay, you help?'

'Cure, can get from Europeans. Yes. But you must live.'

'Nay, you ain't lying?'

He take an angry breath. I look to him, be steadying myself to ask again. But when I only see his face, its owlen grief, I know. His face be like a moon that cannot bear to see. Is like my heart.

So this be how I bring the cure at last to all the Nighted States, save every poory children, young to die. Be how the new America begin, in wars against all hope – a country with no power in a world that hate its life. Be what I seeing, when our Russian boat pull to the nighten waters, as the shore hush from me, drift away all worlds I

628

known. See the shore and see the smoke of Quantico afar, and I comprehend, this all a country, and is mine. Pasha be by me, in his sorrow, talking how he bad for life, and I hold his hand in habit, watch my townie stars, the brushy land beneath their eyes. And I know, inside this final loss, I going to save this place. I be small in all this blackness world, this ship of drunken vampires, but through my hearten wounds, I living yet, and all my love the same. Nor death been ever arguments to me, I know my truth. I know, ain't evils in no life nor cruelties in no red hell can change the vally heart of Ice Cream Star.

ACKNOWLEDGEMENTS

First I'd like to thank my wonderful editors, Craig Pyette, Lee Boudreaux, Bella Pearson, Karen Maine, and especially Juliet Brooke. All of them gave priceless feedback in the revision of the somewhat chaotic 900-page first draft. Juliet was there from the very first stages, did an amazing amount of work, and gave innumerable thoughtful and inspired suggestions. Special gratitude also goes to my always wonderful agent, Victoria Hobbs, who has been the book's best friend from the time when it was only a dozen pages long, and a devoted and brilliant advocate for it. And additional thanks to the book's US agent, the charming and gifted Christy Fletcher.

I'm also grateful for the input of early readers of the book: Paul Bravmann, Matt de la Peña, Jessie Sholl, Michelle Herrera Mulligan, Ellen Tarlow and Gail Vachon.

And most of all, I'd like to thank Howard Mittelmark, who read every version of the book, and was my most trusted advisor at every stage. Howard is one of the greatest editors walking the face of the Earth, or burrowing beneath the Earth's surface, or living at the bottom of the ocean. Plus, dreamy.

www.vintage-books.co.uk